The World's Finest Mystery and Crime Stories

Third Annual Collection

Forge Books by Ed Gorman

Moonchasers and Other Stories

Blood Games

What the Dead Men Say

(as editor, with Martin H. Greenberg)

The World's Finest Mystery and Crime Stories
First Annual Collection

The World's Finest Mystery and Crime Stories
Second Annual Collection

The World's Finest Mystery and Crime Stories
Third Annual Collection

(as E. J. Gorman)

The First Lady

The Marilyn Tapes

Senatorial Privilege

THIRD ANNUAL COLLECTION

The World's Finest Mystery and Crime Stories

*Edited by Ed Gorman
and Martin H. Greenberg*

A TOM DOHERTY ASSOCIATES BOOK

NEW YORK

THE WORLD'S FINEST MYSTERY AND CRIME STORIES:
THIRD ANNUAL COLLECTION

Copyright © 2002 by Tekno Books and Ed Gorman

A Forge Book
Published by Tom Doherty Associates, LLC
175 Fifth Avenue
New York, NY 10010

www.tor.com

Forge® is a registered trademark of Tom Doherty Associates, LLC.

Library of Congress Cataloging-in-Publication Data

The world's finest mystery and crime stories : third annual collection / edited by Ed Gorman and Martin H. Greenberg.—1st ed.
    p. cm.
    "A Tom Doherty Associates book."
    ISBN 0-765-30234-9 (hc) — ISBN 0-765-30235-7 (pbk)
    1. Detective and mystery stories, American. 2. Detective and mystery stories, English. I. Gorman, Edward. II. Greenberg, Martin Harry.

PS648.D4 W65 2002
813'.087208—dc21

2002025034

First Edition: October 2002

Printed in the United States of America

0 9 8 7 6 5 4 3 2 1

To Larry Segriff and John Helfers,
who do 99 percent of the work

Contents

Acknowledgments

Thanks to Jon L. Breen, Edward D. Hoch, Maxim Jakubowski, Thomas Woertche, David Honeybone, and Edo van Belkom, for their informative summaries of the mystery field, and of course, to our editor at Forge Books, James Frenkel, and his able staff.

The Year in Mystery and Crime Fiction: 2001

Jon L. Breen

It has never been so difficult to assign a handy label to the year in mystery fiction. Of course, the specter of September 11 hangs over every attempt to sum up the year. The mystery world reacted to that cataclysm much as did everyone else, with anger, reflection, reassessment, determination, and symbolic acts of community. Despite fears of flying and the possibility of further terrorist attack, Washington, D.C., hosted the Bouchercon as scheduled. What lasting effects, if any, the terrorist acts will have on the narrow world of fictional crime remains to be seen.

You could call 2001 the Year of Change, but we're embarked on a century of change in literary delivery systems. Time will tell what the ultimate effect of the electronic revolution will be on book publishing. On the plus side, new technologies give writers, both established and neophyte, new ways to reach their audience. On the downside, writers and other artists must ponder how intellectual property can be protected in a time of rapid change in modes of delivery.

The New York publishing mainstream continued to show more interest in the blockbuster and less in the standard bread-and-butter mystery novel. As a partial result, a number of writers whose names are familiar from major publishing lists had new novels published through smaller specialist or regional publishers, among them Taffy Cannon, Shelley Singer, Jeremiah Healy, Les Roberts, Ralph McInerny, and Michael Bowen.

Vanity (or more politely, subsidy) publishing used to be a sucker play, but with the relatively inexpensive dissemination of e-books and books-on-demand, writers of genuine talent who are frustrated by the difficulty of breaking into mainstream markets are able to go that route much more economically. In 2000, I reviewed an author-financed on-demand novel for the first time, Daniel Ferry's *Death on Delivery* (iUniverse), and found it a thoroughly professional job that would not have been out of place on an established publisher's list. In 2001 came Thomas B. Sawyer's *The Sixteenth Man* (iUniverse), a novel by a successful television writer that undoubtedly would have found a receptive market in traditional publishing channels if the author had chosen to offer it.

This new flood of inexpensively self-driven publications has the same drawback that can be applied to most of the Internet: the lack of editorial intervention. Good newer writers who could use the help of a strong editor aren't getting it. (You could say that best-selling writers with big-money multibook contracts aren't getting it either—who would deign to edit a six-hundred-pound gorilla?—but that is a problem for another day.)

Change being a constant, now more than ever, I'll call 2001 the Year of the Group Novel. The tradition of multiauthor mysteries goes back to the Detection Club's *The Floating Admiral* (1931), and there have been several examples since, but never, I think, three in one year as in 2001: *Yeats Is Dead* (Knopf), edited by Joseph O'Connor, an Elmore Leonard–style crime comedy by a group of Irish writers, mostly non–genre specialists; *Naked Came the Phoenix* (St. Martin's Minotaur), edited by Marcia Talley, told in turn by a group of prominent female mystery writers; and *Natural Suspect* (Ballantine), devised by William Bernhardt, the comic serial novel of several legal thriller specialists. All the books benefited charity (Amnesty International, breast cancer research, and the Nature Conservancy, respectively); all make entertaining reading, though none is as ultimately satisfactory as a good novel by a single hand.

BEST NOVELS OF THE YEAR 2001

The following fifteen were the most impressive of the crime novels I read and reviewed in 2001. The standard disclaimer applies: I don't claim to cover the whole field, but I challenge anyone to name fifteen better.

J. G. Ballard, *Super-Cannes* (Picador USA). Science-fiction great Ballard provides a genuine detective story as well as an incisive view of dark societal trends in the tale of a sinister state-of-the-art industrial park on the French Riviera. (The late Stanley Kubrick might have made a great movie out of it.)

William Bernhardt, *Murder One* (Ballantine). For legal fiction buffs, the series about Oklahoma lawyer Ben Kincaid is one of the best extant, encompassing humor, extended courtroom action, and ingenious plotting.

Lawrence Block, *Hope to Die* (Morrow). Manhattan private eye Matt Scudder's latest adventure will please equally those who admire traditional detection, fiction noir, and good English prose.

Ken Bruen, *The McDead* (Do-Not/Dufour). Another of the author's satirical, minimalist London police novels. Not for every taste, but for me one of the strongest arguments for Brit Noir.

Michael Connelly, *A Darkness More Than Night* (Little, Brown). Two Connelly characters, L.A. cop Harry Bosch and heart-transplant-recipient and former FBI agent Terry McCaleb (of *Blood Work* [1998]) join forces in a typically complex and enthralling procedural.

David Cray, *Bad Lawyer* (Carroll & Graf/Penzler). A fine specimen of the Big Trial novel from an ostensibly well-known author using a pseudonym. (You might not want to read the jacket copy.)

Val Davis, *The Return of the Spanish Lady* (St. Martin's Minotaur). The best yet in the Nicolette Scott series combines a present-day expedition to recover a World War II Japanese fighter plane with a 1918 reporter's pursuit of a dangerous story. (You *must not* read the jacket copy!)

John Dunning, *Two O'Clock Eastern Wartime* (Scribner). Too long? Yes. Crazy plot? Sure. But I couldn't leave off my list this evocative World War II–era tale, which offers the second or third best use of a radio background in crime fiction.

Evan Hunter and Ed McBain, *Candyland* (Simon & Schuster). The collaboration of a "straight" novelist with his mystery-writing alter ego is a stunt, to be sure, but a successful one.

Val McDermid, *Killing the Shadows* (St. Martin's Minotaur). Who could resist a novel about a serial killer of authors of serial-killer novels? In an exploration of criminal and creative psychology, McDermid even gives samples of each victim's prose.

Joyce Carol Oates (writing as Rosamond Smith), *The Barrens* (Carroll & Graf/Penzler). In a splendid example of dark suspense, Oates provides a chilling exploration of criminal psychology—and the noncriminal characters are pretty twisted, too.

Sara Paretsky, *Total Recall* (Delacorte). Recovered memory therapy and recollections of the *kindertransport* figure in one of the best novels featuring Chicago private eye V. I. Warshawski.

Peter Robinson, *Aftermath* (Morrow). As the title suggests, most of the action of the latest Alan Banks novel occurs *after* a particularly grisly serial killer has been captured.

Steven Saylor, *Last Seen in Massilia* (St. Martin's Minotaur). Some series sleuths never let you down, and the ancient Roman Gordianus the Finder is in that number.

Laura Wilson, *Dying Voices* (Bantam). In a second novel, about a young woman trying to solve the delayed-action murder of her long-gone mother, Wilson reasserts her position as a major new talent.

SUBGENRES

Private eyes. Apart from the characters of Block and Paretsky (see the list of fifteen), there were good cases for Parnell Hall's soft-boiled Stanley Hastings in *Cozy* (Carroll & Graf/Penzler); Ed Gorman's 1950s midwesterner Sam McCain in *Will You Still Love Me Tomorrow?* (Carroll & Graf); and Gary Phillips's Las Vegas sleuth Martha Chainey (not technically a PI but she acts like one) in *Shooter's Point* (Kensington). The Comeback of the Year Award goes to mid-twentieth-century shamus Jack LeVine, who returns after a quarter-century absence in Andrew Bergman's *Tender Is LeVine* (St. Martin's Minotaur). Returning after a shorter hiatus of seven years was R. D. Rosen's baseball player turned private eye Harvey Blissberg in *Dead Ball* (Walker).

Lawyers. Another famous advocate entered the fiction fray with good results: in collaboration with Walt Becker, Robert Shapiro wrote *Misconception* (Morrow), featuring some intriguing issues related to the abortion debate. Series lawyers in solid form included Linda Fairstein's Manhattan prosecutor Alex Cooper in *The Deadhouse* (Scribner); Joe L. Hensley's midwestern Don Robak in *Robak in Black* (St. Martins Minotaur); Jonnie Jacobs's Kali O' Brien in *Witness for the Defense* (Kensington); and Sheldon Siegel's Mike Daley in *Incriminating Evidence* (Bantam).

Police. Besides being a sound procedural, Jill McGown's *Scene of Crime* (Ballantine), about the male/female team of Hill and Lloyd, provides as solid an example of classical puzzle plotting as I encountered during the year. H. R. F. Keating's Inspector Ghote, who now has enjoyed one of the longest careers among series police, returned in *Breaking and Entering* (St. Martin's Minotaur). Other cops in notable action included Paula L. Woods's Charlotte Justice in *Stormy Weather* (Norton); Ian Rankin's John Rebus in *The Falls* (St. Martin's Minotaur); Bill Crider's Sheriff Dan Rhodes in *A Romantic Way to Die* (St. Martin's Minotaur); Jan Burke's Frank Harriman (with wife Irene Kelly in a supporting role) in *Flight* (Simon & Schuster); and P. D. James's Adam Dalgliesh in *Death in Holy Orders* (Knopf).

Historicals. Anna Gilbert's *A Morning in Eden* (St. Martin's Minotaur) is a charmingly written piece of post–World War I romantic suspense from one of the genre's overlooked masters. Max Allan Collins's *The Pearl Harbor Murders* (Berkley) made an amateur sleuth of Tarzan creator Edgar Rice Burroughs. Collins's period PI Nate Heller has a look at the Black Dahlia case in the typically well-researched *Angel in Black* (New American Library). Anne Perry turns her attention to the French Revolution era in the novella *A Dish Taken Cold* (Carroll & Graf/Penzler). Historical series sleuths in good form included Perry's Thomas Pitt in *The Whitechapel Conspiracy* (Ballantine); Peter Tremayne's seventh-century Irish Sister Fidelma in *Act of Mercy* (St. Martin's Minotaur); Laura Joh Rowland's seventeenth-century samurai Sano Ichiro in *Black Lotus* (St. Martin's Minotaur); Robin Paige's Victorian Lord Charles Sheridan in *Death at Epsom Downs* (Berkley); and Lindsey Davis's ancient Roman Marcus Didius Falco in *Ode to a Banker* (Mysterious).

Humor and satire. Wisconsin lawyer Michael Bowen departs from his formal detective novels to skewer Hollywood in *Screenscam* (Poisoned Pen). Straddling humor and history was Ron Goulart's *Groucho Marx and the Broadway Murders* (St. Martin's Minotaur).

Thrillers. The pure thriller is not my usual cup of tea, but conspiring to change my mind were Tess Gerritsen's *The Surgeon* (Ballantine) and Gayle Lynds's *Mesmerized* (Pocket). Also impressive was television writer Thomas B. Sawyer's already mentioned *The Sixteenth Man* (iUniverse).

Psychological suspense. Guy Burt's *The Hole* (Ballantine), a brief and effective novel of a group of students imprisoned by a prankster, was first published in Britain in 1993 and written when the author was a mere eighteen. DeLoris Stanton Forbes's *One Man Died on Base* (Five Star) follows the game-time thoughts of an aging baseball slugger in a psychological study that is less whodunit or whydunit than whathappened.

SHORT STORIES

As the volume in your hand tells you, the mystery short story is alive and well. In the United States, the two venerable digests *Ellery Queen's Mystery Magazine* and *Alfred Hitchcock's Mystery Magazine* continue to be the top periodical markets, joined by the slick but infrequent *Mary Higgins Clark's Mystery Magazine* and a variety of on-line and semipro publications.

In Great Britain, a single journal (*Crimewave*) published both the short-story Dagger winner and two of the other four nominees. Editor Andy Cox's ambitions are modest: "*Crimewave*'s mission is nothing less than the total re-creation of crime fiction. We don't do cosy, we don't do hardboiled, we don't do noir . . . what we do is something entirely different to whatever you've read before. People who have never read crime are about to discover a new universe of fiction in which morality is real but fluid, in which story is central but skewed, in which the traditions of the genre are neither dumped nor subverted, but rather viewed through fresh eyes from a new hill. Meanwhile, lifelong crime fans will be reminded why they turned to crime in the first place: for solidly-made, honest-to-life stories that are only the starting point for a new fiction in which writers make a contract with the reader to provide real plots with real conclusions, not mere vignettes—but who then exploit loopholes and sub-clauses to turn your expectations inside out. Self-indulgent arty-fartiness is out, and so is lazy conservatism; craftsmanship is in, as the only platform strong enough to launch illimitable imagination. In short, *Crimewave* is a celebration of what crime fiction can be, when it stops apologizing for itself, censoring itself, limiting itself, feeling sorry for itself. Our writers are in love with crime fiction's history, and fiercely proud of its future. *Crimewave* is published twice a year in an attractive, creatively designed book format, with color matte laminated covers." (Single copies $12; four-issue subscription $40; *www.ttapress.com.*)

Turning to books, a single separately published short, Mark Twain's 1876 story *A Murder, a Mystery, and a Marriage* (Norton), in book form for the first time, was one of the major scholarly events of the year. Also for the permanent library was *The Selected Stories of Patricia Highsmith* (Norton), an omnibus containing five Highsmith collections: *The Animal-Lover's Book of Beastly Murder, Little Tales of Misogyny, Slowly, Slowly in the Wind, The Black House*, and *Mermaids on the Golf Course*.

Thanks mainly to specialist publishers but with some help from the majors, single-author collections continued to come forth at an unprecedented rate. Among the best of the year from Crippen & Landru were Joe Gores's *Stakeout on Page Street and Other DKA Files*; Ross Macdonald's *Strangers in Town: Three Newly Discovered Stories*, edited by Tom Nolan; and Edward D. Hoch's *The Old Spies Club and Other Intrigues of Rand*. Highlights from Five Star included Edward Wellen's *Perps*, Ed Gorman's *Such a Good Girl and Other Crime Stories*, and John Lutz's *The Nudger Dilemmas*. From elsewhere came Frederic Forsyth's *The Veteran* (St. Martin's) and Ruth Rendell's *Piranha to Scurfy and Other Stories* (Crown). Numerical champ was Max Allan Collins, who had one collection from Crippen & Landru (*Kisses of Death: A Nathan Heller Casebook*) and two from Five Star (*Blue Christmas and Other Holiday Homicides* and *Murder—His and Hers*, the latter in collaboration with wife Barbara Collins).

Anthologists of original stories are not running out of fresh ideas. Among the year's themes were baseball (Otto Penzler's *Murderers' Row* [New Millennium]); erotic noir (Max Allan Collins and Jeff Gelb's *Flesh and Blood* [Mysterious]); summertime (Joseph Pittman and Annette Riffle's *And the Dying Is Easy* [Signet]); the American South (Sarah Shankman's *A Confederacy of Crime* [Signet]); the female bar (Carolyn Wheat's *Women Before the Bench* [Berkley]); history (Mike Ashley's *The Mammoth Book of More Historical Whodunnits* [Carroll & Graf]); romance (Martin H. Greenberg and Denise Little's *Murder Most Romantic* [Cumberland] and Carolyn Hart's *Love and Death* [Berkley]); the Irish (Greenberg's *Murder Most Celtic* [Cumberland]); astrology (Anne Perry's *Murder by Horoscope* [Carroll & Graf]); Sherlock Holmes pastiche (Greenberg, Jon Lellenberg, and Daniel Stashower's *Murder in Baker Street* [Carroll & Graf]); Civil War espionage (Ed Gorman's *The Blue and the Gray Undercover* [Forge]); and cats in the courtroom (Gorman, Greenberg, and Larry Segriff's *Murder Most Feline* [Cumberland]).

Other original anthologies included two devoted to the hard-boiled shamus: the Private Eye Writers of America's *Mystery Street* (Signet), edited by Robert J. Randisi, and *Fedora: Private Eyes and Tough Guys* (Wildside), edited by Michael Bracken. A distinguished publishing imprint celebrated a quarter century's existence in *The Mysterious Press Anniversary Anthology*.

Among the notable reprint anthologies were no less than four from the staggeringly prolific (as editor as well as author) Lawrence Block. *Speaking of Lust* and *Speaking of Greed* (Cumberland House) launched an ambitious deadly-sins series in which the reprinted stories in each volume will be accompanied by a new Block novella on the sin in question. Block also offered a second volume of *Opening Shots* (Cumberland House), in which well-known writers introduce their first stories. And he served as guest editor of Penzler's *The Best American Mystery Stories 2001* (Houghton Mifflin).

For the full story on both anthologies and single-author collections, see Edward D. Hoch's bibliography.

REFERENCE BOOKS AND SECONDARY SOURCES

It was, to put it simply, a banner year for books about crime fiction. Two major additions, both edited by Richard Layman with Julie M. Rivett, were made to the shelf of sources on an enigmatic and endlessly fascinating crime-fiction giant: the 650-page *Selected Letters of Dashiell Hammett 1921–1960* (Counterpoint) and Jo Hammett's brief and extensively illustrated *Dashiell Hammett: A Daughter Remembers* (Carroll & Graf). There was also a new collection from the files of Hammett's greatest *Black Mask* colleague: *The Raymond Chandler Papers: Selected Letters and Non-Fiction, 1909–1959* (Atlantic Monthly), edited by Chandler biographers Tom Hiney and Frank McShane and containing some material not included in earlier compilations.

The year saw first-rate examples of both autobiography (Tony Hillerman's *Seldom Disappointed* [HarperCollins]) and biography (James Sallis's *Chester Himes: A Life* [Walker]) of important crime-fiction writers.

Of more specialized interest is John E. Kramer's *Academe in Mystery and Detective Fiction: An Annotated Bibliography* (Scarecrow).

Collectors Press published two lavishly illustrated coffee-table books that also had informative text from their learned authors, Richard A. Lupoff's *The Great American Paperback* (about paperbacks generally but with an inevitable mystery emphasis) and the ubiquitous Max Allan Collins's *The History of Mystery*. Also combining pictorial magnificence with reference value is *The Paperback Covers of Robert McGinnis* (Pond), compiled by Art Scott and Dr. Wallace Maynard with an introduction by Richard S. Prather.

Fans of broadcast crime will find Michael J. Hayde's *My Name's Friday: The Unauthorized but True Story of* Dragnet *and Films of Jack Webb* (Cumberland), a landmark work.

With all these riches at hand, the most notable secondary volume of the year for this reader was *The Anthony Boucher Chronicles: Reviews and Commentary 1942 to 1947*, Volume I: *As Crime Goes By* (Ramble House), a collection edited by Francis M. Nevins of the renowned critic's columns from the *San Francisco Chronicle*.

Again, see Ed Hoch's bibliography for the whole picture.

A SENSE OF HISTORY

Rue Morgue Press's admirable series of revivals continued with Norbert Davis's 1943 novel *The Mouse in the Mountain*, a cult favorite that lives up to its hype. They also relaunched a formidable specialist in Irish gardening mysteries, Sheila Pim, with three novels: *Common or Garden Crime* (1945), *Creeping Venom* (1946), and *A Hive of Suspects* (1952), only the last of which had previously been published in the United States.

Wildside revived two mystery romances (not involving Charlie Chan) by Earl Derr Biggers, *The Agony Column* (1916) and *Fifty Candles* (1926). Primarily a publisher of fantasy and science fiction, Wildside also offers a dozen volumes by Arthur B. Reeve, creator of early-twentieth-century scientific sleuth Craig Kennedy (once hailed as the American Sherlock Holmes), whose adventures often are borderline sf.

The small publisher Ramble House's main purpose in life is to make available in small-format jacketed paperbacks the works of the unique Harry Stephen Keeler, including some not previously published in English (*The White Circle*, with an introduction by Richard Polt) or in any language (*The Six from Nowhere, The Case of the Flying Hands*, and *Report of Vanessa Hewstone*, the latter two written with Hazel Goodwin Keeler and all introduced by Francis M. Nevins). Also in print for the first time, from the science fiction press Advent, was *Have Trenchcoat—Will Travel*, a sixties vintage mystery novel by sf icon E. E. (Doc) Smith.

Ellery Queen, the most frustratingly unavailable of the form's true masters, made a welcome appearance in the three-novel omnibus *The Hollywood Murders* (Four Walls Eight Windows), including *The Devil to Pay* (1938), *The Four of Hearts* (1938), and (the best EQ Tinseltown case) *The Origin of Evil* (1951).

Paperback reprints of Agatha Christie are obviously not headline news, but the novels featuring her major series characters (Poirot, Miss Marple, the Beresfords) are those most frequently offered to the public. St. Martin's launched a line of nonseries Christies including *The Seven Dials Mystery* (1929), with a new introduction by Val McDermid, and (unintroduced but also welcome) the equally obscure *The Man in the Brown Suit* (1924).

The six novels that made Mickey Spillane's reputation were reprinted in *The Mike Hammer Collection* (NAL), two omnibus volumes, with introductions by Max Allan Collins and Lawrence Block. The latter captures Spillane's appeal as well as anyone: the creator of Mike Hammer wrote comic books in prose form.

AT THE MOVIES

The conventional wisdom is that movies generally had a better year financially than artistically, but notable cinematic crime was copious in 2001. Though Robert Altman's *Gosford Hall*, a classical whodunit in the Agatha Christie tradition, came along at the end of the year to great acclaim, most of the year's output was in the film noir or big caper categories.

The one sure bet for classic status was writer-director Christopher

Nolan's *Memento*, based on a story by Jonathan Nolan. Concerning a man, played by Australian chameleon Guy Pearce, whose lack of short-term memory inhibits his detective work, the story is inevitably told backward and may take a couple of viewings to understand completely. It might take even more return trips to figure out David Lynch's controversial black-and-white interface of dreams and reality in Hollywood, *Mulholland Drive*. Also memorable in the dark tradition were three films with great central performances: *Sexy Beast*, a prime piece of Brit Noir containing one of Ben Kingsley's showiest roles since *Gandhi*, directed by Jonathan Glazer from a script by Louis Mellis and David Scinto; *Training Day*, directed by Antoine Fuqua and written by David Ayer, giving the usually heroic Denzel Washington a chance to play a flamboyantly bent cop; and *L.I.E.*, the uncompromising, unforgiving, but unexploitative NC-17-rated study of a pederast superbly played by Brian Cox, written and directed by Michael Cuesta.

In two masterfully structured caper films that sound like but were not Richard Stark adaptations, Robert DeNiro and Gene Hackman played veteran crooks doing one last job in (respectively) *The Score* and *The Heist*. Though the latter film had the distinctive touch of writer-director David Mamet, the former, directed by Frank Oz from a script by Lem Dobbs, Kario Salem, and Scott Marshall Smith, was even more impressive. A third enjoyable caper was Steven Soderbergh's all-star remake of *Ocean's 11*, written by Stephen W. Carpenter and Ted Griffin.

Other good films in a tough year to pick an Edgar slate: the superb Australian film *Lantana*, directed by Ray Lawrence from Andrew Bovell's screenplay; *Spy Game*, an expert return to classical espionage directed by Tony Scott from a script by David Arata and Michael Frost Beckner; and *The Deep End*, written and directed by Scott McGehee and David Siegel from Elisabeth Sanxay Holding's 1947 novel *The Blank Wall*. And I haven't even mentioned *Harry Potter and the Sorcerer's Stone*, which is (among other things) a whodunit.

AWARD WINNERS FOR 2001

Awards continue to proliferate in the crime fiction field. The Edgars and Daggers—juried rather than subject to an all-comers vote and unrestricted by nationality or subgenre—remain the most prestigious prizes, but all the others have their raisons d'être. Awards tied to publishers' contests, those limited to a geographical region smaller than a country, those awarded for works in languages other than English, and those confined to works from a particular periodical have been omitted. Generally, these were awarded in 2001 for material published in 2000.

Edgar Allan Poe Awards

(MYSTERY WRITERS OF AMERICA)

Best novel: Joe R. Lansdale, *The Bottoms* (Mysterious)

Best first novel by an American author: David Liss, *A Conspiracy of Paper* (Random House)

Best original paperback: Mark Graham, *The Black Maria* (Avon)

Best fact crime book: Dick Lehr and Gerard O'Neill, *Black Mass: The Irish Mob, the FBI, and a Devil's Deal* (Public Affairs/Perseus)

Best critical/biographical work: Robert Kuhn McGregor with Ethan Lewis, *Conundrums for the Long Week-End: England, Dorothy L. Sayers, and Lord Peter Wimsey* (Kent State University Press)

Best short story: Peter Robinson, "Missing in Action" (*Ellery Queen's Mystery Magazine*, November)

Best young adult mystery: Elaine Marie Alphin, *Counterfeit Son* (Harcourt)

Best children's mystery: Frances O'Rourk Dowell, *Dovey Coe* (Atheneum)

Best episode in a television series: Michael Perry, "Limitations" (*Law & Order*, NBC)

Best television feature or miniseries: Michael Chaplin, *Dalziel & Pascoe: On Beulah Height*, based on the novel by Reginald Hill (A&E)

Best motion picture: Stephen Gahgen (based on the original miniseries, *Traffik*, by Simon Moore), *Traffic*

Grand master: Edward D. Hoch

Robert L. Fish Award (best first story): M. J. Jones, "The Witch and the Relic Thief" (*Alfred Hitchcock's Mystery Magazine*, October)

Ellery Queen Award: Douglas G. Greene

Raven: Barbara Peters; Tom and Enid Schantz

Mary Higgins Clark Award: Barbara D'Amato, *Authorized Personnel Only* (Forge)

Special Edgar: Mildred Wirt Benson

Agatha Awards

(MALICE DOMESTIC MYSTERY CONVENTION)

Best novel: Margaret Maron, *Storm Track* (Mysterious)

Best first novel: Rosemary Stevens, *Death on a Silver Tray* (Berkley)

Best short story: Jan Burke, "The Man in the Civil Suit" (*Malice Domestic 9* [Avon])

Best nonfiction: Jim Huang, ed., *100 Favorite Mysteries of the Century* (Crum Creek)

Lifetime Achievement Award: Mildred Wirt Benson

Anthony Awards

(BOUCHERCON WORLD MYSTERY CONVENTION)

Best novel: Val McDermid, *A Place of Execution* (St. Martin's)

Best first novel: Qiu Xiaoling, *Death of a Red Heroine* (Soho)

Best paperback original: Kate Grilley, *Death Dances to a Reggae Beat* (Berkley)

Best short story: Edward D. Hoch, "The Problem of the Potting Shed" (*Ellery Queen's Mystery Magazine*, July)

Best critical/biographical: Jim Huang, ed., *100 Favorite Mysteries of the Century* (Crum Creek Press)

Best anthology/short story collection: Lawrence Block, ed., *Master's Choice 2* (Berkley)

Best fan publication: *Mystery News*, Chris Aldrich and Lyn Kaczmarek, publishers

Lifetime Achievement: Edward D. Hoch

Shamus Awards

(PRIVATE EYE WRITERS OF AMERICA)

Best novel: Carolina Garcia-Aguilera, *Havana Heat* (HarperCollins)

Best first novel: Bob Truluck, *Street Level* (St. Martin's)

Best original paperback novel: Thomas Lipinski, *Death in the Steel City* (Avon)

Best short story: Brendan DuBois, "The Road's End" (*Ellery Queen's Mystery Magazine*, April)

Dagger Awards

(CRIME WRITERS' ASSOCIATION, GREAT BRITAIN)

Gold Dagger: Henning Mankell, *Sidetracked*, translated from the Swedish by Steven T. Murray (Harvill)

Silver Dagger: Giles Blunt, *Forty Words for Sorrow* (HarperCollins)

John Creasey Award (best first novel): Susanna Jones, *The Earthquake Bird* (Picador)

Best short story: Marion Arnott, "Prussian Snowdrops" (*Crimewave 4*)

Best nonfiction: Philip Etienne and Martin Maynard with Tony Thompson, *The Infiltrators* (Michael Joseph)

Diamond Dagger: Lionel Davidson

Ellis Peters Historical Dagger: Andrew Taylor, *The Office of the Dead* (HarperCollins)

Debut Dagger (for unpublished writers): Edward Wright, *Clea's Moon*

Macavity Awards

(MYSTERY READERS INTERNATIONAL)

Best novel: Val McDermid, *A Place of Execution* (St. Martin's)
Best first novel: David Liss, *A Conspiracy of Paper* (Random House)
Best critical/biographical work: Marvin Lachman, *The American Regional Mystery* (Crossover)
Best short story: Reginald Hill, "A Candle for Christmas" (*Ellery Queen's Mystery Magazine*, January)

Arthur Ellis Awards

(CRIME WRITERS OF CANADA)

Best novel: Peter Robinson, *Cold Is the Grave* (Penguin Canada)
Best first novel: Mark Zuehlke, *Hands Like Clouds* (Dundurn Group)
Best true crime: A. B. McKillop, *The Spinster and the Prophet* (Macfarlane Walter & Ross)
Best juvenile novel: Tim Wynne-Jones, *The Boy in the Burning House* (Groundwood)
Best short story: Peter Robinson, "Murder in Utopia" (*Crime Through Time III* [Berkley])
Best crime writing in French: Norbert Spehner, *Le roman policier en Amérique française* (Alire)
Derrick Murdoch Award for Lifetime Achievement: L. R. Wright

Ned Kelly Awards

(CRIME WRITERS' ASSOCIATION OF AUSTRALIA)

Best novel: (tie) Peter Temple, *Dead Point*; Andrew Masterson, *The Second Coming*
Best first novel: Andrew McGahan, *Last Drinks*
Best true crime: Estelle Blackburn, *Broken Lives*
Crime Factory Magazine Readers' Vote: Lindy Cameron, *Bleeding Hearts*
Lifetime achievement: Stephen Knight

Herodotus Awards

(HISTORICAL MYSTERY APPRECIATION SOCIETY)

Best U.S. Historical Mystery: Kris Nelscott (Kristine Kathryn Rusch), *A Dangerous Road* (St. Martin's)
Best International Historical Mystery: Arabella Edge, *The Company: The Story of a Murderer* (Australia, Pan Macmillan)

Best First U.S. Historical Mystery: Joe R. Lansdale, *The Bottoms* (Mysterious)

Best First International Historical Mystery: Betsy Tobin, *Bone House* (U.K., Headline)

Best Short Story Historical Mystery: Charles Todd, "The Man Who Never Was" (*Malice Domestic 9* [Avon])

Lifetime Achievement Award: Lindsey Davis

Barry Awards

(*DEADLY PLEASURES* MAGAZINE)

Best novel: Nevada Barr, *Deep South* (Putnam)

Best first novel: David Liss, *A Conspiracy of Paper* (Random House)

Best British novel: Stephen Booth, *Black Dog* (HarperCollins)

Best paperback original: Eric Wright, *The Kidnapping of Rosie Dawn* (Perseverance Press)

Don Sandstrom Memorial Award for Lifetime Achievement in Mystery Fandom: Marv Lachman

Nero Wolfe Award

(WOLFE PACK)

Laura Lippman, *The Sugar House* (Morrow)

Dilys Award

(INDEPENDENT MYSTERY BOOKSELLERS ASSOCIATION)

Val McDermid, *A Place of Execution* (St. Martin's)

Hammett Prize

(INTERNATIONAL CRIME WRITERS)

Margaret Atwood, *The Blind Assassin* (Doubleday/McClelland & Stewart)

NOTE: The following awards, given in 2000 for works published in 1999, were inadvertently omitted from the Second Annual Collection:

Edgar Allan Poe Awards

(MYSTERY WRITERS OF AMERICA)

Best novel: Jan Burke, *Bones* (Simon & Schuster)

Best first novel by an American author: Eliot Pattison, *The Skull Mantra* (St. Martin's Minotaur)

Best original paperback: Ruth Birmingham, *Fulton County Blues* (Berkley Prime Crime)

Best fact crime book: James B. Stewart, *Blind Eye* (Simon & Schuster)

Best critical/biographical work: Daniel Stashower, *Teller of Tales: The Life of Arthur Conan Doyle* (Henry Holt)

Best short story: Anne Perry, "Heroes" (*Murder and Obsession* [Delacorte])

Best young adult mystery: Vivian Vande Velde, *Never Trust a Dead Man* (Harcourt Brace)

Best children's mystery: Elizabeth McDavid Jones, *The Night Flyers* (Pleasant Company)

Best episode in a television series: Rene Balcer, "Refuge, Part 2" (*Law & Order*, NBC)

Best television feature or miniseries: Steven Schachter & William H. Macy, *A Slight Case of Murder*, based on a novel by Donald E. Westlake (TNT)

Best motion picture: Guy Ritchie, *Lock, Stock and Two Smoking Barrels* (Polygram)

Best play: Joe Di Pietro, *The Art of Murder*. Produced by Jonathan Pollard, George W. George & James N. Vagias.

Grand master: Mary Higgins Clark

Robert L. Fish Award (best first story): Mike Reiss, "Cro-Magnon, P.I." (*AHMM* July–August 1999)

Ellery Queen Award: Susanne Kirk

Raven: The Mercantile Library, Director: Harold Augenbraum

Shamus Awards

(PRIVATE EYE WRITERS OF AMERICA)

Best novel: Don Winslow, *California Fire and Life* (Knopf)

Best first novel: John Connolly, *Every Dead Thing* (Simon & Schuster)

Best original paperback novel: Laura Lippman, *In Big Trouble* (Avon)

Best short story: I. J. Parker, "Akitada's First Case" (*AHMM*, July/August 1999)

Lifetime achievement: Edward D. Hoch

Dagger Awards

(CRIME WRITERS' ASSOCIATION, GREAT BRITAIN)

Gold Dagger: Jonathan Lethem, *Motherless Brooklyn* (Faber & Faber)

Silver Dagger: Donna Leon, *Friends in High Places* (Heinemann)

John Creasey Award (best first novel): Boston Teran, *God Is a Bullet* (Macmillan)

Best short story: Denise Mina, "Helena and the Babies" (*Fresh Blood 3* [Do-Not])

Best nonfiction: Edward Bunker, *Mr. Blue* (No Exit)

Diamond Dagger: Peter Lovesey

Ellis Peters Historical Dagger: Gillian Linscott, *Absent Friends* (Virago)

Herodotus Awards

(HISTORICAL MYSTERY APPRECIATION SOCIETY)

Best U.S. Historical Mystery: Steven Saylor, *Rubicon* (St. Martin's)

Best International Historical Mystery: Gillian Linscott, *Absent Friends* (Virago)

Best First U.S. Historical Mystery: Owen Parry, *Faded Coat of Blue* (Avon)

Best First International Historical Mystery: Clare Curzon, *Guilty Knowledge* (Virago)

Best Short Story Historical Mystery: Margaret Frazer, "Neither Pity, Love nor Fear" (*Royal Whodunnits* [Robinson])

Lifetime Achievement Award: Paul Doherty (a.k.a. Anna Apostolou, Michael Clynes, P. C. Doherty, Ann Dukthas, C. L. Grace, and Paul Harding)

Nero Wolfe Award

(WOLFE PACK)

Fred Harris, *Coyote Revenge* (HarperCollins)

Dilys Award

(INDEPENDENT MYSTERY BOOKSELLERS ASSOCIATION)

Robert Crais, *L.A. Requiem* (Doubleday)

Hammett Prize

(INTERNATIONAL CRIME WRITERS)

Martin Cruz Smith, *Havana Bay* (Random House)

A 2001 Yearbook of Crime and Mystery

Compiled by *Edward D. Hoch*

Collections and Single Stories

BLOCK, LAWRENCE. *Death Pulls a Doublecross*. Norfolk, VA: Crippen & Landru. First separate edition of a story that became chapter one of Block's 1961 paperback of the same title, included as a pamphlet with the limited edition of *The Lost Cases of Ed London*.

————. *The Lost Cases of Ed London*. Norfolk, VA: Crippen & Landru. A limited edition of three novelettes from *Man's Magazine*, 1962–63.

BLYTHE, HAL, & CHARLIE SWEET. *Bloody Ground: Stories of Mystery and Intrigue from Kentucky*. Ashland, KY: Jesse Stuart Foundation. Kentucky mysteries from various sources.

BROWN, FREDRIC. *From These Ashes: The Complete Short SF of Fredric Brown*. Framingham, MA: The NESFA Press. One hundred eleven stories, several criminous, five from *Ellery Queen's Mystery Magazine*. Edited by Ben Yalow.

BURKE, THOMAS. *The Golden Gong and Other Night-Pieces*. Ashcroft, BC, Canada: Ash-Tree Press. Twenty stories, Burke's complete weird tales, including the mystery classic "The Hands of Mr. Ottermole."

CANNELL, DOROTHY. *The Family Jewels and Other Stories*. Waterville, ME: Five Star. Eleven stories from various sources, 1989–98. Introduction by Joan Hess.

CARMICHAEL, MONTGOMERY. *On the Threshold of the Chamber of Horrors*. New York: The Mysterious Bookshop. The first separate edition of a brief Sherlockian parody published in an 1894 issue of *The Illustrated Sporting and Dramatic News*.

CISLER, DAVID N. *The Adventure of the Wish Hounds of Candlemere*. New York: The Mysterious Bookshop. A new thirty two-page Sherlockian pastiche.

COEL, MARGARET. *The Woman Who Climbed to the Sky*. Clarkston, MI, & Mission Viejo, CA: A.S.A.P. Publishing. A single new short story in the author's Arapaho Ten Commandments series. Introduction by Tony Hillerman.

COLLINS, BARBARA, & MAX ALLAN COLLINS. *Murder—His and Hers*. Waterville, ME: Five Star. Nine stories from various sources, 1992–2000, four by Barbara, three by Max, and two collaborations.

COLLINS, MAX ALLAN. *Blue Christmas and Other Holiday Homicides*. Waterville, ME: Five Star. Six holiday mysteries from various anthologies, 1994–2001, three featuring private eye Richard Stone.

————. *Kisses of Death: A Nathan Heller Casebook*. Norfolk, VA: Crippen & Landru. A new novelette and six stories, 1988–2001. (The limited clothbound edition also contains a separate gathering of *Heaven and Heller*, a comic strip by Collins and Ray Gotto.)

CRIDER, BILL. *The Nighttime Is the Right Time: A Collection of Stories*. Waterville, ME: Five Star. Eleven stories, 1991–98, from various sources.

DAVIS, DOROTHY SALISBURY. *In the Still of the Night: Tales to Lock Your Doors By.* Waterville, ME: Five Star. Eight stories from various sources, 1986–98.

DUNLAP, SUSAN. *A Tail of Two Cities.* Norfolk, VA: Crippen & Landru. A new Jill Smith story in a thirteen-page pamphlet included with the limited edition of *The Celestial Buffet.*

———. *The Celestial Buffet and Other Morsels of Murder.* Norfolk, VA: Crippen & Landru. Seventeen stories from various sources, 1978–99, one in its first American publication, a few fantasy. Included are four stories about Jill Smith, two about the Celestial Detective, and one about Kiernan O'Shaughnessy.

EDWARDS, MARTIN. *Where Do You Find Your Ideas?* Chichester England: Countryvise. Twenty-seven short stories, two new, 1991–2001, eight about Harry Devlin. Introduction by Reginald Hill.

ELLISON, HARLAN. *The Essential Ellison: A 50-Year Retrospective.* Beverly Hills, CA: Morpheus International. Eighty-four stories and essays, mainly fantasy but some criminous, including Ellison's two MWA Edgar-winning short stories. Edited by Terry Dowling, with Richard Delap & Gil Lamont.

FORSYTH, FREDERICK. *The Veteran.* New York: St. Martin's. Five new stories and novelettes, most criminous.

GEORGE, ELIZABETH. *Remember, I'll Always Love You.* Clarkston, MI, & Mission Viejo, CA: A.S.A.P. Publishing. A single new novelette in a limited edition. Introduction by Jeffery Deaver.

GORMAN, ED. *Such a Good Girl and Other Crime Stories.* Waterville, ME: Five Star. Eleven stories, four new, 1993–2000.

GOULART, RON. *Adam and Eve on a Raft.* Norfolk, VA: Crippen & Landru. Twelve stories mainly from *EQMM*, five about Scrib Merlin and seven about an unnamed California ad man. With a checklist of the author's mystery novels and short stories.

———. *The Great Impersonation.* Norfolk, VA: Crippen & Landru. A new short story in a pamphlet accompanying the limited edition of *Adam and Eve on a Raft.*

HAMMETT, DASHIELL. *Crime Stories and Other Writings.* New York: The Library of America. Twenty-four stories and novelettes, 1923–34, together with an early typescript of *The Thin Man* and two essays.

HANSEN, JOSEPH. *Blood, Snow, & Classic Cars.* San Francisco: Leyland Publications. A new novella and five stories, two about Hack Bohannon and one each about Lt. Ben Shattuck and Dave Brandstetter.

HENSLEY, JOE L. *Deadly Hunger and Other Tales.* Waterville, ME: Five Star. Eighteen stories, two new, from various sources.

HIGHSMITH, PATRICIA. *The Selected Stories of Patricia Highsmith.* New York: Norton. Sixty-four stories from five previous collections. Foreword by Graham Greene.

HOCH, EDWARD D. *Assignment: Enigma.* Norfolk, VA: Crippen & Landru. A single short story in a pamphlet accompanying the limited edition of *The Old Spies Club,* first published in *EQMM,* 9/10/80, as by "Anthony Circus."

———. *Bouchercon Bound.* Norfolk, VA: Crippen & Landru. A single new short story in a pamphlet distributed to those attending the 2001 Bouchercon in Washington, DC.

————. *The Night People and Other Stories.* Waterville, ME: Five Star. Twenty non-series stories from various sources, 1957–79, one in its first American publication.

————. *The Old Spies Club and Other Intrigues of Rand.* Norfolk, VA: Crippen & Landru. Fifteen stories about Jeffery Rand and his wife, Leila, from *EQMM*, 1971–99.

HORNUNG, E. W. *The A. J. Raffles Omnibus.* Ontario, Canada: Battered Silicon Dispatch Box. All three Raffles collections, plus the short novel *Mr. Justice Raffles* and the drama *Raffles: The Amateur Cracksman.*

JAKES, JOHN. *Crime Time: Mystery and Suspense Stories.* Waterville, ME: Five Star. Twelve stories, 1952–96, one each about series characters Johnny Havoc and Roger, and two about Uncle Pinkerton. Some fantasy. Introduction by Ed McBain.

KURLAND, MICHAEL. *The Infernal Device & Others: A Professor Moriarty Omnibus.* New York: St. Martin's. Reprints of two novels plus a new Moriarty short story.

L'AMOUR, LOUIS. *Off the Mangrove Coast.* New York: Bantam. Nine stories from the 1920s through the 1940s, some criminous, one private eye. Afterword by Beau L'Amour, the author's son.

LEE, WENDI. *Check Up and Other Stories.* Waterville, ME: Five Star. Fourteen stories, one new, 1993–2001, including four about private eye Angela Matelli and three about western sleuth Jefferson Birch.

LEWIN, MICHAEL Z. *The Reluctant Detective and Other Stories.* Norfolk, VA: Crippen & Landru. Twenty-one stories, 1981–2001, one new and some in their first American publication, with a checklist of the author's mystery novels and stories. The limited edition includes a photocopy of notes by the author.

LOVESEY, PETER. *The Butler Didn't Do It.* Norfolk, VA: Crippen & Landru. A single brief puzzle mystery from *The Observer,* 1986, in a pamphlet accompanying the limited edition of *The Sedgemoor Strangler.*

————. *The Sedgemoor Strangler and Other Stories of Crime.* Norfolk, VA: Crippen & Landru. Sixteen stories from various sources, 1998–2001, one new and one in its first U.S. publication.

LUPOFF, RICHARD A. *Claremont Tales.* Urbana, IL: Golden Gryphon. A mixed collection containing two detective stories.

LUTZ, JOHN. *The Nudger Dilemmas.* Waterville, ME: Five Star. Thirteen stories about private eye Alo Nudger, 1978–2000, seven from *Alfred Hitchcock's Mystery Magazine* including Lutz's MWA Edgar winner, "Ride the Lightning."

MACDONALD, ROSS. *Strangers in Town: Three Newly Discovered Mysteries.* Norfolk, VA: Crippen & Landru. An early private eye story and two novelettes featuring Lew Archer, all published for the first time. Edited with an introduction by Tom Nolan. (The limited edition contains a separately bound five-page fragment, "Winnipeg, 1929.")

MATTHEWS, CHRISTINE. *Gentle Insanities and Other States of Mind.* Waterville, ME: Five Star. Fourteen stories from various anthologies, 1992–2000. Foreword by John Lutz.

McBAIN, ED. *McBain Duet: Driving Lessons & Petals. Two Novellas.* Garden City, NY: Mystery Guild. A previously published novella together with a spy novella published for the first time.

MEREDITH, D. R. *A Woman's Place and Other Mysterious Tales*. Waterville, ME: Five Star. Eight stories from various anthologies, 1992–99.

MORTIMER, JOHN. *Rumpole Rests His Case: A Book of Rumpole Stories*. London: Viking. Six new novelettes.

MULLER, MARCIA, & BILL PRONZINI. *Season of Sharing*. Norfolk, VA: Crippen & Landru. A new story about Sharon McCone and the Nameless Detective, in a pamphlet as a holiday gift to the publisher's regular customers.

NEVINS, FRANCIS M. *Night of Silken Snow and Other Stories*. Waterville, Maine: Five Star. Ten stories, two new, including three each about Loren Mensing and Gene Holt, and four about Milo Turner, 1976–2001.

NOLAN, WILLIAM F. *Dark Universe: A Grandmaster of Suspense Collects His Best Stories*. Lancaster, PA: Stealth Press. More than forty horror, SF, and suspense stories published during the past fifty years.

OATES, JOYCE CAROL. *Faithless: Tales of Transgression*. New York: Ecco Press/HarperCollins. Twenty-one stories, one new, many criminous.

O'CALLAGHAN, MAXINE. *Deal with the Devil and Other Stories*. Waterville, ME: Five Star. Fourteen stories, two new, five about Delilah West and two about Emma Hartley.

PERRY, ANNE. *My Object All Sublime*. New York: Mysterious Bookshop. A new short story in a pamphlet as a holiday gift to customers of a Manhattan bookshop.

PRONZINI, BILL. *More Oddments: A Short Story Collection*. Waterville, ME: Five Star. Fourteen stories, 1967–2001, one about the Nameless Detective and two written in collaboration with, respectively, Michael Kurland and Barry Malzberg.

QUILL, MONICA. *Death Takes the Veil and Other Stories*. Waterville, ME: Five Star. Four novelettes about Sister Mary Teresa plus three nonseries stories, 1988–97, mainly from *EQMM*. Introduction by the author under his real name of Ralph McInerny.

RANDISI, ROBERT J. *Delvecchio's Brooklyn: A Short Story Collection*. Waterville, ME: Five Star. Nine private eye stories, 1985–99. Introduction by Max Allan Collins.

RUBINO, JANE. *Knight Errant: The Singular Adventures of Sherlock Holmes*. Ashcroft, BC: Calabash. Three pastiche novellas.

RUSCH, KRISTINE KATHRYN. *Little Miracles and Other Tales of Murder*. Waterville, ME: Five Star. Seven stories from various sources, 1992–2000.

SPARK, MURIEL. *The Complete Short Stories*. London: Penguin/Viking. Forty-one stories, some criminous, four previously uncollected.

SPILLANE, MICKEY. *Together We Kill: The Uncollected Stories of Mickey Spillane*. Waterville, ME: Five Star. Eight stories and novelettes, 1952–98, one about Mike Hammer. Introduction by Max Allan Collins.

STOUT, REX. *By His Own Hand*. Norfolk, VA: Crippen & Landru. First separate edition of an Alphabet Hicks story from *Manhunt* (4/55), in a pamphlet distributed at the Malice Domestic fan convention.

THOMAS, FRANK. *Sherlock Holmes Mystery Tales*. Brooklyn: Gryphon Books. Thirteen new Sherlockian pastiches.

TWAIN, MARK. *A Murder, a Mystery, and a Marriage*. New York: Norton. A single novelette, written in 1876 but unpublished until now. Afterword by Roy Blount, Jr.

WELLEN, EDWARD. *Perps*. Waterville, Maine: Five Star. Twenty-six stories, two new, some fantasy, mainly from *EQMM* and *AHMM*.

WILLIAMS, DAVID. *Criminal Intentions*. London: Robert Hale. Fifteen stories, eight from EQMM, seven from various anthologies.

Anthologies

ASHLEY, MIKE, ed. *The Mammoth Book of More Historical Whodunnits*. New York: Carroll & Graf. Twenty-two new stories.

BARR, NEVADA, presented by. *Malice Domestic 10*. New York: Avon. Fourteen new stories in an annual anthology.

BISHOP, CLAUDIA, & NICK DiCHARIO, eds. *Death Dines at 8:30*. New York: Berkley. Sixteen stories with food themes, all but one new.

BLOCK, LAWRENCE, ed. *Opening Shots, Volume Two: More Great Mystery and Crime Writers Share Their First Published Stories*. Nashville: Cumberland House Publishing. Twenty-four stories, 1953–2001, with a brief introduction by each author.

———, ed. *Speaking of Greed: Stories of Envious Desire*. Nashville: Cumberland House Publishing. Nineteen stories (one a fantasy) from various sources, plus a new novella by the editor.

———, ed. *Speaking of Lust: Stories of Forbidden Desire*. Nashville: Cumberland House Publishing. Eighteen stories from various sources, plus a new novella by the editor.

Blood, Threat & Fears: Four Tales of Mystery and Suspense. Brighton, MI: Avid Press. Four new novelettes and novellas by various authors.

BOSWELL, JOAN, & SUE PIKE, eds. *Fit to Die*. Toronto: RendezVous. Twenty-five new mysteries about sports, fitness, and games by Canadian members of the Ladies' Killing Circle.

BRACKEN, MICHAEL, ed. *Fedora: Private Eyes and Tough Guys*. Doylestown, PA: Wildside Press. Fourteen new stories.

BROWNE, D. L., & KEVIN BURTON SMITH, eds. *Down These Wicked Streets: Seven Tales of Original Detective Fiction*. Wicked Company Writers Community. Seven stories, five new, from a website community crimewriters' group.

COLLINS, MAX ALLAN, & JEFF GELB, eds. *Flesh and Blood: Erotic Tales of Crime and Passion*. New York: Mysterious Press. Eighteen stories, all but one new.

DEAVER, JEFFERY, ed. *A Century of Great Suspense Stories*. New York: Berkley. Thirty-six stories, 1920–98, from various sources.

EDWARDS, MARTIN, ed. *Murder Squad*. East Fourstones, Hexham, England: Flambard. Thirteen stories, eleven new, by seven members of the "Murder Squad," a group of crime writers from the north of England. Introduction by Val McDermid.

FIRKS, DAVID, ed. *The Best of Blue Murder, Volume 1*. Portland, OR: Blue Murder Press. Twenty-nine stories from past issues of the on-line magazine. Introduction by Kevin Burton Smith.

FREED, SARA ANN, & WILLIAM MALLOY, eds. *The Mysterious Press Anniversary Anthology: Celebrating 25 Years*. New York: Mysterious Press. Eighteen new stories by Mysterious Press authors. Foreword by Otto Penzler.

GORMAN, ED, ed. *The Blue and the Gray Undercover*. New York: Forge. Eighteen new spy stories based on events of the Civil War.

————, ed. *The World's Finest Mystery and Crime Stories: Second Annual Collection.* New York: Forge. Forty-one stories and one essay published during 2000, with reviews of the year by Jon L. Breen, Edward D. Hoch, Maxim Jakubowski, and others.

GORMAN, ED, & MARTIN H. GREENBERG, eds. *Pulp Masters.* New York: Carroll & Graf. Five novelettes and a short novel, 1938–77.

GORMAN, ED, MARTIN H. GREENBERG, & LARRY SEGRIFF, eds. *Murder Most Feline: Cunning Tales of Cats and Crime.* Nashville: Cumberland House Publishing. Sixteen new stories involving cats and courtrooms.

GREENBERG, MARTIN H., ed. *Murder Most Celtic: Tall Tales of Irish Mayhem.* Nashville: Cumberland House Publishing. Sixteen stories, all but two new. Introduction by John Helfers.

————, ed. *Murder Most Postal: Homicidal Tales That Deliver a Message.* Nashville: Cumberland House Publishing. Twenty-one stories from various sources. Introduction by John Helfers.

GREENBERG, MARTIN H., JON L. LELLENBERG, & DANIEL STASHOWER, eds. *Murder in Baker Street: New Tales of Sherlock Holmes.* New York: Carroll & Graf. Eleven new stories, together with three Sherlockian essays.

GREENBERG, MARTIN H., & DENISE LITTLE, eds. *Murder Most Romantic: Passionate Tales of Life and Death.* Nashville: Cumberland House Publishing. Twelve new stories.

HART, CAROLYN, ed. *Love & Death.* New York: Berkley Books. Fourteen new stories of crimes of the heart.

HEMMINGSON, MICHAEL, ed. *The Mammoth Book of Legal Thrillers.* New York: Carroll & Graf. Thirty-nine stories, eighteen new.

JAKUBOWSKI, MAXIM, ed. *The Mammoth Book of Pulp Action.* New York: Carroll & Graf. Twenty-three stories and novelettes, 1929–2001, one new.

KAYE, MARVIN, ed. *The Ultimate Halloween.* New York: ibooks/Simon & Schuster. Eighteen stories, ten new. Mainly fantasy but some mystery.

Murder, Mayhem and Mistletoe. Toronto: Worldwide. Four new stories of intrigue and murder during the holiday season, by various authors.

PENZLER, OTTO, ed. *Murderers' Row: Baseball Mysteries.* Beverly Hills: New Millennium Press. Fourteen new stories in the first of a series of sports mystery anthologies. Foreword by Jim Bouton.

————. *Murder on the Ropes: Boxing Mysteries.* Beverly Hills: New Millennium Press. Fourteen new stories in the second of a series.

PERRY, ANNE ed. *Death by Horoscope.* New York: Carroll & Graf. Sixteen new astrological mysteries.

PITTMAN, JOSEPH, & ANNETTE RIFFLE, eds. *And the Dying Is Easy: All-New Tales of Summertime Suspense.* New York: Signet. Twenty new stories.

RANDISI, ROBERT J., ed. *Mystery Street: The 20th Anniversary PWA Anthology.* New York: Signet. Fourteen new stories from the Private Eye Writers of America. Introduction by Robert Crais.

RAPHAEL, LAWRENCE W., ed. *Criminal Kabbalah: An Intriguing Anthology of Jewish Mystery & Detective Fiction.* Woodstock, VT: Jewish Lights Publishing. Twelve new stories. Foreword by Laurie B. King.

SCHOOLEY, KERRY J., & PETER SELLERS, eds. *Iced: The New Noir Anthology of Cold, Hard Fiction.* Toronto: Insomniac Press. Sixteen stories by Canadian writers, 1984–2001, five new.

SHANKMAN, SARAH, ed. *A Confederacy of Crime: New Stories of Southern-Style Mystery.* New York: Signet. Twelve new stories.

STAUDOHAR, PAUL D., ed. *Sports Best Short Stories.* Chicago: Chicago Review Press. Twenty-four stories including a few classic mysteries by Conan Doyle, Ellery Queen, and Leslie Charteris.

STEPHENS, JOHN RICHARD, ed. *Into the Mummy's Tomb.* New York: Berkley. Eighteen stories by well-known writers of the past two centuries, about Egyptian tombs and mummies as seen in fantasy, nonfiction, and detective stories.

VAN THAL, HERBERT, ed. *The Mammoth Book of Great Detective Stories.* New York: Carroll & Graf. Thirty-five stories assembled from the first four of the editor's five-volume series *The Bedside Book of Great Detective Stories,* published in England 1976–81.

WHEAT, CAROLYN, ed. *Women Before the Bench.* New York: Berkley Books. Thirteen new stories of women in the courtroom. Introduction by Linda Fairstein.

Nonfiction

BOUCHER, ANTHONY. *The Anthony Boucher Chronicles. Volume One: As Crime Goes By. Reviews and Commentary 1942–1947.* Shreveport, LA: Ramble House/J&F Publishing. First of three volumes collecting Boucher's book review columns from the *San Francisco Chronicle.* Edited with an introduction by Francis M. Nevins.

COLLINS, MAX ALLAN. *The History of Mystery.* Portland, OR: Collectors Press. A history of detective fiction from its beginnings to the present, illustrated with nearly four hundred book and magazine covers, comic strips, and movie posters.

DERIE, KATE, ed. *The Deadly Directory 2002.* Tucson, AZ: Deadly Serious Press. Information on over 750 mystery-related businesses and organizations.

DOYLE, SIR ARTHUR CONAN. *The True Crime Files of Sir Arthur Conan Doyle.* New York: Berkley. Doyle's accounts of his involvement in two actual crime cases. Edited by Stephen Hines, introduction by Steven Womack.

GILBAR, STEVEN, ed. *L.A. Noir.* Chico, CA: Positive Press. Photographs of Los Angeles scenes, accompanied by brief excerpts from well-known noir novels.

HAINING, PETER. *The Classic Era of American Pulp Magazines.* Chicago: Chicago Review Press. A history, illustrated with hundreds of cover reproductions.

HAMMETT, DASHIELL. *Selected Letters of Dashiell Hammett 1921–1960.* Washington: Counterpoint. Hundreds of letters covering every aspect of Hammett's adult life. Edited by Richard Layman with Julie M. Rivett, introduction by Josephine Hammett Marshall.

HAMMETT, JO. *Dashiell Hammett: A Daughter Remembers.* New York: Carroll & Graf. A biography of Hammett by his daughter. Edited by Richard Layman & Julie M. Rivett.

HAYDEN, G. MIKI. *Writing the Mystery: a Start-to-Finish Guide for Both Novice and Professional.* Philadelphia: Intrigue. Includes interviews with six mystery authors.

HILLERMAN, TONY. *Seldom Disappointed: A Memoir.* New York: HarperCollins. A memoir by the creator of Joe Leaphorn and Jim Chee.

HUANG, JIM, ed. *100 Favorite Mysteries of the Century*. Carmel, IN: Crum Creek Press. A listing, selected by the Independent Mystery Booksellers Association, with comments on each book and additions suggested by booksellers and fans.

LUPOFF, RICHARD A. *The Great American Paperback: An Illustrated Tribute to Legends of the Book*. Portland, OR: Collectors Press. A history of the paperback book with over six hundred full-color cover reproductions, mainly of mystery and crime novels.

MARKS, JEFFREY. *Who Was That Lady? Craig Rice: The Queen of Screwball Mystery*. Lee's Summit, MO: Delphi Books. A biography of the mystery writer, with a checklist of her novels and short stories.

MCCALL, HENRIETTA. *The Life of Max Mallowan: Archaeology and Agatha Christie*. London: British Museum Press. The first full-length biography of Christie's husband.

PENZLER, OTTO. *Clayton Rawson*. New York: The Mysterious Bookshop. One of a series of pamphlets on collecting mystery fiction, containing a descriptive bibliography and price guide.

———. *John P. Marquand's Mr. Moto*. New York: The Mysterious Bookshop. A descriptive bibliography and price guide for collectors.

ROWLAND, SUSAN. *From Agatha Christie to Ruth Rendell: British Women Writers in Detective and Crime Fiction*. New York: St. Martin's. Studies of Christie, Sayers, Allingham, Marsh, James, and Rendell.

SAYERS, DOROTHY L. *Sayers on Holmes*. Minnetonka, MN: Mythopoeic Press. Five Sherlockian essays by Sayers together with a previously unpublished radio script in which Holmes and Lord Peter Wimsey are brought together. Introduction by Alzina Stone Dale.

SCOTT, ART, & DR. WALLACE MAYNARD. *The Paperback Covers of Robert McGinnis*. Boston, MA: Pond Press. A complete listing of the artist's 1,068 paperback cover paintings, with 380 color illustrations, original art, model photos, and preliminary sketches. Foreword by Richard S. Prather.

THOMSON, JUNE. *Holmes and Watson*. New York: Carroll & Graf. A study of Conan Doyle's fictional creations and speculation about their lives.

TRUMPLER, CHARLOTTE, ed. *Agatha Christie and the Orient*. London: British Museum Press. A survey of the author's life and work with its connections to the Middle East.

VAN DE WETERING, JANWILLEM. *Afterzen*. New York: St. Martin's. Meditations on Zen Buddhism combined with autobiographical writing.

Obituaries

DOUGLAS ADAMS (1952–2001). British science fiction author of two futuristic novels about sleuth Dirk Gently, notably *Dirk Gently's Holistic Detective Agency* (1987).

POUL ANDERSON (1926–2001). Well-known science fiction writer who also wrote four mystery novels, 1959–62, as well as several criminous short stories including a Sherlockian pastiche and a science fiction locked-room mystery, "The Martian Crown Jewels."

JACQUELINE T. BABBIN (1921–2001). TV producer who authored two mystery novels with soap opera backgrounds, 1972–89.

PHIL BERGER (1942–2001). Sportswriter who published a single mystery novel, *Deadly Kisses* (1984).

TERENCE CARROLL (19??–2001). British TV reporter who published one crime novel, *Copy Boy* (1962).

BETTY CAVANNA (1909–2001). Author of more than eighty romances and mysteries for teenagers, including two nominated for MWA's Juvenile Edgar Award, in 1970 and 1972.

R(ONALD) CHETWYND-HAYES (1919–2001). British author of more than a dozen novels and two hundred short stories, mainly fantasy but with strong mystery elements as in *Tales from the Haunted House* (1986) and *The Psychic Detective* (1993).

PATRICK COSGRAVE (1941–2001). British author of three novels featuring Colonel Allen Cheyney, 1977–86.

TOM CULLEN (1913–2001). American-born British author of true crime books, including volumes on Jack the Ripper and Crippen.

DAN CUSHMAN (1909–2001). Mainstream writer who began his career with ten adventure-suspense paperbacks, 1951–63.

DAGMAR, stage name of VIRGINIA RUTH EGNOR (1924–2001), who published two spy novels in 1967, both ghost-written by Lou Cameron.

NORA DELOACH (1940–2001). Author of six novels about an African-American mother-daughter sleuthing team, starting with *Mama Solves a Murder* (1994).

KAY DICK (1915–2001). British author and editor who published two suspense novels, 1979–80, under the name of "Jeremy Scott."

GORDON R. DICKSON (1923–2001). Well-known science fiction author who co-wrote a short Sherlockian pastiche, "The Adventure of the Misplaced Hound" (1957), with Poul Anderson.

SOPHIE DUNBAR (1946?–2001). Pseudonym of Gwen Markman, author of six novels, the first five about New Orleans beauty salon owner Claire Claiborne, starting with *Behind Éclair's Doors* (1993).

DOROTHY DUNNETT (1923–2001). Scottish historical novelist whose work included seven suspense novels starting with *Dolly and the Singing Bird* (1968), first published in England as by "Dorothy Halliday."

JULIUS EPSTEIN (1909–2000). Screenwriter and co-author of *Casablanca*, the script of which was published in 1973.

ANDREW GARVE (1908–2001). Best-known pseudonym of British author Paul Winterton, who also wrote as "Roger Bax" and "Paul Somers." A founding member of the Crime Writers Association, he published thirty novels as Garve, notably *No Tears for Hilda*, *Fontego's Folly* (both 1950), *Murder Through the Looking Glass* (1952), *Death and the Sky Above* (1954), and *The Far Sands* (1960), as well as another ten as Bax or Somers.

ANNE GEORGE (19??–2001). Former Alabama State Poet who published five novels about sister sleuths Mary Alice Crane and Patricia Anne Hollowell, starting with the Agatha winner *Murder on a Girls' Night Out* (1996).

RUTH GOETZ (1912–2001). Co-author with her husband August of a three-act suspense play, *The Hidden River* (1957).

Rick Hanson (19??–2001). Author of four mysteries featuring ex-cop Adam McCleet, starting with *Spare Parts* (1994).

Hugh Holton (1946–2001). Chicago police commander who published ten novels about police commander Larry Cole, starting with *Presumed Dead* (1994).

Fred Hoyle (1915–2001). Well-known astrophysicist and science fiction writer whose work included two suspense novels, *Ossian's Ride* (1959) and *The Westminster Disaster* (1978), the latter written with his son Geoffrey.

E. Richard Johnson (1938–1997). Winner of the MWA Edgar Award for his first novel, *Silver Street* (1968), written in prison, followed by ten other novels (1969–90) largely written during his prison years. His death in 1997 went unreported until recently.

William Jovanovich (1920–2001). Well-known publisher who wrote a single suspense novel, *The Money Trail* (1990).

William X. Kienzle (1928–2001). Former priest who wrote nearly two dozen novels about Father Robert Koesler, beginning with *The Rosary Murders* (1979).

Derek Lambert (1929–2001). British author of sixteen suspense novels, 1969–88, who also published eight novels as by "Richard Falkirk" (1971–77), mainly in the Blackstone historical series.

Isobel Lambot (1926–2001). British author of seventeen mystery novels under her own name, notably *Shroud of Canvas* (1967) and *Point of Death* (1969), as well as three as by "Mary Turner" and one as by "Daniel Ingham," most unpublished in the U.S.

Richard Laymon (1947–2001). Fantasy and horror writer who published over three dozen suspense and horror novels, one originally as by "Richard Kelly," as well as a score of short stories in magazines and anthologies.

Jean Mayer Liebeler (c. 1900–1998). Author of a single suspense novel, *You, the Jury* (1944), as by "Virginia Mather."

Robert Ludlum (1927–2001). Best-selling author of more than twenty spy and intrigue novels, three originally published as by "Jonathan Ryder" or "Michael Shepherd." Notable titles include *The Scarlatti Inheritance* (1971), *The Osterman Weekend* (1972), *The Matlock Paper* (1973), *The Gemini Contenders* (1976), and *The Bourne Identity* (1980).

Peter Maas (1929–2001). Best-selling true crime writer, author of *Serpico* and several books on organized crime.

Anthony Mann (1914–2001). British journalist, author of a single suspense novel, *Tiara* (1973).

Abigail McCarthy (1915–2001). Wife of former senator Eugene McCarthy, who cowrote a single suspense novel, *One Woman Lost* (1986), with Jane Muskie.

Gardner McKay (1932–2001). Actor-playwright whose first novel was a thriller, *Toyers* (1999).

Charles Neider (1915–2001). Writer and Mark Twain scholar who wrote a novel about Billy the Kid, *The Authentic Death of Hendry Jones* (1956), filmed as *One-Eyed Jacks*.

Ian Ousby (1947–2001). British author of *Bloodhounds of Heaven: The Detective in English Fiction from Godwin to Doyle* (1976).

Simon Raven (1927–2001). British novelist whose work included four early crime novels, notably *Doctors Wear Scarlet* (1960).

ROBERT H. RIMMER (1917–2001). Novelist whose work included a single suspense novel, *The Zolotov Affair* (1967).

LESLIE SANDS (1921–2001). British TV actor and playwright-novelist, author of *Something to Hide* (1956).

RICHARD SCOWCROFT (1916–2001). Author of a single suspense novel, *Back to Fire Mountain* (1973).

ANTHONY SHAFFER (1926–2001). Playwright and novelist, best known for *Sleuth* (1970), a highly successful play and film which won him the MWA screenwriting Edgar. He wrote two more mystery plays and two novels, one with his twin brother, Peter. The two also collaborated on two novels and short stories under the name "Peter Antony."

ELIZABETH DANIELS SQUIRE (1926–2001). Journalist author of eight mystery novels, starting with *Kill the Messenger* (1990), and winner of the Agatha Award for best short story.

RICHARD MARTIN STERN (1915–2001). Past president of Mystery Writers of America and author of a score of suspense novels, notably *The Bright Road to Fear* (1958), winner of the MWA Edgar for best first novel, and *The Tower* (1973), one of the (two) sources for the film *The Towering Inferno*.

GERALD SUSTER (1951–2001). British horror writer who published a single suspense novel, *The Handyman* (1985).

MARGARET SUTTON (1903–2001). Author of thirty-eight Judy Bolton mysteries for children, 1932–67.

CHARLES TEMPLETON (1915–2001). Author of two suspense novels, 1974–78.

GENE THOMPSON (1924–2001). Radio and TV writer who published four crime novels, three about sleuth Dade Cooley, introduced in *Murder Mystery* (1980).

CAROL THURSTON (1927–2001). Journalist and romance novelist who published a historical mystery, *The Eye of Horus*, in 2000.

EUDORA WELTY (1909–2001). Pulitzer Prize–winning author who occasionally reviewed mysteries, and whose ventures into crime fiction included the novella *The Robber Bridegroom* and the stories "Where Is the Voice Coming From?" and "Old Mr. Marblehall," reprinted in *EQMM*.

MARY WILLIAMS (1903–2000). British author of more than two hundred short ghost stories who also published four suspense novels, 1979–91.

L(AURALI) R. WRIGHT (1939–2001). Well-known Canadian journalist and author of sixteen novels, including the MWA Edgar winner *The Suspect* (1985).

World Mystery Report: Great Britain

Maxim Jakubowski

And we Brits kept on committing murder most liberally both on the page and on screens of assorted sizes throughout 2001. Is it something in the water, maybe? Or in our genes?

In fact, it was another good year for crime, with most major British authors (with the exception of Dick Francis, who, following his wife and collaborator Mary's death appears to have hung up his pen) readying new books, many established talents also remaining active while the neophytes of the last two years mostly confirmed their emerging talent, and in a wonderful spirit of renewal yet another batch of most promising newcomers arrived on the scene. Actually, the fact that many young authors with a generally strong literary sensibility now opt to debut in the genre is a testament to crime writing's widespread appeal and acceptance within the British creative community.

Following the flood of dubious gangster movies of the previous year, this was not a vintage twelve months for British cinema, and the majority of interesting crime and mystery work occurred on television, with the reliable Inspector Frost series continuing, featuring popular British actor David Jason; such a pity that Frost creator R. D. Wingfield is so unprolific and takes half a decade at least between new books. Other popular series were *The Bill*, a gripping adaptation of Boris Starling's *Messiah, The Vice* and much original material written straight for the screen, which the various networks grouped into solid and entertaining seasons. Much awaited is the adaptation of Val McDermid's series featuring Tony Hill, which will see the light of day in 2002, with highly acclaimed actor Robson Green portraying the psychologist; six hours are planned, with the first movie being *The Mermaids Singing*.

The Crime Writers' Association elected Russell James as its chairman, with Lindsey Davis pegged to succeed him a year later. Its awards proved less controversial this year, although many critics lamented major absences on the respective shortlists. Scott Phillips's *The Ice Harvest* claimed the dubious honor of being shortlisted for both the Gold Dagger and the John Creasey First Novel Dagger and lost in both categories. The debut award went to Susanna Jones's *The Earthquake Bird*, with Elizabeth Woodcraft as the only other British writer on the list. The Gold Dagger went to Swedish writer Henning Mankell for his Kurt Wallander novel *Sidetracked*, with Canadian author Giles Blunt getting the Silver consolation prize for *Forty Words for Sorrow*. The gallant losers for the main award were Stephen Booth, Denise

Danks, George P. Pelecanos, and the aforementioned Scott Phillips. The Cartier Diamond Dagger life achievement prize went to veteran Lionel Davidson, another regrettably unprolific author who has not published since the masterly *Kolymsky Heights*. In the short story category all the finalists originated from either issue four of *Crimewave Magazine* or my anthology of historical mystery tales *Murder Through the Ages*. The winner was Marion Arnott, leaving Simon Avery, Susanna Gregory, Lauren Henderson, and Brian Hodge in the starting blocks. In 2002, the CWA will be launching a new Dagger for thrillers, sponsored by the Ian Fleming estate.

On the publishing front, there were no new players, although on the plus side, all the houses featuring crime fiction appeared to prosper with no evident cutbacks. Orion, with judicious editing nous and a helpful wink from the Hachette corporate coffers, rules the roost, adding Harlan Coben, Caroline Carver, and other future big names to a prestigious roster that already included Connelly, Burke, Crais, Hoag, and Rankin, amongst many other major sellers. Allison & Busby strengthened its list and signed up a number of British authors surprisingly dropped by the majors. The merger between Constable and Robinson has made the company a player, having broken Elizabeth Peters through for the first time in the U.K., confirmed Mike Ripley's popularity, launched many new talents including Philip Gooden and David Roberts, and enjoyed success with the collectors for small print run debuts for many of its books. Meanwhile, Penguin lured Pan Macmillan crime editor Beverley Cousins away to refocus its disparate list.

The retail scene saw little change, with much battling over discount and range between the big chains, and doom-laden predictions that the market can't sustain all of them, which was confirmed by the demise at year's end of James Thin, the Scottish group. Meanwhile, the independents battled on despite decreasing ranks, with both the London specialist crime and mystery shops Murder One and Crime in Store surviving rent hikes for the meanwhile.

The second annual edition of Crime Scene, the Film and Literature festival at London's National Film Theatre in July, proved a great success, numbering amongst its guests Steve Buscemi (who attracted personal friends like Paul McCartney, Chrissie Hynde, and Joe Strummer to the opening night), Tami Hoag, Steve Hamilton, and the crème de la crème of British crime writing, including newcomers like Stephen Booth, Jake Arnott, Mark Billingham, and Fidelis Morgan for their first ever appearances at a crime event. A major section of the festival was devoted to Agatha Christie, including a delightful adaptation on stage of one of her radio plays directed by Simon Brett with all thespians involved also being crime writers. It was very much a year of celebration of Christie in the U.K., with actor-director Roy Marsden featuring all her plays in repertoire at Westcliff on Sea and the British Museum presenting an exhibition of her archaeological finds and artifacts. Amongst the plethora of panels at Crime Scene, one attracted great controversy when four out of five reviewers for major newspapers present on stage openly admitted in answer to a question from the floor to deliberately never reviewing historical crime. Needless to say, the row lingered for months on the web, in magazines, and at meetings. Manchester's Dead on Deansgate, organized by Waterstone's with the collaboration of the CWA, had another installment in October, which proved a bit of a damp squib and might prove to be the last edition, having angered many authors through its criteria for selection and lack of books on sale.

Like any year, it was also one of sadness as the British crime writing community learned of the passing of Andrew Garve, Derek Lambert, Isobel Lambot (in particularly forlorn circumstances that could have come from one of her books), critic and academic Ian Ousby, Simon Raven, and Conrad Voss Bark.

Another casualty of 2001 was *Shots Magazine*, which now can be found only on the web, but *Crimewave* and *Crime Time* still appear on a regular basis, with the latter devoting a major portion of each issue to a lengthy dossier (U.S. vs. U.K., Sex, Female Crime Authors, Sherlock Holmes, etc.) and planning a change of formula and extent for 2002.

Once again, a thorough look at a year in books can't help but be a tad repetitive, but what other way of showing the richness and diversity of the current British crime scene? Note that for every book or author cited here, there were at least six times more actually published and enjoyed by a reading public that never tires of crime fiction.

The big names didn't fail, with Ian Rankin's *The Falls* topping the bestseller list, and reissues of his thrillers written years ago as Jack Harvey also making a beeline for the paperback lists. Reginald Hill visited Dalziel and Pascoe again in *Dialogues of the Dead*. Simon Brett continued his new series with *Death on the Downs*. Lee Child's new Jack Reacher novel was *Echo Burning*, set in the U.S., where the British author now lives. John Connolly's third Charlie Parker psycho thriller, *The Killing Kind,* catapulted him into the premier division. Lindsey Davis aired Roman sleuth Falco again in *The Body in the Bathhouse*. Minette Walters investigated the downside of British society in *Acid Row*. The couple who write as Nicci French committed *The Red Room*. Jonathan Gash returned, after a break, to his favorite antihero Lovejoy in *Every Last Cent*. Mo Hayder confirmed her grisly, unsettling talent in her second novel, *The Treatment*. P. D. James took Inspector Dalgliesh into ecclesiastical circles in *Death in Holy Orders*. Bill James struck twice, as *Pay Day* featured Harpur and Iles while inaugurated an impressive new espionage series. Donna Leon's Commissario Brunetti trod the wet Venice streets in *A Sea of Troubles*. Jill McGown, an underappreciated but highly popular author, published *Scene of the Crime*. Peter Robinson's Inspector Banks series took a quantum leap with the striking *Aftermath*. Margaret Yorke came out with *Grave Matters,* and Ruth Rendell was as prolific as ever with *Adam, Eve and Pinch Me*.

There was, notwithstanding the critics, little sign of slowdown in the historical mystery field, with confirmed talents and newcomers crowding at the gates. The ever overactive Paul Doherty released *The Corpse Candle*, a Hugh Corbett yarn, *House of Death*, with Alexander the Great, and, pseudonymously Vanessa Alexander's *The Loving Cup*. Susanna Gregory published the seventh Matthew Bartholomew tale, *An Order of Death*. Bernard Knight's Crowner John series continued with *Tinners Corpse*. Edward Marston further mined olde England in *The Repentant Rake*. Peter Tremayne stuck with medieval Irish nun Sister Fidelma with *Smoke in the Wind*. David Roberts offered the second installment of his Sayers-like midwar series *The Bones Are Buried*. Michael Jecks struck twice with *Tournament of Blood* and *The Sticklepath Strangler*. Meanwhile the indefatigable Anne Perry offered us a Pitt puzzler, *The Whitechapel Conspiracy*, and a Monk tale, *Funeral in Blue,* as well as the second installment of a fantasy series. Alys Clare released *The Chatter of the Maidens*. Alanna Knight stuck to Scotland past in *The Dagger in the Crown*. Deryn Lake continued her bawdy tales of apothecary John Rawlings in *Death in the West Wind*. Fidelis Morgan returned to the colorful world of Restoration England in *The Rival Queens*. Newcomer Elizabeth Redfern scintillated with the literary *Music of the Spheres,* and Hannah Marsh (alias Derek Wilson) offered *A Necessary Evil.*

The new Ian Fleming Dagger Award of course reminds us that Britain has always been a fertile ground for the thriller and the end of the Cold War has not affected the high level of quality of new books in the field, with many authors renewing their inspiration as the master of them all, John Le Carré, repeatedly does. Prominent this year were Geoffrey Archer (the ex–television journalist, not the disgraced politician) with *The Lucifer Network.* Ex-publisher (and boss of mine!) Francis Bennett released the final installment of his East vs. West trilogy *Doctor Berlin*. Henry Porter's second critically acclaimed thriller was *A Spy's Life*. Paul Eddy's *Flint* introduced the eponymous heroine, a modern Modesty Blaise–like tough girl. Colin Forbes published *Rhinoceros*. David Hewson confirmed his talent with *Lucifer's Shadow*. Duo Lury-Gibson brought an imaginative approach to their Internet thriller *Dangerous Data*. Robert Wilson gathered numerous kudos for his Dagger follow-up *The Company of Strangers*. James Harland (Matthew Lynn) mixed high finance with conspiracies in *The Month of the Leopard*. Donald James's hero Russian cop *Vadim* came to the U.S. for a third dark caper, and Peter Millar chose Far East politics as backdrop for *Bleak Midwinter*.

On the reissue front, it was a splendid year with print-on-demand publishers The House of Stratus, despite financial difficulties, republishing the complete works of major crime authors who had fallen into neglect and for which they purchased wholesale literary estates. So the British fan was gifted, between sharply designed new covers, with the previously difficult to find novels of R. Austin Freeman, Freeman Wills Crofts, John Buchan, G. K.

Chesterton, Cyril Hare, Georgette Heyer, Nicolas Freeling, Julian Symons, Sam Llewellyn, Dornford Yates, Henry Cecil, Michael Gilbert, Anthony Berkeley, Sax Rohmer, Mark Hebden, Edgar Wallace, Sapper, Michael Innes, George Markstein, and E. C. Bentley, with and many others to come. The shelves are groaning but the fans are not complaining. In addition, Back In Print Books is reissuing Simon Brett's Charles Paris capers, David Armstrong, Deryn Lake, and Tim Heald. But my personal favorite amongst the year's many reissues is that, by Savoy, of Anthony Skene's *Monsieur Zenith the Albino*, the pulp adventures of one of the villains in the Sexton Blake series and, possibly, the best-produced book of the year. Invaluable.

New writers are the necessary transfusion of blood that keeps the crime and mystery field vigorous and innovative. The year's gem was Malcolm Pryce's *Aberystwyth Mon Amour*, a tale that blends *Chinatown* with Monty Python, a mix of hardboiled clichés, irony, and pathos that was quite unique and, naturally, was overlooked for the awards. Other notable debuts include Danny King's streetwise *The Burglar Diaries*, Caroline Carver's Australian outback thriller *Blood Junction*, Hector MacDonald's clever and deceitful thriller *The Mind Game*, Barbara Cleverly's already collectable *The Last Kashmiri Queen*, Mark Billingham's creepy but effective *Sleepyhead*, Susanna Jones's Japanese *The Earthquake Bird*, Elizabeth Woodcraft's music- and Motown-influenced *Good Bad Woman*, and Jasper Fforde's canny *The Eyre Affair*. Only the future will tell us whether these new writers confirm their talent or, even, remain within the confines of the crime genre.

But debutantes of earlier years as well as journeymen, midlist writers who haven't quite made their way into the top division of British crime through a quirk of commercial fate or marketing aggression rather than any lack of storytelling talent, but nonetheless enjoy fruitful careers and regularly bring new offerings to the marketplace and bookshelves, still form the invaluable core of the year's reading. Fans were left with an embarrassment of wonderful riches as all of the following authors published new novels: Michael Pearce, Chris Petit, Danutah Reah, Cynthia Harrod-Eagles, Robert Barnard, Jerry Raine, Russell James, Julian Rathbone, Mike Ripley, Manda Scott, Michelle Spring, Cath Staincliffe, Alison Taylor, Laura Wilson, Sarah Diamond, Andrew Taylor, Hilary Bonner, Martin Edwards, M. J. Trow, Jake Arnott, Rob Ryan, Ken Bruen, Joolz Denby, Lauren Henderson, Patricia Hall, Robert Goddard, Joyce Holms, Meg Elizabeth Atkins, Jo Bannister, Christopher Brookmyre, Colin Bateman, Paul Charles, Natasha Cooper (as herself and as Claire Layton), Linda Davies, Martina Cole, Denise Danks, Judith Cutler, Matthew Branton, Veronica Stallwood, Stuart Pawson, John Malcolm, Jim Lusby, H. R. F. Keating, Frances Fyfield, Maureen O'Brien, Denise Mina, James Humphreys, John Harvey, Roy Lewis, Frederic Lindsay, Scarlett Thomas, Liz Evans, David Peace, John Baker, Anne Granger, Stephen Booth, David Armstrong, Kate Ellis, Quintin Jardine, Paul Johnston, Morag Joss, Frank Lean, Julie Parsons, and Barbara Nadel. It's a long list and because space is at a premium in this already oversize volume, could have been many times the size. Some of these writers are on only their second jump around the circuit; others have been practicing their craft for years. Some aspire to the bestseller list; others are happy just to please their readership. Their turn in the limelight will come if there is any justice in the world of crime.

Two-thousand one? Another very decent vintage, the butler remarked to the policeman!

World Mystery Report: Australia

David Honeybone

The year down under started with a bang with the launch of *Crime Factory* in February, the first crime magazine to be published in Australia since 1996. The quarterly title fills a huge void and has already developed a strong subscription base and is stocked at bookshops in London and New York.

Authors who had new books published during the year included: Peter Corris (*Lugarno*), Gabrielle Lord (*Death Delights*), Yvonne Fein (*April Fool*), Kerry Greenwood (*Away with the Fairies*), Peter Doyle (*The Devil's Jump*), Lindy Cameron (*Bleeding Hearts*), Marshall Browne (*Inspector Anders and the Ship of Fools*), Jon Cleary (*Yesterday's Shadow*), and Andrew Masterson (*Death of the Author*).

One surprise reprint was *Wake in Fright* (Text), by Kenneth Cook, with a new introduction by Peter Temple. Originally published in 1961, the chilling saga of a young teacher's nightmare stay in a small outback town evokes many of the qualities found in the work of Jim Thompson. The film adaptation featuring a demented Donald Pleasence was released as *Outback* in America.

Some notable overseas crime writers visited Australia during the year. The tartan titan Ian Rankin was a guest at the Sydney Writers Festival in May, and fellow Scot Christopher Brookmyre, together with Florida lawyer turned writer James Grippando, was in Melbourne in August. Others who came to Australia included Minette Walters, John Connolly, and Ken Layne.

In August the annual Ned Kelly Awards for Australian Crime Writing, organized by the Crime Writers Association of Australia, again proved to be a memorable night not least because the event was recorded by ABC television's *Coast to Coast* arts program. Following a spirited questioning of this year's judges as to why they are qualified to judge crime, the winners were announced:

Best First Crime Novel:
  Last Drinks (Allen & Unwin) by Andrew McGahan, a sordid tale of corruption and drinking set in Brisbane.

Best Novel (tie):
  The Second Coming (HarperCollins) by Andrew Masterson.
  Dead Point (Bantam) by Peter Temple.
  This is the third time Temple has won a "Ned" and his legions of fans are awaiting his next book, *In the Evil Day*, with relish.

Best True Crime Book:

Broken Lives (Hardie Grant) by Estelle Blackburn.

Blackburn has spent six years on the book investigating this harrowing account of wrongful imprisonment in Perth. Blackburn also won a Walkley, a prestigious award in Australian journalism, for her work.

Lifetime Achievement Award:

Professor Stephen Knight.

Knight reviewed crime fiction for the *Sydney Morning Herald*, edited numerous crime anthologies, and authored the only reference book on Australian crime writing, *Continent of Mystery* (MUP). He currently teaches English at Cardiff University in the U.K. The award was collected on his behalf by Lucy Sussex, whose Ph.D. is being supervised by Knight.

A new category was the introduction of the Readers Vote, sponsored by *Crime Factory* magazine. The winner was Lindy Cameron for *Bleeding Hearts* (HarperCollins).

In an ironic twist, Peter Carey's multiaward-winning book *True History of the Kelly Gang* was amongst the nominations but failed to place. The general consensus is that he probably doesn't mind. . . .

Sisters in Crime Australia marked its tenth anniversary with SheKilda, the first crime convention in Australia and the first-ever female crime convention in the world. Guest of Honor was that leading exponent of Tart Noir, Lauren Henderson. The English crime writer, who currently lives in New York, made her first trip to Australia and made many new fans. The three-day event was attended by more than 350 crime writers, fans, publishers, and commentators. A highlight of the convention was the Saturday night presentation of the inaugural Sisters in Crime Davitt Award (named after Ellen Davitt, claimed to be the author of the first-ever Australian murder mystery *Force and Fraud*, 1865) for the best crime novel published (in 2000) by an Australian woman crime writer. The guest presenter was the police commissioner of Victoria, Christine Nixon, who gave a great speech and then announced the winner: *Eye to Eye* by Caroline Shaw. Ms. Shaw was unable to accept the trophy in person because she was in Japan writing the third in the Lenny Aaron cat-catcher PI series. Dorothy Johnston's *The Trojan Dog* received a highly commended.

Thanks to the enthusiasm of the twenty-one participating Australian women crime writers, the visiting Queen of Tart Noir, the other expert panel members, and the amazing volunteer brigade, the SheKilda Women's Crime Convention was a huge success.

World Mystery Report: Canada

Edo van Belkom

Two thousand one was another banner year for Canadian mystery writers, but before any mention of individual achievements, a moment must be taken to acknowledge the passing of one of Canada's best-loved and most successful mystery authors.

In February, Laurali Rose Wright, known to her readers as L. R. Wright, and to her friends as "Bunny," died after a long battle with cancer. Born in Saskatoon in 1939, Bunny Wright arrived on the mystery scene in a big way in 1985 when her fourth novel, but first mystery, *The Suspect*, won the Edgar Award for best novel. Since then, numerous novels featuring Karl Alberg and Cassandra Mitchell made her a fixture on the Canadian crime and British Columbia literary scenes. She won two Arthur Ellis Awards for her novels, and served a stint as president of the Crime Writers of Canada in 1992–93. As a final honor, the Derrick Murdoch Award was presented to Bunny Wright for her contributions to Canadian crime writing. The award was presented posthumously by Crime Writers of Canada president Nora Kelly.

The rest of the CWC awards were presented at the Arthur Ellis Awards banquet at the Ontario Club in Toronto, Wednesday, May 23. Peter Robinson came away the big winner with wins in the Best Novel category for *Cold Is the Grave*, and the Short Story category with "Murder in Utopia." Mark Zuehlke won for Best First Novel for *Hands Like Clouds*, while Best Juvenile went to Tim Wynne Jones's *The Boy in the Burning House*. A. B. McKillop's *The Spinster and the Prophet* won for Best True Crime, and the award for Best Crime Writing in French went to Norbert Spehner for *Le Roman policier en Amérique française*.

Peter Robinson was also a winner at the Edgar Awards, winning in the short story category for a different story, "Missing in Action." Veteran novelist Eric Wright was also a nominee in the Best Paperback Original category for his book, *The Kidnapping of Rosie Dawn*.

Elsewhere in awards news: *Cadavre au Sous-Sol*, the French translation of Norah McClintock's young adult mystery, *The Body in the Basement*, was chosen by Communication Jeunesse, a nonprofit group in Quebec dedicated to promoting Canadian books and authors, as best book of the year in the twelve-and-over category; and Toronto writer Peter Sellers won the 2001 *Ellery Queen's Mystery Magazine* Readers' Award. His story "Avenging Miriam" from the December 2001 issue was voted most popular by the magazine's readers.

Canada's only annual mystery conference, Toronto's Bloody Words, gained some international notoriety as it presented the Hammett Award in 2001. The Hammett, presented by the North American branch of the International Association of Crime Writers, recognizes the best work of fiction by a North American writer and was presented to Canadian author Margaret Atwood for her novel *The Blind Assassin*. In other convention news, Bouchercon was awarded to Toronto for 2004.

On the silver and small screens, two more of Gail Bowen's Joanne Kilbourn novels, *A Killing Spring* and *Verdict in Blood*, were filmed as television movies, while Lyn Hamilton's novel *The Celtic Riddle* was optioned as a Movie of the Week for Angela Lansbury's *Murder She Wrote* character, Jessica Fletcher.

And finally, 2001 marked the tenth year of continuous publication of *The Mystery Review*, which has not missed a quarterly publication since 1992.

World Mystery Report: Germany

Thomas Woertche

The German book market was a bit nervous last year, due to the shadow of the new currency, the Euro, which went into effect on January 1, 2002. Evidently this was also true for the crime fiction market. But in general, this little bit of turmoil changed nothing.

On one hand, the regionalization continued: Small publishers like Grafit Verlag of Dortmund, Militzke of Leipzig, and be.bra of Berlin got competitors: no-name publishers which are even smaller, purely regional, and hardly known outside of their respective narrow vicinities. Their output was enormous, but no single book reached nationwide attention, let alone acceptance. This sub-business does seem to be feeding its entrepreneurs, however modestly.

On the other hand, the holes in the bestseller lists left by the four Harry Potter volumes continue to be filled by the usual suspects: Donna Leon, Ingrid Noll, Henning Mankell, Patricia Cornwell, et al. What was true in 2000 was still true in 2001: These are bricks designed as mainstream blockbusters with a tinge of crime, but it seems harder by the year to label them as real crime fiction. In three words: Business as usual.

More business as usual was that the big players continued to integrate their crime program into general fiction. Crime fiction in these lines is modeled and shaped like the bestsellers, so Henning Mankell swept a lot of second- and third-rate Scandinavians into the German market; Andrea Camilleri did the same for Italians. This had sometimes bitter consequences: there was, for example, no Spanish-language author among the top-twenty bestsellers. Result: almost all leading Spanish crime writers, like Andreu Martín and Juan Madrid, had no new books available on the German market. The more crime fiction and fake crime fiction and non–crime fiction are thrown together, the harder the times for crime lines *sui generis*.

There is a general lack of competently edited crime lines. *DuMont noir*, the last line presenting a straight hard-boiled collection (Joe R. Lansdale, Russell James, Derek Raymond, George Pelecanos, James Sallis, et al.) has been closed, since its audience didn't appreciate the line's odd mixture of mismanagement and a too narrow concept of hard-boiled/noir. The result was a general lack of publishing space for internationally renowned writers. Authors like Robert W. Campbell, Lawrence Block, and John Harvey, together with the above mentioned, lost their German-language publishers. Even stars like Elmore Leonard, Carl Hiaasen, and Ian Rankin are having hard times, although they are still published by Bertelsmann.

So the hard-core business was left to the small and middle-sized houses. Maass/Pulp Master of Berlin continues to publish books by Buddy Giovinazzo, Charles Willeford, and Gerald Kersh. Distel-Verlag of Heilbronn continues to take care of the French tradition: Jean-Patrick Manchette, Jean-Bernard Pouy, Sylvie Granotier, et al.

The Swiss publishing house Unionsverlag demonstrated that its concept worked: The line called "UT metro," both in paperback and hardcover, insists on a clear crime line, but at the same time on a wide definition of crime fiction, collecting novels literally from all over the world. Unionsverlag metro featured African writers like Meja Mwangi from Kenya and Mongo Beti from Cameroon, Pablo De Santis from Argentina and Guillermo Arriaga from Mexico (who missed the Academy Award for his script of the internationally praised movie *Amores Perros*), and Celil Oker from Turkey, next to Helen Zahavi (U.K.), Bill Moody, Katy Munger, Walter Mosley, Jerome Charyn, and Stan Jones (U.S.). The concept was a double success: Both audience *and* the critics appreciated the line very much. The year's winner of the Critics Award for Crime Fiction, the Deutscher Krimi-Preis, was Garry Disher from Australia with his cop novel *Drachenmann*—a book that perfectly reflects the basic idea of "UT metro": It *is* genre and it is; thanks to the brilliance of Disher's prose and craft, more than genre.

This win demonstrates the rising general interest in global crime fiction. Ranked second in the international section of 2001's award was Yasmina Khadra's *Herbst der Chimären* (from the Austrian publishing house Haymon). The novel is the third of a trilogy set in civil war–torn Algeria. Khadra is the female pseudonym of a male former army officer who wrote these grotesque, violent, and sarcastic books in order to come to terms with the real horror he was confronted with in his country. They are crime fiction in a very profound sense, and the trilogy ranks among the most important novels of contemporary African literature.

Other authors of 2001 who were likewise well received and established on the German-language market were the Colombian Santiago Gamboa (from Wagenbach), the Chilean Ramón Díaz Eterovic, and the Greek Petros Makaris (both from Diogenes of Zurich). The global landscape of crime fiction is getting wider, but it doesn't exclude Anglo-Americans: Ranked third was *Regenzauber* (from Ullstein) by the excellent genuine crime writer from Boston, Dennis Lehane.

The German-language section voted similarly: Rank one and two were given to novels oscillating between genre and beyond-genre: the Swiss author Alexander Heimann's *Dezemberföhn* (from the tiny but ambitious Swiss Cosmos Verlag) and Friedrich Ani's *Süden oder das Gelöbnis des Gefallenen Engels* (from Knaur). Both authors started writing pure genre; both authors have decided to take a different way now. Rank three only awarded a genre novel in a stricter sense, although it is mere funny one: Jörg Juretzka's *Der Willi ist weg* (from Rotbuch).

Contrary to the critics' poll, the crime writers' award, named the Glauser (in honor of the great Swiss writer of the 1930s), did not reflect the tendencies and debates. It was given to Horst Eckert's *Zwillingsfalle* (from Grafit), a Wambaugh-style cop novel minus Wambaugh's experience and comic approach to a violent reality.

Two thousand one has also seen a conflict arise about the issue of genre and non-genre—or high literature and low literature. Two notorious highbrow authors, Georg Klein and Thomas Hettche, surprised the literary pages with crime novels. Klein's *Barba Rossa* (from Alexander Fest Verlag) transposes an alleged private-eye plot into the Berlin of the near future and tells a surreal story with about every Gothic and German Romantic literary theme. *Der Fall Argobast* by Thomas Hettche (DuMont) is a slightly fictionalized piece of true crime about a legal scandal of the former West Germany back in the 1950s and 1960s. The literary pages were full of cheers.

Klein's novel follows in the footsteps of works written decades ago more radically and more capably by Chester Himes, Jerome Charyn, and Jack O'Connell. Hettche's book simply copies the solid courtroom drama that gained popularity in America in the 1980s and 1990s, but is light-years away from legal thrillers by Scott Turow or true crime masterpieces like *In Cold Blood*.

The crime writers' response followed at once. Astrid Paprotta, known for a well-done serial-killer novel a couple of years ago, presented *Sterntaucher* (from Eichborn), a very German crime novel which urgently wants to be something greater. Unfortunately, it reads like a family drama, perhaps a Dostoyevsky tragedy. It is full of deep insights into the human soul. So deep that it loses all contact with reality and doesn't do the job that real crime fiction is supposed to do, telling reality.

Readers and book buyers were entertained much better by living authors, presented during events like the international crime writers' festivals in Cologne and Bremen and—most important—Frankfurt. Last year's international book fair had global crime fiction as the main event.

And public television has meanwhile discovered the readers' interest in mysteries and thrillers of all kinds and supports it by broadcasting thirty- to forty-five-minute portraits of authors like P. D. James, Manuel Vazquez Montalban, Pieke Biermann, and Alicia Giménez Bartlett.

All in all, the crime fiction landscape continued on in 2001 much as it had in 2000—business as usual.

The Year 2001 in Mystery Fandom

George A. Easter

What can a mystery reader do when he or she isn't satisfied with just reading mysteries anymore and wants to do more in the mystery field? The reader can participate in the various activities of mystery fandom. There are numerous local mystery reading groups, usually supported by local libraries or bookstores. Participation in one of these groups allows the fan to rub shoulders with people of similar interests. And it gives the fan an opportunity to read a wider variety of mystery fiction and to experiment with heretofore unread mystery authors. The fan may want to review mysteries for a local newspaper or other publication. The mystery aficionado may get involved in collecting first editions or mystery books in general, and participate in on-line chat groups such as DorothyL. For someone so enamored with the genre, there comes a time when he or she attends a mystery convention.

MYSTERY CONVENTIONS

There are small, regional mystery conventions, such as LeftCoast Crime, Cluefest, and Malice Domestic, which attract 150-plus writers and several hundreds of fans. They are held yearly and have interesting panel discussions to attend and a book dealers' room crammed full of wonderful mysteries (both new and old) to salivate over and buy. These smaller, regional conventions generally are quite relaxed and there is plenty of time to rub shoulders with authors and other fans. By contrast, the largest mystery convention, the annual Bouchercon, the international mystery convention, is a beehive of activity. At this convention many authors meet with their agents, publicists, and editors. Authors have come to renew contacts or to make new ones. And each evening is jam-packed with special events and award presentations. In 2001 Bouchercon was held in Washington, D.C., at the beginning of November. (Bouchercon 2002 will be in Austin, Texas, in October 2002). It was with some trepidation that approximately 1,600 people attended this year's convention in the wake of the events of 9/11. But everything went off without a hitch and a good time was had by all. Especially memorable was the large contingent that attended from the U.K.—more than thirty British authors, many of whom had never attended such an event before. The Guest of Honor was Sue Grafton, the International Guest of Honor was Peter Lovesey, and the toastmaster was Michael Connelly. Also honored was

Edward D. Hoch, short story writer extraordinaire, the recipient of a Lifetime Achievement Award. You should consider attending one of these events. It can be life-changing. For more information on the conventions, go to one of the many mystery websites, or enter the name of the convention in an Internet search engine.

MYSTERY MAGAZINES 2001

One of the most popular ways that mystery fans keep up with what is going on in the field is by subscribing to one or more mystery magazines. The most popular of the current fan magazines are:

Mystery Scene, published five times a year for a cost of $32.00. Eighty-eight pages of articles and reviews. Heavy emphasis on author contributions. 3601 Skylark Lake SE, Cedar Rapids, IA 52403.

Deadly Pleasures, published quarterly for a cost of $18.00. Eighty pages of articles, reviews, news, and regular columns, including the popular "Reviewed to Death" column. P.O. Box 969, Bountiful, UT 84011 or order at *www.deadlypleasures.com/*

Mystery News, published bimonthly for a cost of $20.00. Newspaper format includes cover interview, columns, articles, many reviews, and listing of current and upcoming books. Black Raven Press, PMB 152, 262 Hawthorn Village Commons, Vernon Hills, IL 60061 or order at *www.blackravenpress.com/*

Mystery Reader's International Journal, published quarterly for a cost of $24.00. Each issue treats a mystery theme. Calendar year 2001 will feature New England Mysteries, Partners in Crime, Oxford, and Cambridge. P.O. Box 8116, Berkeley, CA 94707 or order at *www.mysteryreaders.org/*

Drood Review, published bimonthly for a cost of $17.00. Articles and reviews in a newsletter format. 484 E. Carmel Dr., #378, Carmel, IN 46032 or order at *www.droodreview.com/*

CHANGING OF THE MYSTERY GUARD 2001

Each year the mystery fiction genre experiences a changing of the guard. Longtime mystery fans mourn the deaths of some of the old guard and celebrate the arrival of some very talented newcomers. The year 2001 saw the passing of Hugh Holton, Sophie Dunbar, Carol Thurston, Nora DeLoach, Derek Lambert, E. Richard Johnson, George O'Toole, and Gene Thompson. And it saw the first novels published by future stars Cynthia G. Alwyn, Sallie Bissell, C. J. Box, Gabriel Cohen, K. J. Erickson, Glen David Gold, John Searles, Karin Slaughter, James Swain, and Jess Walter.

The World's Finest Mystery and Crime Stories

Third Annual Collection

S. J. Rozan

Double-Crossing Delancey

SHIRA ROZAN is quickly building to bestseller status with her novels and stories of Lydia Chin and Bill Smith. Rozan writes in a quirky, cutting-edge style all her own, telling tales of the big city that resonate with a humane skepticism appropriate to this nervous moment in our shared history. She has won the Shamus twice and the Anthony once. In "Double-Crossing Delancey," which first graced the pages of the anthology *Mystery Street*, Lydia sets up and takes down an inner-city smooth operator as only she knows how.

Double-Crossing Delancey

S. J. Rozan

I never trusted Joe Delancey, and I never wanted to get involved with him, and I wouldn't have except, like most people where Joe's concerned, I was drawn into something irresistible.

It began on a bright June morning. I was ambling through Chinatown with Charlie Chung, an FOB—Fresh Off the Boat—immigrant from Hong Kong. We had just left the dojo after an early-morning workout. The air was clear, my blood was flowing, and I was ready for action.

"Good work this morning," I told Charlie. I stopped to buy a couple of hot dough sticks from the lady on the corner, who was even fresher off the boat than Charlie. "You keep up that kind of thing, you'll be a rank higher by next year." I handed him a dough stick. "My treat."

Charlie bowed his head to acknowledge the compliment and the gift; then he grinned.

"Got big plans, next year, *gaje*," he declared. "Going to college." In Cantonese, "gaje" means "big sister." I'm not related to Charlie; this was his Chinese way of acknowledging my role as his wise advisor, his guide on the path of life. I tried to straighten up and walk taller.

"Really?" I asked.

Charlie nodded. "By next year," he told me with complete confidence, "my English gets better, also my pockets fills up."

In the dojo, Charlie and I practice kicks and punches on each other. Outside, Charlie practices his English on me.

Sometimes it feels the same.

Nevertheless, I said, "Your English is coming along, Charlie."

"Practice make perfect," he grinned, confiding, "English saying." His eyes took on a distant look. "Maybe can put English saying in fortune cookie, sell to China. Make big money."

Fortune cookies are unknown in China; they were invented by a Japanese man in New Jersey. "Not likely, Charlie. Chinese people are too serious about food."

"You think this, *gaje*?" A bus full of tourists pulled around the corner. Heads hung out windows and cameras pressed against faces. Charlie smiled and waved. "Probably right," Charlie went on. "I go look for one other way, make big money. Maybe import lychee nuts."

I munched on my dough stick. "Lychee nuts?"

He nodded. "In U.S.A., too much canned lychees. Too sweet, no taste, pah!"

"You can get fresh lychees here."

"Saying fresh, but all old, dry, sour. Best lychees, can't find. Import best fresh lychees, sell like crazy."

"You know, Charlie, that's not a bad idea."

"Most idea of Charlie not bad idea! Plan also, import water buffalo. Pet for American children, better than dog."

Sometimes Charlie worries me. I mean, if I'm going to be the guy's *gaje*, I have responsibilities. "The lychees may be a good idea, Charlie. The water buffalo is not."

Charlie, his mouth full of warm, sweet dough, mumbled, "Not?"

"Not."

Charlie hasn't learned to shrug yet. He did what Chinese people have always done: he jutted his chin forward. "If you say, *gaje*. Before invest big money, asking you."

"That's smart."

"Maybe," Charlie grinned wickedly, "brother-in-law also come asking you, now."

"Your sister's husband? He needs advice?"

"Too late, advice. Brother-in-law one stupid shit."

I winced. "Remember I told you there are some words you can learn but not say?"

Charlie's brow furrowed. "Stupid?"

I shook my head.

"Oh." He grinned again, and blushed. "Okay. Brother-in-law one stupid jackass."

I guessed that was better. "What did he do that was stupid?"

"Brother-in-law buying two big crates, cigarettes lighters from China. Red, picture both sides of Chairman Mao." Charlie stopped on the sidewalk to bow elaborately. I wondered what both sides of Chairman Mao looked like. "Light cigarette, play 'East Is Red' same time."

"Sounds great."

"Cost brother-in-law twelve hundreds of dollars. Thinks, sell to tourists on street, make big bucks. When crates come, all lighters don't have fluid, don't have wick."

"Oh, no."

"Brother-in-law complain to guy sold him. Guy saying, 'Why you thinking so cheap? Come on, brother-in-law, I have fluid, I have wicks sell you.' Now brother-in-law sitting home filling lighters all night after job, sticking wicks in. Don't know how, so half doesn't work. Now, sell cheap, lose money. Sell expensive, tourist don't want. Also, brother-in-law lazy jackass. By tomorrow, next day, give up. Many lighters, no wick, no fluid, no bucks for brother-in-law."

My eyes narrowed as I heard this story. Leaving aside Charlie's clear sense that no bucks was about what his brother-in-law deserved, I asked, "Who was the guy your brother-in-law bought these things from, do you know? Was he Chinese?"

"Not Chinese. Some *lo faan*, meet on Delancey Street. Say, have lighters, need cash, sell cheap. I tell brother-in-law, you stupid sh—" Charlie swallowed the word. "—Stupid jackass, how you trust *lo faan* guy with ruby in tooth?"

"Lo faan" means, roughly, "barbarian"; more broadly, it means anyone not Chinese. For emphasis Charlie tapped the tooth at the center of his own grin.

"Charlie," I said, "I have to go. So do you, or you'll be late." Charlie works the eight-to-four shift in a Baxter Street noodle factory. "See you tomorrow morning."

"Sure, *gaje*. See you."

With another grin and a wave, Charlie was off to work. With shoulders set and purposeful stride, so was I.

These clear June mornings in New York wilt fast. It wasn't quite so bright or early, I had accomplished a number of things, and I was sweaty and flagging a little by the time I finally spotted Joe Delancey on Delancey Street.

Delancey Street is the delta of New York, the place where the flood of new immigrants from Asia meets the river of them from the Caribbean and the tide from Latin America, and they all flow into the ocean of old-time New Yorkers, whose parents and grandparents were the last generation's floods and rivers and tides. Joe Delancey could often be found cruising here, looking for money-making opportunities, and I had been cruising for a while myself, looking for Joe.

I stepped out in front of him, blocking his path on the wide sidewalk. "Joe," I said. "We have to talk."

Joe rocked to a halt. His freckled face lit up and his green eyes glowed with delight, as though finding me standing in his way was a pleasure, and being summoned to talk with me was a joy he'd long wished for but never dared hope to have.

"Lydia! Oh, exquisite pearl of the Orient, where have you been these lonely months?"

"Joe—"

"No, wait! Do not speak." He held up a hand for silence and tilted his head to look at me. "You only grow more beautiful. If we could bottle the secret of you, what a fortune we could make." I laughed; with Joe, though I know him, I often find myself laughing.

"Do not vanish, I beg you," he said, as though I were already shimmering and fading. "Now that I have at long last found you again."

"*I* was looking for *you*, Joe."

He smiled gently. "Because Fate was impatient for us to be together, and I too much of a fool to understand." He slipped my arm through his and steered me along the sidewalk. "Come. We shall have tea, and sit a while, and talk of many things." We reached a coffee shop. Joe gallantly pulled open the door. As I walked in past him he grinned, and when he did the ruby in his front tooth glittered in the sun.

I'd once asked him what the story was on the ruby in his tooth.

His answer started with a mundane cavity, the kind all of us get. Because it was in the front, Joe's dentist had suggested filling it and crowning it. "In those days, I was seeing an Indian girl," Joe had said, making it sound like sometime last century. "A Punjabi princess, a sultry beauty with a ruby in her forehead. She gave me one that matched it, as a love token. When the embers of our burning affair had faded and cooled—"

"You mean, when you'd scammed her out of all you could get?"

"—I had Dr. Painless insert my beloved's gift in my tooth, where it would ever, in my lonely moments, remind me of her."

I hadn't fully believed either the ruby or the story, and I thought Joe Delancey's idea of what to do with a love token was positively perverse. But though I'm a licensed private investigator, I'm also a well-brought-up Chinese girl, and I hadn't known the Punjabi princess. I'd just looked at my watch and had some place to be.

Now, on this June morning, Joe waved a waiter over and ordered tea and Danishes. "Tea in a *pot*," he commanded, "for the Empress scorns your pinched and miserly cups." He turned to me with a thousand-watt smile. "Anything your heart desires, oh beauteous one, within the limited powers of this miserable establishment, I will provide. Your money is no good with Joe. A small price to pay for the pleasure of your company."

I wasn't surprised that Joe was buying. That was part of his system, he'd once confided cheerfully. Always pay for the small things. You get a great reputation as a generous guy, cheap.

In Joe's business that was a good investment.

"Joe," I began when the tea had come, along with six different Danishes, in case I had trouble deciding which kind I wanted, "Joe, I heard about the lighters."

"Ah," Joe said, nodding. "You must mean Mr. Yee. An unfortunate misunderstanding, but now made whole, I believe."

"You believe no such thing: The guy's stuck with a garage full of garbage and no way to make up his investment. You've got to lay off the new immigrants, Joe."

"Lydia. My sweet. Where you see new immigrants, I see walking gold mines. And remember, darling, never was honest man unhorsed by me."

"Aha. So you're known around here as 'Double-crossing Delancey' for no reason."

"Sticks and stones." He sighed.

"Oh, Joe. These people are desperate. It's not fair for you to take advantage of them."

"Taking advantage of people is inherently unfair," he reflected, lifting a prune Danish from the pile. "And you can be sure each recently come representative of the huddled masses with whom I have dealings believes *himself*, at first, to be taking advantage of *me*."

"Still," I tried again. "You took twelve hundred dollars from this guy Yee. It's a lot of money."

"Fifteen hundred, with the fluid and the wicks," Joe corrected me. "He stands to make quite a lot more than that, with the right marketing plan."

"Marketing plan? Joe, the guy's a waiter!"

"And looking to better himself. An ambition to be commended."

I sighed. "Come on, Joe. Why don't you pick on someone your own size?"

Joe bit into his pastry. "My ancestors would spin in their graves. Surely you, a daughter of a culture famous for venerating the honorable ancestors, can understand that. This street, you know, is named for my family." I suspected the reverse was closer to the truth, but held my tongue. "It is peopled, now as ever, with newly minted Americans seeking opportunity. For a Delancey, they are gift-wrapped presents, Christmas trinkets needing only to be opened."

"You're a rat, Joe."

"Not so. In fact, I detect in you a deep appreciation of my subtle art."

"You're reading me wrong."

"If so, why are you smiling? My glossy-haired beauty, I make my living reading people. I'm rarely wrong. It's you who're in the wrong profession. You have a great future elsewhere."

"You mean, doing the kind of work you do?"

"I do. With me beside you singing in the wilderness."

I sliced off a forkful of cherry Danish. Joe, by contrast, had his entire pastry in his hand and was gouging half-moon bites from it. "Not my calling, Joe," I said.

"I disagree. You have all the instincts. You could have been one of the greats—and owed it all to me. I'd have been famous, mentor to the renowned Lydia Chin." He sighed, then brightened. "The offer's still open."

"I don't like cheating people."

A gulp of tea, a shake of the head, and the retort: "Thinning the herd, darling. I only take from beggars: people who beg me to."

An old line of Joe's I'd heard before. "I know, Joe. 'You can't catch a pigeon unless he sits still.'"

"Damn correct."

"That doesn't mean he wants to be caught."

"Wrong, oh glorious one. None of the people from whom I earn my bread will ever be rich, the brains to keep away from the likes of me being the minimal criteria for financial success. I at least offer them, though for but a fleeting moment, the warm and fuzzy sense that they might someday reach that dream."

"And you're doing them a favor?"

"Oh, I am, I am. Deep down, they know that fleeting moment is all they'll ever have, and they beg me to give them that. At least that. At most that. Joe, they say in their hearts—"

"Oh, stop it, Joe," I said in my mouth. "I've heard it before. And what about your Punjabi princess? Wasn't she rich?"

"You shock me, my sweet. Surely you cannot favor the grasping retention of unearned, inherited, caste-based wealth?"

"When the other choice is having it conned out of people by someone like you, I might."

"You cut me to the quick, my gorgeous friend. It pains me to feel your lack of respect for my ecological niche. Therefore let's cease talking about me and discuss you. How goes it with you? The detecting business treating you well?"

Joe winked and attacked his Danish. I sipped my tea. Around us bustled people making a living and people taking time out from making a living. I watched them and I watched Joe and finally I spoke. "Well, I have to admit that whoever told me this was no way to get rich was right."

"Wasn't that me?"

"Among others, maybe."

"I know I did. I thought, and think, you had, and have, chosen the wrong path. But enough of that. If the detecting of crime doesn't pay, what ecological niche do you propose to fill?"

I cut more Danish. "Oh, I'm not giving up the investigating business. But I do have to supplement it from time to time."

"And with what?"

"This and that. Nothing fun. A friend of mine came up with an idea this morning that sounded good, but then I thought about it. I don't know."

"And that would be what?"

"Lychee nuts."

"Lychee nuts? You intend to build your fortune on, excuse me, lychee nuts?"

"Well, exactly. He thinks it's a great idea, but I'm not sure. On the one hand, the best fresh lychees are hard to find in the U.S., and very big among Chinese people. You can get them canned, but they don't taste anything like the real thing. The fresh ones they import are third-rate. Premium fresh lychees, the best China has to offer, are very scarce and valuable."

"Really?" Joe sounded thoughtful. "How valuable is valuable?"

"Oh, not worth *your* time, Joe, not in your league. People would pay a lot, but they're expensive to import. You couldn't sell them down here. Just uptown, in the really fancy food shops." The waiter, to my surprise, had not only actually brought us our tea in a pot, but now replaced it with a fresh one. It's sometimes amazing what Joe can convince people to do. I filled both our cups. "You know, all those uptown Chinese doctors and invest-ment bankers, the ones who buy raspberries in January and asparagus in November. They'd pay a fortune, if the lychees were really good. But the import business, I don't think I'm cut out for it."

Lifting his freshly filled cup, Joe asked, "Is there none of this fabulous commodity on offer as we speak in New York, food capital of the world?"

"There's only one shop, actually just down Delancey about a block, that sells the big, premium ones. Really fresh and sweet, perfumey-tasting. Go ahead, make a face. Chinese people think of this stuff like caviar."

"Do they really? Then why not go for it?"

"Oh, I don't know. If I could get my hands on lychees from India, it might be worth it."

"They are thought to be special, Indian lychees?"

"I've actually never had one. They don't export them at all."

"Why not?"

"Some government restrictions, I don't know. But if I could sell those . . . on the other hand, this whole import thing probably isn't right for me."

I finished off my Danish, drained my tea. "You sure you won't recon-sider your marks, Joe?"

Flashing the ruby again, Joe said, "Perhaps if you, oh stunning one, reconsider my offer."

I smiled too. "Not in this lifetime. Well, I tried. Thanks for the snack, Joe. I have to go."

"There are Danishes yet untouched." Joe pointed to the pile of pastries still on the plate.

"I've had enough," I said. "More would be greedy. And I know what happens to greedy people when they get around you."

Joe bowed his head, as Charlie had, to acknowledge the compliment. He stood when I did, and remained standing as I worked my way to the door, but then he sat again. As I left he was ordering more tea and reaching for a blueberry Danish. From the distant, dreamy look in his eyes I could tell he was searching for an angle on the lychee nut situation. I wondered if he'd find it.

• • •

Four days later, on the phone, I heard from Joe again.

"I must see you," he said. "I yearn."

"Oh, please, Joe."

"No, in truth. Actually I can help you."

"Do I need help?"

"You do. Let me provide it."

"Why don't I trust you? Oh, I remember—you're a con man."

"Lydia! This is your Joe! My motives in this instance are nefarious, it's true, but not in the way you think. One: I can be with you, motive enough for any man. Two: We can both make money, motive enough for any man or woman. And three: You can see how smart your Joe is, and perhaps be moved to reconsider my previous offer. Motive enough, by itself, for Joe."

"That one's not likely."

"Let me buy you a refreshing beverage and we can discuss the issue."

It was a soggy afternoon, and I was, as we delicately say in the detecting business, between cases. My office air conditioner thinks if it makes enough noise I won't notice it actually does nothing useful, but I'd noticed. I'd finished paying my bills and had been reduced to filing.

I gave up, locked up, and went out to meet Joe.

Joe's meeting place of choice was a bench in Sara Roosevelt Park just north of Delancey Street. The refreshing beverage was a seltzer for me and an orange soda for him from the cart with the big beach umbrella. Joe's Cheshire-cat smile was not explained until we sat side by side, and with a flourish, he poured into my lap the contents of the paper bag he'd been carrying. The ruby flashed as I picked up one of a pair of the biggest, most flawless, most perfect fresh lychees I'd ever seen.

"Where did these come from?" I marvelled.

"Are you pleased, oh spectacular one? Has not your Joe done grandly?"

"Where did you get them?" I asked again. They were the size of tennis balls, which for a lychee is enormous.

"Sample one, my queen," said Joe.

"May I really?"

"They are for you, to lay at your feet. In the spirit of full disclosure, I admit there were originally three. I tried one myself and am left to conclude only that Chinese tastebuds and Irish tastebuds must have been created with irreconcilable differences."

"You didn't like it?" I bit into the lychee. It was firm and juicy, sweet and spicy, good beyond my wildest lychee dreams. As I dabbed a trickle of juice from my chin, I wondered if Charlie had ever had one like it.

"Your verdict, please," Joe demanded. "Is this the lychee that will make us rich?"

"This is a great lychee, Joe," I said warily. "Totally top-notch, super-duper, one of the best. Where are they from?"

Joe had been leaning forward watching me as though I were a race in which he had bet the rent on a horse. Now he leaned back, laced his fingers behind his head, and stretched his legs. He grinned through the leafy canopy at the blue June sky.

"The Raj," he said. "The star of Empire, the jewel in the crown. These are lychees from India, oh joy of my heart."

I stared. "You're kidding."

He spoke modestly, as befitted a man who had performed a miracle. "Procuring them was not a simple matter, even for your Joe. As you yourself stated so accurately, India does not as a matter of course export its lychees. But having been nearly engaged to a Punjabi princess does have its uses."

"You're not telling me her family still even speaks to you? They're willing to do business with you?"

Joe shuddered. "Heavens, no. Her male relatives would long since have sliced my throat, or other even more valuable parts of my person, had not my princess retained a soft spot for old Joe in her heart of hearts. But not all Indians of my acquaintance bear my former beloved's family good will, and the enemy of my enemy is, after all, my friend."

This was baroque enough to be pure Joe. "So you talked some other, what, Indian of your acquaintance into smuggling these for you? As a way to get back at your princess's family for whatever they were mad at them for?"

"Something like that. More important than those inconsequential details is the fact that there are, apparently, many more lychees where these came from."

"Is that a fact?"

"It is. And the fate of those lychees was quite a topic of conversation between myself and my South Asian acquaintances. We have, I am pleased to say, come close to a meeting of the minds. Of course," Joe paused significantly, "we also discussed remuneration, some serious compensation for their trouble, which will apparently include a certain amount of *baksheesh* to establish a home for blind customs officials."

"Really?" I asked. "How much did you promise them?"

Joe sent me a sideways glance. "I haven't, yet. That's why I needed to speak to you."

"Me? Why?"

"Well, putting aside my need for your mere nearness—"

"Say that again."

"What? My need for your mere nearness?"

"A great phrase, Joe. I just wanted to hear it twice. Go on."

He gave me an indulgent smile. "In any case: It is you and you alone who can set a price on these beauties. One beauty knowing another. What will your uptown Chinese pay? What shall I say we, therefore, will pay?"

"We?"

"We, oh shining vision! You and I! Your dream of riches! We shall reach the golden shore together. Whatever you say they're worth, I shall put up half. No questions asked. If you tell me these things will make us wealthy, then wealthy they will make us." He lifted the remaining lychee from my lap, flipped it high in the air, leaned forward and caught it behind his back. Tossing it again he listed like a sailboat in the wind, then looked around wildly for the lychee as though he'd lost it. Just before it beaned him, he reached up, caught it, and produced it with a flourish. I burst out laughing.

"Do I entertain you?" Joe's eyes shone like the eyes of a puppy thrilled that its new trick had gone over well.

"You do. But what really makes me laugh is the idea of going into business with you."

"But Lydia! This is nearly legit! There's the small matter of Indian export regulations, to be sure, but that aside, just look how far I've compromised my principles. I'm proposing to involve the Delancey name in a venture almost honest, for the sake of this dream, *your* dream. Oh, the ancestors! Surely you can bend your principles too?"

"Joe," I said sweetly, "read my lips. I will not do business with you. Legit or shady, risky or insured by Lloyd's of London. I'm more amazed than I can tell you that you found a source for Indian lychees, but I will not invest in any scheme that comes attached to you."

Joe looked at the lychee in his hand. He flipped it in the air, not nearly as high as before. "Time," he said to it. "She needs time to consider." He caught it, tossed it again. "The idea is new, that's all. Once she's sat with it for a day, the rightness of it will become clear to her. The inevitability. The *kismet*—"

He stopped short as I leaned over and snatched the lychee in middescent. "Thanks, Joe. I have a friend who'll enjoy this." I gave him my brightest smile, not quite a thousand watts but as many as I had. "Good luck with Indian customs." I stood and walked away, leaving Joe looking puzzled and forlorn on a bench in Sara Roosevelt Park.

I had told Joe I wouldn't do business with him. This did not mean, however, that nothing he did was of interest to me. In dark glasses and big floppy hat, I was up and out early the next morning, plying my own trade on Delancey Street.

One thing you could say for Joe: He did not, as did many people in his line of work, yield to the temptation to indulge in layabout ways. Joe's work was despicable, but he worked hard. I picked him up just after nine A.M. and tailed him for nearly three hours, waiting in doorways and down the block while he went in and out of stores, sat in coffee shops, met people on park benches. Finally, at a hole-in-the-wall called Curry in a Hurry, he was joined at a sidewalk table by a turbaned, bearded fellow who drank a *lassi* while Joe wolfed down something over rice. They spoke. Joe shrugged. The other man asked a question. Joe shook his head. Watching them from across the street, I was reminded that I was hungry. Luckily, their meeting was brief. When the turbaned gentleman left while Joe was still wolfing, I abandoned my pursuit of Joe and followed.

After a bit of wandering and some miscellaneous shopping, the turbaned gentleman entered a four-story building on the corner of Hester and Delancey. An aluminum facade had been applied to the building's brick front sometime in the sixties to spiff the place up. Maybe it had worked, but the sixties were a long time ago.

I gave the gentleman a decent interval, then crossed to the doorway and scanned the names on the buzzers. They were many and varied: Wong Enterprises; La Vida Comida; Yo Mama Lingerie. The one that caught my eye, though, was Ganges, Ltd.

That was it for a while. Now I had to wait until Charlie got off work at four. I hoped the staff of Ganges, Ltd., was as assiduous as most immigrants, putting in long hours in the hope of making their fortunes. Right now, having put in some fairly long hours myself, I headed off down Delancey Street in the hope of lunch.

At twenty past four, with Charlie at my side, I was back on the corner of Hester and Delancey, pressing the button for Ganges, Ltd. After the back-and-forth of who and what, the buzzer buzzed and we were in.

Ganges, Ltd., occupied a suite on the second floor in the front, from which the swirling currents of life in the delta could be followed. A sari-wrapped woman in the outer office rose from her desk and led us into the private lair of the turbaned gentleman I had had in my sights. The nameplate on his desk made him out to be one Mr. Rajesh Shah.

"Thank you for seeing us without an appointment, Mr. Shah," I said. I sat in one of the chairs on the customer's side of the desk and Charlie took the other. Rajesh Shah had stood to shake our hands when we came in; now he sat again, eyebrows raised expectantly. His white turban and short-sleeved white shirt gleamed against his dark skin. "I'm sure you're a very busy man and I don't mean to be impolite, popping in like this," I went on, "but we have some business to discuss with you. I'm Lydia Chin; perhaps you've heard of me."

Shah's bearded face formed into an expression of regret. "It is I who find, to my despair, that I am in a position to be impolite. Your name is not, alas, familiar. A fault of mine, I am quite sure. Please enlighten me."

Well, that would be like Joe: giving away as little as possible, even to his business partner. Controlling the information minimizes the chance of error, misstep, or deliberate double-cross. As, for example, what Charlie and I were up to right now.

On a similar principle, I introduced Charlie by his first name only. Then

I launched right into the piece I had come to say. "I believe you're acquainted with Joe Delancey."

Shah smiled. "It is impossible to be doing business in this neighborhood and not make the acquaintance of Mr. Delancey."

"It's also impossible to actually do business with Mr. Delancey and come out ahead."

"This may be true," Shah acknowledged, noncommittal.

"Believe me, it is." I reorganized myself in the chair. "Mr. Delancey recently offered me a business proposition which was attractive," I said. "Except that he's involved in it. I won't do business with him. But if you yourself are interested in discussing importing Indian lychee nuts, I'm prepared to listen."

Rajesh Shah's eyebrows went up once again. He looked from me to Charlie. "The Indian government is forbidding the export of lychee nuts to the U.S.A. This is until certain import restrictions involving Indian goods have been reevaluated by your government."

"I know the U.S. doesn't get Indian lychees," I said. "Like most Chinese people, Indian lychees have only been a legend to me. But Joe gave me a couple yesterday. They were every bit as good as I'd heard." I glanced at Charlie, who smiled and nodded vigorously. "Joe also gave me to understand you had found a way around the trade restrictions."

"You are a very blunt speaker, Miss Chin."

"I'm a believer in free speech, Mr. Shah, and also in free trade. It's ridiculous to me that lychees as good as this should be kept from people who would enjoy them—and would be willing to pay for them—while two governments who claim to be friendly to each other carry on like children."

Shah smiled. "I myself have seven children, Miss Chin. I find there is a wisdom in children that is often lacking in governments. What do you propose?"

"I propose whatever Joe proposed, but without Joe."

"This will not please Mr. Delancey."

"Pleasing Mr. Delancey is low on my list of things to do. You have to decide for yourself, of course, whether the money we stand to make is worth getting on Joe's bad side for."

"As to that, Mr. Delancey may be ubiquitous in this neighborhood, but he is in no way omnipotent."

Charlie had been following our English with a frown of intense concentration. Now his eyes flew wide. I smothered my smile so as not to embarrass him, and made a mental note to teach him those words later.

"Charlie here," I said to Shah, "has some money he's saved. Not a lot of money, I have to warn you, just a few thousand. Joe talked about putting up half: I think you'll have to assume more of the responsibility than that."

Shah gave a thoughtful nod, as though this were not outside the realm of possibility.

I went on, "What we can really bring to the deal is a distribution network. Well," I reflected, "that's probably a little fancy. What I mean is, I assume the cost of bringing these lychees in would be high, and so the sale price would have to be high for us to make a profit."

Rajesh Shah nodded, so I went on.

"Then you couldn't sell them on the street in Chinatown. People down here don't have that kind of money. But in the last few days—since Charlie first proposed this lychee idea, and before I knew about the Indian ones—I've done some looking around. There are a number of stores in fancy neighborhoods that are interested. Because I'm Chinese, they'll assume our lychees are from China. I'm sure you and Joe had already figured out a way to fake the paperwork."

Shah had the grace to blush. Then he smiled. "Of course."

"Well, then," I said. "What do you think?"

"Let me be sure I am understanding you," Shah said. "What you are proposing is that your associate"—a nod to Charlie—"invest his modest sum and receive a return commensurate with that investment. You yourself would act as, I believe the expression is, 'front woman'?"

"I guess it is."

"And you would be receiving, in effect, a salary for this service."

"Sounds right."

"And Mr. Delancey would have no part in any of this."

"That's not only right, it's a condition."

Rajesh Shah nodded a few times, his gaze on his desk blotter as though he was working something out. "I think," he said finally, "that this could be a successful proposition. Mr. Charlie," he asked, "how much of an investment are you prepared to make?"

Since the talk of money had begun, Charlie had looked increasingly fidgety and anxious. This could have been fatigue from the strain of focusing on all this English; it turned out, though, to be something else.

Something much worse.

"Money," he mumbled, in an almost-inaudible, un–Charlie-like way. "Really, don't have money."

Shah looked at me. I looked at Charlie. "The money you saved," I said. "You have money put away for college. We talked about using some of that."

Charlie's face was that of a puppy that hadn't meant to get into the garbage and was very, very sorry. I wondered in passing why all the men I knew thought dog-like looks would melt my heart. His beseeching eyes on mine, Charlie said, "You remember jackass brother-in-law?"

I nodded.

"Brother-in-law takes money for next great idea."

"Charlie. You let you brother-in-law have your money?"

Charlie's chin jutted forward. "In family account."

This was a very Chinese method of keeping money: in a joint account that could be accessed by a number of different family members. I wasn't surprised to hear that Charlie's brother-in-law was able to help himself. But: "He had the nerve? To take the joint money? After the disaster with the lighters?"

Rajesh Shah looked confused. Joe must not have shared the story of his triumphant swindle of jackass brother-in-law. But that wasn't my problem at the moment.

Charlie was nodding. "Brother-in-law have big money-making idea. Need cash, give to cousin."

"And what did your cousin do with it?"

"Cousin not mine. Cousin his," Charlie rushed to assure me. This was a distinction Charlie had learned in America. In a Chinese family the difference is nonexistent: Relations are relations, at whatever distance.

"*His* cousin," I said, my tone reflecting growing impatience. "What did *his* cousin do with your money?"

"Comes from China," he said. "Comes from China, brings . . ."

Charlie petered out. I finally had to demand, "Brings what?" *Brought* what, Lydia, I silently corrected myself. Or, *bringing* what. Even in the face of stress and strain, standards must be maintained. "What, Charlie?"

In a voice as apologetic as his face, Charlie answered, "Bear gall."

I counted to ten. When I spoke, my tone was ice. "Your cousin—no, all right, *his* cousin—brought bear gall from China into the U.S.?"

Charlie nodded miserably.

Rajesh Shah spoke. "Excuse me, I am sorry, please: What is bear gall?"

My eyes still on Charlie, I answered, "It's gooey brown stuff from the gall bladders of bears. Certain uneducated, foolish, ignorant Chinese people think it has medicinal properties. It doesn't, and besides that it's very painful to the bears to have it collected, and besides *that*, it's illegal to bring it into this country."

Charlie stared at the floor and said nothing.

"How much, Charlie?" I asked. "How much did he bring?"

Charlie mumbled something I couldn't hear. Rajesh Shah also leaned forward as I demanded again, "How much?"

Just barely louder, Charlie said, "Four pounds."

"Four pounds!" I exploded. "That could get him put away for twenty years! *And* your jackass brother-in-law. And *you*, Charlie!"

"Me?" Charlie looked up quickly. "I don't know they doing this! Just brother-in-law, his cousin!"

"Tell that to the judge," I said disgustedly.

"Judge?" Charlie's eyes were wide. I didn't bother to explain.

"I say this," Charlie said, shaking his head slowly. "I say, stupid guys, now what you think? Selling bear gall on street? Sign, big characters, 'Bear gall here'? But brother-in-law say, so much bear gall, make twenty thousand of bucks, send Charlie to college. Someone in family get to be smart, then everyone listen smart guy."

"Sounds to me like in your family it's too late for that."

"Excuse me." This was Rajesh Shah again. I frowned and Charlie blushed, but we both turned to him. It was, after all, his office. "I must admit surprise on hearing these numbers. Four pounds of this bear gall can bring twenty thousand dollars, actually?"

"Probably more," I grumbled. "If it's a well-known brand, people will pay close to five hundred dollars an ounce in this country because it's so hard to get. Because it's *illegal*," I snarled in Charlie's direction. "Because you can get *arrested* and put in *jail* for selling it. Or *deported*. Does your brother-in-law know that?"

"Brother-in-law know very little, I think. But say, know guy, going buy. Then brother-in-law, cousin, don't have bear gall, don't get arrested. Jeff Yang, on Mott Street?"

"Jeff Yang?" The words came slowly from my mouth. "Your brother-in-law is dealing with Jeff Yang?"

"Not dealing yet. Doesn't really know guy," he admitted. "Just hear guy buys bear gall."

"Jeff Yang," I said, emphasizing each word, as though I'd just discovered Charlie was a slow learner, "is the scum of the earth. I went to grade school with him, Charlie. I've known him forever. He used to steal other kids' lunch money. He'd sell you his grandmother if he could get a good price. Charlie, listen to me. You will not do business with Jeff Yang. Your brother-in-law, your cousin, *his* cousin, your kitchen god, *nobody* will do business with Jeff Yang. You will go home and flush this disgusting stuff down the toilet immediately."

Charlie looked stricken. I stood. "Well, so much for our plan, Charlie," I said. "Come on. Mr. Shah, I'm sorry we wasted your time."

Shah stood also. Reluctantly, so did Charlie.

"It is unfortunate we cannot do business," Shah said. He smiled in a kindly way at Charlie, then returned his gaze to me. "I must tell you, though, Miss Chin, that my door will continue to be open, if other possibilities occur to you."

"I don't think so," I said. "No offense, Mr. Shah, but I should have known better than to get involved in anything Joe Delancey had any part of. It can only lead to things like this, and worse."

Without a look at Charlie, I swept to the door and yanked it open. I nodded to the woman in the sari, crossed her office, and stomped down the stairs. Charlie, with the look of a beaten pup, followed after.

The dog thing got him nowhere.

I was in my office early the next morning, stuffing papers in files and thinking I should sell my air conditioner to Joe Delancey because it was a con artist, too—or maybe I could palm it off on Charlie's brother-in-law—when the phone rang.

Picking it up, I snapped, "Lydia Chin Investigations," in two languages. Then, because whoever this was might not deserve to be snapped at, I added more politely, "Lydia Chin speaking. Can I help you?"

"I think you can," said a male voice from the other end. "How're you doing, Lydia? This is Jeff Yang."

Maybe the snapping hadn't been such a bad idea.

"Jeff," I said. "Good-bye."

"No," came the instant response. "Not until you hear the proposition."

"I can imagine," I said, because I could. "No."

"You can make money and keep your friends out of trouble," Jeff said. "Or you can not make money, and they can get in trouble. What'll it be?"

An echo in Jeff's voice told me I was on the speakerphone in his so-called office, really a tiny room behind a Mott Street restaurant, and not a very good restaurant at that. Well, two could play that game. I punched my own speakerphone button and dropped into my desk chair.

"Go to hell, Jeff."

"You know you don't mean that."

"I mean so much more than that."

"I'll buy it, Lydia. The whole four pounds."

"I have nothing to sell, especially to you."

"Well, you can stay out of it. Just tell me where to find this guy Charlie and his relations."

"Jeff," I said, "I wouldn't tell you where to find a bucket of water if you were on fire."

"I always liked you, too. Holding your teddy bear hostage until you kissed me was just my way of showing that. Let's do business, Lydia."

"Even if I were inclined to do business with you, Jeff, which would be about two weeks after hell froze over, I wouldn't risk my reputation for whatever piddly sum you're about to offer and then cheat me out of."

"It'll be a good price. In cash. You'll have it at the same time as you turn over the goods."

"No cash, no goods, no thanks. If Chinatown found out I was dealing with you, I'd never have a legit client again."

"I'll send someone else. No one will know it's me."

"Who, Rajesh Shah? Is that who's in your office right now, Jeff? Is that why you have me on the damn speakerphone?"

Jeff ignored my question, a sure way of answering it. "Lydia," he said, "if you do a deal with me, we can keep it quiet. If you don't, I'll do two things. One: I'll spread the word in Chinatown that you *did* do a deal with me, and you can kiss your legit clients good-bye. But that'll be the least of your problems, because two, I'll drop a dime on you, and you'll have to give the Customs people your friend Charlie and his brother-in-law to keep your own ass out of jail."

I was speechless. Then: "What?" I heard my voice, low and shocked. "Jeff, you—"

"Don't tell me I wouldn't, because you know I would. Lychee nuts are about your speed, Lydia. Bear gall is out of your league. Five thousand dollars, by noon."

"*Five thousand dollars?* For four pounds?"

"You're not in a great negotiating position."

"Neither are you. I told Charlie yesterday to flush the stuff down the toilet."

"And you *know*," Jeff said, "you just *know* that he didn't. Five thousand, in the park, noon. Or your reputation is what goes down the toilet. And your friend Charlie goes to jail. Sent there by you."

Charlie in jail, sent there by me. That was an ugly picture, and I wiped it from my mind, replacing it with a vision of Jeff Yang in his back-room office. With Rajesh Shah.

"Ten," I said.

"Five."

"It's Golden Venture brand."

"Wrapped and labeled?"

"One-ounce packages."

The briefest of pauses, then, "Seven-five."

"I hope," I said, "that every ounce you sell takes a year off your life."

"The same to you," Jeff said. "See you in the park at noon."

"You must have missed it: I won't be seen with you, Jeff. Charlie will be there."

"How will I know him?"

"He'll find you. By your smell," I added, and hung up.

I called Charlie at the noodle factory. "I need you to be in the park at noon. With your brother-in-law's package."

Of course Jeff had been right: The package had not gone down the toilet. "Only get half-hour lunch," Charlie said apologetically.

"This shouldn't take long." I hung up.

At noon, of course, I was in Sara Roosevelt Park too. I sat far away from the bench I had stationed Charlie at, half-screened by a hot-dog vendor's cart. I just wanted to make sure everything went all right: I felt responsible for this.

It went without incident. I had shown Charlie a picture of Jeff Yang and he spotted him, followed him until he sat, and then, in a burst of creativity, ignored him, walked to a soda stand, bought himself a Coke, and meandered back to Jeff's bench. He put down the brown-paper bag he was carrying and popped the can open. Charlie and Jeff exchanged a few words of casual conversation, two strangers enjoying a sunny June day. Charlie asked to glance at Jeff's newspaper, and Jeff obliged. Charlie opened the pages of the front section, slipping the back section unopened beneath him on the bench. When he was hidden behind the paper Jeff rose, told Charlie in a friendly way to keep the paper, and then set off down the path, the bag Charlie had arrived with under his arm.

In the early evening of the next day, the light was honey-colored, the sky was cobalt, and the trees were a glorious emerald green as I strolled through the same park, Charlie at my side.

"Rajesh Shah, that man, I see him yesterday night, on Delancey Street," Charlie said.

"Really?"

"Yes. He say, hear you have money now, Charlie. Asking if I want invest in lychees, still. From India."

"What did you do?" I asked, though I was pretty sure of the answer.

"I tell him, have to speak to *gaje*. Say Charlie not investing on own anymore."

"Very good, Charlie. Very, very good."

I had bought us pretzels from a cart and was explaining to Charlie the difference between Kosher salt and the regular kind when a trio of men rose from a bench and stepped into our path.

"Lydia," said Joe, with his thousand-watt smile. Rajesh Shah, in turban and short-sleeved shirt, was on his left, and Jeff Yang, bulging shoulders straining his black muscle tee, was on his right. The dark expressions on their faces wouldn't have powered a nightlight.

"Lydia," Joe said again, holding on his palm a paper-wrapped rectangle the size of a mah-jongg tile. "Oh shining star of the east, what is this?"

I peered at the label around its middle. "You don't read Chinese, Joe? It says, 'Golden Venture Brand Bear Gall, Finest In All China.'"

"Yes, exquisite one," Joe agreed. "But what is it?"

"Prune paste, Joe. The stuff they put in Danishes." I gave him a big smile, too, and this time I was sure I hit a thousand watts.

Charlie, beside me, was also grinning. Shah and Yang frowned yet more deeply. Joe just looked sad.

"Did you try to sell it?" I asked sympathetically.

"Indeed I did. And for my trouble was chased from the back alleys of Chinatown by dangerous men with meat cleavers. The damage to my reputation for veracity in those precincts is incalculable."

"No kidding? Nice side benefit," I said.

"Lydia." Joe shook his head, as though the depth of his disappointment was bottomless. "You have cheated your Joe?"

"Well, I was hoping you were behind Jeff's offer," I admitted, "but I was prepared to cheat Mr. Shah if he was all I could get."

"All the packages are prune paste? There is no bear gall?"

"There isn't, and there never was."

"You set us up?"

"I did."

"Lydia," Joe repeated, in a voice of deep grief. "You set up your Joe?"

"My Joe, my foot. Show some respect. You were setting me up, and I out-set you."

"I?" Bewildered innocence. "But—"

"Oh, Joe. Indian lychees. You know, you keep saying I have all the instincts. I don't, but I figured if I thought like *you*, everything would work out."

"How so, my duplicitous darling?"

"When I turned down your offer, right on that bench over there— which you *knew* I would—I asked myself, what would Joe do if he were turning down an offer from a middleman he didn't trust?" Joe wrinkled his nose at "middleman" but didn't protest. "Joe would try to cut the middle-man out," I said. "So let's see how easy Joe makes it for me to cut *him* out. You led me around for a while the next morning, and finally you let me see you with Mr. Shah."

"I did notice you following me," Joe conceded.

"I should hope so. I couldn't have been more obvious except by wav-ing to you. You really think that's the best I can do? Joe, you show very little appreciation for my ecological niche."

"Touché, fair one. And then?"

"Well, you clearly wanted me to go to Mr. Shah and do a deal, leaving you behind. Then you and he would split whatever cash Mr. Shah was able to con us out of, right? Of course there were never any Indian lychees any more than there was bear gall. But when Charlie and I figured that out, who were we going to complain to? I was the one who'd said importing them was illegal in the first place."

Joe sighed. "So, knowing the sting was on, you stung first?"

"Wouldn't you have?"

"I would indeed. And Mr. Yang, so reviled by you when suggested by Charlie as a purchaser for the nonexistent bear gall, had in fact been sug-gested *by* you *to* Charlie as a name to bring up at the appropriate moment, in order to draw in Mr. Shah?"

Jeff Yang was glowering at Joe's side. I said, "Well, Jeff was perfect for the spot. In a million years Jeff would never risk a nickel of his own on a deal like this. If he did a deal, someone would have to be financing it. I hope," I said to Jeff, "you charged a commission. Something for your trouble."

Jeff Yang's frown became fiercer, and his hands curled into fists. I could feel Charlie next to me watching him, tensing.

Joe sighed. "We're all so very, very disappointed."

"No, you're not, Joe. You're impressed."

"Well," Joe conceded, "perhaps I am. But now, my unequaled Asian mistress of mystery, the game is over. Yes, you have won, and I will proclaim that truth to all who ask. Now is the time to return your cleverly gotten gains so that we can go our separate ways, with no hard feelings."

Charlie's face fell at this prospect.

"You have to be kidding, Joe," I said. "When was the last time you gave back money you'd conned somebody out of fair and square?"

"Ah," Joe said, "but I would not—especially in my amateur days, which status I fear you have not yet left behind—have worked a con on such a one as Mr. Yang." He indicated Jeff Yang, whose fists were clenched, angry frown fixed in place. To emphasize the danger, Joe stepped away a little, Rajesh Shah with him, leaving Charlie and me marooned with Jeff Yang in the center of the pathway. "I fear I will not be able to restrain the good Mr. Yang from putting into play his threatened destruction of your professional reputation, unless we are all satisfied. Not to mention what look like fairly dire designs on your person."

This was, finally, too much for Jeff Yang. The frown exploded into a great bellowing laugh.

Whatever else you want to say about Jeff Yang, his laugh has always been infectious. I cracked up too.

So did Charlie.

Jeff, wheezing from laughter, turned to Joe. "I do have designs on Lydia's person, but not that kind. I've spent my whole life trying to make up for the teddy bear kidnapping incident. I'll do anything she asks. I'm putty in her hands. I'll even pretend to be a big-time Chinatown gangster if Lydia wants me to." He pulled a fan of bills from his pocket and waved them in the air. "I charged ten percent," he said to me. "If I buy you dinner, will you finally forgive me?"

"I'll never forgive you," I said. "But you might as well buy me dinner." I slipped my arm into his. Just before Jeff, Charlie, and I walked off in the golden evening I spoke once more to Joe, who stood openmouthed on the path.

"Oh, and thanks for the lychees, Joe. They were China's finest. From that place on Delancey, right? And do keep in touch with your friend Mr. Shah. When they start growing lychees in India, if they ever do, I'm sure he'll let you know."

Mr. Shah blushed and frowned. But Joe, with a wide smile breaking over his face like sun through clouds, swept forward into a low, graceful bow. He came up with a flourish and a grin. I bowed my head to acknowledge the compliment. The ruby in Joe's tooth flashed in a final ray of light as, with Jeff and Charlie, I turned and walked away.

Ed McBain

Activity in the Flood Plain

ED MCBAIN has had one of those careers that most writers wouldn't even bother daydreaming about. Too darned unlikely that it could ever happen to them. Bestsellers, major hit movies, TV miniseries, even writing a screenplay for Alfred Hitchcock. And always the 87th Precinct novels. If there is a storyline, a story form, a story concept that McBain hasn't used, and mastered, in the 87th books . . . please write the editors of this anthology and tell them about it. And they will stand, the 87th novels, and be read and discussed fifty years from now. They're that good and that enduring as portraits of modern city life in America. Of course, Ed doesn't always write about the tough cops of Isola. His story, "Activity in the Flood Plain," published in *The Mysterious Press Anniversary Anthology,* shows him at his wry best as he tells how love and zoning ordinances just don't mix.

Activity in the Flood Plain

Ed McBain

I moved to East Hadley, Connecticut, because I wanted to get away from memories of the big bad city and a woman named Anita Lopez, who used to pose for me.

I am a portrait painter.

At least, that's how I earn my living. My other paintings rarely sell. Anita was the model for twenty canvases with the collective title *The Mayagüez Suite*. I chose the title because Anita herself was from Mayagüez, which is in Puerto Rico. All twenty abstract paintings showed Anita magnificently nude. I was halfway through the twenty-first canvas when she informed me she was pregnant with the child of the short-order cook at Epstein's Deli, around the corner from where I lived and painted in Manhattan. She told me Max—his name was Max Goldberg—was going to marry her and take her to Israel with him. She told me he was going to open his own delicatessen in Tel Aviv. I gave her the half-finished canvas—there was still a lot of work to be done on the breasts—as an engagement present. Then I began looking for a house in Connecticut.

The house I found was on the banks of the Pasquetuck River. In the Pequot Indian language, Pasquetuck means "White Man Drown in Shallow Water." I told that to the real estate agent who sold me the house, but she didn't laugh. Actually, I have no idea what Pasquetuck means in Pequot or any other Indian language. Anita once told me, in Spanish, that I had no sense of humor. This was before she met Max, whose riotous sense of humor extended to taking a Puerto Rican girl to live in Tel Aviv. But the river that runs past my land is indeed a shallow one, especially during the hot summer months when rain is scarce. It was difficult to imagine the land ever flooding. In fact, when I bought the house, I didn't know my meager two acres were in the so-called flood plain. Arthur Manning was the first person to inform me of this fact.

Arthur was a Westport architect who'd been recommended to me by a sculptor I knew in Manhattan. Arthur told me he was very impressed with my work. Arthur told me he might even ask me to paint his wife's portrait one day. Meanwhile, he warned me that architectural fees for residential alterations usually came to at least twenty percent of the building costs. To design and supervise the construction of a heated, well-lighted fifteen-by-twenty-foot extension at the rear of my house, Arthur was charging me an hourly rate of $125 for his services, plus $50 an hour for drafting fees. He told me that my little studio room overlooking the river would cost me something like $50,000 to $75,000 before all was said and done.

"Your land is in a flood plain," he said. "But that shouldn't be a problem."

He was smoking a pipe. He looked like an architect in a film from the fifties. Blond hair, a somewhat pudgy face, cheeks ruddy from the sudden September chill outside. I had bought the house and moved into it in July, two weeks after Anita Lopez left for the Holy Land. I had hoped to have the extension built before Christmas, but it was already September and I was just hearing about a flood plain.

"What does that mean?" I asked. "A flood plain?"

"It means that no regulated activity—as defined in the Public Inland Wetland and Watercourse Act of the State of Connecticut—shall be permitted in any area designated as wetlands."

"Wetlands," I said.

"Wetlands," Arthur said, and nodded almost reverently.

"And what exactly are wetlands?"

"Wetlands are established areas whose natural and indigenous character is preserved by law," Arthur said. "They can't be encroached upon for any use that would alter the natural character of the land."

"How would my little studio alter . . . ?"

"Your house is within the hundred-year flood plain. That's an area that's expected to be flooded every hundred years."

"Expected?"

"Yes. As calculated by records and charts. There are people who figure all the computations and permutations."

"If it floods only every hundred years," I said, "who gives a damn?"

"They do."

"Who's they?"

"East Hadley's Planning and Zoning Board. But don't worry," Arthur said, puffing on his pipe. "I foresee no difficulties."

Smoking was forbidden in the East Hadley Town Hall offices, on the second floor of which was located the hearing room in which the Planning and

Zoning Board held its regular meeting every Monday night. Three weeks ago, Arthur had submitted his application to the board. Tonight, there was to be a public hearing on it. In addition to our business, the three-man, two-woman board would be addressing three other matters: a modification of conditions for something called the Graham Subdivision, Phase I; a discussion of and decision on conditions for the eleven-lot subdivision called the Graham Subdivision, Phase II; and a discussion of and decision on conditions for the nine-lot subdivision called the Orleans Subdivision.

It seemed to me, and I said so to Arthur, that a mere fifteen-by-twenty-foot extension at the back of an artist's house was hardly in the same commercial league as these big-time subdivisions, and I didn't see why we had to go through all this red tape to get a goddamn permit. He agreed with me.

"But," he said, "you have the misfortune of being in the flood plain, and these people at P&Z take their jobs very seriously. They're only an appointed body, Jamie, but their power is absolute. You can't so much as belch in the flood plain without their permission. The problem is they're all laypeople who aren't sure of the issues relating to the federal mandate from FEMA, the Federal Emergency Management Agency that controls *all* flood plain and floodway activity in the United States."

"In other words, they're well-meaning jackasses," I said.

"Not even well-meaning," Arthur said. "I sometimes think they're opposed to *any* sort of development in the flood plain. Simply because they don't really *know* what's good or what's bad for the environment. Even Cassandra Howell isn't as knowledgeable as she appears to be, believe me."

"Who's Cassandra Howell?"

"Chairperson of the board. She merely *acts* as if she knows where the body's buried. That doesn't mean she has the faintest idea of what the federal mandates require. None of them do. They're just a pack of amateurs infatuated with the scent of their own perfume."

At that moment, Cassandra Howell walked into the room.

You have to understand that I was used to big city girls with their big city looks and their big city ways. Cassandra seemed to me the personification of all things wonderfully suburban. Thirty-three years old, maybe thirty-four, she was tall and supple and brimming with good cheer and autumn-spanked beauty. Her smile was as wide as my river. She was wearing a pleated brown woolen skirt, and brown panty hose, and brown loafers, and a russet-colored turtleneck sweater. Her hair was cut short, as black as a raven's wing.

Arthur leaned closer to me.

"Her husband left her five years ago," he whispered. "Got up one morning, ran off, and was never heard from since. I understand she's a trifle bitter about it."

I sat spellbound, listening as she presented our application to the rest of the board. Her voice sounded like buttered rum.

"We are asked to consider an application for a one-story, fifteen-by-twenty-foot addition in an area which is within the footprint of an existing deck," she said. "The deck will be demolished to make way for the addition."

She was pacing back and forth before the long table at which the one other woman and the three men on the board sat listening attentively. In the audience, seated on uncomfortable folding chairs similar to the one I myself sat upon, were the bored attorneys and contractors representing the three subdivision developers applying for permission to go ahead with their doubtless multimillion-dollar projects.

"Footing work will be necessary for the addition," Cassandra said. "This will require digging. The addition will allow expansion of the existing kitchen and dining area, and it will be approximately eighty feet from the Pasquetuck River. The space between the addition and the river is a combination of lawn and an area vegetated with mature trees and saplings. The lawn slopes slightly downgradient near the house and is flat to the edge of the river. The owner of the property is a portrait painter who plans to use the proposed extension as a studio."

She turned to look out over the audience, as if trying to locate me. Our eyes met. My heart stopped. She turned back to the table again.

"The house and addition are within the hundred-year flood plain," she said. "A flood-zone development permit is required for such activity in the flood plain. It is my recommendation that the board walk the site this coming Saturday in order to assist it in making a decision on petitioner's application to build in the flood plain."

She looked out at the audience again, her eyes grazing mine, walked back to the table, dropped her sheaf of notes on it, and then polled the members of the board.

It was agreed that they would meet on my property at eight A.M. this coming Saturday, the fourteenth day of October.

I was up at the crack of dawn.

I had been advised by Arthur not to interfere with the work of the board. Let them wander the property at will, do not offer them guidance or advice, just stay out of their way. But I showered and shaved and dressed myself in country threads from L.L. Bean, corduroy trousers and a red flannel shirt, wide black suspenders and ankle-hugging boots. I watched from an upstairs window as they traipsed down to the river and then walked back to the house, pacing off distances, talking animatedly among themselves. Cassandra was wearing gray slacks, the bottoms of which were tucked into shin-high yellow boots. She wore a yellow scarf over her coal-black hair. She

wore a short black car coat. She had on no makeup, not even a trace of lipstick. She looked fresh and beautiful and serious and intent as she considered
distances and elevations and God knows what else with the other board
members. I waited until the rest of them had piled into their cars and were
already leaving the property. Then I came out of the house and walked to her
just as she was opening the door on the driver's side of her Jeep.

"Miss Howell?" I said.

She turned. Eyes as dark as a Gypsy dancer's, glowing in the bright
October sun. A blue jay shrieked across the lawn, scaring me half to death.

"I'm Jamie Larson. I'm the petitioner," I said, and shrugged in what I
thought was a boyishly charming manner. This sometimes worked with big
city girls. But this was the country.

"How do you do, Mr. Larson?" she said.

I was holding out my hand to her, but she didn't take it. I yanked it
back. Put it in my pocket.

"Would you like to come in for a cup of coffee?" I asked. "Take the
chill off?"

She was staring at me. Studying my face, searching my eyes. Only the
fate of the entire universe hung in the balance.

"Yes, I think I might," she said. And smiled.

Outside, squirrels rattled through fallen leaves. A lawn sumptuously green
after heavy September rains sparkled in the bright golden sunshine. The leaves
kept falling, twisting on the mildest of autumn breezes. We sat at the kitchen
table sipping coffee, talking about how beautiful it was here by the river, how
tranquil, how seemingly removed from everyday troubles and concerns.

"I used to live in this house, you know," she said.

I looked at her.

"Yes," she said, and nodded. "When Michael and I first moved to East
Hadley, eight years ago. My husband," she explained.

"I didn't realize that."

"Yes," she said. "I know this house well."

"Would you like to walk through it?"

"Well . . ."

"Please," I said. "You must be curious."

"I must admit I am," she said.

"Come then," I said. "Bring your coffee."

I took her into the living room with its huge walk-in fireplace dating
back to the 1800s, and she looked around appraisingly and commented that
the bookcases had been moved, and I said the Carters—the family from
whom I'd bought the house—had probably done that. She said nothing to
this, merely nodded and kept looking at the bookcases as if trying to remember them in their previous location. We went upstairs then, into an area that

used to be one large bedroom, but which the Carters had divided into two smaller rooms to accommodate their two children. She told me they'd mentioned they were going to do that when they were still considering buying the house.

"They used to drive up every weekend from New York," she said. "I never thought they were serious. I thought they were just enjoying the countryside."

"When was that?" I asked.

"I sold it to them four years ago," she said. "I don't really see two bedrooms as an improvement over the original, do you?"

"Well, I guess the renovation was necessary," I said.

"But this used to be a *huge* guest room," she said, and opened her dark eyes wide. "There were windows all along the front here, overlooking the gardens. I had gardens everywhere," she said, somewhat wistfully. "I loved those gardens so much."

"People change things to suit their needs," I said.

"I suppose," she said, and I wondered immediately if I'd said the wrong thing. Would she now begin thinking that here was another city slicker moving into the house she'd lived in and nurtured, only to make changes that would not be improvements over the original?

"Where do you paint now?" she asked.

"In the dining room," I said. "Until I get my studio."

"Can't you paint up here?"

"Well, I use models, you know. I like to keep the upstairs of the house private."

"Are you a good painter, Mr. Larson?"

"There's a big demand for my portrait work," I said. "As for the *other* paintings . . . well . . . I do those to please myself, I suppose. Would you like to see some of them?"

"Yes, I would," she said.

I took her out to the garage where I had racked my most recent work, the twenty abstract nudes premised on the voluptuous figure and form of the former Anita Lopez, now Anita Goldberg, a housewife and resident of Tel Aviv. "I call them *The Mayagüez Suite*," I said, and showed her the first of them, which represented Anita lying on her side like an odalisque nude descending a staircase horizontally.

"Why, it's beautiful!" she said.

"Would you like to have dinner with me next Saturday night?" I asked.

"Why, yes," she said, "that might be nice." And smiled.

Arthur received the letter from the board three days after they walked my property. It read:

Dear Mr. Manning:

In the opinion of East Hadley's Planning and Zoning Board, your proposed plans for expansion of the Larson house located in the floodway and flood plain may have serious implications downstream. We are therefore asking that you submit for our further study and consideration a topographic survey prepared to Class T-2 topographic standards, depicting contours at one-foot intervals, physical improvements, trees twelve inches or larger in diameter, wetlands (delineated by a certified soil scientist), 100-year flood line (from FEMA mapping) and location of the Pasquetuck River. All surveys shall be prepared in compliance with Sections 20-300b-1 through 20-300b-20 of the Regulations of Connecticut State Agencies.

When we are in receipt of this material, we shall promptly schedule another appearance before the board.

The letter was signed by Cassandra Howell, Chairperson. "The topographic surveys will cost you between three and four thousand dollars," Arthur told me. "Plus the soil scientist's fee, which won't be as high. Maybe twenty-five hundred or so."

"The whole damn *addition* won't cost more than seventy-five thousand!" I said.

"They're fighting a war of attrition," Arthur said. "They're hoping if they make it difficult enough, you'll simply pack your tent and go away."

"I just got here," I said. "Order the surveys, Arthur."

"Why don't you just paint in your upstairs bedroom?" he suggested.

"Because I don't want my subjects roaming all over the house," I said. "Order the damn surveys."

My first subject in the town of East Hadley, Connecticut, was an eighty-year-old woman named Hannah Peabody, whose grandchildren had ordered her portrait. I had a difficult time getting her to sit still because all Hannah wanted to do was talk all the time. Or else get up to pee. Hannah peed almost as much as she talked. I had set up a temporary studio in what should have been the dining room, and which would go back to being merely that once the extension was completed. If ever the extension got *started*. If ever the board granted us a permit.

The light was excellent here in the dining room, and the location had the added advantage of being close to the powder room near the entry. Hannah would pop up every five minutes or so and come back some five minutes later, settling again into the chair I'd set up near the bank of windows. When Hannah wasn't peeing, she was talking. I tried to get some painting done in between times.

It was Hannah who told me a little bit about Cassandra Howell's husband who had run away. I welcomed the information; our dinner date was for this coming Saturday night.

"You never would've thought what happened would've happened," Hannah said. "They seemed so much in love. But one day, Michael just upped and left. Like the old joke, you know? Man goes to the grocery store for a pack of cigarettes, never comes back. You'd have thought they were so happy together. But you can't ever tell what's going on in a marriage, can you?"

"Is that really what happened?" I asked. "He went to the grocery store one day . . ."

"Well, no, that's the old *joke*. You don't have much of a sense of humor, do you? What *actually* happened is Michael walked himself to town one afternoon and took either a bus or a train to God knows where, never did get in touch with Cassandra to let her know where he was or what he was doing. Just disappeared from sight. Men do that sometimes, you know. Men are peculiar sometimes. Cassandra sold the house a year or so later. You probably bought it from the Carters, didn't you?"

"Yes," I said. "Why'd she sell it?"

"Bad memories here, I guess. Man leaving her and all. A woman can get used to a lot of things, but not a man leaving her. That's the one thing a woman can't abide. Although, in Cassandra's case, you'd have thought . . ."

Hannah closed her mouth.

"Better get some painting done here, don't you think?" she said.

To my enormous surprise, there was a little French bistro in East Hadley. To my greater surprise, the food there was really very good. It was Cassandra who originally recommended the place—which I found a bit awkward, to tell the truth, but I was after all new in town and she didn't seem at all embarrassed making the suggestion so why get all macho about it?

The place was very romantic. I considered it a good sign that she'd recommended a romantic place. I considered it a further good sign that she was dressed like a wicked big city girl in very high heels and a sophisticated little black dress fashioned to reveal breasts I hadn't expected to be quite so sumptuous and legs I hadn't suspected to be quite so shapely.

The waiter welcomed her like a cousin from Provence. He told me his name was Henri, and recommended a burgundy that cost sixty-eight dollars, which I figured was reasonable if the wine was truly as excellent as he said it was.

We sipped the wine by candlelight. It *was* truly excellent. Edith Piaf oozed from hidden speakers. Cassandra's eyes were sparkling. She told me again how much she'd loved the paintings in *The Mayagüez Suite*, and I told her the long sad story of my ill-fated romance with Anita Lopez who had run off with a delicatesseur and was now Anita Goldberg. She looked at me through the burning candles. I thought for a moment she would lean across the table and kiss me.

Instead, she said, "Why don't you paint *me* sometime?"

"Sure," I said, "I'd be happy to. What sort of portrait were you thinking of?"

"Actually," she said, "I was thinking of a nude."

On the Monday following our dinner date, East Hadley's P&Z Board informed us that the surveys and soil analysis—which together had cost me a mere $6,500—were insufficient for them to make a decision on the proposed addition. They were now asking for an engineer's flood-rise report, based on generally accepted engineering formulae and computing the expected rise in the hundred-year flood elevation due to the construction of a proposed fifteen-by-twenty-foot addition within the flood plain. They also wished a cross section cut through the proposed addition to clearly demonstrate the effect of the addition in relation to the entire flood plain.

"I'd like to say something," I said, and got to my feet. "I'm James Larson, it's my property and my house we've been discussing here since September."

"Sit down, Jamie," Arthur whispered.

"I can understand the Board's reluctance to grant permission for any building that might adversely affect the environment," I said, "but . . ."

"Sit *down*," he whispered again.

". . . . I don't intend building a fast-food joint or a bowling alley on the Pasquetuck. We're talking about a fifteen-by-twenty-foot extension here, a studio for a working artist, eighty *feet* from the river, and so far it's taken us almost two full months—this is almost the end of October already—to get a simple building permit. Meanwhile, this board has cost me close to eight thousand dollars in legal and other professional fees, and I'm *still* painting in my dining room!"

The room went silent. I looked at the members of the board sitting behind their long table on the platform. Cassandra's eyes met mine. She seemed hurt, as if I'd attacked her, personally, when of course I hadn't. Ellen Krieg, the other woman on the board, was in her fifties. She appeared embarrassed by my outburst. Two of the men seemed amused. The third man, bald and wearing a heavy cardigan sweater, stared out at me for a moment, and then said, "I'm Jerry Addison. I must say I tend to agree with you, Mr. Larson. I suppose at times we do seem like a five-star chamber here. The truth is we don't always agree, even among ourselves, but we do try to get the job done."

"I just don't understand this excessive *caution*," I said. "I don't know what this engineer's report will cost me . . ."

"You can figure another three thousand dollars," Arthur said, loud enough for everyone to hear.

"Well, there you are," I said. "The longer this thing drags on . . ."

"Believe me," Addison said, "there are some of us on this board who've been trying to expedite your permit."

"Well, I hope you'll reach a decision soon. If this were New York . . ."

"But it isn't, you see," Cassandra said all at once.

"*If* it were, you'd be staring at a lawsuit."

"Oh Jesus," Arthur whispered.

"Which is just what I'm trying to *avoid* here!" Cassandra said.

"Why don't we just grant the damn permit?" Addison said. "We've studied the plans, we've walked . . ."

"What happens fifty years from now?" Cassandra said. "What happens if we grant this permit, and Mr. Larson tears down the deck, and digs his footings, and puts up his proposed studio—and there's a flood?"

"Oh, for God's sake, Cassandra," Ellen Krieg said. "There won't be any flood, and you know it!"

"What if his studio gets washed away in a flood . . ."

"The river's only three feet deep on his property," one of the men on the board said.

"What if his studio gets carried downstream?" Cassandra insisted.

"No such thing has happened in the past two hundred years!" Addison shouted.

"What if his studio crashes into somebody's living room? What if those downstream people sue the town of East Hadley? Are your children or your children's children going to pay the damages?"

The room went silent.

"Mr. Larson," Cassandra said, "we've asked for an engineer's report. When we receive it, we'll consider your application further." She turned away. "Are the lawyers for DBD Partners Land Tech present?" she asked.

"We're here, Madam Chairperson," a man in a striped suit said, leaping to his feet.

"Are you ready to discuss the proposed lot-line changes for the Farm Hill Road subdivision? Those would be the six lots off Sleepy Hollow Lane."

"We are."

I was still standing.

Cassandra's dark eyes met mine. Locked with mine. There was something like a warning in them.

"Was there anything else, Mr. Larson?" she asked.

"Not right this minute," I said.

"Then thank you," she said, dismissing me.

The next day she called to ask when she might start posing for me.

On Saturday, I painted her nude for the first time.

And went to bed with her that very same day.

"It would seem to me," she said, "that you'd *cherish* the privacy of an upstairs studio."

"How do you figure that?"

We were in my bedroom. On my bed. We were both naked. Half an hour ago, Cassandra had been lying nude on a divan downstairs, posing for me. Now we were in each other's arms.

"I'm assuming I'm not the first model to find her way into your bed . . ."

"Cassandra . . ."

"Please, we're both grown-ups. What I'm saying is that it would surely be more convenient—and less expensive in the long run—to convert one of these upstairs bedrooms into a studio. Then you wouldn't have to tear up the house again . . ."

"I haven't torn it up before."

"Well, the Carters moved those bookcases and converted the guest room . . ."

"To suit their needs," I reminded her.

"It seems to me *your* needs would be satisfied by simply . . ."

"My needs would be satisfied by kissing you right this minute," I said.

"Why are you being so stubborn?" she asked.

"What is it?" I asked. "Have you decided *never* to grant the permit? Are you breaking the news to me gently? Is that it?"

"No, that isn't it," she said. "Anyway, it's not *my* decision alone to make. There are five of us on the board, you know. And by the way, it's unethical of you to ask the *Chairperson* of the board a question like that when she's nude in your bed."

"Naked in my bed," I said. "When you were downstairs on the divan, you were nude. Up here in my bed, you're naked."

"I fail to see the difference."

"Which is why you fail to see the difference between a studio and a bedroom."

"I don't know why you insist on making things so difficult," she said, and sighed deeply. "Why don't you just paint upstairs here, and kiss me the way you said you would?"

"I'll kiss you," I said, "but I won't paint upstairs here."

On Monday evening, November 13, Mr. Samuel McReady of McReady Engineering in New Canaan presented his report to the board. McReady was a tall, white-haired man in his late fifties, I guessed. There was a no-nonsense air about him as he faced the long table behind which sat the heart-stoppingly beautiful Cassandra Howell and the four board members.

"McReady Engineering Associates was retained by Arthur Manning, Architect," he said, "to provide flood-plain computations for a proposed addition to an existing dwelling at 87 Sector Road in the town of East Hadley, Connecticut . . ."

I knew what was in his report. This was hardly suspenseful to me. Cassandra knew what was in it, too. She had been leafing ahead through the typewritten pages as he spoke.

"Based on our computations," McReady said, "the predicted increase in flood elevation due to the decreased flood storage volume within the site is zero point zero zero six feet. That's approximately one-sixteenth of an inch. It is our opinion that this computed rise is negligible."

He looked at the table where the board sat.

He nodded his head for emphasis.

"It is clear," he said, "that the proposed addition lies in the flow shadow of the existing house. The existing house is what defines the hydraulic limitation of the existing flood plain, and the proposed addition will do nothing to alter that capacity. In brief, there will be no adverse effect on flooding due to this proposal. Moreover, it is the conclusion of this report and the opinion of this office that the construction of the proposed addition will have no adverse impacts to the adjoining property owners."

He looked up at the table again.

"Thank you," he said.

"Thank you, Mr. McReady," Cassandra said. "We'll take your report into consideration when making our decision. Was that all for this evening, Mr. Manning?"

Arthur nodded, and was waving away any further discussion. When I got to my feet, he sighed deeply. I was certain the board could hear him all the way up there on the platform.

"Madam Chairperson," I said, "I would merely like to ask that we now bring this matter to a climax as swiftly as possible."

"That is surely a consummation devoutly to be wished," Cassandra said, and smiled, and lowered her eyes to the pages on the table before her.

I painted her again that Saturday, and on Monday morning, Arthur received another letter from the board.

Dear Mr. Manning:

I am sorry to report that East Hadley's Planning and Zoning Board is still of the opinion that your proposed plans for expansion of the Larson house may have serious implications downstream. We are asking, therefore, that you review the plans with the State of Connecticut's Department of Environmental Protection. We have this date mailed the original of the enclosed letter to Mr. Franklin Garth, Director of Inland Water Resources in Hartford. Please contact him at your convenience.

The letter to Hartford read:

Dear Mr. Garth:

The above referenced application is before East Hadley's Planning and Zoning Board. It proposes construction in the floodway.

Because the applicant is insistent, we would appreciate the DEP reviewing the plans and sending us your comments.

Thank you for your consideration.

Both letters were signed by Cassandra Howell, Chairperson.

It began snowing two days before Thanksgiving.

I asked Ralph, the man who plowed my driveway, to shovel off all the walks and the back deck as well. He was a man in his late sixties, weathered and gnarled, and it was a bitterly cold day. Along around eleven, while he was still working out there, I invited him in for a cup of coffee. We sat at the kitchen table, steam rising from the mugs, fat lazy flakes still falling from the sky.

"I hear you'll be putting on another room," he said.

"Well, if we ever get a permit," I told him.

"Will you be planting gardens again?"

"I'm not much of a gardener," I said.

"The Howells had the prettiest gardens," he said. "Ran from the back of the house here almost halfway down to the river. There's good sun this side of the house, you know. Them gardens were really something."

"What happened to them?"

"She tore 'em out after Mr. Howell left. Guess she didn't want anything reminded her of him. Put in a lawn and a deck instead—well, the one I'm shoveling clear of snow today. This was some five years ago," he said. "Before the Carters bought the place."

"Did she need a permit for the deck?" I asked.

I was making a joke. If the chairperson of East Hadley's Planning and Zoning Board, a known pain in the ass when it came to granting permits for any activity in the flood plain, was *herself* considering the construction of a—well, I guess you had to be there.

"Don't suppose she did," Ralph said. "The deck being directly at ground level and all. But who knows how they figure these things? I sure don't."

"I don't, either," I said. "Why'd he leave her, anyway, would you know?"

"Mr. Howell? Well, he always did have an eye for the ladies, you know."

"You think another woman was involved, is that it?"

"Man just ups and leaves without a tip of the hat, I'd say Churchy La Flame, yes."

"Is that what he did? Just walked out one day?"

"So the story goes," Ralph said.

"Walked over to the railroad station . . ."

"Or the bus terminal, whichever."

"Hopped a train to Nebraska or Kentucky, huh?"

"Or River City Junction, Iowa. Wherever."

"With another woman."

"Could be."

"So she tore up all her gardens . . ."

"Is what she done."

". . . and built herself a deck."

"Same one right outside the windows here. Was my cousin Rollie and his crew put it in. Took 'em most of three weeks to finish the job, a good solid deck." He drained his coffee cup, set it back on the table. "Which I better get out there and finish shoveling," he said, "'fore another two inches accumulates. Thanks for the coffee, Mr. Larson."

"Thanks for the good talk," I said.

Cassandra called me the very next day.

"May I come over?" she said.

"Yes," I said.

"Now?" she said.

"Whenever," I said.

She arrived ten minutes later. She was wearing a bulky green turtleneck sweater and a heavy woolen skirt to match, the black car coat over them, a long striped college-boy muffler trailing. She was grinning from ear to ear as she climbed down out of the Jeep. Her short black hair danced in a fierce wind that blew off the river. We kissed.

"I have something for you," she said, and took an envelope from her tote bag. The return address on it was:

STATE OF CONNECTICUT
DEPARTMENT OF ENVIRONMENTAL PROTECTION
BUREAU OF WATER MANAGEMENT

"Read it," she said, and handed the envelope to me.

I unfolded the single sheet of paper inside it. The letter was addressed to Ms. Cassandra Howell.

Dear Ms. Howell:

I am in receipt of your letter to Mr. Garth of the Inland Water Resources Division of the Connecticut Department of Environmental Protection. Your letter references the plans for work within the flood plain portion of the Pasquetuck River in East Hadley as mapped by FEMA and the National Flood Insurance Program Floodway Maps.

The most critical part of the plan includes the installation of a 15' × 20' addition to the existing house structure. This addition is located on the south side of the existing structure, which happens to be on the downstream side of the structure as this river is flowing from north to south at this location. This addition is also located in the flowline "shadow" of the structure.

Construction within such a flowline-shadow area rarely affects water surface profiles. For this reason, an engineer reviewing the placement of the addition does not always have to perform a detailed hydraulic analysis in order to prove that the addition causes no adverse hydraulic impacts.

Mr. Samuel McReady, P.E., states in his hydraulic report that the addition lies within the shadow of the existing structure. I agree with Mr. McReady's conclusion.

In short, this construction will not affect river hydraulics in this section of the river.

If you have any additional questions, please feel free to contact me.

The letter was signed by Jason L. Carpenter III, Supervising Civil Engineer.

"Congratulations," Cassandra said, and kissed me again. "Want to go away together for Thanksgiving?"

I called Arthur with the good news. He told me Cassandra had already called to say our petition would undoubtedly be approved at the Monday meeting after Thanksgiving, and that we could start demolishing the deck and digging the ground for our footings as soon as we had the signed piece of paper in our hands.

That Wednesday night, Cassandra and I left for a little inn in Vermont. The flood plain seemed very far away. We shopped antiques stores and drank mulled cider. We ice-skated on a pond behind the inn and took long walks in a countryside crackling with color. We made love at night in an eaved and shuttered room and slept under down comforters.

In bed on our last night there, cradled in my arms, the wind whistling in the trees outside, she lay awake for a very long while.

"What is it?" I asked.

"A favor."

"Name it."

"Withdraw your application."

"What do you mean? It's about to be *granted*."

"Please withdraw it, Jamie. You don't need that studio. You can paint somewhere else in the house."

The room was silent except for the sound of the insistent wind.

"I don't understand," I said.

"I'll lose the chair," she said. "They'll vote Jerry Addison in as chairman."

"Why would they do that?"

"It was my idea to go to Hartford. Jerry resisted it, he was in favor of granting you the permit all along. But I had to protect the board, don't you see? I wanted to have a higher authority to quote if ever there was any trouble downstream. I didn't want the board to be sued later on."

"But Hartford *okayed* my proposal. I don't see . . ."

"That's just the point. Jerry will use that to prove I was being overly cautious. Wasting everyone's time. An unsuitable chairperson. But if you withdraw your application . . ."

"You can't ask me to do that."

"I am asking you. The board will think I was right all along. They'll think you were the one wasting our time."

"But I wasn't."

"It's what they'll think."

"But I *wasn't* wasting anyone's time. I *wanted* that studio, I *still* want it. I'm a working artist. I need a space where I can work. Cassandra, you can't really be asking me to get involved in the petty politics of . . ."

"I don't want to lose that chair," she said.

"I'm sorry. I can't do it."

"Okay, thank you," she said, and rolled away from me.

In a little while, I heard her even breathing and knew she was asleep.

I lay awake for most of the night.

In the morning, she seemed to have forgotten the harsh words we'd exchanged the night before. We made love in sunlight streaming through the dormer windows. We had breakfast at eleven and then packed our bags and drove leisurely down back roads, stopping at antiques shops and apple stands, discovering town fairs along the way. We did not get back to Connecticut until just before dinner. We ate dinner by candlelight in the dining room of my house, where my paints and easels still stood against one wall.

On Monday evening, November 27, Jerome Addison, the P&Z Board member who'd favored granting me a permit all along, moved that the application of James Larson to conduct a regulated activity in an inland wetland and/or water-course area located at 87 Sector Road as proposed and shown on a plan dated August 11 and revised August 23, be approved. The motion was seconded by Ellen Krieg and was carried unanimously.

All that following week, I painted Cassandra Howell in the nude.

On Monday morning, she left town as suddenly as her husband had.

Every weekday morning, the East Hadley *Herald* ran a report titled "The East Hadley Police Blotter." Among the crimes reported on Tuesday morning, December 5, the day after demolition of my deck began, were the following:

> Two stone statues were reportedly stolen from a residence on Carlyle Street. The two-foot statues of a pig and a dog were stolen separately over the weekend from the front lawn. They are valued at $175 and $250.

Workmen digging footings for an extension to a house on Sector Road reported finding a human skeleton buried some four feet deep. Both workmen are from Brazil and do not speak good English, police said, so an interpreter was brought to the scene to help translate.

A resident on Littlejohn Avenue reported a Compaq laptop and a Datacom computer test cable stolen from a GMC truck parked in the driveway Sunday night. The computer is valued at . . .

On Thursday morning, December 7, the police in Wichita, Kansas, telephoned the police in East Hadley, Connecticut, to say they had arrested a woman driving a Jeep over the posted speed limit on the interstate, and that her driver's license identified her as the fugitive named in East Hadley's all-points bulletin.

Cassandra Howell was returned to Connecticut the very next day, to answer charges of first-degree murder. It seemed that a dental chart obtained from a Dr. Nathan Neuberger, who used to be Michael Howell's orthodontist, matched the teeth on the skeleton the Brazilians had found under my deck.

Since the only cells in town were the two small holding cells at the back of the police station, Cassandra was moved to the county jail over at the county seat. It was there that I went to visit her shortly before Christmas.

She looked pale in her gray prison threads. She wore no makeup, but then she rarely had. She said she was happy I was there. I told her I hoped she didn't think I *wanted* those two Brazilian workmen to find the skeleton under my deck . . .

"Well, *my* deck, to be more accurate," she said, and smiled. "Since I was the one who had it built five years ago."

"What I mean . . . if I'd have known . . ."

"Yes, but of course, you didn't."

"Why'd you kill him, Cassandra?"

"Well, maybe because the son of a bitch was cheating on me, hmm?" she said, and smiled again, and I remembered her smiling up at me that day she accepted my invitation to come in for a cup of coffee. "It got to be too much, Jamie. So one night I confronted him, and he admitted it, and I picked up a bread knife from the kitchen counter . . ."

I could not imagine her picking up a bread knife.

". . . and stabbed him," she said.

I could not imagine her stabbing anyone.

"I buried him at the back of the house," she said, and nodded with a finality that was chilling. "Dug up all the gardens so nobody'd think to question the fresh earth. I loved those gardens so much. But then . . ."

She hesitated.

"I loved *him* so much, too," she said, and nodded again.

The cell went silent. She sat on the edge of her cot like a child in a gray school uniform, her hands folded in her lap, her dark head bent. She did not look up at me. I wanted to see her eyes, but she did not look up. "I had the deck built afterward," she said. "I never in a million years expected anyone would tear it down and go digging for him."

She looked up suddenly. Her eyes were brimming with tears.

"But then you came along, didn't you, Jamie? You and your dear innocent need for a studio."

"Cassandra . . ."

"I'm sorry I had to fight your application so hard," she said. "But I knew if it was ever granted, they'd start digging." She smiled again. Tears were streaming down her face, but she was smiling. "I'm so sorry," she said. "Please forgive me, Jamie. I don't want you to think I deceived you. I wasn't trying to bribe you, Jamie."

"I never thought you were."

"I went to bed with you because you made me feel beautiful and desirable, and I hadn't felt that way in a long while. Not to bribe you, Jamie." She reached out and took my hand. "Was I a good model?" she asked.

"You were a wonderful model," I said.

"Better than Anita Lopez?"

"Better than anyone."

"If only we'd met . . . ," she started.

She shook her head.

"But then . . ."

She shook her head again.

"I'm sorry," she said.

I have lived in that house for a year and a half now.

I have never sold the eight paintings I did of Cassandra Howell, nor have I ever painted another nude. All I do now is portrait work.

Every time it rains, I wonder if the property will be flooded.

Maybe that's why I work in one of the upstairs bedrooms, and not in the new studio at the back of the house.

Carolyn Wheat

The Only Good Judge

A FORMER NYPD staff attorney and public defender, Carolyn Wheat has written novels and stories that are generally concerned with that slippery slope known as the criminal justice system. Her books have great heart and great wisdom, especially when they judge those who would judge others, those who do not seem as concerned with injustice as one might hope. She has twice been nominated for the Edgar Award, and after reading "The Only Good Judge," which first appeared in the legal-themed anthology *Women Before the Bench*, one wonders why she has not won the award yet. But maybe that's just because the best is yet to come . . .

The Only Good Judge

Carolyn Wheat

W hat do you say to a naked judge? I said yes. Averting my eyes from the too, too solid judicial flesh.

I mean, the steam room is a place for relaxation, a place where you close your eyes and inhale the scent of eucalyptus and let go the frustrations of the day—most of which were caused by judges in the first place, so the last thing you want to do while taking a *schvitz* is accept a case on appeal, for God's sake, but there was the Dragon Lady, looking not a whit less authoritative for the absence of black robes, or indeed, the absence of any other clothing including a towel.

She'd been a formidable opponent as a trial judge, and we at the defense bar breathed a sigh of relief when she went upstairs to the appellate bench. The Dragon Lady was one of the great plea-coercers of her time; she could strike fear and terror into the hearts of the most hardened criminals and have them begging for that seventeen-to-life she'd offered only yesterday.

Yes, I said she "offered." I know, you think it's the district attorney who makes plea offers while the judge sits passively on the bench. You think judges are neutral parties with no stake in the outcome, no interest in whether the defendant pleads out or goes to trial.

You've been watching too much *Law & Order*. The Dragon Lady made Jack McCoy look like a soft-on-crime liberal. She routinely rejected plea bargains on the ground that the DA wasn't being tough enough. She demanded and got a bureau chief in her courtroom to justify any reduction in the maximum sentence.

So what was she doing asking me, as a personal favor, to handle a case on appeal? I almost fell off the steam room bench. I was limp as a noodle well past *al dente*, and I'd been hoping to slide out the door without having to acknowledge the presence of my naked nemesis parked on the opposite bench like a leather-tanned Buddha. It seemed the health club equivalent of subway manners: you don't notice them, they won't notice you, and the city functions on the lubrication of mutual indifference.

But she broke the invisible wall between us. She named my name and asked a favor, and I was so nonplussed I said yes and I said "Your Honor" and three other women in the steam room shot me startled open-eyed glances as if to say, who are you to shatter our illusion of invisibility? If you two know one another and talk to one another, then you must be able to see us in all our nakedness and that Changes Everything in this steam room.

They left, abruptly and without finishing the sweating process that was beginning to reduce me to dehydrated delirium. I murmured something and groped my way to the door. I left the Dragon Lady, who'd been there twice as long as I had, yet showed no signs of needing a respite; like a giant iguana, she sat in heavy-lidded torpor, basking in the glow of the coals in the corner of the room. She lifted a wooden ladle and poured water on the hot rocks to raise more steam.

I stumbled to the shower and put it on cold, visualizing myself rolling in Swedish snow, pure and cold and crystalline.

The frigid water shocked me into realizing what I'd just done.

A favor for the Dragon Lady.

Since when did she solicit representation for convicted felons?

Four days later, she was dead.

My old Legal Aid buddy Pat Flaherty told me, in his characteristic way. He always said the only good judge was a dead judge, so when he greeted me in Part 32 with the words, "The Dragon Lady just became a good judge," I knew what he meant.

"Wow. I was talking to her the other day." I shook my head and lowered my voice to a whisper. "Heart attack?"

A sense of mortality swept over me. The woman had looked healthy enough in a reptilian way. I'd noticed her sagging breasts and compared them to my own, which, while no longer as perky as they'd once been, didn't actually reach my navel.

But give me ten years.

"No," Flaherty said, an uneasy grin crossing his freckled face. "She was killed by a burglar."

"Shot?"

"Yeah. Died instantly, they said on the radio."

"Jesus." At a loss for words—and believe it or not, considering how much I'd resented the old boot when she was alive, annoyed at Flaherty for making light of the murder.

Good judge. It's one thing to say that about a ninety-year-old pill who dies in his sleep, but a woman like the DL, cut down in what would be considered the prime of her life if she were a man and her tits didn't sag—that verged on the obscene.

The big question among the Brooklyn defense bar: should we or should we not go to the funeral?

We'd all hated her. We'd all admired her, in a way. I loved the fact that she used to wear a Wonder Woman T-shirt under her black robe. She was tough and smart and sarcastic and powerful and she'd been all that when I was still in high school.

But she'd also been one hell of an asset to the prosecution, a judge who thought her duty was to fill as many jail cells as possible and to move her calendar with a speed that gave short shrift to due process of law.

In the end, I opted to skip the actual funeral, held in accordance with Jewish custom the day after the medical examiner released the body, but I slipped into the back row of Part 49 for the courthouse memorial service two weeks later.

What the hell, I was in the building anyway.

I was in the building to meet Darnell Patterson, the client she'd stuck me with. It had taken me two weeks to get him down from Dannemora, where he was serving twenty years for selling crack.

Twenty years. The mind boggled, especially since he wasn't really convicted of the actual sale, just possession of a sale-weight quantity, meaning that someone in the DA's office thought the amount he had in his pocket was too much to be for his personal use. Since he'd been convicted before, he was nailed as a three-time loser and given a persistent felony jacket.

"It's like they punishing me for thinking ahead," he said in a plaintive voice. "I mean, I ain't no dealer. I don't be selling no shit, on account if I do, the dudes on the corner gonna bust my head wide open. I just like to buy a goodly amount so's I don't have to go out there in the street and buy no more anytime soon. I likes a hefty stash; I likes to save a little for a rainy day, you hear what I'm saying?"

"Yeah," I said. "You're the industrious ant and all the other users are grasshoppers. The law rewards the grasshoppers because they bought a two-day supply, whereas you, the frugal one, stocked up."

"You got that right," he said with a broad smile. "I think you and me's gonna get along fine, counselor. You just tell that to the pelican court and they'll knock down my sentence."

It was conservative economics applied to narcotics addiction. Maybe I could get an affidavit from Alan Greenspan on the economic consequences of punishing people for saving instead of spending. I could hear my argument before the appellate court:

"Your Honors, all my client did was to invest in commodities. He wanted a hedge against inflation, so he bought in quantity, not for resale, but to insure himself against higher prices and to minimize the number of street buys he had to make, thus reducing his chances of being caught. Punishing him with additional time for his prudence is like punishing someone for saving instead of running up bills and declaring bankruptcy."

The more I thought about it, the more I liked it. The appellate judges—"pelicans" in defendantese—had heard it all. They were unlikely to buy the "mandatory sentences suck" argument and they had no interest in hearing the drug laws attacked as draconian, and they sure as hell didn't give a damn about my client's lousy childhood. Supply-side economics had the advantage of novelty.

When I walked out of the ninth-floor pens, I still had no idea why I'd been asked to take Darnell's case. The sentence was a travesty, of course, far outweighing whatever harm to society this man had done, but what was new or unusual about that? And why had the Dragon Lady, of all people, taken such an interest in a low-level crack case?

With her dead, I'd probably never know.

I had no inkling of a connection between the case and her untimely death.

It took the second murder for the connection to become apparent.

The deceased was a district attorney we called the Terminator; that quality of mercy that droppeth as a gentle rain from heaven was completely absent from his makeup. So once again, there were few tears shed among us defense types, and, in truth, a lot of really bad jokes made the rounds, considering how Paul French died.

He fell out a window in the tall office building behind Borough Hall, the same building that housed the Brooklyn DA's office, but not the actual floor the trial bureau was on. Which, in retrospect, should have told us something. What was he doing there? Had he fallen, or was he pushed? And had the Dragon Lady really died at the hands of a clumsy burglar who picked her house at random, or was somebody out to eliminate the harshest prosecutors and judges in the borough of Brooklyn?

His own office called it suicide. Word went around that he was upset when someone else was promoted to bureau chief over him.

Bullshit, was what I thought. I knew Paul French, tried cases against him and was proud to say we were even—three wins for him, three for me, which in the prosecution-stacked arithmetic of the criminal courts put me way ahead as far as lawyering was concerned. And I knew that while he might have enjoyed cracking the whip for a while as bureau chief, it was the courtroom he loved. It was beating the opponent, rubbing her nose in his victory, tussling in front of the judge and selling his case to the jury that got his heart started in the morning. He might have gotten pissed off if someone else got a job he thought should have been his, but no way would that have pushed him out a tenth-story window.

The suicide story was bogus, a fact that was confirmed for me when two cops rang the bell of my Court Street office and said they wanted to discuss Paul French. I invited them in, poured them coffee—Estate Java, wasted on cops used to drinking crankcase oil at the stationhouse—and congratulated them on not buying the cover story. The man was murdered; the only question was which of the fifty thousand or so defendants he'd sent up the river could legitimately take the credit.

The larger and older of the cops opened his notebook and said, "You represented a Jorge Aguilar in September of 1995, is that right, counselor?"

It took a minute to translate his fractured pronunciation. It took another minute to recall the case; 1995 might as well have been twenty years ago, I'd represented so many other clients in so many other cases.

"Jorge, yeah," I said, conjuring up a vision of a cocky, swaggering kid in gang colors who'd boasted he could "do twenty years standing on his head." Despite his complete lack of remorse and absence of redeeming qualities, I'd felt sorry for him. In twenty years, he'd be broken and almost docile, still illiterate and unemployable, and he'd probably commit another crime within a year just so he could get back to his nice, safe prison. He could do twenty years, all right. He just couldn't do anything else.

It took all of thirty seconds for me to disabuse them of the notion that Jorge's case killed Paul French. "Look," I pointed out, "the whole family rejoiced when the kid went upstate. It meant they could keep a television set for more than a week. And he was no gang leader; the real gang-bangers barely tolerated him. So I don't think—"

"What about Richie Toricelli, then?" The older cop leaned forward in my visitor's chair and I had the feeling he was getting to the real point of his interrogation.

"Now we're talking. Toricelli I could see killing Paul French. I'm not sure I see him pushing anyone out a window, though. I'd have expected Richie to use his sawed-off shotgun instead. He liked to see people bleed."

The younger cop gave me one of those "how can you defend those people" looks.

"I was appointed," I said in reply to the unspoken criticism. Which was no answer at all. I wouldn't have been appointed if I hadn't put myself on a list of available attorneys, and I wouldn't have done that if I hadn't been committed with every fiber of my being to criminal defense work.

I'd long since stopped asking myself why I did it. I did it, and I did it the best way I knew how, and I let others work up a philosophy of the job.

Some cases were easier to justify than others. Richie Toricelli's was one of the tough ones.

And if you thought he was a dead loss to society, you ought to meet his mother.

"Tell you the truth," I said, only half-kidding, "I'd sure like to know where Rose Toricelli was when French took his dive."

"She was in the drunk tank over on Gold Street," the younger cop said, a look of grim amusement on his brown face. "Nice alibi, only about fifty people and ten pieces of official paperwork put her there."

"Pretty convenient," I said, hearing the echo of the Church Lady in my head.

"Counselor, you know something you're not telling us?"

I dropped my eyes. A slight blush crept into my cheeks. I hated admitting this.

"I changed my phone number after Richie went in," I said. "For a year, I lived in fear that Rose Toricelli would find some way to get to me. She didn't just blame Paul French for Richie's conviction, she blamed me too."

The older cop cut me a look. Skeptical Irish blue eyes under bushy white eyebrows over a red-tinged nose. I got the message: *You're gonna do a man's job, you need a man's balls. Afraid of an old lady doesn't cut it.*

It pissed me off. This guy didn't know Richie's ma. "You look at her, you see a pathetic old woman who thinks her scurvy son is some kind of saint; I look at her and I see someone who wants me dead and who could very easily convince herself that shooting me is the best way to tell the world her boy is innocent."

"Did she ever make threats? And did you report any of this?"

"Only in the courthouse the day they took Richie away. And, no," I said, anger creeping into my voice, "I didn't report it. I know what cops think about defense lawyers who get threats. You think we ask for it. And I didn't want to look like a wimp who couldn't handle a little old lady with a grudge."

What really chilled me weren't Rose Toricelli's threats to do damage to the sentencing judge, to Paul French, to me—that was standard stuff in the criminal courts. What really had my blood frozen were the words she said to her son as they shuffled him, cuffed and stunned like a cow on his way to becoming beefsteak:

"You show them, Richie. You show them you're innocent. It would serve them right if you hung yourself in there."

For a year after that, I waited for the news that Richie's body had been discovered hanging from the bars. Doing what Mamma wanted, like he always did.

But as far as I knew, he was still alive, still serving his time, which gave him an iron-bar-clad alibi for French's death, so why were the cops even bringing it up?

The question nagged at me even after the cops left. I turned to my computer, supplementing the information I pulled up with a few phone calls and discovered something very interesting indeed.

Once upon a time, Richie Toricelli's cellmate had been Hector Dominguez.

You remember the case. It made all the papers and even gave birth to a joke or two on Letterman. Funny guy, that Hector.

He'd kidnapped his son, claiming the boy's mother was making him sick. A devout believer in Santeria, he accused his ex of working roots, casting spells, that sapped the boy's strength. He said God told him to save his little boy from a mother who had turned witch.

You can imagine how well that went over in the Dragon Lady's courtroom. She gaveled him quiet, had him bound and gagged because he wouldn't stop screaming at his sobbing wife. He hurled curses and threats throughout the trial, bringing down the wrath of his gods on the heads of everyone connected to the proceeding.

The day he was to be sentenced, they found the doll in his cell. Carved out of soap, it wore a crude robe of black nylon and sported a doll's wig the exact shade of the Dragon Lady's pageboy. Out of its heart, a hypodermic syringe protruded like a dagger.

Like I said, a lot of criminal defendants threaten the judge who sends them upstate, but a voodoo doll was unique, even in the annals of Brooklyn justice. The *Post* put it on the front page; the *News* thundered editorially about laxness in the Brooklyn House of Detention; *Newsday* did a very clever cartoon I'd taped to my office bulletin board; and the *Times* ignored the whole thing because it didn't happen in Bosnia.

I really wasn't in the courtroom when Dominguez was sentenced because I wanted to see the show. Unlike the two rows of reporters and most of the other lawyers present that day, I had business before the court. But I had to admit a certain curiosity about how the Dragon Lady was going to handle this one.

The lawyer asked her to recuse herself, saying she could hardly be objective under the circumstances. I could have told him to save his breath; the DL was never, under any circumstances, going to admit she couldn't do her job. She dismissed out of hand the notion that she'd taken the voodoo doll personally; it would play no part, she announced in ringing tones, in her sentencing.

Hector Dominguez was oddly compelling when he began to address the court. His English was so poor that an interpreter stood next to him in case he lapsed into his Dominican Spanish, but Hector waved away the help, determined to reach the judge in her own language.

"You Honor, I know it looking bad against me," he said in his halting way. "I just want to say I love my son with my whole heart. *Mi corazón* is hurt when my son get sick. I want her to stop making him sick. Please, You Honor, don't let that woman hurt my boy. He so little, he so pale, he so sick all the time and it all her fault, You Honor, all her doing with her spells and her evil ways."

The child's mother dabbed at her eyes with a tissue, shaking her head mournfully.

The DL gave Dominguez two years more than the District Attorney's office asked for, which was already two years more than the probation report recommended.

This, she insisted, had nothing to do with the doll, but was the appropriate sentence for a man who tried to convince a child that his loving mother was a witch.

Dominguez's last words to the DL consisted of a curse to the effect that she should someday know the pain he felt now, the pain of losing a child to evil.

The papers all commented on the irony of a man like Hector calling someone else evil. And Letterman milked his audience for laughs by holding up a voodoo doll in the image of a certain Washington lady.

But three years later, when the boy's mother was charged with attempted murder and the court shrinks talked about Munchausen's syndrome by proxy, the attitudes changed a bit. Now Hector was seen, not as a nut case who thought his wife was possessed, but as a father trying to protect his son and interpreting events he couldn't understand in the only context he knew, that of his spirit-based religion.

He was up for parole, and it was granted without much ado. He was free—but his little boy, six years old by now, lay in a coma, irreparably brain-damaged as a result of his mother's twisted ministrations.

By not listening to him, by treating him like a criminal instead of a concerned father, the Dragon Lady had prevented authorities from looking closely at the mother's conduct.

He had shared a jail cell with Richie Toricelli. That had to mean something—but what?

The theory hit me with the full force of a brainstorm: defendants on a train. Patricia Highsmith by way of Alfred Hitchcock.

What if Ma Toricelli, instead of killing the prosecutor who sent her precious Richie upstate, shot the Dragon Lady—who had no connection whatsoever to her or her son? And what if Dominguez, who had no reason to want Paul French dead, returned the favor by pushing French out the window? Each has an alibi for the murder they had a motive to commit, and no apparent reason to kill the person they actually murdered.

The more I thought about it, the more I liked it. I liked it so much I actually asked a cop for a favor. Which was how I ended up sifting through DD5s in the Eight-Four precinct as the winter sun turned the overcast clouds a dull pewter.

I learned nothing that hadn't been reported in the papers, and I was ready to pack it in, ready to admit that even if Ma Toricelli had done the deed, she'd covered her tracks pretty well, when one item caught my attention.

The neighbor across the street had seen a Jehovah's Witness ringing doorbells about twenty minutes prior to the crime. He knew the woman was a Witness because she carried a copy of the *Watchtower* in front of her like a shield.

This was a common enough sight in Brooklyn Heights, where the Witnesses owned a good bit of prime real estate, except for one little thing.

Jehovah's Witnesses traveled in pairs. Always.

One Jehovah's Witness just wasn't possible.

My heart pounded as I read the brief description of the bogus Witness: female, middle-aged, gray hair, gray coat, stout boots. Five feet nothing.

Ma Toricelli to a T.

I wasn't as lucky with the second set of detectives. I was told in no uncertain terms that nothing I had to say would get me a peek at the Paul French reports, so I left the precinct without any evidence that Hector Dominguez could have been in the municipal building when French took his dive.

Still, the idea had promise. I had no problem picturing Rose Toricelli firing a gun point-blank into the judge's midsection and I was equally convinced that in return for the Dragon Lady's death, Hector Dominguez would have pushed five district attorneys out a window. But proving it was another matter.

I pondered these truths as I trudged down Court Street toward home. The sidewalks wore a new coat of powder, temporarily brightening the slush of melting gray snow. Dusk had arrived with winter suddenness, and only the snow-fogged streetlights lit the way. I was picking my way carefully in spite of well-treaded snow boots, my attention fixed on the depth of the chill puddle at the corner of Court and Atlantic Avenue, when the first shot zipped past my ear.

I didn't know it was a shot until the guy in the cigar store yelled at me to get down.

Get down where?

Get down why?

I honestly didn't hear it.

I couldn't even say it sounded like a car backfiring or a firecracker. And I didn't hear the second shot either, although this one I felt.

A sting, like a wasp or a hornet, and blood coursing down my cheek. A burning sensation and a really strong need to use a bathroom. I was ankle-deep in very cold water and couldn't decide whether to keep making my way across the street or run to the shelter of the cigar store. While I considered my options, a black SUV swerved around the corner, straight into the icy puddle, drenching me in dirty, frigid water.

That did it. I turned quickly, wrenching my knee, and hoisted myself onto the curb. I slid at once back into the puddle, landing hard on my backside. A couple of teenagers stopped to laugh, and I suppose it would have been funny if I hadn't been scared out of my mind. Limping and holding my bleeding cheek, I slipped and slid on my way to the amber-lighted cigar store on the corner.

Tobacco-hater that I am, I'd never been inside the cigar emporium before. The scent was overwhelming, but so was the warmth from the space heater on the floor.

The counterman met me at the door, a solicitous expression on his moon face. He was short, with a big bristling mustache and two chins. He reeked of cigar smoke, but I didn't mind at all when he put an arm around me and led me into the sanctuary of his store. He seated me on a folding chair and offered the only comfort he possessed. "Want a cigarillo, lady? On the house."

I started to laugh, but the laughter ended in tears of frustration and relief.

I was alive.

I was bleeding.

I'd been shot at.

The cops were on their way, the cigar man told me, and then he proudly added that he'd seen the shooter's car and had written down the license plate.

The cops, predictably enough, talked drive-by shooting and surmised that a gang member might have been walking nearby when the shots rang out. Since my attention was fully absorbed in not falling into the puddle, King Kong could have been behind me on the street and I wouldn't have noticed.

The second theory was the Atlantic Avenue hotbed-of-terrorism garbage that gets dragged out whenever anything happens on that ethnically charged thoroughfare. Just because Arab spice stores and Middle Eastern restaurants front the street, everything from a trash fire to littering gets blamed either on Arab extremists or anti-Arab extremists.

I have to admit, I was slow. Even I didn't think the shooting had anything to do with my visit to the Eight-Four precinct.

That didn't happen until the next day, when I learned that the car whose license plate the cigar man wrote down belonged to one Marcus Mitchell.

Marcus Mitchell had been royally screwed by Paul French in one of those monster drug prosecutions where everyone turned state's evidence except the lowest-level dealers. People who'd made millions cut deals that had the little guys serving major time for minor felonies, and Mitchell was a guy who had nothing with which to deal.

My own client gave up the guys above him and walked away with a bullet—that's one year and not even a year upstate, a year at Riker's, which meant his family could visit him and—let's be honest here—he could still run a good bit of his drug business from his cell. I know, that sucks, but French was only too happy to get the goods on the higher-ups and made the deal with open eyes. All I did was say yes.

All Marcus Mitchell did was keep his mouth shut, and he did that not out of stubbornness but out of sheer ignorance. He'd been the poor sap caught with a nice big bag of heroin, but the only thing he knew was that a guy named Willie handed it to him at the corner of Fulton and Franklin and told him not to come back until it was all sold.

For this, he got twenty to life. Released after three years on a technicality, but by that time his wife had left him, he'd lost his job, and his parents had died in shame. He had plenty of reason to want Paul French dead.

But why had he taken a potshot at me?

I had taken the day off work, called in shot. It was in the papers, so the judges bought it and told me to take all the time I needed to recuperate, then put my cases over a week. I sipped Tanzanian Peaberry while I felt the blood ooze into the gauze bandage on my cheek and reconsidered my theory.

It was still sound, except for two little things.

One: there were three, not two, defendants on a train.

Two: Ma Toricelli's chosen victim wasn't Paul French—it was the defense lawyer she blamed for her son's conviction. Me.

It went like this:

Ma Toricelli kills the Dragon Lady for Hector Dominguez.

Dominguez kills Paul French for Marcus Mitchell.

Marcus Mitchell tries to kill me for Ma Toricelli.

This time the cops listened. This time they questioned everyone in the building where Paul French died and found several witnesses who described Hector Dominguez to a T. Add that to the description of the bogus Witness, squeeze all three defendants until someone cracked, and the whole house of cards would tumble down.

I went to the arraignment. I was the victim, so I had a right to be there, and besides, I wanted to see firsthand the people who'd tried to end my life in an icy puddle.

When the time came for Ma Toricelli to plead for bail, she thrust her chin forward and said, "She was supposed to be my boy's lawyer, but all she did was look down on him. She never did her job, Your Honor, not from the first day. She thought Richie was trash and she didn't care what happened to him."

I opened my mouth to respond, then realized it made no difference what I said. Even if I'd been the worst lawyer in the world, that didn't give Rose Toricelli the right to order my death. And I'd done a good job for Richie, a better job than the little sociopath deserved.

Perhaps my mental choice of words was what caught my attention.

If I really thought Richie was a sociopath, had I done my best for him? Or had I slacked off, let the prosecution get away with things I'd have fought harder if I'd truly believed my client innocent? It was a hard question. There were cases I'd handled better, but I honestly didn't see Richie getting off if Johnnie Cochran had been his lawyer. Still, my cellside manner could have been improved; I could have at least gone through the motions enough to convince Richie's mother that I was doing my best.

The letter came in due course, as we say in the trade. It was enclosed in a manila envelope with the name of a prominent Brooklyn law firm embossed in the left corner. I had no clue what was inside; I had no business pending with the firm and no reason to expect correspondence from them. I slit the thing open with my elegant black Frank Lloyd Wright letter opener, the one my dad gave me for Christmas two years ago.

Another letter with my name handwritten on the front, no address, no stamp, fell into my hands.

This one's return address was the Appellate Division, Second Department.

It was a message from beyond the grave.

Ms. Jameson:

I'm sure you have had reason to wonder why I asked you in particular to handle the case of Darnell Patterson on remand from this court.

Let us just say that I have had reason to regret the current fashion for mandatory minimum sentences and maximum jail time for defendants who commit nonviolent offenses. While I am not one to condone lawbreaking, I firmly believe in distinctions between those who are truly dangerous to society and those who are merely inconvenient.

Mr. Patterson would appear to fall into the latter category. I trust you will agree with me on this point and use your best efforts on his behalf.

You and I, Ms. Jameson, have seldom seen eye to eye, but those traits of yours that I most deplore, your tendency toward overzealousness and your refusal to "go through the motions" on even the most hopeless case, will prove to be just what Mr. Patterson needs in a lawyer.

I expect you will wonder what brought about my change of heart with respect to low-level narcotics cases.

I also expect you to live with your curiosity and make no effort to trace my change of heart to its roots. Suffice to say that it is a private family matter and therefore is nobody's business but my own.

Once again, I thank you for your attention to this matter.

There was no signature. The Dragon Lady had died before she could scrawl her name in her characteristic bold hand.

The compliments brought a traitorous tear to my eyes—especially since the words weren't true.

Mostly true. I was well-known in the Brooklyn court system as a fighter who didn't give up easily, who didn't back down in the face of threats from prosecutors or judges. The DL had been right to rely on me.

But Richie Toricelli hadn't been. I'd been so disgusted by his crimes, so turned off by his attitude, that I'd given less than my best to his defense. Ma Toricelli, for all her craziness, had a point. I'd phoned it in, done a half-baked job of presenting his alibi witnesses, given the jurors little reason to believe his story over that of the prosecution.

The irony was huge. The DL, of all people, sending me compliments on my fighting spirit while Ma Toricelli planned to kill me for rolling over and playing dead on her son's case. Me bailing on Richie and the Dragon Lady getting religion over a three-time loser who hoarded drugs like a squirrel saving up for winter.

The image of Hector Dominguez's voodoo doll swam before my eyes—the weapon protruding from its soap heart wasn't a knife, but a hypodermic. "May you lose a child to evil," he'd cursed, and perhaps she had. Perhaps reaching out to help Darnell Patterson was a way of atoning for that child. Perhaps she'd finally seen that justice needed a dose of mercy, like a drop of bitters in a cocktail.

I sat like a stone while the letter fluttered to the hardwood floor of my office.

Pat Flaherty had been right after all.

The Dragon Lady *had* become a good judge.

Lawrence Block

Speaking of Greed

PAGE FOR PAGE, Lawrence Block's books give so much pleasure that he recently leapt (after forty-some years of wonderful
novel, short story, and nonfiction writing) onto the *New York Times*
bestseller list. He is a man of many moods, all of them finding
homes in his various series, from the endearing quick-talking
(and -fingered) thief Bernie Rhodenbarr to God's existential
errand boy, the hit man Keller, to his single-man portrait of New
York City life and its citizens, Matthew Scudder. He is one of the
crime writing giants of our time, of that there can be no doubt.
Recently he's turned his hand to anthology editing, and has shown
the same deft touch in picking other authors' stories as he has in
writing his own. "Speaking of Greed" appeared in the anthology
of the same name, edited by Block himself, and is a minor masterpiece of quiet noir, as four men at a card table ponder one of life's
innumerable problems, the question of greed.

Speaking of Greed

Lawrence Block

The doctor shuffled the pack of playing cards seven times, then offered them to the soldier, who sat to his right. The soldier cut them, and the doctor picked up the deck and dealt two cards down and one up to each of the players—the policeman, the priest, the soldier, and himself.

The game was poker, seven-card stud, and the priest, who was high on the board with a queen, opened the betting for a dollar, tossing in a chip to keep the doctor's ante comfortable. The soldier called, as did the doctor and the policeman.

Over by the fireplace, the room's other occupant, an elderly gentleman, dozed in an armchair.

The doctor gave each player a second up-card. The policeman caught a king, the priest a nine in the same suit with his queen, the soldier a jack to go with his ten. The doctor, who'd had a five to start with, caught another five for a pair. That made him high on the board, but he took a look at his hole cards, frowned, and checked his hand. The policeman checked as well, and the priest gave his Roman collar a tug and bet two dollars.

The soldier said, "Two dollars? It's a dollar limit until a pair shows, isn't it?"

"Doctor has a pair," the priest pointed out.

"So he does," the soldier agreed, and flicked a speck of dust off the sleeve of his uniform. "Of course he does, he was high with his fives. Still, it's one of the anomalies of the game, isn't it? Priest gets to bet more, not because his own hand just got stronger, but because his opponent's did. What are you so proud of, Priest? Queens and nines? Four hearts?"

"I hope I'm not too proud," the priest said. "Pride's a sin, after all."

"Well, I'm proud enough to call you," the soldier said. The doctor and the policeman also called, and the doctor dealt another round. Now the policeman was high with a pair of kings. He too was in uniform, and word-lessly he tossed a pair of chips into the center of the table.

The priest had caught a third heart, the seven. He thought for a long moment before tossing four chips into the pot. "Raise," he said softly.

"Priest, Priest, Priest," said the soldier, checking his own cards. "Have you got your damned flush already? If you had two pair, well, I just caught one of your nines. But if I'm chasing a straight that's doomed to lose to the flush you've already got . . ." The words trailed off, and the soldier sighed and called.

So did the doctor, and the policeman looked at his kings and picked up four chips, as if to raise back, then tossed in two of them and returned the others to his stack.

On the next round, three of the players showed visible improvement. The policeman, who'd had a three with his kings, caught a second three for two pair. The priest added the deuce of hearts and showed a four flush on board. The soldier's straight got longer with the addition of the eight of diamonds.

The doctor, who'd had a four with his pair of fives, acquired a ten.

The policeman bet, the priest raised, the soldier grumbled and called. The doctor called without grumbling. The policeman raised back, and everyone called.

"Nice little pot," the doctor said, and gave everyone a down card.

The betting limits were a dollar until a pair showed, then two dollars until the last card, at which time you could bet five dollars. The policeman did just that, tossing a red chip into the pot. The priest picked up a red chip to call, thought about it, picked up a second red chip, and raised five dollars. The soldier said something about throwing good money after bad.

"There's no such thing," the doctor said.

"As good money?"

"As bad money."

"It turns bad," said the soldier, "as soon as I throw it in. I was straight in five and got to watch everybody outdraw me. Now I've got a choice of losing to Policeman's full house or Priest's heart flush, depending on which one's telling the truth. Unless you're both full of crap."

"Always a possibility," the doctor allowed.

"The hell with it," the soldier said, and tossed in a red chip and five white chips. "I call," he said, "with no expectation of profit."

The doctor was wearing green scrubs, with a stethoscope peeping out of his pocket. He looked at his cards, looked at everyone else's cards, and called. The policeman raised. The priest looked troubled, but took the third and final raise all the same, and everybody called.

"Full," the policeman said, and turned over a third three. "Threes full of kings," he said, but the priest was shaking his head, even as he turned over his hole cards, two queens and a nine.

"Queens full," said the priest.

"Oh, hell," said the soldier. "A full house masquerading as a flush. Not that I have a right to complain—the flush would have beaten me just as handily. Got it on the last card, didn't you, Priest? All that raising, and you went in with two pair and a four flush."

"I had great expectations," the priest admitted.

"The Lord will provide and all that," said the soldier, turning over his up-cards. The priest, beaming, reached for the chips.

The doctor cleared his throat, turned over his hole cards. Two of them were fives, matching the pair of fives he'd had on board.

"Four fives," the policeman said reverently. "Beats your boat, Priest."

"So it does," said the priest. "So it does."

"Had them in the first four cards," the doctor said.

"You never bet them."

"I never had to," said the doctor. "You fellows were doing such a nice job of it, I saw no reason to interfere." And he reached out both hands to gather in the chips.

"Greed," said the priest.

The policeman was shuffling the cards, the doctor stacking his chips, the soldier looking off into the middle distance, as if remembering a battle in a long-forgotten war. The priest's utterance stopped them all.

"I beg your pardon," said the doctor. "Just what have I done that's so greedy? Play the hand so as to maximize my gains? That, it seems to me, is how one is intended to play the game."

"If you're not trying to win," said the soldier, "you shouldn't be sitting at the table."

"Maybe Priest feels you were gloating," the policeman suggested. "Salivating over your well-gotten gains."

"Was I doing that?" The doctor shrugged. "I wasn't aware of it. Still, why play if you're not going to relish your triumph?"

The priest, who'd been shaking his head, now held up his hands as if to ward off everyone's remarks. "I uttered a single word," he protested, "and intended no judgment, believe me. Perhaps it was the play of the hand that prompted my train of thought, perhaps it was a reflection on the entire ethos of poker that put it in motion. But, when I spoke the word, I was thinking neither of your own conduct, Doctor, or of our game itself. No, I was contemplating the sin of greed, of avarice."

"Greed is a sin, eh?"

"One of the seven deadly sins."

"And yet," said the soldier, "there was a character in a film who argued famously that greed is good. And isn't the profit motive at the root of much of human progress?"

"A man's reach should exceed his grasp," the policeman said, "but it's the desire for what one can in fact grasp that makes one reach out in the first place. And isn't it natural to want to improve one's circumstances?"

"All the sins are natural," said the priest. "All originate as essential impulses and become sins when they overstretch their bounds. Without sexual desire the human race would die out. Without appetite we'd starve. Without ambition we'd graze like cattle. But when desire becomes lust, or appetite turns to gluttony, or ambition to greed—"

"We sin," the doctor said.

The priest nodded.

The policeman gave the cards another shuffle. "You know," he said, "that reminds me of a story."

"Tell it," the others urged, and the policeman put down the deck of cards and sat back in his chair.

Many years ago (said the policeman) there were two brothers, whom I'll call George and Alan Walker. They came from a family that had had some money and respectability at one time, and their paternal grandfather was a physician, but he was also a drunk, and eventually patients stopped going to him, and he wound up with an office on Railroad Avenue, where he wrote prescriptions for dope addicts. Somewhere along the way his wife ran off, and he started popping pills, and the time came when they didn't combine too well with what he was drinking, and he died.

He had three sons and a daughter, and all but the youngest son drifted away. The one who stayed—call him Jack—married a girl whose family had also come down in the world, and they had two boys, George and Alan.

Jack drank, like his father, but he didn't have a medical degree, and thus he couldn't make a living handing out pills. He wasn't trained for anything, and didn't have any ambition, so he picked up day work when it came his way, and sometimes it was honest and sometimes it wasn't. He got arrested a fair number of times, and he went away and did short time on three or four occasions. When he was home he slapped his wife around some, and was generally free with his hands around the house, but no more than you'd expect from a man like that living a life like that.

Now everybody can point to individuals who grew up in homes like the Walkers' who turned out just fine. Won scholarships, put themselves through college, worked hard, applied themselves, and wound up pillars of the community. No reason it can't happen, and often enough it does, but sometimes it doesn't, and it certainly didn't for George and Alan Walker. They were discipline problems in school and dropped out early, and at first they stole hubcaps off cars, and then they stole cars.

And so on.

Jack Walker had been a criminal himself, in a slipshod amateurish sort of way. The boys followed in his footsteps, but improved on his example. They were professionals from very early on, and you would have to say they were good at it. They weren't Raffles, they weren't Professor Moriarty, they weren't Arnold Zeck, and God knows they weren't Willie Sutton or Al

Capone. But they made a living at it and they didn't get caught, and isn't that enough for us to call them successful?

They always worked together, and more often than not they used other people as well. Over the years, they tended to team up with the same three men. I don't know that it would be precisely accurate to call the five of them a gang, but it wouldn't be off by much.

One, Louis Creamer, was a couple of years older than the Walkers—George, I should mention, was himself a year and a half older than his brother Alan. Louis looked like a big dumb galoot, and that's exactly what he was. He loved to eat and he loved to work out with weights in his garage, so he kept getting bigger. It's hard to see how he could have gotten any dumber, but he didn't get any smarter, either. He lived with his mother—nobody knew what happened to the father, if he was ever there in the first place—and when his mother died Louis married the girl he'd been keeping company with since he dropped out of school. He moved her into his mother's house and she cooked him the same huge meals his mother used to cook, and he was happy.

Early on, Louis got work day to day as a bouncer but the day came when he hit a fellow too hard, and the guy died. A good lawyer probably could have gotten him off, but Louis had a bad one, and he wound up serving a year and a day for involuntary manslaughter. When he got out nobody was in a rush to hire him, and he fell in with the Walkers, who didn't have trouble finding a role for a guy who was big and strong and did what you told him to do.

Eddie O'Day was small and undernourished and as close as I've ever seen to a born thief. He got in trouble shoplifting as a child, and then he stopped getting into trouble, not because he stopped stealing but because he stopped getting caught. He grew up to be a man who would, as they say, steal a hot stove, and he'd have it sold before it cooled off. He was the same age as Alan Walker, and they'd dropped out of school together. Eddie lived alone, and was positively gifted when it came to picking up women. He was neither good-looking nor charming, but he was evidently seductive, and women kept taking him home. But they didn't keep him—his relationships never lasted, which was fine as far as he was concerned.

Mike Dunn was older than the others, and had actually qualified as a schoolteacher. He got unqualified in a hurry when he was caught in bed with one of his students. It was a long ways from pedophilia—he was only twenty-six himself at the time, and the girl was almost sixteen and almost as experienced sexually as he was—but that was the end of his teaching career. He drifted some, and the Walkers used him as a lookout in a drugstore break-in, and found out they liked working with him. He had a good mind, and he wound up doing a lot of the planning. When he wasn't working he was pretty much a loner, living in a rented house on the edge of town, and having affairs with unavailable women—generally the wives or daughters of other men.

The Walkers and their associates had a lot of different ways to make money, together or separately. George and Alan always had some money on the street, loans to people whose only collateral was fear. Louis Creamer did their collection work, and provided security at the card and dice games Eddie O'Day ran. George Walker owned a bar and grill, and sold more booze there than he bought from the wholesalers; he bought from bootleggers and hijacked the occasional truck to make up the difference.

We knew a lot of what they were doing, but knowing and making a case aren't necessarily the same thing. We arrested all of them at one time or another, for one thing or another, but we could never make anything stick. That's not all that unusual, you know. They say crime doesn't pay, but they're wrong. Of course it pays. If it didn't pay, the pros would do something else.

And the Walkers were pros. They weren't getting rich, but they were making what you could call a decent living, but for the fact that there was nothing decent about it. They always had food on the table and money under the mattress (if not in the bank), and they didn't have to work too hard or too often. That was what they'd had in mind when they chose a life of crime. So they stayed with it, and why not? It suited them fine. They weren't respectable, but neither was their father, or his father before him. The hell with being respectable. They were doing okay.

The years went by and they kept on doing what they were doing, and doing well at it. Jack Walker drank himself to death, and after the funeral George put his arm around his brother and said, "Well, the old bastard's in the ground. He wasn't much good, but he wasn't so bad, you know?"

"When I was a kid," Alan said, "I wanted to kill him."

"Oh, so did I," George said. "Many's the time I thought about it. But, you know, you grow older and you get over it."

And they were indeed growing older, settling into a reasonably comfortable middle age. George was thicker around the middle, while Alan's hair was showing a little gray. They both liked a drink, but it didn't have the hold on them it had had on their father and grandfather. It settled George down, fueled Alan, and didn't seem to do either of them any harm.

And this wouldn't be much of a story, except for the fact that one day they set out to steal some money, and succeeded beyond their wildest dreams.

It was a robbery, and the details have largely faded from memory, but I don't suppose they're terribly important. The tip came from an employee of the targeted firm, whose wife was the sister of a woman Mike Dunn was sleeping with; for a cut of the proceeds, he'd provide details of when to hit the place, along with the security codes and keys that would get them in.

Their expectations were considerable. Mike Dunn, who brought in the deal, thought they ought to walk off with a minimum of a hundred thousand dollars. Their tipster was in for a ten percent share, and they'd split the residue in five equal shares, as they always did on jobs of this nature.

"Even splits," George Walker had said early on. "You hear about different ways of doing it, something off the top for the guy who brings it in, so much extra for whoever bankrolls the operation. All that does is make it complicated, and gives everybody a reason to come up with a resentment. The minute you're getting a dollar more than me, I'm pissed off. And the funny thing is you're pissed off, too, because whatever you're getting isn't enough. Make the splits even and nobody's got cause to complain. You put out more than I do on the one job, well, it evens out later on, when I put out more'n you do. Meantime, every dollar comes in, each one of us gets twenty cents of it."

So they stood to bring in eighteen thousand dollars apiece for a few hours' work, which, inflation notwithstanding, was a healthy cut above minimum wage, and better than anybody was paying in the fields and factories. Was it a fortune? No. Wealth beyond the dreams of avarice? Hardly that. But all five of the principals would agree that it was a good night's work.

The job was planned and rehearsed, the schedule fine-tuned. When push came to shove, the pushing and shoving went like clockwork. Everything happened just as it was supposed to, and our five masked heroes wound up in a room with five of the firm's employees, one of them the inside man, the brother-in-law of Mike Dunn's paramour. And it strikes me that we need a name for him, although we won't need it for long. But let's call him Alfie. No need for a last name. Just Alfie will do fine.

Like the others, Alfie was tied up tight, a piece of duct tape across his mouth. Mike Dunn had given him a wink when he tied him, and made sure his bonds weren't tight enough to hurt. He sat there and watched as the five men hauled sacks of money out of the vault.

It was Eddie O'Day who found the bearer bonds.

By then they already knew that it was going to be a much bigger payday than they'd anticipated. A hundred thousand? The cash looked as though it would come to at least three and maybe four or five times that. Half a million? A hundred thousand apiece?

The bearer bonds, all by themselves, totaled two million dollars. They were like cash, but better than cash because, relatively speaking, they didn't weigh anything or take up any space. Pieces of paper, two hundred of them, each worth ten thousand dollars. And they weren't registered to an owner, and were as anonymous as a crumpled dollar bill.

In every man's mind, the numbers changed. The night was going to be worth two and a half million dollars, or half a million apiece. Why, Alfie's share as an informant would come to a quarter of a million dollars all by itself, which was not bad compensation for letting yourself be tied up and gagged for a few hours.

Of course, there was another way of looking at it. Alfie was taking fifty thousand dollars from each of them. He was costing them, right off the top, almost three times as much money as they'd expected to net in the first place.

The little son of a bitch . . .

Alan Walker went over to Alfie and hunkered down next to him. "You did good," he said. "There's lots more money than anybody thought, plus all of these bonds."

Alfie struggled with his bonds, and his eyes rolled wildly. Alan asked him if something was the matter, and Mike Dunn came over and took the tape from Alfie's mouth."

"Them," Alfie said.

"Them?"

He rolled his eyes toward his fellow employees. "They'll think I'm involved," he said.

"Well, hell, Alfie," Eddie O'Day said, "you are involved, aren'tcha? You're in for what, ten percent?"

Alfie just stared.

"Listen," George Walker told him, "don't worry about those guys. What are they gonna say?"

"Their lips are sealed," his brother pointed out.

"But—"

George Walker nodded to Louis Creamer, who drew a pistol and shot one of the bound men in the back of the head. Mike Dunn and Eddie O'Day drew their guns, and more shots rang out. Within seconds the four presumably loyal employees were dead.

"Oh, Jesus," Alfie said.

"Had to be," George Walker told him. "They heard what my brother said to you, right? Besides, the money involved, there's gonna be way too much heat coming down. They didn't see anybody's face, but who knows what they might notice that the masks don't hide? And they heard voices. Better this way, Alfie."

"Ten percent," Eddie O'Day said. "You might walk away with a quarter of a million dollars, Alfie. What are you gonna do with all that dough?"

Alfie looked like a man who'd heard the good news and the bad news all at once. He was in line for a fortune, but would he get to spend a dime of it?

"Listen," he said, "you guys better beat me up."

"Beat you up?"

"I think so, and—"

"But you're our little buddy," Louis Creamer said. "Why would we want to do that?"

"If I'm the only one left," Alfie said, "they'll suspect me, won't they?"

"Suspect you?"

"Of being involved."

"Ah," George Walker said. "Never thought of that."

"But if you beat me up . . ."

"You figure it might throw them off? A couple of bruises on your face and they won't even think of questioning you?"

"Maybe you better wound me," Alfie said.

"Wound you, Alfie?"

"Like a flesh wound, you know? A non-fatal wound."

"Oh, hell," Alan Walker said. "We can do better than that." And he put his gun up against Alfie's forehead and blew his brains out.

"Had to be," George Walker announced, as they cleared the area of any possible traces of their presence. "No way on earth he would have stood up, the kind of heat they'd have put on him. The minute the total goes over a mill, far as I'm concerned, they're all dead, all five of them. The other four because of what they might have picked up, and Alfie because of what we damn well know he knows."

"He was in for a quarter of a mill," Eddie O'Day said. "You look at it one way, old Alfie was a rich man for a minute there."

"You think about it," Louis Creamer said, "what'd he ever do was worth a quarter of a mill?"

"He was taking fifty grand apiece from each of us," Alan Walker said. "If you want to look at it that way."

"It's as good a way as any to look at it," George Walker said.

"Beady little eyes," Eddie O'Day said. "Never liked the little bastard. And he'd have sung like a bird, minute they picked him up."

The Walkers had a storage locker that nobody knew about, and that was where they went to count the proceeds of the job. The cash, it turned out, ran to just over $650,000, and another count of the bearer bonds confirmed the figure of two million dollars. That made the total $2,650,000, or $530,000 a man after a five-way split.

"Alfie was richer than we thought," George Walker said. "For a minute there, anyway. Two hundred sixty-five grand."

"If we'd left him alive," his brother said, "the cops would have had our names within twenty-four hours."

"Twenty-four hours? He'da been singing the second they got the tape off his mouth."

Eddie O'Day said, "You got to wonder."

"Wonder what?"

"How much singing he already done."

They exchanged glances. To Mike Dunn, George Walker said, "This dame of yours. Alfie was married to her sister?"

"Right."

"I was a cop, I'd take a look at the families of those five guys. Dead or alive, I'd figure there might have been somebody on the inside, you know?"

"I see what you mean."

"They talk to Alfie's wife, who knows what he let slip?"

"Probably nothing."

"Probably nothing, but who knows? Maybe he thought he was keeping her in the dark, but she puts two and two together, you know?"

"Maybe he talked in his sleep," Louis Creamer suggested.

Mike Dunn thought about it, nodded. "I'll take care of it," he said.

Later that evening, the Walkers were in George's den, drinking scotch and smoking cigars. "You know what I'm thinking," George said.

"The wife's dead," Alan said, "and it draws the cops a picture. Five employees dead, plus the wife of one of them? Right away they know which one was working for us."

"So they know which direction to go."

"This woman Mike's been nailing. Sister of Alfie's wife."

"Right."

"They talk to her and what do they get?"

"Probably nothing, far as the job's concerned. Even if Alfie talked to his wife, it's a stretch to think the wife talked to her sister."

Alan nodded. "The sister doesn't know shit about the job," he said. "But there's one thing she knows."

"What's that?"

"She knows she's been sleeping with Mike. Of course that's something she most likely wants kept a secret, on account of she's a married lady."

"But when the cops turn her upside-down and shake her . . ."

"Leads straight to Mike. And now that I think about it, will they even have to shake her hard? Because if she figures out that it was probably Mike that got her sister and her brother-in-law killed . . ."

George finished his drink, poured another. "Her name's Alice," he said. "Alice Fuhrmann. Be easy enough, drop in on her, take her out. Where I sit, she looks like a big loose end."

"How's Mike gonna take it?"

"Maybe it'll look like an accident."

"He's no dummy. She has an accident, he'll have a pretty good idea who gave it to her."

"Well, that's another thing," George Walker said. "Take out Alfie's wife and her sister and there's nobody with a story to tell. But I can see the cops finding the connection between Mike and this Alice no matter what, because who knows who she told?"

"He's a good man, Mike."

"Damn good man."

"Kind of a loner, though."

"Looks out for himself."

The brothers glanced significantly at each other, and drank their whiskey.

The sixth death recorded in connection with the robbery was that of Alfie's wife. Mike Dunn went to her home, found her alone, and accepted her offer of a cup of coffee. She thought he was coming on to her, and had heard from her sister what a good lover he was, and the idea of having a quickie with her sister's boyfriend was not unappealing. She invited him upstairs, and he didn't know what to do. He knew he couldn't afford to leave physical evidence in her bed or on her body. And could he have sex with a woman and then kill her? The thought sickened him, and, not surprisingly, turned him on a little too. He went upstairs with her. She was wearing a robe, and as they ascended the staircase he ran a hand up under the robe and found she was wearing nothing under it. He was wildly excited, and desperate to avoid acting on his excitement, and when they reached the top of the stairs he took her in his arms. She waited for him to kiss her, and instead he got his hands on her neck and throttled her, his hands tightening convulsively around her throat until the light went out of her eyes. Then he pitched her body down the stairs, walked down them himself, stepped over her corpse and got out of the house.

He was shaking. He wanted to tell somebody, but he didn't know whom to tell. He got in his car and drove home, and there was George Walker with a duffel bag.

"I did it," Mike blurted out. "She thought I wanted to fuck her, and you want to hear something sick? I wanted to."

"But you took care of it?"

"She fell down the stairs," Mike said. "Broke her neck."

"Accidents happen," George said, and tapped the duffel bag. "Your share."

"I thought we weren't gonna divvy it for a while."

"That was the plan, yeah."

"Because they might come calling, and if anybody has a lot of money at hand . . ."

"Right."

"Besides, any of us starts spending, it draws attention. Not that I would, but I'd worry about Eddie."

"If he starts throwing money around . . ."

"Could draw attention."

"Right."

"Thing is," George explained, "we were thinking maybe you ought to get out of town for a while, Mike. Alfie's dead and his wife's dead, but who knows how far back the cops can trace things? This girlfriend of yours—"

"Jesus, don't remind me. I just killed her sister."

"Well, somebody can take care of that."

Mike Dunn's eyes widened, but he didn't say anything.

"If you're out of town for a while," George said, "maybe it's not a bad thing."

Not a bad thing at all, Mike thought. Not if somebody was going to take care of Alice Fuhrmann, because the next thing that might occur to them was taking care of Mike Dunn, and he didn't want to be around when that happened. He packed a bag, and George walked him to his car, and took a gun from his pocket and shot him behind the ear just as he was getting behind the wheel.

Within hours Mike Dunn was buried at the bottom of an old well at an abandoned farmhouse six miles north of the city, and his car was part of a fleet of stolen cars on their way to the coast, where they'd be loaded aboard a freighter for shipment overseas. By then Alan Walker had decoyed Alice Fuhrmann to a supermarket parking lot, where he killed her with a home-made garrote and stuffed her into the trunk of her car.

"Mike did the right thing," George told Eddie O'Day and Louis Creamer. "He took out Alfie's widow and his own girlfriend, but he figured it might still come back to him, so I gave him his share and he took off. Half a mill, he can stay gone for a good long time."

"More'n that," Eddie O'Day said. "Five hundred thirty, wasn't it?"

"Well, round numbers."

"Speaking of numbers," Eddie said, "when are we gonna cut up the pie? Because I could use some of mine."

"Soon," George told him.

Five-thirty each for Louis Creamer and Eddie O'Day, $795,000 apiece for the Walkers, George thought, because Louis and Eddie didn't know that Mike Dunn had not gone willingly (though he'd been willing enough to do so) and had not taken his share with him. (George had brought the duffel bag home with him, and stashed it behind the furnace.) So why should Eddie and Louis get a split of Mike's share?

For that matter, George thought, he hadn't yet told his brother what had become of Mike Dunn. He'd never intended to give Mike his share, but he'd filled the duffel bag at the storage facility in case he'd had to change his plans on the spot, and he'd held the money out afterward in case the four of them wound up going to the storage bin together to make the split. As far as Alan knew, Mike and his share had vanished, and why burden the lad with the whole story? Why should Alan have a friend's death on his conscience?

No, George's conscience could carry the weight. And, along with the guilt, shouldn't he have Mike's share for himself? Because he couldn't split it with Alan without telling him where it came from.

Which changed the numbers slightly: $530,000 apiece for Alan, Louis, and Eddie; $1,060,000 for George.

Of course we knew who'd pulled off the robbery. Alfie's wife had indeed suffered a broken neck in the fall, but the medical examination quickly revealed she'd been strangled first. Her sister had disappeared, and soon turned up in the trunk of her car, a loop of wire tightened around her neck. Someone was able to connect the sister to Mike Dunn, and we established that he and his clothes and his car had gone missing. Present or not, Mike Dunn automatically led to Creamer and O'Day and the Walkers—but we'd have been looking at them anyway. Just a matter of rounding up the usual suspects, really.

"Eddie called me," Alan said. "They were talking to him."

"And you, and me," George said. "And Louis. They can suspect all they want, long as they can't prove anything."

"He wants his cut."

"Eddie?"

Alan nodded. "I asked him was he planning on running, and he said no. Just that he'll feel better when he's got his share. Mike got his cut, he said, and why's he different?"

"Mike's case was special."

"Just what I told him. He says he owes money he's got to pay, plus there's some things he wants to buy."

"The cops are talking to him, and what he wants to do is pay some debts and spend some money."

"That's about it."

"And if the answer's no? Then what?"

"He didn't say, but next thing I knew he was mentioning how the cops had been talking to him."

"Subtle bastard. You know, when the cops talk to him a few more times—"

"I don't know how he'll stand up. He's always been a stand-up guy before, but the stakes are a lot higher."

"And you can sort of sense him getting ready to spill it. He's working up a resentment about not getting paid. Other hand, if he does get paid . . ."

"He throws money around."

They fell silent. Finally George said, "We haven't even talked about Louis."

"No."

"Be convenient if the two of them killed each other, wouldn't it?"

"No more worries about who'll stand up. Down side, we'd have nobody to work with, either."

"Why work?" George grinned. "You and me'd be splitting two million, six-fifty."

"Less Mike's share," Alan pointed out.

"Right," George said.

They were planning it, working it out together, because it was not going to be easy to get the drop on Eddie, who was pretty shrewd and probably a little suspicious at this stage. And, while they were figuring it all out, Louis Creamer got in touch to tell them he'd just killed Eddie O'Day.

"He came by my house," Louis said, "and he was acting weird, you know? He said you guys were going to pull a fast one and rat us out to the cops, but how could you do that? And he had this scheme for taking you both out and getting the money, and him and me'd split it. And I could see where he was going. He wanted me for about as long as it would take to take you both down, and then it would be my turn to go. The son of a bitch."

"So what did you do?"

"I just punched him out," Louis said, "and then I took hold of him and broke his fucking neck. Now I got him lying in a heap in my living room, and I don't know what to do with him."

"We'll help," said George.

They went to Louis's house, and there was Eddie in a heap on the floor. "Look at this," George said, holding up a gun. "He was packing."

"Yeah, well, he was out cold before he could get it out of his pocket."

"You did good, Louis," George said, pressing the gun into Eddie's dead hand and carefully fitting his index finger around the trigger. "Real good," he said, and pointed the gun at Louis, and put three shots in his chest.

"Amazing," Alan said. "They really did kill each other. Well, you said it would be convenient."

"One of them would have cut a deal. In fact Eddie did try to cut a deal, with Louis."

"But Louis stood up."

"For how long?"

"That was nice, taking him out with Eddie's gun. They'll find nitrate particles in his hand and know he fired the shot. But how'd he get killed?"

"We're not the cops," George said. "Let them worry about it."

We didn't worry much. We looked at who was still standing, and we brought in the Walkers and grilled them separately. They had their stories ready and we couldn't shake them, and hadn't really expected to. They'd been through this countless times before, and they knew to keep their mouths shut, and eventually we sent them home.

A week later they were at George's house, in George's basement den, drinking George's scotch. "We maybe got trouble," Alan said. "The cops in San Diego picked up Mike Dunn."

"That's not good," George said, "but what's he gonna say? They'll throw the dame at him, Alfie's wife, and they got him figured for the sister, too. He'll just stay dummied up about everything if he knows what's good for him."

"Unless they offer him a deal."

"That could be a problem," George admitted.

Alan was looking at him carefully. George could almost hear what was going through Alan's mind, but before he could do anything about it Alan had a gun in his hand and it was pointed at George.

"Now put that away," George said. "What the hell's the matter with you? Just put that away and sit down and drink your drink."

"You're good, Georgie. But I know you too well. I just told you they arrested Mike, and you're not the least bit worried."

"I just said it could be a problem."

"What you almost said," Alan told him, "was it was impossible, but you didn't, you were quick on the uptake. But you knew it was impossible because you knew all along Mike Dunn was where nobody could get at him. Where is he, Georgie?"

"Buried. Nobody's gonna find him."

"What I figured. And what happened to his share? You bury it along with him?"

"I tucked it away. I didn't want the others to know what happened, so Mike's share of the money had to disappear."

"The others are gone, Georgie. It's just you and me, and I don't see you rushing to split the money with your brother."

"Jesus," George said, "is that what this is about? And will you please put the gun down and drink your drink?"

"I'll keep the gun," Alan said, "and I think I'll wait on the drink. Now that Louis and Eddie are out of the picture, you were gonna split Mike's share with me, weren't you?"

"Absolutely."

"Why don't I believe you, Brother?"

"Because you're tied up in knots. Because they grilled you downtown, same as they grilled me, and they offered you a deal, same as they offered me a deal, and we're the Walkers, we're not gonna sell each other out, and if you'd relax and drink your fucking drink you'd know that. You want your share of Mike's money? Is that what you want?"

"That's exactly what I want."

"Fine," George said, and led him to the furnace room, where he hoisted the duffel bag. They returned to the den, with Alan holding a gun on his brother all the way. George set down the bag and worked the zipper, and the bag was full of money, all right. Alan's eyes widened at the sight of it.

"Half's yours," George said.

"I figure all of it's mine," Alan said. "You were gonna take it all, so I'm gonna take it all. Fair enough?"

"I don't know about fair," George said, "but you know what? I'm not going to argue. You take it, the whole thing, and we'll split what's in the storage locker. And drink your fucking drink before it evaporates."

"I'll take what's in the locker, too," Alan said, and squeezed the trigger, and kept squeezing until the gun was empty. "Jesus," he said, "I just killed my own brother. I guess I'll take that drink now, Georgie. You talked me into it."

And he picked up the glass, drained it, and pitched forward onto his face.

The room fell silent, but for the crackling of the fire and, after a long moment, a rumbling snore from the fireside.

"A fine story," said the doctor, "though not perhaps equally engrossing to everyone. The club's Oldest Member, it would seem, has managed to sleep through it."

They all glanced at the fireplace, and the chair beside it, where the little old man dozed in his oversized armchair.

"Poison, I presume," the doctor went on. "In the whiskey, and of course that was why George was so eager to have his brother take a drink."

"Strychnine, as I recall," said the policeman. "Something fast-acting, in any event."

"It's a splendid story," the priest agreed, "but one question arises. All the principals died, and I don't suppose any of them was considerate enough to write out a narrative before departing. So how are you able to recount it?"

"We reconstructed a good deal," the policeman said. "Mike Dunn's body did turn up, eventually, in the well at the old farmhouse. And of course the death scene in George Walker's den spoke for itself, complete with the duffel bag full of money. I put words in their mouths and filled in the blanks through inference and imagination, but we're not in a court of law, are we? I thought it would do for a story."

"I meant no criticism, Policeman. I just wondered."

"And I wonder," said the soldier, "just what the story implies, and what it says about greed. They were greedy, of course, all of them. It was greed that led them to commit the initial crime, and greed that got them killing each other off, until there was no one left to spend all that money."

"I suppose the point is whatever one thinks it to be," the policeman said. "They were greedy as all criminals are greedy, wanting what other men have and appropriating it by illegal means. But, you know, they weren't that greedy."

"They shared equally," the doctor remembered.

"And lived well, but well within their means. You could say they were businessmen whose business was illegal. They were profit-motivated, but is the desire for profit tantamount to greed?"

"But they became greedy," the doctor observed. "And the greed altered their behavior. I assume these men had killed before."

"Oh, yes."

"But not wantonly, and they had never before turned on each other."

"No."

"The root of all evil," the priest said, and the others looked at him. "Money," he explained. "There was too much of it. That's the point, isn't it, Policeman? There was too much money."

The policeman nodded. "That's what I always thought," he said. "They had been playing the game for years, but suddenly the stakes had been raised exponentially, and they were in over their heads. The moment the bearer bonds turned up, all the deaths that were to follow were carved in stone."

They nodded, and the policeman took up the pack of playing cards. "My deal, isn't it?" He shuffled the pack, shuffled it again.

"I wonder," the soldier said. "I wonder just what greed is."

"I would say it's like pornography," the doctor said. "There was a senator who said he couldn't define it, but he knew it when he saw it."

"If he got an erection, it was pornography?"

"Something like that. But don't we all know what greed is? And yet how easy is it to pin down?"

"It's wanting more than you need," the policeman suggested.

"Ah, but that hardly excludes anyone, does it? Anyone who aspires to more than life on a subsistence level wants more than he absolutely needs."

"Perhaps," the priest proposed, "it's wanting more than you think you deserve."

"Oh, I like that," the doctor said. "It's so wonderfully subjective. If I think I deserve—what was your phrase, Policeman? Something about dreaming of avarice?"

"'Wealth beyond the dreams of avarice.' And it's not my phrase, I'm afraid, but Samuel Johnson's."

"A pity he's not here to enliven this conversation, but we'll have to make do without him. But if I think I deserve to have pots and pots of money, Priest, does that protect me from greed?"

The priest frowned, considering the matter. "I think it's where it leads," the policeman said. "If my desire for more moves me to sinful action, then the desire is greedy. If not, I simply want to better myself, and that's a normal and innocent human desire, and where would we be without it?"

"Somewhere in New Jersey," the doctor said. "Does anyone ever think himself to be greedy? You're greedy, but I just want to make a better life for my family. Isn't that how everyone sees it?"

"They always want it for the family," the policeman agreed. "A man embezzles a million dollars and he explains he was just doing it for his family. As if it's not greed if it's on someone else's behalf."

"I'm reminded of the farmer," said the priest, "who insisted he wasn't at all greedy. He just wanted the land that bordered his own."

The soldier snapped his fingers. "That's it," he said. "That's the essence of greed, that it can never be satisfied. You always want more." He shook his head. "Reminds me of a story," he said.

"Then put down the cards," the doctor said, "and let's hear it."

In my occupation (said the soldier) greed rarely plays a predominant role. Who becomes a soldier in order to make himself rich? Oh, there are areas of the world where a military career can indeed lead to wealth. One doesn't think of an eastern warlord, for example, slogging it out with an eye on his pension and a cottage in the Cotswolds or a houseboat in Fort Lauderdale. In the western democracies, though, the activating sin is more apt to be pride. One yearns for promotions, for status, perhaps in some instances for political power. And financial reward often accompanies these prizes, but it's not apt to be an end in itself.

Why do men choose a military career? For the security, I suppose. For self-respect, and the respect of one's fellows. For the satisfaction of being a part of something larger than oneself, and not a money-grubbing soulless corporation but an organization bent on advancing and defending the interests of an entire nation. For many reasons, but rarely out of greed.

Even so, opportunities for profit sometimes arise. And greedy men sometimes find themselves in uniform—especially in time of war, when the draft sweeps up men who would not otherwise choose to clothe themselves in khaki.

As often as not, such men make perfectly acceptable soldiers. There was a vogue some years ago for giving young criminals a choice—they could enlist in the armed forces or go to jail. This later went out of fashion, the argument against it being that it would turn the service into a sort of penitentiary without walls, filled with criminal types. But in my experience it often worked rather well. Removed from his home environment, and thrown into a world where greed had little opportunity to find satisfaction, the young man was apt to do just fine. The change might or might not last after his military obligation was over, of course.

But let's get down to cases. At the end of the second world war, Allied soldiers in Europe suddenly found several opportunities for profit. They had access to essential goods that were in short supply among the civilian population, and a black market sprang up instantly in cigarettes, chocolate, and liquor, along with such non-essentials as food and clothing. Some soldiers traded Hershey bars and packs of Camels for a fraulein's sexual favors; others parlayed goods from the PX into a small fortune, buying and selling and trading with dispatch.

There was nothing in Gary Carmody's background to suggest that he would become an illicit entrepreneur at war's end. He grew up on a farm in the Corn Belt and enlisted in the army shortly after Pearl Harbor. He was assigned to the infantry and participated in the invasion of Italy, where he picked up a Purple Heart and a shoulder wound at Salerno. Upon recovery from his injury, he was shipped to England, where in due course he took part in the Normandy invasion, landing at Utah Beach and helping to push the Wehrmacht across France. He earned a second Purple Heart during the German counterattack, along with a Bronze Star. He recuperated at a field hospital—the machine-gun bullet broke a rib, but did no major damage—and he was back in harness marching across the Rhine around the time the Germans surrendered.

Neither the bullets he'd taken nor the revelations of the concentration camps led Gary to a blanket condemnation of the entire German nation. While he thought the Nazis ought to be rounded up and shot, and that shooting was probably too good for the SS, he didn't see anything wrong with the German women. They were at once forthright and feminine, and their accents were a lot more charming than the Nazis in the war movies. He had a couple of dates, and then he met a blue-eyed blonde named Helga, and they hit it off. He brought her presents, of course—it was only fitting, the Germans had nothing and what was the big deal in bringing some chocolate and cigarettes? Back home you'd take flowers or candy, and maybe go out to a restaurant, and nobody thought of it as prostitution.

He brought a pair of nylons one day, and she tried them on at once, and one thing led to another. Afterward they lay together in her narrow bed and she reached to stroke the stockings, which they hadn't bothered to remove. She said, "You can get more of these, liebchen?"

"Did they get a run in them already?"

"Gott, I hope not. No, I was thinking. We could make money together."

"With nylons?"

"And cigarettes and chocolate. And other things, if you can get them."

"What other things?"

"Anything. Soap, even."

And so he began trading, with Helga as his partner in and out of bed. She was the daughter of shopkeepers and turned out to be a natural at her new career, knowing instinctively what to buy and what to sell and how to set prices. He was just a farm boy, but he had a farm boy's shrewdness plus the quickness it had taken to survive combat as a foot soldier, and he learned the game in a hurry. As with any extralegal trade, there was always a danger that the person you were dealing with would pull a fast one—or a gun or a knife—and use force or guile to take everything. Gary knew how to make sure that didn't happen.

It was another American soldier who got Gary into the art business. The man was an officer, a captain, but the black market was a great leveler, and the two men had done business together. The captain had a fraulein of his own, and the two couples were drinking together one evening when the captain mentioned that he'd taken something in trade and didn't know what the hell he was going to do with it. "It's a painting," he said. "Ugly little thing. Hang on a minute, I'll show you."

He went upstairs and returned with a framed canvas nine inches by twelve inches, showing Salome with the head of John the Baptist. "I know it's from the Bible and all," the captain said, "but it's still fucking unpleasant, and if Salome was really that fat I can't see losing your head over her. This look like five hundred dollars to you, Gary?"

"Is that what you gave for it?"

"Yes and no. I was going back and forth with this droopy-eyed Kraut and we reached a point where we're five hundred dollars apart. And he whips out this thing of beauty. 'All right,' he said. 'I vill hate myself for doing zis, but you haff me over a bushel.' And he goes on to tell me how it's a genuine Von Schtupp or whatever the hell it is, and it's worth a fortune.

"The way he did it, I couldn't come back and say, look, Konrad, keep the picture and gimme a hundred dollars more. I do that and I'm slapping him in the face, and I don't want to rub him the wrong way because Konrad and I do a lot of business. And the fact of the matter is yes, we're five hundred bucks apart, but I could take the deal at his price and I'm still okay with it. So I said yes, it sure is a beautiful picture, which it's not, as anyone can plainly see, and I said I'm sure it was valuable, but what am I gonna do with it? Sell it in Paris, he says. Sell it in London, in New York. So I let him talk me into it, because I wanted the deal to go through but what I didn't want was for him to try palming off more of these beauties on me, because I saw the look in his eye, Gary, and I've got a feeling he's got a shitload of them just waiting for a sucker with a suitcase full of dollars to take them off his hands."

"What are you going to do with it?"

"Well, I don't guess I'll throw darts at it. I could take it home, but what's a better souvenir, a genuine Luger or an ugly picture? And which would you rather spend your old age looking at?"

Gary looked at the painting, and he looked at Helga. He saw something in her eyes, and he also saw something in the canvas. "It's not that ugly," he said. "What do you want for it?"

"You serious?"

"Serious enough to ask, anyway."

"Well, let's see. I've got five hundred in it, and—"

"You've got zero in it. You'd have done the deal for what he offered, without the painting."

"I said that, didn't I? Strategic error, corporal. I'll tell you what, give me a hundred dollars and it's yours."

"Let's split the difference," Gary said. "I'll give you fifty."

"What is it we're splitting? Oh, hell, I don't want to look at it anymore. Give me the fifty and you can hang it over your bed."

They didn't hang it over the bed. Instead Helga hid it under the mattress. "The Nazis looted everything," she told him. "Museums, private collections. Your friend is stupid. It's a beautiful painting, and we can make money on it. And if we can meet his friend Konrad—"

"There's more where this one came from," he finished. "But how do we sell them?"

"You can get to Switzerland, no?"

"Maybe," he said.

The painting, which he sold without ever learning the artist's name—he somehow knew it was not Von Schtupp—brought him Swiss francs worth twenty-eight hundred American dollars. The proceeds bought four paintings from the droopy-eyed Konrad. These were larger canvases, and Gary removed them from their frames and rolled them up and took them to Zurich, returning to Germany this time with almost seven thousand dollars.

And so it went. It wasn't a foolproof business, as he learned when his Zurich customer dismissed a painting as worthless kitsch. But it was a forgiving trade, and most transactions were quite profitable. If he was in doubt he could take goods on consignment, selling in Zurich or Geneva—or, once, in Madrid—and sharing the proceeds with the consignor. But you made more money if you owned what you were selling, and he liked owning it, liked the way it felt. And if there was more risk that way, well, he liked the risk, too.

All his time and energy went into the business. Art was all he bothered with now—there were enough other soldiers making deals in stockings and cigarettes—and he was preoccupied with it, with the buying and selling and, almost as an afterthought, with the paintings themselves.

Because it turned out he had a feel for it. He'd seen something in that first painting of Salome, even if he hadn't realized it at the time. He'd responded to the artistry. Before he enlisted, he'd never been to a museum, never seen a painting hanging in a private home, never looked at any art beyond the reproductions in his mother's J.C. Penney calendar.

He learned to look at the paintings, as he'd never looked at anything before. The more he liked a painting, the harder it was to part with it. He fell in love with a Goya, and held on to it until something else came along that he liked better. Then he sold the Goya—that was the one he took to Madrid, where he'd heard about a crony of Franco's who wouldn't be put off by the work's dodgy provenance.

It was easier to part with Helga. They'd been good for each other, as lovers and as business partners, but the affair ran its course, and he didn't need or want a partner in his art dealings. He gave her a fair share of their capital and went on by himself.

Nothing lasts forever, not even military service. There came a time for Gary to board a troopship headed back to the States. He thought of staying in Europe—he had a career here, for as long as it could last—but in the end he realized it was time to go home.

But what to do with his money? He had run his original stake of cigarettes and nylons up to something like eighty thousand dollars. That was a lot of cash to carry, and it was cash he couldn't explain, so he had to carry it—he couldn't put it in a bank and write himself a check.

But what he could do, and in fact did, was buy a painting and bring that home with him. He chose a Vermeer, a luminous domestic interior, the most beautiful thing he'd ever seen in his life. It hadn't come to him in the usual way; instead, he'd found it in an art gallery in Paris and had been hard-pressed to get the snooty owner to cut the price by ten percent.

On the troopship, squinting at the painting in his footlocker by what little illumination his flashlight afforded, he decided he must have been out of his mind. He'd had all that cash, and now he was down to what, fifteen thousand dollars? That was a lot of money in 1946, it would buy him a house and get him started in a business, but it was a fifth of what he'd had.

Well, maybe he could run it up a little. It would be a week before the ship docked in New York, and there were plenty of men on board with money in their pockets and time on their hands. There were card games and crap games running twenty-four hours a day, and he'd always been pretty good at a poker table.

I suspect you can guess at the rest. Maybe he ran up against some card-sharps, or maybe the cards just weren't running his way. He never knew for sure, but what he did know was that he reached New York with nothing in his kick but the five hundred dollars of case money he'd tucked away before he started. Everything else was gone, invested in straights that ran into flushes, flushes that never came in, and bluffs some other guy called.

You'd think he'd be desolate, wouldn't you? He thought so himself, and was surprised to discover that he actually felt pretty good. If you looked at it one way, he left Germany with eighty thousand dollars and landed in New York with five hundred. But there was another way to see it, and that was that he had five hundred dollars more than he'd had when he left Iowa in the first place, and he'd been shot twice and lived to tell the tale, and he had a Bronze Star to keep his two Purple Hearts company, and he knew as much about women as anybody in Iowa, and more about art. The money he'd had, well, in a sense it had never been real in the first place, and, as for the paintings he'd trafficked in, well, they hadn't been real either. They'd all been stolen, and they had no provenance, and sooner or later they could very well be confiscated and restored to their rightful owners.

He figured he'd done just fine.

"Soldier? Have you finished?"

The soldier looked up, blinked. "More or less," he said. "Why? Don't you like the story?"

"It's a fine story," the doctor said, "but isn't it unfinished? There's a sense of closure, in that our hero is back where he started. That's if he went back to his family's farm, which I don't believe you mentioned."

"Didn't I? Yes, he returned to the farm."

"And to the girl he left behind him?"

"I don't believe there was a girl he'd left behind," said the soldier, "and if there was, well, she'd been left too far behind to catch up with him."

"That must have been true of the farm as well," the priest offered.

The soldier nodded. "That proved to be the case," he said. "He had, as it were, seen Paree—and Madrid and Geneva and Zurich and Berlin, and no end of other places more stimulating than an Iowa corn field. He'd spent two days in New York, waiting for his train, and he'd spent much of it at the Metropolitan Museum of Art and in the galleries on upper Madison Avenue. He stayed in Iowa for as long as he could, and then he packed a bag and returned to New York."

"And?"

"He found a cheap flat, a fifth-floor walkup in Greenwich Village for twenty-two dollars a month. He made the rounds of the art galleries and auction houses until he found someone who was willing to hire him for forty dollars a week. And, gradually, he learned the business from the ground up. From the very beginning he saved his money—I don't know how he could have saved much when he earned forty dollars a week, but he managed. Half of it went into a permanent savings account. The other half went into a fund to purchase art.

"Years passed. Although there was often a woman in his life, he never married, never formed a long-term alliance. Nor did he move from his original apartment in the Village. The neighborhood became increasingly desirable, the surrounding rents went up accordingly, but his own rent, frozen by the miracle of rent control, was still under a hundred dollars a month twenty-five years later.

"His capital grew, as did his collection of prints and paintings. The time came when he was able to open a gallery of his own, stocking it with the works he'd amassed. Rather than represent living artists, he dealt in older works, and on more than one occasion he was offered work he recognized from his time in Germany, stolen paintings he'd brokered years ago. Since then they'd acquired provenance and could be openly bought and sold.

"He's in the business today. He could retire, he'll tell you, but then what would he do with himself? He walks with a cane, and on damp days he feels the pain of his second wound, the rib broken by the machine-gun bullet. It's funny, he says, that it never bothered him once it healed, and now it aches again, after all those years. You think you're done with a thing, he'll say philosophically, but perhaps no one is ever done with anything.

"He's respected, successful, and if I told you his name, which is certainly not Gary Carmody, you might very well recognize it. There were rumors over the years that he occasionally dealt in, well, not stolen goods exactly, but works of art with something shady about them, and I don't mean chiaroscuro. But nothing was ever substantiated, and there was never a scandal, and few people even remember what was once said of him."

"And that's the end of the story," the policeman said.

"Well, the man's still alive, and is any story ever entirely over while one lives? But yes, the story is over."

"And what does it all mean?" the priest wondered. "He was a rather ordinary young man, not particularly greedy, until circumstances created a great opportunity for greed to flourish. Greed led him into a marginally criminal existence, at which he seems to have thrived, and then his circumstances changed, and he tried to change with them. But greed led him to try his hand at poker—"

"Even as you and I," murmured the doctor.

"—and he lost everything. But what he retained, acquired through greed, was a love of art and a passion for dealing in it, and as soon as he could he returned to it, and worked and sacrificed to achieve legitimate success."

"Unless those rumors were true," the policeman said.

"It's a fine story," the doctor said, "and well told. But there's something I don't entirely understand."

"Oh?"

"The Vermeer, Soldier. He was working for nothing and living on less. My God, he must have been scraping by on bread and water, and it would have been day-old bread and tap water, too. Why couldn't he sell the Vermeer? That would have set him up in business and kept him living decently until the gallery started paying for itself."

"He fell in love with it," the policeman offered. "How could he sell it? I daresay he still owns it to this day."

"He does," the soldier said. "It hung briefly on the wall of his room in the farmhouse in Iowa, and for years it hung on a nail in that fifth-floor Village walkup. The day he opened his own gallery he hung it above his desk in the gallery office, and it's still there."

"A lucky penny," the doctor said. "'Keep me and you'll never go broke.' And I'd say he's a long way from broke. I haven't priced any Vermeers lately, but I would think his would have to be worth an eight-figure price by now."

"You would think so," the soldier allowed.

"And he wouldn't part with it. Is that greed, clinging so tenaciously to that which, if he would but let it go, might allow him to reach his goals? Or is it some other sin?"

"Like what, Doctor?"

"Oh, pride, perhaps. He defines himself as a man who possesses a Vermeer. And so it hangs on his crumbling wall while he lives like a church mouse. No, make that like a ruined aristocrat, putting on a black tie every night for dinner, setting the table with Rosenthal china and Waterford crystal, and dining on stone soup. Made, you'll no doubt recall, by simmering a stone in water for half an hour, then adding salt."

"An old family recipe," the policeman said. "But would the painting be worth that much? An eight-figure price—that's quite a range, from ten to a hundred million dollars."

"Ninety-nine," the doctor said.

"I stand corrected. But if it increased in value from fifty thousand dollars to—oh, take the low figure, ten million. If it performed that well, how can you possibly argue that he should have sold it? He may have struggled, but it doesn't seem to have harmed him. Who can say he was wrong to keep it? He's a success now, he's been a success for some years—and he owns a Vermeer."

They fell silent, thinking about it. Then the priest cleared his throat, and all eyes turned toward him.

"I should think," he said, "that at least two of the figures are after the decimal point." He drew a breath, smiled gently. "I suspect Soldier has neglected to tell us everything. It's a forgery, isn't it? That priceless Vermeer."

The soldier nodded.

"By Van Meegeren, I would suppose, if it fooled our Mr. Carmody the first time around. That fellow's Vermeers, sold as the fakes that they are, have reached a point where they command decent prices in their own right. I don't suppose this one is worth quite what that young soldier gave for it half a century ago, but it's a long way from valueless."

"A fake," the policeman said. "How did you guess, Priest?"

"The clues were there, weren't they? Why else would his heart sink when he peered at the painting as it reposed in his footlocker? He saw then by flashlight what he hadn't seen in the gallery's more favorable lighting—that he'd squandered all his profits on a canvas that was never in the same room as Vermeer. No wonder he gambled, hoping to recoup his losses. And, given the state of mind he must have been in, no wonder he lost everything."

"An expert in New York confirmed what he already knew," the soldier said. "Could he have sold it anyway? Perhaps, even as the Parisian dealer, knowingly or unknowingly, had sold it to him. But he'd have taken a considerable loss, and would risk blackening his reputation before he even had one. Better, he always felt, to keep the painting, and to hang it where he would see it every day, and never forget the lesson it was there to teach him."

"And what was that lesson, Soldier?"

"That greed can lead to error, with devastating results. Because it was greed that led him to sink the better part of his capital into that worthless Vermeer. It was a bargain, and he should have been suspicious, but the opportunity to get it at that price led him astray. Greed made him want it to be a Vermeer, and so he believed it to be one, and paid the price for his greed."

"And hung it on his wall," the priest said.

"Yes."

"And moved it to his office when he opened his own gallery. So that he could look at it every day while conducting his business. But others would see it as well, wouldn't they? What did he tell them when they asked about it?"

"Only that it was not for sale."

"I don't suppose it harmed his reputation to have it known that this new kid on the block was sufficiently well fixed to hang a Vermeer on his wall and not even entertain offers for it," the doctor mused. "I'm not so sure he didn't get his money's worth out of it after all."

They fell silent again, and the policeman dealt the cards. The game was seven-card stud, but this time the betting was restrained and the pot small, won at length by the priest with two pair, nines and threes. "If we were playing baseball," he said, raking in the chips, "with nines and threes wild, I'd have five aces."

"If we were playing tennis," said the doctor, who had held fours and deuces, "it would be your serve. So shut up and deal."

The priest gathered the cards, shuffled them. The soldier filled his pipe, scratched a match, held it to the bowl. "Oh, it's your pipe," the doctor said. "I thought the old man over there had treated us to a fart."

"He did," said the soldier. "That's one reason I lit the pipe."

"Two wrongs don't make a right," the doctor declared, and the priest offered the cards and the policeman cut them, and, from the fireside, the four men heard a sound that had become familiar to them over time.

"You see?" said the doctor. "He's done it again. Try to counteract his flatulence with your smoke, and he simply redoubles his efforts."

"He's an old man," the policeman said.

"So? Who among us is not?"

"He's a bit older than we are."

"And isn't he a pretty picture of what the future holds? One day we too can sleep twenty-three hours out of every twenty-four, and fill the happy hours with coughing and snuffling and snoring and, last but alas not least, great rumbling pungent farts. And what's left after that but the grave? Or is there more to come, Priest?"

"I used to wonder," the priest admitted.

"But you no longer doubt?"

"I no longer wonder, knowing that all will be made clear soon enough. But I'm still thinking of greed."

"Deal the cards, and we can do something about it."

"As I understand it," the priest went on, "crimes of greed, crimes with mercenary motives, fluctuate with economic conditions. When and where unemployment is high and need is great, the crime rate goes up. When times are good, it drops."

"That would stand to reason," the soldier said.

"On the other hand," said the priest, "the criminals in Policeman's story fell tragically under the influence of greed not when they lacked money, but when they were awash in it. When there was not so much to be divided, they shared fairly and equally. When the money flooded in, they killed to increase their portion of it."

"It seems paradoxical," the policeman agreed, "but that's just how it was."

"And your corporal-turned-art dealer, Soldier. How does he fit into the need-greed continuum?"

"Opportunity awakened his greed," the soldier said. "Perhaps it was there all along, just waiting until the chance came along to make money on the black market. We could say he was greediest when he bought the fake Vermeer, and again when he realized what he'd done and tried to recoup at the card table."

"A forlorn hope," said the doctor, "in a game like this one, where hours go by before someone deals the cards."

"His money gone," the soldier went on, "he applied himself like a character out of Horatio Alger, but was he any less avaricious for the fact that his actions were now ethical and lawful? He was as ambitious as ever, and there was a pot of gold looming at the end of his rainbow."

"So greed's a constant," said the priest, and took up the deck of cards once again.

"It is and it isn't," the doctor said. "Hell, put down the damned cards. You just reminded me of a story."

The priest placed the cards, undealt, upon the table. By the fireside, the old man sighed deeply in his sleep. And the priest and the soldier and the policeman sat up in their chairs, waiting for the doctor to begin.

Some years ago (said the doctor) I had as a patient a young man who wanted to be a writer. Upon completion of his education he moved to New York, where he took an apartment rather like your art dealer, Soldier, but lacking a faux-Vermeer on the wall. He placed his typewriter on a rickety card table and began banging out poems and short stories and no end of first chapters that failed to thrive and grow into novels. And he looked for a job, hoping for something that would help him on his way to literary success.

The position he secured was at a literary agency, owned and operated by a fellow I'll call Byron Fielding. That was not his name, but neither was the name he used, which he created precisely as I've created an alias for him, by putting together the surnames of two English writers. Fielding started out as a writer himself, sending stories to magazines while he was still in high school, and getting some of them published. Then World War Two came along, even as it did to Gary Carmody, and Byron Fielding was drafted and, upon completion of basic training, assigned to a non-combat clerical position. It was his literary skills that kept him out of the front lines—not his skill in stringing words together but his ability to type. Most men couldn't do it.

When he got out of the service, young Fielding wrote a few more stories, but he found the business discouraging. There were, he had come to realize, too many people who wanted to be writers. Sometimes it seemed as though everybody wanted to be a writer, including people who could barely read. And when they tried their hand at it, they almost always thought it was good.

Was such monumental self-delusion as easy in other areas of human endeavor? I think not. Every boy wants to be a professional baseball player, but an inability to hit a curveball generally disabuses a person of the fantasy. Untalented artists, trying to draw something, can look at it and see that it didn't come out as they intended. Singers squawk, hear themselves, and find something else to do. But writers write, and look at what they have written, and wonder what's keeping the Nobel Commission fellows from ringing them up.

You shake your heads at this, and call it folly. Byron Fielding called it opportunity, and opened his arms wide.

He set up shop as a literary agent; he would represent authors, placing their work with publishers, overseeing the details of their contracts, and taking ten percent of their earnings for his troubles. This was nothing new; there were quite a few people earning their livings in this fashion—though not a fraction of the number there are today. But how, one wondered, could Byron Fielding hope to establish himself as an agent? He had no contacts. He didn't know any writers—or publishers, or anyone else. What would persuade an established writer to do business with him?

In point of fact, Fielding had no particular interest in established writers, realizing that he had little to offer them. What he wanted was the wannabes, the hopeful hopeless scribblers looking for the one break that would transform a drawer full of form rejection slips into a life of wealth and fame.

He rented office space, called himself Byron Fielding, called his company the Byron Fielding Literary Agency, and ran ads in magazines catering to the same hopeful hopeless ones he was counting on to make him rich. "I sell fiction and non-fiction to America's top markets," he announced. "I'd like to sell them your material."

And he explained his terms. If you were a professional writer, with several sales to national publishers to your credit, he would represent you at the standard terms of ten percent commission. If you were a beginner, he was forced to charge you a reading fee of one dollar per thousand words, with a minimum of five dollars and a maximum of twenty-five for book-length manuscripts. If your material was salable, he would rush it out to market on his usual terms. If it could be revised, he'd tell you how to fix it—and not charge you an extra dime for the advice. And if, sadly, it was unsalable, he'd tell you just what was wrong with it, and how to avoid such errors in the future.

The money rolled in.

And so did the stories, and they were terrible. Fielding stacked them, and when each had been in his office for two weeks, so that it would look as though he'd taken his time and given it a careful reading, he returned it with a letter explaining just what was wrong with it. Most of the time what was wrong was the writer's utter lack of talent, but he never said that. Instead he praised the style and found fault with the plot, which somehow was always flawed in ways that revision could not cure. Put this one away, he advised each author, and write another, and send that along as soon as it's finished. With, of course, another reading fee.

The business was profitable from the beginning, with writers sending in story after story, failing entirely to learn from experience. Fielding thought he'd milk it for as long as it lasted, but a strange thing happened. Skimming through the garbage, he found himself coming across a story now and then that wasn't too bad. "Congratulations!" he wrote the author. "I'm taking this right out to market." It was probably a mistake, he thought, but this way at least he got away with a shorter letter.

And some of the stories sold. And, out of the blue, a professional writer got in touch, wondering if Fielding would represent him on a straight commission basis. By the time my patient, young Gerald Metzner, went to work for him, Byron Fielding was an established agent with over ten years in the business and a string of professional clients whose work he sold to established book and magazine publishers throughout the world.

Fielding had half a dozen people working for him by then. One ran a writing school, with a post office box for an address and no visible connection with Byron Fielding or his agency. The lucky student worked his way through a ten-lesson correspondence course, and upon graduating received a certificate of completion and the suggestion that he might submit his work (with a reading fee) to guess who.

Another employee dealt with the professional clients, working up market lists for the material they submitted. Two others—Gerald Metzner was one of them—read the scripts that came in over the transom, the ones accompanied by reading fees. "I can see you are no stranger to your typewriter," he would write to some poor devil who couldn't write an intelligible laundry list. "Although this story has flaws that render it unsalable, I'll be eager to see your next effort. I feel confident that you're on your way."

The letter, needless to say, went out over Byron Fielding's signature. As far as the mopes were concerned, Fielding was reading every word himself, and writing every word of his replies. Another employee, also writing over Fielding's mean little scrawl, engaged in personal collaboration with the more desperate clients. For a hundred bucks, the great man himself would purportedly work with them step by step, from outline through first draft to final polish. They would be writing their stories hand in hand with Byron Fielding, and when it was finished to his satisfaction he would take it out to market.

The client (or victim, as you prefer) would mail in his money and his outline. The hireling, who had very likely never sold anything himself, and might in fact not ever have written anything, would suggest some arbitrary change. The client would send in the revised outline, and when it was approved he would furnish a first draft. Again the employee would suggest improvements, and again the poor bastard would do as instructed, whereupon he'd be told that the story, a solid professional effort, was on its way to market.

But it remained a sow's ear, however artfully embroidered, and Fielding wouldn't have dreamed of sullying what little reputation he had by showing such tripe to an editor. So the manuscript went into a drawer in the office, and there it remained, while the hapless scribbler was encouraged to get cracking on another story.

The fee business was ethically and morally offensive, and one wondered why Fielding didn't give it up once he could afford to. The personal collaboration racket was worse; it was actionably fraudulent, and a client who learned what was going on could clearly have pressed criminal charges against his conniving collaborator. It's not terribly likely that Fielding could have gone to jail for it, but a determined prosecutor with the wind up could have given him some bad moments. And if there were a writer or two on the jury, he couldn't expect much in the way of mercy.

Fielding hung on to it because he didn't want to give up a dime. He didn't treat his professional clients a great deal better, for in a sense he had only one client, and that client was Byron Fielding. He acted, not in his clients' interests, but in his own. If they coincided, fine. If not, tough.

I could go on, but you get the idea. So did young Metzner, and he wasn't there for long. He worked for Fielding for a year and a half, then resigned to do his own writing. A lot of the agency's pro clients were writing softcore paperback fiction, and Metzner tried one of his own. When it was done he sent it to Fielding, who sold it for him.

He did a few more, and was making more money than he'd made as an employee, and working his own hours. But it wasn't what he really wanted to write, and he tried a few other things and wound up out in California, writing for film and television. Fielding referred him to a Hollywood agent, who, out of gratitude and the hope of more business, split commissions on Metzner's sales with Byron Fielding. Thus Fielding made far more money over the years from Gerald Metzner's screenwriting than he had ever made from his prose, and all he had to do for it was cash the checks the Hollywood agent sent him. That was, to his way of thinking, the ideal author-agent relationship, and he had warm feelings for Metzner—or what passed for warm feelings in such a man.

When Metzner had occasion to come to New York, he more often than not dropped in on his agent. He and Fielding would chat for fifteen minutes, and then he could return to Hollywood and tell himself he hadn't entirely lost touch with the world of books and publishing. He had an agent, didn't he? His agent was always happy to see him, wasn't he? And who was to say he wouldn't someday try his hand at another novel?

Years passed, as they so often do. Business again called Gerald Metzner to New York, and he arranged to drop by Fielding's office on a free afternoon. As usual, he waited for a few minutes in the outer office, taking a look at the sea of minions banging away at typewriters. It seemed to him that there were more of them every time he visited, more men sitting at more desks, telling even more of the hopeful hopeless that they had talent in rare abundance, and surely the next story would make the grade, but, sad to say, this story, with its poorly constructed plot, was not the one to bring their dreams to fulfillment. What a story required, you see, was a strong and sympathetic lead character confronted by a problem, and . . .

Di dah di dah di dah.

He broke off his reverie when he was summoned to Fielding's private office. There the agent waited, looking younger than his years, health club–toned and sun lamp–tanned, a broad white-toothed smile on his face. The two men shook hands and took seats on opposite sides of the agent's immaculate desk.

They chatted a bit, about nothing in particular, and then Fielding fixed his eyes on Gerald. "You probably notice that there's something different about me," he said.

"Now that you mention it," Metzner said, "I did notice that." Years of pitching doubtful premises to studio heads and network execs had taught him to think on his feet—or, more accurately, on his behind. What, he wondered, was *different* about the man? Same military haircut, same horn-rimmed glasses. No beard, no mustache. What the hell was Fielding talking about?

"But I'll bet you can't quite put your finger on it."

Well, that was a help. Maybe this would be like soap opera dialogue—you could get through it without a script, just going with the flow.

"You know," he said, "that's it exactly. I sense it, but I can't quite put my finger on it."

"That's because it's abstract, Gerry."

"That would explain it."

"But no less real."

"No less real," he echoed.

Fielding smiled like a shark, but then how else would he smile? "I won't keep you in suspense," he said. "I'll tell you what it is. I've got peace of mind."

"Peace of mind," Metzner marveled.

"Yes, peace of mind." The agent leaned forward. "Gerry," he said, "ever since I opened up for business I've been the toughest, meanest, most miserable sonofabitch who ever lived. I've always wrung every nickel I could out of every deal I touched. I worked sixty, seventy hours a week, and I used the whip on the people who worked for me. And do you know why?"

Metzner shook his head.

"Because I thought I had to," Fielding said. "I really believed I'd be screwed otherwise. I'd run out of money, I'd be out on the street, my family would go hungry. So I couldn't let a penny get away from me. You know, until my lawyers absolutely insisted, I wouldn't even shut down the Personal Collaboration dodge. 'Byron, you're out of your mind,' they told me. 'That's consumer fraud, and you're doing it through the mails. It's a fucking federal offense and you could go to Leavenworth for it, and what the hell do you need it for? Shut it down!' And they were right, and I knew they were right, but they had to tell me a dozen times before I did what they wanted. Because we made good money out of the PC clients, and I thought I needed every cent of it."

"But now you have peace of mind," Metzner prompted.

"I do, Gerry, and you could see it right away, couldn't you? Even if you didn't know what it was you were seeing. Peace of mind, Gerry. It's a wonderful thing, maybe the single most wonderful thing in the world."

Time for the violins to come in, Metzner thought. "How did it happen, Byron?"

"A funny thing," Fielding said. "I sat down with my accountant about eight months ago, the way I always do once a year. To go over things, look at the big picture. And he told me I had more than enough money left to keep me in great shape for as long as I live. 'You could shut down tomorrow,' he said, 'and you could live like a king for another fifty years, and you won't run out of money. You've got all the money you could possibly need, and it's in solid risk-free inflation-resistant investments, and I just wish every client of mine was in such good shape.'"

"That's great," said Metzner, who wished he himself were in such good shape, or within a thousand miles thereof.

"And a feeling came over me," Fielding said, "and I didn't know what the feeling was, because I had never felt anything like it before. It was a relief, but it was a permanent kind of relief, the kind that means you can stay relieved. You're not just out of the woods for the time being. You're all of a sudden in a place where there are no woods. Free and clear—and I realized there was a name for the feeling I had, and it was peace of mind."

"I see."

"Do you, Gerry? I'll tell you, it changed my life. All that pressure, all that anxiety—gone!" He grinned, then straightened up in his chair. "Of course," he said, "on the surface, nothing's all that different. I still hustle every bit as hard as I ever did. I still squeeze every dime I can out of every deal I touch. I still go for the throat, I still hang on like a bulldog, I'm still the most miserable sonofabitch in the business."

"Oh?"

"But now it's not because I *have* to be like that," Fielding exulted. "It's because I *want* to. That's what I love, Gerry. It's who I am. But now, thank God, I've got peace of mind!"

"What a curious story," said the priest. "I'm as hard-pressed to put my finger on the point of it as your young man was to recognize Fielding's peace of mind. Fielding seems to be saying that his greed had its roots in his insecurity. I suppose his origins were humble?"

"Lower middle class," the doctor said. "No money in the family, but they were a long way from impoverished. Still, insecurity, like the heart, has reasons that reason knows nothing of. If he's to be believed, Byron Fielding grew up believing he had to grab every dollar he could or he risked ruin, poverty, and death."

"Then he became wealthy," the priest said, "and, more to the point, came to *believe* he was wealthy and financially secure."

"Fuck-you money," the policeman said, and explained the phrase when the priest raised an eyebrow. "Enough money, Priest, so that the possessor can say 'fuck you' to anyone."

"An enviable state," the priest said. "Or is it? The man attained that state, and his greed, which no longer imprisoned him, still operated as before. It was his identity, part and parcel of his personality. He remained greedy and heartless, not out of compulsion but out of choice, out of a sense of self." He frowned. "Unless we're to take his final remarks *cum grano salis*?" To the puzzled policeman he said, "With a grain of salt, that is to say. You translated fuck-you money for me, so at least I can return the favor. A sort of quid pro quo, which in turn means . . ."

"That one I know, Priest."

"And Fielding was not stretching the truth when he said he was the same vicious bastard he'd always been," the doctor put in. "Peace of mind didn't seem to have mellowed him at all. Did I mention his brother?"

The men shook their heads.

"Fielding had a brother," the doctor said, "and, when it began to appear as though this scam of his might prove profitable, Fielding put his brother to work for him. He made his brother change his name, and picked Arnold Fielding for him, having in mind the poet Matthew Arnold. The brother, whom everyone called Arnie, functioned as a sort of office manager, and was also a sort of mythical beast invoked by Byron in time of need. If, for example, an author came in to cadge an advance, or ask for something else Byron Fielding didn't want to grant, the agent wouldn't simply turn him down. 'Let me ask Arnie,' he would say, and then he'd go into the other office and twiddle his thumbs for a moment, before returning to shake his head sadly at the client. 'Arnie says no,' he'd report. 'If it were up to me it'd be a different story, but Arnie says no.' "

"But he hadn't actually consulted his brother?"

"No, of course not. Well, here's the point. Some years after Gerald Metzner learned about Byron Fielding's peace of mind, Arnie Fielding had a health scare and retired to Florida. He recovered, and in due course found Florida and retirement both bored him to distraction, and he came back to New York. He went to see his brother Byron and told him he had decided to go into business. And what would he do? Well, he said, there was only one business he knew, and that's the one he would pick. He intended to set up shop on his own as a literary agent.

" 'The best of luck to you,' Byron Fielding told him. 'What are you going to call yourself?'

" 'The Arnold Fielding Literary Agency,' Arnie said.

"Byron shook his head. 'Better not,' he said. 'You use the Fielding name and I'll take you to court. I'll sue you.'

" 'You'd sue me? Your own brother?'

" 'For every cent you've got,' Byron told him."

The soldier lit his pipe. "He'd sue his own brother," he said, "to prevent him from doing business under the name he had foisted upon him. The man may have achieved peace of mind, Doctor, but I don't think we have to worry that it mellowed him."

"Arnie never did open his own agency," the doctor said. "He died a year or so after that, though not of a broken heart, but from a recurrence of the illness that had sent him into retirement initially. And the old pirate himself, Byron Fielding, only survived him by a couple of years."

"And your young writer?"

"Not so young anymore," said the doctor. "He had a successful career as a screenwriter, until ageism lessened his market value, at which time he returned to novel-writing. But the well-paid Hollywood work had taken its toll, and the novels he wrote all failed."

They were considering that in companionable silence when a log burned through and fell in the fireplace. They turned at the sound, observed the shower of sparks, and heard in answer a powerful discharge of methane from the old man's bowels.

"God, the man can fart!" cried the doctor. "Light up your pipe, Soldier. What I wouldn't give for a cigar!"

"A cigar," said the priest, thoughtfully.

"Sometimes it's only a cigar," the doctor said, "as the good Dr. Freud once told us. But in this instance it would do double duty as an air freshener. Priest, are you going to deal those cards?"

"I was just about to," said the priest, "until you mentioned the cigar."

"What has a cigar, and a purely hypothetical cigar at that, to do with playing a long-delayed hand of poker?"

"Nothing," said the priest, "but it has something to do with greed. In a manner of speaking."

"I'm greedy because I'd rather inhale the aroma of good Havana leaf than the wind from that old codger's intestines?"

"No, no, no," said the priest. "It's a story, that's all. Your mention of a cigar put me in mind of a story."

"Tell it," the policeman urged.

"It's a poor story compared to those you all have told," the priest said. "But it has to do with greed."

"And cigars?"

"And cigars, yes. It definitely has to do with cigars."

"Put the cards down," the doctor said, "and tell the story."

There was a man I used to know (said the priest) whom I'll call Archibald O'Bannion, Archie to his intimates. He started off as a hod carrier on building sites, applied himself diligently learning his trade, and wound up with his own construction business. He was a hard worker and a good businessman, as it turned out, and he did well.

He was motivated by the desire for profit, and for the accoutrements of success, but I don't know that I would call him a greedy man. He was a hard bargainer and an intense competitor, certainly, and he liked to win. But greedy? He never struck me that way.

And he was charitable, more than generous in his contributions to the church and to other good causes. It is possible, to be sure, for a man to be at once greedy and generous, to grab with one hand while dispensing with the other. But Archie O'Bannion never struck me as a greedy man. He was a cigar smoker, and he never lit a cigar without offering them around, nor was there anything perfunctory about the offer. When he smoked a cigar, he genuinely wanted you to join him.

He treated himself well, as he could well afford to do. His home was large and imposing, his wardrobe extensive and well chosen, his table rich and varied. In all these areas, his expenditures were consistent with his income and status.

His one indulgence—he thought it an indulgence—was his cigars.

He smoked half a dozen a day, and they weren't William Penn or Hav-a-Tampa, either. They were the finest cigars he could buy. I liked a good cigar myself in those days, though I could rarely afford one, and when Archie would offer me one of his, well, I didn't often turn him down. He was a frequent visitor to the rectory, and I can recall no end of evenings when we sat in pleasantly idle conversation, puffing on cigars he'd provided.

Then the day came when a collection of cigars went on the auction block, and he bought them all.

A cigar smoker's humidor is not entirely unlike an oenophile's wine cellar, and sometimes there is even an aftermarket for its contents. Cigars don't command the prices of rare bottles of wine, and I don't know that they're collected in quite the same way, but when a cigar smoker dies, the contents of his humidor are worth something, especially since Castro came into power in Cuba. With the American embargo in force, Havana cigars were suddenly unobtainable. One could always have them smuggled in through some country that continued to trade with Cuba, but that was expensive and illegal, and, people said, the post-revolution cigars were just not the same. Many of the cigar makers had fled the island nation, and the leaf did not seem to be what it was, and, well, the result was that pre-Castro cigars became intensely desirable.

A cigar is a perishable thing, but properly stored and maintained there's no reason why it cannot last almost forever. In this particular instance, the original owner was a cigar aficionado who began laying in a supply of premium Havanas shortly after Castro took power. Perhaps he anticipated the embargo. Perhaps he feared a new regime would mean diminished quality. Whatever it was, he bought heavily, stored his purchases properly, and then, his treasures barely sampled, he was diagnosed with oral cancer. The lip, the mouth, the palate—I don't know the details, but his doctor told him in no uncertain terms that he had to give up his cigars.

Not everyone can. Sigmund Freud, whom Doctor quoted a few minutes ago, went on smoking while his mouth and jaw rotted around his cigar. But this chap's addiction was not so powerful as his instinct for self-preservation, and so he stopped smoking then and there.

But he held on to his cigars. His several humidors were attractive furnishings as well as being marvels of temperature and humidity control, and he liked the looks of them in his den. He broke the habit entirely, to the point where his eyes would pass over the humidors regularly without his ever registering a conscious thought of their contents, let alone a longing for them. You might think he'd have pressed cigars upon his friends, but he didn't, perhaps out of reluctance to have to stand idly by and breathe in the smoke of a cigar he could not enjoy directly. Or perhaps, as I somehow suspect, he was saving them for some future date when it would be safe for him to enjoy them as they were meant to be enjoyed.

Well, no matter. In any event, he did recover from his cancer, and some years later he died of something else. And since neither his widow nor his daughters smoked cigars, they wound up consigned for sale at auction, and Archie O'Bannion bought them all.

There were two thousand of them, and Archie paid just under sixty thousand dollars for the lot. That included the several humidors, which were by no means valueless, but when all was said and done he'd shelled out upwards of twenty-five dollars a cigar. If he consumed them at his usual rate, a day's smoking would cost him $150. He could afford that, but there was no denying it was an indulgence.

But what troubled him more than the cost was the fact that his stock was virtually irreplaceable. Every cigar he smoked was a cigar he could never smoke again. Two thousand cigars sounded like an extraordinary quantity, but if you smoked six a day starting the first of January, you'd light up the last one after Thanksgiving dinner. They wouldn't last the year.

"It's a damned puzzle," he told me. "What do I do? Smoke one a day? That way they'll last five years and change, but all the while five out of six of the cigars I smoke will be slightly disappointing. Maybe I should smoke 'em all up, one right after the other, and enjoy them while I can. Or maybe I should just let them sit there in their beautiful humidors, remaining moist and youthful while I dry up and age. Then when I drop dead it'll be Mary Katherine's turn to put them up for auction."

I said something banal about the conundrum of having one's cake and eating it, too.

"By God," he said. "That's it, isn't it? Have a cigar, Father."

But, I demurred, surely not one of his Havanas?

"You smoke it," he said. "You earned it, Father, and you can damn well smoke it and enjoy it."

And he picked up the phone and called his insurance agent.

Archie, I should mention, had come to regard the insurance industry as a necessary evil. He'd had trouble getting his insurers to pay claims he felt were entirely legitimate, and disliked the way they'd do anything they could to weasel out of their responsibility. So he had no compunctions about what he did now.

He insured his cigars, opting for the top-of-the-line policy, one which provided complete coverage, not even excluding losses resulting from flood, earthquake, or volcanic eruption. He declared their value at the price he had paid for them, paid the first year's premium in advance, and went on with his life.

A little less than a year later, he smoked the last of his premium Havanas. Whereupon he filed a claim against his insurance company, explaining that all two thousand of the cigars were lost in a series of small fires.

You will probably not be surprised that the insurance company refused to pay the claim, dismissing it as frivolous. The cigars, they were quick to inform him, had been consumed in the normal fashion, and said consumption was therefore not a recoverable loss.

Archie took them to court, where the judge agreed that his claim was frivolous, but ordered the company to pay it all the same. The policy, he pointed out, did not exclude fire, and in fact specifically included it as a hazard against which Archie's cigars were covered. Nor did it exclude as unacceptable risk the consumption of the cigars in the usual fashion.

"I won," he told me. "They warranted the cigars were insurable, they assumed the risk, and then of course they found something to whine about, the way they always do. But I stuck it to the bastards and I beat 'em in court. I thought they'd drag it out and appeal the judgment, and I was set to fight it all the way, but they caved in. Wrote me a check for the full amount of the policy, and now I can go looking for someone else with pre-Castro Havanas to sell, because I've developed a taste for them, let me tell you. And I've got you to thank, Father, for a remark you made about having your cake and eating it, too, because I smoked my cigars and I'll have 'em, too, just as soon as I find someone who's got 'em for sale. Of course this is a stunt you can only pull once, but once is enough, and I feel pretty good about it. The Havanas are all gone, but these Conquistadores from Honduras aren't bad, so what the hell, Father. Have a cigar!"

"I don't know why you were so apologetic about your story, Priest," the soldier said. "I think it's a fine one. I'm a pipe smoker myself, and any dismay one might conceivably feel at watching one's tobacco go up in smoke is more than offset by the satisfaction of improving the pipe itself, as one does with each pipeful one smokes. But pipe tobacco, even very fine pipe tobacco, costs next to nothing compared to premium cigars. I can well understand the man's initial frustration, and ultimate satisfaction."

"An excellent story," the doctor agreed, "but then it would be hard for me not to delight in a story in which an insurance company is hoist on its own petard. The swine have institutionalized greed, and it's nice to see them get one in the eye."

"I wonder," said the policeman.

"I know what you're thinking," the doctor told him. "You're thinking that this fellow Archie committed lawful fraud. You're thinking it was his intention to make the insurance company subsidize his indulgence in costly Cuban tobacco. That's entirely correct, but as far as I'm concerned it's quite beside the point. Lawful fraud is an insurance company's stock in trade, and anyway what's sixty thousand dollars on their corporate balance sheet? I say more power to Archie, and long may he puff away."

"All well and good," the policeman said, "but that's not what I was thinking."

"It's not?"

"Not at all," he told the doctor, and turned to the priest. "There's more to the story, isn't there, Priest?"

The priest smiled. "I was wondering if anyone would think of it," he said. "I rather thought you might, Policeman."

"Think of what?" the soldier wanted to know.

"And what did they do?" the policeman asked. "Did they merely voice the threat? Or did they go all the way and have him arrested?"

"Arrested?" cried the doctor. "For what?"

"Arson," the policeman said. "Didn't he say the cigars were lost in a series of small fires? I suppose they could have charged him with two thousand counts of criminal arson."

"Arson? They were his cigars, weren't they?"

"As I understand it."

"And doesn't a man have the right to smoke his own cigars?"

"Not in a public place," said the policeman. "But yes, in the ordinary course of events, he would have been well within his rights to smoke them. But he had so arranged matters that smoking one of those cigars amounted to intentional destruction of insured property."

"But that's an outrage," the doctor said.

"Is it, Doctor?" The soldier puffed on his pipe. "You liked the story when the insurance company was hoist on its own petard. Now Archie's hoisted even higher on a petard of his own making. Wouldn't you say that makes it a better story?"

"A splendid story," said the doctor, "but no less an outrage for it."

"In point of fact," the policeman said, "Archie could have been charged with arson even in the absence of a claim, the argument being that he forfeited the right to smoke the cigars the moment he insured them. Practically speaking, though, it was pressing the claim that triggered the criminal charge. Did he actually go to jail, Priest? Because that would seem a little excessive."

The priest shook his head. "Charges were dropped," he said, "when the parties reached agreement. Archie gave back the money, and both sides paid their own legal costs. And he got to tell the story on himself, and he was a good fellow, you know, and could see the humor in a situation. He said it was worth it, all things considered, and a real pre-Castro cigar was worth the money, even if you had to pay for it yourself."

The other three nodded at the wisdom of that, and once again the room fell silent. The priest took the deck of cards in hand, looked at the others in turn, and put the cards down undealt.

And then, from the fireside, the fifth man present broke the silence.

"Greed," said the old man, in a voice like the wind in dry grass. "What a subject for conversation!"

"We've awakened you," said the priest, "and for that let me apologize on everyone's behalf."

"It is I who should apologize," said the old man, "for dozing intermittently during such an illuminating and entertaining conversation. But at my age the line between sleep and wakefulness is a tenuous proposition at best. One is increasingly uncertain whether one is dreaming or awake, and past and present become hopelessly entangled. I close my eyes and lose myself in thought, and all at once I am a boy. I open them and I am an old man."

"Ah," said the doctor, and the others nodded in assent.

"And while I am apologizing," the old man said, "I should add a word of apology for my bowels. I seem to have an endless supply of wind, which in turn grows increasingly malodorous. Still, I'm not incontinent. One grows thankful in the course of time for so many things one took for granted, if indeed one ever considered them at all."

"One keeps thanking God," the priest said, "for increasingly smaller favors."

"Greed," said the old man. "What a greedy young man I was! And what a greedy man I stayed, throughout all the years of my life!"

"No more than anyone, I'm sure," the policeman said.

"I always wanted more," the old man remembered. "My parents were comfortably situated, and furnished me with a decent upbringing and a good education. They hoped I would go into a profession where I might be expected to do some good in the world. Medicine, for example."

" 'First, do no harm,' " the doctor murmured.

"But I went into business," said the old man, "because I wanted more money than I could expect to earn from medicine or law or any of the professions. And I stopped at nothing legal to succeed in all my enterprises. I was merciless to competitors, I drove my employees, I squeezed my suppliers, and every decision I made was calculated to maximize my profits."

"That," said the soldier, "seems to be how business is done. Struggling for the highest possible profits, men of business act ultimately for the greatest good of the population at large."

"You probably believe in the tooth fairy, too," the old man said, and cackled. "If I did any good for the rest of the world, it was inadvertent and immaterial. I was trying only to do good for myself, and to amass great wealth. And in that I succeeded. You might not guess it to look at me now, but I became very wealthy."

"And what happened to your riches?"

"What happened to them? Why, nothing happened to them. I won them and I kept them." The old man's bowels rumbled, but he didn't appear to notice. "I lived well," he said, "and I invested wisely and with good fortune. And I bought things."

"What did you buy?" the policeman wondered.

"Things," said the old man. "I bought paintings, and I don't think I was ever taken in by any false Vermeers, like the young man in your story. I bought fine furniture, and a palatial home to keep it in. I bought antique oriental carpets, I bought Roman glass, I bought pre-Columbian sculpture. I bought rare coins, ancient and modern, and I collected postage stamps."

"And cigars?"

"I never cared for them," the old man said, "but if I had I would have bought the best, and I can well appreciate that builder's dilemma. Because I would have wanted to smoke them, but my desire to go on owning them would have been at least as strong."

They waited for him to go on; when he remained silent, the priest spoke up. "I suppose," he said, "that, as with so many desires, the passage of time lessened your desire for more."

"You think so?"

"Well, it would stand to reason that—"

"The vultures thought so," the old man said. "My nephews and nieces, thoughtfully telling me the advantages of making gifts during my lifetime rather than waiting for my estate to be subject to inheritance taxes. Museum curators, hoping I'd give them paintings now, or so arrange things that they'd be given over to them immediately upon my death. Auctioneers, assuring me of the considerable advantages of disposing of my stamps and coins and ancient artifacts while I still had breath in my body. That way, they said, I could have the satisfaction of seeing my collections properly sold, and the pleasure of getting the best possible terms for them.

"I told them I'd rather have the pleasure and satisfaction of continuing ownership. And do you know what they said? Why, they told me the same thing that everybody told me, everybody who was trying to get me to give up something that I treasured. You can guess what they said, can't you?"

It was the doctor who guessed. "You can't take it with you," he said.

"Exactly! Each of the fools said it as if he were repeating the wisdom of the ages. 'You can't take it with you.' And the worst of the lot, the mean little devils from organized charities, armored by the pretense that they were seeking not for themselves but for others, they would sometimes add yet another pearl of wisdom. There are no pockets in a shroud, they would assure me."

"I think that's a line in a song," the soldier said.

"Well, please don't sing it," said the old man. "Can't take it with you! No pockets in a shroud! And the worst of it is that they're quite right, aren't they? Wherever that last long journey leads, a man has to take it alone. He can't bring his French Impressionists, his proof Liberty Seated quarters, his Belgian semi-postals. He can't even take along a checkbook. No matter what I have, no matter how greatly I cherish it, I can't take it with me."

"And you realized the truth in that," the priest said.

"Of course I did. I may be a doddering old man, but I'm not a fool."

"And the knowledge changed your life," the priest suggested.

"It did," the old man agreed. "Why do you think I'm here, baking by the fire, souring the air with the gas from within me? Why do you think I cling so resolutely, neither asleep nor awake, to this hollow husk of life?"

"Why?" the doctor asked, after waiting without success for the old man to answer his own question.

"Because," the old man said, "if I can't take it with me, the hell with it. I don't intend to go."

His eyes flashed in triumph, then closed abruptly as he slumped in his chair. The others glanced at one another, alarm showing in their eyes. "A wonderful exit line," the doctor said, "and a leading candidate for the next edition of *Famous Last Words*, but do you suppose the old boy took the opportunity to catch the bus to Elysium?"

"We should call someone," the soldier said. "But whom? A doctor? A policeman? A priest?"

There was a snore, shortly followed by a zestful fart. "Thank heavens," said the doctor, and the others sighed and nodded, and the priest picked up the deck and began to deal out the cards for the next hand.

Clark Howard

The California Contact

VERY FEW WRITERS ever make their reputations—let alone a living—on short stories alone. But while Clark Howard has written a number of excellent novels, his short fiction remains among the finest of his generation. One could base an entire semester-long writing course on one of his short story collections. Here is an example of his brilliance, a twisted tale of murder and revenge at one of America's iconic landmarks. First published in the November issue of *Ellery Queen's Mystery Magazine*, this is Howard at his labyrinthine best.

The California Contact

Clark Howard

The man who walked into the Division Street district station was about thirty, conservatively dressed in suit and tie. A uniformed Chicago police sergeant at the front desk looked up at him. "Help you?"

"Yes, my name is Roger Morton," the man said, smiling self-consciously. "I'm not sure exactly who I should see. I think I overheard a murder being planned last night. . . ."

That was how it began.

Roger Morton, an assistant bank auditor, had attempted to telephone his fiancée at the Los Angeles home of her parents, where she was visiting. He had direct-dialed the number from his apartment. Instead of reaching that number, he had somehow been cut into a call between two men, one in Chicago, one in Los Angeles. He could hear both ends of their conversation, but when he tried to speak to them, they could not hear him. What Roger heard was this:

"It's all set. He'll be at Disneyland on Friday for sure. Do you think you'll have any problem?"

"No. I'll handle it."

"I don't want any screwups. This is one hit that has to be perfect."

"Don't worry about it. If the weather stays like it's been all week out here, I'll have a nice day for it."

"You're lucky. It's been raining for three days here. Listen, as soon as it's over and you're in the clear, call me so I can let my partner know—"

At that point, Roger's connection had dropped out of the call and he heard a dial tone. That had been at eight-fifteen the previous night. It was the third straight night it had rained in Chicago.

•   •   •

The Chicago Police Department's main headquarters was at Eleventh and State streets. It was a thick, gray, dirty building, as shabby as yesterday's thrown-away newspaper, but as formidable as a twenty-year patrol cop. Gusts of wind whipping around the corner from the nearby lake blew street dirt and litter along the sidewalk in front of it. Through its doors, ignoring the blowing trash, flowed a constant stream of policemen, witnesses, victims, lawyers, and suspects. Eleventh and State was the melting pot of Chicago's dark side.

When Roger Morton entered the building, he was met in the lobby by Lieutenant George Ladd of the Organized Crime Unit.

"Mr. Morton, we appreciate your cooperation in this matter," Ladd said. "There are two things we'd like you to do for us if you would. First, we want to get a stenographer and reconstruct as accurately as possible all of the conversation that you overheard. Second, we want you to listen to some voice tapes we have and see if any of them sound like either of the parties you heard talking. Will you do that for us?"

Roger shrugged. "Sure."

It took them an hour working with Roger and a stenographer to elicit and get down on paper as much of the word-for-word conversation as Roger could recall. It wasn't any more than he had told the district detectives; at least, it didn't seem like it to him. But Ladd, who explained to Roger that he was an expert in voice analysis, was interested in every nuance, every inflection of every word, interested even in the pauses between words, the grunts, the pattern of breathing.

"You'd be surprised how unique everyone's voice is," he told Roger after they had finished with the stenographer and were on their way to the audio room to listen to tapes. "Voice patterns may someday be as concretely acceptable for identification as fingerprints. They're already more reliable for detecting lies than a polygraph."

"Fascinating," said Roger. The banking business suddenly seemed very staid and sterile.

The audio room was a network of tape recorders, players, speakers, sound analyzers, modifiers, separators, and a wide variety of other complex and sophisticated equipment. "Have a seat in the audio chair," Ladd said, indicating a cushioned, shell-like leather chair one sat back into, which had delicate, strategically placed speakers in the padding at the top. Roger sat down, liking the chair at once. Ladd selected a reel of tape from a fireproof cabinet and put it on a player.

"This reel contains a series of voices saying various things, most of them unrelated. All of them will sound as if they are speaking over a telephone; some of them, in fact, were; others we have provided with a simulation feature. There are ten-second intervals between each voice. If you recognize any voice, wait until it is finished speaking and then let me know. Okay, here we go."

Presently Roger found himself listening to a hoarse, deep-throated man talking about racehorses. He did not recognize the voice. Next a smoother, more articulate voice spoke briefly about the stock market. Then a flat monotone began talking about sex and the anatomy of a particular woman he'd had it with. Then came a voice speaking in general terms about the federal government.

The next voice had a slight foreign, probably Italian, accent, and was discussing gourmet food. Then a Southern drawl talked about the weather. That was followed by what sounded like a thick African-American voice discoursing on the space program. Then a Midwestern-type voice began describing a musical play he apparently had enjoyed.

"Wait a minute," Roger said. "That sounded like one of them. Can you play that over for me?"

Without a word to interrupt the subject's train of thought, Lieutenant Ladd reversed the reel to the exact place where the voice had begun. Roger listened intently to it a second time.

"That's one of them," he said. "That's the voice at the Chicago end."

"Okay," said Ladd. "Now let me put another tape on and have you listen to it."

They went through the same routine again: a variety of voices saying a variety of things; some briefly interesting, some dull, some ridiculous, some obscene, some foreign-sounding. Then Roger again heard the voice he had identified on the first tape. It said something different this time—but it was the same voice.

"That's it. That's him," Roger said, an edge of excitement in his own voice.

They went through a third tape, this one containing voice impressions of the earlier voices Roger had listened to. Mixed in with those impersonations were the actual voices again, saying still different things, their voices broken up and separated by strange sounds, unusual noises, to distort Roger's hearing process. There was even some brief, obscene language together with heavy breathing, obviously a woman's, to interrupt his concentration.

But when it was all over, he had picked the same voice a third and a fourth time.

Later that day, Lieutenant Ladd met with the chief of detectives, the deputy chief in charge of the Organized Crime section, and his own captain. The captain's name was Dunleavy.

"Any doubt at all about it?" Dunleavy asked Ladd.

"Not in my opinion, Captain," the voice expert said unequivocally. "In three separate tests, he accurately picked out the voice of Gino Cabrisi four times."

The chief of detectives, whose name was Pittman, lighted a long brown cigar and looked at his deputy, Dennis Fraser, who headed up the Organized

Crime Unit. "What's the sheet on Cabrisi, Denny?" he asked, blowing smoke toward the ceiling.

"He's the number-two man in the Midwest combination," Fraser said. "Has personal charge of the Kansas City–Milwaukee–Evansville triangle, as well as all downstate Illinois operations. He's a third-generation Italian-American, Chicago-born, fifty-one years old, married, has a son at Yale, another one at West Point. No police record since the early seventies. Answers directly to Frank Marello, who controls syndicate business in the seven-state area of Wisconsin, Iowa, Missouri, Kansas, Illinois, Indiana, and Michigan. Want more?"

Chief Pittman shook his head and drew in thoughtfully on his cigar. "A man like that, with a son at West Point, a son at Yale, might be pretty vulnerable with a murder-conspiracy charge staring him in the face. So vulnerable, in fact, that he might be willing to trade information for anonymity. We might be able to take down some pretty big fish if we can get some West Coast help on this. But it would have to be very good help." He looked at Dunleavy. "Who's our California contact on organized crime matters?"

"Fellow named Ramm," said the captain. "Charley Ramm. He's a special agent of the California Bureau of Investigation, out of their L.A. office."

"Charley Ramm," the chief mused, frowning slightly. "Sounds familiar. Do I know him from anywhere?"

"Probably not, Chief," said Dunleavy. "You may remember the name from about fifteen years ago. He used to be a fighter. Light-heavyweight. They called him 'Battering' Ramm."

"What happened to him?"

Dunleavy shrugged. "Same thing that happened to a lot of young light-heavyweights back then. He met up with Evander Holyfield and got slaughtered. The Real Deal took him out in the seventh."

"So he quit and became a cop?"

"Right. But there's a story behind it. He had one more fight after the Holyfield go: a ten-rounder with a Hispanic kid named Chula Valdes that the L.A. mob was building up. They offered Ramm a hundred grand to let Chula take him out in the third—in half the time it took Holyfield to do it. That way Chula would look better to the public than Holyfield, and they could build up a big title elimination match between Holyfield and their man. Well, Ramm took the money, went to Vegas, and bet the whole hundred thousand on *himself*. Then he ripped Chula up in one round. After collecting his winnings, he sent the hundred-grand bribe *back* to the mob and went out that same day and joined the Los Angeles Police Department. It was a smart move. Ramm knew the mob wouldn't think twice about putting a hit on a double-crossing fighter, but they'd be very reluctant to kill a rookie cop. And he was right. It pissed them off royally to do it, but they left him alone."

"And he stayed a cop?" the chief asked.

Dunleavy nodded. "Yes, sir. And turned out to be a damned good one, too. Went to night school and got degrees in Criminal Justice and Law Enforcement. In five years he was a detective; in seven a detective sergeant."

"How'd he get with the CBI?"

"The California attorney general's office launched a big investigation into the fight game throughout the state. They asked all the police agencies to loan them any personnel who were familiar with the fight mob. LAPD sent them Charley Ramm. He worked as part of the CBI strike force that ran the syndicate out of professional boxing. When it was all over, CBI asked him if he'd like to stay on permanently. He did. Eventually they made him the Bureau's liaison for all interstate cases involving the mob in California."

"You've worked with him before?" the chief asked.

"Yes, sir. Several times."

"He's a good man?"

"The best, Chief."

The chief paused, pursing his lips, tapping one finger, hesitating just long enough to give the other men in the office the impression that he still had a touch of reservation about the whole thing, and that he was relying on them to do an extra good job in order to reaffirm his faith in them. But finally he said, "All right, bring your California contact in on it. Let's see how much syndicate garbage we can haul on this one. Get moving."

Charley Ramm, the California contact, left his CBI office in the downtown Los Angeles civic center and drove out to East L.A. to see his friend Chula Valdes at the Dos Amigos Gym. Chula was the fighter that Charley had knocked out in a single round after agreeing to throw the fight for the mob. Betting his bribe money at fifteen to one on a first-round knockout, he had come away with a million and a half dollars. Most of it was now in FDIC-insured certificates of deposit in various banks, paying Charley more than enough monthly interest to maintain a Newport Beach condo facing the ocean, and to enjoy a much more upscale lifestyle than your average state cop.

Within a year after Charley had annihilated Chula Valdes in their ESPN main event, Chula had lost two more fights and his career had gone down the tubes. It was then that Charley, who had a hardcore love of boxing, approached Chula and agreed to advance a hundred thousand dollars for Chula to set up the Dos Amigos—Two Friends—Gym. The enterprise had prospered over the years, and the two men had produced several top-rated, popular fighters. They had not, however, come up with a world champion, which was something they greatly desired. In fact, both of them dreamed— literally *dreamed* at night—of having a champion. Some Hispanic or Black kid from East L.A. or Watts that they could pick up, train, groom, and bring along slowly all the way to a title fight. Lightweight, welterweight, middleweight—they didn't care. Just as long as they could nurture and foster a *champion*.

When Charley got to the gym, he found Chula watching a young white fighter spar with one of the Hispanic amateurs they let train there. "Where'd the gringo kid come from?" he asked.

"Trailer trash," said Chula. "Heard about the gym in Preston. Hitch-hiked down when he got out."

Preston was the state reformatory. "How's he look?" Charley asked anxiously. A *white* champion would really be a coup. But Chula shook his head.

"A bleeder. That mayonnaise skin of his is too thin. He's got two nicks already. What are you doing here this time of day?"

"On my way to Disneyland." Charley held up a hand. "Don't even ask, man."

Charley had received by fax the previous afternoon a brief overview of a Chicago P.D. investigation regarding a possible mob hit being set up. At Disneyland, of all places. Lieutenant George Ladd, from the Chicago department, was flying into LAX early that evening and Charley was to coordinate a local investigation with him. Meanwhile, he was going to lay some groundwork of his own.

The two men stood watching the workout. Chula's face was scarred with proud flesh from beatings he had taken. Charley Ramm's own countenance, except for a hooked nose broken twice, was comparatively unmarked. In addition to being a lethal puncher, Charley had also been a slick boxer. Chula had been neither, and looked it.

"How'd the talk go with Marian the other night?" Chula asked.

"Lousy," said Charley. "But we spent the night together."

Chula grimaced. "How could it be lousy if she let you spend the night with her?"

"Spending the night with her was great. It was the talk that was lousy. She thinks reconciliation is a dirty word."

Charley had been married at one time to Marian Barlow, a Pasadena high school teacher. Marian was everything Charley was not: upper-middle-class background, educated, smart dresser, marvelous conversationalist. Their romance had been strictly a case of opposites attracting. They met when she chaperoned at a state government day for students. It was lust at first sight. Two weeks later they drove to Las Vegas and got married in a tacky little wedding chapel with strangers for witnesses. A year later, Marian divorced him.

"You don't need a wife, Charley," she told him at the time. "You need a cook and a call girl. I've been keeping a record. In your average twenty-four-hour day, you spend six hours sleeping, twelve hours chasing bad guys, four hours at that gym fantasizing about finding a boxing champion, and two hours with me. Those two hours with me consist of one hour eating dinner, and one hour of either sex or television, depending on how tired we are. Best thing would be for you to eat out, hire a call girl, and watch TV alone. I've had it with this so-called marriage."

She moved out. Charley had been begging her to give him another chance. She frequently let him come over and spend the night, but adamantly refused to consider remarriage.

"Where's Luis?" Charley asked, looking around for their latest hot prospect, Luis Munoz, a southpaw welter.

"I got him over in the park doing some roadwork," said Chula.

"How's he looking?"

"Ask me later, man. I have to think about it."

Charley left the gym, hoping that Luis Munoz would be the one. He visualized himself working the corner of a welterweight champion of the world.

Charley drove down to the vast Disneyland amusement park in Anaheim and located Ralph Franklin, its chief of security. He briefed Franklin on the investigation and asked for his input on how to handle a tactical surveillance at the park if it came down to that. Franklin shook his head.

"Charley, unless you come up with some kind of personal ID of the target or the shooter, we haven't got a prayer of conducting a successful surveillance. This park covers more than four thousand acres; that's six square *miles*. This time of year, we get a minimum of twenty thousand people a day going in and out—"

"Classify your average visitors for me, Ralph," said Charley.

Franklin ticked them off on his fingers. "One: father, mother, children between six and ten. Two: grandparents and older children between nine and twelve. Three: teenagers, in groups, usually segregated with boys together, girls together. Next: teenagers on dates, usually in groups of four or six. Then: servicemen, usually Marines from Camp Pendleton or sailors up from San Diego, usually in pairs or trios, in uniform, trying to pick up girls. That's about it. Everybody else comes under miscellaneous."

"What about single guys," Charley asked, "alone?"

"We don't get many of those," Franklin admitted. "Hardly anybody visits Disneyland alone."

"A hit man probably would," said Charley. "Would it be possible to put a tail on every male that enters the park alone on a given day?"

"Probably. I could have our entrance security observers radio a description of all unaccompanied males to plainclothes security people in Town Square and along Main Street, U.S.A. Everybody that comes through the front gates has to go across the square and down that street to the Plaza, which branches off to the various sections of the park: Tomorrowland, Fantasyland, Frontierland, and Adventureland. The only other way into the park is the Monorail that runs from the Disneyland Hotel outside the park to Tomorrowland inside the park. Security observers could watch the Monorail station and the Plaza, and radio in to whichever section he enters."

"Okay, I think you'd better get ready to put a plan like that into operation," Charley advised him. "On very short notice, too. I don't have a timeline on this thing yet, but I probably will have later today when a Chicago Police Department officer gets here. I'll be back in touch as soon as I can."

Ralph Franklin shook his head. "What kind of psycho would pick a place like Disneyland for a hit?"

"A smart one," Charley told him.

From Disneyland, Charley drove to Hollywood Park racetrack and went in through the employee entrance. The racing day had already begun, the horses moving from the paddock toward the starting gate for the third race. In the clubhouse section, Charley made his way down to a private box belonging to a smallish, balding man named Casper Dale, who was sitting with his much younger girlfriend.

"Who do you like in the third, Casper?" asked Charley. Dale looked up.

"Saratoga Sweetie, number seventeen. Take a seat, Charley."

Charley stepped into the box and sat down. Dale handed his girlfriend five one-hundred-dollar bills and told her to go place the bet. Charley gave her a fifty of his own to bet; Casper Dale usually knew what he was doing. He was the owner of three card houses in nearby Gardena, where draw poker was legal, the city council having declared by statute that it was a game of skill rather than a game of chance, therefore not gambling per se. Though Dale was not considered an actual mobster, he did pay protection money, and his business kept him close enough to the mob to be privy to insider information. A number of years earlier, Charley Ramm had helped Dale's teenage son get into a treatment program for his heroin addiction instead of going to jail, and Dale was obligated to him for it.

"What's on your mind, Charley?" Dale asked pointedly when they were alone. Charley leaned closer to him.

"There's word out about a mob hit scheduled very soon. You heard anything?"

Dale shook his head, perhaps a little too quickly. "Not a thing."

"You know of any big debtors that someone might want to make an example of?"

The gambler shook his head again. "No."

"Any of the boys been ripped off by anyone lately?"

Another shake of the head.

Charley pursed his lips in thought for a moment, trying to decide if Casper Dale was leveling with him. "How's Eddie doing?" he asked. Eddie was Dale's son.

Dale's expression clouded. "You don't have to remind me that I owe you, Charley. If you were really interested in Eddie, you would have asked about him before you asked about the hit."

Charley looked away, embarrassed. Dale's words had stung. He watched the horses moving into the starting gate for the third race. Saratoga Sweetie looked feisty. Charley turned back to Casper Dale.

"You're right, Casper. I'm sorry."

"Don't let your job make a bastard out of you, Charley."

There was a loud bell, the starting-gate doors flung open, the horses bolted forward, and over the public address system a voice announced, "They're off and running in the third race—!"

Dale's girlfriend returned with their betting slips and the three of them watched the six-furlong race. Saratoga Sweetie ran second.

"We both lose, Charley," Casper Dale said. "Sorry I couldn't give you a winner today."

"You tried, Casper." Charley held out his hand. "No hard feelings?"

"Not this time."

They shook hands and Charley left.

Early that evening, Charley stood in an arrival terminal at LAX and watched as passengers filed off a jet from Chicago. He picked out Lieutenant George Ladd as soon as their sweeping glances met. Cops always recognize other cops. They introduced themselves and went into a concourse cocktail lounge to have a drink. Ladd gave Charley a personal rundown on the case, beginning with Roger Morton walking into the district station to report the conversation he had overheard. Charley shook his head in wonderment.

"Incredible. I know that telephone calls occasionally are cross-connected like that, but to pick up a conversation where a hit is being planned . . ."

Ladd nodded. "Our communications people conferred with the telephone company operations personnel and were told that approximately one in three hundred thousand direct-dialed toll calls might be erroneously cross-connected in the main switching terminal, but most of the time their scrutiny software detects it immediately and corrects it before a third party actually hears any of the conversation already in progress. Only about one out of a thousand of the one out of three hundred thousand *doesn't* get corrected."

"What does that come down to?" Charley asked.

"Two chances in three hundred million calls."

"And out of those two, for the person who got cross-connected to pick up a *mob* conversation, with a hit being planned—incredible. Whoever the target is, somebody up above is sure looking out for him."

"Must be," Ladd agreed. "Because here we sit, trying to figure a way to help somebody we don't even know." The Chicago officer tilted his head slightly. "You have local tactical command of the operation. Any plans yet?"

"Not many," Charley admitted. "Disneyland security has been alerted and a tentative surveillance plan is being worked up. Right now our main problem is to come up with some kind of lead to the ID of the players involved. Were you able to determine any kind of timeline from your information on the conversation that was overheard?"

"Yeah. You aren't going to like it."

"Tell me anyway."

"It'll be Friday."

Charley's mouth dropped open. *"Tomorrow!"*

"Tomorrow," Ladd confirmed. Charley sat back in the booth and stared numbly at his drink. Tomorrow. If true, it was going to be impossible to stop—unless he had a name or a face: the hit man's, the target's, the connection in California who set it up, the mob boss who approved it, an informant who knew about it—*somebody.*

"There's one long shot I can take that might work," he said quietly, as much to himself as to Ladd. "But I need to think it out. Meantime," he told Ladd, "I'd like you to come back to the CBI office and start going through mug-shot books. We have a pretty comprehensive record of hoods who have moved into the L.A. area from Chicago and other places back east. You might recognize a face that you can tie in to that guy Cabrisi whose voice your people were able to ID on the phone call. Who knows, we might get lucky."

"Let's get started then," agreed Ladd.

At the CBI offices, while Ladd scrutinized mug-shot books, Charley got Ralph Franklin on the phone and told him that the hit at Disneyland could possibly be going down the next day. Franklin was as taken aback as Charley had been when Ladd told him, but agreed to assemble the necessary personnel on his security staff and get the park surveillance plan operational before the park opened the following morning. Charley advised him that he and Ladd would be there with a CBI team two hours before opening time.

Charley then briefed his own boss and they pulled up a computer list of CBI agents available at once for special duty. Calls went out to them immediately. The first of those agents to arrive was Rick Larch, a young ex–Navy SEAL. Charley put him in charge of the next three agents who would show up, to form a night surveillance team, with two vehicles, in near proximity to an address in Beverly Hills that he gave to Larch. Then Charley left the CBI offices alone.

He had been mulling over the long shot he had thought of earlier, and decided to do it. He knew it was risky; so was everything else in his life. But this, he concluded, was worse; it was *extra* risky. In his unmarked car, on the way to Beverly Hills, an unfamiliar anxiety began to surface in his emotions. Suddenly he had the urge to talk to Marian. On impulse he called her on his mobile phone.

"Hello—" As usual, Charley thought her voice sounded like caramel syrup would sound if it could make noise.

"Hey, it's me—"

"Charley, if you mention reconciliation," she warned, "I'll hang up and disconnect the phone."

"I won't, I promise," he said urgently. "Please don't hang up."

Marian sensed something in his voice that she was not accustomed to. "Charley, where are you? Are you all right?"

"Sure, I'm fine. Just on my way out to Beverly Hills to see a guy."

"You sound—stressed, or something."

"Just a little tired. Been a long day. Listen, I'm sorry about spoiling the other night. It was a great evening. It's just that sometimes it's so great being with you that I can't resist talking about—well, you know."

"You're going to *have* to resist it, Charley," Marian said firmly. "My mind is made up. Look, we'll always be close friends, Charley. We can even go on being occasional lovers. We just can't be married."

"I know, I know. I guess I'm just afraid some other guy will come along and all that will change. Then I wouldn't have anything."

"Sure you would. You'd have your job. Chula and the gym. Your dream of managing a champion boxer someday. You'd have a lot, Charley." There was an uneasy pause. Then Marian said, "Listen, it's been a long day for me, too. I need to turn in early. Call me tomorrow night, okay?"

"Sure, honey."

If I'm still alive, he thought as they hung up.

Twenty minutes later, Charley pulled up to the gate of an elegant but not opulent mansion set back on high-walled acreage in an exclusive area. He rang an intercom outside the gate. A voice said, "Yes?"

"I'm here to see Mr. Weiskoff. Tell him it's Bat Ramm. I used to be a fighter. I think he'll remember me."

In fact, I know he'll remember me, Charley thought as he waited. Solomon Weiskoff, known as "King" Solomon, was the longtime head of crime syndicate operations in California, Oregon, Washington, and Arizona. It was he who had arranged the fix in Charley's fight with Chula Valdes fifteen years earlier.

After several minutes, the gate opened and one of the King's bodyguards got in the car with Charley and instructed him to proceed along the three-hundred-yard drive back to the mansion itself. At the door, he handed over his Glock automatic and had his body scanned for other weapons with an electronic, hand-held metal detector. Then he was escorted into a richly appointed study where the King sat with his number-two man, a polished, modern-day, business executive type of criminal named Jack Turban. Weiskoff himself looked like a tired old hardware-store salesman. There was a hint of weary amusement in his eyes when he looked at Charley.

"You have any idea how much money you cost me on that Valdes fight?" he asked. After so many years, the question was more rhetorical than anything else. Charley shrugged.

"A bundle, I guess."

"You guess right. Ten, twelve years ago, if you'd walked in here like this, cop or no cop, you wouldn't have walked back out." Then the King himself shrugged as Charley had, and waved absently with one hand. "But that amount is chump change today, what with inflation, taxes, the cost of living. And time, like somebody said, is a great healer." He smiled wryly. "Heals everything but old age, you understand." He gestured for Charley to sit down. "So what is it you want, Battering Ramm?"

"To do you a favor, maybe," said Charley. "There's a mob contract hit scheduled for tomorrow in your territory, and I have a feeling that you don't know anything about it."

The King's eyes narrowed the tiniest fraction—but enough for Charley, who was primed for a reaction, to catch it. And know he was right.

"You have my attention," the King said.

From his pocket, Charley took a cassette tape that he had been given by Lieutenant Ladd and put it on the coffee table. "The voice on this tape has been identified as the same voice heard on a long distance telephone call a few days ago talking to somebody in L.A. to confirm a hit for sometime tomorrow at Disneyland. The voice belongs to Gino Cabrisi, Frank Marello's number-two man in the Midwest. I don't know who he was talk-ing to; I just know it wasn't you, because you wouldn't deal with him, you'd deal directly with Marello because the two of you have equal standing. That's why I don't think you know anything about the hit. Marello might not either."

The King looked over at Jack Turban, giving him permission to speak. "What's your interest in all this, Ramm?" Turban asked.

"I'm CBI liaison to the Chicago police, who picked up information on the call. Basically what I'm trying to do is prevent another California murder."

Turban was about to say something else, but the King held up a hand to silence him. He smiled at Charley. "As taxpayers, we appreciate your diligent devotion to law and order, Agent Ramm. But we are legitimate businessmen and have nothing to do with criminals and murder. I'm afraid we can't help you. But thank you for dropping in."

In less than five minutes, Charley was shown out, his gun returned, and he was accompanied by an escort car until he was beyond the gate and it had closed behind him.

He drove a block, pulled over, and contacted Rick Larch by radio. Larch and the other three members of the night surveillance team were set up on a wooded lot opposite Weiskoff's gate. They had night vision scopes in place and two undercover vehicles parked nearby for tailing.

"Okay," Charley told them, "I want to know everyone who goes in or comes out of that house for the rest of the night. The King will be conduct-ing some serious business, and he *won't* want to do it over the phone. I want a report on my voice mail by six o'clock in the morning."

"You'll have it," Rick Larch said.

•   •   •

Back at King Solomon's mansion, the old mobster turned to look intently at Jack Turban. They had just finished listening to the cassette tape that Charley Ramm had left.

"So, Jacob, what's going on?" he asked.

"I don't know, Sol," his number-two man said. Turban was also Solomon Weiskoff's nephew, the son of his favorite older sister, who had married a General Motors master mechanic named Nathan Turbansky. They had five sons, all of them good boys except the middle one, Jacob. King Solomon had taken Jacob into the rackets to get him away from the rest of the Turbansky family, which was thoroughly respectable and untainted. To keep it that way, Solomon had instructed Jacob Turbansky to change his name to Jack Turban. It was only when Sol was agitated or suspicious about something that he reverted to addressing Turban as Jacob.

"You know this Cabrisi guy, Jacob," the older man said. "You're both on the same level in the national structure of the organization. What do you suppose he's up to?"

"Maybe the whole thing is just some kind of cop setup," Turban suggested. King Solomon grimaced.

"Jacob," he chided, "I'm going to forget you said that." Pondering, he walked about the room. "Why in the name of reason would anyone pick Disneyland for a hit?"

"Maybe that's the only place the target will be," Turban said.

"No," his uncle replied thoughtfully. "A target can always be followed to another place. If it's set in Disneyland, there's a reason for it." Returning to his chair, he rubbed a forefinger along one side of a very crooked nose that had been smashed by a lead pipe decades earlier when he had been a young strongarm thug just starting in the mob. "Jacob, remember about seven years ago when those two young punks from the Valley knocked us off for eight hundred grand in the Denver airport? Eight thousand C-notes in a piece of carry-on luggage. It represented eighty percent of a million in dirty money that we had sent to Frank Marello to be laundered by his Chicago banking connections for a twenty percent fee. Marello's courier brought the clean money to Denver; our courier was supposed to pick it up there. The two young punks pepper-sprayed them in a men's room, used plastic hand-cuffs to cuff them to a toilet stall, and were out of the terminal before any-body could notify airport security." Sol feigned a lapse of memory. "What were the names of those two punks again?"

"Irish Johnny Flynn and Joey Dancer," said Turban.

Didn't even have to think about it, did you, Jacob? the King thought. "As I recall, Dancer got away clean, but our people caught up with Irish Johnny in a Redondo Beach apartment when he went back to get his wife. They blew him away with silencers when he tried to pull a gun. His wife was pregnant, but fortunately she was at the doctor's office at the time and didn't witness it.

Our boys searched the apartment from top to bottom but didn't turn up any part of the money. The only unusual thing they found was in Irish Johnny's pocket: a used all-day pass to Disneyland, dated that same day. Which means what, Jacob?"

"That he was in the park earlier that day," Turban replied.

"Exactly. Nobody's ever found the money, and nobody's ever found Dancer, even though we had people in every part of the country looking for him for two solid years." King Solomon leaned forward and fixed Jack Turban in a level stare. "You don't personally know anything about what's going on here, do you, Jacob?"

"No, Uncle," Turban disclaimed. "Of course not. I'd tell you if I did."

"Yes," the old mobster nodded, "of course you would." He sat back. "All right, here's what you do. Contact the Leper. Have him come over here right away, tonight. Then go down to the office and bring me the file we have on Joey Dancer. The one with the pictures in it. Go."

Jack Turban left the room.

Charley Ramm went back to the CBI office. George Ladd had finished going over the mug-shot books, with no success. Charley spent two hours putting together a CBI team of six agents and briefing them on what was expected the next day at Disneyland. The agent he put in charge of the team was Casey Clay, a young black man who had been a Marine Corps inter-service heavyweight boxing champion. Charley was constantly on him to change his name to Casey Ali and turn pro so that he and Chula Valdes could manage him. But Casey always spurned their offer. "I don't like getting punched in the face, Charley," was his stoic reply every time Charley brought up the subject.

When Charley had his team ready, he sent George Ladd with them to check into the Disneyland Hotel so they could be on the scene for the surveillance operation the next morning. Satisfied that he had everything covered, Charley left the CBI offices to go home.

It took him an hour to drive down to Newport Beach. His condominium apartment building was built over a tenant parking garage. Pulling into his private parking space, he suddenly realized that he was very tired, very stressed. Forlornly, he wished with all his being that Marian would be waiting for him upstairs, as she had been so many nights when they'd been married. How great it would be to sit out on the balcony drinking mugs of hot chocolate with her, listening to the surf, feeling the cool night air begin to chill them, then hurrying inside to get into bed and warm up, make love, and fall asleep in each other's arms.

That was what Charley was fancying in his mind as he walked toward the garage elevator. He was as unalert as a schoolboy in church, did not even notice the figure come up from behind him and drive a brass-knuckled fist against his temple. Charley pitched sideways, where he was hit in the face by a blow from a second man on the other side of him. Blood gushed from his nose. Ex-boxer's instincts rising, he stepped inside the next punch, which he knew would be coming from the first man, and swung blindly, feeling a painful satisfaction as his fist impacted jawbone. At the same time, he twisted and kicked up with one foot, hoping to find the groin of the second man. But the kick missed and, off balance now, he took two more hard punches to the face. Then the blows rained from both directions, to the stomach, rib cage, kidneys. In less than a minute, he was in a heap on the concrete floor. A hand snatched his Glock automatic from its holster and slid it under a parked car. From the indistinct murkiness surrounding his head, he heard a voice growl, "Stay out of Disneyland, cop, or you're gonna end up in Forest Lawn." The threat was followed by a vicious kick to Charley's right ankle.

Covering his head and face with both arms, Charley listened to their footsteps hurry up the stairs to ground level. For a moment he pictured the pastoral serenity of Forest Lawn, a cemetery, and wished he were lying on the soft green grass next to some cool marble headstone. But eventually his pain pulled him back to reality and, raising his head, he saw that he could again focus. Working himself into a kneeling position, he crawled over to the parked car to retrieve his gun. Then, using the car for support, he pulled himself upright and leaned his head forward to rest and steady himself. Blood from his nose streaked down the driver's-side window, making him wonder briefly what the car's owner would think when he came down to go to work the next morning.

In the elevator, Charley left a little blood on the floor, but took off his coat and held it bundled to his face so as not to drip on the carpet in the hall upstairs. Once in his apartment, he went directly to the shower, painfully stripped out of his clothes, and stood under the cold water for ten full minutes. The nosebleed stopped. Getting out, he put on a thick terry-cloth robe, swallowed two codeine tablets, took a couple of face towels, and went into the kitchen for a bucket of ice. With that, a glass, and a bottle of Tanqueray, he went onto his balcony and sat on a chaise longue. While he drank the gin, he used the towels to make ice compresses which he rotated from ankle to face and points in between. The cool ocean air felt good. The codeine began to work. The gin made friends with the codeine.

It was Jack Turban who ordered his beating, he was sure of it. King Solomon would not have done it so quickly and so obviously. It had to have been Turban. He was the only other person who knew Charley was aware of the planned hit.

I'll get the son of a bitch for this, Charley promised himself as he began to go into an ice-drug-alcohol haze. At some point, he went inside and crawled into bed. He went to sleep pretending a pillow he was holding against him was Marian.

•   •   •

At six o'clock the next morning, Charley Ramm's automated wake-up call rang him out of his drugged sleep. When he moved to shut the call off, pain shot through his body. Groaning softly, he pulled the phone onto the bed and pushed a double digit to ring his voice mail. There were three messages. The first was from Marian: "Hi, Charley. Listen, I'm sorry if I cut you short last night. Maybe we can get together this weekend and just try to enjoy each other without any heavy commitments. Let's talk about it later, okay? 'Bye." Good, Charley thought. It sounded like she might be coming around.

The next message was from Chula: "Hey, bro, listen, I don't wanna ruin your day or nothing, but I've decided this kid Luis Munoz ain't going no place with us, man. I've had him doing roadwork in the park every day an' he's always coming back huffing and puffing like a three-pack-a-day smoker. No stamina at all, you know, man? I think he might even have asthma. So keep your eye out for somebody new, okay? Later, man." Damn, Charley thought. He'd practically had the kid winning the welterweight title.

The last message was from Rick Larch on the night surveillance team. "Reporting in, Charley. Five movements at King Sol's place overnight. Jack Turban left about half an hour after you did. Went to a mob-owned real estate office down on Sepulveda. Was inside for about ten minutes, then came out with a file of some kind and returned to the King's place. An hour after he got back, the Leper turned up. He was in the place for about an hour. Then the Leper left and went to his apartment in Santa Monica. Twenty minutes later, Turban left and drove to his home in Bel Air. That was it. Call me if you need me."

Charley sat on the side of the bed, feeling much as he had after the Holyfield fight. For several minutes he carefully massaged some of the stiffness out of his body, and thought about the Leper. No one knew who he really was; he could not be identified by fingerprinting because all of his prints and parts of several fingers had been eaten away by leprosy. A man of about fifty, his disease was in remission, and he had enough finger flexibility left to be an excellent pistol shot. He was believed to have killed at least eleven men for Solomon Weiskoff over the years, but had never been arrested. He used several names and ostensibly lived off the proceeds of an annuity that had been established for him, so even federal tax people couldn't get to him.

What, Charley wondered, had King Solomon learned after Charley left last night that was so important he was throwing the Leper into the mix? Maybe he'd find out, he decided, in a few hours when Disneyland opened for the day. Dragging himself into the kitchen, he made some strong black coffee to help him shave without hacking himself to death.

By eight o'clock, Charley was driving through the security gate at the Magic Kingdom. In Ralph Franklin's office, he found Franklin, Lieutenant George Ladd, and Casey Clay from the CBI team. All were wearing casual sport clothes—jeans, shorts, loose shirts—to conceal weapons and radios. Also present were a dozen members of Franklin's security force, similarly dressed to blend in with the crowd. Six key contact officers were code-named Main Street One, Plaza One, Tomorrowland One, Adventureland One, Fantasyland One, and Frontierland One. Each of them was dressed in a costume in keeping with the theme of their area: Main Street One was an 1890s policeman; Tomorrowland One was an astronaut; Fantasyland One was Robin Hood; Frontierland One was Daniel Boone; Adventureland One was a jungle trader in safari garb; and Plaza One was a park cleanup man with a broom, caddy, and trash barrel on wheels. Special teams of male and female security personnel in street clothes with a touristy look were also assembled.

As Charley briefed everyone on the scant information that he had, fax photographs of the Leper were coming in from CBI headquarters and being distributed to everyone by Franklin. "This man is the only link we have to anyone right now," Charley told the group, "and we don't even know that he'll actually show today—but I *think* he will. Why he'll be here, or who he's after, I can't tell you. But he is a *link*—and right now he's the only one we have. Aside from him, we'll be on any males who come in alone. We can only hope that our scrutiny and alertness will enable us to pick up on whatever's been planned and prevent it from happening. Good luck."

Franklin patted Charley on the back. "I hope our luck is better than yours was last night." He alluded to Charley's bruised and cut face.

"So do I," Charley said.

"Okay, let's get out there and in place," Franklin ordered. "Park opens in twenty minutes."

As Charley had hoped, the Leper was one of the first people to enter the park when it opened. An undistinguished little man, he walked with a slight shuffle because he had lost several toes as well as finger joints to leprosy. With a park guidebook, he sat on a convenient bench in the Town Square park at the beginning of Main Street, U.S.A. He appeared to be studying the guidebook, but was actually watching the entrance gates.

Charley watched the Leper from a tinted window of Disneyland City Hall, across the park, and radioed Casey Clay and Ladd on the platform of the nearby Disneyland Railroad Station. "He's here, Casey," said Charley.

"Got him," Casey affirmed. He pointed him out to Ladd. "He carries a .32 automatic in an ankle holster on his right leg."

"Small piece for a pro, isn't it?" Ladd asked.

"Not when the pro is as accurate as the Leper," Casey replied. "Those stubby fingers of his handle that gun like it's part of him. He's a deadly shot—and he uses magnum loads."

As they talked, a young man in his late twenties also casually entered the park. He did not act suspicious in any way, but he was alone, and, as was done with the Leper, one of Chief Franklin's security observers radioed into Town Square that he was on his way in. Charley and Franklin watched him come in, pause, and look around the square. Presently he located a woman and a little girl standing near a souvenir kiosk and went over to them.

"Casey," said Charley into his radio, "doesn't that guy look like Joey Dancer? Used to be a small-time hood out in the Valley?"

"The guy that dropped out of sight six or seven years ago?" Casey asked. "Was supposed to be on the run from the mob?"

"Yeah. Ripped off a courier or something."

"Could be," said Casey.

"Let's stay close on him, just in case."

"Check."

The man they thought was Joey Dancer walked up to the woman and little girl. "Hello, Edie."

"Hello, Joey."

He knelt down to the child, who was six. "You must be Jennifer. Your mom told me all about you when I talked to her on the phone the other day. You don't know me, but I was a friend of your daddy's—"

"Look, Joey, she didn't know her daddy, either, remember?" Edie said tightly. "Can we please just get on with this?"

Joey stood back up. "Relax, Edie. We can't just rush around. We have to look ordinary. Let's have a little fun first. I haven't had any fun in nearly seven years." He took the little girl's hand. "How about some ice cream to start the day, Jenny? And you call me 'Uncle Joey,' okay?"

Joey Dancer led Jenny and her mother down Main Street. From the bench where he was sitting, the Leper took a small mug-shot photo of Joey from his pocket, studied it briefly, then rose to follow them at a discreet distance.

"Looks like the Leper is tailing Dancer—if it is Dancer," said Casey into his radio. "But who's the woman and the kid?"

"Don't know," Charley answered.

"Who do you want on him, you or us?" Casey asked.

Before Charley could answer, another alert came in from the front gate. "Another male coming in alone. Acting edgy, looking around. Young guy, early twenties, flat-top haircut. Carrying a windbreaker over his right arm, concealing his hand."

"I don't believe this," Franklin muttered to himself. "Most days we don't get three guys alone all day."

"Casey, we'll take the Leper," Charley said into the radio. "You and Ladd hook onto the guy with the windbreaker. Keep in touch."

"Roger."

Moments later, everyone—Dancer, Edie and Jenny, the Leper, Charley and Franklin, and Casey and Ladd—were mixing with the crowd walking leisurely up Main Street, U.S.A., toward the Main Plaza.

Behind all of them, a group of perhaps a dozen people departed Guided Tour Garden, an open-air gathering area just off Town Square park. Gate security, on the alert for lone males, had paid little attention to the group when it entered a few minutes earlier. Now, following a tour guide, it passed beyond Town Square park and up Main Street. One of the group, a stocky man in a Hawaiian shirt, carrying a Disneyland shopping bag for souvenirs, unobtrusively lagged back and stepped into one of the Main Street shops. The group moved on without him.

"I want to go to Fantasyland first!" Jenny said around a mouthful of ice cream.

"You're the boss," said Joey Dancer.

The two led Jenny's reluctant mother across a drawbridge and through a castle wall into the land of Peter Pan, Snow White, King Arthur, Mr. Toad, Dumbo, and a plethora of other marvelous rides and attractions for children.

"I want to ride the circus train!" shouted Jenny.

"Okay with you, Edie?" Joey asked.

"I suppose," said Edie, seeing the excitement in her daughter's face.

Joey put the young girl in a seat on the circus train, and he and Edie sat on a bench where they could watch her. Edie studied Joey in silence for several moments, then asked, "So where have you been hiding all this time?"

"The best place of all," Joey told her. "In prison. When I heard what happened to Johnny, I hopped the first bus out of town. Rode it to Oklahoma City. For a week or so I holed up in a motel, but I kept getting jumpier every day. I knew the mob hadn't found the money in your apartment when they killed Johnny, so they'd be after me. For sure they'd have the word out to spotters in every big city; I knew I'd have to get out of circulation for a while. So I took another bus to this little town about fifty miles away and I stuck up a drugstore in broad daylight." Joey grinned wryly. "Got a hundred and forty bucks. Then I just wandered around town until the law caught me. Took the clods nearly all afternoon. But it worked. A month later I was on my way to a joint called McAlester with six-to-ten-years to do." He shrugged. "I kept out of trouble and did six years and eight months." His expression darkened. "But that McAlester pen is some bad place. I wouldn't do it over again."

"It was still better than what Johnny got," Edie said bitterly.

"I know." Joey took her hand. "I'm sorry about Johnny—"

"Sorry!" Edie snatched her hand away. "You were the one who always got him in trouble! If it wasn't for you and your big ideas, he'd have found an honest job and—"

"Wait a minute!" Joey was stunned. "That's not true, Edie. Johnny was always the leader. I strung along with *him*. He was the only friend I had. But I never planned anything, never thought up any jobs. It was always Johnny, I swear it was."

Edie stared at him, her face wrinkling into a frown of uncertainty. Just then, the Circus Train came back in and she rose abruptly to go meet Jenny.

"Can we go to Sleeping Beauty's Castle now?" the little girl asked happily.

The Leper leaned against the outdoor Welch's Grape Juice Bar and watched the couple and little girl move about Fantasyland. Charley Ramm was just inside the open-air Gift Fair, watching the Leper. The agent code-named Fantasyland One, dressed as Robin Hood, circulated within eye-sight.

The man with the windbreaker had entered Frontierland. The way he was carrying the windbreaker, it was still covering his right hand. Casey used a palm-size radio to immediately advise Frontierland One, who was patrolling the area dressed as Daniel Boone.

Several minutes later, Casey and Ladd met the officer near the River Belle Terrace and watched Windbreaker make his way down to the Tom Sawyer Island Rafts pier. "Looks like he's heading for Tom Sawyer Island," the officer said.

"You ride over on the same raft he does," Casey told Ladd. "We'll cover the pier in case he gets back without you."

Back in Fantasyland, Joey Dancer and Edie Flynn were having a soft drink while Jenny explored Captain Hook's Pirate Ship.

"Look, I know it's been rough for you since Johnny was killed," Joey said. "I knew you were close to having your baby when we planned that job in Denver, and I tried to talk Johnny out of it, but he wouldn't listen to me. He said it was too sweet to pass up. A day didn't go by in McAlester that I didn't wish we hadn't done it, or that I was out to help you. But you've got to believe me, Edie, I never led Johnny astray. I know you loved him, and you know he was my best friend, and I don't like talking against the dead, but it was *always* him that picked the jobs and made the plans, Edie. Always."

Edie Flynn sighed heavily: the hollow, weary sigh of a young woman with burdens beyond her years. "I guess I just don't want to admit that Johnny lied to me so much. He always said it was you. Joey was the bad influence. He had to help Joey out. Joey needed him. It was always you."

Joey shrugged. "He loved you, Edie. I don't blame him for saying that. Guys like Johnny and me, we have to lie to nice girls like you. Otherwise, you wouldn't have nothing to do with us."

Edie locked eyes with him. "You could be lying to me right now for that exact reason."

"I could," Joey admitted. "But I'm not." He took Edie's hand again. This time she did not draw away.

Watching them from the exit of the nearby Dumbo Flying Elephant ride was the Leper.

Watching all of them from the Mad Hatter's Tea Party ride was Charley Ramm.

At the raft pier, Casey Clay and Frontierland One were waiting for Ladd to return. The shifting scrutiny of Casey's eyes glanced downstream to the Mark Twain Steamboat dock, and suddenly stopped. The big paddle-wheeler had just pulled in and passengers were debarking. Among them was Windbreaker.

"Damn!" said Casey, pointing him out to Frontierland One. "He must have lost Ladd on the island. You stay in the area. I'll try to catch up with this guy!"

Windbreaker walked quickly back into Fantasyland. Casey radioed ahead to Fantasyland One; the officer dressed as Robin Hood hurried to intercept their man. But before Robin Hood could do so, Windbreaker rushed up the stairs to the Skyway Ride, and within seconds was in an over-head bucket being transported by cable wire across Fantasyland.

Casey ran up to the security man. "Where does he get off that thing?"

"Tomorrowland," the officer pointed. "It goes through that mountain over there, the Matterhorn, then all the way across Tomorrowland."

"Alert security in Tomorrowland," Casey said. "I'll try to follow him on the ground!"

The CBI agent moved rapidly through the crowd on the ground, watching Windbreaker in the ride above.

"Where has the money been all this time?" Edie Flynn asked.

"Hidden," Joey told her. "Inside the Pirates of the Caribbean ride. Come on, we'll get it."

Holding Edie's hand on one side and Jenny's on the other, Joey Dancer, feeling for all the world like a respectable young family man, led them back to the Plaza and into Adventureland. They walked under the big Swiss Family Treehouse and on to New Orleans Square, to what was arguably the most popular attraction in the park, the fantastic Pirates of the Caribbean ride.

They stood on a ramp to board the wide, flatbed boat that would carry them along the dark waterways where they would see life-size scenes of pirates looting and burning a town, fighting, singing, drinking ale with Victorian wenches, and carrying off their treasure to a great cave.

"We have to get the last seat in the boat," Joey told Edie. They maneuvered along the ramp to the right spot. Other people took the forward seats, and in a moment they were on their way into the dark water tunnel.

Charley watched the Leper take the front seat of the next boat. He himself boarded two seats behind the Leper.

Windbreaker reached the Skyway Terminal in Tomorrowland just ahead of Casey Clay on the ground. Running down the steps, he saw Casey hurrying toward him and reversed direction, rushing up the steps of the nearby People

Mover, a caterpillar-like ride that wound around, over, and through Tomorrowland. From a moving boarding platform, Windbreaker jumped into an empty front car of a departing train. Casey, running after him, barely missed getting into the last car.

Looking back at him, Windbreaker smiled. Casey muttered a curse and radioed all officers. "Windbreaker's on the loose! He's on the People Mover!"

In the Pirates of the Caribbean flatboat, Joey whispered to Edie, "I'll be getting out as the boat passes alongside the pirate treasure cave. The money is hidden in one of the treasure chests. You and Jenny finish the ride, then go around and come back through in the last seat again. I'll get in with you as the boat goes by."

From the boat behind them, the Leper and Charley Ramm both saw Dancer's boat turn a corner. It was momentarily out of sight. When their own boat turned and it came back into view, they both saw that Joey was no longer with Edie and Jenny. They looked around urgently, searching, but Joey was nowhere to be seen in the huge, glittering display of the pirate treasure cave.

Having no viable option, the Leper remained in the boat, continuing to follow Edie and Jenny. Charley did the same.

Edie and Jenny Flynn left their boat and walked around to reenter the Pirates of the Caribbean ride. The Leper followed them. Charley followed him. Back inside, on the loading ramp, Edie and Jenny again got into the rear seat of a boat. The Leper and Charley again took the next boat. This time, the Leper glanced suspiciously back at Charley, remembering that he had been in the previous boat with him.

He's made me, Charley thought.

He saw the Leper bend forward to get the gun from his ankle holster.

The boat started its journey.

In Adventureland, the area security man, dressed as a jungle trader, spotted Windbreaker, who had left the People Mover and was now walking past the Big Game Shooting Gallery. He radioed the location to all other officers, then hurried to keep Windbreaker in sight. The fleeing man looked around anxiously, then quickly headed past New Orleans Square. Ahead of him was the exit of the Pirates of the Caribbean ride.

Adventureland One held back, concealing himself, and radioed the man's movements. Casey Clay, hearing the call, hurried across the Plaza toward New Orleans Square.

In the Pirates of the Caribbean tunnel, Joey Dancer stepped lightly back into the boat with Edie and Jenny. Behind them, the Leper now divided his time between watching Joey and looking back at Charley Ramm behind him.

The lead boat docked and Joey, Edie, and Jenny stepped onto the ramp. Joey now carried a knapsack slung over one shoulder.

"Joey, let's walk faster," Edie said, clutching his hand.

"What's the matter?" Joey asked tensely.

"I just feel funny," she said. "Maybe it's the money."

As Joey, Edie, and Jenny walked toward the exit, the next boat docked and the Leper leaped out and hurried after them at a stumbling but surprisingly rapid speed.

Charley, cut off by several other debarking passengers, fell a short distance behind.

Security Chief Franklin, who had been monitoring the calls from Adventureland One, picked up Casey on his way to New Orleans Square in an electric car.

"Lieutenant Ladd got back from Tom Sawyer Island," he told Casey. "Windbreaker lost him in the woods."

Presently they converged with Adventureland One, Frontierland One, and Fantasyland One on New Orleans Square.

Windbreaker was standing at the exit of Pirates of the Caribbean. His right hand was still concealed by the jacket he carried. Casey Clay and the others spread out to surround him.

Just then, Joey Dancer, Edie, and Jenny came out of the Pirates exit. The Leper stepped directly behind them and pressed his gun just above Jenny's hip.

"You do what I tell you, or I'll blow her kidneys out," he said quietly to Joey and Edie.

Everyone stood stock-still.

"Hold it right there!" a voice shouted from the direction of Sara Lee's Cafe Orleans.

All eyes shifted quickly to the voice. It came from a Navy shore-patrol officer accompanied by two Marine military policemen. They moved with drill-like precision toward Windbreaker and apprehended him. When the jacket was taken from his arm, it revealed a dangling handcuff still locked to his wrist.

"He's a Navy deserter," the officer said as Casey came up and showed his CBI badge. "He escaped from a brig transfer bus by picking his handcuff lock. We'll take charge of him from here."

"You can have him," Casey said, shaking his head in exasperation.

Outside the Pirates exit, the Leper, his gun still pressed against little Jenny's side, looked back at Charley Ramm as he hurried up to them, hand under his jacket on his gun.

"I don't know who you are, mister," the Leper said, "but if you do anything I don't like, I'm gonna kill this kid here. Understood?"

Charley nodded. "Understood."

The Leper scooped Jenny up and carried her. She was trembling in fear. "Just be still, honey," her mother said, trembling just as much.

"Let's move," the Leper said to Joey and Edie. "Right down this street to the Plaza, then straight down Main Street to the entrance. When we get outside, we'll all get into a taxi and go for a little ride. Keep a good grip on that money, punk. Okay, move."

While Charley and the other officers looked helplessly on, the Leper guided his captives through Adventureland toward the Plaza entrance. As they passed the Big Game Shooting Gallery, with its staccato of loud pellet gunfire, one of the shooters there turned from the jungle targets and casually took a long-barreled, silencer-attached Sig revolver from a shopping bag of souvenirs. It was the stout man in the Hawaiian shirt who had come in with the tour group, then straggled away on his own.

Quickly fitting the revolver onto a dead-eye stock that he also took from the shopping bag, he attached the contraption with spring clamps to the inside of his right wrist and lower arm. With the weapon so attached, its potential accuracy was increased to that of a rifle. Quickly the stout man took aim and fired. A .38 caliber, Teflon-coated power slug hit the Leper in the center of the forehead, its shock killing him instantly, its impact causing him to drop Jenny as his body was hurled across a large display counter in front of Far East Imports.

Charley and the others, seeing the Leper fall, looked around frantically for the shooter. But before they could locate him, he fired again. His second shot dropped Joey Dancer.

Covering the gun with the shopping bag, the stout man moved quickly to Dancer's fallen body and snatched up the knapsack of money. Then he dashed out of Adventureland and into the Plaza. Charley and the others, spotting him now, immediately gave chase.

On the Plaza, the stout man leaped aboard one of the double-decker omnibuses that carried passengers up and down Main Street, U.S.A. The bus was heading for the main entrance at Town Square. Charley and the others spread out on both sides of Main Street, hurrying through the crowds, trying to keep up with the bus. Chief Franklin radioed ahead to front-gate security observers, ordering them into position to block the omnibus.

The stout man, seeing that he was being trapped, jumped from the bus in an attempt to escape on foot—but he mistimed his jump and went directly into the path of a horse-drawn trolley. A replica of America's turn-of-the-century trolleys, this one was pulled by a magnificent twelve-hundred-pound white draft horse. The stout man slipped when he hit the cobblestone street and went under the big horse. One of the animal's hooves caught him on the top of the head. He rolled unconscious to the side of the street.

Disneyland security men quickly moved him away.

•　　•　　•

At the park service entrance sometime later, an ambulance pulled in and Joey Dancer, on a stretcher, was put inside. "He's got a bad shoulder wound, but he'll recover," a paramedic said. Charley Ramm and Edie Flynn rode to the hospital with Joey. Casey Clay and Lieutenant Ladd followed behind with the little girl, Jenny.

In the ambulance, Dancer made a full confession to Charley. "The guy that set up the heist in the Denver airport was Jack Turban. He tipped Johnny Flynn about where the two money couriers would meet. For that, he was to get three hundred grand, and Johnny and I were to split five. What I didn't know was that he intended to take it all. But Johnny was smarter than me; he didn't trust Turban from the start, so when we got back to L.A. he decided to hide the bundle in Disneyland and find a way to get Turban's share to him without risking ours. But Turban was ahead of us; he sent two guys to hijack Johnny. I guess Johnny put up a fight and they whacked him; or maybe Turban ordered him killed, I don't know. Anyway, I got scared and split, like I said, and went underground in the McAlester pen in Oklahoma. I got out a week ago."

Charley nodded thoughtfully. "My guess is, Turban was partners with a hood in Chicago named Gino Cabrisi. And you're right when you say Turban probably ordered Flynn killed. You would have been next, but you disappeared too quickly, and too completely."

Charley sat back on the ambulance jump seat. He was frowning. Something didn't fit.

"Okay, now it's seven years later and you get out of McAlester," he said. "Turban and Cabrisi still want the same two things: the eight hundred grand—and you dead. They arrange for a hit man to take care of you and grab the money; that was the guy in the Hawaiian shirt that we caught. But again something goes wrong; a long-distance telephone call between Cabrisi and the hit man is accidentally overheard by a citizen in Chicago who takes the information to the police. Chicago P.D. identifies the voice of Cabrisi and sends one of their Organized Crime men out here to bring me into the case. After I hear the whole story, I'm convinced that Solomon Weiskoff, the one man who can authorize a hit in California, knows nothing about what's going on. So I let him know. He probably remembered the courier hijack—it was *his* money—and suspects that the guy who got away—you—might be coming back. So he sends his own personal killer, the Leper, to Disneyland to do the same thing that Cabrisi and Turban have sent *their* hit man to do: get you and get the money. So we had two killers and one target. Lucky thing for you that we knew who the Leper was; otherwise, you'd be a dead man back there." Charley paused, staring hard at Joey Dancer. "Just one thing doesn't make sense."

"Yeah," Joey Dancer said, as it dawned on him. His expression was half pain, half confusion. "How'd Turban know I was coming back when he didn't even know where I'd been? And how'd he know I'd be at Disneyland?"

Charley did not reply. He didn't want to be the one to tell him. But he didn't have to. Joey turned his eyes to Edie. At once, tears streaked down her cheeks.

"I told them, Joey," she admitted. "Turban had come around after Johnny's funeral. He said he'd make it well worth my while to let him know if you ever contacted me. I—I had always been convinced that it was you who was the bad influence who caused so much trouble in my marriage. So when you called me, I—I contacted Turban and told him all about it. He said for me to go ahead and meet you at Disneyland, that he'd have some men pick you up when we left the park."

"More than likely," Charley told her, "the hit man hired by Cabrisi and Turban was supposed to kill you and your little girl, too. Having to kill the Leper upset his timing. He shot Joey, then rushed to get the money."

"I'm—sorry, Joey," said Edie. "Now I've caused you to get shot and lose all that money—"

"The money doesn't matter," Joey said. "And the bullet hole will heal." He took Edie's hand and turned to Charley again. "What'll I get charged with for this? How much time do you figure I'll have to do?"

Charley studied the young couple. He thought of Marian and how much he wanted her back. After a moment, he shrugged soft-heartedly.

"The most I could probably get you for would be trespassing in the Disneyland pirate cave. I don't know what you'd get for that; ten days, maybe. But I could probably forget about it if you were planning to settle down. Go straight. Get married, maybe." The ambulance pulled up to the hospital and attendants opened the doors. "You think about it," Charley told him. "I'll visit you in a couple of days and we'll talk."

Charley went back to the escort car to join Casey and Ladd, as Jenny ran up to her mother and Joey Dancer.

That evening, Charley was once again sitting in the study of King Solomon Weiskoff. This time, he and the old mobster were sipping Napoleon brandy from lead crystal snifters.

"The guy we caught," Charley said, "is a Milwaukee torpedo named Gus Kowski. He was hired by Cabrisi and briefed by Turban when he got out here. He's agreed to give a full statement implicating both of them in a murder-for-hire conspiracy, in exchange for an agreement that the state won't ask for a death penalty against him for killing the Leper. Your nephew's going away, Mr. Weiskoff."

"Call me Sol," said the King. "You know, I always secretly admired you, Charley Ramm. The way you ripped us off took a lot of moxie. And you're right," he added ominously, "Jacob *will* be going away. Only not like you think."

"That's your business, not mine," Charley said. "I just want to make sure that you and I are square. I don't want to have to watch my back every time I step out a door."

"We're square," the King assured him. "I appreciate you coming to me."

When Charley left Beverly Hills, he felt good, felt refreshed, in spite of his battered face and bruised body. He decided to call Marian.

"Hey, it's me," he said when she answered. "Can I drop over?"

"For a while," she said. "If you promise not to bring up getting married again."

"I promise. Actually, all I want tonight is your lush body."

"Well, that can be arranged. Will I have time to put on my Victoria's Secret outfit and light candles in the bedroom?"

"Only if you hurry," Charley said. He clicked off.

Five minutes later, driving along Hollywood Boulevard, Charley glanced down a side street and saw three skinheads with a young black kid backed up against a building. The black kid was fighting off all three of them. Charley made a quick U-turn and swung around the corner. As he got out of his car, the skinheads turned threateningly toward him. Charley pulled back his coat so they could see the holstered Glock.

"Don't even think about it, assholes," he said. "I've got a badge, too."

The skinheads hurried off down the street.

"Thanks, mister," the black kid said. "They jumped me for no reason."

"They had a reason. You're the wrong shade of white. You were doing pretty good against all three of them. Where'd you learn to fight?"

The kid shrugged. "Here and there."

"What's your name?"

"Marvin Moore."

Charley almost smiled. Marvin Moore. As in Marvin Hagler and Archie Moore, two of the greatest fighters of all time. "What do you weigh, Marvin?"

"Hunnerd and sixty. Why?"

One-sixty. A solid middleweight. "Take a ride with me," Charley said. The kid hung back, suspicious. "I just want you to meet somebody," Charley assured him. "Look, I helped you out, didn't I?"

Marvin got in the car with him and Charley drove away. He dialed his cell phone again.

"Chula," he said when the call was answered, "meet me at the gym in thirty minutes. I want you to meet the future middleweight champion of the world."

Smiling, he turned onto the freeway and headed for East Los Angeles.

In her apartment, wearing less than six ounces of pale pink silk, Marian was lighting candles.

Joyce Carol Oates

Tell Me You Forgive Me?

ONE OF THE MOST CELEBRATED, and sometimes controversial, writers of our time on the planet, Joyce Carol Oates has written virtually every kind of fiction, from prize-winning literary novels to excursions into the darkest kind of horror. It's fun to imagine being her agent. You'd never know what Ms. Oates planned to hand in next. One imagines agent and author have had many lively conversations over her body of work. "Tell Me You Forgive Me?" appeared in *Ellery Queen's Mystery Magazine*'s September/October issue. This novella has all the hallmarks of an Oates classic: dark psychological suspense, characters who are not what they first seem, and an ending that will remain with you long after the last page is turned.

Tell Me You Forgive Me?

Joyce Carol Oates

1.

THE ELMS ELDERCARE CENTER, YEWVILLE, NY. OCTOBER 16, 2000.

To my Dear Daughter Mary Lynda who I hope will forgive me. I am writting this because it has been 40 yrs. ago this day, I saw by the calendar, that I sent you down into that place of horror & ugliness. I did not mean to injure you, Darling. I could not foresee. I was an ignorant & blind woman then, a drinker. I know you are well now & recovered for yrs. but I am writting to ask for your forgiveness?

Darling, I know you are smiling & shaking your head as you do. When your Mother worries too much. I know you're saying there is nothing to forgive, Mother!

Maybe that is not so, Darling.

Tho' I am fearful of explaining. & maybe cant find the words to explain, what was so clear 40 yrs. ago & <u>had to be done.</u>

Its strange for me to write this, & to know that when you read it, these words one by one that take me so long to write, I will be "gone." I am asking Billy (the big Jamaican girl with "cornrow" hair) to abide by my wishes & save this letter for you & I believe she will, Billy is one of the few to be trusted here.

If you wanted to speak to me after reading this, tho', you could not. This seems wrong.

You have forgiven me for that terrible time, Mary Lynda, I suppose. You have never blamed me as another daughter might.

No one ever accused me, I think. Not to my face?

(Except your father of course. & all the Donaldsons. I'm sorry, Mary Lynda, you bear that name yourself, I know! But you are more your Mother's daughter than his, everybody has always said how "Mary Lynda" takes after "Elsie." Our eyes & hair & our way of speaking.)

(I think of your father sometimes. Its strange, I did injury to "Dr. Donaldson" also, yet it never worried me. I thought—He is a man, he can take care of himself. I'm not proud that when I was young if I ceased loving a man, or caring for a woman friend, I seemed almost to "forget" them overnight. I'm not proud of this, Darling, but its your Mother's way.)

So many times this past year, since I have been moved to this wing of the Center, tho' its only across the lawn from the other place—I wanted to take your hand, Darling, and tell you the truth in my heart. Not what you have forgiven me for but something more. Something nobody has guessed at, all these years! But I did not, for I feared you would not love me then. That was why I was so quiet sometimes, after the chemo especially. When I was sick, & so tired. Yet to be forgiven, I must confess to you. So I am writing in this way. A coward's way I know, after I am "gone."

There are things you say in quiet you cant say face to face. I am not going to live much longer, and so it is time.

Last year I think it was April, when the Eagle House was razed, & you came to visit & were "not yourself"—upset & crying—I wanted to tell you then, Darling. & explain about Hiram Jones. (Is that a name you remember?) But I saw you needed comfort from your Mother, not "truth." Not just then.

After 40 yrs.! I have not been downtown to see South Main Street since coming to this place. Since my surgery etc. That part of old Yewville was meant to be "renewed"—but the state money gave out, I heard. So there's vacant lots & weeds between buildings, rubble & dust. The Lafayette Hotel & Midland Trust & the library & post office are still there, but the Eagle House is gone, & the rest of that block.

So I try to picture it in my head. Its only 3 miles from here, but I will never see it, I think.

I know its a childish way to think, he is buried beneath rubble. & his bones are in that debris.

"The Elms" is a good place for me, I think. I'm grateful to you, Darling, for helping me to live here. God knows where I would be living with just Medicare & Social Security! I don't complain like the other "oldsters." Tho' I am only 72, the youngest in this cottage. The oldest is that poor thing Mrs. N. you've seen, blind & with no teeth, "deaf & can't hear" etc. Lately they haven't brought Mrs. N. into the sun room even, which is a pity for her, but a relief to us. She is 99 yrs. old & everybody is hoping she will live to 100—except Mrs. N., she has no idea how old she is or even her name. There are 3 or 4 of us who are "progressing" (as the doctors call it, but this means the disease not us!) & those of us who are "just plain old." I am out of my time element here, because I am still young (in my mind) but the body has worn out, I know Darling its sad for you to see me, your Mother who used to be "beautiful" & vain of it.

Now I am vain of you, Darling. My "M.D." daughter I can boast of to these other old women, the ones who are my friends.

I love the pretty straw hat you brought for me to cover my head, & the bluebird scarf.

Are dead people "lonely" I wonder?

I have been writting—writing?—this damn letter for a week & it gets harder. Like trying to see into the darkness when you are in the light. The future when I will be "gone" is strange to me tho' I know its coming. When some other sick woman will have my room here & my bed.

You'd be surprised, we dont talk much of God here. You'd think so, but no. Its hard to believe in a "universe" inside these walls & lasting beyond a few days' time. Do I have a fear of God's judgement for my sins, somebody might ask. No Darling, I do not. Remember your Grandaddy Kenelly who laughed when "God" was spoken of. It was all just b.s. invented to keep weak people in line, Daddy believed.

Hell, God better believe in me. I'm a man, he'd say.

By that Daddy meant that "man" is more important than "God" because it was "man" who invented God, not the other way around.

Only just I wish I had more courage.

Daddy has been dead a long time but to me he's more real than the people in this place. I talk to him & hear his voice in my head. Since 1959! Thank God, Daddy never lived to be an old man here in "The Elms." Imagine your Grandaddy 100 yrs. old, deaf & blind & not knowing his own name or where the hell he is. He was only 55 when he died—thats young. How Time plays tricks on us. My handsome Daddy always older than me, now he'd be younger. When he died, I mean. I dont think of these things if I can.

Billy says I should not pass away with secrets in my heart. So I am trying, Darling.

Is "Hiram Jones" a name you remember, Darling? Maybe I have asked you this already.

However you were told your Grandaddy died, its best to think it was an accident like a roll of the dice. Nothing more.

Wish I could undo the bad thing that happened to you, Darling.

You were only 10 yrs. old. I cant think why I would send you into that terrible place like I did, to see where that terrible man had got to. I was drinking in those days & missing my father & that caused me to forget my duties as a Mother.

Now its a later time. You are a M.D. like "Dr. Donaldson" & so you know about my case, more than I would know myself. Tho' "oncology" is not your field. (I hate that word, its ugly!) But this is why I am not afraid of dying: when I had my surgery & my mind went out, it was OUT. Like a light bulb switched OFF. When I had you, Darling, I was very young & ignorant & believed I was healthy & went into labor not guessing what it would be, 18 hrs. of it, but afterward I "forgot" as they say but I knew what true pain was & would not wish to relive it. But this, when you're OUT, is different. The 3 times I was operated on, each time it was like "Elsie Kenelly" ceased to exist.

So if you're dead and theres no pain you cease to exist. If theres no pain theres nothing to fear.

Darling, I am a coward I guess. Too fearful of telling you what I have wished to, to beg your forgiveness. I'm <u>sorry</u>.

But in this envelope I am leaving a surprise for you. These ivory dice, remember? From your Grandaddy you didn't know too well. These dice he'd keep in his pocket & take out & roll "to see what they have to tell me"—he'd say. They were Daddy's Good Luck Dice he'd got in Okinowa—Okinawa?—that island in the Pacific where the U.S. soldiers were waiting to be shipped to Japan to fight & a lot of them would have died (Daddy always said) except the war ended with the A-bomb. So Daddy said these were Good Luck Dice for him. He'd toss away his medals but not these. At the Eagle House he'd roll his friends for drinks. 7 times out of 10 he'd win, I swear. The other men didnt know how the hell Willie Kenelly did it but the dice werent fixed, as you will see. Yet Daddy would snap his fingers & sometimes it seemed the dice would obey him, who knows why.

After my mother died we had some happy years, your Grandaddy & me. Maybe Daddy had a drinking problem but thats not the only thing in life, believe me.

Theres something about dice being tossed, if they're classy dice, it makes my backbone shiver even now. As soon as the dice fly out of your hand. & its an important bet, & everybody watching. I hope you will put away these dice for safekeeping, Mary Lynda. They're pure ivory which is why they've changed color. Daddy & I would roll them for fun, & one night he pressed them in my hand (in June 1959, I will always remember) & I knew this must be a sign of something but could not have guessed that Daddy would be dead in 5 weeks.

& Bud Beechum would be dead in about a year.

& Hiram Jones (maybe this is a name you dont remember) would be dead in a few years.

Well! Its too late now, Darling. For any of this, I guess. Even for feeling sorry. Like your Grandaddy said theres nothing to do with dice except "toss 'em."

Your loving Mother "Elsie Kenelly"

2.
YEWVILLE, NY.
APRIL 11, 1999.

A fire. It looked like a fire: not flames but smoke.

Clouds of pale dust-colored smoke drifting skyward in erratic surges, like expelled breaths. In the downtown area of Yewville, just across the river, it looked like.

She was driving to visit her mother in the nursing home. She'd delayed the visit for weeks. Poor Elsie: who'd once been a beautiful, vain woman, with that wavy shoulder-length dark-blond hair, now she was a chemo patient, the hair gone, and what sprouted from her scalp was fuzzy gray like down or mold you had an instinct to wipe off with a damp cloth.

Mary Lynda, no: I don't mind.

I'm lucky to be alive, see?

Mary Lynda, the daughter, wasn't so sure. She was a doctor, and she knew what was in store for her mother, and she wasn't so sure.

She'd had a driver's license for more than thirty years but the fact was, which she could never have explained to anyone: in all those years she'd never once driven in downtown Yewville. She'd managed to avoid South Main Street—the "historic" district—on the western bank of the Yewville River. Not that it was a phobia, it was a conscious choice. (Or maybe, yes, it was a phobia. And it soothed her vanity to tell herself it was a conscious choice.) There were circuitous routes to bring her to other parts of Yewville and its suburbs without any need to navigate the blocks closest to the river; though, from childhood, with the vividness of impressions formed in childhood, she could instantly recall the look of South Main Street: the grandiose Lafayette Hotel with its sandstone facade and many gleaming windows; Franklin Brothers, once Yewville's premiere department store, with its brass flagpole and fluttering American flag; the old stone City Hall, for decades the downtown branch of the Yewville Public Library; Mohawk Smoke Shop, King's Cafe, Ella's Ladies' Apparel, Midland Trust, Yewville Savings & Loan with its luminous clock tower; the Old Eagle House Tavern, gray stone, cave-like inside, with its faded sign in the shape of a bald eagle in flight, wings outspread, talons ready to grip prey. . . . She hadn't seen this sign in forty years but could see it now, swift as a headache. She could hear the sign creaking in the wind.

Old Eagle House Tavern est. 1819.

For some reason, she was going to drive through the downtown today. The "historic" district. Why not? She was curious about the smoke, and what South Main Street looked like after so many years. She'd been there last in 1960. Now, it was 1999. The bridge over the river had been totally changed, of course. Now four lanes, reasonably modern. Her car's tires hummed on the wire-mesh surface. There didn't seem to be any fire, though. No fire trucks or sirens. Main Street traffic was being diverted into a single slow-moving lane overseen by burly men shouting through megaphones. CONSTRUCTION AHEAD. DEMOLITION WARNING. She smelled a powdery-gritty dust, her eyes smarted. Damn: jackhammers. She hated jackhammers. Her heartbeat began to quicken in panic, such loud noises upset her. What was she trying to prove, driving here, when there was no one to prove it to, no witness? She vowed she wasn't going to mention this to Elsie.

I'm not that girl. She was someone else.

The girl had been ten at the time. When she'd gone down into the cellar of the Eagle House that smelled of beer, mildew, dirt. The stink of urine from the men's room. She'd been sent by Momma to see where the proprietor Bud Beechum "had got to."

Now, she was forty-nine years old. She hadn't lived in Yewville for decades. She'd graduated, valedictorian of her high school class, in 1968. She'd gone to college in Rochester and medical school in New York City. She was "Dr. Donaldson"—she had a general practice in Montclair, New Jersey. She was fully an adult, it was ridiculous that Yewville should reduce her to trembling like a child.

In her life away from Yewville, "Mary Lynda" was a name she rarely heard. Among friends and colleagues she was simply "Mary." An old-fashioned name, a name so classic it was almost impersonal, like a title. She liked the formality of "Dr. Donaldson" though it was her (deceased) father's name, too. Both her parents had called her "Mary Lynda" while she was growing up. Never had she had the courage to tell them how much she hated it.

Mary Lynda! Born in 1950, you could guess by the name. Sweet and simpering in gingham, like June Allyson. Crinkly crinoline skirts and pin-curls, weirdly dark lipstick. Don't hurt me, please just love me, I am so good.

Mary Donaldson visited her mother in Yewville two or three times a year. They spoke often on the phone. Or fairly often. Until just recently Elsie had lived by herself but she'd had a run of bad luck in her mid-sixties, health problems, financial problems, so she'd allowed Mary to persuade her to move into The Elms Retirement Village, which was a condominium complex for senior citizens in a semirural suburb of Yewville; when Elsie's health began to deteriorate, she moved into a nursing home on the premises. ("Next move," Elsie quipped, "is out the door, feet first." Mary winced, pretending not to hear.) When Elsie had been younger and in better health, Mary bought her a plane ticket once or twice a year so that she could come visit her in Montclair; they went to matinees and museums in New York; they were judged to be "more like sisters than mother and daughter," as Mary's friends liked to say, as if this remark might be flattering to Mary. Of course it wasn't true: Mary looked nothing like Elsie, who was an intensely feminine woman with a full, shapely body carried upright as a candle, dark blond hair that bobbed enticingly, flirty eyes, and a throaty voice. ("Don't be deceived by Mother's 'personality,' " Mary said. "Mother is a dominatrix." Her friends laughed, no one believed her for an instant.) Well into her mid sixties Elsie could pass for a youthful fifty. Though she'd been a heavy smoker and drinker, her skin was relatively unlined. She'd had only two husbands—Mary's father was the first—but numerous lovers who'd treated her, on the whole, as Elsie said, not too badly. But now, at last, life was catching up with her. Her girlfriends from childhood were white-haired, wrinkled grandmothers, the boys elderly-shrunken, or dead. In her late sixties things began to go wrong with Elsie. She had varicose-vein surgery on her legs. She had surgery to remove ovarian cysts. Arthritis in her lower spine, bronchitis that lasted for weeks in the cold damply windy climate of upstate New York. For much of her adult life she'd been a drinker, joined Alcoholics Anonymous in her early thirties, and quit smoking at about the same time. ("I must have thought I'd live forever," Elsie said ruefully. "Now look!") In fact, Mary was in awe that her mother, who'd taken such indifferent care of herself, who'd avoided doctors for decades, was in such relatively good health for a woman of her generation, and had managed even to keep her bright "upbeat" temperament. *Not a dominatrix, a seductress. Her power is more insidious.*

Driving with maddening slowness on Main Street, Mary thought of these things. And of the past, coiled snaky and waiting (for her? that wasn't likely) beyond the facades of these old, now shabby buildings. The Lafayette Hotel; the ugly discount store that had once been classy Franklin Brothers; the old City Hall which hadn't changed much, at least on the outside; the Mohawk Smoke Shop, still in business, though with a sign in its window ADULT X-RATED VIDEOS; the old Yewville Savings & Loan with the clock tower that had always seemed gigantic, a proud glowing clock face to be seen for miles, though in fact, as Mary now saw, to her surprise, the granite tower was no higher than the second floor of the bank building.

But where was Ella's, and where was King's Cafe, and where was . . . the Eagle House Tavern?

Mary stared, confused. Half the block was being razed. Only the shells of some buildings remained. Stone, and brick. Rubble in heaps. Like an earthquake. A bombing. She was tasting dust, swallowing dust; she steeled herself against the noise of jackhammers, that made her heartbeat race as if with amphetamine. There came a wrecking ball swinging in air like a deranged pendulum, and at once a wall of weatherworn stone collapsed in an explosion of dust.

Go look for him, honey. I'll wait out here.

Mommy, why? I don't want to.

Because I'm asking you, Mary Lynda.

I don't want to, Mommy. I'm afraid . . .

Go on, I said! Damn you! Just see where that bastard has got to.

Mommy's face was bright and hard and her mouth twisted in that way Mary Lynda knew. Her mother had been drinking, it was like fire inside her that could leap out at you, and burn.

Mommy wanted to know where Bud Beechum was, exactly. For he wasn't in the tavern when they came inside. When Mommy pushed Mary Lynda inside. Bud Beechum owned the Eagle House. He'd been a friend of

Grandaddy Kenelly when Grandaddy was alive and he was a friend of Mary Lynda's mother, too. Somehow, the families were friendly. Beechums, Kenellys. Bud Beechum's wife was Elsie's cousin. They'd all been "wild" together in high school. Just to remember those times, they'd start laughing, shaking their heads. The child Mary Lynda was uneasy around Beechum. He had a way of looking at you, smirking and rubbing at his teeth with the tip of his tongue.

Mary Lynda was uneasy around most adult men, except her father and the Donaldsons: They were "different" kinds of people. They were soft-spoken, "nice." When Elsie divorced Timothy Donaldson, she was given custody of Mary Lynda and so Mary Lynda saw her father only on weekends.

Bud Beechum had been dead now for almost forty years. Yet you could imagine his big, chunky bones in the cellar of that old building. His broken-in skull the size of a bucket amid the rubble and suffocating dust.

Mommy, no. Mommy, don't make me.

Mary Lynda, do as you're told.

Mommy's voice was scared, too. And Mommy's fingers gripping Mary Lynda's narrow shoulders, pushing her forward.

It was now that Mary did the unexpected thing: As soon as she was safely past the traffic congestion on South Main, she turned left on a street called Post, and drove back toward the river, and, with an air of adventure, a sense of recklessness, parked in the lot, now mostly deserted and weedy, behind the old Franklin Brothers store.

Dr. Donaldson, why? This is crazy.

She wasn't a woman of impulse, usually. She was a woman who guarded her actions as she guarded her emotions. Not for Mary Donaldson the dice-tossing habits of her charming old drunk of a grandfather Kenelly.

And so it was strange that in her good Italian shoes, in her taupe linen pants suit (Ann Taylor), her hair stylishly scissor-cut, she was parking in downtown Yewville, and hurrying to join a small crowd of people gathered to stare at the destruction of a few old, ugly buildings. Coughing from the dust, and maybe there was asbestos in that dust. Yet she was compelled by curiosity, like the others, most of whom were elderly, retired men, with here and there some woman shoppers, some teenagers and children. (Thank God, no one who seemed to recognize Mary Lynda Donaldson.)

His bones in that rubble. Ashes.

Toxic to inhale!

Of course this was ridiculous. Bud Beechum had been properly buried. Forty years ago.

The Eagle House was being razed, spectacularly. The very earth shook as the wrecking ball struck. "Wow! Fan-tas-tic." A teenaged boy with spiky hair spoke approvingly. His girl snuggled against him, wriggling her taut little bottom as if the demolition of the Eagle House had a private, salacious meaning. Mary saw that the girl was hardly more than fourteen, her brown hair streaked in maroon and green, one nostril and one eyebrow pierced. She was pale, wanly pretty, though looking like a pincushion. Very thin. One of her tiny breasts, the size and color of an oyster, was virtually exposed, her tank top hung so slack on her skinny torso. She wore faded jeans, and in this place of litter and broken glass was barefoot.

That afternoon, Elsie had picked up Mary Lynda from school. She'd driven here. She'd parked her car, the yellow Chevy, in this lot, though closer to the rear of the Eagle House. *Why are we here, Mommy?* Mary Lynda asked. *Because that bastard owes me. He owed your Grandaddy, he's got to pay.* Mary Lynda knew the symptoms: Her mother's eyes were dilated, her hair hung lank in her face. When she hiccupped, Mary Lynda could smell her sweetish-sour breath.

"What's happening here?" Mary asked in the bright, friendly voice of a visitor to Yewville who'd just wandered over from the Lafayette Hotel. The boy with the spiky hair said, with an air of civic pride, "They're tearing these old dumps down. They're gonna build something new." His girl said, smirking, "About time, huh?" Mary had to press her fingers against her ears, the jackhammer was so loud. Such noises enter the soul, and may do permanent damage. She saw that beyond the adjacent lot was an unpaved alley that led toward the river. This was the lot in which her mother had parked that day. Debris was piled on both sides of the alley, some of it Styrofoam of the white-glaring hue of exposed bone. Mary was smiling, or trying to smile, but something was wrong with her mouth. "Ma'am? You okay?" The teenagers were suddenly alert, responsible. You could guess they had mothers for whom they were sometimes concerned. They helped Mary sit down— for suddenly Mary's knees were weak, her strength was gone like water rapidly draining away—on a twisted guardrail. Amid the deafening jackhammer that made her bones vibrate she sat dazed, confused, breathing through her mouth. Her legs were clumsily spread, thank God for the trousers. She was wiping her nose with her fingers. Was she crying? Saying earnestly, "A man was found dead in that building, a long time ago. A little girl found him. Now I can tell her the cellar is gone."

3.
ROCHESTER, NY 1968–BARNEGAT, NJ 1974.

For years she would see a male figure, not fallen but "resting"—prone on the floor, for instance, inside a room she was passing; in the blurry corner of her eye she saw this figure, but had no sense that the figure meant death. Because when she looked, there was no figure, of course. One night, in Rochester, working late in the university library, she was swiftly passing a dim-lit lounge and though it had been eight years since she'd seen Beechum's body in that cellar, and rarely thought of it, now suddenly she was seeing it again, in terrifying detail, more clearly than she'd seen the body at the time. *He's here.*

How'd he come to be here? Always a logical young woman, even in her panic she reasoned that if Bud Beechum's body was actually here in the University of Rochester library, so long as there was no linkage between the body and Mary Lynda Donaldson, a pre-med student, she was blameless, and could not be blamed.

Her instinct was to stop dead in her tracks and stare into the room, yet since she knew (she knew perfectly well) that no one was lying there on the carpet, she averted her eyes and flew past.

No. Don't look. Nothing!

She believed it was an act of simple discipline, fighting off madness. As an adult you took responsibility for your life, you were no-nonsense. High grades at the university, always high grades. She was pre-med after all. Ignore the politics of the era. Assassinations, the Vietnam War, the despairing effort of her generation to "bring the war home." For always in history there have been wars, and destruction, and people dying to no purpose, if not here then elsewhere, if not elsewhere then (possibly) here, count your blessings, Mary Lynda, her mother often consoled her; or maybe it was a mother's simple command, and it made sense. (Elsie had joined AA, Elsie hadn't had a drink stronger than sweet apple cider in years, laughing *Can you believe it?*) So private madness seemed to Mary Lynda the worst nonsense. Stupid and self-hurtful as "dropping acid," or laughing like a hyena (that belly laugh of Bud Beechum's, how she'd hated it) at someone's funeral, or tearing off your clothes and running in the street when you didn't even look good, small breasts and soft hips and tummy, naked. Fighting off madness seemed to Mary Lynda like beating out a fire with a heavy blanket or canvas—"Something anybody could do if they tried."

It was her opinion that both Kennedys could have prevented being assassinated if they'd been more prudent in their behavior. Martin Luther King, too. But she kept this opinion to herself.

One of the men she'd loved, and would live with intermittently for several years in her late twenties, she'd seen lying in the sun in khaki shorts, bare-chested, amid sand and scrub grass at the Jersey shore. She was an intern at Columbia Presbyterian and lived a life far from Yewville and from her mother. Seeing the boy sleeping in the sun, sprawled on the sand, she stared, like one under a spell. She went to him, knelt over him, stroked his hair. The boy was in fact a young man, her age; with long pale lashes and long lank hair women called moon-colored. At Mary's touch he opened his eyes that were sleepy but sharpened immediately when he saw who she was: another man's girl. And when he realized what Mary was doing in her trancelike state, where her hand crept, he came fully awake and pulled her down on top of him, his hands gripping her head. His kisses were hard, hungry. Mary shut her eyes that hurt from the sun, she would see what came of this.

4.
YEWVILLE, NY.
1960–1963.

Those years of Elsie chiding, frightened. *Mary Lynda, talk to me! This is just some sort of game you're playing, isn't it!*

At first they believed her inability to speak might have something to do with her breathing patterns. She breathed rapidly, and usually through her mouth. This precipitated hyperventilation. (Elsie learned to enunciate this carefully: "Hy-per-ven-ti-lation.")

Mary felt dizzy, her eyes "sparked." Her throat shut up tight. If she managed to choke out words they were only a sound, a shuddering stammer like drowning. "Is your daughter a little deaf-mute girl?" a woman dared ask Elsie at the clinic.

For approximately ten months after October 16, 1960, she was mute. And what relief when finally she wasn't expected to speak. They let you alone if you don't talk, they seem to think you're deaf, too. Except for some of the kids teasing her at school it was a time of peace. She'd never been very afraid of children, even of the loud-yelling older boys, only just adults frightened her. Their size, their sudden voices. The mystery of their moods, and their motives. The grip of their fingers on your shoulders even in love. *Mary Lynda, I love you, honey! Say something. I know you can talk if you want to.*

But mostly this was a time of peace. No one would question her words as the police had questioned her, for she had no words. Because she'd ceased speaking, she was surrounded by quiet. Like inside a glass bubble. She carried it with her everywhere, inviolable.

In school where she was *Mary Lynda Donaldson* she occupied her own space. Her teacher Miss Doehler with the watery eyes was very kind to her, always Mary Lynda's desk was just in front of Miss Doehler's desk in fifth and sixth grades. She was *the little girl who'd found the dead man. The dead man!* The man who'd owned the Eagle House Tavern by the river. With the soaring eagle sign that creaked in the wind. When Bud Beechum was killed, his picture was printed in the Yewville paper: the first time in Bud's life, people said. Poor bastard, he'd have liked the attention.

Tavern Owner, 35, Killed in Robbery.

Strange that, in Bud Beechum's picture, he was young-looking, without his whiskers, and smiling. Like he had no idea what would happen to him.

Strange that, when Mary Lynda's throat shut up the way it did, she felt safe. Like somebody was hugging her so tight she couldn't move. Sometimes in the night her throat came open, like ice melting, and then she began to groan, and whimper like a baby, and call "Momma! Mom-ma!" in her sleep. If Elsie was home, and if Elsie heard, she might come staggering into Mary Lynda's room, groggy and scolding. "Oh Mary Lynda, what? What is it *now?*" If Elsie wasn't home, or wasn't wakened, Mary Lynda woke herself up, and tried to sleep sitting up, which was a safe way, generally. Not to put your head down on a pillow. Not to be so unprotected. She stared at the walls of her room (which was a small room, hardly more than a closet) to keep them from closing in.

Always in one of the walls there was a door. As long as the door was shut, she was safe. But the door might open. It might be pushed open. It might glide open. On the other side of the door there might be steep steps leading down, and she had no choice but to approach these steps, for something was pressing her forward, like a hand against her back. A gentle hand, but it could turn hard. A hard firm adult hand on her back. And she would see her own hand switching on a light, and she would see suddenly down into the cellar into the dark. That was her mistake.

5.
YEWVILLE, NY.
OCTOBER 1960–MARCH 1965.

The boy was a Negro, as blacks were then called, with an I.Q. of eighty-four. This was not "severe retardation" (it would be argued by prosecutors), this was not a case of "not knowing right from wrong." Though the boy was seventeen, he'd dropped out of school in fifth grade and could not read, still less write, except to shakily sign his name to a confession later to be recanted, with a protestation of his court-appointed attorney of "extreme police coercion." The case would receive the most publicity any murder case had ever received in Eden County. In some quarters it was believed to be a "race murder"—the boy, Hiram Jones, had brutally killed and robbed Bud Beechum because Beechum was a white man. In other quarters, the case was believed to be a "race issue"—Hiram Jones was being prosecuted because he was a Negro. Because his I.Q. was eighty-four. Because he lived in that part of Yewville known as Lowertown, a place of makeshift wood-frame shanties with tin roofs. Because the testimony of his family that Hiram had been home at the probable time of the murder was dismissed as lies. Because when he'd been arrested by police he had in his possession Bud Beechum's wallet, containing twenty-eight dollars; he was wearing Bud Beechum's favorite leather belt with the silver medallion buckle; Bud Beechum's shoes were hidden in a shed behind the Joneses' house. These items, Hiram claimed he'd found while fishing on the riverbank, less than a mile from the Eagle House. Yet when police came into Lowertown to arrest him, having been tipped off by a (Negro) informant, Hiram Jones had "acted guilty" by trying to run. He'd made things worse by "resisting arrest." Police had had to overpower him, and he'd been hurt and hospitalized, his nose and eye sockets broken, ribs cracked, windpipe crushed from someone's boot. He would speak in a hoarse, cracked whisper like wind rattling newspaper for the remainder of his life.

Always Hiram Jones would deny he'd killed the white man. He would not remember the white man's name, or how exactly he'd been charged with killing him, but he would deny it. He would deny he'd ever been in the Eagle House. No Negroes in Yewville patronized the Eagle House. He would be tried as an adult and found guilty of second-degree murder and robbery, he would be incarcerated while his case was appealed to the state supreme court where a new trial would be ordered, but by this time Hiram Jones was diagnosed as "mentally deficient"—"unable to participate in his own trial"—so he was transferred to a state mental hospital in Port Oriskany where, in March 1965, he would die after a severe beating by fellow inmates.

6.
THE EAGLE HOUSE TAVERN, YEWVILLE, NY.
OCTOBER 16, 1960.

At the bottom of the wooden steps there was a man lying on his side. Like he was floating in the dark. Like he was sleeping, and floating. His arms sprawled. Maybe it was a joke, or a trick? Bud Beechum was always joking. *Hey, I'm kidding, kid,* Bud Beechum would say, in reproach. *Where's your sense of humor?* If he saw you were frightened of him, he'd press in closer. He smelled of beer, and cigarette smoke, and his own body. His stomach rode his big-buckled belt like a pumpkin. He had hot moist smiling eyes and the skin beside those eyes crinkled. He'd been in the Korean War. He boasted of things he'd done there with his "bayonet." He refused to serve Negroes in the Eagle House because, as he said, he owed it to his white customers who didn't want to drink out of glasses that Negroes drank out of, or use the men's room if a Negro had used it. His wife was Momma's cousin Joanie who smelled of talcum. Once at the Beechums' in the old hay barn where kids were leaping into hay and screaming like crazy, bare arms and legs, Bud Beechum laughed at Mary Lynda for being so shy and fearful—"Not like your Momma who's *hot.*" Because Mary Lynda didn't want to run and jump with the others into the hay loft. Bud Beechum teased her pretending to grab at her between the legs with his big thumb and forefinger. *Uh-oh! Watch out, the crab's gonna getcha!* It was just a joke though. Bud Beechum's face was flushed and happy-seeming. So maybe now, lying at the foot of the steps, in this nasty-smelling place with the bare light bulb that hurt her eyes, maybe this was a joke, too. Bud Beechum's head that was big as a bucket twisted to one side like he was trying to look over his shoulder. Something glistened on his head, was it blood?

Mary Lynda was fearful of blood. She began to breathe in a quick light funny way like the breath couldn't get past her mouth. Was Mr. Beechum breathing? Or holding his breath? His mouth was gaping in surprise and something glistened there, too. There was a smell—Mary Lynda's nostrils pinched—like he'd soiled his pants. A grown man! Mary Lynda wanted to run away, but could not move. Nor had she any words to utter. Never had she spoken to Momma's man friend Bud Beechum except shyly in response to a teasing query and that only sidelong, out of the corner of her mouth, eyes averted. You could not. You did not. She stood paralyzed, unable to breathe. She could not have said why she was in this place. Or where exactly this place was. A dungeon? Like in a movie? A cave? It made her think of bats: She was terrified of bats, that got into little girls' hair.

Of the Yewville taverns where Momma went when she was feeling lonely her favorite was the Eagle House because that had been Grandaddy Kenelly's favorite, too. There, Mary Lynda was allowed to play the jukebox. Nickel after nickel. Sometimes men at the bar gave her nickels. Like they bought drinks for Momma. Bud Beechum, too—"This one's on the house." Mary Lynda drank sugary Cokes until her tummy bloated and she had to pee so bad it hurt. If Momma stayed late she slept in one of the sticky black vinyl booths. All the men liked Momma, you could tell. Momma so pretty with her long wavy dark-blond hair and her way of dancing alone, turning and lifting her arms like a woman in a dream.

Mary Lynda had overheard her parents quarreling. Her father's voice, and her mother's voice rising to a scream. *Because you bore the shit out of me, that's why.*

Such words, Mary Lynda wasn't allowed to hear.

Why was this afternoon special? Mary Lynda didn't know. Momma had come to pick her up at school which wasn't Momma's custom. Saying she didn't have to take the damned school bus. They'd come here, and parked in the next-door lot. It would turn out—it would say so in the newspaper—that the front door of the Eagle House was locked, only the back door was open. There were no customers in the bar because it was early: not yet four o'clock. Momma talked excitedly explaining (to Mary Lynda?) that she was in no mood to see Bud Beechum's face. "Just tell him I'm out here, and waiting." Momma repeated this several times. It wasn't clear why Momma didn't want to see Bud Beechum's face yet wanted Mary Lynda to find him, to ask him to come outside so that Momma could talk to him. For wouldn't she have to see his face, then? But this was Momma's way when she'd been drinking. One minute she'd grab Mary Lynda's head and kiss her wetly on the mouth calling her "my beautiful baby daughter," the next minute she'd be scolding. Only fragments of the afternoon of October 16, 1960, would be clear in Mary Lynda's memory. For possibly much of it had been dreamt, or would be dreamt. Her throat began to shut up tight as soon as she'd entered the barroom looking for Bud Beechum who was always behind the bar except now he wasn't. She'd have to look back in the kitchen, Momma said. She wanted to leave but Momma said no. *See where that bastard has got to. I know he's here somewhere.* Mary Lynda saw Bud Beechum, and the thought came to her, *He's dead.* She giggled, and pressed her knuckles against her mouth. The day before, Momma had kept her home from school with an "ear infection"—a "fever." When you have a fever, Momma said, you might become "delirious." You might have wild, bad dreams when you weren't even asleep and you couldn't trust what you saw, or thought you saw. So she'd called Mary Lynda's school and made her excuse. Yet, yesterday, it had seemed to Mary Lynda that Momma kept her home because she was nervous about something. She was edgy, and distracted. When the telephone rang, she wouldn't answer it. She wouldn't let Mary Lynda answer it. After a while, she left the receiver off the hook. She made sure every blind in the house was drawn, and lights were out in most of the rooms except upstairs. When Mary Lynda asked what was wrong, Momma told her to hush.

Already, yesterday was a long time ago.

Mary Lynda was crouched at the top of the steps staring down to where Bud Beechum was lying. Looking like he was asleep. *No. He's dead.* Still, Bud Beechum was tricky, he might wake up at any moment. Maybe it was a trick he was playing on Momma, too. You couldn't trust him. Mary Lynda stood there on the steps so long, not able to move, not able to breathe, at last Momma came to see where she was.

Soft as a whisper coming up behind Mary Lynda.

"Honey? Is something wrong?"

7.
THE EAGLE HOUSE TAVERN, YEWVILLE, NY.
OCTOBER 16, 1960.

He told her to come to the Eagle House at noon, he wanted to see her. He'd leave the rear door unlocked. He was pissed as hell at her not answering the phone, almost he'd come over there and broken down the door and the hell with her little girl or any other witness. So she came by. She saw she had no choice. She parked the Chevy on Front Street, by the Lafayette Hotel. A dead-end street. She wasn't seen walking to the Eagle House through the alley. She wore a raincoat and a scarf tied tight around her head and she walked swiftly, in a way unusual for Elsie Kenelly. She entered by the rear door. At this time of day no one was around. There was a raw, egg-white look to the day. High clouds were spitting rain cold enough to be ice. The clouds would be blown away, and the sky would open into patches of bright blue, by the time she left. The Eagle House wasn't open for lunch; it opened, most days, around four P.M. and it closed at two A.M. Beechum was waiting for her just inside. "About time, Elsie." He was angry, but relieved. She'd come as he had commanded: The woman had done his bidding. He grabbed at her. She pushed him off, laughing nervously. She'd washed her hair and put on crimson lipstick. Perfume that made her nostrils pinch. She'd brought a steak knife, one of that set her mother-in-law Maudie Donaldson had given them, in her handbag but she knew she wasn't brave enough to use a knife. She was terrified of blood, and of the possibility of Bud Beechum wrenching the knife out of her fingers. He was strong, and for a man of his size he was quick. She knew he was quick. And he was shrewd. She would have to say the right things to him, to placate him. Because he was pissed from last night, she knew that. She told him that Mary Lynda had been sick, an ear infection. She told him she was sorry. He squeezed her breasts, always there was something mean in this man's touch. And when he kissed her, there was meanness in his kiss. His beery breath, his ridiculous thrusting tongue like an eel. His teeth that needed brushing. The wire-whiskers she'd come to hate though at one time (had she been crazy?) she'd thought they were sexy, and Bud Beechum was "sexy—sort of." She'd always been curious about this guy married to her cousin Joanie, even back in high school it was said all the Beechum men were built like horses which was fine if you liked horses. Drunk, she'd thought just maybe she might. But only part-drunk, and stone-cold sober, she'd had other thoughts.

Mary Lynda was at school. She'd be at school until three-fifteen.

"Look. I got kids, too. You think I don't have my own kids?"

Now he was blaming her for—what? Mary Lynda? The bastard.

There was the doorway to the cellar. Like a dream doorway. *Pass through to an adventure! But you must be brave.* She laughed, and wrenched her mouth free of his. She was breathing quickly as if she'd been running. She lifted her heavy dark-blond hair in both her hands and let it sift through her fingers as it fell, in that way he liked. She could see in his eyes, dilated with desire, he liked. He led her urgently toward the cellar steps, where a bare light bulb was screwed into a ceiling fixture filmy with cobweb. It was both too bright here and smudged-seeming. It smelled of piss from the men's room in the back hall, and of damp dark earth. All the cellars in these old "historic" buildings were earthen. Things died in these cellars and rotted away. Beechum was talking excitedly, laughing, that warning edge to his voice. He was sexually charged up like a battery. But he didn't like tricky women, he wanted her to know that. He'd hinted at things about her old man she wouldn't want generally known in Yewville. She'd got that, right? He was leading her down the steps, ahead of her, to this place they'd gone before, this was the third time in fact, she was disgusted and ashamed and she pushed him, suddenly pushed him hard, and he lost his balance and fell forward. Elsie's fingers with the painted nails, which were strong fingers, you'd better believe they were strong, at the small of the man's fattish back, and he fell.

He fell hard. He fell onto the wooden steps limp and lumpy as a sack of potatoes, sliding down. Horrible to watch, and fascinating, the big man's body helpless, thumping against the steps that swayed dangerously with his weight. Beechum was six feet three, weighed two hundred twenty pounds at least. Yet now, falling, he was helpless as a giant baby. He lay on the earthen floor, stunned. A groan of utter astonishment escaped his throat. If Beechum wasn't seriously hurt, if he got hold of Elsie now, he'd kill her. He'd beat her to death with his fists. She'd seen a pipe amid a pile of debris. Beechum was writhing, groaning, possibly the bastard had injured his back in the fall, maybe his spine or his neck was broken, maybe the bastard was dying but Elsie hadn't faith this could be so easy. Almost, she was willing—she was wanting—to work a little harder. Her father Willie Kenelly had killed men in Okinawa, gunfire and bayonet, he hadn't boasted of it, he'd said it was Goddamned dirty work, it was hard work, killing was hard work, nothing to be proud of but not ashamed either. That had been his job, and they'd given him medals for it, but in his own mind he'd just done his job. *Do it right, girl, or not at all. Don't screw up.*

She knew. She'd known, making up her mind to drive over here.

Afterward, she wrapped the pipe in newspaper. It was bloody, and there were hairs on it. But nothing had splattered onto her. She would bathe anyway. For the second time that day. She wiped the dead man's mouth roughly, thoroughly, removing all traces of crimson lipstick. She took his wallet, stuffed with small bills. She unbuckled his belt and removed it. She unlaced his shoes. She was feverish yet calm. Whispering aloud, "Now. I want this. These. One, two. The shoe. Three, four. Shut the door. *Don't screw up.*" In a paper bag she carried Beechum's things to her car parked on Front Street beside the Lafayette Hotel. This had been an ideal place to park: a side street above the river, a dead end used mainly by delivery trucks. No one had seen her, and no one would see her. It wasn't yet one P.M. The sky was clearing rapidly. Each morning, as winter neared, the sky was thick with clouds like broken concrete but the wind from Lake Ontario usually dislodged them by midday, patches of bright blue glared like neon. Elsie drove north along the River Road humming the theme from *Moulin Rouge*. It had snagged in her brain and would recur throughout her life, reminding her of this day, this hour. She surprised herself, so calm. *You're doing good, girl. That's my girl.* Why she would behave so strangely within a few hours, bringing her daughter Mary Lynda to the death scene as if to ascertain yes, yes the man was dead, yes it had really happened, yes she could not possibly be to blame if her own daughter was the one to discover the corpse, she would not know. She would not wish to think. *That's right, girl. Never look back.*

She drove the Chevy bump-bump-bumping along a sandy access road to the river, where fishermen parked, but today there were no fishermen. Scrub willow grew thick on the riverbank here, no one would see her. She was a doctor's wife, not a woman you'd suspect of murder. She threw the bloodied pipe out into the river, about twenty feet from shore. It sank immediately, never would it be recovered. Beechum's fat, frayed pigskin wallet Elsie hadn't glanced into, not wanting the bastard's money, the leather belt he'd been so proud of, like the oversized silver buckle was meant to be his cock, and his shoes, his size-twelve smelly brown fake-leather shoes, these items of Bud Beechum's she left on the riverbank for someone unknown to find.

"Like Hallowe'en," she said. "Trick or treat, in reverse."

8.
YEWVILLE, NY.
1959–1960.

She was just so lonely, couldn't help herself. Missing him.

Crying till she was sick. Lost so much weight her clothes hung loose on her. Even her bras. And her eyes bruised, bloodshot.

At first, her husband was sympathetic. In his arms she lay stiff in the terror of a death she'd never somehow believed could happen. *Can't believe it. I can't believe he's gone. I wake up, and it's like it never happened.*

Couldn't help herself, she began dropping by the Eagle House though he wasn't there. Because, each time she entered, pushing through the rear door which was the door by which he'd entered, she told herself *It might not have happened yet.* She told herself maybe he was there, at the bar. Waiting.

The other men, his friends, were there. Most were older than Willie Kenelly had been. Yet they were there, they were living, still. Glancing around at her when she entered the barroom, the only woman. And Bud Beechum behind the bar, staring at her. Elsie Kenelly, Willie Kenelly's girl, who'd married the doctor.

God, they'd loved Willie Kenelly: Nobody like him.

Except : He'd left without saying goodbye.

Short of breath, sometimes. The heel of his big callused hand against his chest. And that faraway look in his eyes. She'd asked her father what was wrong, and he hadn't heard her. She asked again, and he turned his gaze upon her, close up, those faded blue eyes, and laughed at her. *What's wrong with what? The world? Plenty.*

Except he'd given Elsie, one evening at the bar of the Eagle House, those worn ivory dice he liked to play with, he'd brought back from Okinawa. His Good Luck Dice he called them.

"Don't lose 'em, honey."

That had been a clear sign, hadn't it? That he was saying goodbye. But Elsie hadn't caught on.

No one would speak of how Willie Kenelly died. One of the papers, not the Yewville paper, printed he'd "stepped or fallen" off the girder of a bridge being repaired upriver at Tintern Falls; there was water in his lungs, yet he'd died of "cardiac arrest." In any case Willie Kenelly's death was ruled "accidental." But Elsie knew better, her father wasn't a man to do anything by accident.

In the Eagle House that summer, she drank. Few women came alone into Yewville taverns, and never any woman who was a doctor's wife and lived in one of the handsome brick houses on Church Street. Yet Elsie was Willie Kenelly's daughter long before she'd become Dr. Donaldson's wife. She'd gone to Yewville High School, everyone knew her in the neighborhood. Bud Beechum leaned his high, hard belly against the edge of the bar, talking with her. Listening sympathetically. Beechum, greasy thinning dark hair worn like he was still in high school, sideburns like Presley's and something of Presley's sullen expression. And those eyes, deep-socketed, black and moist and intense. Elsie had always thought Bud Beechum was an attractive guy, in his way. By Yewville standards. She remembered him in his dress-up G.I. uniform. He'd been lean then. He'd had good posture then. He'd been fox-faced, sexy. They'd kissed, once. A long time ago in somebody's backyard. A beer party. A picnic. When?

Bud Beechum had liked her father. He'd "really admired" Willie Kenelly, he said. Elsie's father was a guy "totally lacking in bullshit," he said. Elsie's father had been in World War II, as it was called, and Beechum in the Korean War. They had that in common: a hatred of the army, of officers, of anybody telling them what to do. And Willie Kenelly hadn't had a son. When Beechum wiped at his eyes with his fist, Elsie felt her heart pierced.

It was hard for men to speak of loss. Of grief. Of what scared them. Better not to try, it always came out clumsy, crude.

But Elsie could tell Beechum, and her father's friends, that he'd been her best friend, not just her father. He'd loved her without wanting anything from her and without judging her. That had always been his way. Maybe she hadn't deserved it but it was so. She'd seen his body at the funeral director's, and she'd seen his coffin lowered into the ground, and she saw his death reflected in others' eyes as in the draining of color during a solar eclipse, yet still it wasn't real to her. So she found herself drifting to the places he'd gone, especially in the late afternoon as fall and winter came on, as the sun turned the western sky hazy, rust-red, reflected in somber ripples on the Yewville River. Never would Elsie drive to Tintern Falls, never would she cross over that bridge. Never again in her lifetime. And this time, the melancholy time, dusk: Never would she not think of him, waiting at the Eagle House for her. She should have been home with Mary Lynda, her daughter. She should have been preparing supper for her husband. She should have been a wife and a mother, not a daughter any longer.

This was the dangerous time.

Possibly Dr. Donaldson wasn't so sympathetic with his wife's grief as people thought, when they were alone. Between him and the older man there'd been rivalry. Donaldson disapproved of Kenelly's business practices. Kenelly had owned a lumberyard in Yewville, but it hadn't been very prosperous. He gave customers credit and rarely collected. The tarpaper roofs of his sheds leaked, his lumber warped and rotted. When customers came to buy single planks, a handful of spikes, he'd say, airily, "Oh hell, just take 'em." His son-in-law Tim Donaldson was a very different kind of man and after Willie Kenelly's death Elsie began to hate him. Her husband! His teeth-brushing, his bathroom noises, his sighs, his chewing, his frowns, his querying of Mary Lynda: "Did you and Mommy go out in the car today? Did you go shopping? Where?" Tim Donaldson never spoke meanly. Always, Dr. Donaldson spoke pleasantly. As he did at his office with his nurse-assistant, and with his patients, the majority of whom were women. His sand-colored hair was trimmed neatly every two weeks and he was a dignified, intelligent man yet after Willie Kenelly's death his jealousy of the old man quickened. Worse, Kenelly had left several thousand dollars to Elsie and Mary Lynda, without so much as mentioning him in the will. And he'd married Elsie, who hadn't been a virgin! Who'd had a certain reputation in Yewville, as a girl. He'd thought the old man would be grateful to him for that, at least.

One night when he touched Elsie in their bedroom, she shrank from him with a look of undisguised dislike. She began crying, not in grief but in anger. *Leave me alone, you disgust me. I don't love you, I love him.*

Next day, in the dusk of an early autumn, Elsie dropped by the Eagle House for just a single drink. She would stay only a few minutes. But Bud Beechum was alone there, waiting. Seeing her face as she entered the barroom, her eyes snatching at the place where her father should have been. "Elsie! Hey." Beechum spoke almost gently. Elsie saw his eyes on her, she saw how he wanted her.

That first time, she'd been drunk. Beechum shut up the Eagle House early. Running his hands over her, greedy and excited and a little scared. Murmuring, "Oh baby, baby." Like he couldn't believe his good luck. Like he was fearful he'd explode, too soon. He led Elsie down into the cellar. A bare light bulb shone in her eyes, screwed into a ceiling fixture amid cobwebs. There was a smell here of stale beer, a stink of cigarettes. She was sexually aroused as she hadn't been in months. What a strange, dirty thing to do; what a wicked thing to do, instead of preparing supper for a hard-working, hungry husband and a sweet little daughter. Elsie and Bud Beechum laughed like kids, and pulled at each other's clothing. This was high-school behavior, this was teen rock music, oh God how they'd been missing it, these years of being adults.

Somehow it hadn't taken with either of them, adulthood.

Next afternoon, repentant, disgusted with herself, Elsie returned to the Eagle House determined it would be only for a single beer, only so she'd feel less lonely, and she'd take the opportunity to explain to Bud Beechum why yesterday had been a mistake, a terrible mistake, and she hoped he wouldn't think poorly of her . . . but this time, too, somehow it happened that Bud Beechum led Elsie down the unsteady wooden steps into the cellar, to the filthy sofa she recognized as a castoff from her cousin Joanie's living room.

"Bud, no. I can't, Bud. I . . ." Elsie heard her voice, plausible and alarmed, and yet there she was in Beechum's rough embrace, and closing her arms about him another time. *It's just I'm so lonely.*

So it happened that, when Elsie changed her mind about seeing Beechum again, Beechum laughed at her, and said, "Elsie. C'mon. I was there. I remember how it was." He knew and she knew, he'd felt her clutching at him, her helpless thrashing and yearning, he'd seen her tears; and so when she stayed away from the Eagle House naturally he began to telephone her at home, "Hey Elsie, c'mon. Don't play hard to get. This is me, Bud. *I know you.*" When she hung up the receiver he began to drive past the handsome brick house on Church Street. Elsie shouldn't have been surprised, she knew who Beechum was, yet somehow she couldn't believe it: what was happening, spinning out of her control. *I made a mistake, I guess. Oh Daddy.*

When she drove to the grocery store, with Mary Lynda, and she glanced up to see Beechum's car in her rearview mirror, she knew—she'd made a serious mistake.

One evening Elsie stopped her car at the Sunoco station. And Beechum stopped his. And they talked together at the edge of the pavement, Elsie brushing wind-whipped hair out of her eyes, Beechum hunching close in a zip-up jacket, bareheaded. Elsie was talking quickly now. There was a smile she had, a smile girls cultivated for such circumstances, desperate, not quite begging, and Elsie smiled this smile, and told Beechum she'd changed her mind about "seeing him," the mistake had been hers. "See? I'd been drinking. I was drunk." Beechum stared at Elsie, not hearing. She understood that the man was sexually aroused, even now. Her breathy words meant nothing to him, only his arousal had meaning, concentrated in his groin but suffused through his tense, quivering body. She saw it in his eyes, angry and triumphant. For the first time she realized that Bud Beechum, her cousin Joanie's tavern-owner husband, might be dangerous. Like Willie Kenelly, he'd killed men in combat. He'd had the power to kill in his hands, and that power had been sweet. Hoping to placate him, to soften the expression on his flushed, sullen face, Elsie said, almost shyly, "Bud, I just feel wrong, doing this to Joanie. If—" "Screw 'Joanie,'" Beechum said savagely. "This has got nothing to do with 'Joanie.'" Beechum's lips twisted, pronouncing his wife's name. Elsie was shocked at the hatred in his voice. For Joanie? She tried to move away, but Beechum caught her by the arm. His fingers were powerful as hooks. "Your father told me some things, baby," Beechum said suggestively. His breath was warm and beery. "What things?" Elsie asked uneasily. "Things you wouldn't want known," Beechum said, smirking, as if Elsie and her deceased father were co-conspirators in some shame. Elsie asked, "About—what? What?" Beechum said, "How your old man felt about—things. Like, wanting to step in front of a train, or off a bridge. This time he told me—" Elsie lost control and slapped Beechum. The bastard's smug fat face! She was too upset even to scream and when Beechum tried to grab her she wrenched free of him, and ran back to her car. Driving away she trembled with rage, and panic at what was happening to her. *Maligning the dead! Beechum would pay.*

9.

YEWVILLE, NY.
JULY 12, 1959.

The call came late at night: two-twenty A.M. Naturally you'd think it was one of Dr. Donaldson's patients.

Through a haze of sleep, resentfully Elsie heard her husband's calm condescending voice. He loved such late-night calls, obviously; if he didn't, he could leave the damned phone off the hook. (The Donaldsons were sleeping, at this time, in the same bed, of course. Technically, at that time, in the summer of 1959, they were still man-and-wife, with all that implies of marital intimacy and obligation.) Then Donaldson's voice sharpened in surprise. "When? *How?*" Elsie was fully awake in an instant. This was something personal, urgent. And yet there was a thrill to her husband's voice, a quavering she knew meant triumph of a kind, vindication. And when Donaldson put the palm of his hand over the receiver, and said gently, as if he were speaking not to his wife but to his nine-year-old daughter, "Elsie, I'm afraid there's bad news. Your father—in Tintern Falls—" Already Elsie was out of bed, and backing away from him, clumsy as a frightened cow in her aqua nylon nightgown with the lacy straps and bodice, shaking her head. *I already knew. Nothing could hurt me, after this.*

10.

YEWVILLE, NY.
MARCH 29, 1957.

This call, Elsie had been expecting.

"Honey? Your mother has—" (there was a moment's pause, delicate as her father's fingers touching her wrist in that way he had, as if to steady her, or caution her, or simply to alert her that something crucial was being communicated) "—passed away."

Elsie surprised herself, beginning to cry. The tears, the childish sobs, burst from her.

Elsie's father disliked women crying, on principle. But he didn't interrupt Elsie. He let her cry for a while, then told her he was at the hospital if she wanted to come by.

Elsie tasted panic. No, no! She didn't want to see her mother's dead, wasted body, her skin the color of yellowed ivory, any more than she'd wanted to see her mother while the woman was alive, and disapproving of her. "Daddy, I can't. I just can't. I'll come by the house, later."

"Suit yourself, Elsie." Her father laughed, she could imagine him rubbing at his nose, a brisk upward gesture with his right forefinger that signaled the end of a conversation he felt had gone on long enough.

11.
YEWVILLE, NY.
1946–1957.

Elsie and her mother hadn't gotten along. It happened in Yewville sometimes, a girl and her mother, living too close, recoiled from each other, hurt and unforgiving.

Elsie's mother hadn't approved of her. Even her marriage to Dr. Donaldson's son Timothy (as Tim was known at that time in Yewville). Mrs. Kenelly had been furious and disgusted with her youngest daughter since she'd caught Elsie, aged seventeen, with her boyfriend Duane Cadmon, in Elsie's attic bedroom, the two of them squirming partly undressed in each other's arms, French-kissing on Elsie's rumpled bed beneath the eaves. Never would Mrs. Kenelly forgive her for such behavior: being cheap, "easy," soiling her reputation, bringing "disgrace" into the Kenelly household. Elsie, who'd had reason to think her mother would be gone from the house for hours, lay pretzel-sprawled in Duane's grip, in a thrumming erotic haze like drowning, and her eyes sprang open in horror to see, past Duane's flushed face, her pinch-faced mother staring at her with ice-pick eyes. In that instant, Mrs. Kenelly slammed the door, hard enough to make Duane wince. Later, they would have it out. Mrs. Kenelly and Elsie. (Where was Willie Kenelly at such times? Nowhere near. Keeping his distance. He never intervened in such female matters.) Elsie's mother spoke bitterly and sarcastically to her, or refused to speak to her at all, even to look at her, as if the sight of Elsie disgusted her; Elsie slammed around the house, sullen, trembling with rage. "How'd anybody get born, Momma, for Christ's sake," Elsie said, her voice rising dangerously so the neighbors might hear, "you act like people don't do things like Duane and I were doing, well God *damn*, Momma, here's news for you: People *do*."

You didn't talk to your mother like this in Yewville in those days. If you did, you were trailer trash. But here was Elsie Kenelly screaming at her mother. And Mrs. Kenelly screaming back calling Elsie "tramp," "slut," telling her "no decent boy" would respect her, or marry her.

Elsie brooded for weeks, months. Years.

Even after Elsie was married to Tim Donaldson, who'd gone away to medical school in Albany, and was eight years older than Elsie; even after she'd married, not just some high school boyfriend, or a guy from the neighborhood, but a "family physician" with a good income who brought her to live with him on Church Street, still Mrs. Kenelly withheld her approval, as she withheld her love. For that was a mother's sole power: to withhold love. And Elsie recoiled with yet more resentment.

Goddamn, Momma! I married a man of a higher class than you did so maybe you're jealous. My husband's a doctor not a lumberyard owner, see?

She didn't love Timothy Donaldson. But she took pride in being Dr. Donaldson's wife.

After Mary Lynda was born, and Elsie's mother had a beautiful baby granddaughter she wished to see, and to hold, and to fuss over, then Elsie realized her power: to exclude her mother from as much of her life as she could. (Of course, Elsie's father was always welcome in the Church Street house. Invited to "drop by" after work: Anytime!) Though in public when it couldn't be avoided, Elsie and her mother hugged stiffly, and managed to kiss each other's cheek. In Mrs. Kenelly's presence Elsie was lightheaded, giddy. She laughed loudly. She drank too much. *Momma I hate you. Momma why don't you die.*

12.
WOLF'S HEAD LAKE, NY.
SUMMER 1946.

Those evenings at the lake. Where Yewville families went for picnics in the summer. Some of the men fished but not Willie Kenelly who thought fishing was boring—"Almost as bad as the army. Almost as bad as life." He laughed his deep belly laugh that made anybody who listened laugh with him.

Elsie was proud of her dad who'd returned home from the War with burn scars and medals to show for his bravery though he dismissed it all as bullshit and rarely spoke of it with anyone except other veterans. And at such times the men spoke in a way that excluded others. They were profane, obscene. They shouted with laughter. Summer nights, they liked most just to sit drinking beer and ale on the deck of the Lakeside Tavern. Often they played cards (poker, euchre) or craps. These could get to be rowdy, raucous times. The sun set late in summer and so, toward dusk, when the sky was bleeding out into night, red-streaked, bruised-looking clouds, serrated and rough-seeming as a cat's tongue, and the surface of the lake had grown calm except for erratic, nervelike shivers and an occasional leap of a fish, the men would have been drinking for hours, ignoring their wives' pleas to come eat supper. "Daddy, can I?" There was Elsie Kenelly on the deck at her father's elbow teasing him for sips of ale from his glass, or a puff of his cigarette, or asking could she play his hand at cards, just once. Could she take his turn at craps, just once. Elsie in her new white two-piece swimsuit with the halter top, ponytailed dark-blond hair and long tanned legs, nails painted frost-pink to match her lipstick: Elsie was sixteen that summer, and very pretty lounging boldly on the deck against the railing by the men's table, liking the attention her dad gave her, and the other men, which meant more to her than the attention she got from boys her own age. Elsie regarded her good-looking father with pride: how muscled his bare shoulders and his bare, heavy torso, covered in a pelt of hairs, mysteriously tattooed and scarred. She was his girl for life. She blushed and squealed with laughter if he teased her. She bit her lip and came close to crying if he spoke harshly to her. Always it was a risk, hanging by her father, you couldn't predict when Willie Kenelly might speak sarcastically, or suddenly lose patience. He'd come back from the War with an air of speechless rage like a permanent twitch or tic somewhere in his body you couldn't detect, though you knew it was there. You felt it, if you touched him. Yet you had to touch him.

"Sure, honey: Toss 'em."

Willie Kenelly spoke negligently, handing his daughter the ivory dice, as if fate were nothing more than the crudest, meanest chance requiring no human skill. Always she would remember those ivory dice! As the men's eyes move onto her young eager body in the white swimsuit, taking in her snub-nosed profile, the graceful fall of her ponytail partway down her back, Elsie is laughing self-consciously, her heart swelling with happiness, and the excitement of the moment as the dice are released from her hand to tumble, roll, come to rest on the sticky tabletop and there's that anxious moment before you dare look to see what, as your Dad says, the dice have to tell you.

Jeffery Deaver

Beautiful

WALL STREET LAWYER, music teacher, journalist, magazine
editor, Jeffery Deaver's occupations now include bestselling writer.
With major movies being based on his novels, and his own position
staked out on the bestseller list, Deaver brings his own set of skills
and quirks to the suspense novel. If it is even possible, his short stories are more insightful and probing, as evidenced in "Beautiful,"
which, when it first appeared in *Ellery Queen's Mystery Magazine* in
their September/October issue, put a completely different spin on
the stalker story.

Beautiful

Jeffery Deaver

He'd found her already.

Oh no, she thought. Lord, no. . . .

Eyes filling with tears of despair, wracked with sudden nausea, the young woman sagged against the window frame as she stared through a crack in the blinds.

The battered Ford pickup—as gray as the turbulent Atlantic Ocean a few hundred yards up the road—eased to a stop in front of her house in this pretty neighborhood of Crowell, Massachusetts, north of Boston. This was the very truck she'd come to dread, the truck that regularly careened through her dreams, sometimes with its tires on fire, sometimes shooting blood from its tailpipe, sometimes piloted by an invisible driver bent on tearing her heart from her chest.

Oh no. . . .

The engine shut off and tapped as it cooled. The dusk light was failing and the interior of the pickup was dark but she knew the occupant was staring at her. In her mind she could see his features as clearly as if he were standing ten feet away in broad August sunlight. Kari Swanson knew he'd have that faint smile of impatience on his face, that he'd be tugging an earlobe marred with two piercings long ago infected and closed up. She knew his breathing would be labored.

Her own breath coming in panicked gasps, hands trembling, Kari drew back from the window. Crawling to the front hallway, she tore open the drawer of a small table and took out the pistol. She looked outside again.

The driver didn't approach the house. He simply played his all-too-familiar game: sitting in the front seat of his old junker and staring at her.

He'd found her already. Just one week after she'd moved here! He'd followed her over two thousand miles. All the effort to cover her tracks had been futile.

The brief peace she'd enjoyed was gone.

David Dale had found her.

Kari—born Catherine Kelley Swanson—was a sensible, pleasant-mannered twenty-eight-year-old who'd been raised in the Midwest by a loving family. She was a natural-born student with a cum laude degree to her name and plans for a Ph.D. Her career until the move here—fashion modeling—had provided her with both a large investment account and a chance to work regularly in such pampering locales as Paris, Cape Town, London, Rio, Bali, and Bermuda. She drove a nice car, had always bought herself modest but comfortable houses, and had provided her parents with a plump annuity.

A seemingly enviable life . . . and yet Kari Swanson had been forever plagued by a debilitating problem.

She was completely beautiful.

She'd hit her full height—six feet—at seventeen, and her weight hadn't varied more than a pound or so off its present mark of 121. Her hair was naturally golden and her skin had a flawless translucent eggshell tone that often left makeup artists with little to do at photo shoots but dab on the currently in-vogue lipstick and eyeshadow.

People, Details, W, Rolling Stone, Paris Match, the *London Times,* and *Entertainment Weekly* had all described Kari Swanson as the "most beautiful woman in the world," or some version of that title. And virtually *every* publication in the industrialized world that even touched on fashion had run a picture of her at one time or another, most of those pictures appearing on the magazines' covers.

That her spellbinding beauty could be a liability was a lesson she learned early. Young Cathy—she didn't become "Kari" the supermodel until age twenty—longed for a normal teenhood, but her appearance kept interfering. She was drawn to the scholastic and artistic crowds in high school, but they rejected her point-blank, assuming either that she was a flighty airhead or that by applying for the literary magazine or history club or forensic society she was mocking the gawky students in those circles.

On the other hand, she was fiercely courted by the cliquish in-crowd of cheerleaders and athletes, few of whom she could stand. To her embarrassment, she was regularly elected queen of various school pageants and dances, even when she refused to compete for the titles.

The dating situation was even more impossible. Most of the nice, interesting boys froze like rabbits in front of her and didn't have the courage to ask her out, assuming they'd be rejected. The jocks and studs relentlessly pursued her—though their motive, of course, was simply to be seen in public with the most beautiful girl in school or to bed her as a trophy lay (naturally none succeeded, but stinging rumors abounded; it seemed that the more adamant the rejection, the more the spurned boy bragged about his conquest).

Her four years at Stanford were virtually the same—modeling, school-work, and hours of loneliness, interrupted by rare evenings and weekends with a few friends who didn't care what she looked like (tellingly, her first lover—a man she was still friendly with—was blind).

After graduation she'd hoped that life would be different, that the spell of her beauty wouldn't be as potent with those who were older and busy making their way in the world. How wrong that was. . . . Men remained true to their dubious missions and, ignoring Kari the person, pursued her as greedily and thoughtlessly as ever. Women grew even more resentful of her than in school, as their figures changed thanks to children and food and sedentary lives.

Kari threw herself into her modeling, easily getting assignments with Ford, Elite, and the other top agencies. But her successful career created a curious irony: She was desperately lonely and yet she had no privacy. Simply because she was beautiful, complete strangers considered themselves intimate friends and constantly approached her in public or sent her long letters describing their intimate secrets, begging for advice and offering her their own opinions on what she should do with her life.

She grew to hate the simple tasks that she'd enjoyed as a child—Christ-mas shopping, playing softball, fishing, jogging. A trip to the grocery store was often a horror; men would speed into line behind her and flirt merci-lessly. More than once she fled from the local Safeway leaving behind a full grocery cart.

But she never felt any real terror until David Dale, the man in the gray pickup truck. Kari had first noticed him in a crowd of onlookers when she was on a job for *Vogue* two years ago.

People always watched photo shoots, of course. They were fascinated with physiques they would never have, with designer clothes that cost their monthly salary, with the gorgeous faces they'd seen gazing at them from newsstands around the country. But something had seemed different about this man. Something troubling.

Not just his massive size—well over six feet tall with huge legs and heavy thighs, long, dangling arms. What had bothered her was the way he'd looked at her through his chunky out-of-fashion glasses: His expression had been one of familiarity.

As if he knew a great deal about her.

And with a chill Kari had realized that *he* was familiar to *her*, too—she'd seen him at other shoots.

Hell, she'd thought, I've got a stalker.

Then—as he'd realized she was looking at him—something even more chilling had happened. His face had broken into a faint smile of impatience. Meaning, it'd seemed to her: Well, here I am. What are you waiting for? Come talk to me.

At first David Dale would simply appear at photo shoots like the one in

Pacific Grove, parking his pickup truck nearby and standing silently just out-side the ring of activity. Then she began to see him hanging out around the doors of the modeling agencies that repped her. He began to write her long letters about himself: his lonely, troubled childhood, his parents' deaths, his former girlfriends (the stories sounded made-up), his current job as an environmental engineer (Kari read "janitor"), his struggle with his weight, his love of Dungeons and Dragons games, television shows he watched. He also knew a frightening amount of information about her—where she'd grown up, what she'd studied at Stanford, her likes and dislikes. He'd clearly read all of the interviews she'd ever given. He took to sending her presents, usually innocuous things like slippers, DayTimers, picture frames, pen-and-pencil sets. Occasionally he'd send her lingerie: tasteful Victoria's Secret items, in her exact size, with a gift receipt courteously enclosed. She threw every-thing out.

Kari generally ignored Dale but the first time he'd parked his gray pickup in front of her house in Santa Monica, she'd stormed up to it and confronted him. Tugging at his damaged ear, breathing in an asthmatic, eerie way, he ignored her rage and fixed her with an adoring gaze, muttering, "Beautiful, beautiful." Upset, she returned to her house. Dale, however, hap-pily pulled out a thermos and began sipping coffee. He remained parked on the street until midnight—a practice that would soon become a daily ritual.

Dale would dog her on the street. He'd sit in restaurants where she was eating and occasionally have a bottle of cheap wine sent to her table. She kept her phone number unlisted and had her mail sent to her agent's office, but he still managed to get notes delivered to her. Kari was one of the few people in America without e-mail on her computer; she was sure that Dale would find her address and inundate her with messages.

She went to the police, of course, and they did what they could but it wasn't much. On the cops' first visit to Dale's ramshackle condo in a low-rent neighborhood, they found a copy of the state's anti-stalking statute sit-ting prominently on his coffee table. Sections were underlined; David Dale knew exactly how far he could go. Kari convinced a magistrate to issue a restraining order. Since Dale had never done anything exactly illegal, though, the order was limited to preventing him from setting foot on her property itself. Which he'd never done anyway.

The incident that finally pushed her over the edge had occurred last month. Dale also made a practice of following the few men whom Kari had the effrontery to date. In this case it'd been a young TV producer. One day Dale had walked into the man's health club in Century City and had a brief conversation with him. The producer had broken their date that night, leav-ing the harsh message that he would've appreciated it if she'd told him she was engaged. He never returned Kari's calls.

That incident had warranted another visit from the police, but the cops found Dale's condo empty and the pickup gone when they arrived.

But Kari knew he'd be back. And so she'd decided it was time to end the problem once and for all. She'd never intended to be a model for more than a few years and she'd figured that this was a good time to quit. Telling only her parents and a few close friends, she instructed a real estate company to lease her house and moved to Crowell, a town she'd been to several years before on a photo shoot. She'd spent a few days there after the assignment and had fallen in love with the clean air and dramatic coastline—and with the citizens of the town, too. They were friendly but refreshingly reserved toward her; a beautiful face didn't place very high on the scale of austere New England values.

She'd left L.A. at two A.M. on a Sunday morning, taking mostly back streets, doubling back and pausing often until she was sure she'd evaded Dale. As she'd driven across the country, elated at the prospect of a new life, she'd occupied much of her time with a fantasy about Dale's committing suicide.

But now she knew that the son of a bitch was very much alive. And had somehow discovered her new address.

Tonight, huddled in the living room of her new house, she heard his pickup's engine start. It idled roughly, the exhaust bubbling from the rusty pipe—sounds she'd grown all too familiar with over the past few years. Slowly the vehicle drove away.

Crying quietly now, Kari laid her head on the carpet. She closed her eyes. Nine hours later she awoke and found herself on her side, knees drawn up, clutching the .38-caliber pistol to her chest, the same way that, as a little girl, she'd wake up every morning curled into a ball and cuddling a stuffed bear she'd named Bonnie.

Later that morning an embittered Kari Swanson was sitting in the office of Detective Brad Loesser, head of the Felonies Division of the Crowell, Massachusetts, police department.

A solid, balding man with sun-baked freckles across the bridge of his nose, Loesser listened to her story with sympathy. He shook his head, then asked, "How'd he find out you were here?"

She shrugged. "Hired a private eye, for all I know." David Dale was exactly as resourceful as he needed to be when it came to Kari Swanson.

"Sid!" the detective shouted to a plain-clothes officer in a nearby cubicle.

The trim young man appeared. Loesser introduced Kari to Sid Harper. Loesser briefed his assistant and said, "Check this guy out and get me the records from . . ." He glanced at Kari. "What police department'd have his file?"

She said angrily, "That'd be departments, Detective. Plural. I'd start with Santa Monica, Los Angeles, and the California State Police. Then you might want to talk to Burbank, Beverly Hills, Glendale, and Orange County. I moved around a bit to get away from him."

"Brother," Loesser said, shaking his head.

Sid Harper returned a few minutes later.

"L.A.'s overnighting us their file. Santa Monica's is coming in two days. I ran the real estate records here." He glanced at a slip of paper. "David Dale bought a condo in Park View two days ago. That's about a quarter mile from Ms. Swanson's place."

" 'Bought'?" Loesser asked, surprised.

"He said it made him feel closer to me if he owned a house in the same town," Kari explained.

"We'll talk to him, Ms. Swanson. And we'll keep an eye on your house. If he does anything overt you can get a restraining order."

"That won't stop him," she muttered. "You know that."

"Our hands're pretty much tied."

She slapped her leg hard. "I've been hearing that for two years. It's time to *do* something." Kari's eyes strayed to a rack of shotguns on the wall nearby. When she looked back she found the detective was studying her closely.

Loesser sent Sid Harper back to his cubicle and then said, "Hey, got something to show you, Ms. Swanson." Loesser reached forward and lifted a picture frame off his desk and handed it to her. "The snapshot on the left there. Whatta you think?"

A picture of a grinning, freckled teenage boy was on the right. On the left side was a shot of a young woman in a graduation gown and mortarboard.

" 'S'my daughter. Elaine."

"She's pretty. You going to ask me if she's got a future in modeling?"

Loesser laughed. "No, ma'am, I wasn't. See, my girl's twenty-five, almost the same age as you. You know something—she's got her whole life ahead of her. Tons and tons of good things waiting. Husband, kids, traveling, jobs."

Kari looked up from the picture into the detective's placid face. He continued, "You got the same things to look forward to, Ms. Swanson. I know this's been hell for you and it may be hell for a while to come. But if you go taking matters into your own hands, which I have a feeling you've been thinking about, well, that's gonna be the end of your life right there."

She shrugged off the advice and asked, "What's the law on self-defense here?"

"Why're you asking me a question like that?" Loesser asked in a whisper.

"What's the answer?"

The detective hesitated, then said, "The commonwealth's real strict about it. Outside of your own house, even on your front porch, it's practically impossible to shoot somebody who's unarmed and get away with a self-defense claim. And I'll tell you, we look right away to see if the body was dragged inside after it was shot, say, and a knife got put into the corpse's hand." The detective paused then added, "And I'm gonna have to be frank, Ms. Swanson, a jury's going to look at you and say, 'Well, of *course* men're going to be following her around. Moth to the flame. She ought to've had a thicker skin.'"

"I better go," Kari said.

Loesser studied her for a moment, then said in a heartfelt tone: "Don't go throwing your life away over some piece of trash like this crazy man."

She snapped, "I don't *have* a life. That's the problem. I thought I could get one back by moving to Crowell. That didn't work." She replaced the picture of Loesser's children on his desk.

"We all go through rough spots from time to time. God helps us through 'em."

"I don't believe in God," Kari said, rising and pulling on her raincoat. "He wouldn't do this to anybody."

"God didn't send David Dale after you," Loesser said.

"I don't mean that," she replied angrily. She lifted a splayed hand toward her face. "I mean, if He existed He wouldn't be cruel enough to make me look like this."

At eight P.M. a car door slammed outside of Kari Swanson's house.

It was Dale's pickup. She recognized the sound of the truck's door latch.

With shaking hands Kari set down her wine and shut off the TV, which she always watched with the sound muted so she'd have some warning if Dale decided to approach the house. She ran to the hallway table and pulled out her gun.

Outside of your own house, even on your front porch, it's practically impossible to shoot somebody who's unarmed and get away with a self-defense claim. . . .

Gripping the pistol, Kari peeked through the front-door curtain. David Dale walked slowly toward her yard, clutching a huge bouquet of flowers. He knew enough not to set foot on her property and so, still standing in the street, he bowed from the waist, the way people do when meeting royalty, and set the bouquet on the grass of the parking strip, resting an envelope next to it. He arranged the flowers carefully, as if they were sitting atop his mother's grave, then stood up and admired them. Then he returned to the truck and drove into the windy night.

Barefoot, Kari walked out into the cold drizzle, seized the flowers, and tossed them into the trash. Returning to the front porch, she paused under the lantern and tore open the envelope, hoping that maybe Detective Loesser had spoken with Dale and frightened him into leaving. Maybe this was a goodbye message.

But, of course, it was not.

To my most Beautiful Lover—

This was a wonderful idea you had. I mean, moving to the East Coast. There were too many people in California vieing (or whatever/ . . . ha, you know I'm a bad speller!!!) for your love and attention and it means a lot to me that you wanted them out of your life. And quitting your modeling job so I don't have to share you with the world anymore . . . You did that ALL for me!!!!

I know we'll be happy here.

I love you always and forever.

David

P.S. Guess what? I FINALLY found that old *New York Scene* magazine where you modeled those leather skirts. Yes, the one I've been looking for for years! Can you believe it!!!! I was so happy! I cut you out and taped you up (so to speak, ha!!!). I have a "Kari" room in my new condo, just like the one in my old place in Glendale (which you never came to visit—boo hoo!!!) but I decided to put these pictures in my bedroom. I got this nice light, it's very low like candlelight and I leave it on all night long. Now I even look forward to having bad dreams so I can wake up and see you.

Inside, she slammed the door and clicked the three deadbolts. Sinking to her knees, she sobbed in fury until she was exhausted and her chest ached. Finally she calmed down, caught her breath, and wiped her face with her sleeve.

Kari stared at the pistol for a long moment, then put it back in the drawer. She walked into the den and, sitting in a straight-back chair, stared into her wind-swept backyard. Understanding at last that the only way this nightmare would end was with David Dale's death or her own.

She turned to her desk and began rummaging through a large stack of papers.

The bar on West 42nd Street was dim and stank of Lysol.

Even though Kari was dressed down—in sweats, sunglasses, and a baseball cap—three of the four patrons and the bartender inside stared at her in astonishment, one bleary-eyed man offering her a flirty smile that revealed more gum than teeth.

The fourth customer snored sloppily at the end of the bar. Everyone except the snoozer smoked.

She ordered a model's cocktail—diet Coke—and sat at a table in the rear of the shabby place. Ten minutes later, a tall man with a massive chest and huge hands entered the bar. He squinted through the cigarette smoke and made his way to Kari's table. He nodded at her and sat, looking around with distaste at the decrepit bar. He appeared exactly as she'd remembered him from their first meeting. That had been several years ago in the Dominican Republic when she'd been on a photo assignment for *Elle* and he'd been taking a day off from a project he'd been working on in nearby Haiti. When, after a few drinks, he'd told her his line of work and wondered if she might need anyone with his particular skills, she'd laughed at the absurd thought. Still, she'd pocketed his card, which contained the phone number she'd called last night.

"Why didn't you want to meet at my place?" he asked her.

"Because of him," she said, lowering her voice, as if uttering the pronoun alone could magically summon David Dale like a demon. "He follows me everywhere. I don't think he knows I came to New York. But I can't take any chances that he'd find out about you."

"Yo," the bartender's raspy voice called, "you want something? I mean, we don't got table service."

The man turned to the bartender, who fell silent under his sharp gaze and returned to inventorying the bottles of cheap well liquor.

The man across from Kari cleared his throat. With a grave voice he said, "You told me what you wanted, but there's something I have to say. First—"

Kari held up a hand to stop him. She whispered, "You're going to tell me it's risky, you're going to tell me that it could ruin my life forever, you're going to tell me to go home and let the police deal with him."

"Yeah, that's pretty much it." He looked into her flinty eyes and when she said nothing more he asked her, "You're sure you want to handle it this way?"

Kari pulled a thick white envelope out of her purse and slid it toward him. "There's the hundred thousand dollars I promised you. That's my answer."

The man hesitated, then picked up the envelope and put it in his pocket.

Nearly a month after his meeting with Kari Swanson, Brad Loesser sat in his office and gazed absently at the rain streaming down his windows. He heard a breathless voice from his doorway.

"We got a problem, Detective," Sid Harper said.

"Which is?" Loesser spun around. Problems on a night like this . . . that was just great. And whatever it was, he bet he'd have to go outside to deal with it.

Harper said, "We got a hit on the wiretap."

After Kari Swanson had met with him last month Loesser had had several talks with David Dale, urging—virtually threatening—him to stop harassing the woman. The man had been infuriating. He'd appeared to listen reasonably to the detective but apparently hadn't paid any attention at all and, with psychotic persistence, explained how he and Kari loved each other and that it was merely a matter of time until they'd be getting married. On their last meeting, Dale had looked Loesser up and down coldly and then began cross-examining *him*, apparently convinced that he'd asked Kari out himself. That incident had so unnerved the detective that he'd convinced a commonwealth magistrate to allow a wiretap on Dale's phone.

"What happened?" Loesser now asked his assistant.

"She called him."

"Who called who?" the detective snapped.

"Kari Swanson called Dale. About a half-hour ago. She was nice as could be. Asked to see him."

"What?"

"She's gotta be setting him up," Harper offered.

Loesser shook his head in disgust. He'd been concerned about this very thing happening. From the moment when he'd seen her eyeing the department's shotguns he'd known that she was determined to end Dale's stalking one way or another. Loesser had kept a close eye on the situation, calling Kari at home frequently over the past weeks. He'd been troubled by her demeanor. She'd seemed detached, almost cheerful, even when Dale had been parked in his usual spot, right in front of her house. Loesser could only conclude that she'd finally decided to stop him and was waiting for an opportune time.

Which was, it seemed, tonight.

"Where's she going to meet him? At her house?"

"No. At the old pier off Charles Street."

Oh, hell, Loesser thought. The pier was a perfect site for a murder—there were no houses nearby and it was virtually invisible from the main roads in town. And there were stairs nearby, leading down to a small floating dock, where Kari, or someone she'd hired, could easily take the body out to sea to dispose of it.

But she didn't know about the wiretap—and that they now had a clue as to what her plans were. If she killed Dale she'd get caught. She'd be in prison for twenty-five years.

Loesser grabbed his coat and sprinted toward the door. "Let's go."

The squad car skidded to a stop at the chain-link fence on Charles Street. Loesser leapt out. He gazed toward the pier, a hundred yards away.

Through the fog and rain the detective could vaguely make out David Dale in a raincoat, clutching a bouquet of roses, walking slowly toward Kari Swanson. The tall woman stood with her back to Dale, hands on the rotting railing, gazing out over the turbulent gray Atlantic as if she was looking for a boat.

The detective shouted for Dale to stop. The sound of the waves, though, was deafening—neither the stalker nor his prey could hear.

"Boost me up," Loesser cried to his assistant.

"You want—?"

The detective himself formed Harper's fingers into a cradle, planted his right foot firmly in the man's hands, and then vaulted over the top of the chain-link. He landed off balance and tumbled painfully onto the rocky ground.

By the time he climbed to his feet and oriented himself, Dale was only twenty feet from Kari.

"Call for backup and an ambulance," he shouted to Harper and then took off down the muddy slope to the pier, unholstering his weapon as he ran. "Don't move! Police!"

But he saw he was too late.

Kari suddenly turned and stepped toward Dale. Loesser couldn't hear a gunshot over the roaring waves or see clearly through the misty rain, but there was no doubt that David Dale had been shot. His hands flew to his chest and, dropping the flowers, he fell backwards and sprawled on the pier.

"No!" Loesser muttered hopelessly, realizing that he himself was going to be the eyewitness who put Kari Swanson in jail. Why hadn't she listened to him? But Loesser was a seasoned professional and he kept his emotions in check as he followed procedure to the letter. He lifted his gun toward the model and shouted, "On the ground, Kari! Now!"

She was startled by the cop's sudden appearance, but she immediately did as she was told and lay face forward on the wet wood.

"Hands behind your back," Loesser ordered, running to her. He quickly cuffed her hands and then turned to David Dale, who lay on the ground amid the crushed roses, writhing and howling in agony. Kari was saying something, but her face was turned away and Loesser couldn't hear her words. Besides, the detective's attention was wholly on keeping David Dale alive so that Kari would at least avoid a murder conviction.

"Oh God, oh God," the stalker cried.

Loesser pried Dale's hands away from his chest and ripped open his shirt, looking for the entry wound.

But he couldn't find it.

"Where're you hit?" the detective shouted. "Talk to me. Talk to me!"

But the big man continued to sob and shake hysterically and didn't respond.

Sid Harper ran up, panting. He dropped to his knees beside Dale.

"Ambulance'll be here in five minutes. Where's he hit?"

The detective said, "I don't know. I can't find the wound."

The young cop, too, examined the stalker. "There's no blood."

Still, Dale kept moaning as if he were in unbearable pain. "Oh God, no. . . . No. . . ."

Finally Loesser heard Kari Swanson call out, "He's fine. I didn't shoot him."

"Get her up," the detective said to Harper as he continued to examine Dale. "I don't understand it. He—"

"Jesus Christ," Sid Harper's stunned voice whispered.

Loesser glanced at his assistant, who was staring at Kari with his mouth open.

The detective himself turned to look at her. He blinked in astonishment.

"I really didn't shoot him," Kari insisted.

Except . . . *Was* this Kari Swanson? The woman was the same height and had the same figure and hair. And the voice was the same. But in place of the extraordinary beauty that had burned itself into Loesser's memory on their first meeting was a very different face: This woman had a bumpy, unfortunate nose, thin, uneven lips, a fleshy chin, wrinkles in her forehead and around her eyes.

"Are you . . . Who are you?" Loesser stammered.

She gave a faint smile. "It's me, Kari."

"But . . . I don't understand."

She gave a contemptuous glance at Dale, still lying on the pier, and said to Loesser, "When he followed me to Crowell I finally realized what had to happen: One of us had to die . . . and I picked me."

"You?"

She nodded. "I killed the person he was obsessed with: Kari the supermodel. A few years ago, down in the Caribbean, I met a plastic surgeon. His office was in Manhattan but he also ran a free clinic in Haiti. He'd rebuild the faces of natives injured in catastrophic accidents." She laughed. "He gave me his card as a joke—saying if I ever needed a plastic surgeon give him a call. Just trying to pick me up, of course, but I liked it that he was doing volunteer work and we hit it off. I kept his number. When I decided last month I had to do something about Dale, I thought about him. I figured if he could make such badly deformed people look normal, he could make a beautiful person look normal, too. I took the train down to New York and met with him. He didn't want to do the operation at first, but I donated a hundred thousand dollars to his clinic. That changed his mind."

Loesser studied her closely. She wasn't ugly. She simply looked average—like any of ten million people you'd meet on the street and not glance twice at.

Someone whose attractiveness would be found in who she was rather than what she looked like.

David Dale's terrible moaning rose up over the sound of the wind—not from physical pain but from the horror that the beauty that had consumed him for so long was now gone. "No, no, no . . ."

Kari asked Loesser, "Can you take these things off me?" Holding up the cuffs.

Harper unhooked them.

As Kari pulled her coat tighter around her, a mad voice suddenly filled the air, rising above the sound of the ferocious waves. "How could you?" Dale cried, rising to his knees. "How could you do this to me?"

Kari crouched in front of him. "To *you?*" she raged. "What I look like, who I am, the life I lead . . . those things don't have a goddamn thing to do with you and they never did!" She gripped his head in both hands and tried to turn it toward her. "Look at me."

"No!" He struggled to keep his face averted.

"Look at me!"

Finally he did.

"Do you love me now, David?" she asked with a cold smile on her new face. "Do you?"

He scrabbled away in revulsion and began to run back toward the street. He stumbled, then picked himself up and continued to sprint away from the pier.

Kari Swanson rose and shouted after him, "Do you love me, David? Do you love me now? Do you? Do you?"

"Hey, Cath," the man said, surveying the grocery cart she was pushing.

"What?" she asked. The plastic surgery had officially laid "Kari" to rest and she was now using only variations on "Catherine" Swanson.

"I think we're missing something," Carl replied with exaggerated gravity.

"What?"

"Junk food," he answered.

"Oh, no." She too frowned in mock alarm as she examined the cart. Then she suggested, "Nachos'd solve the problem."

"Ah. Good. Back in a minute." Carl—a man with an easy temperament and an endless supply of bulky fisherman's sweaters—ambled off down the snack-food aisle. He was a late-bloomer, a second-career lawyer who was exactly five years older and two inches taller than Cathy. He'd picked her up at the annual Crowell St. Patrick's Day festival ten days ago and they'd spent a half-dozen delightful afternoons and evenings together, doing absolutely nothing.

Was there a future between them? Cathy had no idea. They certainly enjoyed each other's company, but Carl had yet to spend the night. And he still hadn't given her the skinny on his ex-wife.

Both of which were, of course, vital benchmarks in the life of a relationship.

But there was no hurry. Catherine Swanson wasn't looking hard for a man. Her life was a comfortable mélange of teaching high school history, jogging along the rocky Massachusetts shore, working on her master's at BU, and spending time with a marvelous therapist who was helping her forget David Dale, about—and from—whom she'd heard nothing in the past six months.

She moved forward in the checkout line, trying to remember if she had charcoal for the grill. She thought—

"Say, miss, excuse me," mumbled a man's low voice behind her. She recognized his intonation immediately—the edgy, intimate sound of obsession.

Cathy spun around to see a young man in a trench coat and a stocking cap. Instantly she thought of the hundreds of strangers who had relentlessly pursued her on the street, in restaurants, and in checkout lanes just like this one. Her palms began to sweat. Her heart started pounding fiercely, jaw trembling. Her mouth opened but she couldn't speak.

But then Cathy saw that the man wasn't looking at her at all. His eyes were fixed on the magazine rack next to the cash register. He muttered, "That *Entertainment Weekly* there? Could you hand it to me?"

She passed him the magazine. Without thanking her he flipped quickly to an article inside. Cathy couldn't tell what the story was about, only that it featured three or four cheesecakey pictures of some young, brunette woman, which he stared at intently.

Cathy slowly forced herself to calm. Then, suddenly, her shaking hands rose to her mouth and she began laughing out loud. The man looked up once from the pictures of his dream girl then returned to his magazine, not the least curious about this tall, plain woman and what she found so funny. Cathy wiped the tears of laughter from her eyes, turned back to the cart, and began loading her groceries onto the belt.

Max Allan Collins

Unreasonable Doubt

MAX ALLAN COLLINS writes the Nathan Heller series of historical private eye novels that focus on some of the major events and people that helped shape the previous century—everybody from Al Capone to Amelia Earhart. The Hellers are the most important series of its kind being written today—many imitators, no equals. In addition to the Hellers and many other projects, Collins writes an extremely popular series of paperback originals based on tragedies such as the *Titanic*. "Unreasonable Doubt" was first published in *The Mysterious Press Anniversary Anthology*.

Unreasonable Doubt

Max Allan Collins

In March of 1947, I got caught up in the notorious Overell case, which made such headlines in Los Angeles, particularly during the trial that summer. The double murder—laced as it was with underage sex in a lurid scenario that made *Double Indemnity* seem tame—hit the front pages in Chicago, as well. But back home I never bragged about my little-publicized role, because—strictly speaking—I was the one guy who might have headed the whole thing off.

I was taking a deductible vacation, getting away from an Illinois spring that was stubbornly still winter, in trade for Southern California's constant summer. My wife, who was pregnant and grouchy, loved L.A., and had a lot of friends out there, which was one of the reasons for the getaway; but I was also checking in with the L.A. branch office of the A-1 Detective Agency, of which I was the president.

I'd recently thrown in with Fred Rubinski, a former Chicago cop I'd known since we were both on the pickpocket detail, who from before the war had been running a one-man agency out of a suite in the Bradbury Building at Third and Broadway in downtown Los Angeles.

It was Friday morning, and I was flipping through the pages of *Cue* magazine in the outer office, occasionally flirting with Fred's good-looking blonde receptionist—like they say, I was married but I wasn't dead—waiting to get together with Fred, who was in with a client. The guy had just shown up, no appointment, but I didn't blame Fred for giving him precedence over me.

I had seen the guy go in—sixtyish, a shade taller than my six feet, distinguished, graying, somewhat fleshy, in a lightweight navy suit that hadn't come off the rack; he was clearly money.

After about five minutes, Fred slipped out of the office and sat next to me, speaking *sotto voce*.

My partner looked like a balding, slightly less ugly Edward G. Robinson; a natty dresser—today's suit was a gray pinstripe with a gray and white striped tie—he was a hard, round ball of a man.

"Listen, Nate," he said, "I could use your help."

I shrugged. "Okay."

"You're not tied up today—I know you're on vacation . . ."

"Skip it. We got a well-heeled client who needs something done, right away, and you don't have time to do it yourself."

The bulldog puss blinked at me. "How did you know?"

"I'm a detective. Just keep in mind, I've done a few jobs out here, but I don't really know the town."

Fred sat forward. "Listen, this guy is probably worth a cool million—Walter E. Overell, he's a financier, land developer, got a regular mansion over in Pasadena, in the Flintridge district, real exclusive digs."

"What's he want done?"

"Nothin' you can't handle. Nothin' big."

"So you'd rather let me hear it from him?"

Fred grinned; it wasn't pretty. "You are a detective."

In the inner office, Overell stood as Fred pulled up a chair for me next to the client's. As the financier and I shook hands, Fred said, "Mr. Overell, this is Nathan Heller, the president of this agency, and my most trusted associate."

He left out that I wasn't local. Which I didn't disagree with him for doing—it was good tactically.

"Of course, Mr. Heller commands our top rate, Mr. Overell—one hundred a day."

"No problem."

"We get expenses, and require a two-hundred-dollar retainer, non-refundable."

"Fine."

Fred and I made sure not to look at each other throughout my partner's highway robbery of this obviously well-off client.

Soon we got down to it. Overell slumped forward as he sat, hands locked, his brow deeply furrowed, his gray eyes pools of worry.

"It's my daughter, Mr. Heller. She wants to get married."

"A lot of young girls do, Mr. Overell."

"Not this young. Louise is only seventeen—and won't be eighteen for another nine months. She can't get married at her age without my consent—and I'm not likely to give it."

"She could run away, sir. There are states where seventeen is plenty old enough—"

"I would disinherit her." He sighed, hung his head. "Much as it would kill me . . . I would disown and disinherit her."

Fred put in, "This is his only child, Nate."

I nodded. "Where do things stand, currently?"

Overell swallowed thickly. "She says she's made up her mind to marry her 'Bud' on her eighteenth birthday."

"Bud?"

"George Gollum—he's called Bud. He's twenty-one. What is the male term for a golddigger, anyway?"

I shrugged. "Greedy bastard?"

"That will do fine. I believe he and she have . . ." Again, he swallowed and his clenched hands were trembling, his eyes moist. ". . . known each other, since she was fourteen."

"Pardon me, sir, but you use the term 'known' as if you mean in the . . . Biblical sense?"

He nodded curtly, turned his gaze away; but his words were clipped: "That's right."

An idea was hatching; I didn't care for it much, but the idea wasn't distasteful enough to override my liking of a hundred bucks a day.

Overell was saying, "I believe he met my daughter when he was on leave from the Navy."

"He's in the Navy?"

"No! He's studying at the Los Angeles campus of U.C., now—pre-med, supposedly, but I doubt he has the brains for it. They exchanged letters when he was serving overseas, as a radioman. My wife, Beulah, discovered some of these letters . . . They were . . . filth."

His head dropped forward, and his hands covered his face.

Fred glanced at me, eyebrows raised, but I just said to Overell, "Sir, kids are wilder today than when we were young."

He had twenty, twenty-five years on me, but it seemed the thing to say.

"I've threatened to disinherit her, even if she waits till she's of legal age—but she won't listen, Louise simply won't listen."

Overell went on, at some length, to tell me of Louise's pampered childhood, her bedroom of dolls and Teddy bears in their "estate," the private lessons (tennis, riding, swimming), her French governess who had taught her a second language as well as the niceties of proper etiquette.

"Right now," the disturbed father said, "she's waging a campaign to win us over to this twenty-one-year-old 'boyfriend' of hers."

"You haven't met him?"

"Oh, I've met him—chased him off my property. But she insists if we get to know Bud, we'll change our minds—I've consented to meet with them, let them make their case for marriage."

"Excuse me, but is she pregnant?"

"If she were, that would carry no weight whatsoever."

I let the absurdity of that statement stand.

Overell went on: "I've already spoken to Mr. Rubinski about making certain . . . arrangements . . . if that is what Louise and her Bud reveal to us tomorrow evening."

"Tomorrow?"

"Yes, we have a yacht—the *Mary E.*—moored at Newport Harbor." He smiled embarrassedly, the first time he'd smiled in this meeting. "Excuse my pomposity—'yacht' is rather overstating it, it's really just a little forty-seven footer."

Little?

"Louise asked me to invite her and her 'boyfriend' aboard for the evening, with her mother and myself, so we can all get to know each other better, and talk, 'as adults.' "

"And you're going along with this?"

"Yes—but only to humor her, and as a . . . subterfuge for my own feelings, my own desires, my own designs. I want you to explore this boy's background—I don't know anything about him, except that he's local."

"And you think if I turn up something improper in this boy's past, it would matter to your daughter?"

His eyes were so tight, it must have hurt. "If he's the male equivalent of a golddigger, won't he have other girls, other women? That would show Louise the light."

"Mr. Overell, is your daughter attractive?"

"Lovely. I . . . I have a picture in my wallet, but I'm afraid she's only twelve in it."

"Never mind that right now—but you should know there's every possibility that these two young people . . . and twenty-one seems younger to me, every day . . . really *are* nuts about each other. Gollum may not be seeing anybody else."

"But you can find out!"

"Sure, but . . . aren't you overlooking something?"

"Am I?"

"Your daughter is underage. If I catch 'em in the backseat of this boy's jalopy, we can put him away—or at least threaten to."

"Statutory rape?"

I held up two palms, pushed the air. "I know, I know, it would embarrass your daughter . . . but even the threat of it ought to send this rat scurrying."

Overell looked at Fred for an opinion. Fred was nodding.

"Makes sense, Mr. Overell," he said.

Overell's eyes tensed, but his brow unfurrowed some; another sigh seemed to deflate his entire body, but I could sense relief on his part, and resignation, as he said, "All right . . . all right. Do what you think is best."

We got him a contract, and he gave us a check.

"Can I speak with your wife about this matter?" I asked him.

He nodded. "I'm here with Beulah's blessing. You have our address—you can catch her at home this afternoon, if you like."

I explained to him that what I could do today would be limited, because Overell understood that his daughter and would-be future son-in-law were (and he reported this with considerable distaste) spending the day "picnicking in the desert." But I could go out to the Los Angeles campus of the University of California and ask around about Bud.

"You can inquire out there about my daughter as well," he said.

"Isn't she still in high school?"

"Unfortunately, no—she's a bright girl, skipped a grade. She's already in college."

Sounded like Louise was precocious in a lot of ways.

Around ten-thirty that same morning, I entered at Westwood Boulevard and Le Conte Avenue, rolling in my rental Ford through a lushly terraced campus perched on a knoll overlooking valleys, plains and hills. The buildings were terra cotta, brick and tile in a Romanesque motif.

I asked a cute coed for directions to the student union, and was sent to Kerckhoff Hall, an imposing building of Tudor design with a pinnacled tower. I was further directed to a sprawling high-ceilinged room where college kids played Ping-Pong or played cards or sat in comfy chairs and couches and drank soda pop and smoked cigarettes. Among sweaters and casual slacks and bobby socks, I stuck out like the thirty-eight-year-old sore thumb I was in my tan summer suit; but the kids were all chatty and friendly. My cover was that Bud had applied for a job—what that job was, of course, I couldn't say—and I was checking up on him for his prospective employer.

Not everybody knew Bud Gollum or Louise Overell, of course—too big a campus for that. But a few did.

Bud, it seemed, was a freshman, going to school on Uncle Sam. Other first-year fellas—younger than Bud, probably nineteen—described him as "a good guy, friendly, and smart," even "real smart." But several didn't hide their dislike of Bud, saying he was smart-alecky, writing him off as a "wiseguy."

A mid-twenties junior with an anchor tattooed on his forearm knew Bud as a fellow Navy veteran, and said Bud had been a Radio Man First Class.

"Listen," the husky little dark-haired, dark-eyed ex-gob said, "if you're considering him for a job, give him a break—he's smarter than his grades make him look."

"Really?"

"Yeah, when you see his transcripts, you're going find him pulling down some low junk, so far this year . . . but it's that little skirt's fault. I mean, they don't let dummies into pre-med around here."

"He's got a girlfriend distracting him?"

The gob nodded. "And it's pretty damn serious—she's a young piece of tail, pardon my French, built like a brick shithouse. Can hardly blame him for letting his studies slide."

"Well, I hope he wouldn't be too preoccupied to do a good job—"

"No, no! He's a right fella! Lives at home with his mom and stepdad—he's an assistant scoutmaster, for Christ sakes!"

"Sounds clean cut."

"Sure—he loves the outdoors, always going hiking in the mountains up around Chatsworth, backpacking out into the desert."

"His girl go in for that?"

"They go everywhere together, joined at the hip . . . don't give me that look, buddy! I mean, haven't you ever had a female lead you around by the dick?"

"No," I said, and when he arched an eyebrow, I added, "Does my wife count?"

He grinned at me. "Does mine?"

A table of girls who were smoking and playing pitch allowed me to pull up a chair for a few questions; they weren't very cute, just enough to make me want to bust out crying.

"I don't know what a cute guy like that sees in ol' Stone Face," a blonde with blue eyes and braces said. I liked the way she was getting lipstick on her cigarette.

"Stone Face?"

"Yeah," a brunette said. She wasn't smoking, like her friends, just chewing and snapping her gum. "That Overell gal's got this round face like a frying pan and's got about as much expression."

"Except when she giggles," a redhead said, giggling.

All the girls began to giggle, the blonde saying, "Then she really looks like a dope!"

"She laughs at everything that idiot says," the brunette said. "They hang onto each other like ivy—it's sickening."

That was all I learned at the college, and the effort took about three hours; but it was a start.

Pasadena was the richest city per capita in the nation, and the residential neighborhood where the Overells resided gave credence to that notion—mansions with sunken gardens, swimming pools and tennis courts on winding, flower-edged, palm-flung streets. The white mission-style mansion at 607 Los Robles Drive, with its well-manicured, lavishly landscaped lawn, was no exception.

Mrs. Overell was younger than her husband by perhaps ten years, an attractive dark-blonde woman whose nicely buxom shape was getting a tad matronly. We sat by the pool watching the mid-afternoon sun highlight the shimmering blue surface with gold. We drank iced tea and she hid her feelings behind dark sunglasses and features as expressionless as the Stone Face with which those coeds had tagged her daughter.

"I don't know what I can tell you, Mr. Heller," she said, her voice a bland alto, "that my husband hasn't already."

"Well, Mrs. Overell, I'm chiefly here for two reasons. First, I can use a photo of your daughter, a recent one."

"Certainly." A tiny smile etched itself on the rigid face. "I should have thought of that—Walter carries a photo of Louise when she was still a child. He'd like to keep her that way."

"You do agree with this effort to break off Louise's relationship with this Gollum character?"

"Mr. Heller, I'm not naïve enough to think that we can succeed at that. But I won't stand in Walter's way. Perhaps we can postpone this marriage long enough for Louise to see through this boy."

"You think he's a male golddigger, too?"

She shrugged. "He doesn't come from money."

"You know where he lives? Have an address?"

"He's here in Pasadena."

I couldn't picture a wrong side of the tracks in this swanky burg.

"No, I don't have an address," she was saying, "but he's in North Fair Oaks . . . where so many coloreds have moved in."

I had been met at the door by a Negro butler, who I supposed had to live somewhere.

But I didn't press the subject. I sipped my tea and offered, gently, "If your daughter is willing to wait to marry this boy till her eighteenth birthday . . . which I understand is many months from now . . . perhaps what you ought to do is humor her, and hope this affair cools off."

The blue and gold of the sun-kissed pool shimmered in the dark lens of her sunglasses. "I would tend to agree with you, Mr. Heller. In time she might come to her senses of her own volition. But Walter is a father who has not adjusted to losing his little girl . . . she's our only child, you know . . . and I do share his concern about the Gollum boy."

"That's the other reason I wanted to speak with you, directly," I said, and—delicately—I filled her in on my notion to catch the two in flagrante delicto. I wanted to make sure she wouldn't mind putting her daughter through the public embarrassment a statutory rape accusation would bring.

Another tiny smile etched itself. "We've gotten quite used to Louise embarrassing us, Mr. Heller."

Mrs. Overell thought I might have trouble catching them, however, since they so often went hiking and camping in the West San Fernando Valley—like today. That would be tough: I was used to bagging my quarry in backseats and motel rooms.

As it turned out, Mrs. Overell was able to provide a snapshot, filched from her daughter's room, of both Louise and her beau. They were in swimsuits, at the beach on towels, leaning back on their elbows smiling up at the camera.

Louise had a nice if faintly mocking, superior smile—not exactly pretty, and indeed round-faced, but not bad; and she was, as that ex-gob had so succinctly put it, built like a brick shithouse. This girl had everything Jane Russell did except a movie contract.

As for Bud, he was blond, boyish, rather round-faced himself, with wire-rimmed glasses and a grin that somehow lacked the suggestion of cunning his girlfriend's smile possessed. He had the slender yet solid build so often seen in Navy men.

I spent another hour or so in Pasadena, which had a sleepy air of prosperity spawned by the many resort hotels, the formidable buildings, the pretentious homes, the bounteous foliage. The North Fair Oaks section did seem to have more than its share of colored residents, but this was still nicer than anywhere I'd ever lived. With the help of a service station attendant—the private detective's best friend in a strange city—I located the home of Dr. Joseph Stomel, married to Bud's mother, Wilhilmina. But I had no intention of talking to anyone there, as yet. This was strictly a point of reference for the eventual tailing of Gollum.

That was Friday, and between the college and the Pasadena run, I'd earned my hundred bucks. I spent all day Saturday with my wife, and friends, enjoying our premature summer vacation.

Then I went back to work Saturday night, though I looked like a tourist in my blue sportshirt and chinos. The camera I had with me was no tourist's Brownie, however, rather a divorce dick's Speed Graphic loaded with infrared film and the world's least conspicuous flash.

It was around ten o'clock when I turned right off State Highway 55, my rental Ford gliding across the low-slung spit over the mouth of an inlet of landlocked Newport Bay, dotted by sails, glistening with moonbeams, dancing with harbor lights. Seaside cottages clustered along the bay shore, but grander dwellings perched on islands in the lagoon-like bay, California-style Riviera-worthy stucco villas, a suitable backdrop for the fleet of yachts and other pleasure crafted moored here.

My behind was moored in a booth in the Beachfront Café, a chrome-heavy diner with a row of windows looking out on the dock and the peaceful, soothing view of lights twinkling and pleasure crafts bobbing on the moon-washed water. I ate a cheeseburger and fries and sipped coffee as I kept watch; I had a perfect view of the sleek cruiser, the *Mary E.* A few lights were on in the boat, and occasional movement could be made out, but just vague shapes. No different than any number of other boats moored here, gently rocking.

Overell had told me that he and his wife would be entertaining their daughter and her beau aboard the cruiser, having dinner, talking out their problems, perhaps even coming to some sort of understanding. What I had in mind was to follow the young lovers when they left this family powwow. Since Bud lived at home with his mom, I figured the couple would either go to some lover's lane to park, or maybe hit a motel. Either way, my Speed Graphic would collect the evidence needed to nail Bud for statutory rape. It's not elegant, but it's a living.

Around eleven I spotted them, coming down a ladder, stepping onto the swaying dock: Bud and Louise. Hazel-haired, taller than I'd imagined her, she did have an admirable top-heavy figure, which her short-sleeved pale blue sweater and darker blue pedal pushers showed off nicely. Bud wore a yellow sportshirt and brown slacks, and they held hands as they moved rather quickly away from the boat.

I was preparing to leave the café and follow them up to the parking lot, and Bud's car—Mrs. Overell had given me the make and color, and I'd already spotted it, a blue Pontiac convertible, pre-war, battered but serviceable—only, they threw me a curve in addition to Louise's.

The couple were heading up the ramp toward the café!

Absurdly, I wondered if they'd made me—impossible, since they hadn't seen me yet—and I hunkered over my coffee as the lovebirds took a couple of stools at the counter, just about opposite my window booth.

At first they were laughing, at some private joke; it seemed rather forced—were they trying to attract attention?

Then they both ordered burgers and fries and sat there talking, very quietly. Even a trained eavesdropper like me couldn't pick up a word. Perhaps they'd had a rough evening with her folks, because periodically one would seem to be comforting the other, stroking an arm, patting a shoulder, reassuringly.

What the hell was going on? Why did they need a burger, when presumably that luxury cruiser had a well-stocked larder? And if they wanted to get away from her parents and that boat, why hang around the dock? Why not climb in Bud's convertible and seek a burger joint that wasn't in her parents' watery backyard?

Such thoughts bobbed like a buoy in my trained snoop's mind as the couple sat at the counter and nibbled at their food. It was a meal any respectable young couple could down in a matter of minutes. But forty-five minutes later, the two were still sitting on those stools, sometimes picking at barely eaten, very-cold-by-now food, often staring soulfully into each other's eyes. Every other stool at that counter had seen at least three customer backsides in the same span.

I was long since used to boring stakeout duty; but it was unnerving having my subjects so near at hand, for so long a time. I finally got up and went to the men's room, partly to test whether they'd use that opportunity to slip away (again, had they made me?), and partly because after three cups of coffee, I needed to take a piss.

When I got back, Bud and Louise were still sitting on their stools, Louise ever so barely swivelling on hers, like a kid in a soda shop. Frustrated, confused, I settled back into my booth, and glanced out the window, and the world exploded.

Actually, it was just the *Mary E.* that exploded, sending a fireball of flame rising from the cruiser, providing the clear night sky with thunder, hurling burning debris everywhere, making waves out of the placid waters, rocking the pier.

Rocking the café patrons, too, most of them anyway. Everyone except the employees leapt to their feet, screaming, shouting, running outside into a night turned orange by flame, dabbed gray by smoke.

Almost everyone—Bud and Louise were still just sitting at the counter, albeit looking out the window, numbly.

Me, I was on my feet, but then I settled back into the booth, trying to absorb what I'd seen, what I was *seeing*. I knew my client was dead, and so was his wife—two people I'd spoken to at length, just the day before—as that cruiser was already a listing, smoking shambles, sinking stern first into the bay's eighteen feet.

Finally, the couple headed outside, to join the gathering crowd at the water's edge. I followed them. Sirens were cutting the air, getting closer, closer.

Louise was crying now, hysterical, going from one gaping spectator to another, saying, "My father was on that boat! My mother, too! Somebody save them—somebody rescue them . . . somebody has to rescue them!"

The boyfriend remained at the side of the stricken girl as she moved through the crowd, making her presence blatantly known, Bud's boyish face painted with dismay and shock and reflected flames.

I went to my rental car and got my Speed Graphic. I wouldn't even need the flash—plenty of light.

Snagging shots of the dying boat, and the distraught daughter and her beau, I heard the speculation among the boating-wise onlookers, as to the explosion's cause.

"Butane," one would say.

"Or gasoline," another would say.

But this ex-Marine wasn't so easily fooled.

Butane, hell—I smelled dynamite.

Before long, the Coast Guard arrived, and fire trucks, and police from nearby Santa Ana and Orange County Sheriff's Department personnel. The chief of the Newport Beach Police showed, took over the investigation, questioned the tearful, apparently anguished Louise Overell and promptly released her, and her boyfriend.

Pushing through the bustle, I introduced myself to the chief, whose name was Hodgkinson, and told him I was an investigator who'd been doing a job for Walter Overell.

"A job related to what happened here tonight?" the heavyset chief asked, frowning.

"Very possibly."

"You suspect foul play?"

"Oh yeah."

"Where are you staying, Mr. Heller?"

"The Beverly Hills Hotel."

That impressed him—he didn't realize it was a perk of my security work for the hotel. "Well, obviously, Mr. Heller, I'm gonna be tied up here quite a while. Can you come by the station tomorrow sometime? Tomorrow's Sunday—make it Monday. And if I'm not there, I may be back out here."

"Sure. Why did you let those two kids go?"

"Are you kiddin'? We'll be dredging her parents' scorched corpses outa the drink before too long. It's only decent to spare that girl the sight of that."

Only decent.

Sunday I took my wife to the beach at Santa Monica—she was only a few months pregnant and still looked great in a swim suit. Peggy was an actress and recently had a small role in a Bob Hope picture, and even out here her Deanna Durbin-ish good looks attracted attention.

She ragged me, a little, because I seemed preoccupied, and wasn't terribly good company. But that was because I was thinking about the Overell "Yacht Murder" (as the papers had already starting calling it). I had sold my crime scene photos to Jim Richardson, at the *Examiner*, by the way, for three hundred bucks. I was coming out way ahead of the game, considering my client and his wife had been blown to smithereens the night before.

Call it guilt, call it conscience, call it sheer professionalism, but I knew I hadn't finished this job. Walter Overell deserved more for that two-hundred-buck retainer—just like he'd deserved better from that shrewd sexed-up daughter of his.

So on Monday, bright and early, looking like a tourist in sportshirt and chinos, I began looking. What was I looking for? A slip of paper . . . a slip of paper in the desert . . . sounds worse than a needle in a haystack, but it wasn't. I found the damn thing before noon.

Chatsworth was a mountain-ringed hamlet in the West San Fernando Valley that used a Wild West motif to attract tourists, offering them horseback riding and hiking trails, with the ocean and beaches and desert close at hand for lovers of the outdoors—like that Boy Scout Bud Gollum and his bosomy Campfire Girl.

The guy behind the counter in the sparse storefront at the Trojan Powder Company looked a little like Gabby Hayes—white-bearded, prospector-grizzled, in a plaid shirt and bib overalls. But he had his original teeth and a faint British accent, which took him out of the running for playing a Roy Rogers or Gene Autry sidekick.

This was the owner of the place, and he was looking at the photo I'd handed him, taking a closer look than he had at the Illinois PI badge I'd flashed him.

"That young woman will never drown," he said, with a faintly salacious smile.

"I'm not so much interested whether you recognize her tits as if her face is familiar—or her boyfriend's."

"I recognize the whole batch of them—both faces, both bosoms, for that matter. The girl didn't come in, though—she sat out in their convertible—a Pontiac, I believe. I could see her right through the front window."

"Did he make a purchase?"

"I should say—fifty sticks of dynamite."

Jesus, that was a lot of dinah.

"This is fresh in my memory," the proprietor said, "because it was just last Friday."

Day before the boat blew up.

"Can anybody stroll in here and buy that stuff?"

"It's a free country—but back in the early days of the war, when folks were afraid of saboteurs, city and county officials passed an ordinance, requiring purchasers to sign for what they buy." I liked the sound of that. "Can I see the signed receipt?"

Bud had not signed his own name—"R.L. Standish" had purchased the fifty sticks of dynamite—but I had no doubt handwriting experts would confirm this as the Boy Scout's scrawl.

"Some officers from Newport Beach will be along to talk to you," I told him.

"Fine—what about reporters?"

"Good idea," I said, and used the phone.

Examiner editor Richardson paid me another C-note for the tip, and the proprietor of the Trojan Powder Company earned his own fifty bucks of Mr. Hearst's money for providing the exclusive.

I found Chief Hodgkinson at the Newport Beach dock, where the grim, charred wreckage had been surfaced from the depth of eighteen feet—about all that remained was the black blistered hull. The sun was high and golden on the waters, and the idyllic setting of stucco villas in the background and expensive pleasure craft on either side was turned bizarre by the presence of the scorched husk of the *Mary E.*

Seated in the Beachfront Café across from the blue-uniformed, heavyset chief, in the same booth I'd occupied Saturday night, I filled him in on what I'd discovered up Chatsworth way. He excused himself to pass the information along to a couple of DA's investigators who would make the trip to the Trojan Powder Company.

When the chief returned, bearing a plate with a piece of pecan pie with whipped cream, he sat and ate and shared some information.

"Pretty clear your instincts were right about those kids," he said gruffly but good-naturedly. "It's just hard to believe—patricide *and* matricide. Only in California."

"The late Walter Overell was supposedly worth around a million. And, like I told you, he was threatening to cut his daughter off, if she married her four-eyed romeo."

"What made you think to go looking for that sales receipt, Mr. Heller?"

"I knew they'd gone 'picnicking' in the San Fernando Valley, and a college pal of Bud's said the loving couple liked to hike up around Chatsworth. Plus, I knew if Bud had been a Radio Man First Class in the war, he had the technical knowhow to rig a bomb. Hell, Chief, Saturday night, you could smell the dynamite in the air—and the murder."

He nodded his agreement. "It's as cold-blooded a crime as I've ever come across. We found thirty-one sticks of unexploded dynamite in the galley, crude time-bomb thing, rigged with wire and tape to an alarm clock—second of two charges. Bulkhead kept the larger one from goin' off. Which was lucky."

"Not for the Overells."

"No, the smaller bundle of dynamite was enough to kill 'em plenty dead," he said, chewing a bite of pecan pie. "But it wasn't enough to cover up the rest of the evidence."

"Such as?"

"Such as what the coroner discovered in his autopsies—before the explosion, both Mom and Dad had been beaten to death with a ball-peen hammer we found aboard the ship . . . That there was no water in their lungs backs that theory up."

"Jesus—that is cold."

A young uniformed officer was approaching; he had a wide-eyed, poleaxed expression. "Chief," the young cop said, leaning in, "somebody's here and wants to talk to you—and you won't believe who it is."

Within a minute, a somber yet bright-eyed Louise Overell—in a short-sleeved, cream-colored, well-filled sweater and snug-fitting blue jeans—was standing with her hands fig-leafed before her.

"Hello, Chief Hodgkinson," she said, cheerfully. "How are you today?"

"Why, I'm just fine," he said.

"I'm doing better . . . thanks," the blue-eyed teenager said, answering a question Hodgkinson hadn't asked. "The reason I'm here is, I wanted to ask about the car."

"The car?"

"My parents' car. I know it was left here in the lot, and I thought maybe I could drive it back up to Flintridge . . . I've been staying up there, since . . . the tragedy."

"Excuse me," I said, getting out, and I flashed the chief a look that I hoped he would understand as meaning he should stall the girl.

"Well," the chief was saying, "I'm not sure. I think perhaps we need to talk to the District Attorney, and make sure the vehicle isn't going to be impounded for . . ."

And I was gone, heading for the parking lot.

Wherever Louise went, so surely too went Bud—particularly since another driver would be needed to transport the family sedan back to the Flintridge estate.

Among the cars in the gravelled lot were my own rental job, several police cars, Bud's Pontiac convertible, and a midnight blue '47 Caddy that I just knew had to have been Walter Overell's.

This opinion was formed, in part, by the fact that Bud Gollum—in a red sportshirt and denim slacks—was trying to get into the car. I approached casually—the boy had something in his left hand, and I wanted to make sure it wasn't a weapon.

Then I saw: a roll of electrical tape, and spool of wire. What the hell was he up to?

Then it came to me: while little Louise was keeping the chief busy, Bud was attempting to plant the tape and wire . . . which would no doubt match up with what had been used on the makeshift time bomb . . . in Overell's car. When the chief turned the vehicle over to Louise, the "evidence" would be discovered.

But the Caddy was locked, and apparently Louise hadn't been able to provide a key, because Bud was grunting in frustration as he tried every door.

I just stood there, hands on my hips, rocking on my heels on the gravel. "Is that your plan, Bud? To try to make this look like suicide-murder, planned by ol' Walter?"

Bud whirled, the eyes wild in the boyish face. "What . . . who . . . ?"

"It won't play, kid. The dynamite didn't do its job—the fractured skulls turned up in the autopsy. You're about two seconds away from being arrested."

That was when he hurled the tape and the wire at me, and took off running, toward his parked convertible. I batted the stuff away, and ran after him, throwing a tackle that took us both roughly down onto the gravel.

"Shit!" I said, getting up off him, rubbing my scraped forearm.

Bud scrambled up, and threw a punch, which I ducked.

Then I creamed him with a right hand that damn near broke his jaw—I don't remember ever enjoying throwing a punch more, though my hand hurt like hell afterward. He dropped prayerfully to his knees, not passing out, but whimpering like a little kid.

"Maybe you aren't smart enough for pre-med, at that," I told him.

Ambling up with two uniformed officers, the chief—who had already taken Louise into custody—personally snapped the cuffs on Bud Gollum, who was crying like a little girl—unlike Louise, whose stone face worked up a sneery pout, as she was helped into the backseat of a squad car.

All in all, Bud was pretty much a disappointment as a Boy Scout.

The case was huge in the California press, the first really big crime story since the Black Dahlia. A grand jury convicted the young lovers, and the state attorney general himself took charge of the prosecution.

My wife was delighted when we spent several weeks having a real summer's vacation, at the expense of the state of California, thanks to me being a major witness for the prosecution.

I didn't stay for the whole trial, which ran well into October, spiced up by steamy love letters that Louise and Bud exchanged, which were intercepted and fed to the newspapers and even submitted to the jury, after Bud's "filth" (as the late Mrs. Overell would have put it) had been edited out.

The letters fell short of any confession, and the star-crossed couple presented themselves well in court, Louise coming off as intelligent, mature and self-composed, and Bud seeming boyishly innocent, a big, strangely likable puppy dog.

The trial took many dramatic twists and turns, including a trip to the charred hulk of the *Mary E.* in drydock, with Louise and Bud solemnly touring the wreckage in the company of watchful jurors.

Not unexpectedly, toward the end of the trial, the respective lawyers of each defendant began trying to place the blame on the other guy, ultimately requesting separate trials, which the judge denied.

After my wife and I had enjoyed our court-paid summer vacation, I kept up with the trial via the press and reports from Fred Rubinski. All along we had both agreed we had never seen such overwhelming, unquestionably incriminating evidence in a murder case—or such a lame defense, namely that Walter Overell had committed suicide, taking his wife along with him.

Confronted by the testimony of handwriting experts, Bud had even admitted buying the dynamite, claiming he had done so at Walter Overell's request! Medical testimony established that the Overells had died of fractured skulls, and a receipt turned up showing that Bud had bought the alarm clock used in the makeshift time bomb—a clock Bud had given Louise as a gift. Blood on Bud's effects was shown to match that of the late Overells.

And on, and on . . . I had never seen a case more open and shut.

"Are you sitting down?" Fred's voice said over the phone.

"Yeah," I said, and I was, in my office in the Loop.

"After deliberating for two days, the six men and six women of the jury found Bud and Louise not guilty."

I almost fell out of my chair. "What the hell?"

"The poor kids were 'victims of circumstance,' so says the jury—you know, like the Three Stooges? According to the jury, the Overells died due to 'the accident of suicidal tampering with dynamite by Walter Overell.'"

"You're shitting me . . ."

"Not at all. Those two fresh-faced kids got off scot free."

I was stunned—flabbergasted. "How could a jury face such incontestable evidence and let obvious killers go free?"

"I don't know," Fred said. "It's a fluke—I can't imagine it ever happening again . . . not even in California."

The trial took its toll on the lucky pair, however—perhaps because their attorneys had tried to pit Bud and Louise against each other, the girl literally turned her back on the Boy Scout, after the verdict was read, scorning his puppy-dog gaze.

"I'm giving him back his ring," she told the swarming press.

As far as anybody knows, Louise Overell and Bud Gollum never saw each other again.

Nine months after her release, Louise married one of her jailers—I wondered if he'd been the guy who passed the love letters along to the prosecution. The marriage didn't last long, though the couple did have a son. Most of Louise's half-million inheritance went to pay for her defense.

Bud flunked out of pre-med, headed east, married a motordrome rider with a travelling show. That marriage didn't last long, either, and eventually Bud got national press again when he was nabbed in Georgia driving a stolen car. He did two years in a federal pen, then worked for a radio station in the South, finally dropping out of public view.

Louise wound up in Las Vegas, married to a Bonanza Air Lines radio operator. Enjoying custody of her son, she had a comfortable home and the security of a marriage, but remained troubled. She drank heavily and was found dead by her husband in their home on August 24, 1965.

The circumstances of her death were odd—she was naked in bed, with two empty quart-sized bottles of vodka resting near her head. A loaded, cocked .22 rifle was at her feet—unfired. And her nude body was covered with bruises, as if she'd been beaten to death.

Her husband explained this by saying, "She was always falling down." And the Deputy Coroner termed her cause of death as acute alcoholism.

I guess if Walter Overell dynamited himself to death, anything is possible.

AUTHOR'S NOTE: Fact, speculation and fiction are freely mixed within this story, which is based on an actual case and uses the real names of the involved parties, with the exception of my fictional detective, Nate Heller, and his partner Fred Rubinski (the latter a fictionalization of real-life private eye, Barney Ruditsky). I would like to acknowledge my research associate, George Hagenauer, as well as the following works: *The California Crime Book* (1971), Robert Colby; *For the Life of Me* (1954), Jim Richardson; *"Reporters"* (1991), Will Fowler; and the Federal Writers' Project California guide.

Nancy Pickard

Lucky Devil

SINCE THE MID-1980S, Nancy Pickard has been in the van-
guard of writers dedicated not only to making the traditional mystery novel more relevant to our time, but also to imbuing it with
elegance, style, and wit. That, anyway, is one aspect of her writing
career. The other is to bring new depth to the straight suspense
novel, which she has done with a feminist sensibility that informs
her work but does not overwhelm it. She does both brilliantly, and
her output has shown it with each new book. Fortunately, she also
finds time to write the occasional short story as well, like "Lucky
Devil," which was first published in *Malice Domestic #10*.

Lucky Devil

Nancy Pickard

It's not fair.

Except for the beautiful part, *none* of what happened to me is fair.

I've tried to grasp whatever larger, cosmic reason there may be for it all, but high-flown philosophy is not my forte. "Josie's of a practical nature," my mother used to say to me, and heaven knows she was right about that. If I am anything, it is down-to-earth. At the moment, I am damnably so.

My name, as you may know from newspaper accounts, is Josephine Taylor. I am sixty-three years old, widowed for so many years it feels as if I was never married. I live alone, I am a cashier at a bank. I don't suppose it takes an Einstein to read that description and get a pretty good idea of me as I am. And yes, I'm a bit of a fuss-budget. I've always liked things to be logical and orderly, from my checkbook to the books I check out of the library. I suppose if you want to read a little loneliness between the lines, I can hardly argue. It is true that somehow the days of my life have always seemed longer than the chronology of my years. In my forties I began to sense the inevitable dying of my cells, the daily, dusty walk toward death. My family are long-lived, however; I felt sure I would follow the example of my hardy parents and not die until my eighties.

Imagine my surprise when it happened sooner than that!

Medical death, they call it, and they termed my survival a miracle. No doubt you've heard similar stories, though none, I'll wager, quite like mine. Perhaps you have even experienced it yourself, but not as I did, I feel safe to say. As for skeptics, I would remind them that it was I, not they, who experienced it, and so they may not presume to speak for me. I know I was truly dead, with no qualifying adjectives like "medical" to soften it for our rational minds. I *died* on that mild September night, and now I am regrettably alive.

I was murdered.

• • •

"Lovely weather," my neighbor called out to me on that fateful Thursday evening when I stepped out of our apartment building for my nightly stroll. It was, indeed, a lovely twilight, soft and warm as only certain autumn nights can be, with a cloudless sky turning gracefully to a vast, dark blue.

"Hello, Esther," I greeted her, and then her dog. "Captain."

She was seated on a bench, with the big yellow Labrador lying at her feet. At the sound of my voice, he wagged his tail. His leash was loosely wrapped around Esther's left hand, which was no guarantee that she could hold him back if he decided to bolt. He's a friendly creature, but he has been known to charge pedestrians, so I always gave him a wide berth.

"I hope you'll be careful, Josie, dear. You'll walk under streetlights, won't you?"

"I'll be careful."

I was not afraid to walk alone in our neighborhood, but it was comforting to know there was at least one person in the world who would notice if I failed to return before dark.

I felt so weary that night. My shoulders ached and I probably slumped a bit. No doubt my head was down and my eyes were looking at my feet as I shuffled away the dreariness of the day.

"You were an inviting target," police officers told me afterward. "You were just the sort of person they like to prey upon: an older woman, not paying any attention to where she's going or who's around her."

And then, to top it off, I had my purse with me, as I always do, because it holds my keys. I also like to carry a little change in case I decide to stop at the Baskin-Robbins for a caramel sundae.

"Really, Mrs. Taylor," my lawyer chided me later. "You might as well have worn a sign that said 'Rob Me.'"

Perhaps the "experts" were not, after all, surprised by the assault on me. But the victim certainly was. Oh, it was so quick, so startling, so utterly terrifying!

He jumped out at me, grabbed the strap of my purse and tried to jerk it away from me. When he did that, he jerked my arm, too, catching me off balance. I began to fall. At that point everything slowed down. Slowly, I fell, so slowly it seemed I had time to study the cement in the pavement below me, to see its cracks, its gritty surface rising to meet me. All the while, I *knew* with a sickening awareness that this was going to be a very bad fall. I would be hurt; it would damage me.

But it didn't hurt at all.

It merely killed me.

Instantly, as my head struck the sidewalk, I felt a tremendous *whoosh*, as if I were being sucked out of my body, into the air above me. I'm sure you've heard similar reports, so I will not bore you with the familiar details, except to confirm that it is true what you have heard. Suddenly I was above myself, watching people running toward me and then bending over me. I saw the backs of their heads. I saw my own face! What surprises me even now is that I felt such loving sympathy for that poor pale woman lying so pitifully there on the pavement, with her blood trickling into the street.

Poor dear Josephine, I thought, tenderly.

I hovered there above. I watched an ambulance arrive and paramedics rush my limp body into it. They seemed outwardly calm, inwardly frantic.

"Get a move on!" the eldest of them muttered to himself.

I wanted to tell them not to bother.

A tall thin man I recognized from the neighborhood shook his head and looked touchingly dejected. "It's too late for her," I heard him say, and I wanted to comfort him.

Don't be sad, I wanted to say.

I even watched my assailant run away, and observed him being pursued by strangers who had come to my aid. They yelled at him, they were furious on my behalf. I started to follow them, to see if they'd catch him, but suddenly I didn't have time for that. Quicker than an instant I was gone from there, sucked further from earth. Down a tunnel I fell like Alice, down and down. I promised I wouldn't bore you with the details, but it is important for me to tell just a little more of what happened next. I became abruptly aware of a wonderful, bright light, and I tumbled into it. And suddenly everything was beautiful, peaceful, happy, more lovely than anywhere on earth, more peaceful than the stillest pool. I felt more happy than the happiest day that anyone has ever known.

I have died, I thought with wonder.

But then I felt a pulling again, as if forces were trying to suck me back into the world I had left. I fought it. I wept, crying, "No, please, I don't want to go back."

The next thing I knew I was hovering over my body again. This time I was hooked up to machines that registered no life in me. Doctors and nurses pummeled my thin body as if they could pound it back to life.

No! I tried to yell at them. *I won't come back!*

But I couldn't resist the gravity of existence. I whirled back into my body. Then came awful pain. I knew I was alive again. I opened my eyes.

"She's alive!" they shouted joyously, as if they'd done me a favor.

I wept for days.

There have been so many thousands of reports of after-death experiences that no one doubted my travelogue of heaven. They were interested. They called in their friends to hear it. A few of them took notes.

It was only when I insisted I had been murdered that I encountered resistance.

"What do you mean, he murdered you?" The police smiled at the very idea. "He can't very well have killed you, not if you're here to complain about it. Now can he, Mrs. Taylor?"

My lawyer said in her condescending way, "He can't be tried for murder. You're alive, you see."

This attitude is illogical of them. If they believe I died, how can they deny the corollary truth of my homicide?

A judge was sympathetic but curt.

"Be grateful that he'll wind up in jail at all, Mrs. Taylor," he advised me. "You are fortunate there were witnesses to apprehend him. He'll be punished for assaulting and robbing you, you may be sure of that."

But I am not grateful.

Having experienced a beautiful world of truth and justice, I know the boy should face the rightful consequences of his earthly actions. He is old enough to be tried as an adult for murder. This is a death penalty state. If people would only behave rationally, the boy could be given a fresh start in life, by dying.

"Even if I wanted to prosecute him," the prosecutor has said to me, "there is no such law on the books. Our society has no provision for dealing with the murderers of victims who don't *stay* dead."

He seemed to find that amusing.

The injustice of it all weighs upon my mind as I heal in my body. It all seems so unfair to the boy and me. He will only continue to degenerate here on earth. As for me, I am cheated of that paradise I was privileged to glimpse. I miss it terribly, as one might miss a beloved home; I long with all of my soul to return to it. Before I was murdered, life seemed barely endurable. Now it feels more barren than ever; now I cannot tolerate the thought of the years that lie before me until my next death. I want so badly that bliss which I tasted for that sweet short time.

Others have come back from such experiences claiming they were assigned a mission in life.

I was told nothing like that.

But I believe I do have a special mission.

The boy is out on bail. He has already returned to this neighborhood. Through the week I have unobtrusively observed his comings and goings. I am waiting for the right moment to present itself. I have seen him swagger, I have watched him brag to his friends. I am hopeful for him.

I plan to help him tonight.

He must be alone.

It must be fully dark outside, with no one near us.

I will approach him, holding in front of me one of the two small guns that my father left to me.

"You?" the boy will say, smirking until he sees the gun and the loving determination on my face. "Hey!"

"Stand still," I will order him.

Then I will take the second gun from the pocket of my cardigan sweater. I will hold it out to him and say, "Take this."

He will look puzzled and obscurely frightened, but he will take the gun.

"It's loaded," I will assure him.

He will begin to smile, possibly even raising his gun to me.

"What the hell?" he may ask, for the last time.

"I want you to kill me," I will direct him. "I will count to five. If you don't shoot me by the time I get to five, I will shoot you. One . . ."

He will look blank, stupid.

"Two."

I will aim at his heart.

"You're crazy!" he will exclaim.

But by the time I reach the count of four, he will shoot me in order to save himself. As I die, my little gun will fall to the ground. The boy will run away, but that won't matter. Everyone will know whom to suspect in my death.

The prosecutor will arrest the boy, who will attempt to tell his strange story, which no one will believe. They will say, "That poor lady carried a gun to protect herself against you. You killed her to keep her from testifying against you." Then they will try and convict him for his true crime: murder. And at last he will be privileged to face the heavenly consequences of his crime.

It isn't fair!

Nothing happened as I planned it.

Tonight, when I handed the gun to the boy, he looked bewildered, just as I knew he would, and he looked vaguely frightened, too.

"I will count to five," I told him.

It was then that the big yellow dog came bounding out of nowhere, lunging playfully at my legs. I fell forward against the boy. It was *my* gun that went off, firing at him rather than his gun firing at me.

Oh, the lucky young devil!

"Justifiable," the police have assured me. "Obviously he was trying to silence your testimony. Of course, you had to protect yourself."

Of course.

And so it is I who am still alive and the boy who is dead. Perhaps even now he is savoring the bliss of that heaven where all is forgiven. I'm sure he thanks me.

I have not given up hope for myself, however.

There will be other ways of going home again, and perhaps some other boy to whom I may give a fresh start.

Brendan DuBois

The Star Thief

BRENDAN DUBOIS has written various kinds of fiction, all of it good, some of it brilliant. Despite writing numerous fine novels, including the wonderfully evocative *Resurrection Day*, which examined an alternate history where the Cuban Missile Crisis erupted into full-fledged war, he is best known for his short fiction, which always has one or two twists that you never see coming. Along with Clark Howard, he is, with good reason, the preeminent crime story author of his generation. His story "The Star Thief," published in the March issue of *Alfred Hitchcock's Mystery Magazine*, concerns two brothers, one good, one evil, or is that the other way around? With DuBois, the only sure thing is that whatever the circumstances, a story by him is always worth reading.

The Star Thief

Brendan DuBois

Mick Sloan checked the time as he washed his hands at the bathroom sink. Damn. Because of the nonsense of the past several minutes, he'd have to forgo breakfast this morning, and he had a busy day planned, a quite busy one, and he could have used a good meal. He glanced up at the bathroom mirror and caught a glimpse of the bathtub behind him, and the foot that was sticking out. The foot had on a black sock and a polished black shoe. When he was done washing his hands and had cleaned out the crusty red stains from underneath his fingernails, he quickly went to work, wetting down all of the bathroom towels in cold water and going back over to the tub. The man in the tub had a blue blazer on, red necktie, and a hotel nametag that said KENNY. As he draped the towels over the man's body, Mick said, "Sorry about that, Kenny, but if you hadn't been so damn noisy, we could have avoided all of this."

When he was done, he went into the room and flipped on the air conditioner, as high as possible, and drew the shades against the early morning Florida sun. With any luck Kenny hadn't told anyone where he was going, and right now, luck was what Mick needed. He rubbed at the smooth skin on his jaw as he packed his few belongings. That's where the problem had started, when he had shaved off his beard and had gotten his hair cut. Kenny had gotten suspicious about his entering the room—since he looked so different from the previous day—and had started asking questions. Mick was never one for answering questions, especially from the guys in the world like Kenny, and when the pushing started, Mick pushed right back and escalated, right to a full exchange.

He flipped on the television set for one last look. That had always been his talent, he thought. Other guys would dilly-dally, think of the different options, think of what was right, and while all that thinking was going on, Mick was getting the job done.

On the television screen was the picture he'd been waiting for, from the NASA Select channel. The space shuttle *Columbia*, on its pad, getting ready for a launch in seven hours.

A lot could happen in seven hours.

He looked down at the open knapsack. Inside was his 9mm Smith & Wesson, two extra clips, and a U.S. Army Model V anti-personnel hand grenade nestled among his shorts and polo shirts. The hand grenade was a bit of an overkill, but he was never one to go into a situation underarmed.

Not his style. He zipped the knapsack and left the room, and hung a DO NOT DISTURB sign on the outside door handle. He looked up at the morning sky. Clear. If he were lucky, the weather would hold, the maid wouldn't come to this room, and he'd get to the Kennedy Space Center with no problems.

He thought of the dead hotel security man in his room. Sure. Luck.

At what age did it start, he wondered, when he knew he was different? He wasn't sure, but it had to have been when his younger brother started getting older, and when his mother and father had started yapping after him when they saw how successful his brother was becoming. How come you're not more like your brother? He doesn't get into trouble like you, he doesn't get bad grades like you, the teachers don't send notes home about him, yadda yadda yadda.

So what. He didn't particularly like his younger brother, but he didn't particularly dislike him, either. Their house was a small Cape in a forgotten corner of Vermont, and Dad and Mom both worked at the local marble quarry—Dad manhandling the cutting equipment, Mom balancing the books in the company's office. He and his brother shared an upstairs bedroom, with Mom and Dad in the other bedroom. Early on they had come to an agreement over the room—an imaginary line ran down the center, and if everyone stayed on their own side, things were fine.

On his side were piles of clothes, magazines about cars and motorcycles, and posters of Richard Petty. On his brother's side was a bookshelf and plastic models, carefully put together and painted, made up of jet planes and rockets. There was a single poster on the wall, a big map of the moon.

One night he watched his brother sitting up in bed doing his homework on a laptop table he had made from scrap lumber. He was on his own bed reading a girlie mag he had hidden inside a motorcycle magazine. He looked over at the grim expression on his brother's face and said, "What are you working on?"

"Algebra."

"Is it fun?" he asked, knowing what the answer would be.

"No, I hate it!" his brother said. "It's all letters and symbols. Numbers I can understand. I can't understand letters in math."

"So why are you doing it?"

"Because I have to, that's why."

He laughed. "Kiddo, let me tell you a little secret. That's all crap they slop at you, all the time, in church, in school, and at home. You don't have to do a thing you don't want to do, ever."

"You do if you want to go places."

Another laugh. "The game's rigged, little brother. You think a couple of guys like us are going anywhere? Face it, when we were born here, we were set for life. That's the plan. Grow up and go to high school, marry your local sweetheart, and march into the quarry to cut stone for another generation. That's the plan, and I'm having no part of it. All your schoolwork ain't gonna make a difference."

"You have another plan?"

He winked, turned the pages of the magazine. "Sure, and it has nothing to do with them. I'm gonna do what I want no matter what, and I get what I want. That's it. Simple and to the point."

His brother smiled. "I think I'll stick with algebra."

It was cool enough in the morning air that he didn't have to flip on the air conditioning in the car. He got onto Route A1A in Cocoa Beach and headed north, up to the Cape. Traffic was light, and he went by the T-shirt emporiums, fast food joints, motels, hotels, and other stores. On one sign outside a hotel black letters hung in the morning air, like they were advertising the early bird dinner special. This message said GOOD LUCK COLUMBIA.

Right, he thought. Luck.

He followed the curve of the road as it went up the coast past cube office buildings with names of aerospace companies: Rockwell, Boeing, Lockheed Martin. Beyond the office parks was a long stretch of flat, dusty land and then a cruise ship terminal with huge ships moored at docks that looked like skyscrapers tilted on their sides. Up ahead the horizon was a bit muddy, but he thought he could make out the gantries and buildings of the Kennedy Space Center. As he drove, he kept his speed at a constant fifty-five even though he was passed on the left and right by other cars and drivers who didn't care as much as he did. His foot flexed impatiently on the accelerator, but he kept his cool. No way did he want to stand out, this close to the prize. Which is why when he got into Cocoa Beach, he had gotten his hair cut and shaved his beard. Didn't want to look like a freak on this morning.

A schoolbus passed him and then another. Of course, cutting his hair and shaving his beard had done exactly the opposite—it had gotten him noticed, had gotten him face-to-face with someone who didn't back down, and while he was heading north on this fine Florida highway, back at his hotel room Kenny was resting in his bathtub. Maybe Kenny wasn't sleeping with the fishes, but it was pretty close.

Route A1A became Route 528, and after a few miles there was an intersection, for Route 3, and he took a right, heading north. Traffic was getting heavier and the road was four lane, and he still couldn't believe how flat everything was. The grass was green and the brush and the trees were ugly, with sharp points and odd knobs, and nothing looked particularly attractive. His different business interests had brought him to this state off and on during the past few years, before he started getting tired, but he had never really gotten the feel of the place. Everything seemed too bright, too new, too plastic.

Traffic was thicker as the houses and businesses began thinning out. Taillights flickered as cars and trucks slowed. He looked ahead. There was an American flag flapping in the breeze next to a full-scale Mercury-Redstone rocket complete with Mercury capsule on top. Two similar setups had lofted Shepard and Grissom into space back in 1961. He couldn't tell from this distance if the rocket were real or just a mock-up. But he was sure of one thing: the sign welcoming him to Gate 2 at the Kennedy Space Center, and the armed guards standing next to the guard shack.

He reached over and unzipped the top flap of the knapsack and waited.

At some time in their brotherly relationship after a few raucous battles, they had made a vow never to rat out each other to their parents, which is why he never really bothered to hide what he did from his younger sibling. One night, swaying a bit because of his drinking and high on what he had just done, he stood in the dim light of a reading lamp over his bed, emptying his pockets onto the frayed bedspread. Crumpled and grease stained bills fluttered into a pile, with pictures of Washington, Lincoln, Hamilton, and Jackson staring up at him.

There was a noise in the bedroom, and he turned. Another light came on, and his little brother rolled over, rubbing at his eyes.

"What's up with that?" younger brother asked.

Not that he ever cared what his younger brother thought about him, but still, he felt proud of what he had done. "What's up?" he said, speaking clearly, not wanting the words to slur. "What's up is that I'm working my way to my new career, that's what. See that?" He picked up a fistful of the bills and said, "See? This is what the old man earns in a week, kissing butt and going up to that stinking quarry. Right here, and I earned this in one night, just one night."

Younger brother rubbed at his eyes again. "How did you get all that money?"

He laughed. "How else? Somebody had it and I took it. Nothing more than that. A thief, that's what I am, and a damn good one." Of course there was more than just being a thief. There was the feeling of going into that gas station, next county over, and seeing the fear in the attendant's face, the fear that made him feel strong, like he counted. The money was just extra. That thrill was what mattered, and he could hardly wait to try it again.

Younger brother shook his head. "That's wrong, and you know it."

"Nope," he said. "What was wrong was being born in this stinking town and having your whole life laid out for you. You can do what you want, but I'm not following the blueprint. I'm doing my own thing."

"Neither am I," his brother said bravely. "I'm not following the blueprint, either. I'm doing the same thing you are, except I'm not going to jail."

He sat down heavily on the bed, started flattening out the crumpled bills. "Sure," he said. "You're going to college and then to the moon. Make sure you send me some green cheese when you get there."

Younger brother switched off his light. "If whatever prison you're in takes packages, I'll send some along."

For a moment he thought about going over and pounding the crap out of him—he had learned long ago that putting a pillow over his head muffled his screams so their parents didn't hear a thing—but he was tired and slightly drunk and he wanted to count his money, his wonderful money, the only thing that counted.

At the gated entrance Mick pulled his hand out of his knapsack—silently saying to himself, test number one approaching—and he held up the vehicle pass with the drawing of the shuttle and the mission number on the outside.

Shazam, he thought, as the guard merely waved him through and he was in, joining another line of cars, heading north.

I'll be damned, he thought. Maybe we can pull this off after all.

He stayed on the narrow two lane road, heart thumping as he realized that with each passing second he was getting closer and closer to making it all happen. He passed a sign that said SHUTTLE LAUNCH TODAY, and he found himself speeding up. Close, it was getting close.

Then the road came to an overpass and a large sign pointed to the left, saying SPACEPORT USA. He made a left-hand turn, and after another couple of minutes of driving, the roadway bordered on each side by low drainage ditches, he saw the Spaceport USA tourist facility on his left. It was a collection of low white buildings with a fullsize space shuttle mock-up front and another sign at the entrance that said GODSPEED COLUMBIA AND HER CREW.

The parking lots next to the buildings were all named after shuttles, and he didn't particularly care which lot he ended up in. But in the end he followed orange vest clad parking lot attendants, who waved him along. He pulled his rental car in next to a minivan and got out, knapsack in hand. He decided to leave the keys in the ignition.

He followed the other people, who were streaming into an open doorway that was half-hidden near the Spaceport buildings, the visitors' center for the Kennedy Space Center. It felt odd being with these friends and family members, for only the special ones were here today, the ones with connections. The early morning sun was quite hot, and off to the left was a place called the Rocket Garden, with about a half dozen rockets, held up by wires and cables, reaching to the bright Florida sky. He wanted to go over to the garden and poke around, but first things first. There was a little paperwork to take care of.

Inside the office—called Room 2001 by someone with a sense of humor—was a set of counters with signs overhead indicating lines for visitors and industry representatives. He went to an open space at the counter and whispered, "Time for test number two," and as he went up to the woman, he carefully put his free hand in the knapsack, around the handle of his 9mm.

"Can I help you?" asked a woman at the counter, and Mick smiled. By God he knew it was a stereotype and cliche and all that, but he loved women from the South. They wore too much makeup and too much jewelry and their clothes were either too tight or cut too short, and he loved it all. This one was a redhead with long painted fingernails and a short yellow dress that exposed an impressive amount of freckled cleavage. Mick wished he had more time to spend with this woman, but wishes wouldn't do much today.

"Yes, you can," he said. "I should be on the visitors' list. Mick Sloan."

"Well, let's see," she said, drawing out her Southern drawl, and Mick couldn't stop grinning, though he did keep his hand on his pistol. As before, first things first, and if things went bad, and getting out of here meant taking this pretty young thing as a hostage, that's what he'd do. No hard feelings. Just what had to be done.

She looked up at him and smiled. "Very well, Mr. Sloan. You're on the list." She passed him a stuffed cardboard folder bordered in orange. "Here's your official press kit for the mission." Then she passed over a small pin that showed a drawing of the shuttle and letters underneath: LAUNCH GUEST.

"Make sure you wear this pin at all times, and follow the directions of your guide," she said. "Oh, and here's the mission patch. It must have fallen out of the press kit."

She slid the mission patch across the counter and then stopped, smiling. "Why, look here. One of the astronaut names here is Sloan. Same as yours. A relative?"

Mick picked everything up and kept on smiling. "Yes, you could say that. A relative."

Another night, another job, and his younger brother was complaining, something about being waked up every time he got in, and he decided to do something about it. Which he did. A few minutes later younger brother was huddled in his bed whimpering, and he sat on his own bed rubbing his sore knuckles.

He sighed. "Just what in hell is your problem, anyway?"

The face rose up, eyes reddened, cheeks wet. "What do you mean?"

"You know what I mean. You're so big on doing things for yourself, studying hard, spending time at the library. Hey, you do what you do, and I'll do what I do to get along. We both want out of this town. You just leave me be."

"But it's wrong and you know it," younger brother said, stammering.

"Says who? And what makes you so smart anyway? You think you're so cool, so above it all? You're just a whiny little chicken. Hell, you think you're going to the moon, first time you go up in an airplane, you'll wet yourself."

"I will not!"

"Sure you will. You don't have guts for anything, whether it's talking back to the old man or telling the old lady that I pound on you every now and then. Face it, little brother, you don't have what it takes to do anything."

Now he was sitting up in bed, tears still rolling down those chubby cheeks. "Yes, I do so have it, and I'll prove it to you!"

He laughed, started to get undressed for bed. "That'll be the day."

Mick stood among the metal shapes in the rocket garden, waiting. The sun had risen even higher, heating everything up even more. Large birds—pelicans? buzzards? vultures?—hovered around in the humid air. Around him were the shapes and little plaques, marking the rockets and their missions. Scout. Redstone. Titan. Jupiter. All of them now resting and slightly rusting, some held up by cables. A couple of boys went racing through, dodging the shapes of the rockets, and he felt like grabbing them by the scruffs of their necks, telling them to be silent in such a holy place. But it probably wouldn't be worth it. The last time he let his temper loose poor ol' Kenny back at the hotel had paid a pretty steep price.

There was a deep growling noise, and then, one after another, buses rolled up by the sidewalk. He joined the crowds of people lining up and he got on, making sure his lapel button was visible. The other passengers were good-natured but a bit solemn, knowing what they were about to witness: six other human beings—friends and family—strapped to the top of one of the most explosive structures in history, to be violently propelled into a place that could kill you within seconds of being exposed without protection.

He sat alone, which suited him, while other people quietly talked about the weather, about scrub scenarios, about missions in the past and missions for the future. A woman escort stood up at the front of the bus and gave a little talk as they made their way back to the highway. She identified herself as a worker at the Cape, described briefly what she did—something to do with the shuttle processing facility—and explained some of the ground rules. Stay in the grandstands. No wandering off. Remember your bus number, and return to the bus immediately after launch. If there is any kind of emergency—she didn't say *Challenger*, but then again, she didn't have to—also return immediately to the bus.

And all while she talked, he kept his knapsack with his weapons firmly in his lap.

•   •   •

In the bedroom he got dressed, putting on bluejeans, black T-shirt, and black leather jacket. His little brother watched him from behind his little desk, where he was making a model of some damn rocket or something.

"Another night out with the boys?" his brother asked.

"Yep," he said, looking in the mirror, combing back his hair. "That it is."

"And what's it tonight? A gas station? A convenience store? Mugging a couple of college kids from Burlington?"

There. Hair looked great. "Oh, whatever opportunity comes our way."

Younger brother put down his model. "I want to come along."

He started laughing, so loud that he put his hand against his mouth, so that their parents downstairs couldn't hear him. His brother glared at him, saying, "I'm serious. Honest to God, I'm serious."

"Oh please," he said. "What makes you think I'll take you along? Huh? And why do you want to go along anyway?"

His younger brother started putting away some of his modeling tools. "Because I want to prove to myself that I can do it." He rolled his eyes. "I hate to say it, but you were right. I know I can be afraid, really afraid, and if I'm going to learn to fly and get into the air and go into space, I need to control my fear. I figure if I go along with you and can do that, I really can do anything."

He opened the top drawer of his bureau, reached to the back where he always hid a pack of Marlboros behind a couple of pairs of dress socks. "Okay. If you go along, maybe that helps you in your queer little quest. What's in it for me?"

Younger brother's eyes were young, but they were sharp. "Because maybe I will get scared, so scared that I cry and maybe even wet myself. You'd like that, wouldn't you?"

Now, that was a point. He turned to his younger brother and said, "Yeah, I would like that. All right. You want in? You're in."

Now he was in the VIP viewing area, set up against the Banana River. To the left was a huge building, a new museum highlighting the Saturn V rocket and the moon missions. Grandstands rose near a fence adjacent to the riverbank, and three flagpoles had been set up. An American flag flapped in the breeze from one, a flag for the shuttle *Columbia* from another, and a NASA flag from the third. Sweat was trickling down the back of his neck and his arms. Jesus, it was hot. He wished he had a hat.

Buses in the parking lot behind the grandstands grumbled, their diesel engines still on, and lines began to form at the stands for souvenirs, ice cream, and water. Mick slowly climbed to the top of one of the grandstands. People were walking up and down taking seats, and some popped up umbrellas to give themselves a little shade. Loudspeakers announced that it was T-minus three hours and counting, and so far, everything was a go. There were two televisions set up in front of the grandstands, showing the live feed from the NASA channel, but the glare from the morning sun washed out the picture. A digital countdown clock flipped the numerals backwards as the countdown proceeded; he had never seen time move so slowly.

He sat down, put the knapsack down next to him, put his hand inside to touch his weapons. He rummaged around inside for a moment and pulled out a pair of binoculars. He looked across the river, focusing in until he saw the gantry complex. Launch pad 39B. Set up against the gantry was the space shuttle, the orange fuel tank, bright against the slight haze, flanked by the twin solid rocket boosters and the stubby wings of *Columbia*. His throat tightened at seeing it in person, not watching it on CNN or C-SPAN, and as he thought about who was now inside, waiting for launch, he had to turn away for a moment.

Next to him sat two young boys accompanied by their parents. While mom and dad fussed over sunscreen, cameras, and water, one boy said to the other, "I see it! There's the shuttle, *Columbia*!"

The older brother corrected him. "Nate, the whole thing is the space shuttle. *Columbia* is the orbiter. Remember that, okay? If you want people to think you know something about space, you gotta know the right names. Okay?"

"Okay," the boy said, and Mick watched as the two brothers quietly began holding hands as the announcer kept track of the countdown. For a moment he wanted to talk to them, to ask them what it was like, to be two brothers who got along, but this was their day. He didn't want to disturb them.

A convenience store was the target this night, set deep along one of the many rural back roads that connected the small Vermont towns in this part of the county. His buds Harry and Paul had put up a fuss when he'd brought along his younger brother, but he said, "Hey, this is my night, and I say he goes along. You guys got a problem, you can ride with somebody else."

Considering how well things had gone the past few months, Harry and Paul had grumbled some more and had shut their mouths. Except Paul had said, "You're the weirdo who wants to go to the moon, is that right?"

"Yep," his brother said, and Harry and Paul and even he himself had started laughing. He said, "One day maybe the moon, but not tonight. Let's get it on."

He drove by a convenience store called Liar's Paradise and saw one car parked at the side. The clerk's, probably. He made a U-turn farther up the road and came back, parked at the side also. "Harry, Paul, go in and get some stuff. Come back and tell us who's there."

"'Kay," they said and left. It was quiet inside the car as he sat behind the steering wheel, his younger brother in the rear seat. His brother cleared his throat. "How long, do you think?"

"Just a couple of minutes," he said, his mouth growing dry with excitement, the idea that in a very short while he was going inside to steal something from someone, someone he didn't even know.

His brother cleared his throat again. Nervous, wasn't he? He said, "You know, the two of us, we have a lot in common."

"Yeah," he said, tapping the steering wheel with both hands. "Parents who weren't bright enough to move somewhere with better jobs."

"There's something else. We both have drive, that's what. We both want to get out of this town. I want to do it legally, you want to do it illegally. Except for that, we're the same."

"Oh, shut up, will you?" as Harry and Paul came out, laughing. Harry had a beer in his hand, and Paul had a small package. They got into the car, and Harry said, "Piece of cake. Female clerk maybe sixteen or seventeen. That's it."

"Great." He popped open the glove compartment and took out a .38 revolver. "Give me five minutes, then pull up to the front door." After stepping outside he said, "Paul, what the hell do you have there?"

"Something for your brother," Paul said, giggling, tossing over a package of disposable diapers.

More laughter, and then he went into the store. He turned and his brother was right behind him. He wasn't laughing.

Mick took a deep breath as the countdown went into a preplanned hold. He looked around at the crowd noticing the low conversations, the anxious looks at the gantry and the shuttle a couple of miles away. It was hard to believe that he was actually looking at it, looking at a spaceship. For that's what it was no matter how officious it sounded. The damn thing out there was a spaceship, ready to go, and he was about to see the launch.

If everything went well, of course. He began to pick out faces and such. There. That guy leaning against the fence with the binoculars who wasn't spending much time looking at the launch site. The guy and the gal by the souvenir stand, standing there chatting like they were just there to get some sun, not to see a shuttle launch. And the two guys within a few yards of him in the grandstand who casually looked his way every few minutes. All of them muscled, all of them too casual, and all seeming to share a handicap, for what looked like hearing aids were in their ears.

He shifted the knapsack in his lap, made sure his weapons were within easy reach.

"This is shuttle launch control," came a voice over the loudspeaker, echoing slightly. "The preplanned hold has been lifted. All systems remain go. The count has resumed at T-minus nine minutes and counting. T-minus nine minutes to today's launch of *Columbia*."

People in and around the grandstand applauded and cheered, and after a few seconds Mick found himself joining them.

• • •

Inside the store it was just as Paul and Harry had described. Long rows of chips, canned goods, and other stuff, coolers for beer and drinks, a closed restroom door, and a counter with the girl standing behind it. Younger brother seemed to take a deep breath and stood close, too close, and he said quietly, "Back off, will you? You're crowding me."

His brother went down a row, between chips and soft drinks, and he smiled at the girl. She was in her teens, short red hair and a bright smile that faded quickly when he took the revolver out.

"We'll make this quick and easy, girl, but it's up to you," he said. "Everything in the register. Now."

Immediately she burst into tears, and then she punched open the register drawer and started pulling out bills. "Please—please—" It was like she couldn't finish a sentence. My, how he enjoyed those tears, enjoyed that sense of power going through him, knowing that she would have to do anything and everything he wanted, all because of that hunk of iron in his fist. Without it he was nothing, but with it, for this girl clerk on this night, he was a god.

"Now now," he said, waving the revolver for emphasis. "Under the drawer, too, where you keep the extra bills." She passed the bills to him, and he extended his fingers, just so he could touch her skin, and then—

"Hey!"

He turned, seeing that everything was wrong, everything was wrong, the door to the restroom was open and a large man with a handlebar mustache and one pissed-off expression on his face had his brother in a headlock with a folding knife to his throat. His brother was gurgling, his face red, and the guy started out, "If you want to see your friend here let loose, then—"

He didn't listen to the rest of the speech. Paul and Harry had pulled up to the door, honked the horn, and he was outside and in the front seat just as they were pulling away. Paul said, "Your brother, man, what's going on—"

And he had said, "Go, damn it! Just get the hell out of here!"

Mick hadn't felt this way in a long time, the sheer energy of the moment, knowing that everybody in this crowd was looking and hoping and praying in one direction, to that gantry and spaceship on the other side of the river. In front of him some people had umbrellas up against the heavy sun, but when the countdown fell below five minutes, they put them away so as not to block the view of their neighbors. He was surprised at how damned considerate they were.

"T-minus two minutes and counting for today's launch of *Columbia*," the echoing voice said. "Everything still a go for launch. Launch control has advised *Columbia* crew to close and lock their helmet visors. T-minus one minute and forty-five seconds."

Then one and then another and then four or five more people stood up as if they were in a giant, open-air cathedral, and Mick joined them. Beside him the two boys were straining up, trying to see over the heads in front of them, and then they climbed up on the next step of the grandstand. The older of the two had a pair of binoculars in his chubby fists, keeping view of the shuttle, while the other one seemed to be saying the Hail Mary in a faint whisper.

"T-minus one minute and counting."

Mick hung his knapsack from one shoulder while bringing up the binoculars, trying to focus on what was going on, but he found to his dismay that his hands were shaking. Everything he had ever done in his life, and now, now his hands couldn't keep still! He let the binoculars drop around his neck on their strap.

"T-minus thirty-one seconds and counting. *Columbia's* on-board computers now in command as we begin auto-sequence start. T-minus twenty seconds and counting . . ."

And who could have believed, when it all was sorted out, that his brother wouldn't give him up!

No matter the threats, the pleading, the arguments, younger brother had stayed in juvie detention not saying a thing, not saying one word. Only once did he have a chance to speak to him, and his brother's words were to the point: "Guess you think I'm brave now, huh?"

"Jesus, you're an idiot," he said.

"Maybe I am," his younger brother said, his voice calm. "But I'm my own idiot. Maybe I just want to prove that I can do something that scares me so much. Something that I can use later on. Maybe that's why I'm here."

"You think our parents and the cops are going to believe you? That you were robbing that store with some guys you met on the street? Why haven't you given me up?"

His younger brother shrugged. "Why haven't you told them?"

"I have!" he said. "I've told them that I was there, but that damn store clerk is too scared to testify. And her dad, the guy with the knife at your throat, he didn't get a good look at me. And that's why you're still here, stupid. Why don't you do the smart thing?"

A secret little smile. "I am doing the smart thing. I'm showing you that I can make it, that I'm brave enough to do anything I want. Even if it's being a thief like you."

Mick found he could not breathe as the countdown went on and on, each passing second feeling like another stone added to his shoulders.

"T-minus ten, nine, eight, we have a go for main engine start . . . we have a main engine start . . ."

The crowd about him went "ooooh" as the bright flare of red and orange blew out from the bottom of the gantry, and then ". . . three, two, one . . ."

An enormous cloud of steam and smoke billowed out as the solid rocket boosters lit off, and Mick could hardly hear the PA system as the man said: ". . . liftoff, we have a liftoff of space shuttle *Columbia* as she embarks on a nine day mission for space science . . ."

It was like a dream, a dream he had seen in his mind's eye over and over again, as the winged shuttle rose from the pad, rotating as it headed up into the Florida sky. For a few seconds the ascent was silent as the sound waves rushed at a thousand feet per second to the grandstand. Then the noise struck, rising in a crescendo, a thundering, rippling noise that seemed to beat at his chest and face. For the first second or two the shuttle seemed to climb at an agonizingly slow pace, but then it accelerated, from one heartbeat to the next, rising up and up.

Around him people were yelling, cheering, clapping. Most had binoculars or cameras or camcorders against their faces, but Mick was satisfied to watch it roar up into the sky with his own naked eyes, the exhaust moving out behind the bright engine flare of *Columbia* like a pyramid of smoke and steam.

His cheeks were suddenly wet, and he realized he was crying.

For his younger brother, everything that could have gone wrong, went wrong.

His stay at the juvenile detention center was extended, and then extended again, due to his fights with other detainees. He walked away from a counseling group and spent three days on the outside before being recaptured.

And when he eventually got home, his eyes seemed tired all the time, like he had seen so very much in such a short time. Younger brother had to sleep with a light on, and he had put up a fuss until his brother said quietly, "I'll fight you for it. Trust me, I'll whip your ass."

So the light stayed on, and he had a terrible time sleeping every night, for every time he closed his eyes, he saw that scene back in the convenience store where he'd abandoned him.

In just a very short while, the shuttle had climbed until all he could make out was the base of the orange fuel tank, and the flames coming from the three main engines and the two solid rocket fuel boosters. Then came a pair of bright flares of light and smoke, and another "ooooh" from the crowd.

The PA announcer calmly said, "Booster control officer confirms normal separation of the boosters. All systems aboard *Columbia* are performing well."

More cheers, as the engine noise finally began to fade away. And then another announcement: "Three minutes and five seconds into the flight, *Columbia* is traveling at thirty-six hundred miles per hour and is seventy-nine miles downrange from the Kennedy Space Center and fifty miles in altitude. All systems continue to perform nominally."

He wiped the tears from his cheeks, kept on staring up, his neck beginning to ache, and he knew he would keep on looking as long as possible.

It began to get even worse. His younger brother had put away his books, had gotten hooked up with some friends he made in the juvenile detention center, and his parents began coming down hard on him, the older brother. One night, his father—never one to do much of anything—got drunk and belted him around the living room. "You fool!" he shouted. "What the hell did you do? Huh? Bad enough that you have to grow up to be such a loser, you had to take him along for the ride, too? Is that it? Is it?"

So his father had tossed him out of the house, at age seventeen. A year later, after stumbling by on one low-rent job after another, he had joined the military.

By now all he could see was a bright dot of light as *Columbia* surged out across the Atlantic. The PA announcer said, "*Columbia* is now two hundred miles downrange from the Kennedy Space Center and is sixty-seven miles in altitude. All systems still performing well."

He looked down, just for a moment. At the gantry a large cloud of smoke and steam was slowly drifting away. Around him people started leaving the viewing stands, laughing and chattering. He smiled as he saw the two boys, still holding hands, walk away with their parents.

When he looked up again, the dot of light was gone. *Columbia* and her crew were in orbit.

Years later he had met up with his younger brother. The talk had been strained, for whatever little things they'd had in common were now gone. They had both left their small Vermont town, and while he had lived on military bases in the States and Europe, younger brother had gone around the country doing things he would not explain. Though he had a good idea of what was going on, could tell from the hard look about his brother's eyes.

At their very last meeting he had paid their bar bill and said, "Please, can I ask you something?"

"Sure," younger brother said. "Go ahead."

He had stared down at a soggy cocktail napkin, afraid of what he was going to say next. "Will you . . . will you forgive me for what I did, back there?"

His younger brother looked puzzled. "Back where?"

"At the convenience store. When I left you behind . . . I've always felt bad about it, honest. I abandoned you and . . ." He couldn't speak, for his throat felt like it was swelling up so much it could strangle him.

His brother shook his head, picked up a toothpick. "That was a long time ago. I went in that store of my own free will. Forget it, all right? Just forget it."

But he could never do that.

• • •

Mick was now sitting alone in the grandstand seats. All the other launch guests had streamed back to the buses, which had grumbled away, heading back to the visitors' center. He sat there alone, the knapsack in his lap. He took a deep breath. It had all worked out. He had had his doubts, but it had all worked out.

Then one man appeared and then another. Joined by a woman and another man. They all had weapons in their hands, and they slowly came up the grandstand, flanking him. He stood up, carefully put his knapsack down, and then kicked it aside. He would no longer need it.

"On your knees and turn around, now!" one of the men shouted. He did as he was told and felt something light begin to stir in his chest. The long run was over. He had finally seen what he was destined to see. Finally.

The handcuffs were almost a comfort around his wrists. Maybe later he'd tell them about Kenny back at the hotel, but not right now. One of the men leaned into him and said, "The name is Special Agent Blanning, Mick, I've been following your trail for years. For murder and bank jobs and everything in between, across eight states. And you know what? When you said you would give yourself up if you could see a damn shuttle launch in person . . . well, I never would have believed it."

"Glad to make you a believer, Agent Blanning. Sometimes you just get tired of running. And could I ask one more favor to close out the day?"

The FBI agent laughed as they went down the grandstand. "Sure. Why not. You've just made my day."

So he told him. As they led him away, Mick looked back once again at the empty gantry, where all his hopes and dreams had once rested.

So, damn it, this is what it was like! In all those years in the service of his country, in the air force, he'd found an aptitude he never knew existed. He had hit the books while on the government's dime and had actually enjoyed it. The air force was also damn short of pilots. He'd tested out positive for flight training, and from there he kept on climbing that ladder, getting higher and higher, from flying regular jets to test piloting to even applying for the astronaut service, can you believe it.

But all the while, as he climbed the ladder, that little weight was on his shoulders, calling him a fraud, calling him a usurper, calling him a thief. And when word came in from the FBI about what his younger brother wanted, well, he thought it would croak any chance of flying into orbit.

But, Jesus, here he was, floating in the shuttle flight deck, his stomach doing flip-flops and his face feeling puffy from adjusting to micro-gravity, and out of one of the aft viewing windows, there was Africa, slowly turning beneath him. There were so many things to do, so many tasks to achieve, and still, he could not believe he was here, that he had made it.

Fraud, the tiny voice whispered. You don't belong here. You stole this. You stole this from your brother.

"Ah, *Columbia*, Houston," came a voice inside his earpiece.

The mission commander, floating about ten feet away, toggled the communication control switch at his side. "Go ahead, Houston."

"Greg, a bit of early housekeeping here. We've got a message for Tom."

He pressed down his own communication switch. "Houston, this is Tom. Go ahead."

"Tom . . . message is that your package has been safely picked up."

He nodded, knowing that his brother was now in custody, now faced trial, and life in prison, all because of what he'd agreed to. He had a flash of anger, thinking that this was his brother's revenge, to spoil this mission and whatever career he had with NASA.

"Ah, Tom . . ."

"Go ahead, Houston."

"Another message, as well. Just one word."

His mission commander was staring at him like he was thinking, what in the world is going on with you and this mission?

"I'm ready, Houston."

The words crackled in his earpiece. "Message follows. Forgiven. That's it, Tom. One word. Forgiven."

"Ah, thanks, Houston. Appreciate that."

"Okay. Greg, we're ready for you to adjust the Ku-band antenna, and we want to check the cargo bay temperatures . . ."

He turned, pretended to look for something in the storage lockers. He knew he would experience many things in this trip to space, from adjusting to the micro-gravity, to assisting in the experiments, to actually seeing how it was to live up here in earth orbit.

But he'd never thought he'd learn that, in space, tears in the eyes have no place to go.

Bill Pronzini

Chip

BILL PRONZINI has spent much of his career creating a Balzacian series about a private detective named Nameless. He writes with the same rue, disappointment, and love about San Francisco and its environs that Balzac brought to his work set in Paris. While Pronzini claims to have written the "last" Nameless novel, one hopes that he'll reconsider and grace us with another one soon. In the meantime, we can still look forward to his short stories, like this brief stunner. "Chip" was published in issue #71 of *Mystery Scene Magazine*, and it tells of the family ties that bind, cutting a father to the quick.

Chip

Bill Pronzini

John Valarian felt as he always did when he came to St. Ives Academy—a little awkward and uncomfortable, as if he didn't really belong in a place like this. St. Ives was one of the most exclusive, expensive boys' schools on the east coast, but that wasn't the reason; he'd picked it out himself, over Andrea's objections, when Peter reached his eighth birthday two years ago. The wooded country setting and hundred-year-old stone buildings weren't the reason, either. It was what the school represented, the atmosphere you felt as soon as you entered the grounds. Knowledge. Good breeding. Status. Class.

Well, maybe he didn't belong here. He'd come out of the city slums, had to fight for every rung on his way up the ladder. He hadn't had much schooling, still had trouble reading. And he'd never been able to polish off all his rough edges. That was one of the reasons he was determined to give his son the best education money could buy.

He climbed the worn stone steps of the administration building, gave his name to the lobby receptionist. She directed him up another flight of stairs to the headmaster's office. He'd been there once before, on the day he'd brought Peter here for enrollment, but he didn't remember much about it except that he'd been deeply impressed. This was only his third visit to St. Ives in three years—just two short ones before today. It made him feel bad, neglectful, thinking about it now. He'd intended to come more often, particularly for the father-son days, but some business matter always got in the way. Business ruled him. He didn't like it sometimes, but that was the way it was. Some things you couldn't change no matter what.

The headmaster kept him waiting less than five minutes. His name was Locklear. Late fifties, silver-haired, looked exactly like you'd expect the head of St. Ives Academy to look. When they were alone in his private office,

Locklear shook hands gravely and said, "Thank you for coming, Mr. Valarian. Please sit down."

He perched on the edge of a maroon leather chair, now tense and on guard as well as uncomfortable. The way he'd felt when he got sent to the principal's office in public school. He didn't know what to do with his hands, finally slid them down tight over his knees. His gaze roamed the office. Nice. Books everywhere, a big illuminated globe on a wooden stand, a desk that had to be pure Philippine mahogany, a bank of windows that looked out over the central quadrangle and rolling lawns beyond. Impressive, all right. He wouldn't mind having a desk like that one himself.

He waited until Locklear was seated behind it before he said, "This trouble with my son. It must be pretty serious if you couldn't talk about it on the phone."

"I'm afraid it is. Quite serious."

"Bad grades or what?"

"No. Chip is extremely bright, and his grades—"

"Peter."

"Ah, yes, of course."

"His mother calls him that. I don't."

"He seems to prefer it."

"His name is Peter. Chip sounds . . . ordinary."

"Your son is anything but ordinary, Mr. Valarian."

The way the headmaster said that tightened him up even more. "What's going on here?" he demanded. "What's Peter done?"

"We're not absolutely certain he's responsible for any of the . . . incidents. I should make that clear at the outset. However, the circumstantial evidence is considerable and points to no one else."

Incidents. Circumstantial evidence. "Get to the point, Mr. Locklear. What do you *think* he did?"

The headmaster leaned forward, made a steeple of his fingertips. He seemed to be hiding behind it as he said, "There have been a series of thefts in Chip's . . . in Peter's dormitory, beginning several weeks ago. Small amounts of cash pilfered from the rooms of nearly a dozen different boys."

"My son's not a thief."

"I sincerely hope that's so. But as I said, the circumstantial evidence—"

"Why would he steal money? He's got plenty of his own—I send him more than he can spend every month."

"I can't answer your question. I wish I could."

"You ask him about the thefts?"

"Yes."

"And?"

"He denies taking any money."

"All right then," Valarian said. "If he says he didn't do it, then he didn't do it."

"Two of the victims saw him coming out of their rooms immediately before they discovered missing sums."

"And you believe these kids over my son."

"Given the other circumstances, we have no choice."

"What other circumstances?"

"Chip has been involved in—"

"Peter."

"I'm sorry, yes, Peter. He has been involved in several physical altercations recently. Last week one of the boys he attacked suffered a broken nose."

"Attacked? How do you know he did the attacking?"

"There were witnesses," Locklear said. "To that assault and to the others. In each case, they swore Peter was the aggressor."

The office seemed to have grown too warm; Valarian could feel himself starting to sweat. "He's a little aggressive, I admit that. Always has been. A lot of kids his age—"

"His behavior goes beyond simple aggression, I'm afraid. I can only describe it as bullying to the point of terrorizing."

"Come on, now. I don't believe that."

"Nevertheless, it's true. If you'd care to talk to his teachers, his classmates . . ."

Valarian shook his head. After a time he said, "If this has been going on for a while, why didn't you let me know before?"

"At first the incidents were isolated, and without proof that Peter was responsible for the thefts . . . well, we try to give our young men the benefit of the doubt whenever possible. But as they grew more frequent, more violent, I *did* inform you of the problem. Twice by letter, once in a message when I couldn't reach you by phone at your office."

He stared at the headmaster, but it was only a few seconds before his disbelief faded and he lowered his gaze. Two letters, one phone call. Dimly he remembered getting one of the letters, reading it, dismissing it as unimportant because he was in the middle of a big transaction with the Chicago office. The other letter . . . misplaced, inadvertently thrown out or filed. The phone call . . . dozens came in every day, he had two secretaries screening them and taking messages, and sometimes the messages didn't get delivered.

He didn't know what to say. He sat there sweating, feeling like a fool.

"Last evening there was another occurrence," Locklear said, "the most serious of all. That is why I called this morning and insisted on speaking to you in person. We can't prove that your son is responsible, but given what we do know we can hardly come to another conclusion."

"What occurrence? What happened last night?"

"Someone," Locklear said carefully, "set fire to our gymnasium."

"Set fire—my God."

"Fortunately it was discovered in time to prevent the fire from burning out of control and destroying the entire facility, but it did cause several thousand dollars' damage."

"What makes you think Peter set it?"

"He had an argument with his physical education instructor yesterday afternoon. He became quite abusive and made thinly veiled threats. It was in the instructor's office that kerosene was poured and the fire set."

Valarian opened his mouth, clicked it shut again. He couldn't seem to think clearly now. Too damn quiet in there; he could hear a clock ticking somewhere. He broke the silence in a voice that sounded like a stranger's.

"What're you going to do? Expel him? Is that why you got me up here?"

"Believe me, Mr. Valarian, it pains me to say this, but yes, that is the board's decision. For the welfare of St. Ives Academy and the other students. Surely you can understand."

"Oh, I understand," Valarian said bitterly. "You bet I understand."

"Peter will be permitted to remain here until the end of the week, under supervision, if you require time to make other arrangements for him. Of course, if you'd rather he leave with you this afternoon . . ."

Valarian got jerkily to his feet. "I want to talk to my son. Now."

"Yes, naturally. I sent for him earlier and he's waiting in one of the rooms just down the hall."

He had to fight his anger as he followed the headmaster to where Peter was waiting. He felt like hitting something or somebody. Not the boy, he'd never laid a hand on him and never would. Not Locklear, either. Somebody. Himself, maybe.

Locklear stopped before a closed door. He said somberly, "I'll await you in my office, Mr. Valarian," and left him there alone.

He hesitated before going in, to calm down and work out how he was going to handle this. All right. He took a couple of heavy breaths and opened the door.

The boy was sitting on a straightback chair—not doing anything, just sitting there like a statue. When he saw his father he got slowly to his feet and stood with his arms down at his sides. No smile, nothing but a blank stare. He looked older than ten. Big for his age, lean but wide through the shoulders. *He looks like I did at that age,* Valarian thought. *He looks just like me.*

"Hello, Peter."

"Chip," the boy said in a voice as blank as his stare. "You know I prefer Chip, Papa."

"Your name is Peter. I prefer Peter."

Valarian crossed the room to him. The boy put out his hand, but on impulse Valarian bent and caught his shoulders and hugged him. It was like hugging a piece of stone. Valarian let go of him, stepped back.

"I just had a long talk with your headmaster," he said. "Those thefts, the fire yesterday . . . he says it was you."

"I know."

"Well? Was it?"

"No, Papa."

"Don't lie to me. If you did all that . . ."

"I didn't. I didn't do anything."

"They're kicking you out of St. Ives. They wouldn't do that if they weren't sure it was you."

"I don't care."

"You don't care you're being expelled?"

"I don't like it here anymore. I don't care what the headmaster or the teachers or the other kids think. I don't care what anybody thinks about me." Funny little smile. "Except you, Papa."

"All right," Valarian said. "Look me in the eyes and tell me the truth. *Did* you steal money, set that fire?"

"I already told you I didn't."

"In my eyes. Up close."

The boy stepped forward and looked at him squarely. "No, Papa, I didn't," he said.

In the car on the way back to the city he kept seeing Peter's eyes staring into his. He couldn't get them out of his mind. What he'd seen there shining deep and dark . . . it must've been there all along. How could he have missed it before? It had made him feel cold all over; made him want nothing more to do with his son today, tell Locklear he'd send somebody to pick up the boy at the end of the week and then get out of there fast. Now, remembering, it made him shudder.

Lugo was looking at him in the rear view mirror. "Something wrong, Mr. Valarian?"

At any other time he'd have said no and let it go at that. But now he heard himself say, "It's my son. He got into some trouble. That's why I had to go to the school."

"All taken care of now?"

"No. They're throwing him out."

"No kidding? That's too bad."

"Is it?" Then he said, "His name's Peter, but his mother calls him Chip. She says he's like me, a chip off the same block. He likes the name, he thinks it fits him too. But I don't like it."

"How come?"

"I don't want him to be like me, I wanted him to grow up better than me. Better in every way. That's why I sent him to St. Ives. You understand?"

Lugo said, "Yes, sir," but they were just words. Lugo was his driver, his bodyguard, his strongarm man; all Lugo understood was how to steer a limo, how to serve the mob with muscle or a gun.

"I don't want him in my business," he said. "I don't want him to be another John Valarian."

"But now you think maybe he will be?"

"No, that's not what I think." Valarian crossed himself, picturing those bright, cold eyes. "I think he's gonna be a hell of a lot worse."

Donald E. Westlake

Come Again?

YOU NAME IT, Donald E. Westlake's written it. If he didn't invent the comic mystery, he re-invented it. If he didn't invent the hard-boiled crime novel told from the criminal's point of view, he raised it to new levels of both style and substance with his Parker series, which recently made a welcome comeback with the novel titled *Comeback*. And so on. His writing talents don't just lie in the fiction arena either. His film writing has attained near-mythic status, and includes a wonderfully dark script for *The Stepfather* and an Academy Award–nominated script from Jim Thompson's *The Grifters*. And if that's not enough, he's also one of our best short story writers. In "Come Again?" he handles wry humor as deftly as anyone, bringing together a boorish tabloid reporter hot on the trail of the story of the century, only to find a real-life situation he couldn't have made up in his wildest imaginings. Published in *The Mysterious Press Anniversary Anthology*, it's a showcase of his best work yet.

Come Again?

Donald E. Westlake

The fact that the state of Florida would give the odious Boy Cartwright a driver's license only shows that the state of Florida isn't as smart as it thinks it is. The vile Boy, execrable expatriate Englishman, handed this document across the rental-car counter at Gulfport-Biloxi Regional Airport and the gullible clerk there responded by giving him the keys to something called a Taurus, a kind of space capsule sans relief tube, which turned out on examination in the ghastly sunlight to be the same whorehouse red as the rental clerk's lipstick. Boy tossed his disreputable canvas ditty bag onto this machine's backseat, the Valium and champagne bottles within chattering comfortably together, and drove north.

This was not the sort of assignment the despicable Boy was used to. As by far the most shameless and tasteless, and therefore by far the best, reporter on the staff of the *Weekly Galaxy*, a supermarket tabloid that gives new meaning to the term degenerate, the debased Boy Cartwright was used to commanding teams of reporters on assignments at the very peak of the tabloid Alp: celebrity adultery, UFO sightings, sports heroes awash in recreational drugs. The Return of Laurena Layla—or, more accurately, her nonreturn, as it would ultimately prove—was a distinct comedown for Boy. Not an event, but the mere anniversary of an event. And not in Los Angeles or Las Vegas or Miami or any of the other centers of debauchery of the American celebrity world, but in Marmelay, Mississippi, in the muggiest, mildewiest, kudzuest nasal bowel of the Deep South, barely north of Biloxi and the Gulf, a town surrounded mostly by De Soto National Forest, named for a reprobate the *Weekly Galaxy* would have loved if he'd only been born four hundred and fifty years later.

There were two reasons why Boy had drawn this bottom-feeder assignment, all alone in America, the first being that he was in somewhat bad odor at the *Galaxy* at the moment, having not only failed to steal the private psychiatric records of sultry sci-fi-pic star Tanya Shonya from the Montana sanitarium where the auburn-tressed beauty was recovering from her latest doomed love affair, but having also, in the process, inadvertently blown the cover of another *Galaxy* staffer, Don Grove, a member of Boy's usual team, who had already been ensconced in that same sanitarium as a grief counselor. Don even now remained immured in a Montana quod among a lot of Caucasian cowboys, while the *Galaxy*'s lawyers negotiated reasonably with the state authorities, and Boy got stuck with Laurena Layla.

But that wasn't the only reason for this assignment. Twenty-two years earlier, when Boy Cartwright was freshly at the *Galaxy*, a whelp reporter (the *Galaxy* did not have cubs) with just enough experience on scabrous British tabloids to make him prime *Galaxy* material, just as despicable in those days but not yet as decayed, he had covered the trial of Laurena Layla, then a twenty-seven-year-old beauty, mistress of the Golden Church of Sha-Kay, a con that had taken millions from the credulous, which is, after all, what the credulous are for.

The core of the Golden Church of Sha-Kay had been the Gatherings, a sort of cross between a mass séance and a Rolling Stones world tour, which had taken place in stadiums and arenas wherever in rural America the boobs lay thick on the ground. With much use of swirling smoke and whirling robes, these Gatherings had featured music, blessings, visions, apocalyptic announcements, and a well-trained devoted staff, devoted to squeezing every buck possible from the attending faithful.

Also, for those gentlemen of discernment whose wealth *far* exceeded their brains, there had been private sessions attainable with Laurena Layla herself, from which strong men were known to have emerged goggle-eyed, begging for oysters.

What had drawn the younger but no less awful Boy Cartwright to Laurena Layla the first time was an ambitious Indiana D.A. with big eyes for the governorship (never got it) who, finding Laurena Layla in full frontal operation within his jurisdiction, had caused her to be arrested and put on trial as the con artist (and artiste) she was. The combination of sex, fame, and courtroom was as powerful an aphrodisiac for the *Galaxy* and its readers then as ever, so Boy, at that time a mere stripling in some other editor's crew, was among those dispatched to Muncie by Massa (Bruno DeMassi), then owner and publisher of the rag.

Boy's English accent, raffish charm, and suave indifference to putdowns had made him a natural to be assigned to make contact with the defendant herself, which he had been pleased to do, winning the lady over with bogus ID from the *Manchester Guardian*. His success had been so instantaneous and so total that he had bedded L. L. twice, the second time because neither of them could quite believe the first.

In the event, L. L. was found innocent, justice being blind, while Boy was unmasked as the scurrilous Galaxyite he in fact was, and he was sent packing with a flea in his ear and a high-heel print on his bum. However, she didn't come off at all badly in the *Galaxy*'s coverage of her trial and general notoriety, and in fact a bit later she sent him the briefest of thank-you notes with no return address.

That was not the last time Boy saw Laurena Layla, however. Two years after Muncie it was, and the memory of the all-night freight train whistles there was at last beginning to fade, when Laurena Layla hit the news again for an entirely different reason: She died. A distraught fan, a depressingly overweight woman with a home permanent, stabbed L. L. three times with a five-and-dime steak knife, all the thrusts fatal but fortunately none of them disfiguring; L. L. made a lovely corpse.

Which was lucky indeed, because it was Boy's assignment on that occasion to get the body in the box. Whenever a celebrity went down, it was *Galaxy* tradition to get, by hook or by crook (usually by crook), a photo of the recently departed lying in his or her casket during the final viewing. This photo would then appear, as large as physically possible, on the front page of the following week's *Galaxy*, in full if waxen color.

Attention, shoppers: Next to the cash register is an intimation of mortality, yours, cheap. See? Even people smarter, richer, prettier, and better smelling than you die, sooner or later; isn't that news worth a buck or two?

Getting the body in the box that time had been only moderately difficult. Though the Golden Church of Sha-Kay headquarters in Marmelay—a sort of great gilded banana split of a building with a cross and a spire and a carillon and loudspeakers and floodlights and television broadcasting equipment on top—was well guarded by cult staff members, it had been child's play to Mickey Finn a staffer of the right size and heft, via a doctored Dr Pepper, borrow the fellow's golden robe, and slip into the Temple of Revelation during a staff shift change.

Briefly alone in the dusky room with the late L. L., Boy had paused above the well-remembered face and form, now inert as it had never been in life, supine there in the open gilded casket on its waist-high bier, amid golden candles, far too much incense, and a piped-in celestial choir oozing out what sounded suspiciously like "Camptown Races" at half speed. Camera in right hand, he had reached out his left to adjust the shoulder of that golden gown to reveal just a bit more cleavage, just especially for all those necrophiles out there in Galaxyland, then it was *pop* goes the picture and Boy was, so far as he knew, done with the lovely late lady forever.

But no. It seemed that, among the effects Laurena Layla had left behind, amid the marked decks, shaved dice, plastic fingernails, and John B. Anderson buttons, was a last will and testament, in which the lady had promised her followers a second act: "I shall Die untimely," she wrote (which everybody believes, of course), "but it shall not be a real Death. I shall Travel in that Other World, seeking Wisdom and the Way, and twenty years after my

Departure, to the Day, I shall return to this Plane of Existence to share with You the Knowledge I have gained."

Twenty years. Tomorrow, the second Thursday in May, would be the twentieth anniversary of Laurena Layla's dusting, and an astonishing number of mouth-breathers really did expect her to appear among them, robes, smiles, cleavage, Wisdom, and all. Most if not all of those faithful were also faithful *Galaxy* readers, naturally, so here was Boy, pasty-faced, skeptical, sphacelated, Valium-enhanced, champagne-maintained, and withal utterly pleased with himself, even though this assignment was a bit of a comedown.

Here was the normally moribund crossroads of Marmelay, a town that had never quite recovered from the economic shock when the slave auction left, but today doing its best to make up all at once for a hundred and fifty years of hind teat. The three nearby motels had all quadrupled their rates, the two local diners had printed new menus, and the five taverns in the area were charging as though they'd just heard Prohibition was coming back. Many of the Sha-Kay faithful did their traveling in RVs, but they still had to eat, and the local grocers knew very well what *that* meant: move the decimal point one position to the right on every item in the store. The locals were staying home for a couple days.

Boy traveled this time as himself, a rare occurrence, though he had come prepared with the usual array of false identification just in case. He was also traveling solo, without even a photographer, since it wasn't expected he'd require a particularly large crew to record a nonevent: "Not appearing today in her Temple of Revelation in the charmingly sleepy village of Marmelay, Mississippi . . ."

So it was the truth Boy told the clerk at the Lest Ye Forget Motel, unnatural though that felt: "Boy Cartwright. The *Weekly Galaxy* made one's reservation, some days ago."

"You're a foreigner," the lad in the oversize raspberry jacket with the motel chain's logo on its lapel told him, and pointed at Boy as though Boy didn't already know where he was. "You're French!"

"Got it in one, dear," Boy agreed. "Just winged in from jolly old Paris to observe the festivities."

"Laurena Layla, you mean," the lad told him, solemn and excited all at once. Nodding, he said, "She's coming back, you know."

"So one has heard."

"Coming back tomorrow," the lad said, and sighed. "Eight o'clock tomorrow night."

"I believe that is the zshedule," Boy acknowledged, thinking how this youth could not have been born yet when Laurena Layla got herself perforated. How folly endures!

"Wish I could see it," the lad went on, "but the tickets is long gone. Long gone."

"Ah, tickets," Boy agreed. "Such valuable little things, at times. But as to one's room . . ."

"Oh, sure," the lad said, but then looked doubtful. "Was that a single room all by yourself?"

"For preference."

"For this time only," the lad informed him, speaking as by rote, "the management could give you a very special rate, if you was to move in with a family. Not a big family."

"Oh, but, dear," Boy said, "one has moved *out* from one's family. Too late to alter that, I'm afraid."

"So it's just a room by yourself," the lad said, and shrugged and said, "I'm supposed to ask, is all."

"And you did it very well," Boy assured him, then flinched as the lad abruptly reached under the counter between them, but then all he came up with was some sort of pamphlet or brochure. Offering this, he said, "You want a battlefield map?"

"Battlefield?" Boy's yellow spine shriveled. "Are there public disorders about?"

"Oh, not anymore," the lad promised, and pointed variously outward, saying, "Macunshah, Honey Ridge, Polk's Ferry, they're all just around here."

"Ah," Boy said, recollecting the local dogma, and now understanding the motel's name. "Your Civil War, you mean."

"The War Between the States," the lad promptly corrected him. He knew *that* much.

"Well, yes," Boy agreed. "One has heard it wasn't actually that civil."

In the event, Boy did share his room with a small family after all. In a local pub—*taa*-vin, in regional parlance—he ran across twins who'd been ten years old when their mother, having seen on TV the news of Laurena Layla's demise, had offed herself with a shotgun in an effort to follow her pastoress to that better world. (It had also seemed a good opportunity for her to get away from their father.) The twins, Ruby Mae and Ruby Jean, were thirty now, bouncing healthy girls, who had come to Marmelay on the off chance Mama would be coming back as well, presumably with her head restored. They were excited as all get-out at meeting an actual reporter from the *Weekly Galaxy*, their favorite and perhaps only reading, and there he was an Englishman, too! They just loved his accent, and he loved theirs.

"It's one P.M.," said the musical if impersonal voice in his ear.

Boy awoke, startled and enraged, to find himself holding a telephone to his head. Acid sunlight burned at the closed blinds covering the window. "Who the hell cares?" he snarled into the mouthpiece, which responded with a rendition of "Dixie" on steel drum.

Appalled, realizing he was in conversation with a *machine*, Boy slammed down the phone, looked around the room, which had been transmogrified overnight into a laundry's sorting area, and saw that he was alone. The twins had romped off somewhere, perhaps to buy their mother a welcome-home pair of cuddly slippers.

Just as well; Boy was feeling a bit shopworn this morning. Afternoon. And that had been the wake-up call he must have requested in an optimistic moment late last night. Most optimistic moments occur late at night, in fact; realism requires daylight.

Up close, the banana-split Temple of Revelation appeared to have been served on a Bakelite plate, which was actually the shiny blacktop parking area, an ebony halo broadly encircling the temple and now rapidly filling with RVs, tour buses, pickup trucks, and all the other transportations of choice of life's also-rans.

And they were arriving, in their droves. Whole families, in their Sunday best. Sweethearts, hand in hand. Retired oldsters, grinning shyly, made a bit slow and ponderous by today's early-bird special. Solitaries, some nervous and guarded in hoods and jackets too warm for the weather, others gaudily on the prowl, in sequins and vinyl. Folks walked by in clothing covered with words, everything from bowling teams and volunteer fire departments to commercial sports organizations and multinational corporations that had never given these people a penny. Men in denim, women in cotton, children in polyester. Oh, if Currier and Ives were alive in this moment!

Boy and the rental Taurus circled the blacktop, slaloming slowly among the clusters of people walking from their vehicles toward the admission gates. Show or no show, miracle or nix, revelation or fuggedabahdid, every one of them would fork over their ten bucks at the temple gate, eight for seniors, seven for children under six. Inside, there would be more opportunities for donations, gifts, love offerings, and so on, but all of that was optional. The ten-spot at the entrance was mandatory.

Everyone here was looking for a sign, in a way, and so was Boy, but the sign he sought would say something like VIP or PRESS or AUTHORIZED PERSONNEL ONLY. And yes, there it was: MEDIA. How modern.

The media, in fact, were sparse in the roped-off section of parking lot around to the side of the banana split, where a second entrance spared the chosen few from consorting with the rabble. Flashing his *Galaxy* ID at the golden-robed guardian of the MEDIA section, driving in, Boy counted two TV relay trucks, both local, plus perhaps half a dozen rentals like his own. Leaving the Taurus, Boy humped onto his shoulder the small canvas bag containing his tape recorder, disposable camera, and a folder of the tear sheets of his earlier coverage of Laurena Layla, plus her truncated note of gratitude, and hiked through the horrible humidity and searing sun to the blessed shade of the VIP entrance.

It took two golden-robers to verify his ID at this point, and then he was directed to jess go awn in an keep tuh the leff. He did so, and found himself in the same curving charcoal-gray dim-lit corridor he'd traversed just twenty years ago when he'd gotten the body in the box. Ah, memory.

Partway round, he was met by another fellow in a golden robe, next to a broad black closed metal door. "Press?" this fellow asked.

"Absolutely."

"Yes, sir," the fellow said, drew the door open, and ushered him in.

With the opening of the door, crowd noises became audible. Boy stepped through and found himself in a large opera box midway down the left side of the great oval hall that was the primary interior space of the temple. Raised above auditorium level, the box gave a fine view of the large echoing interior with its rows of golden plush seats, wide aisles, maroon carpets and walls, battalions of lights filling the high black ceiling, and the deep stage at the far end where L.L. used to give her sermons and where her choir and her dancer-acolytes once swirled their robes. The sect had continued all these years without its foundress, but not, Boy believed, as successfully as before.

The stage looked now as though set for some minimalist production of *King Lear*: bare, half-lit, wooden floor uncovered, gray back wall unlit, nothing visible except one large golden armchair in the exact center of the stage. The chair wasn't particularly illuminated, but Boy had no doubt it would be, if and when.

Below, the hall was more than half full, with the believers still streaming in. Sharing the box with Boy were the expected two camera crews and the expected scruffy journalists, the only oddity being that more of the journalists were female than male: four scruffy women and, with Boy, three scruffy men. Boy recognized a couple of his competitors and nodded distantly; they returned the favor. None of them was an ace like himself.

Ah, well. If only he'd succeeded in that Montana sanitarium. If only Don Grove were not now in a Montana pokey. If only Boy Cartwright didn't have to be present for this nothingness.

The con artists who ran Sha-Kay these days would no doubt produce some sort of light show, probably broadcast some old audiotapes of Laurena Layla, edited to sound as though she were addressing the rubes this very minute rather than more than twenty years ago. At the end of the day the suckers would wander off, very well fleeced and reasonably well satisfied, while the fleecers would have the admissions money, fifty or sixty thousand, plus whatever else they'd managed to pluck during the show.

Plus, of course, TV. This nonevent would be broadcast live on the Sha-Kay cable station, with a phone number prominent for the receipt of donations, all major credit cards accepted.

No, all of these people would be all right, but what about poor Boy Cartwright? Where was his *story*? "The nonappearance today in Marm—"

And there she was.

It was done well, Boy had to admit that. No floating down into view from above the stage, no thunderclaps and puffs of smoke while she emerged from a trapdoor behind the golden chair, no fanfare at all. She was simply *there*, striding in her shimmering golden robe down the wide central aisle from the rear of the hall, flanked by a pair of burly guardians to keep the faithful at bay, moving with the same self-confidence as always. Most of the people in the hall, including Boy, only became aware of her with the amplified sound of her first "Hosannas!"

That had always been her greeting to her flock, and here it was again. "Hosannas! Hosannas!" spoken firmly as she nodded to the attendees on both sides, her words miked to speakers throughout the hall that boomed them back as though her voice came from everywhere in the building at once.

It was the same voice. That was the first thing Boy caught. It was exactly the same voice he'd heard saying any number of things twenty years ago, *hosannas!* among them as well as *oh yes!* and *more more!*

She's lip-synching, he thought, to an old tape, but then he realized it was also the same body, sinuous within that robe. Yes, it was, long and lithe, the same body he well remembered. The same walk, almost a model's but earthier. The same pitch to the head, set of the shoulders, small hand gesture that wasn't quite a wave. And, hard to tell from up here, but it certainly looked like the same face.

But not twenty years older. The same age, or very close to the same age, twenty-seven, that Laurena Layla had been when the fan had given her that bad review. The same age, and in every other respect, so far as Boy could tell from this distance, the same woman.

It's a hologram, he told himself, but a hologram could not reach out to pat the shoulder of a dear old lady on the aisle, as this one now did, causing the dear old lady to faint dead away on the instant.

She's real, Boy thought. She's returned, by God.

A chill ran up his back as she ran lightly up the central stairs to the stage, the hairs rose on his neck, and he remembered all too clearly not the body in the box but the body two years before that, as alive as quicksilver.

She stopped, turned to face her people. Her smile was faintly sad, as it had always been. She spread her hands in a gesture that welcomed without quite embracing, as she always had. "Hosannas," she said, more quietly, and the thousands below thundered, "Hosannas!"

Boy stared. Gray sweat beaded on his gray forehead. His follicles itched, his clothing cramped him, his bones were gnarled and wretched.

"I have been away," Laurena Layla said, and smiled. "And now I have returned."

As the crowd screamed in delight, Boy took hold of himself—metaphorically. You are here, my lad, he reminded himself, because you do not believe in this crap. You do not believe in any of the crap. If you start coming all over goose bumps every time somebody rises from the dead, of what use will you be, old thing, to the dear old *Weekly Galaxy?*

Onstage, she, whoever she was, whatever she was, had gone into an old routine, feel-good mysticism, the basic tenets of Sha-Kay, but now delivered with the assurance of one who's been there and done that. The faithful gawped, the TV crews focused, the second-string stringers from the other tabs wrote furiously in their notebooks or extended their tape recorders toward the stage as though the voice were coming from there, and Boy decided it was time to get a little closer.

Everyone was mesmerized by the woman on the stage, or whatever that was on the stage. Unnoticed, Boy stepped backward and through the doorway to the hall.

Where the golden guardian remained, unfortunately. "Sir," he said, frowning, "were you going to leave already?"

"Just a little reconnoiter, dear," Boy assured him.

"I'm not supposed to let anybody past this point," the guardian explained, looking serious about it.

This was why Boy never went on duty without arming himself with, in his left trouser pocket, folded hundred-dollar bills. It was automatic now to slide hand in and C-note out, the while murmuring; "Just need a quieter location, dear. Those TV cameras foul my recorder."

The reason employees are so easy to suborn is that they're employees. They're only here in the first place because they're being paid for their time. Whatever the enterprise may be, they aren't connected to it by passion or ownership or any other compelling link. Under the circumstances, what is a bribe but another kind of wage?

Still, we all of us have an ass to protect. Hand hovering over the proffered bill, the guardian nevertheless said, "I don't want to get in any trouble here."

"Nothing to do with you, old thing," Boy assured him. "I came round the other way."

The bill disappeared, and then so did Boy, following the long curved hall toward the stage. More and more of the temple layout he remembered as he moved along. Farther along this hallway he would find that faintly sepulchral room where the body had been on display, placed there because crowd control would have been so much iffier out in the main auditorium.

That last time, Boy had had no reason to proceed past the viewing room, which in more normal circumstances would have been some kind of offstage prep area or greenroom, but he knew it couldn't be far from there to the stage. Would he be closer then to *her*?

The likeness was so uncanny, dammit. Or perhaps it was so canny. In any event, this Laurena Layla, when close to people, kept moving, and when she stopped to speak she kept a distance from everyone else. Could she not be observed up close for long? If not, why not?

Though as Boy came around the curving hallway his left hand was already in his pocket, fondling another century, there was no guard on duty at the closed greenroom door; a surprise, but never question good fortune. In case the undoubted sentry was merely briefly away to answer mother's call, he hastened the last few yards, even though the brisk motion made his brain-walnut chafe uncomfortably against the shell of his skull.

The black door in the charcoal-gray wall opened soundlessly to his touch. He slipped through; he pulled the door shut behind him.

Well. It did look different without a coffin in the middle. Now it was merely a staging area, dim-lit, with the props and materials of cultish magic neatly shelved or stacked or hung, waiting for the next Call. A broad but low-ceilinged room, its irregular shape was probably caused by the architectural requirements of the stage and temple that surrounded it. That shape, with corners and crannies in odd shadowed places, had added to the eeriness when Boy and his Hasselblad had been in here twenty years ago, but now it all seemed quite benign, merely a kind of surrealistic locker room.

There. The closed door opposite, across the empty black floor. That was the route Boy had not taken last time, when the viewers of the remains had been herded through the main temple and over the stage, past many opportunities to show their sorrow and their continued devotion in a shall we say tangible way, before they were piloted past the dear departed, out the door Boy had just come in, and down the long hall to what at this moment had been converted into the VIP entrance.

After a quick glance left and right, reassuring himself he was alone and all the stray dim corners were empty, he crossed to that far door, cracked it just a jot, and peered one eyed out at what looked like any backstage. Half a dozen technicians moved about. A hugely complex lightboard stretched away on the right, and beyond it yawned the stage, with Laurena Layla—or whoever—in profile out there, continuing her spiel.

She looked shorter from here, no doubt the effect of the high-ceilinged stage and all those lights. The golden chair still stood invitingly behind her, but she remained on her feet, pacing in front of the chair as she delivered her pitch.

How would it all end? Would she sit in the chair at last, then disappear in a puff of smoke? A trapdoor, then, which would make her devilish hard to intercept.

But Boy didn't think so. He thought they'd be likelier to repeat the understated eloquence of that arrival, that L. L. would simply walk off the stage as she'd simply walked onto it, disappear from public view, and come . . . here.

She would not be alone, he was sure of that. Determinedly alone onstage, once free of the suckers' gaze, she would surely be surrounded by her . . . acolytes? handlers?

Boy had his story now. Well, no, he didn't *have* it, but he knew what it was: the interview with the returned L. L. The *Galaxy* had treated any number of seers and mystics and time travelers and alien abductees with po-faced solemnity over the years, so surely this Layla would understand she was in safe hands when she was in the hands—as he certainly hoped she soon would be—of Boy Cartwright. The question was how to make her see his journal's usefulness to her before her people gave him the boot.

The old clippings; the thank-you note. Waggle those in front of her face, they'd at least slow down the proceedings long enough to give him an opportunity to swathe her in his moth-eaten charm. It had worked before.

His move at this point was to hide himself, somewhere in this room. This was where he was sure she would travel next, so he should conceal himself in here, watch how the scam proceeded, await his opportunity. *Snick*, he shut the stageward door, and, clutching his canvas bag between flaccid arm and trembling ribs, with its valuable cargo of clippings and thank-yous, he turned to suss the place out.

Any number of hiding places beckoned to him, shady nooks at the fringes of the room. Off to the right, in a cranny that was out of the way but not out of sight of either door, stood two long coatracks on wheels, the kind hosts set up for parties, these both bowed beneath the weight of many golden robes. Don one? At the very least, insert himself among them.

As he hurried toward that darkly gold-gleaming niche, a great crowd-roar arose behind him, triumphant yet respectful, gleeful yet awed. Just in time, he thought, and plunged among the robes.

Dark in here, and musty. Boy wriggled backward, looking for a position where he could see yet not be seen, and his heel hit the body.

He knew it, in that first instant. What his heel had backed into was not a sports bag full of laundry, not a sleeping cat, not a rolled-up futon. A body.

Boy squinched backward, wriggling his bum through the golden robes, while the crowd noise outside reached its crescendo and fell away. He found it agony to make this overworked body kneel, but Boy managed, clutching to many robes as he did so, listening to his knees do their firecracker imitations. Down at mezzanine level, he sagged onto his haunches while he pushed robe hems out of the way, enough to see . . .

Well. *This* one won't be coming back. In this dimness, the large stain across the back of the golden robe on the figure huddled on the floor looked black, but Boy knew that, in the light, it would be a gaudier hue. He felt no need to touch it, he knew what it was.

And who. The missing sentry.

I am not alone in here, Boy thought, and as he thought so he was not; the stageward door opened and voices entered, male and female.

Boy cringed. Not the best location, this, on one's knees at the side of a recently plucked corpse. Hands joining knees on the floor, he crawled away from the body through the robes until he could see the room.

Half a dozen people, all berobed, had crowded in, Laurena unmistakable among them, beautiful, imperious, and a bit sullen. The others, male and female, excited, chattered at her, but she paid them no attention, moving in a boneless undulation toward a small makeup table directly across the room from where Boy slunk. They followed, still relieving their tension with chatter, and she waved a slender forearm of dismissal without looking back.

"Leave her alone now."

This was said clearly through the babble by an older woman, silver-haired and bronze-faced in her golden robe, who stood behind the still-moving Laurena, faced the others, and said, "She needs to rest."

They all agreed, verbally and at length, while the older woman made shooing motions and Laurena sank into a sinuous recline on the stool at the makeup table. Boy, alert for any eruption at all from anywhere, trying to watch the action in front of him while still keeping an eye on every other nook and cranny in the entire room—a hopeless task—watched and waited and wondered when he could make his presence, and his news, known.

The older woman was at last succeeding in her efforts to clear the area. The others backed off, calling final praises and exhortations over their shoulders, oozing out of the room like a film in reverse that shows the smoke go back in the bottle. Boy gathered his limbs beneath him for the Herculean task of becoming once more upright, and the older woman said, "You were magnificent."

Laurena reached a languid arm forward to switch on the makeup lights, in which she gazed upon her astonishingly beautiful and pallid face, gleaming in the dim gray mirror. "What are they to me?" she asked, either to herself or the older woman.

"Your life," the older woman told her. "From now on."

Outside, the faithful had erupted into song, loud and clamorous. It probably wasn't, but it certainly sounded like, a speeded-up version of "We Shall Overcome."

Laurena closed her striking eyes and shook her head, "Leave me," she said.

Boy was astonished. An actual human being had said, "Leave me," just like a character in a vampire film. Perhaps this Laurena *was* from the beyond.

In any event, the line didn't work. Rather than leave her, the older woman said, "This next part is vital."

"I know, I know."

"You'll be just as wonderful, I know you will."

"Why wouldn't I be?" Laurena asked her. "I've trained for it long enough."

"Rest," the older woman urged. "I'll come back for you in fifteen minutes." And with that, at last, she was gone, leaving Laurena semi-alone, the raucous chorus surging when the door was open.

Boy lunged upward, grabbing for handholds among the robes, knees exploding like bags full of water. His first sentences were already clear in his mind, but as he staggered from concealment, hand up as though hailing a cab, movement flashed from off to his left.

Boy looked, and lunging from another hiding place, between himself and the stageward door, heaved a woman, middle-aged, depressingly over-weight, in a home permanent, brandishing a stained steak knife from the five-and-ten like a homicidal whale.

Good God! Have they *both* come back? Is there hope for Ruby Mae and Ruby Jean's mom after all?

Laurena's makeup mirror was positioned so that it was the whale she saw in it first, not Boy. Turning, not afraid, still imperious, she leveled her remote gaze on the madwoman and said, "What are you?"

"You *know* who I am!" snarled the madwoman, answering the wrong question. "I'm here to finish what my mother started!"

And in that instant Boy knew everything. He knew that the roused chorus in the temple auditorium meant that cries for help would go for naught. He knew that escape past the madwoman out that door toward the stage was impossible. He knew that he himself could make a dash for the opposite door, the one by which he'd entered, but that Laurena, by the makeup table, would never make it.

But he knew even more. He knew the scam.

However, what he *didn't* know was what to do about it. Where, in all this, was poor Boy's story? Should he zip out the door, report the murders, have *that* scoop? Should he remain here, rescue the maiden without risk to himself and in hope of the usual reward, have *that* scoop (and reward)? (The "without risk to himself" part tended to make that plan Plan B.)

How old was she, *that* was the question, the most important question of all. Answer that one first.

"Dears, dears, dears," he announced in his plummiest voice, swanning forward like the emcee in *Cabaret*, "play nice, now, don't fight."

They both gaped at him. Like a tyro at the game arcade, the madwoman didn't know what to do when faced with two simultaneous targets. She hung there, flat-footed, one Supphose'd shin before the other, knife arm raised, looking now mostly like a reconstructed dinosaur at the museum, while Lau-rena gave him a stare of cool disbelief and said, "And who are *you*?"

"Oh, but, dear, you must remember me," Boy told her, talking very fast indeed to keep everybody off balance. "Dear old Boy, from the *Galaxy*, I still have your thank-you note, I've treasured it always, I brought it with me in my little bag here." Deciding it would be dangerous to reach into the bag—it might trigger some unfortunate response from the dinosaur—he hurtled on, saying, "Of course, dear Laurena, one had to see you again, after all this time, *report* our meeting, tell the world we—"

The penny dropped at last, and now she *was* shocked. "You're a *reporter*?"

"Oh, you do remember!" Boy exulted. "One *knew* you would!"

"You can't stop me!" the madwoman honked, as though she hadn't been stopped already.

But of course she could reactivate herself, couldn't she? Boy told her,

"One did not have the pleasure of meeting your mother, dear, I'm sorry to say, but one did see her in custody and at the trial, and she certainly was forceful."

Whoops; wrong word. "And so am I!" cried the madwoman, and lumbered again toward Laurena.

"No no, wait wait wait!" cried Boy. "I wanted to ask you about your mother." As the madwoman had now halved the distance between herself and the shrinking Laurena, Boy felt an increasing urgency as he said, "I *wrote* about her, you know, in the *Weekly Galaxy*, you must have seen it."

That stopped her. Blinking at Boy, actually taking him in for the first time, a reluctant awe coming into her face and voice, she said, "The *Weekly Galaxy?*"

"Boy Cartwright, at your service," he announced with a smile and a bow he'd borrowed from Errol Flynn, who would not have recognized it. "And as a reporter," he assured her, "I assure you I am not here to alter the situation, but simply to observe. Madam, I will not stand in your way."

Laurena gawked at him. "You won't?"

"Good," the madwoman said, hefted her knife, and thudded another step forward.

"But *first*," Boy went hurriedly on, "I do so want to interview Laurena. Very briefly, I promise you."

They both blinked at him. The madwoman said, "Interview?"

"Two or three questions, no more, and I'm out of your way forever."

"But—" Laurena said.

Taking the madwoman's baffled silence for consent, Boy turned to Laurena. "The silver-haired party was your grandmother," he said.

Managing to find reserves of haughtiness somewhere within, Laurena froze him with a glare: "I am not giving *interviews*."

"Oh, but, dear," Boy said, with a meaningful head nod toward the madwoman, "*this* exclusive interview you will grant, I just know you will, and I must begin, I'm sorry to say, with a personal question. Personal to *me*. I need to know how old you are. You *are* over twenty-one, aren't you?"

"What? Of course I—"

"Honest Injun?" Boy pressed. "One is not a bartender, dear, one has other reasons to need to know. I would guess you to be twenty-five? Twenty-six?" The change in her eyes told him he'd guessed right. "Ah, good," he said with honest relief.

"That's right," the madwoman said.

They both turned to her, having very nearly forgotten her for a few seconds, and she said, "People don't get older in heaven, do they?"

"No, they do not," Boy agreed.

Laurena said, "What *difference* does it make?"

"Well, if you were twenty-one, you see," he explained, "you'd be *my* daughter, which would very much complicate the situation."

"I have no idea what you're talking about," Laurena said, which meant, of course, that she had every idea what he was talking about.

Now he did dare a quick dip into his bag, and before the madwoman could react he'd brought out and shown her his audiocassette recorder. "Tools of the trade, dear," he explained. "No interview without the tape to back it up."

Laurena finally began to show signs of stress, saying, "What are you *doing*? She's got a knife, she's going to *kill* me!"

"Again, darling, yes," Boy said, switching on the machine, aiming it at her. "Just so soon as I leave, at the end of the interview." Because now at last he knew what his story was, he smiled upon her with as much fondness as if she *had* been his daughter—interesting quandary *that* would have been, in several ways—and said, "Of course, in your answers, you might remove our friend's *reason* for wanting to kill you all over again."

Growling, the madwoman bawled, "Nobody's going to stop me! I'm here to finish what my mother started!"

"Yes, of course, you are, dear," Boy agreed. "But what if your mother *did* finish the job?"

The madwoman frowned. "What do you mean? There's Laurena Layla right there!"

"Well, let's ask her about that," Boy suggested, and turned attention, face, and recorder to the young woman. "I must leave very soon," he pointed out. "I only hope, before I go, you will have said those words that will reassure this lovely lady that her mother did not fail, her mother is a success, she can be proud of her mother forever. Can't she, dear?"

Laurena stared helplessly from one to the other. It was clear she couldn't figure out which was the frying pan, which the fire.

To help her, Boy turned back to the madwoman. "You *do* trust the *Galaxy*, don't you?"

"Of course!"

"Whatever this dear child says to us," Boy promised, "you will read in the *Galaxy*. Trust me on this."

"I do," the madwoman said with great solemnity.

Turning to the other, Boy said, "Dear, five million readers are waiting to hear. How was it done? Who are you? Time's getting short, dear."

Laurena struggled to wrap her self-assurance around herself. "You won't leave," she said. "You couldn't."

"Too bad," Boy said with a shrug. "However, the story works just as well the other way." Turning, he took a step toward the hall door as the madwoman took a step forward.

"Wait!" cried the former Laurena Layla.

Lauren Henderson

Dark Mirror

LAUREN HENDERSON'S heroine Samantha Jones has been described as "wonderfully politically incorrect" and "the dominatrix of the British crime scene." In other words, one cool woman. Lauren herself enjoys travel, reading, and keeping her audience breathless while they await her next novel. Until that day comes, they can lose themselves in the twists and turns of "Dark Mirror," a complex story about two sisters whose lives have intertwined until not even they can figure out who's who. It was published in the anthology *Murder Through the Ages*, and was a finalist for the Crime Writers' Association's Golden Dagger Award.

Dark Mirror

Lauren Henderson

for my sister Lisa

L ast night I couldn't sleep. I thought once Terry was gone, sent away, I would sleep again. That was what he said, and he's a doctor, a psychiatrist, so he should know. But he was wrong. I lie awake next to him, listening to his steady breathing, and he never seems to be aware that I am wide awake, staring at the ceiling. Nor does he ask me about it next morning, though he must surely notice the dark shadows under my eyes. Or perhaps he doesn't see them either.

There was a time I thought that he knew everything. He behaved as if he did. That was why I married him.

Last night, lying awake, I didn't toss or turn. I never have. I get out of bed every morning and see that the sheets on my side of the bed are hardly rumpled. I was always the quiet one. One of you two has to be, our mother said: how else am I to tell the pair of you apart?

I didn't move at all. I lay still on the bed, remembering, for some reason, that terrible evening when they came to take Terry to the asylum. I should have felt relieved when it happened, but I didn't; I was just very tired, nearly tired to death. That was the most terrible time of all, that evening. Even worse than when they found that doctor stabbed to death and we were identified as having been in his apartment around the time that it happened. (When I say "we," I don't mean both of us, of course. That's the shorthand twins use. I mean one of us.)

And of course people knew who we were. We ran the little kiosk down in the foyer of the building. Everyone knew us. And I don't mean both of us, either; I mean one of us. No one knew we were identical twins. They thought we were one girl, a girl called Terry. It was a little game we played, a silly harmless game. And we had been dating him, too, that doctor who was killed. Both of us.

That was another game. It didn't mean anything; neither of us cared for him, not in that way, not seriously. But he was clever. Most men didn't guess that there were two of us, the lively one and the quiet one. But he did. And he preferred one of us. He said some hateful things about the other, the one he didn't like. That was a hard thing to do, an unnecessary, cruel thing. It was why he was killed. And there are many worse reasons for killing people.

That evening when I came out of our bedroom, for some reason the first thing I saw was the mirror. It hung on the opposite wall and it reflected the sofa back at me. Terry was sitting there, still talking; she hadn't yet seen me, and her eyes were bright, her expression taut with that intensity I always envied. I never felt things the way Terry did. I wasn't passionate like her.

She was leaning forward as if she were talking to someone sitting next to her, but there was no one there. On the back of her head was the smart, fashionable little black hat with the sparkles that I loved, but whenever I tried it on it didn't look right somehow. I had never worn it out. Whenever I saw it on Terry I would think: You see, it looks fine! And I would see people turn in the street to look at her admiringly. But I knew that it didn't suit me. I couldn't carry it off.

Terry was wearing her favorite black dress; she had many, but this was the one she chose for important occasions when she wanted to give herself confidence. I thought she looked very beautiful. It was unusual for me to feel detached enough from her to be able to comment on how she looked, because it felt like I was passing a judgment on my own appearance. But that night, for some reason, I could.

I saw myself in the mirror too, above Terry's head. Only the top part of my body, to just below my breasts, then the angle of the mirror cut me off; I was floating on the wall like a picture, in my white dressing gown, my hair pulled back because it needed to be washed. It makes me nostalgic for her just to remember the characteristic way her head moved, its quick nods as she talked, agreeing with what she was saying, confirming it with every little assent of her head. But her words were mad, crazy words.

He was right, she was crazy. I saw it clearly then for the first time.

She was saying that she was me, Ruth; she wasn't Terry. That no one had ever wanted Terry, it was always Ruth whom the men had wanted. That there was something wrong with Terry, something bad, and everyone knew it. I stood watching her and it was like my heart was being torn out of my body to hear her say those things about herself.

I knew she didn't have to be that way, you see. I had memories of her from when we were younger, or even just a short time ago, before things went so wrong, before that man, that doctor, was so cruel to her. All the times we'd laugh and joke together, over milkshakes when we were small, in the local drugstore, then cocktails, later, both of us sipping drinks through straws, perfectly happy, telling stupid jokes we'd heard a thousand times and laughing at them fresh, because we were so happy like that, just telling each other stupid, silly, girls' jokes. Oh, she could be different. It was as if no one wanted to see it.

Why had she got this way? That was something he could never tell me. He just said that she was bad and I was good. And he made it sound necessary, fixed in stone, almost as if she had to be bad so that I could be the good one. Yet he couldn't explain why. I didn't question him at the time. I had to have something to believe in with Terry gone. But that's not much of an excuse.

Still, looking at her then, I could see that he was right about one thing. She was crazy. Up till that moment I had denied it. I had tried to protect her. I told the police that we had spent the night together, the night that doctor was killed, that neither one of us had left our apartment. And as long as I stuck to my story, though one of us had been identified as being over at that doctor's place, we were both safe.

What could they do? she said. They couldn't arrest both of us. And she was right. They couldn't. But they were sure it was me or her. Terry said it must have been someone else who killed the doctor and of course I believed her. The police didn't. They made us go to him to let him look at what was going on inside our heads. To shrink them, Terry said. I was cross with her when she put him down, because I was in love with him then and I loved all his tests too, the psychiatric tests to see if you were crazy or not. The ink blots were such fun. It was like being a kid again, playing silly games. And it was wonderful just to sit and talk to him. He was pretty young, but in his white coat and his office with all the scientific charts, it was as if he knew everything that had ever happened, everything you felt. It was a release to me. I trusted him.

Terry was in love with him too, of course. We always fell for the same men. Or was it that she always fell for the ones I liked?

I'll never be able to ask her now.

There were all these men in the room, too. I hadn't noticed them at first, I hadn't taken my eyes off Terry. But then they moved—not much, but enough so that I became aware of their presence.

They all turned to look at me. All but one. I was standing just inside the room, almost in the doorway. She saw them turn, too, and she followed the line of their glances, her head darting in a jerky movement that was very like the convulsive little nods she had been making. She stopped talking in mid-sentence, and our eyes met in the mirror. I can't describe what I saw in hers.

Desperation, maybe. A terrible sadness. Because of course my presence there contradicted everything that she had just been saying, the comforting story she had been telling herself.

Looking at me, she knew that I was Ruth and she was Terry. There was the evidence, in black and white. Like the clothes we were wearing.

All I could say was: "I'm sorry, Terry." And my voice sounded so help-less I hated myself for it.

I never was sure why she called herself Terry. I preferred Teresa, her given name. In fact, I would have liked to have been called that myself. It was such a pretty name, much prettier than Ruth. But it used to amuse me, telling people that I shared a flat with Terry, because some of them would think I meant a man, Terence, and they could see I wasn't married. I had no ring. They would look so shocked for a moment. Then they would look at me, and realize I wasn't that kind of girl, and summon up the nerve to ask who I meant.

Terry still didn't say anything. Suddenly I hated the quiet, hated it. But I couldn't think of anything to say. I should have gone to her, then, sat down next to her, put my arms around her; told her I was here and everything was all right. But I couldn't. Maybe I was still scared of her.

He said later that she had been trying to drive me mad, to make me think that I was the one who had killed that doctor. And yes, it had been terrible those last two weeks. I couldn't sleep; I cried all the time, holding my head, trying to remember doing something that I simply hadn't done. But she didn't mean to drive me mad. She was just crazy, and she was trying to pre-tend to herself that she hadn't done it. I know that. Terry is part of me. I know how her mind works. People think I don't notice things because I'm quiet and sweet and she's the clever, talkative one, but they're wrong. I do see things; I can see what people are like. And no matter what he said, I know that Terry would never, never have hurt me.

It's not fair to expect him to have realized that, though. How could he? He looked in from the outside and thought my life was in danger, and he loved me, so he wanted to protect me. I do understand. But he says now that all his concern, his worry, was on my behalf, and that, I think, is hypocritical. After all, Terry had already killed one man for preferring me to her, and telling her that she was crazy. And here he was, telling her the same thing, a doctor too, just like the other one. No one's going to persuade me that he wasn't a little scared for himself as well.

Although the men around us were silent, I could hear their breathing. It was uneven, nervous. Their presence filled the room, not just their physical bod-ies but the intensity with which they were watching us. It felt somehow as if they had always been there, but only now had decided to reveal themselves. He was one of them, and he fitted in perfectly. All of them were wearing dark suits, except for the one sitting by the table who never took his eyes off Terry; I don't know how I'm so sure about that, for I never took my eyes off her either, but I am. He had very short hair and was all in white, like me. White tunic, white trousers. A hospital uniform. For a moment, aware as I was of Terry's beauty, her likeness to me but also her detachment, he seemed to be another reflection of myself, as still and white as I was, concentrating on her as much as I did. For from the moment I came through the door I never moved, and nor did he, sitting there like a statue.

Then, all of a sudden, Terry's face began to work, distorting itself into something that I recognized. She jumped up and picked up an ashtray off the table, throwing it directly into the mirror. And what she could see in the mirror, apart from herself of course, was me, in my white dressing gown. It was as if she were aiming at me, at my reflection, at us together. But not at me, not at the real Ruth. That's very important to realize. It was that picture of us together she couldn't bear. Even he didn't notice the meaning of that—the significance, as he would put it. But I saw it, and I understood. It wasn't me, Ruth, she hated. It was the way people saw the two of us together.

Of course she hit the mirror bang in the middle with that ashtray; she was always the one who could throw straight. It shattered into pieces. And she did too, from that moment. There was a rush of people, of bodies, motion released. I had to turn my head away from where the mirror had been, now just an empty frame, to see her in the flesh, and when I did she was in the arms of the man in white, sobbing, crumpled, the black hat slipping from her head, no longer beautiful or anything I could put a name to.

He came to me and put his arm around me. I clung to him, my arms clumsily round the dark material of his suit, as Terry was clinging to her warder in his white coat, and we stood there, frozen, dark and light, light and dark, the two pairs of us. But I wasn't crying.

When I woke up I was in my nightdress. He must have taken my dressing gown off and put me to bed with a tranquilizer. And he was sitting on the bed, smiling at me. It was all right now, that's what his smile said. He went to get a breakfast tray, and brought it straight back; he had had it all ready and waiting. I sipped my coffee, smiling into his face, and he said, "Tell me something, Miss Collins?" and I said, "What?" and he said, "How do you come to be so much more beautiful than your sister?" and I smiled at him again, my best smile.

All that smiling . . . That's where it stops. That's where it should have stopped.

I miss her so much. I can't tell him; he would think I was crazy.

I don't mean that literally, of course. I'm the sane one. But he wouldn't understand it, and that would worry him. After all, he would say, she tried to drive you insane, to make you think you killed that doctor; she fed you sleeping pills, told you that you had nightmares until you believed her and started dreaming them for yourself; she told me all those lies about you and in the end, already over the edge, she pretended that she was you, and that you were her, the one who should be committed.

And what would I say? Yes, I know, but . . . but . . .

It's how I feel, I can't express it properly. I was never good with words. Terry was the articulate one. When we were out with boys she would dazzle me and them with her wit, her sense of humor, and I would sit there, silent and jealous but proud of her at the same time. Everything she said seemed to sparkle, while in my mouth it would have been banal. But it was me they walked home, me they lingered with outside the front door, me they rang up and, halting, shy, asked out. Gradually, I learnt that this would be the pattern, and so when we went out together I would be able to sit there, quiet, waiting for my turn later on. But now I wish I had tried to express myself, practiced on them as she did, because I can't manage to explain to him how I still feel about her. I can only think about it like this, rambling away. I'm sure I'm not making much sense.

No, that's not right. I am making sense. I don't know why I just thought that. It's something I say quite often, after I've talked for longer than usual, because it makes their expressions change, the men who are listening. Their faces soften, they smile at me in that kind reassuring way I'm used to, and I feel again in the right place to be.

But I am making sense. I wish I had a friend to talk to about this. Terry was the only friend I ever wanted; my twin, my sister, she was all I had and all I needed. I always imagined us married, living next door to each other, as close as we could be, popping in and out of each other's houses all the time, swapping recipes we'd cut out from magazines, our children playing together in the backyard.

When I was going to see him—for "consultations," as he called them—he was so calm and professional I felt that I could tell him anything. I expect it's only natural that now we're married, that's all changed. But in a strange way I miss the tests, those ink blots, the machine that he connected up to me that would tell if I were lying or not, the graphs it made with its pen. It was all so scientific. And then there was the reassurance that although he was a mind doctor, he was a proper one as well. (He explained that to me when I asked, so nicely, not as if I were ignorant because I didn't know you could be both.) It was as if he had all the bases covered, just in case.

That building, where we had our kiosk in the entrance hall, was full of doctors. They all had offices there, consulting rooms. We called practically every man who passed "Doctor," automatically: it was quicker, and it helped if you forgot one of their names. And it's strange, rather ironic, to think about it now, but at the time, there was something very comforting about working in that particular building, with all of those doctors; it made me feel very safe, knowing that if you hurt yourself, you couldn't be in a better place for it to happen.

I don't think he realized how much it would hurt me for Terry to be committed. I don't think he had the least idea. He saw it as a rescue, with himself as my knight in shining armor. And he was, that's true. I mustn't forget that. She was pulling me down with her into her craziness. But he thought that he could just split us apart cleanly, and keep me separate from what was going on in her head.

Sometimes I wish I'd never seen Terry like that. He says it was necessary for my sake, to prove to me once and for all that she was the mad one of the two of us. It's not that I forget what it was like, those last days when she really was crazy. In fact, I remember it all very sharply, more and more every day. My terrible doubts of her, and of myself, the times when I held my head and cried with fear of my own nightmares, that moment when she asked me if I would ever betray her, and said that if I did she didn't know what she would do. I turned and saw her standing in the shadows under the window in her black dress, her face hidden and her voice metallic, monotonous, and she frightened me.

But I would never have betrayed her, never, no matter what. She didn't need to scare me to make sure.

She couldn't understand that. Maybe she thought I had already betrayed her, with those boys, and then the men—him—because I was the one they liked; but that wasn't my fault! I couldn't help it. When we were first double-dating, I was sure it was her they would want, she was so bright and funny and quick. It was as much of a surprise to me as to her that it was Ruth, not Terry, who got the phone calls and the proposals. And if I came to learn that this was the way it was, I still didn't change, I just went on behaving in the same way. You can't blame me for that, Terry, can you? Just for going on the same?

Looking back on that morning—the day after they had taken her away, when he brought me in the breakfast tray and asked me why I was so much more beautiful than my sister—I feel sick for smiling. It seems so false, to do that at Terry's expense, as if I were laughing at her. It was a betrayal. And it wasn't even true that I was the more beautiful one. We were so alike, physically at least. We could fool anyone at first. Later, as people got to know us, we found it more difficult to act each other. Sometimes they would look puzzled, or ask us if we were in a bad mood, or feeling well.

That was the moment when something split, or at least when we realized something had split; not being able to slip so easily into being each other. It seemed too important to be ourselves. If I'm honest, I'll admit that I didn't want to act like Terry. I preferred being me, what it brought me. I was frightened that if I could be like her on occasion, witty, funny, that I would always have to be that way. Oh, I enjoyed how it felt, making people laugh; in fact it wasn't that difficult. But I could see the change in their attitudes as well. They thought I was hard, tough. That I could take care of myself. And they hardened too, they weren't so kind, so gentle, so reassuring.

It made me feel lonely and I wanted to be Ruth again, sweet Ruth who men automatically wanted to look after.

I feel lonely now all the time. Even with him. The behavior that seemed so natural to me before, when I had Terry to compare myself with, now seems—I don't know, not false, exactly, but somehow unreal. As if now I'm acting a part. Of course, I don't work at the booth any longer, so I'm alone during the day. I miss it sometimes, which is silly of me; think how serious his work is, and here I am complaining I don't still sell cigarettes and magazines, instead of look after his house and make it nice for him! We go out a lot in the evenings, to dinner, to a show, or dancing. . . .

I miss her like a part of my body that's been amputated. As if he had cut her away with his scalpel. He had to do it, I know he did. He was saving me.

I went to see her yesterday. I didn't tell him, because I knew that he would have argued me out of it. I was expecting to feel detached, as I had the last time I saw her. In fact I hoped I would feel that way. I wanted to be able to say goodbye to her, my mad sister, to put her memory to rest.

But instead, when I saw her I felt as if I were whole again for the first time since they took her away. She wasn't mad at all, she was Terry, Terry when we were small and she was still shy like me. Her face was scrubbed, and she wore one of those coarse white gowns tied at the back with strips of cloth; she looked very pure and beautiful, like an angel, apart from her eyes, which darted around the room the whole time. They weren't mad, though, just frightened. My darling sister Terry, frightened of me. I wanted to bawl like a baby. But I knew it wasn't really me she was scared of, it was this place, and what was in her head. She still loved me, Ruth. I know she did.

Gradually she was able to look at me for longer and longer periods, like a bird learning to trust a human. I cried. She stroked my hair as if she were comforting a child. She knew who I was, she called me Ruthie as she did when we were children, and I called her Tessie. She didn't know who Terry was; she'd changed her name when we were sixteen, declaring Tessie was too girlish, too silly. But now Terry was a stranger to her.

We talked about our childhood, and how happy we were. It's true, we were very happy. We hugged each other as tightly as always, talking about our time at school, children we had known there.

But when we reached our memories of the time that we were fifteen, sixteen, her face started to crumple up as if I'd hit her. She just kept saying, "I love you, Ruthie," over and over again, as if it was the most important thing in the world to her, holding my hand all the time.

My clothes were a source of wonderment to her. They are to me, too. People who knew me before would hardly recognize me. I'm very smart now; we are very social. His work with the police has brought him fame—he says, modestly, that it's only notoriety—and we are invited to plenty of parties. People are fascinated with me, since they all know the story—our story, Terry's and mine. They are rarely bold enough to ask me questions, but they stare at me in a way I don't like, as if, on his arm, smiling—that smile again—I am living proof of his success, his professional skill. I suppose that I am.

After a while I found that the smarter I dressed, the more unapproachable I looked. It was a form of self-protection, and he encourages me to spend money on clothes. He likes to see me smart, which is strange, because when he fell in love with me, I was dowdier than she was. Even when Terry and I wore matching outfits, which we often did, she was always the chic one. Now, however, I am learning to dress well, because it pleases him. I wear what she would have worn, I carry myself like her.

Terry touched my hat, my hair, delicately, as if I would crumble if she didn't use the lightest movements. I had meant to dress in something bright to visit her but I didn't have the heart for it, and I was wearing a black crepe dress, very simple, with a belted waist and exaggeratedly padded shoulders. Terry ran her fingers shyly along my sleeve. She whispered something. "What, darling?" I said. She put her head up a little and murmured, "Dark, dark . . ."

After an hour they said I had to go. I had thought before that I couldn't cry any more, but I was wrong, and they almost had to pull us apart. Terry was crying too, "Don't go, Ruthie, don't go," she kept saying. They led me out of the room with two men holding her back, not forcefully, but so she couldn't move. It took me another hour to collect myself enough for the journey back.

Since then I haven't been able to get the image of her out of my head. I always thought that the most important person in the world to me would be my husband, and then my children. That's how it's supposed to be. But there must be something wrong with me, because the most important person in the world for me will always be Terry, no matter what she has done or tried to do. She's my twin, my other half. Why did it take me so long to understand that? And how does he possibly think that I can just split myself off from her and pretend that she never even existed? How does he dare?

In that bedroom she and I shared, I was happier than I have ever been with him. I was myself. With him I don't know who I am. But I know who he thinks I am: the good one, the good sister. He thinks I am better than any woman in the world because he has cut the bad part of me away with his scalpel. Well, he's wrong.

Our beds were next to each other, with a rug between them, just like his and mine are now. Sometimes at night Terry and I would reach out and hold hands till we fell asleep. Or we would talk for hours, rambling away, talking about nothing at all, just to hear the sound of our own voices. We invented codes for grunting to each other when we were small and too tired or lazy to talk: one grunt for "yes," two for "no," three for "I don't know," four and five I don't remember, but six was "I love you." Why, we used them the night before it happened. I will never be that happy again.

I can't undo what's happened, what I've done. I took something from Terry without really knowing what I was doing, but that doesn't excuse me. I took it all and there was nothing left for her.

We were at dinner, just the two of us, the night I had come back from seeing her in that awful place, and my head was still spinning. Suddenly I found myself picturing Terry with that doctor. I wondered how many times she stabbed him. Isn't that ridiculous? It was a pair of scissors she used. No one heard it happen, so there can't have been that much noise. I know I shouldn't think about it, that it's morbid; that's what he says when I mention her name, that it's not good for me to remember, because it's morbid. But sometimes I can't help it.

What did she feel when she was doing it? And was it easy? Because somehow I picture it as having been very easy, the scissors sliding into him like a knife into butter. Because he would have been taken by surprise, unsuspecting. Thinking, you see, that she was me . . .

I look more like Terry now. More and more, at smart dinner parties, the words that come out of my mouth, the jokes, the questions, are hers. He doesn't seem to notice. Maybe he thinks that because I'm the good sister, anything I do must be right. How amusing it would be if that were true.

At dinner I had the strangest thought. It would have made her laugh; she loved odd things. I thought: Wouldn't it be a neat pattern if Terry killed someone because he loved me and not her, and then if I killed someone too for exactly the same reason? Because he loved me and not her? It's more interesting that way, don't you think, more interesting than if I killed someone for preferring her to me. That's just complete symmetry, which is too perfect to be real. After all, even Terry and I aren't perfectly identical. If you know us well you can see that her eyebrows are slightly lighter than mine, slightly more arched, for instance. Or that my nose has a little kink in it where I broke it when I was four, falling over on the school playground, running to get to her.

But no one has ever known us that well. Except each other, of course.

It was just a stupid thought. But I wished Terry had been there to laugh at it with me. Or that I was back in that place with her.

You know, I wouldn't care what the place was like if we could be together. No matter how badly they treated us, how uncomfortable and scratchy those white gowns might be. I wouldn't care about anything else but being with her. Nothing at all. Not even what I would have to do to get there.

(This story is based on the film *The Dark Mirror*, by Robert Siodmak, with Olivia de Havilland as both Ruth and Terry. The story begins at the end of the film.)

Jon L. Breen

The Adventure of the Cheshire Cheese

FEW CRITICS are also first-rate writers of fiction. One of the few exceptions is Jon L. Breen, whose work as a reviewer, short story writer, and novelist is all equally distinguished. If you have any doubts about the statement after reading his incisive and thorough introduction on the mystery year in review, read "The Adventure of the Cheshire Cheese" and you'll wonder why you ever had any doubts in the first place. In this marvelous short story, first published in *Murder in Baker Street*, Breen proves he is up to the master's level and more as Sherlock Holmes wraps up a seemingly inconsequential mystery with graver than expected results.

The Adventure of the Cheshire Cheese

Jon L. Breen

"Watson," said Sherlock Holmes, "I believe you have been known to frequent the Cheshire Cheese from time to time. Perhaps you can enlighten our American friend as to the reason for his reception there."

Holmes's deference to me was a mixed blessing, surprising, gratifying, and unnerving all at once. He had already regaled our unexpected late-evening visitor to the Baker Street rooms with his usual string of remarkable observations—that Mr. Calvin Broadbent was an American, that he had arrived in England three days earlier and had been troubled on his crossing by seasickness, that his comfortable financial status had suffered recent reverses, and that he had just come from a disturbing experience at the venerable Fleet Street tavern most famous for its association with the Great Lexicographer, Dr. Samuel Johnson. Of course, Holmes had explained his deductions with the usual exasperating offhandedness. Some of the points seemed elementary in retrospect (that four-day-old New York newspaper in our guest's coat pocket, the fraying at the cuffs of his expensive jacket, his obvious air of agitation) and others remarkably lucky guesswork (that stain on his waistcoat and the sawdust clinging to his shoes). Now my friend was offering me the chance to contribute more to the elucidation of our visitor's problem than admiring cries of "Amazing, my dear fellow." Fortunately I would not disgrace myself completely.

Mr. Broadbent was an energetic, well-spoken, tastefully dressed young man of less than thirty. His manner was respectful and polite, with only the lightest seasoning of that brashness we often associate with his countrymen. The story he had told us, delivered in meticulously crafted sentences in a surprisingly pleasant and cultured American accent, was a remarkable one indeed.

"I'm a member of the Ichabod Crane Club in New York," he began. "Oh, I'm sure you've never heard of it, but it's a pretty long-established literary society. The somewhat whimsical name came from a character in the works of Washington Irving."

" 'The Legend of Sleepy Hollow,' I believe," Holmes remarked. "A schoolmaster bedeviled by the Headless Horseman, was he not?"

"Why, yes, that's right." The young man appeared surprised and impressed. I had long since ceased to marvel at the arcane knowledge at my friend's command.

"We are a club of intellectuals, you might say, mostly but not entirely writers and journalists, certainly appreciators of the finer things in life. We gather every six weeks or so in a good Manhattan restaurant to share a meal and a fine vintage and listen to a lecture that is improving or entertaining or, at the best of times, both. How many members turn out depends upon the lecturer, and we've found to bring out the full membership, there's nothing like a visiting Englishman. Charles Dickens was a great success—that, I hasten to say, was well before my time—and so was Oscar Wilde a few years back. So when his tour managers offered us a chance to hear Algernon Fordyce, naturally we jumped at the chance."

Holmes and I glanced at each other meaningfully but said nothing. The old Fleet Street hack Fordyce was hardly in a class with Dickens or Wilde.

"As chairman of the program committee, I had the duty and honor of playing host to the guest lecturer and his wife in my home during his stay in New York. My circumstances have given me a unique ability to offer this hospitality. I am a bachelor and enjoy a small private income, though as you rightly observed, Mr. Holmes, recent reversals in the stock market have somewhat reduced it.

"Unfortunately, the morning after Mr. Fordyce spoke to our society— and he was a great speaker, let me tell you, well worth the fee his agency charged us—he was stricken with a sudden and mysterious illness. At first, we thought it would pass after a few days' rest, but it did not. Mr. Fordyce was my invalid houseguest for three weeks, with all manner of medical specialists in and out. Try as they might, they could do nothing for him, and one tragic morning Mr. Fordyce passed away."

"We read of his death in the *Times*," I said. "A sad event."

"It was indeed. Of course, I did my best to comfort his widow and help her with what arrangements needed to be made."

"What was determined to be the cause of death?" Holmes asked.

"There was disagreement on that point among the medical men. The death certificate listed heart failure as the cause, and I have no reason to doubt it."

"Nor do I," said Holmes dryly. "But what caused the heart to fail? I seem to remember that poisoning was suspected." Clearly, I reflected, Holmes had been reading about the case in papers other than the *Times*.

"It's true that one of the doctors was convinced Fordyce had been poisoned, but I assure you there was no basis for that. Who would have poisoned him? His wife loved him, was prostrate with grief. My servants I can vouch for entirely, and they would have had no motive. No one else, save his doctors and a highly respectable nurse, came near the man during his stay in my house. I'm sure the cause of his death was natural."

"As I recall," said Holmes, "Mrs. Fordyce is some years younger than her husband."

"Yes, that is true, but completely devoted to him. You could not possibly be around them in those last sad days of his life and doubt that. Now, in order for you to understand my problem, I must speak of my own relationship with Fordyce. In those waning days of his life, we became great friends. Though he grew steadily weaker day by day, his mind remained clear, and the discussions we had of literature and sports and art and politics served to take his mind off his affliction. He had come to America not only to lecture but to write of his experiences. He hadn't the strength to produce those articles about America his London editors had contracted for, but he did continue writing verse in an increasingly unsteady scrawl to the very end.

"One day as I sat by his bedside—his exhausted wife was sleeping at the time, the poor dear—we came to talk of our clubs. I told him about the Ichabod Crane and the few other Manhattan clubs of which I'm privileged to be a member. Fordyce belonged to several in London, but the one he mentioned with the most fondness was called the 1457 Club, or simply the Fourteen Club for short. This club, he told me, met every month at one of his favorite London haunts, an old tavern called the Cheshire Cheese. Does either of you gentlemen know of the 1457 Club?"

While I could think of several clubs that had their meetings at the Cheese—St. Dunstan's, the Johnson Club, the Rhymers' Club, the amusingly named Soakers' Club—I obviously did not know them all, and the 1457 or Fourteen Club was unfamiliar.

"Can't say that I do," I replied. I glanced toward Holmes, who remained impassive.

Broadbent went on, "He told me more about the meeting place than he did the club, if truth be told. He said the Cheshire Cheese was a famous tavern that dated back hundreds of years and had long been a gathering place for journalists and writers and barristers. I remember he called it 'a storied inn where Dr. Johnson is still a living presence.' But I was much more curious about the oddly named 1457 Club. I asked him many questions about it, and it seemed to amuse him to keep me in the dark. What, I wondered, did the 1457 signify? Was it part of a street address?"

"Rather a high number for a street address," I said. "Don't you think so, Holmes?" My friend did not answer. "More likely to be a year, I should think."

"That's what I decided," Broadbent said. "I wondered what had happened in the year 1457 that could be the basis for a club. It was not an especially eventful year, and the possibilities I suggested only made Fordyce laugh. I found it frustrating, but after all, he was dying, not I, so let him take what pleasure he could. As he grew more and more ill, he began to realize that he would never again enter Wine Office Court and share drink and good fellowship with his friends. To staunch his melancholia, he wrote in those last days of his life one final poem, a sonnet in tribute to the Cheshire Cheese. He asked me to deliver the sonnet in person to a meeting of the Fourteen Club in the event he could not do so himself. I, of course, reassured him that he would recover, but by that time I was certain he would not."

"You've come all the way to London for a sentimental gesture, Mr. Broadbent?" Holmes inquired.

Broadbent smiled ruefully. "Not entirely. He told me something else about the club, not what it was devoted to or what the 1457 meant, oh, no, not that, but something that would be of more practical importance. Fordyce said that several members of the Club owed him large sums of money, which in the event of his death he wanted me to collect for the welfare of his widow. That there were no written records of these debts seemed to me most odd, but he assured me his debtors were honorable men who would surely volunteer them to me once they were assured by my reading of the sonnet that I had appeared as his posthumous representative."

"That would be honorable indeed," Holmes murmured, "to insist on paying an unrecorded debt to a dead man. And where is Mrs. Fordyce now? No doubt she has returned to England?"

Broadbent seemed a bit uncomfortable as he said, "She has remained in New York."

"That seems odd, doesn't it?" I ventured. "Surely she would want to be with friends and family at such a time."

"Ah, she has little family left, I fear, and she quite likes America. I assured her I would collect the moneys owed and bring them back to her."

"Thus your visit tonight to the Cheshire Cheese," Holmes prompted.

"Yes. Fordyce told me when the Fourteen Club would be holding its regular meeting and assured me that I would be made welcome once I mentioned his name. I must confess when I entered, I was subject to some disconcerting stares, not impolite precisely but—well, I gather the crowd is mostly made up of regulars."

"It's a conservative place," I told him, "mindful of tradition and the old ways of doing things. The clientele is suspicious of strangers and resistant to change, any kind of change. I remember when they imported a lemon-squeezing machine from your country, Mr. Broadbent. The controversy was enormous. It was intended to be a simple labor-saving device, but you should have heard some of the cries of outrage."

"They were a bit more friendly when they realized I was an American. Someone shouted out, 'He'll want a serviette then!' I can't imagine what that meant."

"What you would call a napkin, Mr. Broadbent," Holmes explained.

"Provision of such luxuries is not automatic in London eating houses as I understand it is in your country."

"I see. They thought I'd want to see Dr. Johnson's table, the right hand table in the left hand room, just after the entry. They showed me a copy of Joshua Reynolds's portrait of Johnson and a picture depicting Johnson saving Oliver Goldsmith from his landlady. They pointed out to me the portraits of past waiters that were the most prominent non-Johnson paintings on the walls—honoring waiters in that way seems to me a most civilized custom, and I said so, but I was struggling to control my impatience to complete my business. Finally, after my guided tour of the ground floor, I asked where I might find the Fourteen Club and was directed to the upstairs room where they were meeting. There are so many little rooms in that place, a stranger could easily find himself lost. Once I found the Club and told them why this foreign stranger was in their midst, they were most hospitable. I described to them Fordyce's last days in my house, tried to express how much the Cheshire Cheese and the Fourteen Club meant to him, and told them Fordyce had insisted that I read them his final sonnet. They of course were eager to hear it." Broadbent probed in his coat pocket and pulled out a crumpled sheet of paper. "This is a fair copy of the sonnet, made by me from Fordyce's original, which was barely legible."

Holmes glanced at the poem for a moment and passed it over to me. This is what I read:

> "The weary trav'ler back from foreign port
> Up Fleet Street strolls full up with memories
> Of jolly times at Ye Olde Cheshire Cheese,
> Down dark and narrow old Wine Office Court.
> No Great Fire singed the treasured seat
> Upon which good Will Shakespeare came to sit
> Or scorched that storied bar even a bit
> From which Boswell his source of fame would greet.
> End your meal with pudding; have some more,
> Remembering the chops that went before,
> And how Scotch, Irish, claret, port, or gin
> Unlock tongues the more you let them in.
> Oh, Fourteen Club, declare loud if you please
> Your love of golf at Ye Olde Cheshire Cheese."

"As I read the first four lines," Broadbent declared, "I was certain I saw tears in the eyes of some of the club members. They seemed truly moved by Fordyce's reverence for their meeting place. But as I read on, their expressions began to harden. They looked at each other in consternation, even anger. And when I was finished, I was denounced as an impostor and summarily asked to leave the premises. My demands for an explanation fell on deaf ears.

Such was their outrage, I feared some of them, one very large person in particular, might do physical damage to me if I did not flee at once. I had not even had dinner. Mr. Holmes, your reputation as an elucidator of mysteries is well known all over the world. Can you tell me where I went wrong, how I offended these clubmen? And can you make any suggestion how I might collect Algernon Fordyce's unwritten debts for the benefit of his brave widow?"

Holmes looked at our visitor with a somewhat unsympathetic expression. He appeared about to say something but held his tongue. It was then he referred to my sometime patronage of the Cheshire Cheese and passed the torch to me.

"Mr. Broadbent," I said gently, "at least the reference to golf tells you to what pastime this club is apparently devoted. But the sonnet has a few errors in it, I fear."

"Errors? What do you mean?"

"To begin with, the Great Fire of 1666 *did* destroy Ye Olde Cheshire Cheese, and it was rebuilt the following year. Legend has it that Shakespeare and Ben Jonson frequented the place in earlier years, but no seat the Bard of Avon sat upon can have survived. Secondly, the pudding for which the Cheshire Cheese is famous is not a sweet that comes at the end of the meal but rather a meal in itself. They serve it on Wednesdays and Saturdays, and its size ranges from fifty to eighty pounds. Under its flaky crust you'll find rump steak, kidneys, oysters, larks, mushrooms. It's a lovely dish, makes me hungry just talking about it. When it's cooking on a breezy day, they say you can savor its aroma as far away as the Stock Exchange."

"Spare us your raptures, Watson," Holmes said.

"Quite so. The point, Mr. Broadbent, is that you would not follow a chop with that pudding, no, indeed. It is by no means a dessert as the sonnet implies." I cleared my throat. "I must point out some other problems of nomenclature. No patron of the Cheshire Cheese would refer to Scotch, Irish, or gin."

"Why on earth not?" Broadbent cried in seeming outrage. "The place is a tavern, is it not?"

"Yes, but if you want Scotch, you simply ask for whiskey; if you want Irish whiskey, you must ask for Cork; and gin is never referred to as anything but rack."

"How on earth would I be expected to know that?" Broadbent demanded.

"You wouldn't," said Holmes, "but Algernon Fordyce certainly would. Do you have any more observations, Watson?"

"Ah, no, I believe that's all." And quite enough, I would have thought.

"I have only a couple of points to add. What was Boswell doing at the Cheese?"

"Holmes," I remonstrated, "surely Dr. Johnson would not have gone to the Cheese without Boswell."

"Ah, good old Watson, you are my Boswell, and a better one no man could hope for. But history is against you on this point. Boswell knew Johnson in his old age, years after he lived nearby the Cheese. Boswell makes no mention of the place in his life of Johnson, and as far as anyone knows, he never went there. And the reference to golf in the sonnet may suggest the meaning of the club's name."

"Fourteen Club," I cried. "Could it be named after the fourteenth hole on some golf course?"

"What then do you do with the fifty-seven?"

I thought about it for a moment, reluctant to abandon my theory. "Someone could have a total of fifty-seven strokes through fourteen holes, could he not?"

"A remarkable round," Broadbent murmured.

"No," said Holmes, "the reference is, as you thought, to a year. And one thing happened in the year 1457 that is significant in the history of golf. James II of Scotland issued an edict banning the game on the grounds that it was distracting men from the improvement of their archery, which was vital for military purposes. Knowing this, who would form an organization called the 1457 Club? Keen golfers? I think not. More likely those who hate the game of golf."

"But, Holmes," I objected, "surely the name could have been adopted ironically by lovers of golf."

"Could have been, yes, but since everything else in Algernon Fordyce's poem appears designed to embarrass the man he asked to deliver it, I shall stay with my first hypothesis. Declaring love of golf in that sonnet would be the final insult to the membership of a golf haters' club, the one most certain to bring about the banishment of Mr. Broadbent."

"I don't understand this," Broadbent cried. "Why would Fordyce perpetrate this hoax on someone who only tried to help him?"

"He would not," Holmes replied sharply.

Ignoring Holmes's implication, our visitor said, "And how can I hope to collect those debts?"

"Don't you see? Those supposed unwritten debts are a fiction. Tell me one thing, Mr. Broadbent."

"Yes?"

"Who was administering the poison that slowly drained the life from Algernon Fordyce. Was it you? Was it his wife? Or did you take the duty in turn?"

"Mr. Holmes," our visitor cried, "that is a monstrous suggestion."

"It was a monstrous act. What poison precisely did you use? Any of several might have achieved the desired effect of misleading the physicians. Oh, you needn't answer. It's merely professional curiosity. Probably you covered your tracks sufficiently to ensure that my 'monstrous suggestion' will never be made in an American law court."

Despite this pessimistic assertion, Holmes would cable his conclusions to Wilson Hargreave, his friend on the New York Police Bureau, shortly after Broadbent departed 221B.

"When Fordyce realized what was happening," Holmes continued, "that his young wife had fallen in love with a much younger man, that he was being slowly poisoned, he realized it was too late to get help from the outside world as a captive in your house. But he at least managed one very good joke on you, sending you across the Atlantic on a wild-goose chase."

"You presume a lot from just a poem, Mr. Holmes," Broadbent said, "however inaccurate."

"Ah, but there's that one final clue in the poem."

"Another clue, Holmes?" I said.

"It's staring us all in the face, and you needn't be a habitué of the Cheshire Cheese to interpret it. Look at the first letter of each line of the poem. Do they spell out anything?"

Broadbent and I both looked.

"T, U, O, D, N," I read.

"That spells nothing!" our visitor said.

"Try reading from the bottom," Holmes snapped. "Do you see it now, Broadbent? You are found out!"

David B. Silva

Dry Whiskey

DAVID B. SILVA is best known for dark suspense and horror, though his stories are often crime pieces at heart. Among his recent works are a series of science fiction thriller novels with the renowned actor Kevin McCarthy. While horror takes many forms, it is difficult to combine with a mystery story, something that Silva accomplished quite effectively in "Dry Whiskey," a somber story of melancholy and remorse in a style reminiscent of John Steinbeck. It was first published in *Cemetery Dance* magazine.

Dry Whiskey

David B. Silva

When I was a boy, I would look at my father and see everything right with the world. He seemed bigger, then. At the end of the day, he would come in from the fields with his shirt slung over his shoulder and the sun at his back, and every muscle in his body would be perfectly defined. I looked up to him back then, like most boys looked up to their fathers. And I had wanted to grow up to be the man he was.

The rub of it is . . . time has a way of changing the order of things.

My father started drinking nearly twelve years ago, not long after my mother died of ovarian cancer. At first, though I was only eleven at the time, I thought I had understood: anything to help forget that bone-thin skeleton, that rictus smile that she had become just before her death. It was an image that had haunted me for a long time afterward. And I imagined it was an image that had never stopped haunting my father.

That was the thought going through my mind as I sat in the truck, staring at the house. How could things change so much in just ten or twelve short years? It was mid-morning. The sun was already high in the sky, and there was a dark shadow enclosing the front porch. I stared a while longer, then climbed out of the truck and closed the door.

By the time I made it to the front steps, my father had come out of the house, dragging himself across the porch like a man who had been ill for a long time now. The screen door bounced off the jamb behind him. He fell into one of the rattan chairs my mother had bought, hawked up a wad of phlegm and sent it flying over the porch railing. "What're you doing here?" he asked.

"Just thought I'd come by and see how you're doing. That's all."

"Yeah?" He scratched at the stubble on his chin, which had been growing for better than a week by the look of it. It hadn't been all that long ago that the first signs of gray had begun to sneak in. Now, it was almost *all* gray. "Well, I'm doing okay. Anything else?"

"Heard you were in town last night."

"Believe I was."

"Heard you got booted out of the Forty-Niner."

"Did I?"

"That's what Len Dozier says."

My father nodded slightly, as if that sounded close enough to the truth to suit him. Then he buried his face in his hands and let out a slow breath of air that seemed like an effort to control something inside that he found frightening. When he looked up again, I was reminded of the fact that this was the morning after. His coloring was ashy, his eyes bloodshot.

"I might have," he said. "I don't exactly remember."

"How'd you get home?"

"Drove."

He thought maybe he had taken Buzzard Roost Road, which was the long way home no matter how you figured it. But he really couldn't be certain. He might have gone down Old Forty-Four and across. To be honest, he finally confessed, he couldn't recall much of anything about last night. "Things get a little fuzzy after I stopped at the Forty-Niner."

He stared down at his hands then, silently, with that look of shame that I'd seen cross his face a thousand times before.

"Have you eaten breakfast yet?" I asked.

"Uh-uh."

"Then let's get some food in you, okay?" I cooked him up some eggs and bacon and poured him a cup of strong, black coffee. We sat at the table in the kitchen. For a while we talked about the drought that had settled over the state the past four years, wondering how much longer it was going to go on. It hadn't proved to be as bad as the '77–'78 drought yet—*that* one had been the worst in the state's history—but summer was here now and it was going to be a long time before we were likely to see any new storms move through.

After breakfast, I cleared the dishes off the table, and placed them in the sink. "I've gotta be going, Pa."

"You working today?"

"Len needs a hand repairing his tractor."

"Well, you go on, then."

"Are you gonna be all right?"

"I'll be fine."

He walked me to the front porch, the suspenders hanging loosely around his waist, his gait a bit shorter, a bit slower than it generally was when he had had a belly full of whiskey to move him along. Outside, there were shimmering waves of heat rising off the bed of my father's old pickup, and in the distance, you could see a mirage in the crease between two brown hills.

It looked a little like a pond. But there hadn't been a pond there in nearly five years now. Not since before the drought.

My father had let the farm go to hell after my mother had died. It had always been a small farm: four fifty-acre parcels, about two hundred acres altogether. It sat near the base of the foothills, with South Cow Creek flowing lazily along its southern border. He leased out two of the parcels: one for grazing, the other for beehives in the winter months when the bees were dormant and there wasn't much call for pollinating. He had his own small herd, too, about twenty head of cattle, and that was pretty much it.

I stopped at the foot of the steps, wanting to be on my way and feeling a little guilty for it.

"You looked yet?" he asked me.

"No, Pa."

"You gonna?"

"Sure." I didn't know when this routine had first started. Like everything else, I suppose it was around the time that my mother had died. Definitely sometime after he had started drinking. I was used to it by now, and I guess because nothing had ever come of it, it seemed more like a routine than a real concern. But I gave the front end of his truck an honest look anyway.

He drove an old Chevy flatbed with aluminum running boards and an unpainted, right front fender. The fender had been replaced several summers back after he'd clipped a fence post—trying to avoid a jackrabbit, he claimed. The rest of the truck was in fairly decent shape, considering its age.

Something was wrong with the front end, though. I noticed that almost immediately. The bumper, which was second-hand scrap he had brought home from the junkyard and painted off-white, had been smashed up against the front grille. It looked as if someone had taken a sledge hammer to it. Just above the bumper, the lens of the headlight was broken, its mounting ring dangling loosely off to one side. If that weren't enough, there was also a good-size depression in the top of the left fender, where it looked as if the metal had been crimped at a weak spot almost directly over the wheel well.

Last night, on his way home, my father had hit something. "Jesus."

"What is it?" he asked.

I ran my fingers across the bumper. There was a dark stain that looked as if something had spilled over the top edge and had run down the white paint. It was shaped like a waterfall, with a mix of thick-and-thin lines flowing unevenly, top to bottom. At first thought, it looked like a kid might have taken a black Magic Marker to it. But when I looked closer, I realized the color was brownish-red. It hadn't been done by any Magic Marker. It was a blood stain. "Oh, God."

"What?"

"You did it, Pa. You finally did it." I looked up at him, and he was standing at the edge of the porch with an arm wrapped around the post like it was the only thing holding him up. His face had turned ashen, and for the first time this morning, there was a hint of sobriety behind his eyes. "The bumper's smashed, and there's some blood, Pa. You hit something last night."

I spent most of that afternoon at Len Dozier's place, working on his tractor. We got it up and running some time around four, so I stopped by the market in Kingston Mills, picked up a couple of steaks, some potatoes, a sixty-four-ouncer of Coke, and headed back to my father's place. When I had left, he had been sitting at the kitchen table, staring vacantly into his half-empty cup of coffee. It was only a matter of time, I figured, before the coffee was replaced by whiskey, and if that had already happened, it was a good bet I was going to find him passed out cold on the living room couch.

But that's not where I found him.

He was sitting on the front porch, next to a pile of plastic bags filled with bottles and cans. I climbed out of the truck with the grocery bag in one arm, and as I closed the door, I watched him toss an empty whiskey bottle into the air. It sailed a good fifteen or twenty feet, landed smack-dab in the middle of a feeding trough with *loomix* stenciled across the side, and then shattered with the harsh sound of a bottle landing in a recycling bin.

"What are you doing, Pa?"

He didn't bother to look up. As I went through the gate, he popped the tab off a can of Budweiser, dumped the contents out through an opening between the porch slats, then crushed the can and tossed it in the direction of another pile only a few feet away. It fell short, making almost no sound at all.

"Pa?"

When he finally did look up, his face was drawn and haggard, and though I had seen him like this before, this time was different. This was not a man who had hung one on while I had been gone. It was a man who had looked at himself in the mirror and had been frightened by what he had found.

"Pa, what's the matter?"

He stared at me a moment, something apparently aching silently inside him. "You ever meet Lloyd's kid?"

"Joey Egan?"

He nodded.

"Yeah, a couple of years ago, I think. When I was helping with Four-H."

"He died last night," my father said mechanically. He took a bottle of Johnnie Walker Black Label out of the plastic bag next to him, gazed fondly at the label, then unscrewed the top and emptied out the whiskey. "It was a hit-and-run, off Buzzard Roost Road. He was on his way home after the school dance."

"Are you sure?"

"It was in this morning's paper," he said. Then he sent the empty bottle sailing across the yard, end over end. A spattering of sunlight glittered off the glass just before the neck of the bottle landed against the side of the trough and fell apart before my eyes. I'm not sure I even heard the sound it made. It seemed a thousand miles away just then.

"Maybe it wasn't you," I said.

"You're forgetting the blood on the bumper, Will."

"Yeah, but . . . Jesus, don't you remember anything from last night?"

"Not after I left the bar." He pulled another bottle out of the bag, poured the liquid down an opening between the slats, and flung it in the direction of the front gate this time. It landed short, in a soft mound of dirt where my mother had once planted a bed of wild violets and Shasta daisies, even some brown-eyed susans. *Just because we live on a farm*, she had said, *doesn't mean we can't have a little color around the place.* The bottle kicked up a cloud of dust that lazily drifted away on the evening breeze.

I plopped down in a chair next to him. "So what now?"

"You can join me if you want." He handed over a six pack of beer.

The farm sat at the west end of a valley. It was a little past five now, the last week of May. The shadows from the hills were beginning to lengthen, and I could feel the coolness of evening coming on. I popped the top off the first of the cans, poured out the contents, and began my participation in a ritual that took nearly an hour before it was finished.

We never discussed calling the police. I suppose we should have at least discussed it. But what was the point? It wasn't going to change the fact that there was blood on the front end of my father's pickup. And it wasn't going to bring little Joey Egan back, either.

In a strange way, though, what had happened had already started to bring my father back. He had been hiding inside a bottle for a long, long time, but suddenly it looked as if he might at last come out and show himself. If he did, I didn't want to risk losing him again.

We barbecued the steaks on an old grill out back that night. We had planned to eat outside at the picnic table under the dogwoods, but the mayflies were swarming, so we ended up inside at the kitchen table instead. It wasn't until we had finished the meal, and I had poured him a cup of coffee that I noticed his hands were shaking.

"Are you all right?"

He nodded, appearing unaffected. "The booze is wearing off. That's all."

"You sure?" He looked warm, beads of sweat spattered across his forehead, and weary. Though I had seen him looking much worse after an all-night bender.

"I'll be fine."

"You want me to stay tonight?"

"No, you go on home. I'll be all right."

I stacked the dishes in the sink, wiped my hands off on a kitchen towel, then turned around and stared at him. When you're a kid, you never think about your father as being old. I wasn't a kid anymore, of course. But I had thought of him as an old man for a good many years now, and I wondered briefly when it was that I had become the father, and he the son. And I wondered how much longer he was going to be with me.

"I'll come by in the morning," I said.

"No need."

"Just to check to see how you're doing."

"If that's what you want."

Joey Egan's funeral was held three days later. He was buried in a family plot in the Black Oak Cemetery on the outskirts of town, next to his mother, who had died of pneumonia the year before. After the services, I drove my father home and stayed with him that night, because I was afraid he might start drinking again. He hadn't shed a tear since the day my mother had died. But in the truck, on our way out of Black Oak, he broke down and started a long, painful crying jag.

More than just his drinking, I guess I worried about him doing something crazy that night.

The next morning, my father woke up with a hangover.

He came dragging into the kitchen sometime around nine, his eyes bloodshot, his brain apparently pounding unmercifully at the inside of his skull. He stopped at the sink, shading his eyes against the morning sun, and took a drink of water right out of the faucet. It was the one-hundred-and-seventeenth straight day without rain, and while the well hadn't gone dry, it sometimes took a while before anything came out of the spout.

"How's bacon and eggs sound?" I asked.

He shook his head guardedly. "Nothing for me, thanks."

"You gotta eat something." I had already tossed some bacon in the skillet. He hadn't been eating much of anything since the accident, and I had promised myself not to let him get away with it again. But he looked like the man of old this morning, like a man coming out of a stupor: ragged and foul and slightly out of touch with his surroundings. I didn't think he was going to be able to keep his food down even if he tried. "Christ, you didn't go on another drunk last night, did you?"

He looked up at me, his lips dry and chapped, his face expressionless. "You know I didn't. You were here all night, weren't you?"

"Then what the hell's the matter with you?"

"It's a dry drunk," he whispered hoarsely. He wiped his hands across the front of his undershirt, where one strap of his overalls was unfastened and hanging loosely.

"It happens sometimes," he said. "When you've been drinking as long as I have."

"All the more reason to get some food in your stomach."

"Maybe." He shut off the faucet and moved to the table, where he sat down a little gingerly, and let out a half-hearted sigh. "I saw Joey Egan last night," he said.

"Joey's dead, Pa."

"He came into my room and stood over my bed. There was a mess of cuts and scratches all over his face. Looked like some fool had taken the business end of a pitchfork to him. And I think his left arm was broken. It looked that way at least."

"It was a dream, Pa."

"No, it wasn't no dream. He knew how your ma died."

"Everyone knows she had cancer. That's no secret."

"But the cancer ain't what killed her, Will."

We had never talked about my mother's death, but she had been sick for a good many months before she died. For a long time afterward, my father had always said that it was the consumption that got her. I guess it was less painful for him to think of it that way.

"I couldn't stand to watch her suffer," he said.

"What did you do, Pa?" He looked up at me, a man whose rounded shoulders reflected the heavy weight they had been carrying, and suddenly I understood everything. All the nights at the Forty-Niner. The way he had pulled back from me after she had died. The way he had pulled back from everyone. I understood it all. "You killed her, didn't you?"

"I . . . I placed a pillow over her face," he said softly.

"Jesus."

"She was in so much pain . . ."

His bottom lip began to tremble, then suddenly he broke down and cried for the second time in less than a week. I sat next to him, my arm draped over his shoulders, feeling helpless. Guilt carried a heavy price, and my father, I suspected, had been paying a hefty markup for a long, long time.

After a while, he caught himself and took in a deep breath. "I'm all right," he said uncertainly. He stared out the kitchen window, off to the distance, where a small dust devil had kicked up and was swirling across the open field like a child swirling finger paints across a paper canvas. I had never noticed the burden in his face quite the way I noticed it just then. Here was a man who had been killing himself for years with booze, and now he was killing himself without it. I wondered if I had ever really known my father, if anyone had ever really known him.

"Things'll be all right once the booze wears off," I said weakly. "You hear?"

He nodded.

I gave him a pat on the back. "You sure you don't want anything to eat?"

"Later," he said.

I left him around eleven that morning. He was sitting in a chair on the front porch, staring out across the barren terrain, his mind a million miles away. I had gotten myself a six-week stint up in Oregon, hauling trees out of a private co-op that was selectively logging its land, and I reminded him about the job.

"I'll be back in six weeks. Okay, Pa?"

"I ain't going nowhere," he said.

"Six weeks," I repeated. As I drove out the dirt driveway, I caught a glimpse of him in my rearview mirror. There was something standing next to him, something I couldn't quite make out. And the man, himself, was hardly recognizable. A man so completely different from the man of my early childhood that I felt a little rattle of uneasiness run through me. What had happened to him? What had happened to the man who had been as strong as an ox, who had put up the barn by himself one summer, using a block-and-tackle, who had been able to stack a hundred bales of hay in a day and still have the energy to shoot some hoops out back under the last vestiges of twilight? What the hell had happened to that man?

He had grown old, I wanted to tell myself.

He had grown old and alone and empty.

But there was more to it than that.

He had also grown frightened.

I called him twice while I away was in Oregon. Under the circumstances, I guess I should have called more often. But that picture of him in my rearview mirror had been haunting me like a ghost. I kept thinking I had caught a glimpse of little Joey Egan standing next to him on the porch. That Joey had been that *something* I couldn't quite recognize, and that he had had one hand on my father's shoulder as if he were trying to hold him down.

The first time I called, the phone rang relentlessly, maybe as many as a dozen times, before my father finally picked it up. "No more," he said sharply. "You hear me? You call me one more time and I swear I'll come out to Black Oak myself and dig up your goddamn remains. You hear me? I'll feed 'em to the damn buzzards and that'll be the end of it."

"Pa, it's me."

There was a sudden, surprised silence on the other end. Then, quietly: "Will?"

"Yes."

"Oh, Christ. Will? That really you? Where are you?"

"I'm in Oregon, Pa. What's going on there? What's all the shouting about?"

"Oregon . . . ," he mumbled, in nearly a whisper. And for a moment, I thought he had gone back to the bottle again. In fact, I was certain that was exactly what he had done.

"You've been on a drunk, haven't you, Pa?"

"What's my boy doing in Oregon?"

"Listen to me. You've been drinking again, haven't you?"

Then the line went dead.

I called him back within seconds, my hands shaking almost uncontrollably as I fumbled with the phone. What the hell was going on? He had sounded like a man on the verge of self-destruction. I couldn't even be certain he had recognized me. Maybe he wasn't drinking again, but if it wasn't the booze I had heard, I hated to think what it might have been.

The phone rang thirty, maybe forty times without an answer. Eventually, I hung up and tried to convince myself that I had probably disturbed his sleep, that I must have caught him in the middle of a bad dream, and that there was nothing to worry about. He had been tired, was all. The call had wakened him and *that's* why he had sounded so crazy, because he'd still been half-asleep.

It was nearly three weeks later before I was finally able to get hold of him again. I was due to head back to Kingston Mills the next morning. I'm not sure what I expected him to sound like after that first call. Still a little crazy, I guess. But he didn't sound crazy, and he didn't sound like a man who would be dead in a few short hours. He sounded like a man who had finally forgiven himself.

"Is everything all right there?" I asked.

"I'm finally dry," he said serenely.

"What?" I thought I could hear something in the background that sounded dry and brittle, something that made me think of autumn leaves and sand through an hourglass. And then he chuckled.

"I think the booze is wearing off," he said. "My head's clearing up. It's been a long time since I've seen things this clearly."

"Look, Pa, I'm coming home tomorrow. Are you gonna to be all right till then?"

"Fine," he said. "I'm gonna be just fine."

I don't remember what I said in return. But I remember holding the phone in my hand after he had hung up, and being overwhelmed with a strange jumble of emotions. It had been years since I had felt close to my father, and suddenly I was terrified that I might never have a chance to feel close to him again.

Early the next morning, I left Oregon, arriving at the farm shortly after one o'clock in the afternoon. His pickup was parked out front, in the same spot it had been parked the day I had discovered the blood on the bumper. There was a layer of dust a quarter of an inch thick across the hood, and it was nearly impossible to see through the windshield into the cab. The pickup had sat there like a dinosaur for nearly two months now. In the back of my mind, I suppose I knew it would eventually be buried under that dust like an old desert ghost town. But at the time, I didn't give it much thought.

The front door to the house was unlocked. It had been left slightly ajar, and just inside there was a strange wind-cut pattern of sand and dust scattered across the hardwood floor. Kingston Mills had gone a hundred-and-fifty-nine days without rain, and the dust, it seemed, was no longer content to stay outside.

"Pa?"

In the kitchen, I discovered a pyramid-shaped pile of dirt in the sink, maybe five or six inches high. One of the faucet handles had been broken off. It was lying on the lip of the drain, partially buried by the dirt. I took hold of the other handle, turned it, and watched a slow, steady stream of dirt sift lazily out of the spout.

"Pa?"

I found him, or some general semblance of him, in his bedroom at the back of the house. He was lying in bed, on top of the sheets, his hands folded peacefully across his stomach. He was dressed in the same clothes he had worn nearly every day of his life since my mother had died: an old pair of work boots worn at the heels, a pair of blue-jean overalls with one unfastened strap hanging loosely at his side, and of course, the long johns he always wore come hell or high water.

Underneath, there was very little left of the man I remembered. Something had happened to him in the few short weeks that I had been gone, something I didn't think I was ever going to be able to understand. Maybe it had something to do with the drought—after all, the well *had* gone dry. Or maybe it had something to do with all those damn bottles he had tossed off the front porch the night he went dry. The booze had kept him going for a good many years. Maybe without it, the well of his soul had gone dry, too. I don't know. All I know is that the man I discovered at the back of the house was all dust and bones.

He looked as if he had been dead a very long time. I had spoken with him last night, but here he was now, less than twenty-four hours later: skeletal hands peeking out from beneath his shirt-sleeves; teeth bared in a dreadful, lipless grin; eyes no more than dark, empty sockets.

Like the flowers my mother had planted out front, after an unquenchable thirst, my father had simply shriveled up and died.

There's a prayer from The Book of Common Prayer that reads: *Earth to earth, ashes to ashes, dust to dust, in sure and certain hope of the Resurrection unto eternal life.* I find myself often thinking back to these words.

My father was buried in the Black Oak Cemetery, two rows over from Joey Egan. A bunch of the guys from the Forty-Niner came by the house afterward, drank a little beer, and talked about the good times they'd had together. Mostly, though, they seemed to stare off into the distance, reflecting on things that I suppose I will never be privy to.

Late in the afternoon, Lloyd Egan pulled me aside and told me about a man they had locked up in Sparks, Nevada. They had caught him robbing a small Mom and Pop liquor store and during the interrogation, he had confessed to Joey's hit-and-run. He had leaned across the seat to roll down the passenger window, he said, and his car had drifted onto the shoulder, and . . . and there was Joey, turning around, his eyes bright and surprised, just as the car made impact. The man had stopped and gotten out and realized the boy was dead. Then he had gotten back into the car and had driven off. It had apparently been haunting him ever since.

Lloyd took a swig of his beer, and gazed off into nothingness, looking like he was on the verge of tears. I put my arm around him, tried to comfort him, and then led him back into the kitchen, where someone was telling a story about the time my father had had a few too many and had gone home and tried to shoe one of the steers.

Several days later, a storm moved in off the Pacific and dropped nearly five inches of much needed rain across the north state. It was the beginning of the end of the drought. But it had come too late for my father.

To this day, I don't know what it was he hit coming home from the bar that night. It could have been a deer or a cow, I suppose. But it wasn't Joey Egan, and I'm grateful for that, grateful beyond description.

I still think back to those times when I was a boy and he would come in from the fields with his shirt slung over his shoulder and every muscle of his body taut and perfectly defined. And like most boys, there are still the times when I wish I could have grown up to be that man.

The shame of it is . . . I don't think I ever really got to know who he was.

Wolfgang Burger

Countdown

IT IS A PLEASURE to welcome several new and talented foreign authors to this year's volume. This story is by Wolfgang Burger, an author who has been writing novels and short stories in Germany for several years. After reading this extremely short, razor-sharp vignette, you'll know that the idea of noir is alive and well in Europe, too, and sometimes coming from amazing places. "Countdown" was first published in an anthology called *Karlsruhe 2000*, named for the town where it was published, and we're pleased to be able to reprint it here in the United States.

Countdown

Wolfgang Burger

There she sits in complete symmetry on her chair like a raven in fear. Her old-fashioned handbag on her knees, she's staring at me like a girls'-school teacher at the Ministry of Education.

I give Schneider a sign, I think for the next five minutes I can take care of myself.

"Now, Mrs. Fischlein, what can I do for you?"

She swallows, opens her mouth and closes it again. Nothing is to be heard.

"I have to repeat, I've got very little time, Mrs. Fischlein. Five minutes, we said. So please . . ."

"I'm so sorry. It's such a long story . . ."

I'm too hard on her. She's going to cry, and then this will take even longer.

"Please, Mrs. Fischlein."

She nods, she swallows, she nods. Oh, dear God, this is never going to end. I will ring for Schneider and let him kick her out. But look: she is opening her mouth. The black bird is speaking.

"Look, doctor, the story goes like this. I had a little daughter. Miriam. My husband died so early, you understand, and she was then my one and only. You understand?"

"Up to now, I can follow you pretty good."

Four minutes left.

"And to my Miriam a bad misfortune happened. She was in the second class, when she found a syringe in the schoolyard. It was from a junkie, you understand, from a heroin junkie. And she was so little then, she was only seven at the time, and she took it home, and I had to leave her alone some afternoons, because I had to go to work, you understand? But it wasn't that nobody looked after her, there was a waitress, Mrs. Augustin, but she had a vacation that day, or she was ill, I don't know. And Miriam played hospital with her teddy, and then she pricked herself with that needle."

She looks so lamentable. I'm nodding as optimistically as I can. Three minutes left.

Calmness. I think, she's lost her voice again, but then she whispers:

"And the guy that needle was from had AIDS!"

Well, not so nice.

"I'm really sorry, Mrs. . . . . How is your daughter? I really hope she didn't infect herself?"

She sniffs. Now she's going to cry, I'm sure. And she will rip her handbag to pieces, if she keeps pulling it the way she does. Should I give her a handkerchief? No. She's only sniffing a little.

"She died. Two days ago I buried her."

Now she's actually crying. But well, it's of course a really sad story about her little daughter, that's true.

"I'm really sorry, Mrs.—ahm—Fischlein. Really. But you've got only two minutes left. So what can I do for you in this case?"

"Well, you see, doctor. I thought so much about all these things. Miriam was ill such a long time, she was seventeen when she died, and I had such an awful lot of time to think about, you know. Someone must be guilty for such bad luck, don't you think? There must someone responsible, or not?"

Maybe. Not my problem. What's wrong with this damned handbag?

Only one minute left.

"First I thought, that junkie was guilty. And I went to the park behind the slot. But then I saw, these guys are ill, they don't know what they are doing. Then I read books, and at last I went to the police. It was difficult, they actually didn't want to talk to me. But then I found one, I met an inspector. I think he has children as well. That man told me that they can't catch the dealers. They always catch the small fish, he said, but never the big ones, the bosses, he said. That they know them all, but are not able to prove anything. And then, at last, he told me your name, doctor."

Shit. Bloody fucking shit.

"And then I thought, now, as Miriam is dead, and I took care of her for such a long time, finally I even had to leave my job to take care of her, and now I won't find another, at my age. And then I thought that you will not hide this time again, and if the police won't catch you, then why not me?"

This woman is really funny, I'm sure going to laugh myself to death. Schneider must come. Where is that damned buzzer?

"And that's why I'm here now, doctor. It was not so easy for me, you know. Specially to find a bomb that fits into a handbag was a real, real hard job for me as an old woman."

Robert Barnard

Old Dog, New Tricks

ROBERT BARNARD is often thought of as a "traditional" suspense writer. But if that's true, one has to wonder which tradition that would be. You want puzzles, he's done puzzles, and brilliant ones; you want comedies, he's given us several superlative ones; you want moody stories of middle age, he's even given us a few of those. He's a pro's pro and has long deserved a much wider audience in America than the one he has now. With stories like "Old Dog, New Tricks," published in *Ellery Queen's Mystery Magazine* in March, he's sure to get it.

Old Dog, New Tricks

Robert Barnard

I was beginning to get worried about my man. That's one thing that gets most of us hopping mad about a man: you just get him trained up, everything to your liking, and suddenly he goes through a midlife crisis, has a career move, or sinks into a rut of depression. And you have to start all over again.

In the case of my man it was a career move, though the other two played their part, too. He was fifty-five, and, as is normal in Norway, the police retired him. He decided to take me with him, and that was all right by me, though I'd always enjoyed the excitements and the perks of police work. At nine I was, let's say, mature myself, and Svein (my man) told everyone I was beginning to make mistakes. That was a reference to an incident at Bergen Airport, where I missed a packet of marijuana because the young American college boy had a bag with the remains of his roast beef airline dinner in his other pocket. Okay, it was an error—a bad one. But did he have to go on about it? I was consumed with worries about his approaching retirement at the time.

Anyway, Svein set up as a security consultant. Instead of just going home with him at night, he and I were in that flat together all day. Just like a married couple when the man retires—finding they get on each other's nerves twice as much when they are twice as much together. Of course, I soon got him trained as to when I wanted my meals, when and how long my walks were to be. Training a man is something some dogs make a great fuss about, but I've never found it difficult. The problem was the boredom.

I had been used to a life full of incident. Every day there was something different—training, public displays, airport and dockyard duties, even the occasional chase. But the truth is, there's hardly any crime in Norway, and what there is can be easily dealt with by the police (who spend most of their days pen–pushing or testing drivers who may be a millimeter over the alcohol limit). Dragsville. Svein put a brass plate on his front door, got an entry in the Yellow Pages, and sat down to wait for the customers to knock, ring, or make contact on the Internet.

And waited. And waited.

That is no life for a dog. As the great philosopher dog Heidegger (fl. Trondheim 1920s) said: "Excitement is the opium of the canine." A life of food and walks and watching bad programs on television was not for me. And I should have mentioned that there was only Svein and me together in the flat. His wife Unn had walked out on him about eight years previously. She'd moved in with a bank clerk. That's how exciting she found Svein. It would have been less insulting if she'd moved in with a bus conductor. Svein didn't seem to mind, though. He sent her cards for her birthday and Christmas.

"Well, old man," Svein would say to me periodically (nine is *not* old), "business is slow, isn't it?"

No, it was not slow. It was nonexistent.

So that was my situation. Svein and me mooching around the flat most of the hours God sends, me heaving deep sighs periodically and dreaming of my old, thrilling days (exaggerating that side of it a bit) in the police force, sometimes waking up with my paws going like the clappers as if I was in the middle of a thrilling chase. Svein, meanwhile, was doing—well, pretty much the same, actually, though I think what he dreamed about was more, well, personal. His boredom and frustration were all his own fault. Security consultant in Norway! You might as well go on a hunt for bones in a vegetarian colony.

Except that . . . It occurred to me that if business showed no sign of coming to us, we didn't have much option but to go in search of it. And, inevitably, in that search I was going to have to take the lead. As the great social philosopher dog Karl said (fl. Kristiansand ca. 1968): "From each according to his abilities, to each according to his needs." Svein's and my needs were pretty much equal, but there was no question in my mind as to who had the abilities.

I really couldn't see anything of interest turning up in the Minde district of Bergen: too normal, conventional, middle-middle class. Upper-middle might yield some interesting results, but would they be in our line? We were hardly equipped to tackle large-scale tax evasion or company fraud, and in any case, what had either to do with a security consultant? It seemed to me in every way better to start lower down the social scale. Or, perhaps better still, to make no prejudgments about where suitable crime was likely to turn up, and start in the center of the city. That was where it was all happening, if anything of a criminous nature was happening in Bergen at all. We needed to case the fish market, the park at Nordnæs, all the buildings that made up the university.

In the mornings I began pulling Svein in the direction of the garage. After about four mornings he got the message.

"Bored with your usual walks, are you, boy? Can't say I find them much of a turn-on, either. Let's have a trip to town."

Training tells. Eventually.

At first we stuck to the parks and open areas: Nordnæs park, out on the promontory, and Nygårdsparken, up near the university. We did the first on the first day, the second on the second. I made it clear to Svein, clear as his hazy mind could ever grasp, that I was now a police dog again. This was being on duty, not being bent on pleasure. To that end, I ignored a great many extremely attractive bitches who made "Come up and sniff me some time" gestures in my direction. "Some *other* time, doll," my demeanor told them, as I scurried purposefully off.

The pickings in both parks were meager: I identified dropping-off places for drugs, two or three in each park. But what could be done with that information by a security consultant? Svein shook his head dubiously, because I think he knew what I was thinking. The police probably had exactly the same information from their own dogs, my mates and my successors, in whom I had perfect confidence (we dogs, unlike human beings, do not denigrate our professional colleagues and successors). Anyway, the Bergen police do not pay retired policemen for information. What we needed to start the business rolling was information that was in some way saleable.

After a bit, as Svein got the general idea, we began to do a fairly systematic search and mapping of the central area.

Of course Svein quite often saw people he knew from his thirty-odd years in the Force—local notables, former colleagues, petty criminals. Quite often, I too had them on my computer database—not under "widdles" or "turds," which I would categorize as the pleasure part of my detective work, but under such headings as "work," "crime," "bigwigs," and so on. Every time my memory was stirred, I inserted the appropriate disk and called up the relevant information. Only my computer was all in my head, and needed no cumbersome machinery. The Lord Dog made us dogs well!

One such encounter occurred on the fourth day, as we were walking along Bryggen from Håkonshallen towards the Fish Market. I got the scent fifty meters away, and my mental computer said: pipe tobacco, ripe socks, fish-consumer. As we walked along, Svein spotted him too (he being dependent on sight, having no nose to speak of) and he took the man by the hand.

"Well, well. . . . It *is*, isn't it? . . . *God dag* Kjetil! How are things going with you?"

"Mustn't grumble," said Kjetil Myklebust, in a voice that said that grumbling was precisely what he did much of the time. "Just about surviving on my police handout."

"Don't talk about it," said Svein. "Takes a bit of getting used to, doesn't it, being permanently off-duty?" Myklebust had been stationed at the central branch, so Svein, at Fana, had not had a great deal to do with him in his working life. Still, there was a degree of fellow feeling, as was usual with the newly retired.

"Life can get boring," agreed Myklebust. "Is that mutt one of your old sniffer dogs?"

"Yep! Old faithful Loyd."

Myklebust twisted up his face.

"Wouldn't fancy having one of them around me all the time. A cat's company, but it doesn't give you the same amount of trouble. Those old dogs take all your time feeding them and exercising them, and the rest of the time they just lie around getting mangier and mangier."

I began to pull Svein over the road, to where the office of Molde Kreditkassen bank presented a likely object of criminal interest. My dislike of Mylkebust had been instant. There are worse old coppers than Svein, obviously. I, a dog in his prime, described as lying around getting mangy. And placed below a cat, as being more trouble than we're worth. "The less trouble, the less the value," said Beauty, a family dog (Tromsø, 1977–89) whose homely philosophy has been passed down from generation to generation and has penetrated the thinking of the whole Norwegian canine population.

Over the next few days we continued our search and reconnaissance around the central area of Bergen, striking particular gold in the train and bus stations (always fruitful areas, but with many quite new smells accumulated in the six months since I had retired from the Force), and less predictably around Grieghallen and the Rasmus Meyer Samling—the concert hall and the art gallery (arty types—don't ever get involved with them: feeding unreliable, walks almost nonexistent). Nothing, however, carried with it any suggestion of future profit. I don't say that Svein was reduced to feeding me on the sort of dry meal you mix with water. The police paid better pensions than *that*. But I certainly noticed he was buying the cheaper sort of tin.

It was, in fact, five days after our first meeting with Kjetil Myklebust, when we were doing the areas around the station, that we saw him again. I got his smell first, of course (normally I love ripe socks, but not his), then raised my head and saw him: he was slouching around further along Kong Oscars gate, going into doorways, slipping down side alleys, then reappearing. I made sure, by a judicious timing of tiddles and sniffs, that he was in the street when we approached. Eventually Svein recognized him (how can I get across to him that he needs long-sight glasses?).

"Kjetil! You again! Still at a loose end?"

He looked annoyed.

"Not at a loose end at all. I've always been a city man. Couldn't be anything nicer or more interesting than casing the city streets."

Hmmm. Bergen is the rainiest city in Europe. You'd have to be a bit of a masochist to enjoy casing its streets.

"Well, at least I've got Loyd to give me an excuse," said Svein.

"Who the devil needs an excuse? I do what I feel like doing, and I can do without an excuse that brings fleas and leaves hairs everywhere."

I pulled Svein on, then paused outside the offices of the Ålesund Sparebank, squeezing out of my bladder urine that I didn't know I had. Eventually even Svein had to get the message.

"You know," he said softly, as we continued on our way, "I wouldn't mind betting Kjetil's up to something."

Oh brave new world, that has such human brains in it! I'd decided that when I first got his scent in Kong Oscars gate, and I'd had wisps of suspicion on that first encounter back in Bryggen.

That evening, when we got home, Svein cooked himself one of his boring meals (bought-in kjøtt-kaker that tasted like meat-flavored cardboard), leaving, as always, something for me (big deal), and then settled down in his chair. After a while, he went over to the telephone table and brought back the Yellow Pages. He puzzled over these for some time, then put them aside.

"Must be a new company," he said, seeming mystified. Then he cheered up. "But then, it would be."

If he was puzzled, I was, too. Did he think Kjetil Myklebust was going to advertise his services? I began to worry about brain softening. I had heard that this happened to a lot of policemen soon after they retired from the routine slog work that was the only thing we thought men (in which I include women, of course) capable of.

My doubts were increased when we sighted Myklebust for the third time. We were casing the streets around Mariakirken, and this time both of us spotted him at once, lurking around several intersections away. We started towards him, but a moment or two later he caught sight of us and darted away down a back alley. "The man who decamps at the sight of us is either a dog-hater or is up to no good" (Police Dog Morse, fl. 1990). Or, in this case, both. Svein slackened pace, but I tugged him forward. Away we went, across the little-trafficked streets, until we got to his corner. There it was: a small branch of Vestlands Landsbruksbanken. I didn't feel I needed to urinate to press the point home.

"Looks like I was right," said Svein pensively. "Looks like Kjetil's gone into the security business as well."

I could have wept. The dolt! The dunderhead! The stupid old thickie! I sat there, looking up at him, and then I did the only thing I could think of doing: I threw back my head and howled.

Now, I never howl. It's a thing a lot of dogs do, and they find it useful, but I've usually got my way by more subtle means. But faced with his thick-headed idiocy I just howled and howled, going on and on.

I must have had a lot of unused howl in me.

Eventually a man came to the door of the Vestlands Landbruksbank. I looked at him. Middle-aged, twinkling eye, comfortable girth. I thought he could be useful. I stopped howling at once.

"Oh," he said, grinning at Svein. "I was going to ask you if you'd mind moving him along a bit, but he seems to have stopped of his own accord."

"I just can't understand him," said Svein, scratching his head. "He never howls."

"Well, he seems to have been making up for lost time."

"He's a former police dog. A howler would be no use to us in the Force." An idea seemed to strike him (wonder of wonders!). "By the way, I can't say I admire your security arrangements."

"Security arrangements?"

"The chap you're employing seems to have no idea of how to keep a low profile. I presume you're in with other small banks as well, are you? Either he lurks around these banks in a very obvious way, or—like today— he scuttles off, drawing attention to himself. I know him of old, both of us being retired coppers, but I'd have thought he'd have learned how to do a discreet bit of obbo when he was in the Force."

The man looked at him, frowning.

"We don't employ any private security firm. On the other hand . . . Look, could you come inside?"

"Sure," said Svein. "I'll tie up Loyd."

"Oh, bring him in. We're very dog-friendly here." He probably thought I was his only chance of getting an intelligent audience.

It was a very small branch of an insignificant bank. The manager had an office at the back, but a lot of the time, one suspected, he was serving at the counter. He introduced himself as Stig Bjørhovde, settled us (or rather Svein) into a chair, then served us coffee from a gently steaming percolator.

"You see," he said when we were settled, "your words struck a chord. Because there've been several raids on small banks recently—tiny branches of Bergens Privatbank or, like us, banks that don't loom large on the national scene, but need to have a presence in the major cities."

"I see," said Svein, and I hoped he was beginning to.

"So of course we've been alerted by the police, but they can't do much in the way of surveillance, and we've discussed upping our own security by getting a private firm."

"Well, if you do, I hope you'll consider us—," began Svein. And then he stopped, dumbfounded by a thought. "Where have the most recent robberies been?"

"At Molde Kreditkassen round the corner on Bryggen and the Ålesund Sparebank in Kong Oscars gate."

"My God! But that's impossible!"

Impossible? Oh come on, Svein. There's not much crime around in Norway, but if anybody knows about it, and knows about the best way of committing it without getting caught, it's an experienced copper.

"The man mentioned—," prompted the manager gently.

"But he's an old copper, like me," said Svein, his expression totally bewildered and upset. "I thought he was using his golden handshake to set up a security business, like me."

"But you've seen him lounging around the banks I've mentioned."

Miserably, Svein nodded. Perhaps loyalty between colleagues is not so rare in the human species as I've suggested. The silly thing is, Svein had never liked Kjetil: I knew that from his body emanations every time they'd met. If I'd had the same reactions to another dog, I'd have first snarled a warning, and if he didn't back off, we'd have had a brief set-to to establish my superiority.

Anyway, the upshot was that the manager, Bjørhovde, rang around the banks that had been robbed, got guesstimates of the raider's height, weight, and age (he always wore a reversed Balaclava helmet with slits for the eyes), and began the business of setting up additional security for all small branches. And that additional security was us.

Being on obbo, waiting for something that *might* happen with no guarantee that it will, is always boring. Svein and I got to the Vestlands Landsbruksbank well before opening and sat in the manager's office all day, Svein reading all the Bergen newspapers until it seemed that no event of whatever insignificance could have escaped his earnest, slow-reading eye. The manager was in and out, serving customers with his assistant on first opening, then again around midday, and at any other time when there were more than two customers. He had alerted us to the really slack times, and at last, on cue, during one of those, I got my first rush of adrenaline for months.

"This is a holdup."

The words sound even more ridiculous in Norwegian than they do in American English. The door to the manager's office had been left slightly open ever since we took up our stations there. I prowled in its direction, waiting for a sign from Svein. We wanted to catch him with the money, of course. Svein kept his eyes on the closed-circuit TV.

"Put your hands above your head. . . . Now put the keys on the desk. . . ."

And so the spiel went on. Talk about passé. And it was only when the cash was in his bag and he was backing out and nearly at the main door, gun still pointing, that Svein, all tense and giving off sweaty signals, at last said:

"Go."

I got to him ten paces into the street outside and three paces from his car. I got him in the leg, and when he howled and staggered I threw myself at his neck with a mental "Pardon my mange" and had him in the gutter by the time that Svein ran up to us. The Bergen police, of course, arrived three-quarters of an hour later, but they did have a couple of my old mates with them, so it all ended very pleasantly. Kjetil Myklebust is currently in a low-security prison making furniture for sale to high-minded persons with little regard for their own comfort.

So now we have work—an income-generator, as Svein rather grandly calls it. I got a great deal of kudos out of the whole matter, and I could very easily have changed my man and upgraded my whole lifestyle if I'd wanted to. On the other hand, if I joined Bergen's one big security firm I'd probably spend a lot of my time alone in big, drafty warehouses, or in a pound with a collection of dogs of inferior lineage and limited conversation. No thanks.

After all, I knew Svein. Okay, you can't teach an old man new tricks. And he had all the usual drawbacks that men do have: flatulence, beery smells, hair loss, a periodic tendency to tidy up and take away all the things a dog most cherishes. But when all's said and done, Beauty was right: no trouble, no joy. She wasn't thinking of us dogs, of course, but of men. And she said something else, in her homespun way. They give you an awful lot to put up with, but in the end they're dog's best friend.

Ruth Rendell

The Wink

WHILE RUTH RENDELL has never been quite as popular in America as she has been in Europe, her influence can certainly be felt on American writers. An entire generation of suspense novelists—as opposed to mystery novelists—have incorporated her style and approach to what the British call "chillers." She writes novels and stories of desperate people, the sort of people who take readers into a darkness rarely seen in most mystery fiction. Great spiritual turbulence animates most of her novels. Say what you like about them, the one thing most everyone agrees on is that her books are difficult to forget. Sometimes too difficult. If the idea of plunging into one of her novels sounds a bit daunting, perhaps you'd like to try one of her shorter works. Here, then, is "The Wink," which first appeared in *Ellery Queen's Mystery Magazine* in February, in which body language does much more than just talk.

The Wink

Ruth Rendell

The woman in reception gave her directions. Go through the day room, then the double doors at the back, turn left, and Elsie's in the third room on the right. Unless she's in the day room.

Elsie wasn't, but the Beast was. Jean always called him that, she had never known his name. He was sitting with the others watching television. A semicircle of chairs was arranged in front of the television, mostly armchairs but some wheelchairs, and some of the old people had fallen asleep. He was in a wheelchair and he was awake, staring at the screen where celebrities were taking part in a game show.

Ten years had passed since she had last seen him, but she knew him, changed and aged though he was. He must be well over eighty. Seeing him was always a shock, but seeing him in here was a surprise. A not unpleasant surprise. He must be in that chair because he couldn't walk. He had been brought low, his life was coming to an end.

She knew what he would do when he saw her. He always did. But possibly he wouldn't see her, he wouldn't turn round. The game show would continue to hold his attention. She walked as softly as she could, short of tip-toeing, round the edge of the semicircle. Her mistake was to look back just before she reached the double doors. His eyes were on her and he did what he always did. He winked.

Jean turned sharply away. She went down the corridor and found Elsie's room, the third on the right. Elsie, too, was asleep, sitting in an armchair by the window. Jean put the flowers she had brought on the bed and sat down on the only other chair, an upright one without arms. Then she got up again and drew the curtain a little way across to keep the sunshine off Elsie's face.

Elsie had been at Sweetling Manor for two weeks, and Jean knew she would never come out again. She would die here—and why not? It was clean and comfortable and everything was done for you and probably it was ridiculous to feel as Jean did, that she would prefer anything to being here, including being helpless and old and starving and finally dying alone.

They were the same age, she and Elsie, but she felt younger and thought she looked it. They had always known each other, had been at school together, had been each other's bridesmaids. Well, Elsie had been her matron of honor, having been married a year by then. It was Elsie she had gone to the pictures with that evening, Elsie and another girl whose name she couldn't remember. She remembered the film, though. It had been Deanna Durbin in *Three Smart Girls*. Sixty years ago.

When Elsie woke up she would ask her what the other girl was called. Christine? Kathleen? Never mind. Did Elsie know the Beast was in here? Jean remembered then that Elsie didn't know the Beast, had never heard what happened that night, no one had, she had told no one. It was different in those days, you couldn't tell because you would get the blame. Somehow, ignorant though she was, she had known that even then.

Ignorant. They all were, she and Elsie and the girl called Christine or Kathleen. Or perhaps they were just afraid. Afraid of what people would say, would think of them. Those were the days of blame, of good behavior expected from everyone, of taking responsibility, and often punishment, for one's own actions. You put up with things and you got on with things. Complaining got you nowhere.

Over the years there had been extraordinary changes. You were no longer blamed or punished, you got something called empathy. In the old days, what the Beast did would have been her fault. She must have led him on, encouraged him. Now it was a crime, *his* crime. She read about it in the papers, saw about things called helplines on television, and counselling and specially trained women police officers. This was to avoid your being marked for life, traumatized, though you could never forget.

That was true, that last part, though she had forgotten for weeks on end, months. And then, always, she had seen him again. It came of living in the country, in a small town; it came of her living there and his going on living there. Once she saw him in a shop, once out in the street, another time he got on a bus as she was getting off it. He always winked. He didn't say anything, just looked at her and winked.

Elsie had looked like Deanna Durbin. The resemblance was quite marked. They were about the same age, born in the same year. Jean remembered how they had talked about it, she and Elsie and Christine-Kathleen, as they left the cinema and the others walked with her to the bus stop. Elsie wanted to know what you had to do to get a screen test and the other girl said it would help to be in Hollywood, not Yorkshire. Both of them lived in the town, five minutes' walk away, and Elsie said she could stay the night if she wanted. But there was no way of letting her parents know. Elsie's parents had a phone, but hers didn't.

Deanna Durbin was still alive, Jean had read somewhere. She wondered if she still looked like Elsie or if she had had her face lifted and her hair dyed and gone on diets. Elsie's face was plump and soft, very wrinkled about the eyes, and her hair was white and thin. She smiled faintly in her sleep and gave a little snore. Jean moved her chair closer and took hold of Elsie's hand. That made the smile come back, but Elsie didn't wake.

The Beast had come along in his car about ten minutes after the girls had gone and Jean was certain the bus wasn't coming. It was the last bus and she hadn't known what to do. This had happened before, the driver just hadn't turned up and had got the sack for it, but that hadn't made the bus come. On that occasion she had gone to Elsie's and Elsie's mother had phoned her parents' next-door neighbors. She thought that if she did that a second time and put Mr. and Mrs. Rawlings to all that trouble, her dad would probably stop her going to the pictures ever again.

It wasn't dark. At midsummer it wouldn't get dark till after ten. If it had been, she mightn't have gone with the Beast. Of course, he didn't seem like a Beast then, but young, a boy really, and handsome and quite nice. And it was only five miles. Mr. Rawlings was always saying five miles was nothing, he used to walk five miles to school every day and five miles back. But she couldn't face the walk and, besides, she wanted a ride in a car. It would only be the third time she had ever been in one. Still, she would have refused his offer if he hadn't said what he had when she told him where she lived.

"You'll know the Rawlings, then. Mrs. Rawlings is my sister."

It wasn't true, but it sounded true. She got in beside him. The car wasn't really his, it belonged to the man he worked for; he was a chauffeur, but she found that out a lot later.

"Lovely evening," he said. "You been gallivanting?"

"I've been to the pictures," she said.

After a couple of miles he turned a little way down a lane and stopped the car outside a derelict cottage. It looked as if no one could possibly live there, but he said he had to see someone, it would only take a minute and she could come, too. By now it was dusk, but there were no lights on in the cottage. She remembered he was Mrs. Rawlings's brother. There must have been a good ten years between them, but that hadn't bothered her. Her own sister was ten years older than she was.

She followed him up the path, which was overgrown with weeds and brambles. Instead of going to the front door, he led her round the back where old apple trees grew among waist-high grass. The back of the house was a ruin, half its rear wall tumbled down.

"There's no one here," she said.

He didn't say anything. He took hold of her and pulled her down in the long grass, one hand pressed hard over her mouth. She hadn't known anyone could be so strong. He took his hand away to pull her clothes off and she screamed, but the screaming was just a reflex, a release of fear, and otherwise useless. There was no one to hear. What he did was rape. She knew that now—well, had known it soon after it happened, only no one called it that then. Nobody spoke of it. Nowadays the word was on everyone's lips. Nine out of ten television series were about it. Rape, the crime against women. Rape, that these days you went into court and talked about. You went to self-defense classes to stop it happening to you. You attended groups and shared your experience with other victims.

At first, she had been most concerned to find out if he had injured her. Torn her, broken bones. But there was nothing like that. Because she was all right and he was gone, she stopped crying. She heard the car start up and then move away. Walking home wasn't exactly painful, more a stiff, achey business, rather the way she had felt the day after she and Elsie had been learning to do the splits. She had to walk anyway, she had no choice. As it was, her father was in a rage, wanting to know what time she thought this was.

"Anything could have happened to you," her mother said.

Something had. She had been raped. She went up to bed so they wouldn't see she couldn't stop shivering. She didn't sleep at all that night. In the morning she told herself it could have been worse, at least she wasn't dead. It never crossed her mind to say anything to anyone about what had happened; she was too ashamed, too afraid of what they would think. It was past, she kept telling herself, it was all over.

One thing worried her most. A baby. Suppose she had a baby. Never in all her life was she so relieved about anything, so happy, as when she saw that first drop of blood run down the inside of her leg a day early. She shouted for joy. She was all right! The blood cleansed her and now no one need ever know.

Trauma? That was the word they used nowadays. It meant a scar. There was no scar that you could see and no scar she could feel in her body, but it was years before she would let a man come near her. Afterwards she was glad about that, glad she had waited, that she hadn't met someone else before Kenneth. But at the time, she thought about what had happened every day; she relived what had happened, the shock and the pain and the dreadful fear, and in her mind she called the man who had done that to her the Beast.

Eight years went by and she saw him again. She was out with Kenneth, he had just been demobbed from the Air Force and they were walking down the High Street arm-in-arm. Kenneth had asked her to marry him and they were going to buy the engagement ring. It was a big jewellers they went to, with several aisles. The Beast was in a different aisle, quite a long way away, on some errand for his employer, she supposed, but she saw him and he saw her. He winked.

He winked, just as he had ten minutes ago in the day room. Jean shut her eyes.

When she opened them again, Elsie was awake.

"How long have you been there, dear?"

"Not long," Jean said.

"Are those flowers for me? You know how I love freesias. We'll get someone to put them in water. I don't have to do a thing in here, don't lift a finger. I'm a lady of leisure."

"Elsie," said Jean, "what was the name of that girl we went to the pictures with when we saw *Three Smart Girls?*"

"What?"

"It was nineteen thirty-eight. In the summer."

"I don't know, I shall have to think. My memory's not what it was. Bob used to say I looked like Deanna Durbin."

"We all said you did."

"Constance, her name was. We called her Connie."

"So we did," said Jean.

Elsie began talking of the girls they had been at school with. She could remember all their Christian names and most of their surnames. Jean found a vase, filled it with water, and put the freesias into it because they showed signs of wilting. Her engagement ring still fitted on her finger, though it was a shade tighter. How worried she had been that Kenneth would be able to tell she wasn't a virgin! They said men could always tell. But of course, when the time came, he couldn't. It was just another old wives' tale.

Elsie, who already had her first baby, had worn rose-colored taffeta at their wedding. And her husband had been Kenneth's best man. John was born nine months later and the twins eighteen months after that. There was a longer gap before Anne arrived, but still she had had her hands full. That was the time, when the children were little, that she thought less about the Beast and what had happened than at any other time in her life. She forgot him for months on end. Anne was just four when she saw him again.

She was meeting the other children from school. They hadn't got a car then, it was years before they got a car. On the way to the school, they were going to the shop to buy Anne a new pair of shoes. The Red Lion was just closing for the afternoon. The Beast came out of the public bar, not too steady on his feet, and he almost bumped into her. She said, "Do you mind?" before she saw who it was. He stepped back, looked into her face, and winked. She was outraged. For two pins she'd have told Kenneth the whole tale that evening. But of course she couldn't. Not now.

"I don't know what you mean about your memory," she said to Elsie. "You've got a wonderful memory."

Elsie smiled. It was the same pretty teenager's smile, only they didn't use that word teenager then. You were just a person between twelve and twenty. "What do you think of this place, then?"

"It's lovely," said Jean. "I'm sure you've done the right thing."

Elsie talked some more about the old days and the people they'd known and then Jean kissed her goodbye and said she'd come back next week.

"Use the shortcut next time," said Elsie. "Through the garden and in by the French windows next door."

"I'll remember."

She wasn't going to leave that way, though. She went back down the corridor and hesitated outside the day-room door. The last time she'd seen the Beast, before *this* time, they were both growing old. Kenneth was dead. John was a grandfather himself, though a young one, the twins were joint directors of a prosperous business in Australia, and Anne was a surgeon in London. Jean had never learned to drive, and the car was given up when Kenneth died. She was waiting at that very bus stop, the one where he had picked her up all those years before. The bus came and he got off it, an old man with white hair, his face yellowish and wrinkled. But she knew him, she would have known him anywhere. He gave her one of his rude stares and he winked. That time it was an exaggerated, calculated wink, the whole side of his face screwed up and his eye squeezed shut.

She pushed open the day-room door. The television was still on but he wasn't there. His wheelchair was empty. Then she saw him. He was being brought back from the bathroom, she supposed. A nurse held him tightly by one arm. The other rested heavily on the padded top of a crutch. His legs, in pajama trousers, were halfbuckled and on his face was an expression of agony as, wincing with pain, he took small tottering steps.

Jean looked at him. She stared into his tormented face and his eyes met hers. Then she winked. She winked at him as he had winked at her that last time, and she saw what she had never thought to see happen to an old person. A rich dark blush spread across his withered face. He turned away his eyes. Jean tripped lightly across the room towards the exit, like a sixteen-year-old.

Paul Lascaux

Fire Works

PAUL LASCAUX is the pseudonym of Paul Ott. Born in 1955, he grew up in Goldach on the shores of Lake Constance and in St. Gallen, Switzerland, and has lived in Berne since 1974. During the past twenty-five years he has had various articles published in several newspapers and magazines, as well as several literary works. He has written crime novels and short stories for the past fifteen years, most set in the city of Berne and the neighboring villages and countryside in Canton Berne. It seems that there is a fair, if not overwhelming, market for short fiction in European newspapers. Because of this, many of the authors who write for them have mastered the difficult art of the short-short story. "Fire Works," translated from his collection *Europa Stirbt,* is a paradigm of the form in a thousand words.

Fire Works

Paul Lascaux

Just after the charwoman emptied the last wastepaper basket, switched off the light and locked the office door behind her, the first flame wriggled and squirmed amongst the paper in the filing cabinet. It stilled its most urgent hunger on the thin card of the folders. The flimsy sheets of the job applications seemed to invite the flame's burning caresses. Its tongue licked at the correspondence and engulfed them within seconds, leaving only flakes of black, crumbling ash in its wake.

It had started at the letter N and had reached the end of the alphabet minutes later. Searching for more food, it flowed out of the cabinet, raced along the plastic cables and, with destructive energy, penetrated the computer. Only then did the alarm, triggered by the acrid smoke of burning wiring, begin to scream, and the sprinklers added to the destruction by drowning everything within range, whether damaged or not.

When the fire brigade arrived at the scene they found the offices of Mäder & Co., Employment and Personnel Advisors, in a state of utter devastation. None of the records could be saved; the company would have to close down operations for some time to come. A single, singed photo floated on the surface of the ankle-deep water. It showed the face of a woman around forty, whose smile showed a faint trace of bitterness. A fireman took the picture home with him; the eyes reminded him of a famous painting.

"Are enterprise and vision your strong points? Our client—a company in the metal industry near Berne—has reorganized and restructured to suit modern requirements. For a new department in their company we have a vacancy for an OFFICE MANAGER/ESS FOR FINANCES, CONTROLLING AND HUMAN RESOURCES.

Qualifications required: Long-term experience in personnel management, A-level education and additional training in bookkeeping/controlling. Enterprise and innovation, initiative and independence, but also team spirit and flexibility. Age: 25 to 40."

How many times had Laura read adverts for job vacancies, in which people over forty weren't welcome? She had just celebrated her forty-second birthday and had been presented with a diploma for an advanced training course, which put her qualifications now well up to management level. And yet for months she had been trying to find work. Refusal followed refusal, most of them couched in oh so polite terms, "Unfortunately we must inform you that, on studying the many applications we received, we have selected a candidate more suited to the advertised vacancy. This by no means questions your qualifications blah blah blah . . ."

Laura threw *The Job Advertiser* angrily into the corner, where it landed with a thud in the kitty litter.

The despair that had been growing deeper each day had begun to leave traces on her face. Laura set about hiding her worry-lines and red-rimmed eyes beneath her makeup—she had an appointment in the afternoon. She had been invited to go for an interview at Careers For Women at 5 p.m. The personnel manageress hadn't wanted to give her any false hopes on the telephone, but at least she'd been invited to call. You never knew, maybe something would come of it.

Arriving a few minutes early, Laura sat in the boss's reception room, where a young girl was getting ready to leave, while dealing with a telephone call. She was apparently one of those "friendly, purposeful, personable secretaries, capable of working under pressure," who were, if you believed the vacancy columns, so common these days. In Laura's opinion, she seemed just another snotty, superficial and irritable typist, who barred the door to that crucial office beyond.

She had often been stopped by loud-mouthed bimbos and she hated them all for the humiliation she was made to feel. Laura introduced herself while, in front of the building, a young kid in a flashy, leased sportscar bombarded the neighborhood with annoying techno noise while he waited for the typist.

Laura's concentration on the discussion that followed was slowly lost in an uncontrollable fury at the society for whom only youth and a carefree lifestyle counted. Ignorance and arrogance, wherever she looked!

Barbie Doll left the reception without a parting glance and locked the door behind her. Laura was now imprisoned with a stranger who was making her wait even longer. Laura stood up and tiptoed to the filing cabinet. Opening her handbag, she removed a small vial, unscrewed the lid and quickly placed it between the job applications. Then she sat down again and tried to calm her hammering heart.

•　　•　　•

When the manageress finally emerged from her office and asked her to enter, she could tell just from the elegantly dressed woman's critical glance that she didn't stand a chance. The woman got quickly to the point. Although she apologized several times and assured Laura that it wasn't her fault, there was simply nothing she could do with women above a certain age, except commiserate with them. They just weren't wanted anymore. Other, more pressing values counted these days. But Laura could hear no trace of pity in the other's voice.

She left the office having achieved nothing. She went to a bar which was on her way home. There, at least, she could talk to men about other subjects—to men who found her attractive no matter what her age was, and who took her mind off "purposeful, personable" secretaries.

Laura heard the wail of the fire engine's siren as she sipped her second dry martini. She smiled and, unusually for her, ordered a third glass.

They found Careers For Women burnt to the ground. There was nothing left to save and the soggy pulp of ashes and extinguisher foam stuck to the firemen's boots as they went about their work.

A fireman picked up a charred photograph and took it home with him. Only the top half of the picture was undamaged, the nose, the eyes, forehead and hair. Then he looked into the eyes, recognized them and knew that this would not be the last fire.

Nancy Springer

Juggernaut

NANCY SPRINGER is a lifelong fiction writer, author of thirty-one volumes of mythic fantasy, children's literature, mystery, suspense, short stories, and poetry. A longtime Pennsylvania resident, she teaches creative writing at York College of Pennsylvania. In her spare time she is an enthusiastic, although not expert, horseback rider, and a volunteer for the Wind Ridge Farm Equine Sanctuary, a home for horses that have been rescued from neglect or abuse. She lives in Dallastown with a phlegmatic guinea pig and a psychotic cat. Given these varied interests, it was only natural that she would eventually write a mystery story, and what a story it is. "Juggernaut" first appeared in the June issue of *Ellery Queen's Mystery Magazine*.

Juggernaut

Nancy Springer

G ood Lord, why am I doing this?"
Marietta whispered, teetering on
her platform heels, immobilized at the door of the hotel ballroom. On a logical level she knew exactly why she was there: Five murdered men, that was
why. Despite her scarlet flirty-skirted dress and the "Temptress Red"
Shampoo-It-Away hair dye covering her gray, Marietta Becker was on duty,
her badge tucked into her capacious purse. Just doing her job. But on a
woman's gut level . . . good grief, a singles dance? With a disco ball, of all
things, wheeling a slow juggernaut in the middle of the ceiling and hurling
spangles of confusion onto the women seated at the circular tables, the men
standing in the shadows, a few couples awkwardly clinched on the dance
floor? Snowed under by those silver sequins of reflected light, Marietta froze
at the edge of enormity: Lord, she'd been married almost as long as she'd
been a cop; she didn't venture to places like this. "What am I *doing* here?"
she complained aloud.

"Honey," answered a woman about her age crowded next to her in the
Art Deco doorway, "I ask myself that selfsame question every blessed week."
Marietta hadn't expected the other women, who should regard her as com-
petition, to speak with her, but she tried not to show her surprise as she
turned. "Really?"

"Sure. But it beats sitting home alone." Prim in a business suit, the
woman slapped a nametag onto her blazer above her left breast. First name
only, of course: Pat. She asked Marietta, "Your first time?"

"Yes."

"Well, come sit with us. Smile," Pat coached, leading the way into the
disco-starred darkness of the dance.

Following, Marietta felt men's glances slide over her like soap. With her
teeth bared, she peered through the polka-dot gloom. In front of her, the

linen-draped tables seemed to float like white lily pads at the edge of a black and shining dance-floor lake. Centered on each table, candles burned—for romance, or for a wake? Somewhere in this room, most likely, smiled a murderer.

Five victims had been found so far, all male. One from Harrisburg, two from York, one from Carlisle, one from Williamsport, for God's sake. All over the map in more ways than one. A young black college professor, a middle-aged Pennsylvania Dutch truck driver, a Greek Cypriot fish-sticks salesman, an unemployed Latino suspected of drug trafficking, and a retired Army master sergeant. They were such a disparate collection of stiffs that only the M.O. marked them as the victims of a serial killer. "The Crusher," the news called him.

"You want to face the dance floor?" Pat asked Marietta, offering a chair at an angle to one of the tables.

"Sure."

Sitting, Marietta slipped into her purse the card they had given her when she had paid to get in: HeartSong Singles, Attend Six Dances Get the Seventh Free. The card that had been found in the wallets of two of the five Crusher victims. Names of two others had been found on the mailing list, but that was strictly departmental info, Marietta's captain had warned. What about the fifth victim? she had asked. Married, he'd told her with a look that told her to butt out, it was not her case, she was just there to carry the purse. Bill was doing the work, and where the heck was he?

"So, Mary," Pat said, glancing at Marietta's nametag, "what's the story, morning glory?"

"Oh, uh, the usual." Marietta had not thought she would need a cover story.

Pat nodded. "He dumped you for a younger woman?" Marietta had to force herself to nod and smile. She was here as a single, she reminded herself—but no, it couldn't happen, her husband would never dump her. George wasn't very affectionate, but that was just because he worked too hard. Sometimes, like the last couple of days, their work schedules were so off whack they didn't even see each other. She hadn't gotten to tell him about this assignment—but that was probably just as well. She never knew what was likely to make him hit the ceiling. The idea of her dressing up and dancing with other men might do it, even though it was just her job and he'd been happy for her when after twenty years of parking meters and traffic detail she'd been promoted to undercover. He hadn't minded her putting herself into danger playing Muggable Mary.

Huh. Nobody better try to snatch the purse tonight. In it were guns, handcuffs, radio, all the equipment Bill might need if he found out anything. Some sort of kinky homo sex motivation, Homicide thought. They profiled the Crusher as a blue-collar male, hefty enough to muscle his victims into some sort of machine press to torture and kill them, strong enough to dump the bodies afterward. Bill had to be hugging his gun. Where was he? They kept it so dark in here it was hard to tell, especially with that stupid disco ball slinging snowflakes of light in her eyes. Marietta scanned the straggle of men around the dance floor—funny, most of the women, at the tables, were chatting with one another, while most of the men stood staring in parallel, not speaking. And what a selection of men—round men in fuzzy sweaters, edgy men in suits, cadaverous old men in pleated slacks and crepe-soled shoes, men trying to look sporty in Nikes and collared T-shirts, a black guy in dreadlocks, a Don Johnson pretender in a *Miami Vice* hat, for God's sake, and a ponytailed biker type in leathers; lean men and teddy-bear men and bearded men and boyish men, and—*and I'd like to get to know every one of them*, Marietta realized, surprising herself. *I like men. All kinds.*

And she felt a stab of guilt at the thought, as if she'd been unfaithful. Throughout her years of marriage, she'd trained herself not to look at other men. Being at this singles dance was doing strange things to her.

But getting into character, that was part of the job, wasn't it? Part of going undercover?

A tall gray-haired man headed toward her. She stiffened in anticipation; would he ask her to dance? But he walked past her without a glance, stopped at the next table, and spoke to a tawny young woman in a very abbreviated dress. Together they walked to the dance floor.

A hefty blond woman in a make-me-look-slim-please black tunic sat down on Marietta's other side. "Hi, I'm Deb," she said to Marietta. "Yo, gang," she called past Marietta toward Pat. "Wearing your shoes out dancing?"

A general chuckle ensued. Marietta glanced over her shoulder. The table had filled with women about her age, some round, some skinny, some comfy and some dressed to kill, all kinds, and Marietta imagined the men looking them over the way she had looked over the men, thinking, wow, I like them all.

She watched a fat man dancing with a perfectly endowed blonde half his age. Marietta wanted to dance. The deejay was playing "Crocodile Rock," damn it, and she never got to dance; George hated dancing, it had been years . . . She demanded, "When *do* they ask us to dance?"

Quite a lot of laughter erupted, and Deb patted her hand. "You're new, right?"

"Is it that obvious?"

"Honey, everybody starts the same way," Pat said. "The old guy in the suspenders, by the water cooler," she added, "if he asks you to dance, say no. He puts his hand on your butt."

"You're brave, coming by yourself," Deb said.

Deb seemed nice, Marietta thought at the same moment as she finally spotted Bill talking with the bartender. Stalking a murderer. Was it the distinguished-looking older man with the younger woman, or the bald guy dancing with yet another young girl, this one willowy and vaguely reminiscent of an Afghan hound? Or was it the guy in the *Miami Vice* hat, or the leather-clad biker, or the fat man? Inspired, Marietta turned to Deb.

"A friend told me about the dance. Guy named Bob. Fortyish, overweight, beer belly, balding." This was the most recent murder victim. "You know him?"

Deb laughed. "Honey, you have just described half of the guys here."

The deejay announced, "Paul Jones time."

"Now you get to dance," Pat told Marietta. "Sort of."

Paul Jones, it turned out, was not a person, but a mixer worthy of a milk shake. Coached by Pat, Marietta joined the women on the dance floor, under the slow swirling of the disco ball. The women circled widdershins around a smaller circle of men moving clockwise. When the music changed, Marietta stopped opposite a reasonably handsome man about her own age. He looked straight at her, then reached for the woman next to her, who was younger and thinner.

Huh. Marietta stood out, feeling very much like the leftovers pushed to the back of the fridge. She wasn't the only one; with her stood a woman from her table. Muriel, said her nametag, its i dotted with a heart, which seemed out of all keeping with her. Arrow-slim and straight, Muriel looked perma-pressed all over despite the wrinkles shirring her face. "Just like high school," she commented crisply, with a hard glance at some men slumping nearby, ignoring the leftover women, blankly staring at the couples on the dance floor.

Under the disco ball, the Paul Jones juggernaut wheeled again. This time Marietta slow-danced with halitosis incarnate, escaping gratefully when the music changed. The next go-round she was leftovers. Bill, she noticed, had joined the staring men on the sidelines, ignoring her like the others. Marietta danced next with an attractive man her age who inched his hand toward her butt. She grasped his arm and hoisted it. "Oh, is that the way it is," he complained. Her next partner, a nerdy youngster, seemed to regard her as a maypole to circle around. Eventually the ordeal ended, and she fled to her seat.

"That Bob you mentioned," Deb asked, rejoining her, "is he married?"

Only the fact that she had completely forgotten about Bob kept Marietta from blowing her cover by knowing too much. She had to think, and thinking saved her. "I, uh, don't know him that well. I guess not, since he came here."

"Oh, we have our married singles," Deb said wryly.

"But why? I mean, how do they get in?"

Everyone smiled at her naïveté. "Nobody checks," put in the straight-arrow older woman, Muriel. Something about her starchiness made Marietta peg her as a librarian or a head nurse. "People come, people go, nobody cares."

"You can tell when they're married," said Pat. "They come from someplace far away. They want your phone number, but they won't give you theirs."

"Sometimes I think the married ones are the only ones actually trying to connect," said Muriel almost wistfully.

"What's *with* all those guys who just stand and stare?" Marietta asked. "What are they looking at?"

"Easy. They're looking at the boobs bouncing," Muriel said, her tone so undisguisedly bitter that, without meaning to, Marietta gave her a shocked look. Muriel returned the glance, opaque, expressionless. Deb saw, apparently, and interceded.

"Do we seem like the witches in *Macbeth?*" she asked lightly. "Capering in circles?"

"Well, it's hard to keep smiling year after year," Pat put in. "I mean, the brains and experience at this table . . . Deb, you're a lab tech when you're not at the Little Theater, right? And I'm a wellness administrator, Judy drives a truck for UPS. Sue has her own graphic arts business, Muriel is a physician—one of the first female gynecologists in the state."

"Wow," Marietta said on cue, although she was still trying to figure out what a wellness administrator was.

"And there's an astronomer who joins us sometimes," Pat continued, "and a movie producer, and—oh, some others who drop out and in, people do that a lot at these singles things. But the point is, the men . . ." Pat seemed to have mislaid the point.

"Boobs," Muriel summed up tersely.

Men were boobs? All men looked for in a woman was boobs? Both of the above?

"What do you do, Mary?" Pat asked.

"I, um, I'm in civil service."

"Postal?"

"Yes. Frequently." They laughed, and talk moved on. Marietta saw that Bill had moved to the dance floor, with the willowy blonde for his partner. The evening blurred. She no longer hoped to dance. With her back to the table she watched the dancers, she watched more men and a few women arriving insouciantly late, she watched the slow wheeling of that dreadful disco ball, hearing snatches of womentalk all around her.

". . . a few drinks before they get here, then more at the bar . . ."

". . . only four grams of fat."

"Premarin and, what's the name of that other stuff that makes you keep having your period till you're ninety?"

". . . do you believe for one moment that guys would get annual dickograms?"

". . . so sweet until we started going steady, and then it was like Dr. Jekyll and . . ."

". . . can't wait to get home and take them off." Muriel's crisp voice. "The adhesive irritates my skin."

". . . in a big hurry, get it in before they need Viagra . . ."

"Three hours of brisk walking a week . . ."

". . . had sex the day he left me."

The deejay announced, "Time for our second Paul Jones of the evening, folks." Marietta stayed where she was, watching the others get up and form their circle on the floor. Deb, the peacemaker. Pat, so very much the businesswoman. Muriel, brittle and correct and very, very erect, her breasts under her well-fitted shirtwaist dress as pointed as her discourse and nearly as unyielding. This woman had boobs that did not bounce. Not at all.

Beyond her, yet another latecomer male stood in the doorway. He turned toward Marietta, and his glance passed right over her.

Marietta gasped and grabbed at the table as if she were falling. It was her husband.

There he stood with the other men, staring without expression at the dancers. Her George, in the shirt and tie she had bought him for his birthday.

But—it couldn't be. He was working. He always worked late on—

On singles dance nights.

Oh, God.

For several seconds, all of Marietta's cognitive processes quite simply stopped. When they started again, they proceeded logically and quite coolly; it was this levelheadedness in a crisis that made Marietta a good cop, if anyone would notice. George must not see her, she realized. Because she was undercover, and also because she was his wife, he must not know she was here—but he had not noticed her so far. She sat in near darkness, with her hair dyed and her face masked by way more makeup than she usually wore, and anyway, nothing is more invisible than a middle-aged woman; he probably would not notice her as long as she did not call attention to herself. Better not move.

For the next several moments she sat blending into her environment, watching George watch the boobs bounce, and feeling a cold, covert fury building, building, hardening like an iceberg in her. She had not known she possessed such silent fury.

I hate men. All of them.

"You didn't go out for the Paul Jones?" It was Deb, returning along with the others.

Marietta shook her head.

"You can't get tired already, girl."

Marietta shook her head again. "That man," she said, fixated on George, "I know him. He's married."

Peripherally she saw heads swivel; she had the attention of the whole table. Pat asked, "Which one?"

"In the blue shirt and tie set. Just came in. Name's George."

"George? Oh, yes." It was Muriel. "I know him. He's a regular."

Marietta felt her ice-coolness go glassy sharp. She turned to Muriel. "His wife is the nicest woman," she stage-whispered across the table. "But she had a mastectomy. I guess he's not getting what he wants at home."

This was a lie told for a reason. She watched Muriel's face, but it revealed nothing.

"Did he see you?" Deb asked.

"No, and I don't want him to. I have to get out of here. It's going to be bad enough facing him and his wife . . ."

"I'll ask him to dance." Deb heaved her black-clad bulk up. "Most of them will dance if you ask them. Anyway, I'll distract him for a minute. You make a run for it."

"Thanks, Deb."

"I guess we won't be seeing you again?" Pat asked as Deb waddled across the room.

"I guess not. No big loss."

"Yes, it is."

"Not for me, I mean. I . . ." She let the thought trail away.

Muriel completed it for her in a voice as dry as dead thistles in winter. "You had hoped for something more from the heart."

"Right." Marietta looked Muriel straight in the eye, appraising her, then turned away. "Well, I gotta go."

Ducking out the door, Marietta clutched in her mind like a talisman the memory of the deadly bleakness in Muriel's stare.

She thought about George. All the years she had spent cleaning up the popcorn he dropped down the sofa cushions when he was watching TV, sleeping with his snore in her ear, cooking homemade french fries for him. Her husband, a regular. Here. Wearing that shirt and tie.

May he fry in hell.

She wondered whether the men who had been killed were the kind who watched, or the kind who groped, or both.

She wondered which other woman, or women, at that table were carrying pistols in their purses.

Darting across the too-brightly lighted hallway, she found refuge in the ladies' room. After making sure she was alone, she reached into her purse and pulled out one of the boy-toys in there. She pressed a button to activate a vibrator hidden inside Bill's belt, alerting him that she needed to talk with him.

"There's a guy who knows me in there," she told him in the safety of the parking lot a few minutes later.

"Well, let's call it off for tonight, then. I'll talk with the captain. Crusher be damned, I don't see any guys in there who look like they can bench-press me. I don't feel like I'm getting anywhere."

No wonder he wasn't getting anywhere, Marietta thought as she settled into her car to wait, as she watched Bill drive away. Guys didn't talk to one another the way women did. And anyway, Bill was operating on the wrong premise. Maybe she ought to have suggested to him that a mammography machine was quite a powerful kind of press, and that two or more women working together could maneuver a guy into it very nicely, thank you.

But nah. He'd just laugh at her. And anyway, she wanted to wait and see.

It wouldn't happen tonight, probably. Not if they had any sense of caution. But the chill, furious beauty of Marietta's situation, she considered, was that she didn't have to do a thing about George except smile as usual. Keep cleaning up the popcorn, sleeping through the snore, boiling the oil for his precious fries. Smile, and have faith in the force she had set in motion.

Hazily Marietta thought of a glacier grinding its massive, icy way down a lonesome valley of betrayed dreams, then of gigantic wheels turning with monstrous pressing power. Once upon a time there had been a huge, heavy cart that had borne the idol of some Hindu god, crushing the faithful beneath its implacable tread. She wondered what deity they had been worshiping, poor fools. Wondered whether it had been the incarnation of love.

Peter Lovesey

Star Struck

PETER LOVESEY is another British author who has excelled at a variety of forms in the mystery and suspense genres. He can be tart, taut, amusing, sentimental, and bloody—all with equal skill and ease. His novels have somewhat overshadowed his work as a short story writer. But a collected works volume will someday be in order and then the mystery world will be able to see what an important short story writer he really is. The innocuous subject of newspaper horoscopes gets its comeuppance from this master of the short form in "Star Struck," when a hungry reporter decides to change fortune to suit his fate, instead of the other way around. Published in the anthology *Death by Horoscope*, "Star Struck" shows Lovesey's ear for dialogue and his neat way with a plot in fine form.

Star Struck

Peter Lovesey

On that September evening the sun was a crimson skull cap, and a glittering cope was draped across the sea. I was leaning on the rail at the end of the pier where the fishermen liked to cast. By this time they had all packed up and gone. A few unashamed romantics like me stood in contemplation, awed by the spectacle.

I wasn't aware of the woman beside me until she spoke. Her voice was low-pitched, instantly attractive. She was wearing what looked like a cloak.

"I can already see a star," she said.

"Jupiter," I answered.

"For sure?"

"Certainly."

"Couldn't it be Venus? Venus can be very bright."

"Not this month. Venus is in superior conjunction with the sun, so we won't see it at all this month."

"You obviously know," she said.

"Only enough to take an interest." This was true. I'm no expert on the solar system.

"This is an ideal place to stand," she said. "It's my first time here."

Up to now I hadn't looked at her fully. All my attention had been on the sky. Turning, I saw a fine, narrow face suffused with the strange crimson light. Dark, straight hair worn long and loose. She could have modelled for Modigliani. "I thought I hadn't seen you here before. Did someone recommend it?"

Her eyes widened. "How did you know?"

"A guess."

"I don't think so. You must be intuitive. I always read my horoscope in the local paper, the *Argus*. This week, it said Friday was an evening to go somewhere different that gives a sense of space. I couldn't think of anywhere that fitted better than this."

"Nor I." The polite response. Privately I haven't much time for people who take astrology seriously.

As if she sensed I was a skeptic, she said, "It's a science, you know."

"Interesting claim."

"The zodiac doesn't lie. If mistaken readings are made, it's human error. Anyone can call himself an astrologer, and some are charlatans, but the best are extremely accurate. I've had it proved again and again."

You don't cast doubt on statements like that—not when they're made by a beautiful woman you've only just met. "Right. If it has a good result, who cares? You came here and saw this wonderful sunset."

Only later, hours later, still thinking about her, did I realize what I should have said: *Did the horoscope tell you what to do next?* The perfect cue to invite her out for a meal. I always think of the lines too late.

She'd made a profound impression on me—and I hadn't even asked what her name was.

Idiot.

I played the pier scene over many times in the next few days. She'd spoken first. I should have made the next move. Now it was too late unless I happened to meet her again. I went back to the pier and watched the next three sunsets. Well, to be truthful I spent most of the time looking over my shoulder. She didn't come.

I couldn't concentrate on my job. I'm a subeditor on the *Argus*—yes, the paper she mentioned. My subbing was so bad that week that Mr. Peel, the editor, called me in and pointed out three typos in a single paragraph. "What's the matter with you, Rob? Get your mind on the job, or you won't have a job."

Still I kept thinking about the woman in the cloak. I can't explain the effect she had on me. I'd heard of love at first sight, but this was more like infatuation. I'm thirty-two and I ought to be over adolescent crushes.

It took a week of mental turmoil before I came to my senses and saw that I was perfectly placed to arrange another meeting. The one thing I knew about her was that she read—and acted on—her horoscope in the *Argus*. My paper.

The horoscopes were written by a freelance, some old darling in Tunbridge Wells. The copy always arrived on Monday, banged out on her old typewriter with the worn-out ribbon. Vacuous stuff, in my opinion, but as a writer she was a pro. The word-count was always spot on. Not a word was misspelled. Each week I transferred the text to my screen almost without thought.

This week I would do what I was paid to do—some subediting.

First, I looked at last week's horoscopes for the phrase my mysterious woman had mentioned. One entry had it almost word for word. *Go somewhere different on Friday. A sense of space will have a liberating effect.* She was an

Aquarian. Finally I knew something else about her. She had a birthday in late January or the first half of February.

I picked up the piece of thin paper that had just come in from Tunbridge Wells with this week's nonsense. Aquarians had a dull old week in store. *A good time for turning out cupboards and catching up with odd jobs.* I can improve on that, I thought.

"Saturday," I wrote, "*is the ideal time for single Aquarians to make a rendezvous with romance. Instead of eating at home in the evening, treat yourself to a meal out and you may be treated to much more.*"

One word in my text had a significance only a local would understand. There is a French restaurant called Rendezvous on one of the corners of the Parade, above the promenade. I was confident my lady of the sunset would pick up the signal.

The day after the paper appeared, I wasn't too surprised to read a huffy letter from The Diviner—as our astrological expert in Tunbridge Wells liked to be known to readers. It was addressed to the Editor. Fortunately Mr. Peel's secretary Linda—who is wonderfully discreet—opened it and put it in my tray before the boss saw it. Was the newspaper not aware, The Diviner asked in her letter, that each horoscope she wrote was the result of many hours of study of the dispositions and influences of the planets? In seventeen years no one had tampered with her copy. The mutilation of last week's piece was a monstrous act of sabotage, the most appalling vandalism, calculated to undermine the confidence of her thousands of loyal readers. She demanded a full investigation, so that the person responsible was identified and "dealt with accordingly." If she was not given a complete reassurance within a week she would speak to the proprietor, Sir Montagu Willingdale, a personal friend, who she knew would be "incandescent with fury."

Rather over the top, I thought. However, I valued my job enough to concoct an abject letter from Mr. Peel stating that he was shocked beyond belief and had investigated the matter fully and found the perpetrator—who it turned out was a schoolboy on a work experience scheme. This hapless boy had mistakenly deleted part of the text on the computer and in some panic improvised a couple of sentences. The copy had gone to press before anyone noticed. "*Needless to say,*" added, "*the boy on work experience will not be experiencing any more work at the* Argus *office.*" And I added more grovelling words before forging Mr. Peel's signature.

After that inspired piece of fiction, I just hoped the risk I'd taken would produce the desired result.

You have to be confident, don't you? I booked a table for two on Saturday evening at the Rendezvous, a decent place with French cuisine at reasonable prices and a good wine list.

They opened at seven and I was the first in. The manager consulted his reservations book and I stood close enough to see he had plenty of names as well as mine.

"I expect you're busy on Saturdays," I said.

"Not usually so busy as this, sir. It's a bit of a mystery. We're popular, of course, but this week we were fully booked by Thursday lunchtime. It's like Valentine's Day all over again."

I hoped so.

Before I was shown to my seat, others started arriving, men and women, mostly unaccompanied, and nervous. I knew why. I was amused to see how their eyes darted left and right to see who was at the other tables. I would have taken a bet that they all had the same birth sign.

Never underestimate the power of the press.

In the next twenty minutes, the restaurant filled steadily. One or two bold souls at adjacent tables started talking to each other. In my quiet way, I was quite a matchmaker.

Unfortunately none of the women resembled the one I most hoped to see. I sat sipping a glass of Chablis, having told the waiter I would wait for my companion before ordering.

After another twenty minutes I ordered a second glass. The waiter gave me a look that said it was about time I faced the truth—I'd been stood up.

Some of the people around me were already on their main course. A pretty redhead alone at a table across the room smiled shyly and then looked away. She was a charmer. Maybe I should cut my losses and go across, I thought.

Then my heart pumped faster. Standing just inside the door handing her cloak to the waiter was the one person all this was set up for. In a long-sleeved blue velvet dress with glitter on the bodice, she looked stunningly beautiful.

I practically walked on air across the room, but at a fair speed, before anyone else made a move.

"You again?" I said. "We met at the end of the pier a few days ago. Do you remember?"

"Why, yes! What a coincidence." Her blue eyes shone with recognition—or was it joy that her star sign had worked its magic?

I said I was alone and suggested she join me and she said nothing would please her more. Brilliant.

At the table we went through the preliminaries of getting to know each other. Her name was Helena and she worked as a research chemist at Plaxton's, the agricultural suppliers. She'd moved down from Norfolk three years ago, when she got the job.

"Helena—that's nice," I said.

"Actually I wish it was plain Helen. I have to keep telling people about the 'a' at the end."

I told her I've lived in the area all my life. "As a matter of fact, I'm a journalist."

"How exciting. Is that with a magazine?"

"Newspaper."

"Which one?"

"Which Sunday paper do you take?"

"The *Independent*."

"You've probably read some of my stuff, then. I'm a freelance." A departure from the truth, but I didn't want to mention the *Argus* in case she got suspicious.

"Should I know your name?" she asked.

"From my by-line in the papers, you mean? I don't suppose so," I answered with modesty. "It's Rob—Rob Newton."

"It sounds familiar."

"There was a film star. Called himself Robert. Dead now."

"I know! Bill Sikes in *Oliver Twist*."

"Right. And Long John Silver in *Treasure Island*. He cornered the market in rogues."

"But you're no rogue, I hope?"

"No film star, either." Actually I'm rather proud of my looks.

"What brought you here tonight? Do you come regularly?"

This innocent-sounding question was not to be answered lightly. I knew she was serious about this astrology nonsense.

"No," I answered, trying my best to summon up an otherworldly look. "It was quite strange. Something mysterious, almost like an inner voice, seemed to be urging me to make a reservation. And I'm so pleased I acted on it. After we spoke at the pier, I really wanted to meet you again."

She made no comment. Her eyes told me I'd got it right.

The waiter came over, and, flushed with the success of my stratagem, I ordered champagne before we looked at the menu. Helena said something about dividing the bill, but I thanked her in a lordly fashion and dismissed the idea. After all, I had my own words to live up to: *you may be treated to much more.* The champagne was just the beginning.

"How about you?" I asked after we'd ordered. "What made you come here tonight?"

"It was in the stars." She could look otherworldly, too.

"Do you really believe they have an influence?"

She said, her eyes shining with conviction, "I'm certain of it." But she didn't mention the *Argus* horoscope directly.

After the meal, we walked by the beach and looked at the stars. It was one of those magic late summer nights when they look like diamonds scattered across a black velvet cloth. Helena pointed to the group of ten that formed Aquarius, her own constellation, the water bearer. Personally, I have a real difficulty seeing any of the constellations as shapes, but I pretended I could make it out.

"Let me guess," she said. "Are you an Aquarian also?"

I shook my head. "Capricorn—the goat."

She giggled a little at that.

"I know," I said. "Goats get a bad press. But I'm well behaved, really."

"Pity," she said, and curled her hand around my neck and kissed me. Just like that, without a move from me.

I had to be true to the stars, didn't I? I took her back to my flat and treated her to much more. She was a passionate lover. And I am a bit of a goat.

We went out each night for the next week, clubbing, skating, the cinema and the theater. We always ended at my place. It should have been perfect and it would have been if I'd been made of money. Aquarians are supposed to associate with water, but it was champagne all the way for Helena. She had expensive tastes, and since that first evening she didn't once offer to go halves. It was very clear she expected to be treated to much more—indefinitely.

On the Friday it all turned sour.

We'd been to London because Helena wanted a meal at the Ivy, and the Royal Ballet after. I should never have agreed. I was already overdrawn at the bank and paying for everything with plastic, trying not to think what next month's statement would amount to. Even so, I was horrified at how much it all cost. She didn't even offer to pay her train fare.

"Another day over," she said with a sigh, in the train at the end of the evening. Nothing about the ballet.

"Enjoyed it?"

"So where shall we go tomorrow?"

I said in as reasonable a tone as I could manage, "How about a night in for a change?"

"*Saturday night?* We can't stay in."

"Why not? I've got pizzas in the freezer and plenty of beer."

"You're joking, I hope."

"We can rent a video."

"Come off it, Rob."

"I've got no choice," I admitted. "After tonight I'm cleaned out." Which should have been her cue to treat *me* for a change.

"You mean you can't afford to take me out?"

"It's been an expensive week, Helena."

"You don't think I'm worth it? Is that what you're saying?"

"That doesn't come into it. I think you're terrific. But I can't go on spending what I haven't got."

"You're a freelance journalist. You told me. The national papers pay huge money just for one article."

At this stage I should have told her I was only a lowly subeditor on the *Argus*. Stupidly I didn't. I tried bluffing it out. "Yes, but to earn a fat fee I have to have a top story to sell. That can mean months of research, travel, interviewing people. It's the old problem of cash flow."

"Get away," she said. "You're a typical Capricorn, money-minded, with the heart and soul of an accountant. I bet you keep a cashbook and enter it all in."

"That isn't fair, Helena."

She was silent for a time, staring out of the train window at the darkness. Then she said, "You've been stringing me along, haven't you? I really thought you and I were destined to spend the rest of our lives together. I gave myself to you, body and soul. I don't throw myself at any man who comes along, you know. And now you make me feel cheap, keeping tabs on every penny you spend on me. It puts a blight on all the nice things that happened."

"What a load of horseshit."

"Pig!"

When we reached the station she went straight to the taxi rank and got into a waiting cab. I didn't see her again. I walked home, more angry with myself than her. All my ingenuity had gone for nothing. I'd really believed I was making all the running when in reality I was being fleeced. A fleeced goat is not a pretty sight.

At least I didn't have to fork out for her taxi fare.

I forgot about Helena when I started going out with Denise. Do you remember the redhead who smiled at me in the Rendezvous? She was Denise. I saw her in a bus queue one afternoon and there was that double-take when each of us looked at the other and tried to remember where we'd met. Then I clicked my fingers and said, "The restaurant."

We got on well from the start. I was completely open with her about my bit of improvised astrology-writing in the *Argus*, and she thought it was a good laugh. Denise laughed a lot, which was a nice change. She admitted she always read her horoscope and had gone along that Saturday evening—"just for a laugh"—in the hope of meeting someone nice. Such openness would have been impossible with Helena, who was so much more intense. I told Denise all about Helena, and she didn't mind at all. She said any woman who expected the guy to pay for everything wasn't living in the real world. To me, that was a pretty good summing-up of Helena.

"Was she out of a job, or something?" Denise asked.

"No. She has a good income, as far as I know. She's a scientist, a research chemist, with Plaxton's, the agricultural people."

"You wouldn't think a scientist would believe in star signs."

"Believe me, she takes it very seriously. She said astrology was a science."

Denise giggled. I don't think we discussed Helena again for some time. We had better things to do.

At work, I'd been keeping a lookout for letters postmarked Tunbridge Wells, just in case The Diviner decided to write back to Mr. Peel, but nothing came in except her weekly column—which of course I set in type without adding so much as a comma. My brown-nosing apology had done the trick. I continued with my boring subbing, looking forward to Friday evening, when I had another date with Denise. So when a package in a manila envelope arrived for The Diviner, care of the *Argus*, I did what I routinely do with all the other stuff that is sent to us by people wanting personal horoscopes, or advice about their futures—readdressed it to Tunbridge Wells and tossed it into the mailbag.

On our date, Denise told me she'd had an ugly scene with Helena. "It was last Monday lunchtime, in the sandwich stop in King Street. I go there every day. I was waiting in line and felt a tap on on my arm. She said, 'You're Rob Newton's latest pickup, aren't you?'—and made it sound really cheap. I shrugged and looked away and then she told me who she was and started telling me you were—well, things I don't want to repeat. I tried to ignore her, but she kept on and on, even after I'd bought my baguette and drink and left the shop. She was in a real state. In the end I told her there was nothing she could tell me I didn't know already. I said I had no complaints about the way you'd treated me."

"Thanks."

"Ah, but I only made it worse. Talking about you *treating* me was like a trigger. She wanted to know what my birth-sign is. I didn't say I was Aquarius, but she said I must be, and started telling me about the astrology piece she'd read in the *Argus*. I said, 'Listen, Helena, before you say any more, there's something you should know. Rob works for the *Argus*. He wrote that piece himself because he fancied you and knew you were dumb enough to believe in astrology.' That really stopped her in her tracks."

"I can believe it."

"Well, it's time she knew, isn't it? She's a damaged personality, Rob."

"What did she say?"

"Nothing after that. She went as pale as death and just walked away. Did I do wrong?"

"No, it's my fault. I ought to have told her the truth at the time. As a good thing she knows. Her opinion of me can't get any lower."

I woke on Saturday to the sound of my mobile. Denise, beside me, groaned a little at the interruption. "Sorry," I said as I reached across her for it. "Can't think who the hell this is."

It was my boss, Mr. Peel. "Job for you, Rob," he said. "Have you heard the news?"

I said, "I've only just woken up."

"There's been a letter-bomb attack. A woman in Tunbridge Wells. She's dead."

"Tunbridge Wells isn't local," I said, still half asleep.

"Yes, but it's a story for the *Argus*. The dead woman is The Diviner, our astrology writer. Get there fast, Rob. Find out who had anything against the old dear."

I could have told him without going to Tunbridge Wells.

The police arrested me last Monday morning and charged me with murder. I've told them everything I know and they refuse to believe me. They say I had a clear motive for killing the old lady. Among her papers they found a copy of the letter to Mr. Peel complaining about her column being tampered with and demanding that the person responsible was "dealt with accordingly." They spoke to Linda, Mr. Peel's secretary, and she confirmed she'd passed the letter to me. Also in the house at Tunbridge Wells they found my reply with my poor forgery of Mr. Peel's signature. They say I was desperate to keep my job and sent the letter and must have sent the letter bomb as well. Worst of all, a fingerprint was found on a fragment of the packaging. It was mine.

I told them why I handled the package when it arrived at the *Argus* office addressed to The Diviner. I said I now believe the bomb was meant for me, sent by Helena under the mistaken impression that I was the writer of the astrology column. I said I'd gone out with her for a short time and she was a head case. I also told them she's a scientist with access to agricultural fertilizers, which any journalist would tell you can be used to make explosives. She's perfectly capable of constructing a letter bomb.

To my horror, they refuse to believe me. They've interviewed Helena and of course she denies any knowledge of the letter bomb. She says she stopped going out with me because I'm a pathological liar with fantasies of being a top London freelance. Do you know, they believe her! They keep telling me I'm the head case, and I'm going to be remanded for a psychological assessment. My alteration to the astrology column proves that I'm a control freak. Apparently it's a power thing. I get my kicks from ordering people to do pointless things—and from sending letter bombs to old ladies.

Will nobody believe I'm innocent? I swear everything I've just written is true.

Jac. Toes

Known unto God

BORN IN 1950 in The Hague, the Netherlands, Jac. Toes enjoyed a restless youth that was followed by an even stormier career as a sailor in the Merchant Navy. Later, he graduated from the University of Nijmegen with a degree in literature and linguistics. He has taught secondary education in various colleges, and in 1980 founded the broadcasting station Radio City. He is the author of several crime novels, including *Twin-Tracks* and *Settling Accounts*, both nominated for the Golden Noose, the Dutch award for best crime novel, and *Fotofinish*, which won the Golden Noose for best crime novel of 1997. He is currently a full-time novelist who also works as a scriptwriter for various Dutch media. In "Known unto God," published in the Netherlands newspaper *Algemeen Dagblad*, he examines the plight of the reformed criminal who, no matter how hard he tries, just can't seem to leave his old life behind.

Known unto God

Jac. Toes

1

It was quiet at the cemetery, as usual. Only men lie buried there, as orderly as when they marched into combat at the battle of Arnhem. I parked the Mazda at the entrance.

I jogged from graveyard to graveyard; from dead villagers to missionaries, hidden deep in the wood, and back past the Liberators. A round of the dead, to celebrate my New Life once again.

The warmth from weeks of sunshine still lingered under the trees, but a dense blanket of cloud now made the air clammy. I started to loosen up my muscles. From head to ankles, dribbling, turning, shrugging, in measured doses. Discipline. Leaning against the railings I stretched my calf muscles. I voiced my affirmations to an oak's crown.

"I jog loose-limbed and at ease, under my own steam."

I was still mumbling my maxims as a BMW crunched to a halt on the gravel beside me.

With one heel pressed to my bum I watched as her dark blue court shoes appeared below the car door, followed by a pair of tanned calves and a skirt that was hastily smoothed down.

The woman inspected the surroundings, gave me an absent-minded smile and took a bouquet of lilies from the back seat. Her passenger got out on the other side, a man with wavy grey hair and a bull-like physique. Twice her age, lord and master. He too looked around first and then nodded towards me, a signal that he had noticed me.

"Come on, my dear."

He had a voice to match. Deep and impatient. He pushed open the gate to the cemetery. The woman followed. Pilgrims of war, I thought, paying their respects to the grave of a father, uncle or grandfather. Not holiday-makers.

Holidays. Oh, all that emptiness didn't appeal to me, a black hole that always swallowed up more money than I possessed. No, holidays weren't for me, they would endanger my New Life. For the past year I had spent my days off running, the aim being to do the marathon inside three hours. That morning the program stipulated intensive hill training.

I watched the woman leave. Her white suit stood out sharply against the immaculate green lawn between the graves. When the man stopped suddenly, she wobbled slightly on her high heels. For a brief moment she glanced back to see whether I had noticed her unsteadiness.

I darted through a gap in the rhododendrons and started running, fast.

A few minutes later I was forcing myself up a hill along a zigzag path, accelerating powerfully after each hairpin bend. Reaching the top I still had some breath left, enough to storm the next hill at a higher pace. After half an hour the sweatband around my forehead was drenched, salt stung my eyes. But still I didn't lapse into a pounding gait. I continued to run in a supple way, almost soundlessly. I completed my round of the dead with a long sprint. Arriving at the car park as unexpectedly as ever, I broke through the green undergrowth and began to slow down, then did a few slow laps to acclimatize.

The door of my car was open, a worn pair of jeans protruded from the opening. I stopped abruptly.

"Hey!"

A young male body shot upright, pony-tail bobbing. Under one of his arms he had wedged a handbag. My car radio glinted in his other hand.

Rumbled, he grinned, but his eyes were alert.

"Easy, man!"

I shot a glance at the BMW. The side window was a pile of splinters next to the front wheel. He stepped forward threateningly.

"Keep going, man, piss off."

Suddenly his grin grew slack. Only then did I recognize him.

2

Kammeling—an old hand! Kammeling, who had let himself get caught napping by his old buddy!

Kammeling was a rat—just like I used to be, once. A desperate little rat, living in constant fear of losing the way to dealer and dope. I was the one who had initiated him into the world of easy pickings. Handbags, cigarette vending machines, cars, within six months he was an all-round petty criminal. Fulltime. Nickname Kammetje.

He held the car radio triumphantly aloft. The wires dangled uselessly.

"That old heap of yours wasn't even locked, man!"

He kicked the door shut. I stared at him silently.

"Okay, okay, here, take it," he said magnanimously, and held the radio out towards me.

I attempted to take it, but he withdrew his hand at the last moment and held it high above his head. I made a lunge that he parried by turning away.

The man and the woman must have seen our strange dance. They popped up suddenly behind Kammeling, between our cars.

The man remained motionless for a few seconds. His eyes darkened when he spied the handbag. With a curse he kicked away the pile of glass splinters and rushed forward. There was no escape for Kammeling. The strap on the handbag broke, the contents spilled onto the ground, a diary, a purse, a mobile phone.

"I'll phone 911," I said quickly and grabbed the phone.

"Take it easy, man," Kammeling said. His voice still sounded indignant, but the bragging tone had disappeared.

The man grabbed him by his ears with both hands, and brought his head down hard against his rising knee. Kammeling held his hands to his face and collapsed in a heap.

The man turned around. In two strides he had reached the rose-bed where he pulled a stake out of the ground. Kammeling fended off the first blow with his fists, but the second hit him squarely across the back of his head.

While the man was landing another blow, the 911 operator answered. Did I require fire, police or ambulance? I couldn't get a word out, frozen, paralyzed by the explosion of violence.

The man kept on laying into Kammeling, powerfully and purposefully. And all the time the woman was standing close by him, watching in fascination, with her mouth half-open, as if she could not decide whether to encourage the man or call him to order. Only when Kammeling stopped moving did I thrust the mobile into her hands.

"Stop it," I cried. "That's enough, mate, do you want to kill him?"

For a moment it seemed as though the man was going to lunge at me. He hesitated and looked towards the woman who was speaking animatedly into the phone. When she pointed an angry finger at the BMW, he allowed the stake to be taken away from him.

"Bloody bastard," he said to Kammeling, and walked around to the other side of the car.

While the woman stuffed her things hastily into her handbag, he got in unhurriedly. She gestured towards me with her head before turning the ignition.

"Get out of here!"

Kammeling's mouth was opening and shutting as though he was having difficulty breathing. When I bent over him he opened his eyes and looked anxiously at the stake, which I was still holding. In the distance a police siren was tearing the silence to shreds.

"Let me go," he lisped. "Please."

3

Arriving home, first of all I brought my log book up to date. Time and tempo, heart rate and recovery rate, the graph displayed an agreeably upward trend. I hesitated at *particulars*. The incident with Kammeling. I wrote down: *None*.

Even so, I could not shake off the image of Kammeling's bloody face, and his mouth moving mechanically like that. Not even with a cold shower.

I emerged from the bathroom sweating, and stretched out on an airbed on my balcony. Breathe in, breathe out, as I had learned to do, all the way to my toes and the tips of my fingers, giving free passage to the life force. The tension flowed out of me, but when I stood up my feet were ice cold.

Kammeling's pleadings for me to stop, his panic-stricken glances at the stake I'd managed to remove from the man's grasp. Had he been hit so hard that he had lost his mind? It was as if he thought that I had beaten him up. When, on the contrary, he ought to be grateful to me, it was thanks to me he was still alive—if he *was* still alive. The man had laid into him as if he were cleaving a tree-stump. And that woman! She just stood there as though she were at a boxing match. Obsessed, almost horny. And me, why did I run away? Should I have stayed with Kammeling? Garbage, fuck all that shit, especially someone else's. I had chucked the stake into the bushes near some traffic lights. My old survival instincts were still alive and kicking.

But what about the couple, that greying tycoon and his chic wife? They were bound to wonder whether or not Kammeling had anything on them. Would he be able to recall the BMW's license plates? I'd never taught him to do that, the contents were what it was all about, the packaging was irrelevant. Maybe he hadn't even got a good look at the man, as he'd lashed out so suddenly.

Only when drops of rain started detonating onto the cement edge of the balcony did I get up and have a look at that afternoon's training schedule. A steady long-distance run. It would have to be the park, I decided, even though it was the dogs and the tourists who ran the show there.

I opened a carton of fruit juice and glugged down the contents. Oh, what the heck, Kammeling, bloody junkie, exploiting the dead. Go to hell.

I plowed along with difficulty in the silently falling rain, a warm bath that brought no relief. On the way back I bought the evening paper and read it on my balcony. The incident had just made the *News in Brief* column. An unknown man had been admitted to intensive care in a coma with serious head injuries. The police were appealing for witnesses, interviewing the victim was out of the question for the time being.

For the time being. Good. Perhaps his brain cells had been smashed to smithereens. People who wake up from a coma often have no recollection of the last few hours before their accident, sometimes of entire days. I resisted the impulse to phone the hospital. That evening I was tired early, but was only able to get to sleep after raiding the drinks cabinet.

It was after midnight when the front doorbell pierced my slumber.

I opened my eyes immediately. Kammeling had talked, it had begun.

I stayed perfectly still and waited until the bell was rung again.

Commandingly long rings.

I reconciled myself to the inevitable and opened the door.

Standing in front of me was the woman from the BMW. She was still wearing that crazy suit, now creased and torn.

"I'm Isadore," she said.

When I stood to one side she came in immediately.

4

"I want to thank you."

She drew an uneven breath and took off her sunglasses. Even by the dim glow of the hall light I could see that she had been crying. In the living room she sank onto the settee.

"He's still alive," she said.

My empty glass stood on the table. I held up the bottle inquiringly and poured her a generous shot of whisky.

She raised her glass and took a long swig.

This was followed by a heartfelt, "The bastard!" I wasn't sure whether she was still referring to Kammeling.

"Henri completely lost his rag," she continued. She clasped the bottle and poured herself some more.

"Did you—have you been to the police yet?"

I sat down next to her and shook my head. She didn't seem to notice that I was only wearing my boxer shorts.

"Henri said: that bastard had no respect for the dead," she continued. "Scum like that aren't worthy of the freedom his father died for."

I nodded, although I myself was doing my level best to leave the past where it belonged.

"Henri gets very hostile. He says we're still at war," she said. "Only now the foe is practically invisible, criminal riffraff. And nobody realizes it."

"Except Henri—," I said. "And you then? Had a spat too?"

I pointed to the torn slit in her skirt. She brushed a few spatters of mud from her ankles.

"Where his daddy's concerned, Henri has no self-control," she said. "Thank God we're staying at a hotel, so he has to exercise some restraint. He—"

She sniffed loudly.

"Each of us is fighting our own private war," I remarked.

She searched for a paper tissue in her handbag. A few fifty-Euro bank-notes fluttered down. I picked them up and laid them beside her glass.

"Keep them," she said.

Did she lose her balance on purpose after this, so that she was forced to support herself against my thigh? She gave my muscles a quick pinch.

"Hard," she concluded approvingly. "You're in fine fettle, Balthus—"

"How do you know my name?" I asked. "And my address?"

"Henri's in security. He has friends all over the place. In the police force too, old mates. Anonymous naturally. Your license plate was enough."

She emptied her glass and leaned forward, with both hands on my thighs.

"All's fair in love and war," she said with a quick laugh. "After all, you haven't been to the police station, have you, even though you saw every-thing? We're on the same side Balthus, we're allies."

She devoted ample time to the sealing of our alliance, with an aban-donment that caught me unawares. I submitted without protest: it wasn't often I came across allies like this! When I saw her to the door she took the bottle and the glass with her.

"For the journey," she explained, again with that vague smile which she probably used to wangle a lot of things.

I watched her go, from my balcony. The night air smelt sour, as though the rain had washed the town with a new detergent.

In the room it was as if nothing had happened, but in my bed I discov-ered her handbag, with its broken strap.

Perhaps that's why I wasn't surprised when the doorbell rang again at five A.M. I opened the door, yawning. The first plainclothes policeman barked his identification. The other three pinned me against the wall without a word.

Before I had a chance to ask what they thought they were doing, snatching an innocent member of the public from his bed, they dragged me down the stairs, handcuffed and blindfolded.

Half an hour later I was sitting in a surprisingly cold police cell.

The duty officer had just pushed the sandwiches and a beaker of lukewarm coffee through the hatch, when Bollander came to get me from the cell. Interrogation on an empty stomach, a classic form of harassment.

He had me put on a paper overall and took me to an interrogation room, where Hanson was waiting. The pair had grown more pasty-faced this past year. And meaner. Bollander didn't beat about the bush.

"Are you going to make a statement right away or do we have to go through all the usual bullshit first, Balthus?"

Hanson pushed the file, which he had flicked halfway through, to one side. I recognized the code of my dossier on its spine.

I shrugged my shoulders. They exchanged a knowing glance. Hanson threw a packet of cigarettes down on the table.

"Smoke?"

I shook my head.

"Who's a healthy boy, then," observed Bollander.

"I've been clean for a year now," I said, although I had resolved to remain silent. "I've said goodbye to the scene, I'm a respectable citizen just like you."

He sniffed.

"D'you know what they say at AA? 'My name's Dickhead and I'm an alcoholic.' Repeat it at every meeting, even if they've been dry for ten years."

A patrol car tore out of the station yard. Bollander waited until the siren had died away.

"Did you have a score to settle with Kammeling? An old one?"

"Who?"

Hanson sighed loudly.

"That necrophiliac junkie you beat to a pulp," Bollander said. "Or did you two have a territorial problem? Was the cemetery your patch?"

He pointed to my dossier.

"Timing always was your strong point, wasn't it? You'd hit on visitors to a hospital, a swimming baths, or the theater. You never took any risks, you knew they'd always be gone for an hour or so."

"That was then."

"Do you know Kammeling?"

I made a dismissive gesture.

"You knew the whole scene after all," he insisted.

"The turnover rate is pretty quick," I said. "Junkies come and go."

Hanson began to sweat, even though all he was doing was leaning backwards, observing me intently. He was the body language specialist. I stretched.

"You were seen. Yesterday morning. At the spot where the dastardly deed took place," Bollander whispered, as if he was divulging a secret. "At the scene of the crime."

"I confess: my mortal coil is visible to the naked eye."

Hanson turned to Bollander.

"So, the usual bullshit it is, then."

I bowed my head and cut myself off from the barrage of questions they fired at me for the rest of the morning.

And the afternoon. And the evening.

Mr. De Koude, my solicitor, was waiting in his official car. He could be proud of me. I'd finally followed the advice he used to give me so often; when the cell door opens, shut your mouth. De Koude was the sort of solicitor who was particularly keen on suspects remaining silent.

"A paper-thin dossier this time," he said. "An anonymous telephone call, that's all they had. Without a murder weapon and witnesses they haven't got a hope. And the good news is still to come."

He slapped me on the shoulder.

"According to the latest information, Kammeling is waking up. Once his memory starts working again, he can get you off the hook immediately."

He dropped me off at home and stuck his thumb up as he drove away.

In the bathroom I tore the paper overalls from my body and took a long shower.

I had stayed silent, because of Isadore, but even more because of the fifty-Euro banknotes that she had allowed to escape from her bag. There would have to be more where they came from, I decided. I had done their dirty work for them after all. And now that Kammeling was coming round she would have an extra reason for maintaining our alliance.

A phone began bleeping somewhere. I went to the living room but the sound was coming from the bedroom.

From her handbag.

When she heard me check in on her mobile, Isadore gave a sort of sob.

"Oh, at last you're there," she said. "I've been so worried about you."

"Everything's fine," I said. "I've just been released. The police haven't a shred of—"

She didn't let me finish.

"Henri has gone completely apeshit," she said. "He's just heard that the guy is coming to. I couldn't stop him. I drove after him."

"Where are you now?"

"At the hospital."

Henri was right, there was a secret war raging. And if I didn't act quickly I would be back in the firing line again. As a civilian casualty.

"I'm on my way," I said.

I raced to the hospital, and dumped the Mazda just outside the entrance. The porter came running out of his lodge, gesticulating, but I pushed him aside. Kammeling was my life insurance and I only had the one.

Intensive Care was on the top floor. I sprinted through the hall and dashed into the stairwell. Hang in there, Kammetje, your old buddy is on his way. He's coming to save you, and especially himself. I stormed up the staircase and thrust open the door.

Isadore stood in the hallway, concealed in a recess.

"Where is he?" I panted.

She put her finger to her lips and pointed to a door, which was ajar.

I found Kammeling in the far corner, behind a screen. He was half sitting-up, with his eyes open and waved a weak hand at me. A drip swung back and forth as he did so. Next to his bed a monitor displayed his heart rate.

"Hey there, Kammetje, thank God you made it."

He nodded tiredly.

"The fuzz were round here like a flash," he said. "I already told them everything, this morning."

He closed his eyes for a second.

"Sorry Balthus, it's sink or swim."

"That's why I'm here Kammetje. That bloke who did for you is around here somewhere. He's looking for you—"

His heart rate remained steady, as he whispered: "Sure, Balthus, but it wasn't him who—"

I grabbed hold of the end of his bed.

"What?"

"We both know it wasn't."

"Are you stitching me up?" I cried. "Has Henri been to see you?"

He slumped down a bit further.

"Of course, Balthus, and you can't touch me anymore. You used to really be someone, in those days I would have told any amount of lies for you, but now—"

I shook his bed.

"Bastard, what did he offer you?"

Kammeling grinned, as far as the tube in his nose would allow him. I jerked at his bed, but two hands grabbed hold of my upper arms.

"Easy, Balthus."

Behind me stood Bollander and Hanson. I turned back to Kammeling in confusion. On the monitor next to his bed the alarm started to sound. His heart rate soared as he pointed at me with a shaky finger.

"That's him," he gasped.

In the lift, Bollander and Hanson stood very close to me, even though I was handcuffed.

"A stake has been found, Balthus. With your prints on it and Kammeling's blood. And you'd hidden the woman's handbag in your bed. And two witnesses have come forward—"

The lift doors opened. On the other side of the hall, Isadore and Henri emerged from the florist's, arm in arm. Isadore carried an enormous bouquet and just for a moment I thought she smiled at me.

I stood stock-still but Bollander dragged me on.

"That Englishman over there, salt of the earth," Bollander said. "He scoured the entire town looking for Kammeling. Sacrificed his days off to give a statement. He saw everything. Now there's a man who knows the meaning of the words, civic duty. And to think he was only here to visit the grave of his father."

Lillian Stewart Carl

The Eye of the Beholder

LILLIAN STEWART CARL writes what she calls "gonzo mythology" fantasy novels, as well as mystery and romantic suspense novels. While growing up in Missouri and Ohio, she began writing at an early age, and she has continued all her life, even while traveling to Europe, Great Britain, the Middle East, and India, among other places. Her short fiction has appeared in several anthologies. "The Eye of the Beholder" was first published in *Death by Horoscope*. It is a subtle, effective tale of the way superstition can influence a person's life, and the troubles that can arise because of it.

The Eye of the Beholder

Lillian Stewart Carl

By the time Jake turned into the driveway the bombs were already falling. He stood beside the car and watched the flashes play along the bottom of the clouds like lightning. It was going to rain again—the wind was gusty, damp, scented with earth, weighing down the collar of his uniform. But lightning? No. The Luftwaffe was hammering the shipyards at Bristol again.

Not that he could do anything about it, not now. He stabbed his cane into the mud. The movement jolted the patchwork that was his gut and he winced. He should be glad he was out of it, safe, tucked away at this old house in the Somerset countryside. He should be glad to be alive.

The conical shape of Glastonbury Tor stood in black outline against the distant fiery glow. Jake had crawled like a worm along the dark, narrow roads to get from there to here. He could've flown those few miles in seconds.

He felt again the throb of his Spitfire, full throttle, nose up, the patterns of fields and roads falling away behind him and clouds streaming over the wings—he'd break free of earth and cloud alike and see the stars strewn across the night sky, constellations marching from horizon to horizon—the sound of his engines, of his thoughts, would be lost in the mighty vastness. . . . He crash-landed in his own present.

He'd drunk too much scrumpy cider in Glastonbury, Jake told himself. The Brits hadn't been joking, it was powerful stuff.

The surrounding trees creaked and thrashed in the wind. Cold rain sifted down on his face. Awkwardly he felt his way up the unlit steps and opened the front door of the house. Once a butler had answered this door. Now Jake was greeted by the acrid hospital smell of disinfectant and overcooked cabbage.

A musical feminine voice asked, "Did you enjoy your leave?"

He looked around. There was the one bright spot in this dark, cold, wet, besieged country. Nurse O'Neill. Bridget. Tonight the starched wings of her cap contained her tightly-bound red hair. Last night, during her birthday party, her hair had tumbled down over her shoulders and he'd caught a flowery whiff more intoxicating than any alcohol.

"I'd have enjoyed my leave a lot more if you'd come along," he told her with a smile. "Country boys like me, we need native guides."

"You manage well enough, I'm thinking."

Jake could see her breath leaving her parted pink lips. He leaned forward. "All those narrow lanes, night coming on fast—I was expecting a Roman soldier or a medieval knight to step out in front of me."

"I shouldn't be surprised to see one myself, not here."

"The car heater was acting up. Feel my hands." He grasped her warm hands with his icy ones.

She pulled hers away, but not very quickly. "You're thinking it's cold? Just you wait, it's autumn now, winter's round the bend . . ."

"Well, well, well." Harry Davenport's nasal bray echoed from the high ceiling.

Bridget's face went rigid and she stepped back abruptly. She hasn't done anything wrong, Jake told himself. I'll be damned if I'll let anyone make her feel like she's done something wrong.

Harry's nose and teeth thrust forward like a predator's. A red scar creased one cheek. "So you fancy foreigners like yourself, is that it, Bridget? Can't resist our Yank's Hollywood handsome face? No accounting for tastes, is there? But then, I hear beauty is in the eye of the beholder."

"And handsome is as handsome does." With a tart glance at Jake, Bridget walked off down the hall toward the kitchen.

Harry's dark beads of eyes followed her. Jake stepped in front of him. "She told you last night she wasn't interested."

"Why should I be interested in her, she's nothing but a bog-trotter's daughter." Harry pivoted on his crutch and started heaving himself up the staircase, one thudding step at a time.

Jake wanted to shout after him, *Pick on someone your own size.* But the other airmen were already Harry's favorite targets, like Taffy with his Welsh accent and tin ear, and serious, literal-minded Dicky.

Jake took off his coat. Outside a rush of wind threw raindrops like shrapnel against the mahogany panels of the door. The fanlight was blocked by cardboard. The marble flooring of the entrance hall would have gleamed if it hadn't been smudged by muddy footprints—and if more than two bulbs of the chandelier had been lit.

This was a hell of a place, Jake thought, and amended, had been a hell of a place. Now the carved wood and marble trim was roughly boxed in. Now pale rectangles on the wallpaper were the ghosts of paintings taken away for safekeeping. Anthony Jenkins-Ashe was trying to preserve his ancestral home. He'd told Jake his family had lived at Lydford Hall for centuries.

Jake had grown up in a bungalow in Kansas City and was hardpressed to name his grandparents. While the other airmen might call the elderly estate owner "Dotty Andy," Jake found him both educational and entertaining—not least because he refused to let anyone call him "My lord" or "his lordship" or however a baronet was supposed to be addressed.

Jake pulled a paper-and-twine-wrapped package out of his coat pocket and headed for the back parlor that was now Andy's sole domain. He knocked. After a long moment Andy's reedy voice answered, "Come."

The room was cold and dark. A small fire provided the only light. The old man would rather strain his eyes than close the blackout curtains, even though tonight his view was of blank darkness. His chair sat on the hearth, so close to the fire that the flames illuminated the hills and furrows of his face as harshly as the folds in his old tweed suit. He was scraping the mud off a boot.

"Have you studied Herodotus?" Andy asked. " 'In peace, children inter their parents; war violates the order of nature and causes parents to inter their children.' "

He was thinking of his son, dead at Dunkirk. "I was scheduled for a classics seminar," Jake answered. "Then the war started, and suddenly history and literature seemed mighty useless."

"Useless? No, history and literature are never useless. Glastonbury, now, is proof of that."

"It's an interesting little town with a heck of a history—I looked at some of the books while I was waiting for the clerk to fill your order. Here you go." Jake handed over the package.

Andy put the boot down next to his rack of pipes and used his knife to cut the twine. "Thank you, Pilot Officer Houston. Very kind of you."

"Seems only fair, I was using your car."

"The car belongs to the hospital now. There's a war on." Paper rustled and Andy held two books to the firelight.

Jake squinted at their spines—*The Company of Avalon* by Frederick Bligh Bond and *The High History of the Holy Grail*. Those names were vaguely familiar, which was more than he could say of most of Andy's books. He'd barely heard of heraldry and astrology and DeBrett's Peerage before he'd come here.

With a weary sigh Andy stacked the books by his chair, next to his omnipresent notebook and pen, and picked up the boot again. "Please, sit down."

Jake glanced over his shoulder, but Bridget was probably back under Matron's watchful eye. He pulled up a footstool and lowered himself onto it. The wind whistled a low note in the chimney and rain streamed down the windows. "Did you get out for your walk this afternoon? Find any more Roman ruins?"

"Perhaps a trace or two by the Brue, between the bridge and the apple orchard. If this rain ever lets up I'll give you a tour. Although we're unlikely to see any improvement so late in the year. It's the equinox, you know. Virgo giving way to Libra . . . What is that commotion? Are they playing cricket in the gallery again?"

Voices spoke urgently in the distance. Footsteps drummed overhead. A door slammed. "I don't think so," Jake answered. "I'll take a look."

He got up, opened the door, and peered out. Now several voices were talking at once. Foggy Dewar was stumping along the hall as though he was working his way through deep mud. "What's happened?" Jake called.

"Another poor sod's bought it. Randy last week and now . . ." Foggy disappeared around the corner.

Hell, Jake told himself. Losing a colleague on the mend was worse than losing him in the midst of battle.

Behind him Andy said quietly, "Fate can be cruel, can't it? Damnable war, too many young men lost."

Jake agreed, but he didn't see any way of stopping the war other than sacrificing even more men. With a half-salute to Andy, he followed Foggy toward the library.

Its double door was clotted with his fellow patients. Using his cane, Jake levered himself high enough to see Doc Skelton, the flight surgeon, kneeling on the floor. "Yes, he's dead. Has been for over an hour."

A murmur ran through the group. Jake pushed his way through the gathered men until he could see Bridget. She was standing alone next to the massive Victorian desk. Her normally rosy cheeks were pasty white and her arms were laced across her chest.

Skelton stood up and brushed off his trousers. He turned toward the door, shoulders coiled and head down like a bull searching for a china shop. "As you've no doubt noticed, gentlemen, his head's been bashed right in, by that bit of sculpture, I should think. He was murdered."

Murdered. Jake's mind tripped over the word and went sprawling. In the sudden silence he could hear the wind howling outside, rain sluicing down the tall windows behind the heavy black curtains, and the ragged breaths of the men around him. Then someone swore, softly. Each airman inched a bit farther away from the man he was standing next to and Jake found himself popped like a cork into the library.

Stretched out on the bare planks of the floor lay Dicky Richardson. A rust-red puddle pillowed his head and his blond hair was mottled with crimson. His face was as white and still as the plaster cast on his left arm. His blue eyes looked purple. Maybe, Jake thought, they'd stared yearningly into the sky so long they'd bruised.

A fist-sized lump of gray stone lay between Dicky and the desk. Even in the dim light Jake could see the half-dozen drops of blood spattering its weathered surface.

He braced himself on his cane. Dicky. He'd liked Dicky, even though the man had no sense of humor. Which was hardly reason to murder him.

So what, then, would be enough reason to murder him? Or anyone, for that matter? Hadn't there been enough death already? Jake looked up at Bridget. She bit her lip, and for just a moment fear dulled her eyes.

"Has anyone been seen going into or coming out of the library in the last hour?" asked Skelton. "Save Nurse O'Neill, who fetched me."

Some of the men looked off into space, some at the floor, some at each other. No one answered.

"Has anyone had a row with Richardson, lent him money, anything of that nature?"

Silence.

"Right. Houston?" Skelton pronounced it "Hooston," like everyone except Andy, who knew better, and Bridget, who'd asked.

Reluctantly Jake turned away from her. "Sir?"

"You were on leave."

"Yes, sir."

"When did you get in?"

"Fifteen minutes ago. Maybe twenty."

"Anyone see you?"

"Yes, why?"

"Because it appears you're the only person in the house who couldn't have done Richardson here in. He died whilst you were away."

"Twig and I've been playing cards all evening," said Epsom, his moustache bristling.

Foggy added quickly, "I've been reading, Taffy looked in on me."

Harry's voice overrode the others. "A bit hard to sneak up on a chap and bash him when you're lumbered with a bloody great crutch, isn't it?"

"No one here is incapacitated," Skelton told him.

Jake nodded. "And the wind is noisy enough to hide footsteps."

"Very observant," said Harry acidly.

Matron thrust her way through the door, parting the men with her cantilevered bosom like a ship's bow parting the waves. A clean white sheet hung from her arm. "I phoned for the police, but the line's dead. A tree's gone down in the storm, I expect. Good job the electricity's from our own generator. I've sent the orderly with the car round by West Pennard, in case the road's blocked or the bridge over the Brue is awash."

"Slow going, but needs must," said Skelton.

Taffy asked, "What if the orderly's the murderer?"

"Then he'll be in the hands of the police, won't he?" Matron beckoned to Bridget. "Come along, Nurse."

"Aren't you going to pick him up and lay him out properly?" asked Foggy.

Skelton shook his head. "The police will want to see him like this."

The women unfolded the sheet, stretched it out over Dicky's body like a canopy, then lowered it. His outstretched arm and hand lay at an angle to his torso and Bridget bent down to pull the fabric over them. She looked like a ministering angel in a Renaissance manuscript, Jake thought . . . "Wait a minute. What's he holding?"

Skelton brushed Bridget aside, knelt, and inspected the tightly curled fingers of Dicky's right hand. "A pen. His fingers have ink on them. Was he writing something?"

Jake walked the dozen paces to the desk. A bottle of ink stood in the center of the blotter, its lid beside it. Next to that lay a partly crumpled piece of paper. When he smoothed it out Jake saw several smudges looking like badly-drawn hieroglyphs straggling across its top. The only words he could read were "Lydford" and "suspected t . . . ," the rest of the word trailing away and ending in a blotch. The letter "B" nestled beside another blotch.

"Dicky was left-handed," said Bridget at his shoulder. "He was learning to use his right, but still I was writing the letters home to his mum."

"This one he wanted to write himself," Jake said, handing the paper to Skelton.

"Lydford," Skelton read aloud. "Suspected, followed by a word beginning with T. Another word beginning with B. Anyone have any idea what he was on about?"

Jake looked back at the men crowding the door. Funny how clear his mind was now, the last vapors of the cider burned away. He saw each face as clearly as a dial on his control panel. Everyone's expression ranged from puzzled to blank except for Twig's and Harry's.

It was, of course, Harry who spoke up. "The word is traitor. A suspected traitor."

"Traitor?" Matron repeated.

"Out with it, man," ordered Skelton.

Harry drew himself up, the center of attention. "Last night, after the party for Nurse O'Neill, Dicky said he suspected someone here of handing information to the Nazis."

"Too much to hope he gave you a name?" Jake asked, wondering whether Harry's sneer had made his face look like a gargoyle's even before it was scarred.

"He started to do, then was interrupted when Matron called lights-out."

"Harry's having us on, isn't he?" Taffy's freckled face peered over his neck brace like a fox from his hole. "He was always having Dicky on, Dicky being such an easy target and all—positively gullible at times."

"No," said Twig, shuffling forward. "I heard what Dicky said, too. He had evidence of a traitor at Lydford Hall."

Jake exchanged a look with Skelton. The doctor knew as well as he did that Twig was a former divinity student who made George Washington look like a liar and a cheat.

"B." Skelton repeated reflectively. "That might be the initial of a name. The person Richardson suspected."

"It's bleeding obvious, isn't it?" demanded Harry. "B as in Bridget. Bridget O'Neill. She's the traitor."

Jake stepped forward, his fist already raised. "Why you . . ."

"Steady on," murmured Skelton.

Bridget's slender body swayed. Jake thought she was going to fall back against the desk and changed course. But she caught herself. The look she shot toward Harry would've disintegrated anyone made of flesh and blood.

"Think," Harry went on. "She found Randy dead last week, didn't she? Lying in the bathroom, not a mark on him. She's the one goes about with tablets and injections—what if she slipped him a few grams of poison?"

"Pilot Officer Randolph had two broken femurs," said Matron, stepping closer to Bridget. "The cause of death was a pulmonary fat embolism."

"Are you questioning my competence?" demanded Skelton.

Harry plunged on. "And today Bridget finds Dicky."

"I'm a nurse," said Bridget. "My job is watching the patients."

"So she watches well enough she catches Dicky writing a letter that'll expose her for what she is. You said yourself, Tex, normally she'd be writing his letters for him, but this one he was writing on his own."

"My name isn't Tex," Jake said. "And it's bleeding obvious to anyone with half a brain that just because Dicky wanted to keep his suspicions to himself doesn't mean he suspected Brid—Nurse O'Neill. Unless you planted the whole idea in his mind to begin with, as another of your stupid jokes. Maybe you wanted to get back at her because she refused your advances."

"And accepted yours?" asked Harry.

Matron shot a swift look at Bridget, who suddenly grew very interested in her shoes.

"No," Jake snapped. "There's nothing between us."

Harry's voice was taking on the same shrill note as the sound of the wind in the chimney. "She's a foreigner, just like you are. Worse. She's Irish. Ireland's sitting out the war. It's not only letting the side down, it's filthy with Nazi sympathizers who'd do anything, commit any crime, to defeat us."

Jake wanted to reach out and pry Bridget's fingernails loose from where they were sunk into her palms, but he didn't dare touch her. Was that what frightened her, that Harry's constant slanders about her homeland would eventually stick? "America's not in the war, either," he said. "Are you accusing us of being a fifth column, too?"

Harry made a dismissive gesture that was almost an obscene one. Jake doubled his fist again. He'd knock the chip off the man's shoulder whether he was wounded or not.

Skelton stepped between them. "Stop it. We're getting nowhere with this. The police have been notified, they'll sort it."

"She needs locking up," said Harry, pointing his crutch at Bridget. "In the linen closet or pantry, so she'll keep. The police'll take her away, and good riddance."

Frowning, Matron took Bridget's arm. "We'll sit in my room and have ourselves a cuppa, won't we? Come along."

With a look over her shoulder at Jake—whether pleading for help or warning him to keep out of it, he couldn't tell—Bridget let herself be led away. The police, he thought. The police might well take Harry's accusations seriously. Everyone in the country was damned touchy right now. And with Hitler's armies poised right across the Channel, who could blame them? But if Bridget was arrested, no matter how quickly she was cleared, she'd have a blot on her record dark enough to cost her not only this job but any other one. That wasn't right.

Not that Dicky's death was right, Jake told himself, not by a long shot.

"The rest of you lot, clear off!" directed Skelton.

The other men shuffled away silently, burdened by deep and discomforting thought. With one last glare over his shoulder, Harry brought up the rear.

Bridget hasn't done anything wrong, Jake told himself. I'll be damned if I'll let anyone make her feel like she's done something wrong. . . . Skelton was looking at him, waiting for him to leave, too. He wanted to lock up the room.

"Sir," Jake said, "sir, you said yourself I couldn't be the murderer. Let me stay here, look the place over, see if I can come up with something that'll exonerate Nurse O'Neill. The evidence against her is no more than prejudice and coincidence."

"You rather fancy Nurse O'Neill, do you, Houston?" Skelton allowed himself a thin smile. "But yes, you could well be quite correct about coincidence. And the prejudice as well, sadly, although you have to recognize that we have our backs to the wall just now, which does rather alter one's viewpoint."

"Yes sir. I understand. Just give me until the police come."

"Very good then. I'd hate to lose Nurse O'Neill."

"Just one thing, sir. Do you have a copy of the roster—a list of . . ." Jake almost said "inmates," ". . . patients and staff both?"

"The initial B, is that it?" Skelton reached into his breast pocket, pulled out a small notebook, and tore off a page. "There you are. You have one thing on your side, Houston—we discharged a group of patients last week and several staff are on leave, so there aren't many people here tonight."

"And I have one thing working against me. Time. Thank you, sir. I'll do my best."

"Lock up when you've finished." With a firm nod, Skelton walked across to the doorway and pulled the double doors shut behind him.

Jake turned in a slow circle, trying to see the familiar room with new eyes. The library had been his sanctuary against the outside darkness both literal and figurative. He'd spent many hours here, reading and writing letters and listening to Andy's half-baked but always interesting musings—*the fault, my lad, is not in ourselves but in our stars.* Now the comforting smell of books, paper and ink with an afterglow of mildew, was overwhelmed by the reek of mortality.

Between the books the shelves were cluttered with Andy's collection of art and artifacts—a bust of Athena, a set of apothecary's scales with a stuffed dove nestling in one bowl, a model ship, a Roman amphora. Several of his rolled-up maps lay on the mantel . . . Andy. After he looked over the library he'd talk to Andy. If the old man had just come in from his daily walk maybe he'd seen or heard something.

Jake leaned up against the desk and unfolded Skelton's list. Of course Skelton himself might be the murderer. While it was stretching it a bit to think a doctor would kill one of his own patients, if Skelton was the traitor then he'd have a motive to kill. Assuming Dicky actually had reason to suspect a traitor. As much as Jake wanted to think the entire scenario was another of Harry's malicious jokes, he couldn't see how a joke would lead to murder. Neither could he see Harry himself killing Dicky, more's the pity.

And what information would a traitor find at Lydford Hall, anyway? Killing off a few recuperating airmen wouldn't damage the war effort.

He read down the list, looking for names beginning with B. No, Skelton's first name was Trevor, for what that was worth. Matron was Geraldine White. The orderly was William Graves. . . . Someone named William was often nicknamed Bill, but Jake couldn't remember hearing anyone ever call him that.

The Brits with their mania for multiple names. Harry wasn't the only one who called Jake "Tex," even though the closest he'd ever been to Texas was Tulsa. His surname was Houston, that was enough. At least Tex was better than some of the others' nicknames, which made them sound like characters in a Wodehouse comedy—Epsom Downs, Foggy Dewar, Twig Smallwood, Taffy Evans. Harry Davenport should've been "Sofa," Jake supposed. But then, no one liked Harry well enough to give him a nickname.

Jake glanced down at Dicky's shrouded shape. He was—had been—a big man. Jake had often wondered how he managed to pleat himself into a cockpit. Now he was no more than a pile of meat to be disposed of. If he owed Bridget the truth, Jake told himself, then he owed Dicky, too.

He looked at the list. Dicky's name was Donald Richardson—not that he'd have been writing about himself. The only "B" on the list besides Bridget was Twig, whose name was Bernard. Even if he could believe Twig was a spy and traitor, which he didn't, Jake knew the man had only to keep his mouth shut about Dicky's suspicions and every one else would've discounted Harry's wild story as just that.

Jake folded the paper into his pocket. The storm seemed to have eased a bit—at least the wind was moaning rather than howling and the rain was more a patter than a roar. A draft played along the floor, stirring the edge of the sheet and exposing Dicky's clenched hand. Jake shivered. From the cold, he assured himself. The fire inside the massive fireplace with its marble mantelpiece had died down, not that it had been very big to begin with. Looking into that fire Jake could see burning cities, exploding flak, Spitfires spiraling down into the cool but unforgiving water of the Channel. He'd sat in the pub in Glastonbury staring into its fire and seeing the same visions. The pictures weren't in the fire at all, were they, but in his own mind.

The small stone—the murder weapon—lay on the floor. Jake knew what it was, a lion's head from Glastonbury Abbey that usually sat on the desk. Andy had rescued it from a spoils heap when he was helping with the excavations before the war. The first war.

And that, realized Jake, was where he'd heard the name on one of Andy's books. Frederick Bligh Bond had been the archaeologist in charge of the excavations. He'd been discredited in later years for saying the spirits of dead monks had told him where to dig.

Painfully Jake lowered himself down beside the sculpture. Except for the flecks of blood the stone looked all right, not damaged at all. Andy wouldn't be happy one of his prized possessions had been used to kill someone. He'd had a wooden pedestal made especially for that lion's head. . . . Jake glanced back at the desk. The pedestal and the sculpture had stood on the edge of the desk. Now the pedestal was lying on its side.

Cursing both the feeble light and his own injuries, Jake sat down on the floor and leaned as close as he could to the sculpture. Yes, it was spattered with a few drops of blood. But several drops lay on the floor as well. And as far as he could tell not one strand of hair clung to that rock, not one blood smear. What if it wasn't the murder weapon at all?

He clambered clumsily to his feet and peered down at the bottom edge of the desk. Yes, beside it lay a long triangle of clean wooden plank. The desk had been moved, very recently. And there—yes. The upper corner, closest to where the sculpture had stood, was sticky. The color of drying blood blended with the cherry wood so well it was almost invisible. But the two strands of blond hair that were matted in the sticky patch were apparent enough, if anyone looked.

Jake let himself down into the desk chair. That was it. Dicky hadn't been hit with the sculpture at all. He'd pitched forward for some reason, hitting his head on the corner of the desk. A sudden jolt could've both moved the desk and toppled the sculpture. Then, dazed, Dicky could've crawled a few paces and then collapsed. Head wounds bled profusely. When Dicky's head hit the floor blood spattered all around.

Jake supposed an autopsy would show that the indentation in Dicky's head was sharply angled, not rounded, to fit the corner of the desk but not the sculpture. Which was all well and good, except for one very important point. Unlike Harry, Foggy, or Jake himself, Dicky had been perfectly steady on his feet. Why had he fallen? Had he been knocked over in a struggle?

The door behind him burst open and Jake jumped, jamming his belly into the arm of the chair. The pain shot stars and comets across the room. When they cleared he saw Harry standing in front of him, wearing a triumphant smirk and holding out a piece of paper. On the whole, Jake thought, he'd rather have the stars and the stitch in his side. "What do you want?"

"I found this in the sideboard in the dining room. Dicky and I both saw Bridget put it there last night. I daresay he had himself a look after the party. Perfectly damning evidence against your little Irish . . ."

Jake lashed out with his cane, striking Harry across his good shin. He cried out, dropped the paper, and staggered backward to crash heavily against one of the bookcases. Several books fell to the floor.

Apologizing silently to the books, Jake leaned over and picked up the paper. On it was drawn a circle with lines radiating out from the center. Other lines angled across them. Letters and symbols were grouped in different sections. *Oh, for the love of . . .*

"What's all this?" demanded Skelton from the doorway.

Harry's words came in staccato bursts, like a machine gun. "Bloody Yank tripped me up. Found proof that O'Neill is the traitor. Some sort of navigation chart. Guiding the Jerry bombers to Bristol. Maybe more. An invasion plan."

"This is perfectly innocent," Jake told them both. "It's not even Bridget's handwriting."

Skelton levered Harry away from the bookcase and draped him over his crutch. Then he took the paper from Jake's hand. "Whose handwriting is it, then?"

"It's Andy's. He cast her horoscope for her—her birthday was yesterday, remember?" Jake reached down and picked up one of the books that had slid to his feet. He opened it. Across the top of the flyleaf, in calligraphy worthy of a diploma, was written, *Anthony Jenkins-Ashe, Lord Brue.* He handed the book to Skelton. "You don't see penmanship like that anymore."

"A horo-what?" asked Skelton, looking from the book to the drawing and back again.

"A horoscope's a way of predicting the future by charting where certain constellations were in the zodiac on the day someone was born. Like in the Bible, when the three wise men follow a special star to Bethlehem. Astrology's just a mathematical game, if you ask me, but Andy believes in it. He told me he knew he'd never see his son again because he read it in his horoscope, and that made his death easier to accept."

Skelton shook his head doubtfully. "Spiritualism?"

"No, he's not claiming he can communicate with the dead. He's claiming he can predict, maybe even control . . . Oh, hell." Jake suddenly remembered the purchase order he'd given the bookshop owner in Glastonbury, signed with just the one word, *Brue*. That was another of Andy's topics, how titles were based on landscape features. *Anthony Jenkins-Ashe, Lord Brue.*

He could see it all now, and he didn't like what he was seeing. "I remember reading an English history book when I was a kid, the author kept referring to Robert Dudley, Earl of Leicester, as both 'Dudley' and 'Leicester.' I thought he was talking about two different people. What I didn't think was that Dicky's 'B' could be Andy. But he always tried to call Andy by his title, didn't he? If he was referring to him in a letter he'd call him 'Brue.' "

Skelton leaned over and pulled the letter closer. "Yes, the word could be 'Brue,' right enough. Richardson may well have thought this, this horoscope business was something underhanded. He borrowed Andy's books, he'd recognize the handwriting."

Jake looked at the sheet laid so carefully over Dicky's body. Blood from the puddle on the floor was seeping through, staining the white linen with a brownish-red blotch. Dicky had been prepared to die for his country in battle. Even here he'd thought he was helping his country by turning in a traitor.

Harry kicked petulantly at the books lying at his feet. "Who's saying this horoscope rubbish isn't underhanded? Maybe the traitor isn't O'Neill—I'll reserve judgment on that—but what about Dotty Andy, eh? He's out and about the countryside every day, isn't he, always writing in that notebook of his, always at his maps. I shouldn't be a bit surprised if he is helping the enemy, him and his supernatural bunkum. The Nazis believe in the occult, don't they? Everyone knows that!"

"It doesn't follow that because Andy's interested in astrology he's a traitor!" Jake spat.

"I've said before and I'll say again," insisted Harry, "that there's something seriously wrong with that man. Wrong enough to sell us all out. Wrong enough to murder Dicky here."

Jake heaved himself to his feet and with his cane started pushing the fallen books into a pile. "Look. I don't think Dicky was murdered at all. He fell against the desk—see, how it's been moved? And there's blood and a couple of hairs on the corner. The sculpture fell over when the desk was pushed. Andy wasn't even here."

Skelton inspected the desk. "I see. Very good."

"So how did he fall, eh?" Harry asked.

"I don't . . ." Beside the book that lay next to the door were several little brown lumps. Jake slowly knelt next to them, but he already knew what they were. He picked up first one lump and then another, rubbing them between his fingers. His heart dived like a rudderless airplane.

"What do you have there?" asked Skelton.

"Bits of mud and leaf mold."

"Someone tracked it in from the outside, I expect."

Jake looked out the door. Footprints smudged the entrance hall, but he didn't see any between there and here. Only the suggestive little clots of mud, as though someone had put a pair of muddy boots down just inside the door. Put them down because they had to do something in the library.

Gritting his teeth, Jake pulled himself up. "I have to talk to Andy."

"Right," said Skelton. "I'll come along, shall I? No, Davenport, I'll see to it."

Jake could feel Harry's glower on the back of his neck as he and Skelton knocked on Andy's door. Again the old man's voice said, "Come."

He was still sitting by the fire, holding a rolled paper across his knees. The scent of tobacco smoke hung in the air and a ghostly wisp of it wafted across the silvery pale rectangles of the windows. The storm had passed, and the moon and the stars were starting to peek through the clouds. A full moon was a bomber's moon, Jake thought. Under the full moon no blackout could hide a target. Only camouflage could do that, making factories look like fields and gun emplacements like barns.

"I hope we're not intruding," Skelton said.

"Not at all," returned Andy. "Please, sit down."

Jake sat on his stool. With a sharp glance at Jake, Skelton moved Andy's clean boots aside and pulled up a light chair.

"Have to valet myself, don't you know," Andy explained. "There's a war on. Mustn't complain."

"Too many young men lost," Jake said quietly, repeating the words Andy had dismissed him with earlier. "Were you thinking of your son? Or were you thinking of someone else?"

Andy's face sagged as though pulled down by a heavy weight.

"You put your dirty boots down inside the library door," Jake went on. "What happened? Why is Dicky—Pilot Officer Richardson—why is he lying there dead?"

The dying fire crackled. Skelton's chair squeaked. Andy said slowly and precisely, "Upon returning from my walk, I wished to consult a reference book. When I pushed open the door of the library I saw Richardson sitting at the desk. He was muttering and splashing ink about, having a spot of bother, I expect, writing with his right hand and holding the paper steady with his left. I asked him if I could be of assistance. He crushed the paper, leapt from the chair, and spun round as though I'd shot him."

"Ah," said Skelton softly.

"Then he went positively ashen and toppled over, striking his head on the desk. I dropped my boots and hurried forward to help, but he propelled himself across the floor away from me. And then he collapsed, quite dead.

Quite. Horribly. Dead." Andy closed his eyes. One bright teardrop traced a zigzag path down the creases in his cheek.

Skelton nodded. "Richardson was still convalescing. Leaping up in alarm like that caused his blood pressure to plummet. He blacked out briefly. Rotten luck he fell against the desk."

"Rotten luck he hadn't been taking Harry's spitefulness with a grain of salt, the way the rest of us have," Jake said. "You never looked at the letter he was writing, Andy?"

"Read another man's private correspondence? I should hope not!"

"Why didn't you fetch Matron or me as soon as it happened?" Skelton asked.

"Ah. Well then . . ." Turning away from the fire, Andy drew his fragile body to attention. "I've been sitting here having a smoke and thinking it all over. I've decided I should put you in the picture. The full picture. You see, Richardson had one of my maps unrolled on the desk beside him, held open with one of my notebooks. He'd found both there in the library. I'm a bit disappointed that he'd take it upon himself to read them, but I imagine the other gentlemen's talk of 'Dotty Andy' and the like had piqued his curiosity."

"Not to say his suspicions," muttered Jake.

"Yes, his suspicions. What was he thinking, do you suppose? That I was making maps to guide the German bombers? An appalling misconception, if so, for I've been doing the exact opposite."

"I beg your pardon?" Skelton asked.

Andy's face struggled with several expressions, doubt, distress, determination. "I didn't tell you Richardson had been injured—had been killed—because I knew there'd be a lengthy investigation that would in all likelihood draw me away from Lydford tomorrow. Tomorrow being the equinox. Virgo is moving into Libra, you see. That segment of the zodiac must be walked."

"The zodiac," repeated Jake.

"I've hesitated to speak of it openly. Look what happened to Bligh Bond when he spoke of his spirit guides—he was removed from his position, completely discredited, left to die in shocking obscurity." Andy shook his head. "But personal considerations aside—and they must be put aside in wartime, mustn't they?—I had an even better reason for keeping my own counsel. While Richardson and Davenport had the wrong end of the stick in regard to my loyalty, in one area they were quite correct. Loose talk must be avoided. The more people who know about the zodiac and the importance of the equinoctial walk, the more opportunity the enemy will have to hear of it, to realize its importance, and to try to destroy it!"

Jake groped for solid facts. "You didn't tell anyone Dicky was dead because you were afraid you'd have to explain why he was startled, even frightened of you. And then you might be prevented from—walking?"

"Richardson was suspicious of the horoscope you made for Nurse O'Neill," said Skelton. "But what's all this about a zodiac?"

"Have a look." Andy handed over the rolled paper. Jake opened it up and turned it to the firelight. Skelton leaned closer.

Jake had no trouble recognizing a map of Somerset. Or of this part of Somerset, at least. There was Glastonbury, West Pennard, Street, the River Brue, Lydford itself. But on top of the usual lines of roads and field boundaries were drawn black borders, in some places interconnecting, in others enclosing angular shapes. One at the bottom of the paper, beyond Charlton, looked like a rough approximation of a dog—or a lion.

"The symbols are quite distinct, really, once you know where to look," Andy assured them. "The Glastonbury Zodiac has been marked out by hills, trackways, watercourses, and the like. It was rediscovered very recently, by Katherine Maltwood whilst she was researching the quest for the Holy Grail as enacted here in Somerset. The chance of such patterns being found on the ground randomly, patterns that harmonize so closely with those in the sky, is on the order of 149,000,000 to 1 against."

Skelton looked at Jake. Jake looked at the map. Only by a stretch of his imagination could he see any likeness to real objects in the indicated shapes.

But Andy's eyes were shining with his vision. "This house was built betwixt Virgo and Libra. At the equinox. But the Glastonbury Zodiac uses the dove of peace instead of the traditional symbol for Libra, the scales. See, there it is in the center of the circle, just above Barton St. David. St. David's symbol, you'll remember, is the dove. And Glastonbury itself is in Aquarius, the beginning of the year, which here is not a water-bearer but a phoenix rising from the ashes. How better could the ancients have signaled to us the importance of this site in wartime than by using such symbols?"

He'd put together a string of coincidences the same way Harry had done with his evidence, Jake told himself. Give either of them a map of Missouri and they'd find Mickey Mouse between Kansas City and St. Joseph. "I've flown over this area. You can't miss the Tor and the square of the ruined abbey, but I've never seen any of these outlines."

"One always sees patterns in the earth," Skelton cautioned.

"But the Temple of the Stars is a pattern in time as well as space," said Andy. "It's the world's greatest feat of engineering, repeating in the natural forms of the earth's surface the patterns of the stars themselves. For the earth and heavens are linked, and the forces of one affect the other. As above, so below."

"You mean streams, roads, and so forth were engineered to form the shapes of the zodiac?" asked Jake. "But streams and roads change course. People build bypasses, that sort of thing."

"Who's to say whether the minds of the surveyors are being directed by planetary forces? The Roman road to the east, for example, the Fosse Way, has a kink in an otherwise dead-straight stretch just at Virgo's clasped hands. Hands clasped in prayer, no doubt."

"Planetary forces." Skelton was looking dazed, but then, he wasn't used to talking to Andy.

Not that Jake wasn't starting to wonder if he were experiencing some bizarre after-effect of the cider. "So this zodiac was built by the Romans?"

"Oh no, it's much older than that. Older than the ancient temples of Stonehenge and Avebury. Once we believed in such spiritual matters and were sustained by them. Now we place our trust in rationality and science, and look where we are—bombs are raining down upon our cities!"

Muted lights flashed across Andy's windows. A car. More than one car. The police. Jake looked over at Skelton.

With a grimace almost of embarrassment, Skelton stood up. "Your Lordship, would you be so kind as to join me in the entrance hall? I'm afraid the local authorities must be told about Pilot Officer Richardson's—tragic accident."

"Yes, yes, of course." But Andy made no move to get up. The light in his eyes winked out and his face went cold and bleak as moorland beneath a sleet storm.

Jake got to his feet, watched Skelton walk out of the room, then turned back to Andy. His symbols were only shapes in the fire, in blotches of ink— or in blood. But he saw those symbols because he had to. "Why do you need to walk over part of the zodiac pattern tomorrow, Andy? What are you trying to do?"

"I'm hoping to raise the powers of England's ancient soil, the soil from which we sprung, to repel a German invasion. Some prayer is a laying on of hands. This is a laying on of feet."

"A prayer? Or a magical rite?"

"Both," Andy replied. "Even such an enlightened Renaissance prince as Elizabeth the Great kept an astrologer, John Dee. He lived here at Glastonbury. Here he raised the power that repulsed the Spanish invasion of the Armada."

The ships of the Armada were dispersed by a sudden storm, Jake knew, but he'd always thought Dee was a charlatan.

"And here, in the Vale of Avalon, is where Britain's greatest warrior, Arthur, was laid to rest. Because in life he, too, walked the zodiac, and so defeated the invading barbarian hordes at Mount Badon."

Jake didn't mention that the invading Angles were the ancestors of the English, and that they won their war in the next generation.

"During the eighteenth century Glastonbury became, briefly, a spa. People came to drink the healing waters of Chalice Well. How many of them were then inspired to walk through the countryside and, however unaware, trace the zodiac? Soon afterwards Napoleon threatened to invade England, but never did so."

Jake could only shake his head in something between astonishment and admiration.

"This evening, this accident—fate can be cruel and capricious—perhaps it's written in the stars that England should fall." Andy looked up, his face twisted in pain. "And yet fate is balanced by free will, isn't it? Jake, my lad, you've told me your date of birth, you're an Aries, active and courageous. Why else would you volunteer to fight here when your own country isn't at war?"

"A lot of people volunteered," said Jake.

"But you are here now. If you could possibly see your way clear to volunteering one more time, to making one more effort for your old and beset mother country . . ."

Jake looked down at the map he was still holding.

"The notebook beside my bed, the pages devoted to Virgo and Libra," Andy went on, his voice winding tighter and tighter. "They list the exact paths to take, the places where you must stop and make small offerings—a bit of food, a drop of wine or beer, a flower. The going isn't difficult, you'd manage quite well even with your cane. Jake, I know you're thinking I'm daft, but . . ."

He'd come this far, thought Jake, from the Great Plains of America to the antique landscape of Somerset. He'd offered to lay down his life. Why shouldn't he lay down his feet, too? What difference would a few more steps make?

According to Andy, a big difference. If he didn't walk the zodiac tomorrow, Jake asked himself, would the Germans invade? If he did, would they stay back? And he answered, no one would ever know what was cause and what effect. If you see the future and then do something to alter it, then it wasn't the future that you saw. The future, like much of the past, was a matter of perception.

If Andy wanted to perceive meaningful symbols in the spilled blood, the death in war, of so many young men, let him. The tragedy wasn't that a troubled old man saw symbols where there were none but that the unimaginative minds of people like Dicky couldn't see symbols at all.

Jake said, "I'd be honored to walk the zodiac in your place."

"Thank you." For a moment Andy went limp with relief. Then he pulled himself together, stood up, seized Jake's free hand, and wrung it between his own. "Most kind. Very good of you."

"Seems the least I can do," Jake said with a wry smile.

Brisk male voices echoed from the entrance hall. Bridget hurried down the corridor and stopped in the door. Her voice was music compared to the crow-like clamor of the others. "Doc Skelton just told us what happened. Andy, I'm so sorry."

Andy's skin crinkled in Jake's hand like the paper of the map. Inside his tweeds he seemed very old, very small, sucked dry. But still he summoned up a hint of a twinkle. "Thank you, Nurse O'Neill. You and Pilot Officer Houston make quite a handsome couple, don't you know? Did I tell you, Nurse, that your horoscope predicts a long happy marriage to an Aries? Houston here is an Aries."

Jake opened his mouth to protest. But the words were spoken—the die was cast. He stole a glance at Bridget.

A log collapsed in a shower of sparks and a sudden flame shot upwards. But the rosy glow in Bridget's face, he decided, wasn't from the fire. Releasing Andy's hand, he slipped his arm around her waist and told himself that some prophecies just might be self-fulfilling.

She leaned against him. Together they watched Andy walk, slowly but as erect as a soldier, out the door and down the hall.

"Thank you, Jake," Bridget murmured. "I was seeing myself sacked and deported. But that poor old man, now, will they be sending him to a home?"

"This is his home," Jake told her. "And sometimes I think he's more sane—and more sober—than anyone else in this crazy world."

"Do you now? With him reading the future in the stars and all? Or is he reading the past this time round?"

"A bit of each. Here, let me show you." Jake unrolled the map and angled it so she could see. "The storm's lifted. I think we should take a walk tomorrow morning, follow some of these paths and have us a picnic in honor of your birthday. The exercise will do me good, shake out the knots in my side."

She eyed the distorted shapes of the zodiac, her head tilted, then turned her face up to Jake's. "I'd like that. Especially if you're after explaining it all to me."

"I'll try," Jake assured her. "I'll try."

The flare of light from the fireplace died down. Shadows oozed in from the corners of the room, but still the windows gleamed faintly. An airplane droned overhead, making the panes of glass reverberate. Jake looked toward them. Even though he couldn't see the Tor he imagined it reaching toward the stars, steady, solid, reassuringly permanent, a bridge between earth and heaven.

Bridget took his cool hand in her warm and capable one and tugged him toward the door. "Let's get on with it, then. There's a war on."

"Yes," he said. "All we can do is get on with it."

Mary Jane Maffini

Blind Alley

MARY JANE MAFFINI is a lapsed librarian and former co-owner of Prime Crime Mystery Bookstore in Ottawa, and author of the Camilla MacPhee mystery series published by Rendezvous Crime. Her quirky characters show up in *Ellery Queen's Mystery Magazine*, where we found the story that follows, and in *Storyteller Magazine* as well as several Canadian crime anthologies. "Cotton Armour" in *The Ladies' Killing Circle* won the 1996 Crime Writers of Canada Arthur Ellis Award for Best Short Story. She was a finalist in 1999 for Best First Novel and Best Short Story. She is the current president of the Crime Writers of Canada and is hard at work on her fourth novel. In "Blind Alley," published in *EQMM* in November, a child takes center stage, and tackles a crime that strikes a bit too close to home.

Blind Alley

Mary Jane Maffini

It was one of Mummy's bad days.

The living room drapes were closed and the lights turned off. You couldn't see Mummy tucked in the wing chair. The smoke from her cigarette curled toward the ceiling, so probably she was leaning back with her eyes closed. I hoped she wasn't biting her lips.

I noticed her blue Belvedere package and her gold lighter matched the upholstery. The living room is French Provincial. I was training myself to observe details.

I didn't try to tiptoe in to give Mummy a kiss.

On bad days, the rules were simple. Stay out of sight and stay out of trouble. Today would be a good opportunity to work on my detecting skills.

Daddy had already left for the office. The Lincoln was gone from the garage and a Rothmans butt was lying on the garage floor. Another detail, but perhaps not very useful. I picked it up in case Mummy's day started to improve. She might decide to take the DeSoto to Antoine's Style Shoppe and get upset about the cigarette butt. That's why Dinah and I never mind picking up after Daddy.

Dinah was locked in her bedroom with pin curls in her hair. I could still smell the Breck shampoo in the bathroom. She was busy planning how to dance with Kenny Wedgewood at the hop on Saturday night. It was Thursday and time was running out.

Mummy never came into the kitchen on bad days, and Sadie was off, so I didn't have to worry about Cream of Wheat. I ate a lot of Frosted Flakes right out of the box, for energy. Then I drank a big glass of Orange Crush. Daddy would call that a chaser.

I never could get braids right without Sadie, so I put my hair in ponytails. I left off the ribbons. Detectives shouldn't have to wear bows.

Because it was the end of August, all my friends were busy getting ready for school. There was no one to investigate with. I would have to spend the day away from Havelock Street where our neighbors didn't understand that a detective has a job to do. What was the use of having those big maple trees if no one was ever allowed to climb in them while they were hunting for clues?

At least it wasn't raining. This was the sunniest day we'd had in weeks. It looked like a good day to go downtown. I'd have to walk, but it was just a mile. I planned to get myself a roadster when I was older. And a sidekick. Everyone always laughed at that. People didn't realize the importance of girl detectives.

Carleton Street was jammed. Mostly mothers taking kids to get new outfits for school. Afterwards, the lucky ones would get a milkshake.

Tommy Bork, the meanest boy in our whole school, went by with his mother and father. "I'm getting a leather binder," he said.

"Maybe you should ask for a brain instead," I said.

Dinah was always telling me I would have less trouble if I just kept my big mouth shut. I didn't believe Tommy was getting a leather binder. Mummy used to say the Borks were terribly common.

I hoped Mummy would have at least one good day before school started. Daddy wouldn't know how to buy school clothes, although maybe he'd be okay for colored pencils and Hilroy scribblers. But he could send his secretary, Miss Merkely. Miss Merkely looked just like a model. She'd think a leather binder was a good idea. I planned to show her the beautiful blue one with navy trim at McLeod's Bookstore. I could keep my detecting notes in that binder. My Big Chief notebook looked too kiddish. And another good thing, Miss Merkely always took me to The London Grill for a chocolate sundae. Miss Merkely would get a sundae, too, and say how much fun it was to talk girl talk.

Unless I got into trouble, which was so easy to do, most adults didn't notice me. They might say, "There's that Chalmers girl, no, not the pretty one, the chubby one, what's her name?" People thought I was too young to understand things, which I definitely was not. But as a girl detective, I didn't want them to pay attention.

I decided to play hopscotch. Hopscotch didn't require any equipment, just a piece of chalk. Sadie always said I needed to get more exercise and anyway it was an excellent way to look for clues without anyone noticing. That morning, the best watching was at the California Fruit and Confectionery Store at the corner of Edward Street. Everyone passed by there. Mr. Sabatino didn't mind if I played hopscotch under the awning.

I was on the lookout for people stealing chocolate bars. I had some suspects. I knew Mr. Sabatino would give me one of his big wide smiles when I showed him the evidence. He'd be surprised because he didn't know I was a detective. He was always nice to me and sometimes would give me an Aero bar. Maybe because I didn't swipe the mints from the glass jars the way Tommy Bork did. Or maybe because Daddy was his landlord. He would pat my head and squeeze my shoulders. I wasn't used to people touching me, but Mr. Sabatino was nice. Dinah says men should be tall, dark, and handsome, like Daddy. Mr. Sabatino looked like a big pillow with ears, and he made me want to smile. He was the only person I knew with a shiny head. And he smelled like peaches.

When it got hot, I decided to practice surveillance. The alley beside the California Fruit and Confectionery Store was the best lookout, especially in the space behind the garbage bins. It was dusty and stinky, but still an excellent detecting spot. From one side, I could see the entrance to the parking lot behind the building. Daddy always parked his Lincoln there next to Miss Merkely's Chevy BelAir convertible. Mr. Sabatino kept the California Fruit and Confectionery Store truck up by the entrance. I liked the truck because it had bananas painted on the side, where it said, *We're a Good Bunch.* From the lookout spot you could see everyone who passed by on Carleton Street. The parking lot is surrounded by buildings, so the alley is the only way in or out of it. That was handy for a detective.

People often snuck their cars into the parking lot. Tommy Bork's father's blue Ford was on the side, blocking the alley. I wrote the license number in my Big Chief notebook. Mr. Sabatino hurried back and forth three or four times taking boxes and bags to the truck for home deliveries later. Someday, I was going to ask if I could go with him. I thought I could gather lots of clues, because Mr. Sabatino's truck went everywhere and it had no doors on it. He didn't spot me behind the garbage cans. I wrote that in my notebook, too. *Surveillance skills improving.*

Not much was happening in the alley, so after a while I got bored and went to see Mr. Sabatino. The California Fruit Store was a good place to practice details, because it was full of strange things, such as chocolate-covered ants. That week there were three gigantic bunches of bananas hanging from hooks in the ceiling. Mr. Sabatino said they came all the way from Brazil by boat. There were huge wooden barrels with yucky things floating in them. Mr. Sabatino said they were black olives from Greece and when I got older I would be crazy about them.

The store smelled of old fruit and there were always flies buzzing. The twirling ribbons of flypaper would have been pretty if they didn't have dead flies stuck on them. Mummy would never allow flypaper in our house.

Even though Mr. Sabatino offered me a banana and something he called a nectarine, I decided to move on. I'd never tasted a nectarine and anyway, it was time to do a report on the morning.

Daddy's office had gold letters on the door. *Chalmers Insurance* in big letters and *Trusted Advice for Three Generations* a bit smaller.

It was boiling out by afternoon, but Miss Merkely was wearing new fall clothes, a reversible tartan skirt and a yellow Banlon sweater with her cultured pearls. Her patent leather pumps had very high heels and she swayed when she walked. Dinah always said the word for blondes like Miss Merkely was glamorous. She always wore Chanel No. 5. She looked like Mummy in her wedding picture, only Mummy had dark hair and red lipstick.

Miss Merkely kept a bowl of humbugs between her telephone and her typewriter. She gave me as many as I wanted. Sometimes she let me use the typewriter. It was a Remington and it had been in my grandfather's office since 1911.

Today Miss Merkely's eyes were red. She was blowing her nose and hiccupping. Something sad must have happened because she kept talking about the baby. Maybe a sick cousin or something.

Daddy was always very nice to Miss Merkely. He would give her the afternoon off if she needed it. Daddy kept telling her not to worry because he could take care of things. I knew he would. Daddy takes care of things for all of us.

They didn't notice me because Miss Merkely was sobbing so much she shook. Or maybe my surveillance skills were much better. It was not a good day to stay at Daddy's office.

I went back to my hopscotch game, this time in the shade in the alley. I could get the rock where I wanted it. I hardly ever stepped on the lines. I was a good hopper. But I must have been concentrating too hard on clues because I slipped on the gravel and scraped my knee. I bit my lip hard because detectives shouldn't cry when they're on the job. Mr. Sabatino was carrying boxes to the truck when he spotted me. He took off his apron and used it to wipe my knee. "You should wash that cut in the bathroom and put a little iodine on it," he said.

I hated iodine because it stung more than any cut, so I just said okay. Tommy Bork went tearing along Carleton Street towards the store just at that minute and Mr. Sabatino rushed back to the door, waving his arms. He forgot his apron. I didn't want it to get dirty in the alley so I picked it up for him. I would get a huge smile for that. I got some water from the sink in the store bathroom and cleaned the rest of the gravel from my knee.

When I went back outside, I heard Tommy Bork yelling at Mr. Sabatino. He said things so rude that I could never even repeat them. I ducked behind the garbage bin in case Tommy caught me alone in the alley. Anything could happen then. It would be harder to convince anyone I was a detective if I had a skinned knee *and* a black eye.

Just when I thought it was safe to stick my head out, I saw Daddy rush by. I hadn't even seen him come in! It must have been when I was washing my knee. I would have asked him to help me get past Tommy Bork, but he looked like he had a lot on his mind. I could tell by the way he wore his hat. He might have been very angry that the Borks' car was blocking his way, or maybe something bad had happened at the office. He tossed his cigarette on the gravel near the bins as he crunched past and looked straight forward.

The insurance business had lots of ups and downs. Dinah and I were not supposed to ask about them because Daddy needed to relax with a gin and tonic and not be pestered with questions from small fry. In the evening he had Kiwanis and Rotary and the Lion's Club, so that wasn't the best time, either. I reached out and picked up his cigarette butt.

Tommy Bork's parents passed me on their way to the car. They had a ton of parcels for their spoiled brat. Tommy saw me step out from behind the garbage bins. Darn. Now I had lost my best hiding spot. "You just wait," he said, lowering his voice so his parents couldn't hear him. He stuck his tongue out.

"You look better that way," I said. I was betting he wouldn't knock me down in front of his parents. They kept walking toward their Ford. Suddenly Mrs. Bork started screaming. She hurried past me out of the parking lot, scattering her parcels. A minute later, Mr. Bork raced behind her. He was the color of glue.

"Call an ambulance," Mr. Bork kept yelling. I ran back down the alley to the parking lot to see what the fuss was about.

Miss Merkely was lying on the ground. Her neck was twisted in a funny way and her string of cultured pearls was broken. There was a strange stain all down the concrete wall and a red puddle spreading behind her head. I dropped beside her. I didn't even feel my skinned knee.

She was out cold. I slid Mr. Sabatino's apron behind her head to keep her beautiful blond hair out of the gravel. "Don't worry, Miss Merkely, I'll look after your pearls," I said, holding up both broken parts of the necklace. I tried shaking her shoulders to wake her. Then a policeman took my arm and made me come away. He was very kind and told me to be a big girl.

The sound of sirens was getting really loud.

It must have been a robber, people on the street said, or a tramp. I didn't think we had robbers or tramps in our town.

The next time I saw Miss Merkely she was on a stretcher with her face covered. You could just see her patent leather shoes with the high heels. People lined up on the sidewalk to watch. The pushing and shoving started as some men carried Miss Merkely into an ambulance. More policemen were making people keep back. One of them said, "Move along, folks. Show's over."

I thought Mr. Sabatino might know what was happening. It was crazy inside the California Fruit and Confectionery Store. Ladies were crying, everyone was talking at once. Kids were stealing chocolate bars. A policeman was yelling at people to be calm. Mr. Sabatino was flopped on the chair behind the cash register with his head in his hands, crying loudly. Someone gave me a hard shove and I tripped and crashed into a smelly barrel of olives. I dropped most of Miss Merkely's pearls and they slid under the front counter, where I couldn't reach them. All I had left was the short piece with six pearls. I think that Tommy Bork was the one who pushed me.

Another policeman took our names and told us to go home. He smiled when I explained I was a detective. "What are you looking for? It has to do with Miss Merkely, doesn't it? I saw her."

His face got kind of cloudy. "Your parents might be worried about you. We'll let you know if we need your help."

"All right," I said, "I have everything written in my notebook."

Mummy had already gone to bed, although she wasn't asleep because I could hear Nat King Cole on her record player and I could smell a fresh cigarette. She didn't answer her door.

Even after such a terrible day, Daddy still had to go to his Rotary Club because he was the president. Dinah stayed on the phone all evening talking to Marilyn Myers about whether to wear bobby sox to the hop. Sadie was still off. No one would say anything to me about Miss Merkely. Some people on the street had told me she died. I needed to know if it was true.

My throat hurt.

I made myself two Swanson TV turkey dinners. It was dark when the policeman came to my house. He had a man in a suit with him. I was happy to be able to talk to them without any interruptions.

"We'd like to know what you saw today," the man in the suit said.

"Everything. I record details in my notebook."

I noticed them look at each other even though they pretended not to.

"Why do you write in this notebook?"

"I'm working on my detecting skills."

For some reason the man in the suit kept chewing his lip. That must have hurt. The policeman seemed to have a problem with a bad cough.

"Did you see anything suspicious?"

I took a minute to think. "What do you mean by suspicious?"

"I mean, was anyone in the alley who shouldn't have been there?"

"Oh, yes. Tommy Bork ran in and out after stealing mints from Mr. Sabatino. His father parked his car there and he's *not* supposed to. Mrs. Bork went in and out like she owned the place."

"And the man from the fruit store?"

"Of course, Mr. Sabatino has to load his truck. That's okay. He pays rent." I tried not to sound like I thought the policeman was asking stupid questions. "He was very upset about the Borks' car. I think he needed to move in a hurry and he couldn't get out because of them."

The policeman wrote that down. "How do you know he was upset?"

"He was yelling and he had big perspiration patches under his arms."

They nodded at each other. I hoped those Borks were going to get a ticket.

"Anyone else? Anything suspicious?"

I closed my eyes to think but I didn't remember anyone suspicious.

"No."

"And you are sure?"

"Of course, I wrote everything down." I showed him my Big Chief notebook. I wished it were a leather binder. I bet they wouldn't smile at that.

They flipped through the pages. Then they said they needed to take the notebook away.

"So you didn't see anyone else come out of the alley? Or go in?"

I'd already said I would have noticed anything suspicious. "No one. Who are you looking for?"

The man in the suit stood up and patted my head. I didn't like that. The policeman said, "Thank you, Detective. Your notes will help a lot."

"Is Miss Merkely going to be okay?" I asked.

On Friday the California Fruit and Confectionery Store was closed. The awning was still rolled up. The door was locked. I pressed my nose to the window. The lights were off inside. You could smell that some things were starting to go bad. Probably those nectarines. The big bunches of bananas still hung there. I thought I heard flies buzzing on the flypaper. Dinah would say that was my overactive imagination.

Someone had broken a window with a rock. I bet it was Tommy Bork.

Lots of people kept stopping outside the California Fruit Store and pointing and talking. Some of the people sounded angry. Some of the mothers pulled at their children and hurried away. As soon as one bunch left, another crowd pushed in. Tommy Bork said that Mr. Sabatino had been arrested. He said his ma always knew there was something greasy about that guy.

I didn't think it was fair. A lady in a brown hat told me they had a lot of evidence against Mr. Sabatino and that should be a lesson to all of us.

"A lesson about what?" I asked, but she didn't answer me.

I never even suspected Mr. Sabatino could hurt Miss Merkely. Kill her. I didn't see any evidence. That meant I was not such a good girl detective after all. After that, I didn't even want to try.

I got the blue leather binder *and* a reversible tartan skirt for school. Mummy got a silky black mink coat that went right to her ankles! Daddy stopped going to Rotary meetings. Instead he would take Mummy to the country club. I could hear Mummy laughing through the window as they climbed into the Lincoln. Daddy hired a new secretary, but she was not glamorous and she didn't have humbugs. Dinah spent all her time in her room giggling with Marilyn Myers. They kept the door closed, which wasn't fair.

I was not allowed to go to Miss Merkely's funeral. I didn't think that was fair, either. I wouldn't dare tell anyone, but I missed Mr. Sabatino a lot. I will never understand how he could have done such a terrible thing.

For a long time afterwards, I could smell Miss Merkely's Chanel No. 5 on the six pearls I had left.

John Vermeulen

Canon

JOHN VERMEULEN is a Belgian crime and mystery author who has had a very busy year, with two new mystery novels published, a play written and produced, and a cookbook, proving that mystery writers have extremely varied and diverse interests. However, he did find the time to write "Canon," a diabolical take on modern-day marriage, and on how far some couples will go to get away from each other. First published in *Dodelijke Paringsdans (Deadly Mating Dance)*, a single author collection, it stands with the best any American or British writer has to offer.

Canon

John Vermeulen

With a gesture of resentment Joyce pushed the off-button on the remote control. The television picture lit up for an instant as if that unexpected intervention had startled it and then it shrank to a small pin-prick of light that slowly faded.

You should be able to do the same with people, Joyce thought while she shut the *TV Guide* and put it on a neat pile with the other magazines. Switch them off when they bored or irritated you, just make them disappear.

She got up and walked over to the other side of the room where Werner had his study corner. Frowning, with his chin resting on his fist he was reading a file by the light of the desk lamp. "It's half past eleven," she said. "Are you coming to bed?"

Without looking up he answered: "You don't have to wait up for me."

She never needed to wait for him to go to bed, not for years. He found satisfaction in his files and sales graphics.

She left the light on so she would stay awake. He counted on her being asleep by the time he came to bed, so she would leave him alone. Werner was a real wet blanket in bed. And things had not improved when he was promoted to the brewery's sales manager. He was a social climber. For someone from a proletarian background without diplomas he had already achieved a great deal at the age of 43, but he had still higher aspirations. His intelligence and his education did not, however, match up to his ambition. He had to twist and turn to prove himself.

Half an hour later she heard him stumble around in the bathroom. Joyce kept her eye on the bathroom door. His change of expression when he saw that she had waited for him did not escape her. His face showed a discouraging and humiliating glimpse of indifference.

He got into bed in his somewhat clumsy way, pulling the blanket partly off her, exposing her right breast. A beautiful breast, exactly right in shape and firmness, just as her entire body was exactly right. Joyce was a couple of years younger than him and in great shape. But Werner gave her looks as much attention as he would a dummy.

He kissed her perfunctorily on her cheek and reached for the light switch. Joyce took his hand and pulled it back with soft compulsion, putting it on her breast. There it remained, cold and motionless, as if he was grasping a piece of plastic. She felt under the blanket and her hand slid down his pajama trousers. She kneaded and caressed him in order to make him come to life. But it did not work, he remained limp and lifeless.

Maybe she should ask Tally to teach her some tricks. Her friend Tally who worked in a sauna. Sometimes she envied Tally who could get stuck into horny guys every day as much as she liked and was paid handsomely for it.

Hardly surprised she asked: "You really don't feel like it again?"

"I'm dead tired," he declared. "I want to go to sleep."

She knew he meant *try* to go to sleep. Very often he got up at night to smoke and drink coffee. Strong black coffee which made his restlessness even bigger. He demanded that she would always leave a full thermos in his study corner.

She pushed his hand between her legs, but he pulled it back immediately as if she disgusted him. Then she sat up brusquely. "This is simply insulting," she stated. "Do you think I'm dirty, do I smell?" She looked at him with a searching glance, an angry frown between her dark eyebrows. "Or have you discovered that you feel more attracted to men or something of the sort?" Her voice sounded almost hopeful. That at least she would be able to understand.

She had started to talk louder and he pointed, frightened, at the wall.

"To hell with the neighbors!" Joyce snapped. "They may know what a nonentity you are!" Suddenly she lowered her voice. As if a thought had suddenly struck her she asked: "Do you finally have a mistress?"

"I wouldn't even have the time for that," Werner answered wearily. He was clearly fed up with the entire conversation.

"Do you want me to find a lover?" she tried.

"Go ahead," he answered.

He sounded as if he could not care less, but she knew that was a lie. Jealousy was one of the few emotions still left in him. He was enormously possessive. And Joyce was his possession. She would not mind getting rid of him, but she was dependent on him. She had never learned to support herself. Furthermore, Werner already owned a couple of houses and some land, and she did not want to give all that up. She found that she had a right to it. For years she had sacrificed all sorts of pleasures because Werner looked twice at every penny before spending it.

She looked down on his angular face with the sunken eyes and the sharp lines around the corners of his tightly shut mouth. It was a hard face, on which single-mindedness and frustration fought to get the upper hand.

I hate you, she thought.

She switched off the light and turned her back on him. She heard him sigh and turn around as well, away from her.

Her thoughts strayed back to her friend. Tally had once suggested that she could come and work for her. At the time the idea had seemed absurd, she in a sauna, pawing strange men. Now the idea did not seem so silly after all. The thought even attracted her in a way so close to perversion that it made her shiver slightly. Heaven knew she could use the money. Werner curtailed her allowance, making it impossible for her to buy anything for herself without having to beg him on her knees for it, so to speak.

The bastard! she thought, startled by the term of abuse which surged up naturally from her mind to the surface.

She lay awake for over an hour, ignoring the restless tossing and turning of her husband beside her. She only fell asleep when she had definitely decided to call up Tally the next morning.

She did not call, she went there.

Sauna Aphrodite was situated in a quiet neighborhood with modern houses. Seen from the outside it looked like an unsuspecting institute. And that is what it was for the ones who did not know the ropes. There were three real saunas, a solarium, and a small bar for the usual clients, who often came there with their wives and children. And then there were two massage rooms. What went on behind the closed doors of these rooms was something between the client and the girl.

Joyce had been there before to have a chat with Tally who sometimes had nothing to do for an hour or so. They had met one another a long time ago during a holiday at the seaside, and because they both lived in Brussels they had kept in touch.

As always Tally looked smart in her starched white coat, which made her look like a nurse. After they had talked awhile Tally asked: "What's on your mind?"

Joyce looked pensively at the other. Tally had a friendly, open and beaming face that invited one to confidentiality. "I want to have a go at it," she said. "I mean that I want to work here, or at least see how it goes."

Tally did not seem surprised. "You know how it goes," she said.

"Of course, I got the picture. But isn't it also a matter of uh . . . technique?"

Tally got up energetically. "Come on," she requested. "A good client is now in the shower. His name is Freddie. He won't mind if I use him for a demonstration."

Joyce hesitated. "I can't just . . ."

"If you want to work here you had better take the bull by the uh . . . horns immediately. She giggled, seeing the other one's face. "Now don't pretend you're a pantywaist. You're not fooling me!"

Funnily enough Joyce did not even feel awkward when she stood in the massage room a little later on and watched how Freddie took off his bathrobe and lay down on the table on his belly. Her friend took off her white coat. She was not wearing anything underneath but her panties. While Joyce watched she started massaging the man's thighs and calves with seasoned movements. She acted so naturally that Joyce never had the feeling something exceptional was going on. She did not even hesitate when her friend asked her to join in. She even chuckled when Tally winked at her while she demonstrated how she could make the man squirm with pleasure.

Later on, when the client had gone Tally asked: "Well?"

Joyce asked reluctantly: "Do you sometimes do more, I mean, do you let yourself be . . ." She was silent.

"It's up to you how far you want to go," the other dodged. "Although you'd better prevent some client from complaining to the boss." She put her hand on Joyce's arm. "You get used to it pretty quick," she said.

"Yeah, I suppose so . . ." Her thoughts made a spring. She wondered how Werner would react if he were to know what she had been up to here today. Very possible that the cold fish would not survive the shock.

"Ask your boss when I can start work," she said.

Normally Joyce stopped working at four, but it often happened that a client came in at the last moment, whom Joyce "served" if Tally was busy. In addition, she had a long bus ride home. In the beginning Werner hardly noticed that she came home a little later. He often left the factory late himself. If she was not there he buried himself in his work and forgot the rest. As long as he found his coffee and his cigarettes.

One day he brought a good customer home with him to discuss some business. Joyce knew that he was bringing someone with him for supper, but precisely that day she came home even later than usual and Werner and his customer had already gone. It was after midnight when he showed up, smelling heavily of alcohol. Something that hardly ever happened, because he could not carry his liquor.

She had waited up, but against all expectations he did not make a scene. Instead he ignored her as if she did not exist. Somewhat unsteadily he stumbled about the house, spreading pieces of clothing everywhere. At last he made himself comfortable on the couch. Helped by the alcohol he started snoring right away.

Joyce looked down on him with distaste. The color of his skin was even more sallow than usual, his mouth hung open a little and he drooled. The way he was lying there, she could easily do away with him, she conceived, and automatically her glance shifted to the rifle above the fireplace. At the same time she took a step backwards recoiling from her own line of thought. She went to the bedroom, confused. She locked the door behind her, something she had never done before. It seemed as if she fled from ghosts.

When Werner came home the following night, he pretended nothing had happened. He ate quickly and without appetite, his thoughts were elsewhere as usual. Only when she poured the coffee did he suddenly say: "You've got your hair differently."

"I've been to the hairdresser's," she replied, immediately wondering why she sounded on the defensive.

"Hairdressers are expensive," he remarked.

"I had some money left over from last month."

"So? I thought you could never make ends meet?"

"I still had some discount coupons left and I . . . dammit, go to the devil!" she suddenly burst out. She ran out of the house, leaving him flabbergasted.

When she came home one hour later he was working and did not even look up.

Over the next days Joyce noticed that Werner kept paying her more attention. He spied on her when he thought she did not notice. It was as if he suspected that something peculiar was the matter with her.

After a while she asked, harsher than intended: "Why are you staring at me all the time?"

With an expression on his face that she could not identify, he answered: "You've changed."

She was surprised that he had even noticed. "Is that so?" she said expectantly.

"You use mascara, something you seldom used to do. And you smell different."

Never before had she known him to be so observant. "I've bought another brand of soap," she explained. In order not to rouse suspicion she had bought the same soap to use at home as she washed herself with in the sauna several times a day. She thanked her lucky stars that she had been so cautious.

"The stuff that you put on your eyelashes isn't cheap, is it?"

"It costs an arm and a leg," she replied with malicious pleasure. "Each time you don't feel like eating I can save some money, and that mounts up very nicely." She looked defiantly at him.

Yet, he let it pass. Shrugging his shoulders he left the table.

Two weeks later he took her to a party given by the brewery. Joyce would rather have stayed at home, but Werner simply insisted that she would accompany him. It was not becoming for an executive to go without his wife, he believed.

At first she actually had a good time. She enjoyed the attention of a couple of talkative gentlemen, whom she vaguely knew from a similar occasion in the past, and she was beginning to hope that it would turn out to be a pleasant evening. Until a latecomer arrived and made the smile on her face freeze up.

He was a tall, reasonably handsome man. He looked round the room in the way newcomers do when they are looking for familiar faces. Before she had come to her senses and turned her head the other way, he spotted her. Despairingly, she still hoped that he would not recognize her, but that hope was in vain. She froze when she saw a streak of surprise on his face. For one terrible moment she feared that he would come and talk to her. However, he immediately shifted his gaze from her and walked up to the bar. While she absent-mindedly took up the thread of the conversation with her company, she noticed that the newcomer was handed a drink and then positioned himself at the bar in such a way that he could keep an eye on her. Pensively he stared in her direction.

"Who's that man who just came in?" she asked the tubby production manager next to her, who had gone out of his way for over an hour now to keep her entertained. "That tall guy with dark hair at the bar."

"Herman Bleys," he answered. "He was the only other candidate for the job of sales manager. Your husband jockeyed him." He turned to another man in the group. "Are they talking to one another again?" he asked.

The other chuckled. "They're certainly not sleeping together," he reasoned. When he saw that Joyce raised an eyebrow in amazement he quickly added: "Sorry, Mrs. Raskin, company jokes . . ."

Joyce was not listening anymore. Her thoughts wandered. When she looked round, she saw that Werner was wrapped up in a lively conversation with the manager of the factory a little further on. He was making large gestures and articulating excessively as if he was talking to a deaf-mute. He did not look in her direction.

She decided to be one step ahead of chance. After having excused herself from her company, she walked straight up to Herman Bleys. When she stood in front of him, he said a little mockingly: "Hello, Sylvia." He pointed to his glass. "Can I order you a drink?"

"A screwdriver, please." She had already had a couple of those, but she could use some tranquilizers.

"I was quite surprised," Bleys said. "Apparently sauna hookers don't always tell their clients the truth."

"I'm not . . . ," she lowered her voice, "a hooker!"

"Well, that depends how you look at it, I would say."

She half emptied her glass and looked pensively at him. She asked: "And what do you intend to do now with your tremendous discovery?" Her breezy tone was in flat contradiction with her state of mind.

"The situation offers some interesting possibilities," Bleys admitted. "Especially, if we presume that saint Werner Raskin isn't informed about the nature of your professional activities."

For a while she looked at him without answering. The ice cubes tinkled against her glass. When she discovered that this was caused by the trembling of her hand she emptied her glass and put it down. At last she asked: "Are you planning on blackmailing me?"

"Don't be so melodramatic, this is supposed to be a pleasant evening." His smile was charming, but his eyes looked calculating.

She said: "I have to go back to my company."

He nodded with excessive understanding. Almost casual he said: "I'll see you at your work on Thursday."

"Don't take it to heart," Tally said when she had told her the whole story. "If that guy wants to rat on you, he'll have to give himself away, and he won't."

"I don't trust him," Joyce said unhappily. "Bleys will almost certainly want to use me to take action against Werner." She was really worried. Even more so because for the past couple of days she had the feeling that she was being watched. In fact she very much liked the idea of quitting work for a while, until things had cooled down. But she did not want to lose the income, and besides the work held an exciting sort of attraction over her. It was a compensation for the colorless drag of her life with Werner. She had enjoyed playing with fire until the moment she had met Bleys at that party.

"Act as if nothing has happened," Tally advised her. "He's the weakest party, because in the end he has to pay for what you do."

"If he doesn't make me pay this time!"

Tally sighed. "Here's what we'll do, when he comes I'll entertain him. And I'll do such a good job that he'll forget all about you."

"That would work with any other man," Joyce said. "But not with him." She startled when the door bell rang.

Tally went to open the door. When she came back, she said: "It's your friend. I'm sorry, but he doesn't want anything to do with me, he only wants to deal with you."

Joyce stood up resigned. "It has been great knowing you," she said.

Werner let in his visitor and closed the glass door of his office behind him. Nervously he asked: "Have you discovered anything?"

The other dropped wearily into a chair. Instead of answering he asked: "Do you mind if I smoke?" He searched in his pockets. Snapping on his lighter he said: "Anyway she doesn't have a lover, at least not as far as I've been able to tell." He lit his cigarette and inhaled deeply as if he badly needed it.

"Is that so?" Werner said. He seemed more disappointed than relieved. "Then what does she have?"

"Work." The private eye took another long puff from his cigarette.

"Work? What kind of work?" The telephone rang. Werner picked up the receiver to stop the ringing and immediately put it back down again.

The private eye carefully said: "I'm afraid you're not going to like the answer."

"You don't have to spare me," Werner said wryly.

"She works in a sauna, Sauna Aphrodite. Here's the address." The private eye handed Werner a calling card.

Not understanding Werner asked: "What in heaven's name does she do there, clean up or something?"

"After hours, maybe." The man chuckled ironically as if he thought that the other was making a bitter joke.

Werner started to get enraged. "Dammit, man, what are you trying to tell me?"

The other stopped chuckling. He sighed wearily. "Your wife . . . ," he made a face, "your wife gives men what they call a 'relax massage.'"

Werner stared at the other in disbelief. "Joyce . . . ?"

The private eye bent forward to flick the ashes off his cigarette. "It's not a bad job," he stated. "It pays very well and they don't have to tire themselves out, well mostly not. If I were a woman I wouldn't have to think twice!" He looked up at Werner who seemed to have forgotten he had a visitor. His eyes were glassy. "Is there anything else I can do for you, Mr. Raskin?"

Werner struggled back to reality. "Keep watching her," he said. He spoke as if he was being strangled. "You report every step she takes to me!"

Joyce closed the door of the massage room behind her and leaned against it. She looked at Herman Bleys. Naked he looked a lot less attractive than with clothes on. He was not fat, but his body looked flabby and puffy, as if he had no muscles under his skin.

Slowly she said: "The wife of your boss and enemy; this situation must give you a very special kick!"

Smiling he said: "Just start your work."

"And if I don't feel like it?"

His smile faded. "How afraid are you actually of Werner?" he informed.

Joyce sighed and started taking off her coat. "It was just a rhetorical question," she said. "I presume you want a free treatment as well?"

"Oh, no." He smiled again. "I'm even willing to pay you more than usual, because you'll have to give me something different than I'm used to here." He put out his hand to her. "Do the best you can," he said.

Werner got into his car and took a map of Brussels out of the glove compartment. He looked up the address the private eye had given him and drove off. A quarter of an hour later he came to Aphrodite. He parked his car a little further down the street and turned off the engine. For almost five minutes he just sat there, staring into nothing, his hands contorted round the steering wheel. He then got out of his car and walked woodenly to the sauna.

A car was parked in front of the sauna and it seemed vaguely familiar, but Werner did not pay any notice. With his finger on the bell he hesitated. He did not know what he would do or say if he was confronted with his wife. Probably nothing at all. He just wanted to see with his own eyes what the private eye had told him.

He rang the bell.

A young, blonde woman answered the door. She gave him a friendly welcome. "Never been here before?" she stated inquisitively.

Werner shook his head. The mere question already annoyed him. He looked round, but there was nobody else to be seen.

"My name is Tally." Suddenly the woman looked insecure, as if she sensed the almost tangible aura of hostility that surrounded Werner. Less fluent than usual she told him the possibilities and the prices.

"I'll take a massage then," Werner said, picking the only word that had really sunk in.

She showed him the showers, took him to a cubicle, and gave him a towel. "When you're ready just go in." She pointed to an open door. "I'll be right with you." Then she left him alone.

Werner just stood there with the towel in his hands, weak-kneed and feeling ridiculous. Then he heard voices, a man's and a woman's voice, talking to one another sotto voce. The sound came from behind the closed door of the second massage room.

Silently he walked up to the door and listened intently. He could only make out a word now and then, yet he recognized Joyce's voice almost immediately.

The towel dropped to the ground and he took an awkward step backwards, as if he planned on bashing the door down. For a few seconds he stood there without moving, his fists clenched, the arteries in his forehead throbbed, fighting the desire to scream out helplessly in anger.

He then heard how the man started to pant heavily and suddenly uttered a low, bestial groan as if he was being tortured. It remained silent for a moment and the talking started again, livelier than before.

Werner turned round and walked away. He found the exit blindly and ran to his car. Before he got in he threw up in the gutter. The convulsive violence of his stomach had a soothing effect on his nerves. When it was over he at least felt capable of driving back to the factory.

He locked himself up in his office, where he sat brooding on his feelings of revenge. He harbored that lust for revenge, because it meant a balm on his wounded ego.

After a long time he pushed back his chair and stood up to walk over to the window. Brooding, he stared at the busy traffic on the road below him that ran past the factory. A couple of workers dressed in dust-coats were unloading the parts of a new packing machine from a truck.

He pulled the window open and listened to the noise of the traffic. But it did not drown the panting and moaning in his mind. His imagination just went on trying to think up images to go with it, revolting, nauseating images.

A car got out of the traffic jam and turned off to the parking lot of the factory. It was a similar car to the one he had seen at the sauna. There were thousands of cars like that, yet the association gave Werner a shock.

The car maneuvered backwards between a row of other cars, and Herman Bleys got out.

Werner closed the window and sat back in his chair. A moment later Herman Bleys knocked and walked into the office.

Werner forced his attention on the here and now. With great difficulty he remembered the order he had given the other that morning. It involved prospecting at a restaurant under construction, but when he tried to call to mind the name of the restaurant he could think of nothing else than Aphrodite. He bypassed that singe in his memory by asking: "Have you talked to the owner of the restaurant?"

"He's abroad, we'll have to be patient for a couple of days."

His voice had a strange undertone that alarmed Werner. Having great difficulty in concentrating he looked at Bleys. He hated that guy's guts, with his fine diplomas, who always tried to give him the push. And he knew damned well that the feeling was mutual. Behind his back Bleys called him a social case whose incompetence had earned him promotion, and Werner had recently found that out. Even now he saw the usual distrust and hostility in the other one's eyes. But there was something more. Ridicule? Contempt? He thought of Bleys's car. For one terrible moment he wondered if it had been him he had heard panting and moaning in the massage room.

His face must have reflected the horror, because all of a sudden Bleys looked surprised. More curious than concerned he asked: "Are you feeling alright?"

Werner took a deep breath and straightened his back. "I'm overworked," he explained. "Something most people here won't suffer from too easily."

Bleys turned round and walked over to the door. With his hand on the doorknob he said over his shoulder: "You should take a relaxing massage from time to time . . ."

He went out and very softly closed the door behind him.

That evening Werner came home quite late. He had stayed in the office, thinking, long after everybody else had gone home.

Joyce was watching some cultural program. When she heard him come in, she shouted without taking her eyes off the screen: "I've made spaghetti, there's still some left that you can heat up."

Without answering he slowly walked up to her armchair. He stared at her until she looked up.

When she saw the expression on his face she suddenly looked worried. "What's the matter?" she asked. "Have you been drinking again?"

The sickening aversion that had supplanted his earlier anger almost gave him the urge to really spit on her. All he did, however, was stare at her witheringly until she lowered her eyes. Whereupon he turned round on his heels and retired to his study corner. With shaking hands he opened the vacuum bottle filled with coffee that waited there for him.

"Spaghetti," he mumbled. "Blast!"

One terrible moment Joyce thought that Bleys had given her away. What she had seen in Werner's expression was worse than hate. Then she dismissed the idea again. Bleys would not waste his trump in such a stupid way. But maybe Werner had spied on her. She knew that he sometimes spied on his own staff while they were doing their job in the city.

Anxiously she went to bed, avoiding looking in Werner's direction.

Somehow she had dozed off when she was brutally wakened some hours later. Werner had pulled the blankets off her. He took her by the arm and dragged her out of bed heavy-handedly so that she landed on her back on the floor with a loud bump. Then he kicked her hard in the stomach and the side. He only stopped when she screamed.

"Get out!" he yelled furiously. "Out of my bedroom, you dirty bitch!"

Wincing with pain she crawled away from him on hands and knees. In the living room she lay on the carpet.

After a while the pain in the places where Werner had kicked her subsided. She hauled herself onto the sofa. She got cold, but she did not dare go to the bedroom for a blanket.

It was obvious now that Werner knew everything. She was shocked and frightened by his reaction, and yet she did not regret what she had done. It even pleased her that he seemed so deeply hurt. But she was scared too.

She thought about Bleys. She hated that shifty slicker. But they had a mutual enemy.

When she heard Werner getting up the next morning she pretended to be asleep. He stayed away from her. She got up when the front door shut behind him.

She felt terrible, but after she had taken a shower and drank a few cups of strong coffee she felt a little better.

She called Aphrodite to tell them that she was not coming. Instead of Tally the boss answered the phone and his reaction was unexpectedly gruff. Already two clients had phoned who came especially for her and if she thought she could fool him she had better stay away altogether. With those words he hung up.

Joyce took a couple of aspirins and lay back down on the sofa. She thought about Bleys again. Tired from the sleepless night and stupefied by the aspirins she dozed off.

Later on, the telephone woke her up. Unwillingly she got up, dazed and unsteady.

It was Bleys. "I'm in the Aphrodite," he said. "And you're not here."

"How sad . . ." She looked at her watch and was surprised to see that it was already midday. Making a sudden decision she asked: "Do you have my address?" He had. "Come over," she said. "I want to talk to you." She hung up without waiting for his answer.

He arrived twenty minutes later. When she let him in he looked round in suspicion as if he suspected some trap.

Joyce took off the bathrobe she had put on straight away and showed him the bruises where Werner had kicked her. She asked: "What do you think now of that bastard?"

She saw that calculating look she knew so well appear in his eyes. "So he knows," he stated.

"Are you disappointed?"

He pulled his gaze from her body and looked her in the eyes. Calmly he said: "I have nothing against you, but I had some matters to settle with that son of a bitch and I saw some interesting possibilities in your escapades. And I still do."

At least now he seemed to be honest. She asked: "Why don't we work together? We could both benefit from it." She put the bathrobe round her shoulders.

He asked: "Do you have something to drink for me?"

She pointed at the bar. "Serve yourself."

While he poured himself a whisky and soda he said: "There's more to you than meets the eye." He obviously drank without pleasure, as if he only performed a ritual to save face.

Joyce said: "Something broke in me last night."

"Really?" He looked at her over the brim of his glass, expectantly and still calculating.

"I want to do something for which I need your help."

"Go on."

"I want him dead," she said flatly.

They met two days later in a pub on the other side of town, because Bleys wanted to avoid being seen together by people they knew.

He handed her a small bottle with a yellow-brownish liquid. "Nicotine," he explained, "pressed out of very expensive cigars."

Joyce looked at the bottle with awe before putting it into her handbag. "You just put it into his coffee," Bleys said. "He will hardly taste it, at the most there'll be a somewhat bitter aftertaste. And even the most ambitious detective will think no harm of it when a neurotic like Werner suddenly gets a heart attack and dies."

Joyce looked pensively at him. She said: "You know, I sometimes get the impression you've done all this before."

"I read a lot and I have a good memory," he answered with a joyless smile.

She let it pass. The only thing that mattered was that she would get rid of Werner.

"Herman Bleys!" Werner spat out the name as if he tasted something filthy. "That damned bastard!"

"He has met her twice outside the Aphrodite," the private eye stated coolly. "Once at your place and once in Café Des Arts in—"

"At my place!" Werner burst out. "So they are having a relationship as well?!"

"Let us say that all the facts point in that direction," the private eye said. He put his notebook in his inside pocket.

"That's enough for me," Werner said almost inaudibly. "That's enough for me . . ."

Later, when the siren of the factory wailed to indicate that work was over, Werner signalled Bleys to come into his office.

He had to force himself to talk to the man in a normal tone. As casually as possible he asked: "Are you in a hurry to go home? The new packing machine is operative since this afternoon and the board is about to have an official introduction. You're invited as well."

Bleys sighed wearily, but he reconciled himself to the inevitable. Together with Werner he walked downstairs.

Their footsteps echoed hollowly in the big, desolate room while they walked over to the new machine.

"There's nobody here yet," Werner remarked. "But we can already have a look. I've seen this thing run this afternoon, it's really worthwhile."

The machine consisted of a man-sized vertical reel with thick plastic foil, and a platform on which huge stacks of beer cans turned round on their pallet in order to be wrapped in plastic automatically. Further there was a metal rod that flew to and fro to lead the foil.

Werner opened the door of the switchboard and pushed a red button. The machine came to life. It made quite a lot of noise and he had to raise his voice to be understood. "Do you know what happens when we don't shut it off?" he asked. "That stupid thing keeps wrapping until the reel is empty or until the layer of plastic has become so thick that the whole thing jams. Look here . . ." He pointed at a spot close to the floor beside the switchboard.

When Bleys came closer and bent forward, unsuspecting, Werner suddenly pushed him hard. Bleys tripped forward and made the expected mistake to automatically reach for the swishing rod so his legs would not get caught in the turning parts. He gave a cry when his arms were almost dislocated. The next moment the first layer of plastic was already wrapped round him. He started to turn with the pallet, his back pressed against the cartons filled with cans, while he struggled to get free. The plastic tore and his arms were free when the second layer came and again he got caught. Two more times he managed to get almost free, and then he was so exhausted that he did not have the strength anymore to tear the tough synthetic material. His mouth grew fixed in a soundless scream of dread when it got covered by a tight layer of plastic by the machine.

Werner watched how the other one was mummified with transparent foil at high speed. It took a while before he could tear himself away from the fascinating image of the other one's face buried beneath a growing layer of synthetic material. But at last he turned round and walked to the exit of the factory.

Behind him the machine kept on turning.

Joyce was home and that surprised Werner. He had expected that she would have left, out of fear or shame. It was better this way, now he did not have to go looking for her.

She was busy in the kitchen and even if she got startled when he came in she did not show it.

He leaned against the jamb of the kitchen door and watched as she rubbed the spotless sink time and again.

"Stop that!" he suddenly snapped sharply.

Joyce froze. She put down the dishcloth and slowly turned round. She was pallid and her eyes were swollen.

Once again Werner felt the aversion coming over him in nauseating waves. Taking a deep breath he said: "Bleys is dead, I killed him."

For a moment it looked like she was going to faint, but she managed to pull herself together. She uttered a muffled sound, cleared her throat and tried again: "Why . . . ?"

His angular face distorted maliciously. "As if you don't know!" He pointed at the vacuum bottle on the kitchen table. "Is that my coffee?"

She nodded blankly.

He poured himself a cup and carefully tasted it. "Boiling hot," he commented. He put down his cup and looked at Joyce.

She looked caught out, he thought. He looked around for something he could use as a weapon. When he did not find anything right away he hit her full in the face with his fist. She fell backwards against a cupboard, but she remained standing. Staring at him with eyes opened wide in disbelief she felt her split lip. He hit her again on the same place, releasing part of his bottled up rage in the blow that stunned her.

When she regained consciousness she was lying on the bed on her back. Her wrists and ankles were tied with electric wire to the sides of the bed. He had gagged her to prevent her from screaming.

When she lifted her throbbing head with great difficulty she saw the shotgun. It was fastened to the backs of two chairs with the end of the barrel half a meter from her stomach.

Werner was standing beside the bed with his hands akimbo. His face seemed made out of stone when he looked down on her. "The gun is loaded with a cartridge," he said. "The trigger is tied to the chair with a leather lace from your sneakers. The lace is soaked with water. When it dries, it will shrink and I have set the trigger very sensitively. I estimate that it'll take round an hour before the shot will go off. I grant you that time so you can think about your sins . . ." His voice trembled as if he could hardly keep himself under control. After a while he went on: "A shot in the stomach is lethal, but I've been told that it takes a long time before you're dead and that it hurts like hell . . ."

Joyce did not move. She just stared at him. The gag soon became red with the blood from her lip. Her eyes radiated only pure hate.

It left him cold. He went out of the bedroom and shut the door behind him.

He switched on the stereo and put on a record of Vangelis. The somewhat unearthly music suited the occasion perfectly. Then he went into the kitchen.

The cup of coffee had got tepid. He tasted it. Joyce had always made great coffee, he had to say that much for her. From now on he would have to do that himself. He finished his cup.

The aftertaste was more bitter than usual.

Margaret Coel

A Well-Respected Man

MARGARET COEL'S background as a graduate student at both the University of Colorado and Oxford University helped prepare her to write powerful and poetic novels about Jesuit priest John Aloysius O'Malley and Arapaho attorney Vicky Holden. Just when you thought nobody could do anything fresh with the Native American novel, she's taken it to a whole new level. Her story "A Well-Respected Man" first appeared in the anthology *Women Before the Bench*, and has her series character racing to find a killer before an innocent man is put on trial. Been done before, you say? Reserve judgment until you finish this one.

A Well-Respected Man

Margaret Coel

The jangling noise grew louder, like a siren closing in from a far distance. Vicky Holden groped for the alarm clock on the nightstand and pressed the button. The noise continued. Struggling upright in the darkness, one elbow cradled in the pillow, she reached for the phone on the far side of the clock.

"Vicky, that you?" A man's voice, the words rushed and breathless. "Oh, man, I thought you wasn't there. They got me locked up in jail."

"Who is this?" Vicky said. She heard the sleepiness in her own voice. The luminous numbers on the clock showed 5:22.

"Leland Iron Wolf." Another rush of words. "You gotta get me outta here."

An image flashed into Vicky's mind: lanky frame about six feet tall; cowboy hat pulled forward, shading the dark, steady eyes that took in the world on its own terms, thick black braids hanging down the front of a western shirt. Leland was about twenty-five years old, the only grandson of Elton Iron Wolf, one of the Arapaho elders. The old man had raised the boy after his parents were killed in an accident. Vicky had never heard of Leland in any kind of trouble.

"What happened?" she asked, fully awake now.

Words tumbled over the line: the police on the Wind River Reservation arrested him an hour ago. He was still sleeping, and there they were, outside pounding on the front door. They turned him over to the sheriff, and next thing he knew, he was in the county jail.

Leland hesitated. Vicky heard the sound of incomprehension in the short, quick breaths at the other end of the line. Finally: "They think I shot the boss. Killed him. *Nokooho.*"

Crazy indeed, Vicky thought. Killers did crazy things, but Leland Iron Wolf . . . He was not a killer.

"Who was shot?" she asked.

"Jess Miller. My boss over at the Miller ranch. I hired out there a couple months ago."

Vicky knew the place—a spread that ran into the foothills west of Lander. The same spread that Jess Miller's father and grandfather had worked. The family was well respected in the area. Over the years, they had occasionally hired an Arapaho ranch hand.

"What happened?" She was out of bed now, phone tucked under her chin as she switched on the light and began rifling through her clothes in the closet.

"How the hell do I know?" Impatience and desperation mingled in Leland's voice. "I rode in from doctoring calves and picked up my pay at the office in the barn. The boss was alive and kickin', his same old mean self when I left."

"What time was that?" Vicky persisted.

"About seven, almost dark. You gotta get me outta here, Vicky." The words sounded like a long wail.

Vicky understood. For an Arapaho accustomed to herding cattle on open ranges, warrior blood coursing through his veins, there was nothing worse than to be locked behind bars. It was death itself.

"I'm on my way." She tossed the jacket and skirt of her navy blue suit onto the bed. Then an ivory silk blouse. "Don't say anything until I get there—understand?"

"Hurry," Leland said.

Vicky pushed the disconnect button, then tapped in the numbers of the sheriff's office and asked for Mark Albert, the detective most likely handling the case. He picked up the phone on the first ring.

"This is Vicky Holden," she told him. "I'm representing Leland Iron Wolf."

"Figured you'd be the one calling." Sounds of rustling paper came over the line.

Vicky ignored the implication that only an Arapaho lawyer would take an Arapaho's case. She said, "What do you have?"

"Evidence that Leland Iron Wolf murdered one of the county's prominent citizens."

"Have you questioned him?"

"We Mirandized him, counselor, and he said he was gonna call a lawyer." The words were laced with sarcasm.

Vicky drew in a long breath, struggling to keep her temper in check. "Give me the details."

"Donna Miller, that's the wife, found Jess's body in the barn last evening about eight o'clock. Shot in the chest, right in the heart, to be precise. Shotgun that killed him was dropped outside the barn."

Vicky said, "Leland left the ranch at seven."

"Mrs. Miller says otherwise." Vicky flinched at the peremptory tone.

Mark Albert was a tough adversary. "The missus was in the kitchen around eight o'clock. Looked out the window and saw Leland going into the barn. Couple minutes later she heard a gunshot and ran outside. That's when she found her husband."

Vicky could feel the knot tightening in her stomach. *His same mean old self*, Leland had called his boss. She said, "What's the motive, Mark?"

"Oldest motive in the world. Cash." A little burst of laughter sounded over the line. "Jess Miller paid Leland in cash every Friday evening. Wife says Indian ranch hands always preferred cash to checks . . ." The unspoken idea hung in the quiet like a heavy weight: local bars prefer cash. "Besides," the detective hurried on, "that's probably the way of Jess's daddy, and his daddy before him. Old families have their own ways of doing things. Point is, the cashbox is gone."

"A lot of people must have known about the cash," Vicky said.

Mark Albert didn't say anything for a moment. Then: "There's something else. We got some good prints off the shotgun. They look like Leland's. We'll have confirmation in a few hours."

Vicky stared out the bedroom window at the dawn glowing red and gold in the eastern sky. Prints. Motive. Opportunity. Mark Albert had them all, but that didn't mean Leland Iron Wolf was guilty.

"When's the initial hearing?" she heard herself asking.

"Monday, one o'clock, county court."

"I want to talk to Leland right away."

"You know where to find him."

The metal security door slammed behind her as Vicky followed the blue-uniformed guard down the concrete hallway. A mixture of television noise, rap music, and ringing phones floated from the cell block at the far end of the hallway. Odors of detergent and stale coffee permeated the air. The guard unclipped a ring of keys from his belt, unlocked a metal door, and shoved it open. Vicky stepped into a small, windowless room. "Wait here," the guard ordered, closing the door.

Vicky dropped her briefcase on the table that took up most of the room. She shivered in the chill penetrating the pale-green concrete walls. Leland had been locked up how many hours now—two? three? He would be going crazy.

The door swung open. Leland stood in the doorway, eyes darting over the windowless walls, arms at his sides, hands clenched hard into fists. He had on a bright orange jumpsuit that looked a couple of sizes too large for his wiry frame. His black hair, shiny under the fluorescent ceiling light, was parted in the middle and caught in two braids that dropped down the front of the orange jumpsuit. He started into the room, shuffling, halting, glancing back.

Vicky held her breath, afraid he would turn around and hurl himself against the closed door. "Tell me what you know about Miller's death." She kept her voice calm, an effort to hold the young man in the present. She sat down and extracted a legal pad and pen from the briefcase.

Leland sank into the chair across from her. He was quiet a long moment, calling on something inside of him. Finally, he said, "Somebody shot him is all I know."

"He was alive when you left the ranch?"

Leland's head reared back. The ceiling light glinted in the dark eyes. "You don't believe me?"

"I had to ask." Silence hung between them a moment. "Where did you go?"

Leland shifted in the chair and shot a glance at the closed door. "Just drove around."

"Drove around?"

"I had some thinkin' to do."

Vicky waited. After a moment, Leland said, "I got the chance to manage a big spread down in Colorado. They need a real good, experienced cowboy, so a buddy of mine workin' there give the owner my name. I gotta decide if I'm gonna leave . . ." He exhaled a long, shuddering breath. "Grandfather don't have nobody but me, and he don't have much money, you know. If I go down to Colorado, it's gonna be real hard on him."

Vicky swallowed back the lump rising in her throat. Leland had just confirmed the motive. With several thousand dollars, Elton Iron Wolf could get along for a while and Leland could move away. She pushed on: "Did you stop anywhere?"

The young man was shaking his head. "I think best when I'm just movin', you know." A glance at the walls looming around them. "I drove up to Dubois and back. Got home about ten."

Vicky made a note on the pad. *Dubois. No alibi.* She looked up. "Look, Leland." She was searching for the words to soften the blow. "I'm going to level with you. Mrs. Miller says she saw you going into the barn just before her husband was killed. The detective says your fingerprints are probably on the shotgun."

A mixture of surprise and disbelief came into the young man's face. "My prints are all over that shotgun. I took it out a couple days ago after some coyotes been killin' the calves."

"Who knew you used the gun?" Vicky persisted.

"The boss's kid, Buddy. He rode out with me. Got a real kick outta watching me pick off a coyote. Helps out on the ranch when school's out. Pretty good cowboy for fifteen years old."

"Any other ranch hands?"

Leland gave his head a quick shake. "That's it. Me and the boss and sometimes the kid. We pretty much took care of things. Boss didn't like a lotta people around, pokin' into his business was the way he put it. Him and his wife and those two kids, they liked their privacy."

"Two kids?"

"Boy's got a sister, Julie. She's thirteen. Real pretty little thing. See 'em comin' down the road together after the school bus let 'em off. Just the two of 'em, like they was each other's best friend. Good kids. Real quiet like their dad."

"You said Jess Miller was mean."

Leland nodded. "Yeah, he could be mean all right, if he didn't like the job you was doin'. About the only time he had much to say was if he wanted to lay you out. Rest the time, he kept to hisself. Tended his own business."

Vicky could feel the jitters in her stomach: prominent rancher who minded his own business, close family, Indian ranch hand with fingerprints all over the murder weapon and a motive to help himself to the cashbox. Selecting the words carefully, she said, "You may have to stay in jail a while, Leland. Just until I can get to the bottom of this."

Leland blinked hard. "What're you gonna do?"

"You'll have to trust me," she said with as much confidence as she could muster.

The sounds of organ music resounded through the church as Vicky slipped into the back pew. Ranchers in cowboy shirts and blue jeans and businessmen filled the other pews. There were only a few women. Vicky recognized some of the mourners: the mayor, the chamber of commerce president, the owner of the steakhouse on Main Street, all friends of Jess Miller. She wondered if the murderer was among them. What had she expected to find by coming here? She was grasping, grasping for some way to clear Leland.

At the hearing, the county attorney had trotted out what he called "a preponderance of evidence," and she had been left to argue that there was some other explanation. "I look forward to hearing it," the judge had said. Then he'd denied bail and remanded Leland to the county jail.

Vicky exhaled a long breath and turned her attention to the Miller family in the front pew: the small woman dressed in black, a black lace veil draping her head, the thin-shouldered boy with sandy hair, the dark-haired girl throwing nervous glances from side to side.

The organ music stopped abruptly, leaving only the hushed sounds of whispering and shifting in the pews. A minister in a white robe mounted the pulpit, eyes trained on the family below. He cleared his throat into the microphone and began a flat, perfunctory talk: fine man in our community, cut down in his prime, loving wife and children, devastated by death. The heavens cried out for justice.

After the service concluded, Vicky kept her place, watching the mourners file past the family, nodding, shaking hands. Suddenly the boy wrenched himself sideways, and Vicky noticed the gray-haired woman approaching him. She bent over the pew, trying to get his attention, but he kept his head averted, as if the woman were not there. She moved tentatively toward the girl, then the mother. Both kept their heads down, and finally the woman moved away. She reached into a large black bag and pulled out a white handkerchief, which she dabbed at her eyes as she exited through a side door.

Vicky hurried out the front entrance and made her way around the side of the church to the parking lot. The woman was about to lower herself into a brown sedan. "Excuse me," Vicky called, walking over.

The woman swung around, surprise and fear mingling in her expression. She pulled the car door toward her, as if to put a shield between herself and the outside world.

"I didn't mean to startle you," Vicky said. "You must be a friend of the family."

The woman shot a nervous glance at the businessmen and cowboys filing toward the rows of cars and trucks in the lot. "I would say that family has few real friends," she said. "I came for the children." Slowly she reached a hand around the door. "Elizabeth Shubert. Lander High counselor."

"Vicky Holden." The other woman's hand was as smooth and cool as a sheet of paper. "I represent Leland Iron Wolf."

"I thought that might be the case." Elizabeth Shubert gave her head a slow shake. "I don't believe Leland is capable of murder."

"You know him?" Vicky heard the surprise in her voice.

"I knew him when he was at the high school. A fine boy."

"Mrs. Shubert . . ."

"Miss," the woman interrupted.

"Would you be willing to talk to me?"

The woman sank into the front seat and peered through the windshield. A line of vehicles waited to turn into the street. The hearse that had been parked in front of the church was pulling away. A black limousine followed, three heads bobbing in the backseat. "I shouldn't be talking to you," she said after a moment. "I must get back to school."

Vicky gripped the edge of the door to keep it from shutting. "Miss Shubert, Leland faces a first-degree murder charge. He's innocent." She hesitated. All she had was an instinct that this woman knew something. She plunged on: "Is there anything you can tell me, anything at all, that might help him?"

Elizabeth Shubert was quiet. She reached up and tucked a strand of gray hair into place, her eyes fixed on some point beyond the windshield. "Come to my house at four-thirty." She gave the address. "White house on the corner. You can't miss it."

Vicky leaned into the bell next to the blue-painted door. From inside came a muffled sound, like the tingling of a xylophone, followed by hurried footsteps. The door flung open. Elizabeth Shubert stood back in the shadow of the front hallway, allowing her gaze to roam up and down the street. "Come in, come in," she said, a hushed tone.

When they were seated in the living room, Vicky said, "I couldn't help but notice the way the family reacted as you extended your condolences."

Elizabeth Shubert picked up the flower-printed teapot on the table between them and poured the steaming brown liquid into two china cups. Handing a cup and saucer to Vicky, she said, "I'm sure they must blame me for . . . well, for what happened."

"For Jess Miller's murder?"

"Oh, no." The woman sat up straighter. One hand flew to her throat and unadorned fingers began crinkling the collar of her white blouse. "For what happened before. You see, I was worried about Buddy and Julie. Whenever there's a precipitous drop in grades and a change in personality, well, naturally, you wish to inquire as to the reason."

Vicky shifted forward. She held the other woman's gaze. "When did this occur?"

"Well, it's not as if they were brilliant students, you understand." Elizabeth Shubert made a little clicking noise with her tongue. "Average, I would say. But they were going along as usual until recently. Several teachers reported they were both flunking classes."

"What about the personality change?"

"Well, not so much the boy." The woman rested her eyes on a corner of the living room for a moment. "Buddy's always been a loner. Tends to his own business. Perhaps he seemed a little more withdrawn and morose lately, but, frankly, I attributed that to the poor report. The change was in Julie. Such a quiet, nice girl until . . ."

Vicky waited, one hand wrapped around the china cup in her lap.

"It's hard to explain," the woman went on. "Julie became very outgoing, I would say. Yes, very aggressive and pushy. You could hear her shouting in the halls. She was distracting in class, giggling and cutting up and generally making a nuisance of herself. She was sent to my office four times in the last two weeks. Well, I thought it was just an adolescent phase." The woman leaned forward and set her cup and saucer on the table. The china made a little rattling noise. "It was more than that."

"How so?"

"The way she flaunted herself. Deliberately provocative, I would say. The tightest, shortest skirts, the lowest-cut tops, that sort of thing." The woman looked away again, then brought her gaze back. "Believe me, girls can be very brazen these days, but this was not like Julie Miller. It was as if suddenly she had become someone else."

Vicky set her own cup and saucer on the table. "What did you do?"

"I'm not certain I did the right thing." The woman spoke slowly, remembering. "I called Mr. and Mrs. Miller last week and asked for a meeting. I was terribly concerned about the children, you see."

"Yes, of course. What did the parents say?"

"The parents? Well, Mrs. Miller said nothing. She remained silent through the entire meeting. She just sat there, never taking her eyes from her husband. He did all the talking. He was very upset. Accused me of violating their privacy. Said he would tend to his own children. If they were having problems, he would straighten them out, and I should stay out of their business. And that's not all." Elizabeth Shubert looked away again, pulling the memory out of a shadowed corner. "He threated to bring a lawsuit against me."

"A lawsuit!" Vicky felt a jolt of surprise. "On what possible grounds? That you were concerned about his children?"

"That I had defamed his family." The woman gave a little shudder. "It was ridiculous, of course. But I don't mind telling you, it frightened me. I don't want any trouble with the school district. You see, I'm due to retire next year, and I'm a woman of modest means." She glanced around the living room: the worn sofa and chairs, the faded doilies on the armrests, the gold carpet criss-crossed with gray pathways. "Mr. Miller was a well-respected man, and he was very angry. Unfortunately, he must have thought Buddy had told me something because . . ."

She stopped. Her hands were clasped now into a tight ball in her lap. "Oh, dear." A tremor had come into her voice. "I shouldn't be telling you this. It's exactly what Mr. Miller warned me against. I have no proof of anything." She gripped the armrests and started to lift herself out of the chair, a motion of dismissal.

"Please, Elizabeth." Vicky moved to the edge of her own chair. "What happened to Buddy after the meeting?"

The woman sat back into the cushions. A muscle twitched along the rim of her jawline. Finally, she said: "Mr. Miller punished the boy."

"You mean, he beat him?" A coldness rippled along Vicky's spine. In her mind, she saw the widow and mother, head lowered under a black lace veil. A silent woman. Had she finally had enough? Had she finally decided to protect her children?

"I have no proof," Elizabeth Shubert was saying. "But the boy was absent for two days after the meeting. When he came back, he had a note from his mother saying he'd been home with a cold. But I didn't believe it, not for a minute."

"Did you report this to social services?"

Elizabeth Shubert was rubbing her hands together now. "I took the steps I believed necessary. I called Buddy into my office. I told him of my suspicions. He said his father was a fine man, that I shouldn't say bad things about him, that his father would sue me for defaming the family. He used almost the same words his father had used, and I remember thinking, *This poor boy has been brainwashed.* But I had no proof. Nothing. Nothing." The woman shook her head; moisture pooled at the corners of her eyes. "Oh, I know I should have reported my suspicions, but what good would it have done? Jess Miller was an upstanding citizen from a very old family. No one would have believed me."

Vicky didn't say anything. She was wondering if Donna Miller had reached the same conclusion: no one could stop her husband.

The woman was crying softly now. "Excuse me," she said, half stumbling to her feet. She disappeared through an alcove. In a moment she was back, blowing her nose into a white handkerchief.

Vicky got to her feet. "You must tell the sheriff what you've told me," she said.

"Oh, I did." An aggrieved note came into the woman's voice. "I called the sheriff the minute I heard about the murder. Not that it did any good." She gave a little shiver.

"What do you mean?"

"I'm sure Mrs. Miller and the children denied everything. They probably said I was a meddling old lady. That's why they rebuffed me today at the church."

"What if . . . ," Vicky began, slowly giving voice to the shadowy idea at the back of her mind, "Donna Miller shot her husband to protect her children."

Elizabeth Shubert nodded. "That thought has been tormenting me."

Outside, Vicky sat behind the wheel of her Bronco trying to arrange the pieces into a picture that made sense: a well-respected man, a perfect family with a cancer eating at its heart, a mother who knew when Leland Iron Wolf would pick up his pay and who must have known he had recently used the shotgun. She could have waited until Leland drove off, then gone to the barn, shot her husband—in the heart, Albert had said. She wore gloves, so Leland's prints were the only prints on the gun. After she had hidden the cashbox, she had called the police. But who would believe it? Certainly not Mark Albert.

Vicky slammed one fist against the edge of the steering wheel. Leland Iron Wolf was about to spend the rest of his life in prison for a murder he didn't commit. He trusted her, and she had come up with nothing. Nothing but a sense of what had happened, a vague and unprovable theory. She rammed the key into the ignition. The engine growled into life, and she pulled into the street, turned right, and headed west. She intended to pay a condolence call on the grieving family.

Vicky drove under the wooden arch with the letter M carved in the center. She passed the cars and trucks parked in front of the red-brick ranch house and stopped in the driveway that ran from the house to the barn. As she let herself out, she glanced about, then made her way to the front door.

"What do you want?" Donna Miller stood in the doorway, a small woman with sloped shoulders and sunken chest. She looked at Vicky out of red-rimmed eyes, the most notable feature in a narrow, plain face. Her hair was streaked with gray and brushed to one side, as if it had simply been put out of the way. She was still in the black dress she had worn to the church earlier. A hum of voices came from inside the house.

"I'd like to talk to you," Vicky said. She had already told the woman that she represented Leland Iron Wolf.

"I have nothing to say to you. I have guests." Donna Miller glanced over one shoulder at the knots of people floating past the entry. Vicky glimpsed Buddy and Julie standing together in the shadows near the staircase.

"I've spoken to Elizabeth Shubert," Vicky persisted.

"Elizabeth Shu . . ." The thin lips tightened on the name. "That woman has no right to . . ." Suddenly she moved backward. "Come in." As Vicky stepped inside, the woman nodded toward the door on the other side of the staircase. "We'll talk in there," she said. The boy and girl had disappeared.

The room was small, with a desk against one wall and two upholstered chairs pushed against the opposite wall. Thick, gauzy curtains at the window gave the air a grayish cast. Donna Miller closed the door and sank back against it. "I know the ugly rumors that woman has spread. The sheriff's looked into them and found them completely false."

"Mrs. Miller," Vicky began, struggling against the sense of hopelessness rising inside her. What did she expect? That this woman would incriminate herself? She pushed on: "Leland Iron Wolf has been charged with a murder we both know he did not commit."

"I don't know what you're talking about." There was a rigid calmness to the woman. She stared at Vicky out of gray, blank eyes. "The sheriff has conducted a thorough investigation. He has arrested my husband's murderer."

"What kind of man was your husband?" Vicky asked, taking a different tack.

The woman blinked, as if she were trying to register the meaning of the question. "He was a very fine man. Ask anyone in the area. He was well respected." She tilted her head toward the closed door and the muffled sound of conversations coming from the main part of the house.

"What about your children?"

"My children? They're very well adjusted, ask anyone." Another tilt of the head toward the door. "They were fortunate to grow up on the ranch. They're very close. They never needed other friends. They had each other."

"How did your husband treat them?"

"What right do you have to ask these questions?" Donna Miller said, a shrillness in the tone that seemed to surprise her. She straightened herself against the door. "He was wonderful to the children, of course. He protected them. He protected all of us in our kingdom." One hand fluttered into the room. "He always called the ranch our kingdom where we could do things our own way." A waviness had come into her voice, a hint of tears. "We could live the way we wanted, with no outsiders telling us what we could do."

Vicky waited for the woman to go on, but Donna Miller had sunk into silence. At any moment, Vicky knew, the woman would tell her to leave. She took a chance: "He abused the children, didn't he? He beat your son. And your daughter?" Vicky caught her breath, a sharp lump in her chest. *Such a nice quiet girl. A complete change in personality.* "What did he do to your daughter, Mrs. Miller?"

"That woman has no right to speak such filth."

"You decided it had to end," Vicky said. "You wanted to protect your children."

"No!" The word came like a cry of agony from a lonely, faraway place. "Go away. Go away and leave us alone."

Suddenly the door swung open against the woman. She stumbled, off balance, and Vicky grabbed her elbow, steadying her. Buddy stood in the doorway, a tall, gangly boy with light hair flopping over his forehead. Behind him was Julie in a tight, black dress with a neckline that dipped into the cleft of round, firm breasts. The boy reached back, grabbed his sister's hand and pulled her into the room. Then, he closed the door.

Turning to his mother, he said, "What's going on? I seen this lady talking to Miss Shubert in the church parking lot. Is she a cop?"

The mother shook her head. "This is Leland's lawyer. She's just getting ready to leave. You and Julie go on out and talk to people."

"Don't you worry, Mother. I'll take care of this. I'll protect you now, just like I told ya." The boy stepped forward, shielding both women. His eyes fixed on Vicky's. "That Indian killed my father and he's gonna get what's comin' to him. You best be goin' now."

Vicky stared at the boy, the narrowed shoulders pulled square, the chin jutting forward in shaky confidence. She had it all wrong. It wasn't Donna Miller who had killed her husband, it was the son. Not until afterward, after the terrible deed had been done and Jess Miller lay dying in the barn office, did his wife summon the courage to protect her child. And now, Vicky realized, her only hope was that Buddy would insist upon protecting his mother.

"I know what happened, Buddy," she said, choosing the words carefully, threading a pathway for him to follow to a logical conclusion. "Your mother killed your father, didn't she?"

A little cry of anguish came from the woman. Vicky pushed on: "She said she saw Leland going to the barn, but that's a lie. It was dark at eight o'clock, and there are no lights between the house and barn. The sheriff is putting it all together. He's talked to Miss Shubert."

The woman was sobbing now, and Julie had dropped her face into both hands. Moisture seeped through the girl's slim fingers. The boy turned toward them. "Don't worry," he said again, a tremor in his voice. "I'll take care of you."

Slowly he turned back. He pushed back the hank of hair that had fallen forward. A vein pulsated in the center of his forehead. "Me, I could take it, 'cause I'm a man," he said. "But he was always hitting Mom, see, and she's just a little lady. Then he started . . ."

He hesitated. His eyes went blank, as if he could no longer take in the reality. "He started hurting Julie, see. And no sheriff or social worker was gonna come out here and tell Jess Miller to stop. Nobody's gonna tell Jess Miller what he can do in his kingdom. That's what he always said. So I took the shotgun that ranch hand had shot off, and I put a stop to it."

Vicky felt a sharp pang of relief and with it, something else—a hot rush of anger that burned at her cheeks and constricted her throat. "All of you were willing to send an innocent man to jail for the rest of his life," she said, the words choked with rage. She backed to the desk and picked up the phone. "I'm going to call the sheriff's office."

She punched in the numbers. From somewhere in the house came the muffled voices of mourners, the clap of a door shutting. She listened to the electronic buzz of the phone ringing on Mark Albert's desk, her eyes on the family huddled together, shoulders touching, hands entwined. Everything seemed suffused with sadness.

"Detective Albert." The voice boomed into her ear, jarring her back to herself.

"One moment," she said, barely controlling the tremble in her voice. She cupped one hand over the mouthpiece and, looking beyond the boy and girl, children yet, she caught the woman's eyes. "Mrs. Miller," she said, "you'll want to call a lawyer for your son."

Val McDermid

The Girl Who Killed Santa Claus

VAL MCDERMID has won numerous crime-writing awards, including the Crime Writers Association's Golden Dagger. She has created three distinctly different series and has of late begun writing longer stand-alone novels such as *A Place of Execution*, which are raising her to bestseller status in both England and America. In "The Girl Who Killed Santa Claus," published in *Ellery Queen's Mystery Magazine* in January, a young heroine does just that, with surprising results.

The Girl Who Killed Santa Claus

Val McDermid

It was the night before Christmas, and not surprisingly, Kelly Jane Davidson was wide awake. It wasn't that she wanted to be. It wasn't as if she believed in Santa and expected to catch him coming down the chimney onto the coal-effect gas fire in the living room. After all, she was nearly eight now.

She felt scornful when she thought back to last Christmas when she'd still been a baby, a mere six-year-old who still believed that there really was an elf factory in Lapland where they made the toys; that there really was a team of reindeer who magically pulled a sleigh across the skies and somehow got round to all the world's children with sackloads of gifts; that she could really write a letter to Santa and he'd personally choose and deliver her presents.

Of course, she'd known for ages before then that the fat men in red suits and false beards who sat her on their knees in an assortment of gaudy grottoes weren't the real Santa. They were just men who dressed up and acted as messengers for the real Father Christmas, passing on her desires and giving her a token of what would be waiting for her on Christmas morning.

She'd had her suspicions about the rest of the story, so when Simon Sharp had told her in the playground that there wasn't really a Santa Claus, she hadn't even felt shocked or shaken. She hadn't tried to argue, not like her best friend Sarah, who had gone red in the face and looked like she was going to burst into tears. But it was obvious when you thought about it. Her mum was always complaining when she ordered things from catalogs and they sent the wrong thing. If the catalog people couldn't get a simple order right, how could one fat man and a bunch of elves get the right toys to all the children in the world on one night?

So Kelly Jane had said goodbye to Santa without a moment's regret. She might have been more worried if she hadn't discovered the secret of the airing cupboard. Her mum had been downstairs making the tea, and Kelly Jane had wanted a pillowcase to make a sleeping bag for her favorite doll. She'd opened the airing cupboard and there, on the top shelf, she'd seen a stack of strangely shaped plastic bags. They were too high for her to reach, but she'd craned her neck and managed to see the corner of some packaging inside one of the bags. Her heart had started to pound with excitement, for she'd immediately recognized the familiar box that she'd been staring at in longing in the toy shop window for weeks.

She'd closed the door silently and crept back to her room. Her mum had said, "Wait and see what Santa brings you," as if she was still a silly baby, when she'd asked for the new Barbie doll. But here it was in the house.

Later, when her mum and dad were safely shut in the living room watching the telly, she'd crept out of bed and used the chair from her bedroom to climb up and explore further. It had left her feeling very satisfied. Santa or no Santa, she was going to have a great Christmas.

Which was why she couldn't sleep. The prospect of playing with her new toys, not to mention showing them off to Sarah, was too exciting to let her drift off into dreams. Restless, she got out of bed and pulled the curtains open. It was a cold, clear night, and in spite of the city lights, she could still see the stars twinkling, the thin crescent of the moon like a knife cut in the dark blue of the sky. No sleigh or reindeers, though.

She had no idea how much time had passed when she heard the footsteps. Heavy, uneven thuds on the stairs. Not the light-footed tread of her mum, nor the measured footfalls of her dad. These were stumbling steps, irregular and clumsy, as if someone was negotiating unfamiliar territory.

Kelly Jane was suddenly aware how cold it had become. Her arms and legs turned to gooseflesh, the short hair on the back of her neck prickling with unease. Who—or what—was out there, in her house, in the middle of the night?

She heard a bump and a muffled voice grunting, as if in pain. It didn't sound like anyone she knew. It didn't even sound human. More like an animal. Or some sort of monster, like in the stories they'd read at school at Halloween. Trolls that ate little children. She'd remembered the trolls, and for weeks she'd taken the long way home to avoid going over the ring-road flyover. She knew it wasn't a proper bridge like trolls lived under, but she didn't want to take any chances. Sarah had agreed with her, though Simon Sharp had laughed at the pair of them. It would have served him right to have a troll in his house on Christmas Eve. It wasn't fair that it had come to her house, Kelly Jane thought, trying to make herself angry to drive the fear away.

It didn't work. Her stomach hurt. She'd never been this scared, not even when she had to have a filling at the dentist. She wanted to hide in her wardrobe, but she knew it was silly to go somewhere she could be trapped so easily. Besides, she had to know the worst.

On tiptoe, she crossed the room, blinking back tears. Cautiously, she turned the door handle and inched the door open. The landing light was off, but she could just make out a bulky shape standing by the airing cupboard. As her eyes adjusted to the deeper darkness, she could see an arm stretching up to the top shelf. It clutched the packages and put them in a sack. Her packages! Her Christmas presents!

With terrible clarity, Kelly Jane realized that this was no monster. It was a burglar, pure and simple. A bad man had broken into her house and was stealing her Christmas presents! Outrage flooded through her, banishing fear in that instant. As the bulky figure put the last parcel in his sack and turned back to the stairs, she launched herself through the door and raced down the landing, crashing into the burglar's legs just as he took the first step. "Go away, you bad burglar!" she screamed.

Caught off balance, he crashed head over heels down the stairs, a yell of surprise splitting the silence of the night like an axe slicing through a log.

Kelly Jane cannoned into the banisters and rebounded onto the top step, breathless and exhilarated. She'd stopped the burglar! She was a hero!

But where were her mum and dad? Surely they couldn't have slept through all of this?

She opened their bedroom door and saw to her dismay that their bed was empty, the curtains still wide open. Where were they? What was going on? And why hadn't anyone sounded the alarm?

Back on the landing, she peered down the stairs and saw a crumpled heap in the hallway. He wasn't moving. Nervously, she decided she'd better call the police herself.

She inched down the stairs, never taking her eyes off the burglar in case he suddenly jumped up and came after her.

Step by careful step, she edged closer.

Three stairs from the bottom, enough light spilled in through the glass panels in the front door for Kelly Jane to see what she'd really done.

There, in the middle of the hallway, lay the prone body of Santa Claus. Not moving. Not even breathing.

She'd killed Santa Claus.

Simon Sharp was wrong. Sarah was right. And now Kelly Jane had killed him.

With a stifled scream, she turned tail and raced back to her bedroom, slamming the door shut behind her. Now she was shivering in earnest, her whole body trembling from head to foot. She dived into bed, pulling the duvet over her head. But it made no difference. She felt as if her body had turned to stone, her blood to ice. She couldn't stop shaking, her teeth chattering like popcorn in a pan.

She'd killed Santa Claus.

All over the world, children would wake up to no Christmas presents because Kelly Jane Davidson had murdered Santa. And everyone would know who to blame, because his dead body was lying in her hallway. Until the day she died, people would point at her in the street and go, "There's Kelly Jane Davidson, the girl who murdered Christmas."

Whimpering, she lay curled under her duvet, terrible remorse flooding her heart. She'd never sleep again.

But somehow, she did. When her mum threw open the door and shouted, "Merry Christmas!" Kelly Jane was sound asleep. For one wonderful moment, she forgot what had happened. Then it came pouring back in and she peered timidly over the edge of the duvet at her mum. She didn't seem upset or worried. How could she have missed the dead body in the hall?

"Don't you want your presents?" her mum asked. "I can't believe you're still in bed. It's nine o'clock. You've never slept this late on Christmas morning before. Come on, Santa's been!"

Nobody knew that better than Kelly Jane. What had happened? Had the reindeer summoned the elves to take Santa's body away, leaving her presents behind? Was she going to be the only child who had Christmas presents this year? Reluctantly, she climbed out of bed and dawdled downstairs behind her mum, gazing in worried amazement at the empty expanse of the hall carpet.

She trailed into the living room, feet dragging with every step. There, under the tree, was the usual pile of brightly wrapped gifts. Kelly Jane looked up at her mum, an anxious frown on her face. "Are these all for me?" she asked. Somehow, it felt wrong to be rewarded for killing Santa Claus.

Her mum grinned. "All for you. Oh, and there was a note with them as well." She handed Kelly Jane a Christmas card with a picture of a reindeer on the front.

Kelly Jane took it gingerly and opened it. Inside, in shaky capital letters, it read, "Don't worry. You can never kill me. I'm magic. Happy Christmas from Santa Claus."

A slow smile spread across her face. It was all right! She hadn't murdered Santa after all!

Before she could say another word, the door to the kitchen opened and her dad walked in. He had the biggest black eye Kelly Jane had ever seen, even on the telly. The whole of one side of his face was all bruised, and his left arm was encased in plaster. "What happened, Dad?" she asked, running to hug him in her dismay.

He winced. "Careful, Kelly, I'm all bruised."

"But what happened to you?" she demanded, stepping back.

"Your dad had a bit too much to drink at the office party last night," her mum said hastily. "He had a fall."

"But I'm going to be just fine. Why don't you open your presents?" he said, gently pushing Kelly Jane towards the tree.

As she stripped the paper from the first of her presents, her mum and dad stood watching. "That'll teach me to leave you alone in the house on Christmas Eve," her mum said softly.

Her dad tried to smile, but gave up when the pain kicked in. "Bloody Santa suit," he said. "How was I to know she'd take me for a burglar?"

Susanna Gregory

The Trebuchet Murder

SUSANNA GREGORY'S historical mysteries with Dr. Matthew Bartholomew are marked by clear, concise writing; a fascinating historical period (the fourteenth century); and engaging insights into how crimes were solved in that period. Gregory has written several other books, both fiction and nonfiction. She is presently doing research on marine pollution at Cambridge University, which is where she completed her Ph.D. "The Trebuchet Murder," which first appeared in *Mystery Through the Ages*, has Dr. Bartholomew trying to figure out which of three candidates for a university position would want it badly enough to kill for it.

The Trebuchet Murder

Susanna Gregory

ELY HALL AT THE UNIVERSITY OF CAMBRIDGE, 1380.

Brother Edmund set down his pen and used both hands to rub his aching back. As Prior Richard's secretary, it was Edmund's duty to make notes on the meeting currently taking place in Richard's chamber. The meeting comprised a trio of eager young men and Richard himself, and had been going on all morning. Edmund was tired of writing down questions and answers, his eyes stung from the smoking candle, and his shoulders were cramped from hunching over his work. The clerk glared at the three young men, as though they were personally responsible for his discomfort.

The young men in question had applied to Ely Hall in the hope of being appointed its next Professor of Theology. A month before, old Brother Henry had choked on his dinner and died, leaving his colleagues not only shocked by the suddenness of his death, but a teacher short in the middle of term. Therefore, Prior Richard, Ely Hall's warden, was obliged to find a replacement as quickly as possible.

Ely Hall was the college at the University of Cambridge where the Benedictine Order sent its most promising students, and Edmund knew that Richard was taking his responsibilities very seriously; it would not do to appoint the wrong man. The grey-haired but still energetic prior grilled the young hopefuls relentlessly, probing the quickness of their minds and their ability to grasp complex arguments under pressure. The candidates looked as exhausted by the interrogation as Edmund felt, but the clerk knew that Richard was conscientious, and that he was simply working hard to ensure the college he loved appointed the best man.

The prior paused, leaning back in his chair to allow the three men to draw breath and collect their thoughts. Taking the opportunity to stand and flex his sore shoulders, Edmund studied the candidates as they sat uneasily on the hard wooden bench in front of him.

First, there was Brother Luke, a slightly balding fellow in his late twenties, who already had the soft, dissipated appearance resulting from too many good dinners. His face was dominated by protuberant blue eyes, and his manner was gentle and almost diffident. Luke had penned two short essays on creationism that had been favorably received by his fellow academics, but Edmund was more impressed that the Archbishop of Canterbury had written to Richard personally, to say that Luke showed great promise as a scholar and should be given the chance to prove himself at Ely Hall.

The second candidate was a Frenchman, Brother Jean, whose books were well known, even by undergraduates. His long, awkward limbs and large, bony hands made him seem ungainly, an appearance accentuated by the fact that the Benedictine habit he wore was rather too small for him. It was also the blackest garment that Edmund had ever seen, and he supposed Jean had ordered it re-dyed especially for his interview, but that the dyer had done a poor job. At breakfast that morning, Jean had revealed a wry sense of humor that Edmund found amusing. The clerk hoped Richard would choose Jean over the other two.

Finally, there was Brother Bravin, who sniffed constantly and was always wiping his long, dripping nose on a piece of linen. Despite his unprepossessing appearance, Bravin preened like a peacock. He was fastidiously clean, and his immaculate habit fitted him perfectly, a stark contrast to Jean's. As far as Edmund could tell, Bravin had no qualifications at all that rendered him suitable for the post. He had written nothing of note, and his replies to Richard's probing questions were hesitant and superficial. And there was the letter of recommendation he had brought with him from his abbot, in which the latter praised Bravin's genius and worth. Edmund regularly corresponded with the abbot over business matters and knew very well that the signature at the bottom of Bravin's testimonial had been forged: it was obvious that Bravin had written the glowing letter himself.

Richard did not allow them respite for long, and was soon back to his questioning. But eventually, when Edmund was so tired and stiff from writing that his whole body seemed to burn with fatigue, Richard indicated that the ordeal was over, and summoned a lay brother to conduct the three candidates to the refectory for some much needed refreshment. When they had gone, Richard slumped in his chair and rubbed his eyes. His normally neat hair was awry, and he looked weary and dispirited. Flexing stiff fingers, Edmund poured him some wine.

"I wish Brother Henry had not choked on those oysters," the prior said, as he took a substantial swallow from the goblet. "Then I would not be in this predicament."

Edmund was surprised that Richard should consider appointing a new master as a "predicament."

"But Henry was old and was no longer a good teacher. His death has provided you with an opportunity to hire a younger, better man. And what a choice! Jean is already famous for his excellent scholarship, while Luke comes recommended by the Archbishop of Canterbury himself. Either one will be an asset to Ely Hall."

Richard gave a smile that was without humor. "True. But I am obliged to offer the position to Bravin."

Edmund's jaw dropped in horror. "But why? He is no scholar, and, as I told you last night, I am sure he forged that letter from his abbot."

Richard's smile became a grimace. "Bravin may not be scholarly, but he is cunning. He went to wealthy Catherine Deschalers, who provides Ely Hall with much of its funding, and ingratiated himself with her. We are obliged to take her wishes into consideration."

"Then tell her Bravin would not be good for Ely Hall," said Edmund, failing to see why Richard should listen to the demands of the forceful but often misguided Catherine. Everyone knew she changed her mind more rapidly and frequently than the direction of the wind, and Edmund was sure she could be persuaded to accept Jean or Luke instead. "She will want what is best for the institution that costs her so much money each year. Tell her Bravin is a fraud."

"I tried," said Richard wearily. "But Bravin anticipated me. He had already spun her some tale about an illness that left his abbot without the use of his right hand, hence the difference in the signatures that you observed."

"Then we will have to rely on Brother Thomas to help us," said Edmund, thinking fast.

"Thomas is the bishop's agent, and the bishop will not want a man like Bravin appointed. I dislike Thomas because he is greedy and ambitious, but even *he* would not approve of a forger elected to Ely Hall."

Richard finished his wine, then held out his goblet to be refilled. "Again, Bravin anticipated me. He promised Thomas preferential treatment for any students he sent to Ely Hall, and even intimated that he would make such students' examinations easier, to ensure their success."

Edmund was shocked. "But we are a reputable institution. We do not want accusations of favoritism and cheating levelled at us!"

Richard laid a comforting hand on Edmund's shoulder, then walked to the window. Edmund followed him, and they stood side by side to gaze into the Market Square below. It was a fine spring day. The sky was blue, dotted with bright white clouds, and the market was alive with activity as vendors shouted the prices of their wares: chickens, cloth, wine, goats, bread and ribbons.

"You are right, Edmund," said Richard softly. "But my hands are bound by Catherine and her money and by Thomas and his influence with the bishop. Bravin will be our next Professor of Theology."

Edmund continued to gaze out of the window. Suddenly, the colors of the market did not seem so vibrant, and the warmth went out of the dancing sunlight. It was a poor world, he thought, when worthy men like Luke and Jean were thwarted by liars and frauds like Bravin, and good, upright men like Richard were powerless to prevent it from happening.

The following day, thick grey clouds covered the sky, promising rain. Edmund attended church, then walked home in a gloomy frame of mind, thinking about the machinations of Bravin and the damage his appointment would do to Ely Hall.

As he approached the college, he saw Prior Richard talking with two people. He recognized the bald head and the false smile of Thomas, the bishop's man, while the other person was the wealthy Catherine Deschalers. Catherine was a thin, big-boned woman, whose fortune allowed her to indulge her taste for bright clothes; that day she wore a scarlet cloak edged with ermine.

"The decision is made," Thomas announced as Edmund drew closer. "We think Bravin is the best candidate. You will draw up the appropriate deeds appointing him today, and we will tell him the good news when they are ready."

"On what grounds do you choose Bravin?" demanded Edmund, ignoring the warning glance shot at him by Richard for his impertinence. "Jean is a brilliant scholar, while Luke comes recommended by the Archbishop of Canterbury. How can Bravin compare to them?"

"He is our choice," replied Thomas sharply. "He has also promised to favor any students I send him. The bishop will like that, I am sure."

"And I think he will make a better professor than the others," added Catherine. "He has also promised to teach me to read—something you have never offered to do."

Before Edmund could say he would teach her himself if she would reconsider her decision, she had raised the hem of her skirts above the muck of the High Street and flounced away. He watched her go, a tall, pinched woman wrapped in her billowing scarlet cloak. He opened his mouth to plead with Thomas, but fell silent when the door opened and the three candidates emerged. He hated seeing the nervous anticipation on the faces of Luke and Jean, and felt a surge of contempt when he saw the secretive smile that played around the corners of Bravin's mouth, as if the man already knew he had won. Bravin dabbed his ever-dipping nose fussily, and addressed Richard.

"You promised to show us around Cambridge this morning, Father. I would like to see the town that may become my home."

"I have a headache," said Richard sharply. Edmund knew the prior never suffered from headaches, and realized that he simply could not bear to spend time with the gloating Bravin and the two men who were to be disappointed.

"And I am rather busy for walking today," said Thomas. He smiled at Bravin. "But visit me later, and I will answer any questions you might have."

Edmund saw Luke and Jean draw their own conclusions from that exchange. It was obvious that some arrangement had been made between Bravin and the bishop's man, and Jean and Luke were too intelligent not to guess what. Luke's rounded features broke into a worried frown, while Jean pursed his lips in disapproval.

"When might we expect a decision about the appointment?" he asked coolly. "Today?"

Thomas nodded. "Later today."

"Good," said Luke with a wan smile. "The waiting is the hardest part. But it would be worth the anxiety if I were successful: a post like this would give me the opportunity to write something truly worthwhile."

"I prefer teaching," said Jean, almost wistfully. "There is something noble about taking a new mind, then opening it to the wonders of learning."

Bravin regarded him in supercilious amusement. "Anyone with any sense would delegate teaching to his senior students, thus leaving him time to do what interests him. That is what all the other masters do."

"Not all," said Edmund, nettled by his attitude. "Prior Richard does his own teaching."

"Prior Richard will soon retire," said Bravin carelessly. "And then Ely Hall will be under the control of younger, abler men who will change it for the better."

Edmund was appalled by Bravin's brazen confidence, and was not pleased when Richard issued a curt order that Edmund should show the visitors the sights of Cambridge.

"We have heard a lot about the colleges, and would like to see them for ourselves," said Luke shyly, when Edmund hesitated, no more happy with the prospect of Bravin's company than Richard had been.

"And the libraries," added Jean eagerly. "We would like to see the libraries."

"I would rather see the taverns," said Bravin drolly. "I imagine that is where most of the important business is conducted."

"Show them the libraries, Edmund," said Richard, giving Bravin a glance of disapproval as he walked away.

Reluctantly, Edmund led Bravin, Luke and Jean along the High Street, pointing out the grand edifices that formed Cambridge's powerful colleges. King's Hall was large and magnificent, Michaelhouse small and elite, Gonville shabby and sprawling. Among them were the religious foundations, and friars belonging to the Dominican, Franciscan, Gilbertine and Carmelite orders scurried along the dirty streets as they went to and from their lectures. Pardoners and tradesmen mingled among them, along with the rough soldiers who prevented the unruly scholars from fighting with the equally quarrelsome townsfolk.

Eventually, Edmund's tour led them to the castle, which dominated the northern part of the town. By then, the day had grown greyer, as if it were matching Edmund's mood. The window shutters of the nearby houses were closed against the gloomy weather, and the only thing that moved under the bleak shadow of the fortress was a stray dog. Tucked below one of the sturdy curtain walls were the remains of a wooden contraption, forlorn and neglected.

"What is that?" asked Bravin, immediately interested in the heavy stone weights and the complex mess of ropes, pulleys and struts.

"A trebuchet," replied Edmund curtly. "It is an instrument of war, and not something to pique the interest of scholars—especially Benedictines, who have forsworn the bearing of arms."

"Nothing should be beyond the interest of a scholar," lectured Bravin pompously, running his hands over the lethal structure in a way that indicated he considered weapons more appealing than the libraries they had visited. "Tell me how it works."

Edmund sighed irritably, reluctant to spend longer in the company of the odious Bravin than was absolutely necessary. "A trebuchet has a long pivoted arm. As you can see, there is a basket of stones (the counterweight) at the short end, and a sling at the long end. To fire it, you fill the sling with missiles—"

"What kind of missiles?" demanded Bravin, fascinated.

"Anything," replied Jean before Edmund could answer, indicating that his learning had not been restricted to theology. "During a siege, a trebuchet can hurl stones at walls, or fling dead animals and burning pitch into castles."

"Really?" asked Bravin keenly. "How does the mechanism fire?"

"The weight of the stones at the short end makes the long arm fly through the air, discharging the sling's contents," answered Luke, not to be outdone by Jean. "It is actually just a big catapult."

Edmund frowned in puzzlement. "Why do you two know so much about weapons?"

"I was a soldier before I took the cowl," explained Jean.

"And, as an eldest son, I was taught such things before I relinquished my birthright to my younger brother," said Luke. "I understand how weapons work, but have no desire to see them in action. Spilt blood is something I find repellent; in fact, it makes me swoon." He blushed suddenly, and looked as if he wished he had not made such a confession to people he barely knew.

"Even a monk should not be so squeamish," said Bravin disdainfully, studying the old machine. "I am not."

Edmund had long since tired of Bravin's offensive company, and longed to return to the warm fire in Richard's chamber and be about his normal duties. The prior allowed him a good deal of freedom, but even so, there was a limit to the amount of time the secretary could spend with visitors when there was work to be done—and it would take him several hours to draft the document that would make Bravin's appointment legal.

"Be careful with that machine," he said, as he left them to explore the rest of the town for themselves. "It is unstable and should have been dismantled years ago."

"It is an interesting monument," contradicted Bravin. "It should not be hauled away and consigned to some peasant's fire. It should remain here to be an object of interest for visitors."

This began a spirited debate among the trio, and Edmund left them to it, retracing his steps along the High Street until he reached Ely Hall. Shortly after he arrived, it began to rain. Thatched roofs and plaster-fronted buildings turned dark and dirty in the deluge, and the leaves of trees shuddered and quivered as raindrops pattered onto them. Huge puddles formed across the muddy morass that was the High Street, and people scurried around them, anxious to complete their business and return to their homes. Edmund was glad to be indoors.

He spent the rest of the morning working on Bravin's letter of appointment. At noon, Thomas arrived to inform him that Catherine had been unable to restrain her pleasure regarding Bravin's success. She lived near the trebuchet, and had spotted Bravin inspecting it with Jean and Luke. She had hurried outside to tell Bravin of his good fortune. It was a tactless, inappropriate way of making the decision public, but typical of Catherine.

"I assume Bravin accepted the offer?" asked Edmund hoping that he had not.

"He did," replied Thomas. A sudden harshness in his voice caused Edmund to glance at him in surprise. "And he had even prepared a little speech laying out his conditions. He delivered it there and then, by the trebuchet."

"Conditions?" asked Edmund, puzzled. "What do you mean?"

"I mean that he has given his future duties some thought. I would not have recommended him had I known he would immediately demand more pay and a bigger room."

Edmund might have told the bishop's man that such behavior was only to be expected from a character like Bravin, but he held his tongue and Thomas left. A few moments later, Prior Richard returned from visiting some parishioners, wet and out of sorts. While Edmund mulled wine, he mentioned Catherine's indiscretion in telling Bravin the "good" news.

"I know," said Richard with a sigh. "I happened to see them when I was out. I guessed from her gestures and their reactions—Bravin's satisfaction and the others' dismay—that she had been unable to restrain herself."

"It is unfortunate," said Edmund. "I was still hoping she would see Bravin is unworthy, so we could have Jean instead."

Richard shook his head slowly. "It is too late. We are stuck with Bravin now."

A little later, in the early afternoon, a lay brother burst into the chamber. Richard's silver brows drew together in annoyance at this lack of manners.

"Father Prior!" the man gasped. "Bravin is dead."

"Dead?" asked Richard, startled.

"He was playing with the trebuchet when it collapsed and crushed him."

"So, we will not have a charlatan as our Professor of Theology after all," remarked Edmund, as he followed his prior out into the rain.

Bravin was indeed dead. The trebuchet's counterweight had been held in place with a badly rotted rope, and it appeared that Bravin's tampering had been the last straw: it had snapped, depositing the heavy basket of stones cleanly on Bravin's head. His skull had been squashed flat, although the one feature that had somehow survived the accident was the long nose with its reddened end. It dripped even in death, as rain pattered onto it and then slid into the bloodstained grass below.

"I told him to be careful," said Edmund, gazing dispassionately at the mess. "The machinery is old and dangerous; he should not have displayed such a morbid interest in it."

"Who found him?" asked Richard, crossing himself as he regarded Bravin with the compassion Edmund would have expected from a gentle man like the prior.

A scruffy soldier stepped forward. "Me. I often check the trebuchet to make sure vagrants are not hiding in it—it is a popular place for them to shelter when it rains."

"What happened?" asked Richard. "Did you witness the accident yourself?"

The soldier shook his head. "Bravin was alone, as far as I know, and all the shutters of the nearby houses are closed against the bad weather, so I doubt anyone saw it happen. But we all know the trebuchet is unstable: it is an accident just waiting for a curious and careless man."

Richard sketched a brief benediction at the corpse and instructed Edmund to remain with it while he returned to Ely Hall to summon pallbearers. Edmund knelt in the mud, trying to ignore the chilly rivulets of rain that ran down his neck as he muttered his prayers. It was not long before his colleagues arrived, bringing a crude stretcher and a sheet with which to cover the body. Edmund watched them struggle to free the corpse from its grisly position, then lift the virtually headless Bravin onto the stretcher. It was an ugly sight, and Edmund turned away, sickened.

As they walked along the High Street, one of Bravin's arms flopped out to trail lifelessly along the ground. Edmund stooped to ease it under the sheet again, but as he did so, he noted that the hands were filthy, and that under the dirt were moon-shaped crescents of blood. Since Bravin has been so fastidious, it was odd his hands should be muddy. Curious Edmund told the pall-bearers to stop and looked more closely.

It was clear to Edmund that Bravin had clawed at something or someone before he died. Since the load that landed on Bravin's head would have killed him instantly, Edmund could only suppose that such a struggle had happened before that—in which case, Bravin's death might not have been an accident after all. Edmund rubbed his chin thoughtfully. Who had fought with Bravin and why? The obvious answer was that it was Luke or Jean, angry because Bravin had inveigled himself into the post with his sly charm.

Leaving the others to carry Bravin to the church, Edmund walked back to the trebuchet and inspected it more closely. The ancient rope that had supported the counterweight had clean bright ends, indicating that they had been cut rather than had frayed, and the wet grass was more damaged than it should have been from a few people inspecting Bravin's remains. It seemed to Edmund that a fight had taken place, which had resulted in the ground's being churned. As he knelt to look at the rope again, something glinting in the grass caught his eye: it was a knife with a blade that was spotted with blood. Thoughtfully, Edmund put it in his scrip and walked to the church.

When he arrived, candles had been lit, filling the gloomy interior with a soft golden light. His colleagues had removed Bravin's wet habit, and were preparing to dress the body in a shroud. Edmund asked them to wait, then inspected the corpse for further signs of violence.

He found them in the shape of some small cuts in the middle of Bravin's back. At first, he thought they were injuries suffered when the trebuchet had collapsed, but then he matched the tiny triangular indentations to the blade of the knife he had found. There were also some red marks on Bravin's neck, and muddy patches at knee-height on his habit. While his colleagues listened in horror, Edmund told them what he had deduced: someone had seized Bravin from behind, which accounted for the red marks around his neck; Bravin had struggled and scratched his assailant, and it was therefore the killer's blood that formed the rings under Bravin's fingernails; and the muddy hands and knees indicated that Bravin had been shoved forward on the ground, leaving the killer to slash the rope that held the counterweight. Death occurred when the stones landed on his head.

One monk suggested a different scenario: that Bravin had been held at knifepoint first, then had escaped to struggle and the rope sliced by accident. Edmund shook his head, pointing out that Bravin had muddied his hands *after* he had scratched his assailant—the blood would not have been under his nails if they were already filled with dirt.

He left the monks preparing Bravin for his burial, and went to tell Richard about his discoveries. The gentle prior was predictably appalled.

"I do not believe you," he said in a hushed voice. "Bravin must have bloodied his nails when he tried to claw his way from under the trebuchet."

"He was killed instantly," Edmund pointed out. "His head was crushed almost flat."

"Then these so-called knife injuries occurred earlier—before he came to Cambridge."

Edmund shook his head. "They are fresh wounds."

Richard shuddered. "This is dreadful. We must tell the sheriff."

Edmund disagreed. "We do not want the townsfolk accusing us of harboring a murderer in our midst: there will be a riot. And we do not want that drunken sot of a proctor—the University's law and order officer—investigating, either. I will do it."

"You?" asked Richard startled. "Why you?"

"Because I will be discreet, and I will not harm Ely Hall's reputation," replied Edmund. "And anyway, we only have two possible culprits. It will not be too difficult to decide whether Luke or Jean is the guilty party."

"What makes you think it is either?" asked Richard.

"Because they are the ones who were wronged by Bravin's underhand tactics. Both are more deserving than Bravin, and they know it. Anger and frustration has led one of them to have his revenge."

"Then you had better solve this mystery quickly, Edmund," said Richard softly. "Because with Bravin dead, we will appoint Luke or Jean in his place, and I do not want a murderer teaching my students."

Edmund left Prior Richard and went to find Jean and Luke. Virtually all Ely Hall's students were lingering in the church to stare at the corpse of the man who had almost been appointed to teach them. Among the onlookers was Jean, who stared dispassionately at the sheeted figure. Edmund noticed that the rain had caused the black in his newly dyed habit to run, and that his bony hands were deeply stained with it. Jean saw that Edmund had observed the marks, and scrubbed self-consciously at them. Edmund thought the Frenchman should have paid more and had the garment dyed properly: it would have been cheaper in the long run.

"Bravin should not have shown such a perverse fascination with instruments of death," said Jean harshly, to hide his embarrassment. "God did not want such a man teaching his novices."

"There is nothing to suggest his death was God's work," replied Edmund. "Indeed, all the signs suggest he was murdered." He regarded Jean intently, trying to determine his reaction to such a statement. But the Frenchman merely nodded.

"Bravin was not a pleasant person."

"Where were you when he met his death?" asked Edmund bluntly.

Jean did not seem surprised by the question. "I was sitting alone in this church. I was disappointed by the decision to appoint him rather than me, and I wanted solitude."

"Were you disappointed enough to kill him?" asked Edmund.

Jean gave a half-smile. "Yes, I was, but I did not do it. Look elsewhere for your murderer, Edmund. But do it quickly. I leave Cambridge at dawn tomorrow."

There was no more to be said, so Edmund looked around for Luke. However, Luke was not among the spectators in the church. Edmund walked outside, and saw the portly monk perched on an ancient tombstone, oblivious of the drizzle that still fell. Luke's hands were unsteady, and his face pale and wan.

"You are the only Benedictine not gawking at Bravin's mortal remains," said Edmund, wondering why the man looked so ill. Was it his guilty conscience? "Why such a lack of curiosity? It is not every day you can view a man killed by such bizarre means."

"I have already told you that the sight of blood makes me weakheaded," replied Luke. "I could not look on such a sight without swooning; I feel sick even thinking about the manner of his death."

"He was murdered," said Edmund in a soft voice. "It seems someone did not want him to become our new theologian."

Luke nodded slowly. "I can see why. Catherine and Thomas clearly realized their mistake after appointing the man. You should have seen their faces when Bravin made his little speech accepting the post."

"They were pleased with their choice," said Edmund. "They wanted him."

"They were not pleased," contradicted Luke. "Bravin immediately declared he would show no favoritism to any students Thomas might send him, and then claimed he would be too busy to teach Catherine to read. After all they did to secure his appointment, I am not surprised one of them ordered him killed."

"You think Thomas or Catherine killed him?" asked Edmund, startled by this new information. Thomas had mentioned Bravin's speech, but he had failed to indicate that the contents had been personally objectionable.

Luke sighed. "You think that either Jean or I made an end of him. I confess, I would have enjoyed doing so. The man was one of the most unpleasant people I have ever met, but I would not have chosen a way that involved such a spillage of blood."

"Then where were you at the time of his murder?" asked Edmund, not sure what to believe.

"Walking alone by the river. I was disgusted that Ely Hall had chosen Bravin, and wanted to be alone. No one saw me, and I cannot prove I had no hand in his death. You will just have to believe me. But I recommend you look to Catherine or Thomas for your culprit. There is nothing so dangerous as a powerful person who finds he—or she—has been cheated."

Edmund walked away, his head bowed in thought. Whom should he believe? Jean and Luke had good reason to want Bravin dead, and both had demonstrated a knowledge of the trebuchet and its workings: either would have known which rope to cut to ensure Bravin was killed. And neither man had an alibi for the crucial time. Was Luke exaggerating his dislike of blood? Was he pale because he had killed a man, not because he had an aversion to the sight and thought of violence? Why did Jean plan to leave Cambridge so soon? Was he merely leaving a place that had disappointed him, or was he fleeing the scene of his crime before justice could be done?

And what about Luke's claim—that Catherine and Thomas's favored candidate had already turned against them and had no intention of giving them what they thought they were owed? Had one of them killed him? Edmund decided there was only one way to find out, and walked briskly along the High Street to Catherine's house.

When Edmund was admitted to Catherine's solar—a pleasant chamber on the upper floor with glass windows and a merrily crackling fire in the hearth—he found Thomas already there, comfortably seated on a cushioned bench near the fire. Prior Richard was there, too, giving them the grim details that Edmund had uncovered regarding the manner of Bravin's death.

"It is a pity so many people know Bravin was murdered," Thomas was saying. "It would have been best for everyone if we could have buried him quickly and claimed he had a fatal seizure when given the good news."

"It would have been wrong to hide such a wicked crime," said Richard sternly. "Edmund is already hunting for the killer, although I confess I am not optimistic about his chances of success. I have questioned the people who live near the trebuchet whether they saw or heard anything, but they all claim the rain had driven them indoors with the shutters fastened."

"So no one witnessed anything?" asked Edmund, disappointed. "What about you, Catherine? Did you hear anything? Your house is very close to the scene of the murder."

"I can tell you nothing," she replied. "I saw Bravin with the two other candidates at the trebuchet this morning, and I desperately wanted to tell him of his success. With Thomas at my heels, I rushed out to tell him, but saw no killers lurking."

"You should have waited before you gave him the news," admonished Thomas. "Then we might have learned what kind of man he was before we made our final decision."

"So I see, with hindsight," retorted Catherine irritably. "But before his little speech, I thought him a charming man. However, as soon as he learned of his success, he showed his true colors."

"He made it clear he would renege on the promises he made us," explained Thomas, turning to Richard and Edmund. "We would have remonstrated with him, but it started to rain, and we had no wish to be wet as well as insulted. We left him admiring the trebuchet with Jean and Luke."

"And that was the last you saw of him?" asked Edmund.

"Yes," snapped Catherine. "Why? Do you think we killed him?"

"The killer chose a good place for his crime," said Thomas, ignoring her outburst. "He selected a lonely spot on a bleak day when most people were indoors. He is a clever man."

"Or woman," said Edmund.

"I confess to loathing the man after his nasty words," said Catherine, "but I did not kill him."

"How long was it after his speech that Bravin was killed?" asked Edmund, wondering whether Catherine had time to recruit a killer—an easy feat given the number of mercenaries who haunted the town—or whether her temper had led her to kill him herself. She was a large woman, bigger than Bravin, and certainly strong enough to fight and overpower him.

"Almost immediately," replied Thomas. He saw Edmund's eyebrows rise questioningly, and hastened to explain how he knew such a thing. "At least, I imagine so. It was not long after we left Bravin that we heard the soldier raise the alarm when he found the body."

Was Thomas telling the truth? Edmund wondered. Or had he and Catherine gone together to kill Bravin? Had Thomas fought with Bravin until Catherine had drawn the knife? He looked at Thomas's cloak, carefully folded across the bench. He saw it was damp, but could not tell how long the dampness had been there. As he left the solar, he surreptitiously took a fold of Catherine's distinctive scarlet cloak between his finger and thumb, and had one answer at least. He walked back to Ely Hall with his head bowed in thought.

He had four suspects for the murder. Luke and Jean wanted Bravin dead because they thought they should be Professor of Theology. Meanwhile, Thomas and Catherine were certainly capable of dispatching a man who had crossed them. Edmund rubbed his temples tiredly. Unless someone confessed, he suspected there was no hope of ever solving the crime. And if he were unsuccessful, it was possible that a murderer would come to live at Ely Hall, or that a murderer would play a major role in the way it was run. Neither possibility was attractive to Edmund. He took a deep breath, and began to review all his evidence again, piece by piece, until he began to detect a pattern.

Before he made his thoughts public, Edmund needed to revisit Bravin's corpse in the church, and he wanted to ask a few questions of the people who lived near the trebuchet. Ignoring the objections of the monks who were keeping vigil by Bravin's remains, he inspected the hands and arms closely. Then he visited the houses, hoping that Richard may have missed someone, and that there might yet be a witness to the events that took place at the trebuchet that day.

By the time he had his answers, it was dusk, and vendors desperate to sell the last of their wares before nightfall jostled and pushed him as he returned to Ely Hall. He was so engrossed in his thoughts that he barely noticed them. He barely noticed Thomas either and had walked right past the bishop's man before he heard the insistent greeting. Thomas was buying a pie from a baker, reaching out to inspect them before he made his purchase.

"I was saying that this has worked out rather well," said Thomas loudly, apparently offended at being ignored by a mere secretary. As he stretched out one hand to pass a coin to the baker, his wide sleeve fell away, giving Edmund the opportunity to inspect his arm. The clerk smiled to himself; Thomas was not as clever as he imagined. "Bravin's behavior made it clear that we were wrong to have chosen him. Now he is dead, we can have Luke or Jean."

"We told you not to appoint him," said Edmund. "He was a cheat, who wrote his own testimonial and forged the signature of his abbot. How could you have considered such a man in the first place?"

"We only had your word that the signature was false," said Thomas stiffly, unwilling to shoulder too much blame for the near-disaster. "To begin with, he seemed an amiable man who would prove to be exactly what we wanted."

"A puppet," said Edmund harshly. "Just like poor Brother Henry, his predecessor."

"Yes," said Thomas bluntly, eating his pie. "It is a pity those oysters killed Henry. He was an excellent man to approach for favors." He inclined his head and went on his way, leaving Edmund staring after him thoughtfully.

Much later that night, when most of Ely Hall's residents were sleeping, Edmund sat with Richard in the prior's office. They held goblets of mulled wine in their hands, and their feet were stretched towards the fire as they sat in companionable silence.

"So, how have you fared in tracing our killer?" asked Richard, staring into the yellow flames that leaped in the hearth.

"I know his identity, and I know how he committed the crime," replied Edmund evenly.

Richard stared at him in astonishment. "Who? How?"

"The killer grabbed Bravin around the neck, then drew a knife. The culprit has scratches on his arms, where Bravin struck out with his nails."

"We all saw the blood on Bravin's fingers," mused Richard. "He must have fought hard."

"Like a cat," agreed Edmund. "But he was subdued when the killer produced a knife. Then the killer pushed him towards the trebuchet, prodding him in the back with the blade. When Bravin was below the trebuchet, the killer shoved him forward, so that he fell on his hands and knees, which became muddy. Finally, the killer cut the rope that held the counterweight. Death was instant."

"I suppose that is one mercy," said Richard. "He did not suffer. So, who is the killer? Luke or Jean?"

"I was obliged to add two more suspects to my list," said Edmund, declining to reveal his conclusions before he had outlined his reasoning. "Thomas and Catherine also had cause to want Bravin dead."

"Thomas and Catherine are the killers?" asked Richard, appalled. "But that cannot be true! I have known them for years! You have made some dreadful error in your investigation."

"The killer could not have been Jean. He had dyed his habit for his interview, but the rain made the cheap dye leak. Jean's hands were covered in the stuff, and had the killer been him, then some dye would have been present on Bravin's body. This afternoon, I inspected Bravin's corpse very carefully, but there was nothing: Jean is innocent."

"Luke, then?" asked Richard. "He did it."

"Luke has a strong aversion to blood. I thought he had feigned it, so that we would not suspect him, but he confessed to his weakness *before* Catherine had told Bravin of his success. That means he had admitted to his weak stomach *before* he had a motive to kill Bravin."

"Perhaps he anticipated Bravin's victory, and was already plotting his murder," suggested Richard. "He may be lying about this fear of blood."

Edmund disagreed. "He was white and shaking when I found him outside the church, because even the thought of Bravin's crushed head made him sick. But more revealing is the fact that his weakness forced him to give up his inheritance, because he knew he could not protect his estates by fighting. I imagine that was why he became a monk. His fear of blood is real enough: it was responsible for the loss of his birthright."

Richard sipped his wine. "So you are left with Thomas and Catherine. But Thomas is a confidant of the bishop, while Catherine is . . . well, a woman."

"I felt Catherine's cloak—that horrible scarlet thing—when I visited her this afternoon. It started to rain after Bravin made his speech but before he died. If she had killed him, her cloak would have been wet. It was quite dry."

"Thomas, then?" asked Richard.

"Thomas's cloak was damp, but he had walked to Ely Hall to inform me that Catherine had told Bravin the 'good' news, and then returned to Catherine's house—in the rain. I expected his cloak to be wet. However, I saw his arms when he reached out to buy a pie in the High Street. There were no scratches on them, and so I concluded he was innocent, too."

"Who, then?" cried Richard, exasperated. "I do not like playing these guessing games."

"You do not need to guess the killer's identity," said Edmund softly. "You already know it. You murdered Bravin."

"Me?" asked Richard, startled. "How in God's name did you arrive at that conclusion?"

"Several reasons. The killer was a man who visited the houses near the trebuchet to ensure there were no witnesses to his crime—as you did. You were lucky there were none, or you would have been obliged to kill again, to hide the first murder."

"This is outrageous," said Richard, shaking his head.

"You arrived here drenched and unsettled just after Bravin was killed—I saw you myself. You said you had been visiting parishioners, and I had assumed it was Bravin's appointment that was distressing you. But it was the fact that you had murdered Bravin that rendered you quiet and thoughtful. And you were soaked."

"So?" asked Richard. "It was raining. What do you expect?"

"You were wet because you had killed Bravin under the trebuchet, not because you were visiting parishioners in their warm, dry homes."

"This is not evidence," warned Richard. "It is conjecture."

"You sent *me* to show the three candidates around the town, because you said you had a headache. We both know you never suffer from headaches. It was a ploy to delay my writing of the documents that Bravin was to sign—you wanted him dead before anything was made legal."

"Again, conjecture. Not evidence."

Edmund ignored the interruption. "Therefore, I deduce that you had decided to kill him *before* Catherine told him of his success and he made his speech—an incident you told me you witnessed, incidentally, and which forced you to act sooner. You went to some trouble to ensure that the death looked like an accident, and I suspect your horror was genuine when I told you it was murder."

"This is all gross speculation . . ."

"You also personally questioned the soldier who found Bravin's body, to ascertain that he had seen or heard nothing to incriminate you," Edmund went on relentlessly. "You must have been relieved to learn that he had not."

"This is not evidence," said Richard again. "You can prove nothing."

Edmund reached out and pulled up the sleeve of Richard's habit, revealing numerous angry scratches on the prior's forearms. "But this is evidence," he said softly. "This is where Bravin fought you. You are a gentle man. Why did you kill him?"

"Because I love Ely Hall," replied Richard simply, no longer denying his guilt. "I did not want a charlatan teaching the novices in my care. Can you blame me?"

"No," said Edmund. "But you should have let me do it. I would not have left a trail of clues as you did."

"You are much better at murder than me," agreed Richard ruefully. "When poor Henry ate those bad oysters, no one considered for a moment that you had deliberately poisoned them."

Edmund sighed. "But I did not kill Thomas and Catherine's puppet merely so that they could appoint another in Henry's place. I hope there is never a next time, but if there is, you should leave the killing to me."

Richard smiled wanly at his secretary, then changed the subject. 'So, shall we have Luke or Jean as our new professor?'

"Jean, I think," replied Edmund, sipping his wine. "We do not want a protégé of the Archbishop of Canterbury here to tell tales of monks murdered by their priors. I hope Catherine and Thomas have learned from their experiences and will fall in with our plans this time."

Richard nodded. "They will. Now, why did you say Luke could not have been the killer?" he asked, settling back in his chair and staring at the fire. "Is there any reason why *he* should not hang as Bravin's killer?"

"No reason at all," said Edmund, raising his goblet in a comradely salute to his prior.

Carolyn Hart

Turnaround

CAROLYN HART, like Nancy Pickard, has overhauled the American cozy in many different ways, making the genre not only more fun than it used to be, but also more important. While she gives cozy and traditional readers what they want, she also gives them something they may not have expected—a shrewd eye for society and a subtle yet cutting wit. Wit is not the focus of the story chosen for this year's volume, however, but greed, jealousy, ambition, and wrath certainly are. "Turnaround," published in *Malice Domestic #10*, is a microcosm of treachery, cross and double-cross, and revenge, proving that there is no such thing as a fair play murder.

Turnaround

Carolyn Hart

Damn. She'd forgotten the tickets! Leigh Graham Porter swerved her silver Jag into the alley that ran behind the houses. She parked by the stone wall next to the gate. She'd slip quietly up to the house and get them without Brian knowing. It would be so much more fun tonight to hand the tickets to Brian. He would open the folder, lift them out, two tickets to Tahiti, and then his lips would curve into that lazy, crooked, sensuous smile. That moment would cap a romantic evening at The Ivy, the wonderful restaurant where he'd proposed to her four years ago today.

Leigh was smiling as she walked through the gate of the bougainvillea-draped wall. All right, she was proud to have Brian Winslow—tall, blond, athletic, thirtyish Brian—as her third husband. Whenever she saw her first husband at parties, he with his much younger trophy wife, dark-eyed seductive Courtney, Leigh and Hal exchanged cordial smiles of mutual understanding.

Youth was all that mattered in Hollywood, but she and Hal were still surviving. Leigh's body was Jane Fonda hard. No one would ever guess that she was past fifty, her black hair lustrous, her face smooth, her wide-set green eyes glowing with health and success. She continued to sell screenplays for enough money to afford Brian and a turreted house in Beverly Hills and a sprawling Palm Springs hacienda. To remember the long ago lean years, she'd kept her first little house in Topanga Canyon, and it was still a favorite retreat, especially to spend moonlit nights there with Brian. She walked a little faster, tendrils of vine brushing against her designer jeans. Perhaps she'd call in sick, skip the script meeting, stay home with Brian this morning. She was almost to the terrace when she heard his voice. She smiled indulgently. He always carried the portable phone outside with him and stretched out in the hammock to make calls. Yes, he was a creature who loved all comforts. But so was she.

". . . you shouldn't call here. I know. Yes, she's gone, but what if she ran late? Let's not take any chances now, Holly. We're so close . . ."

Leigh stopped behind the hibiscus. Brian was on the other side. He could not be more than a few feet away, his deep voice achingly familiar, and that softness when he said—

"I love you, too. Of course I do. Trust me, it's going to work out . . . No, there's no chance of failure. It's all set. Then I'll be free."

Leigh crossed her arms against her body, struggled to breathe.

"Don't worry. Thursday night at the Topanga Canyon house. She thinks I'm meeting her there." He spoke briskly. He might have been describing a train connection.

Leigh felt the warm track of tears down her cheeks.

"You don't need to know about that, Holly. I've got a deal with a friend. One shot and it's over. I've got it all figured out. I'll have an alibi that can't be broken. A car wreck. She's going to get to the house about seven-thirty. When she arrives, the door will be open. She'll think I'm already there and walk in and that will be that. Then we'll be together forever. God, I love you . . ."

Leigh edged softly away from the terrace, her goal the kitchen door. Brian never came into the kitchen. Rosa wouldn't be there yet; she didn't come to work until ten. Leigh reached the door, stepped inside. She took off her shoes, held them in her hand, ran up the back stairs in her stocking feet. When she reached her office, she hurried to her desk, looked down at the blinking Caller ID: Holly Fraser and a Valley number. She reached for a pen, repeating the number over and over in her mind. The light blinked off and the name and number disappeared as Brian deleted the listing.

In only a moment Brian's Porsche—the Porsche she'd bought him for his birthday—roared down the drive to the street. Leigh's face was hard. She knew Brian loved that car. He must really be willing to make a sacrifice to wreck his Porsche.

Her eyes traveled to her desk calendar. Today was Tuesday. According to Brian, she had two days to live.

She began to pace, the way she always worked, waiting for fragments of thoughts to swirl into a pattern. They always did for her. Critics lauded the brilliance of her plots. Thursday night . . . the canyon house . . . a hired killer . . . but what if . . .

Leigh was aware of admiring glances from men at nearby tables and the icy jealousy of their women. She knew she looked especially lovely, her dark hair in a soft French roll, the kind that teased a man to loosen it and let it fall, her hard body alluring beneath the silver sheath dress. She sparkled like a many faceted diamond. Brian, of course, puffed with satisfaction, smugly certain that her uncommon iridescence grew out of passion for him.

He flipped open the ticket folder. "Tahiti! Leigh, you're unbelievable."

Was there a tinge of regret in his deep voice? Why hadn't he asked for a divorce? But Leigh knew the answer to that. She'd never been a fool, and the prenuptial agreement accorded him nothing if there was a divorce. Brian would be a very rich widower.

Leigh's lips curved in a merry smile. She picked up her champagne glass. "Brian, I have something even more special for you." Her exhilaration came not from champagne, but from the intoxication of danger.

He quirked a blond brow, leaned forward, his eyes full of warmth.

Her smile never wavered. "I've written a script that will be perfect for you—"

His eyes widened and his mouth parted. She'd let him read lines in her scripts, but she'd never made an effort to help him audition. Why should she? Why expose him to the temptations of hungry young actresses willing to barter body and soul for any perceived advantage? And a recommendation to be in a Leigh Graham Porter film was to die for.

"—and tomorrow morning I'll make a video and take it to Cameron Bachman with the script."

Cameron Bachman was currently the most successful movie director in the business.

Leigh held out the fluted glass. "To us. Forever."

Brian hesitated for only an instant, then his glass clicked against hers. He didn't repeat the toast.

The videocam was set up beside the desk. Leigh leaned against the desk. "Here's the story. You're in love with this girl. You've loved her forever. But you quarreled. She ran away and married a bandleader. He's abusive. You hear about her problems, how she's shown up at her sister's house with a bruised face, even been to the E.R. Anyway," Leigh waved her hand, "you've gotten in touch with her, she knows you care. You'd planned to meet her at your sister's house just before dark. Your sister gets called out of town. The girl's scared to be alone with you in case her husband finds out. So," Leigh pulled loose a sheet of script, "here's your sides. Let's see what you can do." Her voice was crisp now, businesslike, professional. "I'll do the voiceover." She slipped on her tortoiseshell-rimmed glasses and picked up the script. Not, of course, a script that she'd written on her computer. It was an easy matter to drive to Pasadena, find a Kinko's that rented use of computers. She'd worn a red wig, baggy gray sweats, and paid cash. She reached out, adjusted the angle of the camera, turned it on, then casually leaned back against the desk, one hand behind her to flip on the tape recorder. One finger rested lightly on the Stop key. "Okay, Brian. Lots of emotion. Let's go."

EXT. CITY STREET—NIGHT

To establish—

EXT. PHONE BOOTH—NIGHT

Jarvis runs to booth, quickly punches out number, looks over his shoulder as if fearful.

JARVIS

It's me. Listen, plans have changed. She's going out of town. Meet me there, seven-thirty.

EILEEN (*v.o., filtered*)

I can't. He'll . . .

JARVIS

We'll have a wonderful night, just you and me. And next week, we'll be together.

EILEEN (*v.o., filtered*)

I—I want to be with you—

JARVIS

I love you. Don't disappoint me. I've got to go. Don't call me. Someone's . . .

She took two takes, then clapped her hands. "Brian, you are so *good.* Cameron will be blown away. I'll take the script and videotape to his office this afternoon."

Thursday morning Leigh's eyes glowed like a cat's as Brian walked to the garage with her. As she slipped behind the wheel, he tangled a finger in her dark hair. "Hell, I wish you didn't have to go to the damn production meeting."

Leigh smiled up at him, touched his cheek with her finger, drew it down slowly to his lips. "I could call in, say I was sick."

His eyes flared just for an instant. His laugh was hearty. "Not you, Leigh. You don't want them making decisions about your script without you there."

"As if I'd have any choice," she said dryly.

"Besides," his tone was rueful, "the guys'll kill me if I don't show up to play."

"Oh, yes, today's your regular game." Yes, she remembered that well. Every Thursday morning, Brian played doubles at the Beverly Hills Country Club. "And you're right. I can't miss this meeting." She smiled at him. "How well you know me." Yes, she was a fighter. Often if a studio bought a screenplay then changed its mind and the script went into turnaround, she used every contact she had to find the screenplay a new home. Soon he would know just how hard she was willing to fight for whatever belonged to her, including her life. "All day I'll be thinking about tonight. I'll see you at the canyon house."

She parked in the alley, waited until it was past time for Brian's tennis to start. In her office, she carried the tape player and the portable phone to a window overlooking the drive. She'd hear the Porsche if he returned early. She was taking no chances. Her lips moved in a cold smile. Brian thought he wasn't taking any chances. Ah, to be young and to live and learn.

She punched in the numbers.

A breathless voice, a sweet young voice, answered. "Hello."

Leigh pushed the button and the carefully edited tape ran:

"It's me. Listen, plans have changed. She's going out of town. Meet me there, seven-thirty. We'll have a wonderful night, just you and me. And next week we'll be together. I love you. Don't disappointment me. I've got to go. Don't call me. Someone's . . ."

"Brian, what—"

Leigh clicked off the phone.

Leigh took her time in the office. She found the sides, tucked one into her purse, tore the rest into shreds, flushed them down the toilet.

Leigh left the production meeting early, drove back to Beverly Hills. Brian wouldn't leave the house until after seven. He'd time the car wreck for around seven-fifteen. There would be a wait for the cops to come. But later, no one could ever suggest he'd been in Topanga Canyon. As alibis went, it was clever.

Leigh turned the Jag into their drive shortly after seven. She left the car running. The Jag was blocking the drive, but that wouldn't occur to Brian. She ran up the front steps, unlocked the door, flung it open, shouting, "Brian, Brian!"

He was coming down the stairs. He stopped and stared at her, his handsome face slack with shock.

"Brian, I've got the most wonderful news. I had a call from Cameron. He caught me just before I was leaving for the canyon. But that doesn't matter. You know how he is." She threw up both hands in exasperation. "He always has to do things at once. And his way. He'll audition you tonight. At his house. This may be your chance!"

She turned south on the San Diego freeway. Traffic was heavy. Finally, she reached 5 South, but rush hour traffic stalled them for more than an hour. "He lives to hell and gone." Her tone was irritated. "But he gave me directions. He's back in the hills down near Laguna. You concentrate on your lines."

Brian practiced.

Leigh listened in rapt admiration. Occasionally, she made a suggestion. She drove as dusk turned to darkness. She turned off the 5, took a road into the hills, a twisting, hairpin road that skirted canyons. It was almost ten when she finally gave up. She stopped at the side of the road, got out her cell phone, scrabbled through her purse. "Damn, I thought I had his number. And it's unlisted. Oh Brian, I'm so sorry. I'll call first thing in the morning. I have his number in my Rolodex. Cameron's a good guy. He'll understand." A trill of laughter. "He knows I have the world's lousiest sense of direction."

Brian didn't laugh.

Leigh held the muscle relaxant tablets in her hand. One or two? One should be enough. Be damned awkward if there were an overdose. Using the back of a spoon, she ground the pill into white powder, scraped the powder into a wineglass. She poured in champagne, stirred, carefully set that glass at the front of the tray on the left side. She didn't fill the second glass quite so full.

She waited a few minutes, then carried the tray upstairs and knocked on Brian's door. She opened it.

Brian swung around, his face tight with irritation. He wouldn't keep those boyish good looks frowning like that. She noted his blue silk pajamas. Yes, she'd given him time to change. He'd tossed his gray slacks onto the sofa. "Brian"—Leigh stretched out his name like a dramatic festival tattoo—"I brought champagne to celebrate. Tomorrow will be the most unforgettable day of your life."

She handed him the glass on the left, picked up the nearby glass, raised it high. "To tomorrow and the new life of Brian Winslow."

The glasses clicked with a light chime. They drank.

In her room, Leigh changed unhurriedly from her silk tee and beige jeans into a long-sleeve black turtleneck, black jeans, black sneakers. She tucked money and a driver's license into her pocket. It took a moment to find a pair of gloves, since neither the society nor the climate required them. But there were soft doeskin driving gloves tucked in a winter coat she'd bought for location shooting in New York. She glanced at the clock. Just past midnight.

Brian's door was closed. She didn't bother to knock. She opened the door. He was sprawled on his back across the foot of his bed, mouth wide, breathing stertorous. She moved quickly, snatched up his slacks with her gloved hands. "Sweet dreams, little man." She checked the pockets, a tight frown thinning her mouth. Where was the sides he'd practiced? Not in the pockets. She glanced around the room, saw the sheet lying on the bedside stand. She grabbed it up, carried it to the bathroom, ripped the page into tiny pieces, flushed them away.

Leigh drove past the turnoff to the cliff road twice. On her third pass, reassured by the silence and the dark, she turned onto the narrow, rutted, twisting road. Always before, the rustic, almost hidden entrance had appealed, the gateway to privacy and adventure. Now her heart thudded uncomfortably. Once on the road, she was trapped by anyone coming in after her. No one should come, of course. She'd considered parking along the road and walking up. But it was almost a mile to the house, and someone might see the parked car, note the license plate. If all went well, she could be up and down the road in a quarter hour at the most.

Leigh drove without lights, easing the car up the twisting road, using the moonlight as her guide. At the top of the grade she paused, studying the dark house. No lights, no movement. She turned into the drive, carefully turned and backed until the car was facing downhill. If she had to hurry . . .

She turned off the motor, listened to the swish of the pines and the crash of the waves far below. Her hands gripped the steering wheel. She should move now, this instant, hurry from the car, run across the graveled drive, up the steps to the redwood deck. Still she sat.

An owl hooted. What was that crackling sound? She jerked her head so quickly her neck hurt. Her heart thudded. Oh, God. She could scarcely hear above the roar in her ears. Slowly she sorted out the sounds, the crash of the waves, the sough of tree limbs, the rustle of shrubbery.

Leigh held tight to the wheel. She wanted desperately to turn on the motor and careen down the canyon, away from this pocket of dark and quiet, this isolated house and the malevolence that seemed so near. But she had no choice. There was no turning back.

She opened the door, slipped out of the car, leaving the door a little ajar. She forced herself to walk quickly. The faster she moved, the sooner she could be out of here. She carried Brian's trousers in one hand, a small pocket flashlight in the other. She didn't need the flashlight. Moonlight bathed the deck, turning the dark windows to patches of silver.

The front door stood open. That's what Brian had planned, the open door and her stepping inside. One step, another, Leigh moved like a shadow across the deck. She eased open the screen door, stepped into the living room. She flicked on the flashlight and stared across the shining expanse of wood—she'd always been pleased with the white pine floors, such a dramatic contrast to the red cypress of the walls—at the body sprawled only a few feet away. The blood spatters were stark and ugly against the shell-pink dress and white wood floor. The young woman lay on her back, thrown there by the force of the shot. Blond hair curved against a lace-white cheek. Dead green eyes stared emptily into eternity.

Leigh shuddered. She struggled to breathe, heard her own voice, high and stricken, "No, no, no . . ." She'd not realized how terrible this would be. She flung out her arms, the light of the flash dancing crazily around the dark room. Brian's trousers slapped against the door frame. She looked at the gray worsted slacks, then turned her head toward the murdered woman. Her hand steadied, light spilling over the still form.

That could be her body. That would be her body if she hadn't overheard Brian's clever plan. This woman had known. This woman had been willing for her to die. She owed her nothing.

Hands shaking, the trousers dangling in front of her, Leigh walked toward the body. Averting her eyes from the dead white face, she leaned forward, swiped the pants against that bloodied chest.

A click.

She froze. What was that sound? She jerked the flashlight around the room. Nothing moved. The dark shadows behind the furniture might harbor a thousand screaming devils of her imagination, but there was no one in this room except her and the forever still body.

All right, all right. God, how long had she been here? Too long. Time to move now. Fast. She hurried across the room to the wet bar, stepped behind, stuffed the trousers beneath the sink.

She didn't glance again toward the body. Everything was done now. Let Brian reap what he had sown. She clattered across the deck and down the stairs, ran to the car.

Three weeks later Leigh carried the *Times* to her favorite chair by the pool.

SCREENWRITER'S HUSBAND
CHARGED IN CABIN DEATH

Brian Winslow, husband of Oscar-winning screenwriter Leigh Graham Porter, was charged with first-degree murder today in the shooting death April 4 of Holly Fraser, a young actress he met while filming an unsuccessful TV pilot two years ago.

Winslow's attorney entered a plea of Not Guilty. Winslow is accused of shooting Fraser, 26, at the Topanga Canyon home owned by his wife. No motive has been established, and police said Winslow and Fraser had remained friends after the filming.

Winslow claims he spent the evening of the murder in the company of his wife. Porter has not responded to interview requests. However, intimates of the writer have said that Porter was shocked by her husband's statement. According to friends, Porter was home alone that evening and didn't see her husband. Further, Porter expressed surprise at his story of an audition for one of her scripts. She told a friend that she'd never written a script suitable for her husband. Porter is reported to have said that she didn't believe Winslow would shoot anyone. However, Winslow remains jailed, as he has been unable to post the $100,000 bail and Porter has declined to post bail.

Although police have not released details of their investigation, there is reason to believe . . .

Leigh dropped the paper on the wicker table, picked up her espresso, and reached for a script on the glass-topped table. The harder she worked, the easier it was to push away the memory of those dead green eyes.

• • •

The plain manila envelope was tucked into the mailbox when Leigh returned from the studio the next evening. She frowned as she picked it up. It was too light to be a script. It was amazing how often hopeful writers cornered her at cocktail parties, tucked scripts into the mailbox. What a bore. But this envelope couldn't hold much. Her name was written in a flowing script. That was all.

She carried the envelope into the kitchen, sniffed. Hmm. Rosa was such a good cook. What would it be this evening? She glanced at the note on the kitchen block. Dove casserole and rice. She poured a glass of Chablis, almost tossed the envelope into the wastebasket, shrugged, opened it.

A photograph dropped onto the pale yellow tiles of the cooking island.

Leigh's eyes widened. Her breath stopped. A hard pressure filled her chest. The wineglass slipped from her fingers, shattering on the red tile floor. Leigh stared at the picture, the telling, damning, hideous picture: the dark walls, the white floor, the dead girl, her open eyes, the blood that had welled across her pink dress, and Leigh leaning down, swiping Brian's gray trousers against the body. The flashlight pointed down toward the body, but Leigh's face was clear and distinct, her eyes hard, cheekbones jutting, lips pressed into a thin line.

Nausea welled in Leigh's throat. A wave of heat swept her. She crumpled the slick eight-by-ten photograph and shuddered. She'd thought herself alone with death, but she had not been alone. Someone watched, watched and waited, and when the moment was perfect, held the camera rock steady and pressed the button. There'd been no flash. But there need not have been, not with high-speed film and the right lens aperture.

Fear washed over her. Where had this film been developed? Who had seen it? But there had likely been a casual explanation of publicity stills for a local playhouse. Who would ever question any kind of pose in this town? No doubt the film was taken to a one-hour photo shop and a false name given, the prints paid for with cash. Who would remember after time passed?

The negative.

A pulse quivered in Leigh's throat. The negative didn't matter. Any number of copies could be made from a photograph now. So, no matter how much she paid, there could always be copies in reserve.

Paid.

That was the point of this photograph, wasn't it?

Whirling, she grabbed the envelope, the unmarked plain manila envelope, ripped it open. Nothing. The envelope was empty. Reluctantly, she spread out the crumpled photograph, turned it over. Nothing on the back. In a frenzy, she ripped the photo into tiny pieces, carried them to the sink, hunted for matches. There had to be some matches somewhere—

The phone rang.

Leigh stared at the bright lemon portable phone.

Another peal. Another.

Stiffly, she reached out, picked up the receiver, pushed the button. She held the phone to her ear. She didn't speak. She knew who was calling, who had to be calling. It didn't matter when the envelope was delivered. The photographer—no, be plain, be honest, she told herself—the murderer, the friend Brian had asked to murder her, had only to park down the street, waiting until her silver Jag turned into the drive, allowing her time enough to find the envelope, open it, see the hellish picture.

The whisper was slow in coming. "Photography is an art, isn't it, Leigh?"

She stared at the Caller ID bar: *Unavailable.*

"Don't you like my picture?" The whisper was sexless, ageless, a wisp of sound.

Her throat was so dry, it hurt to talk. She pushed out the words, dropped them like steel balls into a cavern. "What do you want?"

"You get right to the point, I see. Very well. But I'll give you time to think about the future. Oh, say, until tomorrow. There's a pay phone at the Rite-Aid on Canon not far from your house. Be there at ten o'clock in the morning."

Leigh stared at her reflection in the shiny plate glass of the Rite-Aid. She looked old, her eyes bloodshot, her face pasty. She'd lain wakeful most of the night. When fatigue pulled her into sleep, she'd jerked awake at every sound, and in her mind a photograph expanded, grew larger and larger, until all she could see was dead staring eyes. She leaned against the plastic side of the pay phone, smelled that essentially California mixture of car fumes, gasoline, and eucalyptus, and waited.

How much money would he want? What else could she do but pay up? If she told the truth to the police, she was an accomplice to murder. A lizard slithered along the rock wall by the hedge. Accomplice? More than that. Though it seemed only fair. But the police didn't care about fair.

The phone rang. Leigh yanked up the receiver.

The whisper was as insubstantial as fog, but the words permeated her soul. "You're guilty of murder."

"No." The denial burst from her. "You were going to kill me. You were going to kill me!"

"You could have called the police."

Leigh felt her body shrink and tighten. That's what everyone would say.

"But you didn't." The whisper was silky. "Somehow you found out what was planned. I was waiting. I heard the footsteps running across the deck. As soon as she stepped inside, I shot. As you'll discover, it isn't easy to do. I wanted to get it over with. If I'd waited a minute, seen her better . . . But I didn't. Of course, after I shot, I had to be sure you were dead. Imagine my surprise—"

"Stop it." Leigh's voice rose. "Stop whispering!"

"Oh, I don't have much more to say." The whisper was even lighter, fainter. "The minute I saw the dead girl, I knew what had happened. I knew who she was, but it was too late. Too late for her and for Brian. But not too late for me. I knew you must have arranged for her to come. But I knew you wouldn't stop there."

Leigh's fingers tightened around the sticky receiver.

"I was sure you'd implicate Brian. That meant putting some kind of physical evidence in the house. I took a chance and went to get a camera."

Thoughts whipped in her mind: . . . left and came back . . . how far could he live . . . he could have stopped, bought one . . . no way of knowing . . .

"How much do you want?" She tried to keep her voice even, but it cracked as she spoke. She was afraid, so damn afraid.

A husky laugh. "I don't want money, Leigh."

A car squealed out of the parking lot, the fumes choking her. Leigh didn't move. She stared at the black metal box.

"Brian and I had a deal. No one would ever suspect me of shooting you, and no one would ever suspect him of shooting a man quite unknown to him. I was to shoot his bête noire, he was to shoot mine. He was to have an unbreakable alibi at the time of your death. I will have an unbreakable alibi this coming Saturday night."

"You're out of your mind." She began to shake. She had a sudden sharp clear memory of Robert Walker and Farley Granger in the classic *Strangers on a Train*. But this was so much worse. She'd never planned anyone's death. She pushed away the picture of the girl's dead green eyes. That hadn't been her plan. Holly died because of Brian and this nameless creature with the hideous whisper.

Soft laughter. "Aren't we all for living in La-La Land? But it's quid pro quo, Leigh. You'll do quite as well as Brian. Now," the whisper was brisk, "when you get home, go down to the alley. There's a backpack inside your gate. You'll find detailed instructions in it. Who you are going to kill and when."

"I can't." Leigh's chest squeezed.

"You can. You will." The whisper was cold and determined. "A final note, Leigh, don't try to be clever. You can't find me. There are too many people who want this man dead. His wife. His son. His daughter. His ex-mistress. His business partner. And I've made it easy for you. You'll find the gun in the backpack. Zero hour? Saturday night, Leigh, nine o'clock."

The connection broke.

Leigh gripped the receiver. She struggled to breathe. Pay phone. The killer sent her here so she couldn't see the number on Caller ID . . .

Leigh scrabbled in her purse, her fingers desperately seeking coins. She found one, two, jammed them into slots, punched ★69. There was a pause, a squeal, a recorded voice, "Call return service is not . . ."

Oh damn, damn, damn.

•   •   •

Leigh stared at the blue nylon backpack lying in deep shade next to the oleander. It held death. She didn't want to touch it, not ever. But she had to . . . She wore gardening gloves, carried the pack at arm's length into the garage to a worktable. She unbuckled the plastic snaps, pulled out a manila envelope. She left the gun in the dark interior. It was hard to open the envelope with her clumsily gloved hands. A studio portrait slipped to the cement floor. Leigh creased the picture as she picked it up.

Sunlight spilled through the window above the work-bench. She studied the face. An Alan Alda type, but tougher, harder, with a sensuous mouth and combative eyes. Across the bottom, scrawled in a bold masculine script, was the inscription and name, *Love, Jake.*

She pulled two sheets of paper, both computer generated, from the envelope and a driver's license with her photograph. The name on the license was Ellen Vorhees and the address was in Long Beach. On one sheet was a map of an elegant backyard with a legend identifying sites, with a star by the Fortune Teller booth near the swimming pool. The second sheet contained instructions.

Leigh read swiftly, picking out the important facts. Saturday night the county bar association was having a fundraising carnival at a house three streets from her home. Jake Garrison was volunteering as a swami in the fortune-telling booth from eight-thirty to nine-thirty.

And:

The back flap of the tent will be unfastened. At nine o'clock, pull aside the flap, shoot Jake, drop the gun, meld into the crowd. You may be able to slip away down the alley. If not, the police will take names and IDs. You'll have one. But no one will ever find Ellen Vorhees. You will receive the photograph you desire in the next mail. Good hunting.

Jake Garrison. Attorney at law. Personal injury lawyer specializing in medical malpractice. Facts welled from his law firm's website, so many that Leigh didn't try to absorb them all. She found everything she needed to know about his wife, Ingrid; his son, Bobby; his daughter, Tina; his partner, Ray Porter. She found their ages, histories. And phone numbers.

Leigh tilted back her chair and stared at the screen. If she were the Whisperer, she wouldn't have included herself among the suggested villains.

Who hates medical malpractice lawyers?

Leigh shot a glance at the clock. She'd been at her computer ever since she got home from the pay phone, almost four hours. Her eyes ached, her head throbbed. The time, so little time, how could she find out in time . . . All right, all right. She had to narrow the search, set up parameters. She could rule out lawsuits against hospitals and HMOs. It had to be personal. Someone who had been damaged, perhaps irrevocably, by Garrison. Or, better yet, someone close to trial who might believe his death could make a difference. Yes, that was the route to take.

Leigh ended up with four names: a doctor who operated while high on drugs, a doctor who amputated the wrong leg, a doctor who misdiagnosed ovarian cancer, and a doctor whose liposuction patient died. Four names . . . Leigh rubbing her aching head and stared at the list. Abruptly, she jolted back her chair, ran down the hall to Brian's room. She grabbed the doorknob, flung the door open, hurried to the bath. Flicking on the light, she crossed to the medicine cabinet, opened it. She reached up, grabbed a handful of plastic vials.

Oh shit, yes. There it was. A painkiller after his knee surgery. Prescribed by Dr. Annabelle Smith. The same Dr. Annabelle Smith who had amputated a left leg instead of a right. Yes, yes, yes! Hello, Whisperer.

Leigh called Dr. Smith's home number at shortly after five. Voice mail picked up. Leigh didn't identify herself. If she'd found the Whisperer, no identification was needed. "Hello, Annabelle. I've been giving some thought to our conversation earlier today. I haven't yet informed Jake Garrison. I won't unless we can't make a deal. I suggest we get together at ten o'clock tonight at my house. You bring the picture and film. I'll have the backpack. Fair exchange. We both walk away with no hard feelings. See you then."

Ten o'clock came and went, of course. Leigh didn't expect Dr. Smith to respond to her summons. Not at the stated time. But she felt certain Dr. Smith would come very late, long after the appointed hour, when she should be deep in sleep. And easy to kill.

The house was dark and quiet. The only light came from security lights in the trees. It was just before three o'clock in the morning. Leigh waited in the deep shadow at the end of the patio, curled in a dark wicker chair. She had a good view of the back gate and the side yard. Her hair was tucked beneath a navy ball cap. She wore a black sweater, jeans, dark sneakers. She sipped a cup of strong black coffee, not that she was likely to drift into sleep. She felt oddly calm and perhaps a little exhilarated. This afternoon she'd been in a deadly box. Now she had a chance. If Dr. Smith was the Whisperer . . . Leigh shook her head impatiently. It couldn't be a coincidence, the doctor's trial set to begin next month and her name on Brian's medicine bottle. Dr. Smith was the Whisperer, smart, cunning, careful, dangerous, and a gambler. The Whisperer would come tonight, prepared to kill. Leigh sipped her coffee and waited, the gun heavy on her lap. Occasionally, she reached down to touch the heavy twine she'd tied to the switch that would turn on the patio lights.

The gate creaked. The squeal had to be unnerving to the doctor. Metal hinges scraped. A dark figure moved cautiously on the path, a small carryall in one hand.

Leigh watched, part of her mind at a distant remove, admiring the grace and stealth of the approach, part of her mind boring toward the moment when the lights would come on. Not yet. Not yet. Wait until the intruder was at a disadvantage. Leigh's hand gripped the twine. Wait, wait . . .

Enough light spilled down from the trees to illuminate the intruder's dark cap, black sweater, saggy black cardigan, shiny vinyl gloves, skintight black bike pants. No wonder she hadn't heard a car. Annabelle—surely they were on a first name basis now—had probably parked nearby. Her car must have a bike rack.

Annabelle stopped at the base of a tree with a limb that stretched over the second-story sun porch. She opened the carryall, pulled out a rope ladder. Dropping the small bag, she took a step nearer the tree, flung the ladder up. It took two tries before the hooks caught.

Leigh's hand tightened on the twine, yanked. Light blazed on the patio.

Annabelle froze on the rope ladder, halfway to the limb.

"Stay there." Leigh's voice was as sharp and hard as the click of a safety catch. She held the gun in both hands, aimed it.

Annabelle hung on the ladder, twisting to look down. The cap made her broad face look heavy. Burning dark eyes that slitted into fury. The long thin mouth quivered.

"Come down slowly. Yes, that's right. Put your hands up." Leigh was poised to shoot. She didn't want to. Not here. But if she had to . . .

The vinyl-gloved hands lifted, shiny in the lights of the patio. The hands of a killer.

Leigh watched those deep-socketed, furious eyes. "Don't move." The carryall—a blue canvas gym bag—lay near Annabelle's feet. "Shove the bag with your foot."

Cautiously, Leigh eased close enough to snag the bag with her foot. She felt the hardness of a gun, gave a quick glance, felt the tightness ease out of her shoulders. Triumph almost made her giddy. She was in charge now. She had the only weapon. Now to get Annabelle into the garage . . . Her mind shied away from the next moment. But she had no choice. A quick shot. She'd already spread big black garbage sacks on the cement floor. The rest would be hard, getting the body into the trunk, driving to a remote area of the San Gabriel Mountains, dumping the grisly load. There was a road near the Mount Wilson Observatory . . . There would be no connection between her and a body found there.

"Walk up to the garage. I'm right behind you." And in a hurry, a big hurry.

Annabelle slowly moved ahead of her. "I'll make a deal. I've got the picture—and the negative—in my car."

"Too little too late, Annabelle." They were at the side door to the garage. "Open the door." Leigh's hands tightened on the gun.

Annabelle grabbed the knob and pulled. "It's stuck."

Leigh prodded her with the gun. They were almost there, almost inside the garage. Impatiently, she pressed nearer. "Turn it—" Leigh never finished.

Annabelle's right hand plunged into her cardigan pocket and out and up.

Leigh glimpsed the needle, felt a sharp, hot prick in her neck. In her last moment of life, Leigh squeezed the gun, heard the shots, knew that Annabelle fell as she herself sagged into oblivion.

Bill Crider

Out like a Lion

BILL CRIDER has written so well in so many genres, it's difficult to believe he isn't better known. His Sheriff Rhodes mysteries are his most popular novels, but the wise reader will also search out his suspense novels and his westerns as well. Like many crime writers of his generation, he is a regional writer in the sense that his Texas environment always plays an important role in his work. Every writer needs to branch out, however, and in "Out Like a Lion," Crider turns a wry eye toward Hollywood during the 1930s, when moviemaking (much like today) was more low-finance and high-return than high art. Published in *Death by Horoscope*, his story shows what happens when a Leo oversteps his bounds, which leads to murder.

Out like a Lion

Bill Crider

Frank Packard, star of several sword-and-sandal epics at Gober Studios, was not wearing sandals. He wasn't carrying a sword, either. Instead he was wearing a garterbelt, nylons, cotton panties, and a bra.

He might have gotten away with it if he'd been in costume for a movie, but he wasn't. He was in his garage, about to get into his car. He'd told his wife he was tired of living a lie.

His wife was a starlet at Gober Studios, and she didn't mind living a lie at all, not as long as she kept getting parts. So of course she called Mr. Gober, and Mr. Gober called me.

"Goddammit, Ferrel!" Gober said. He always begins his conversations with me that way. I've never figured out why.

"Goddammit, Ferrel! You've got to stop him! *The Roaming Roman* opens next week!"

I asked who I had to stop, and he told me. I hung up, got in my 1940 Chevy, and caught up with Packard before he managed to get more than five blocks from home. He didn't want to go back, but when I explained that he'd never get to hang around with a cast of thousands of guys wearing togas again, he decided to give the straight life another try.

A job well done, I thought as I drove to my office. I'm a licensed private detective, and I take regular cases now and then, but being on retainer to Gober Studios pretty much assures that I'll never be without work. In fact, by the time I got back to my office and sat down to wonder how much of a bonus Gober would pay me, the phone rang again.

"Goddammit, Ferrel," Mr. Gober said, "get out here! Sidney's killed Howard Steele!"

•   •   •

Howard Steele had been a heavily-decorated hero of the war in the Pacific, fighting his way across a series of small islands and singlehandedly wiping out machine-gun nests, picking off snipers, and raising Old Glory on whatever little hill was handy.

When he came back to the States, the newspapers were full of photos of his rugged, handsome face, and Mr. Gober, who loves publicity, signed him to be Gober Studio's new star.

It turned out that Steele was rugged and handsome, all right, and he photographed even better than he looked. But he couldn't act a lick. His line readings made the kids in high school plays look like Laurence Olivier. Mr. Gober never let a little thing like that stop him, however. The Tarzan movies were doing all right for RKO, and they had a hero who didn't have much to say, so Gober had one of his hacks create a jungle hero named Karg, who had even less to say than Johnny Weissmuller. Gober had plans for a whole series of movies with titles like *Jungle Peril, Jungle Flames, Jungle Terror,* and on and on.

As it happened, Steele looked great in a loin cloth, a lot better than Weissmuller, who'd put on a few pounds since his first Tarzan movie and these days was wearing what looked like a pair of leather boxer shorts to help cover his paunch. The Karg movies were a hit and were among the studio's biggest money-makers, not just because they attracted huge audiences but because they could be filmed in a hurry and on the cheap on the studio's back lot, with a fake jungle. Plenty of scenes of authentic jungle animals were spliced into the film, but I doubt that they fooled anyone over the age of eight.

I never knew where the authentic stuff came from. Probably some guy shot it on safari and sold it to Gober for a couple of hundred bucks. The same scenes turned up in nearly every movie—the same giraffes running across the veldt, the same crocs slithering into the river, the same elephants trumpeting—but no one ever complained. Maybe nobody cared.

The only real animal that ever appeared in the movies was Sidney, who was a lion, or so Gober claimed. It was hard to tell. Sidney was pretty much fangless and clawless, and whenever there was a big fight between him and Steele, which was just about every movie, Steele had to work hard to make it look as if there was a real struggle going on. Sidney himself never seemed to work up much interest. The technicians juiced up the soundtrack with roars and growls, and audiences never seemed disappointed, but I knew for sure that Sidney hadn't killed anybody. Sidney couldn't maul a mouse.

I pulled my wheezing crate up to the studio gatehouse and old Ray waved me through. He'd seen me often enough to know I belonged there.

I drove on back to the lot that served as the jungle. There were plenty of cars parked around, but no police yet. No reporters, either. Gober didn't believe in calling them until everybody got together and settled on the story Gober wanted told to the cops and the papers.

When I walked onto the set, one of the first people I saw was Anna

Lonestar. I'd always thought she was the real reason for the success of the Karg pictures. She was as regal as a lioness, her auburn hair touched with gold highlights, and when she put on one of those skimpy jungle outfits to play Karg's wild jungle love, well, there wasn't a guy in the theater whose eyes didn't bug out just a little.

She wasn't wearing the costume at the moment, I was sorry to see.

Instead she was wearing jodhpurs and a tight white shirt with a red scarf tied around her throat, but it didn't matter. She was the one you looked at, no matter what she was wearing. Whatever star quality is, she had it by the truck load.

Standing beside her was Doctor Christopher Benton, her astrologer. Everywhere that Anna Lonestar went, Dr. Benton was sure to go. I wasn't sure where the "doctor" came from. Maybe he was a doctor like Georgie Jessel was a general. Not that I cared. Everybody in Hollywood has a con going, and one more didn't much matter.

Mr. Gober wasn't there, of course. He didn't like to mingle with the talent. But his flunkies were there, running around and telling everybody to keep quiet until the word came down from the top. The crew was there, too, of course: grips and stagehands and lighting technicians. George Zenko, the director, was there, and a guy who had to be the producer. I didn't know him, but you can always spot a producer when there's trouble. He's the one who's sweating buckets.

So naturally it was the producer who buttonholed me. He was about five-six or -seven, which made him the same height as most of the stars he worked with, not counting Steele, who was a genuine six-footer.

"You're Ferrel, right?" the producer said.

I admitted that I was.

"I'm Anderson. The producer."

I said I'd figured that out.

"You gotta do something," he said. "This is going to cost us an arm and a leg. The picture was almost in the can, and now Steele's dead. It's going to be hard to finish the picture without him, but it can be done. We'll just cut in some shots from the earlier pictures. Nobody'll notice. The publicity from this could kill us, though. We can't have people thinking there's a killer lion on the set. We could get sued."

Anderson didn't seem too worried about Steele, so I said, "Something's already killed your star."

"Yeah. It was the lion. Come on. I'll show you."

I followed him into the fake jungle. A bunch of the others trailed along behind, but I didn't look to see who was there. It sounded like quite a lot of them.

The trees looked even less like jungle trees in real life than they did in the movies. They were real enough, but some of them had broad rubber leaves stuck on them to make them look more tropical, and of course there were vines everywhere. The vines weren't real. They were mostly ropes, disguised to look like vines. When it came to swinging from tree to tree, ropes were much safer than vegetation.

A lot of the plants growing by the trees needed water. There's not as much rain in Southern California as there is in the jungle.

It wasn't noisy like a real jungle. There were no birds calling, no monkeys howling. All those sounds are added to the movie later, like the scenes with the real animals.

Howard Steele was lying not far from one of the trees. Overhead in the crotch of the tree was the house where Karg and the lovely Kiela, portrayed by Anna Lonestar, lived. The treehouse was very solid, put together with nails and screws even if everything was supposedly tied in place with vines.

But while Steele was lying under the tree, he didn't look as if he'd fallen from the treehouse.

He looked as if he'd been mauled by a lion.

"We should have warned him," Benton said, and I turned around to look at him.

"Warned who?" I asked. "About what?"

He had a cherubic face, except that cherubs don't have beards. He also had lots of curly black hair that was turning gray and didn't quite cover the bald spot in the middle of his head. He wore a black suit, white shirt, narrow black tie, and he was holding a beat-up black hat, which I suppose he'd removed out of respect for the dead. He looked more like an out-of-work rabbi than an astrologer.

"We should have warned Steele," Benton said. "About his impending doom."

"Yes," Anna Lonestar agreed. Her voice was as much a purr as anything. It sounded even better in person than it did on the screen. I felt the little hairs on the back of my neck stand up.

"How could you have known?" Anderson asked, but I already knew the answer he'd get. Anna never worked with anyone whose horoscope Benton hadn't cast.

"It was in the stars," Benton said. He really talked like that: *impending doom, in the stars.* "He was an Aries, of course, ruled by Mars, as his success in the late war would attest. Pure raw energy! But that success is long past. His natal chart shows Neptune conjunct Mars in the eighth house. And his Sun was in the twelfth house."

He looked at me as if I'd have some idea of what he meant, but of course I didn't.

Anderson probably didn't, either, but he said, "That's malarkey. Don't give me that cheap newspaper crap."

Benton looked pained, as if he had to deal with skeptics all the time, which he probably did. He said, "Horoscopes that you might see in magazines and newspapers are not entirely 'crap.' But they usually look only at the Sun sign. Real astrology, such as I practice, is much more complex. It looks at all the planets, both in the present and in the birth chart. It—"

"Yeah, yeah, yeah," Anderson said. "But what good does that do us?"

I was wondering the same thing, but I was curious. So I said, "What about Miss Lonestar's horoscope?"

"She, of course, is a Leo," Benton said.

So she not only looked like a lioness; she was one. Anna smiled as if it should have been obvious to anyone.

"Her magnetic personality," Benton went on, "is typical of the Leo. It draws people to her. People love her. She has millions of fans because her natural warmth comes through on the screen."

"OK," I said, but I wasn't convinced.

I thought she had millions of fans because of the way she looked in that skimpy jungle outfit, especially after a swim, and there was a swim in every movie. Besides, I was a Leo, too, and I'd never been accused of having a magnetic personality. The only thing that stuck to me was lint.

"What was that you were saying about Steele's Sun being in the eighth house?" I asked. "What does that have to do with anything?"

"The twelfth," Benton said. "Not the eighth. It means that Steele was killed by—"

"A lion!" someone screamed.

I looked into the trees over Benton's shoulder, and there came Sidney.

He looked pretty bedraggled, like a giant alley cat wearing a moth-eaten fur that someone had found in the attic and thrown away. His mane was as scraggly as Benton's beard, and he stared around near-sightedly with his watery old eyes.

I heard lots of pounding feet at my back as people fled from the ferocious maneater.

Not everyone was running away. Benton and Anna Lonestar stood their ground. A stagehand and a script girl were still there, along with the director, George Zenko, and a guy who looked as if he might be dressed for safari: Randall Curry, Sidney's trainer. And of course Anderson was there. Lions don't scare producers. They have to deal with actors and directors all the time.

"Get out your roscoe," Anderson told me.

"Roscoe?" I said.

"Your gat, idiot. Your heater."

He'd been watching too many of Gober's gangster pictures. I said, "My gun?"

"Yeah, your gun. Get it out."

"I don't carry a roscoe."

"You're a detective and you don't carry a gat?"

"I've never needed one," I said.

"Well, you need it now. That's a rogue beast over there."

Sidney was standing there watching us hopefully, as if he thought one of us might have a case of tuna for him. His chain was hanging from his leather collar.

"I don't think I need a gun for Sidney," I said.

"What about you, Curry?" Anderson asked. "Don't you have a whip or something?"

"I'd never use a whip on Sidney," Curry said. "He's gentle as a lamb."

"Sure he is," Anderson said. "Why don't you go over there and see how gentle he is."

"That might not be prudent," Curry said. He looked down at Steele. "Considering the circumstances."

"I'll go over," Anna said, with what I guessed must be typical Leo bravery, except that I, as the other Leo on hand, wasn't feeling particularly brave. Maybe she just didn't think Sidney was dangerous.

Anderson grabbed her arm.

"Oh, no, you don't," he said. "We can't risk it. Ferrel goes. That's what Mr. Gober pays him for."

Sidney walked over and looked down at Steele's body. He bent his head to sniff.

"For God's sake, Ferrel," Anderson said. "Stop him before he takes a bite!"

I didn't think Sidney would bite anyone, even a dead man, so I started over to him. He looked up at me quizzically, and I said, "Hey, Sidney. How's it going?"

Sidney, naturally enough, didn't answer. He just stood there until I took his chain. I looked at the end of the chain, saw a broken link, and then led the docile lion over to Curry.

"He's all yours," I told the trainer.

Curry took the chain and looked at Anderson.

"Get him out of here," Anderson said. "And be sure he doesn't get loose again."

As Curry led Sidney away, I said, "Who found the body?"

"I did," the stagehand said, his voice sad.

He was a big guy with dirty blond hair, and he wore blue denim overalls, the kind with a bib. There was even a little loop to hang a hammer in.

"Who are you?" I asked.

"Roger Ruggles. I was supposed to do a little work on the house, and when I came back here, I found Steele lying there."

"What about Sidney?"

"He was standing over the body. When I tried to check on Steele, the lion growled at me. I was afraid he'd tear me apart, so I left to find Mr. Zenko."

"That right, Zenko?" I asked.

"Is right," he said.

He was from Russia, I think, or somewhere like that. He directed westerns, jungle yarns, and detective tales with equal facility, which is to say, not much. But he worked fast, and he worked cheap. That was the kind of director Gober liked.

I went over to have a better look at Steele. No matter what anyone said, I didn't believe he'd been killed by Sidney. Sidney was just a scapegoat. Or a scapelion.

As I knelt down, I said, "Anybody on the set have a reason to kill Steele?"

I couldn't see any faces, but I could almost feel people freezing up behind me.

"You don't need to ask questions like that, Ferrel," Anderson said. "You know better than that."

"I thought you didn't want it to be the lion."

"Better the lion than somebody on the set. We don't need a scandal like that. And we won't have one, because I'm beginning to think Steele fell out of the treehouse."

"Not with these marks on him," I said.

Now that I could see them better, I could tell they'd been made with something that had ripped the skin and flesh away from the bone. No wonder Steele looked as if he'd been mauled by a lion. He'd been mauled, all right.

"He wasn't killed by the lion," Anna said, using that voice again.

I was pretty sure she was correct, but I said, "How do you know?"

"The stars," Benton said.

I remembered that he'd been interrupted before he could answer my question about the Sun and the eighth house, or maybe it was the twelfth. So I asked him again.

"You're very astute," Benton said. "I would like to cast your horoscope some day."

"Sure," I told him. "But first, what about that Sun business?"

"The eighth house is the house of death," Benton said. "And Mars and Neptune in the eighth house could indicate a violent death surrounded by mysterious circumstances. Things here are therefore not what they appear to be."

I could have told him that. But I hadn't.

"Furthermore," Benton went on, "the twelfth house is the house of self-undoing, and the Sun in the twelfth house implies that Steele may have somehow played a part in his own death."

I'd sort of figured that out, too.

"And finally," Benton said, "the Sun in the twelfth house suggests that

Steele had hidden enemies. The lion was not Steele's enemy. He was killed by a human being."

I had a feeling he was right on the money. I said, "What was Steele doing out here anyway? Why wasn't he waiting in his trailer?"

I stood up and turned around as I asked. No one was looking at me. They were all looking at the script girl, who was blushing. I didn't know that there was anyone in Hollywood who could do that. It made her look very young and innocent, which was probably deceptive. There are plenty of young people in Hollywood. I wasn't so sure about innocent.

"What's your name?" I asked her.

"Martha Varner," she said.

"You knew Mr. Steele?"

She nodded.

"How well?"

She didn't answer, but then she didn't have to. I didn't know anything about astrology, but Benton had said Steele was an Aries. I knew a little about rams. I also knew a little about Howard Steele.

"Couldn't you have had a little privacy in the trailer?" I asked. "Why meet here?"

She still didn't feel like answering, and Anderson said, "Leave her alone, Ferrel. What happened was that Steele was going to meet her in the tree-house and he climbed up and fell back down. That's the way Mr. Gober would want it, and that's the way we'll play it. I'll go call the cops and give them the story."

"I don't think so," I told him. "It's pretty clear that's not the way it happened."

"Who pays your retainer?" Anderson asked.

He knew the answer, so I didn't bother to tell him. I said, "You might be able to pay a doctor to swear to a false cause of death, but there are too many witnesses for you to keep it quiet."

"They all work for the same boss," he said. "And so do the cops if we want them to. We'll keep it quiet."

Maybe it would've worked, but I wasn't going to let it.

"I'm not keeping quiet," I said. "Not about murder."

"Murder? What are you talking about? He fell, that's all."

That wasn't all, and he knew it. We all knew it. But I was the only one who said it.

"He didn't fall. You can see that. We all can."

"You're right," Anderson said. He was getting desperate, I guess. "Sidney did it. Look at those claw marks."

Back to the lion again. There were claw marks on Steele, all right, but Sidney hadn't made them.

"Were you and Steele playing footsie?" I asked Martha Varner.

"I wouldn't call it that," she said, still blushing.

"But you were fooling around."

"Maybe just a little. He was so handsome."

She looked at Steele's mangled body, and tears ran down her cheeks.

Benton either didn't notice her grief or didn't care. He said, "Mars conjunct Neptune in the eighth house can also indicate a possible sexual scandal or confusion."

I was beginning to wonder if there was anything that Mars and Neptune *couldn't* suggest. I said to Martha, "Was there anyone on the set who thought he had a claim on you?" I asked.

She started sobbing as she tried to answer, but I could make out that she said, "No."

I wasn't sure she was telling the truth. I looked around. One of our little party was missing.

"What happened to the stagehand?" I asked.

Zenko pointed at the trees and said, "He went thataway."

I thought he'd been reading too many western scripts. I also thought I should've been watching Ruggles more closely. After all, I'd thought for the last ten minutes that he was the killer. I took off into the trees after him.

A stagehand wearing overalls with a hammer loop, but no hammer? I'd wondered from the beginning what had happened to it. They don't call them claw hammers for nothing. I suspected that Ruggles had used his to beat Steele and rip away his flesh, and I also thought he'd used it, along with a chisel, to break Sidney's chain and set him free, hoping to throw the blame for Steele's death on the old lion.

I pounded through the underbrush, slapping branches out of the way and trying to keep my legs from tangling in vines. I hadn't gone far when I heard someone behind me. I turned and saw Anna Lonestar.

"You don't know the jungle," she said, as if reciting a line from one of her movies. Her voice was no longer a purr.

"I can follow a trail," I said.

"Then you should be going that way," she told me, and pointed off to the right. Sure enough, there was a broken branch that I'd missed.

"Do you know something about Steele that I should know?" I asked.

"The stagehand wasn't jealous of him," she said, which surprised me.

"Roger was jealous of the girl," she continued, which should have surprised me, but didn't.

"You mean that Steele would swing on any vine that happened to be handy."

"That's one way to put it. Neptune was in the eighth house, remember? Come along."

She started off in the direction she'd pointed, and I followed. It wasn't long before we came to the fake river and pool where the swimming scenes were filmed. I was hoping Anna might dive in, the way she had in *Jungle Menace*. She wasn't wearing her skimpy jungle get-up, but I thought she'd look just swell in a wet shirt and jodhpurs.

She didn't jump in. She got a running start, grabbed a vine, and swung across. When she hit the other side, she turned around and looked over at me.

"Come along," she said, purring again.

I would have followed that voice anywhere. I spotted a vine, trotted over, and made a leap. The next thing I knew, I was sailing out over open water, and my hands were slipping on the vine.

I hoped there weren't any real crocodiles around, not that I thought there was much of a chance.

I didn't fall in the water, but I slid so far down the vine that when I hit the other side, I landed on my knees instead of my feet and skidded through the undergrowth on my stomach. I knew I'd ruined a good pair of pants, a jacket, a shirt, and a tie.

I struggled to my feet and tried to knock some of the dirt and mashed plants off my pants. Anna was already loping down a trail, so I stopped cleaning myself and followed.

It wasn't long before we came to a clearing that held a village of huts made of wood and straw. I remembered it from several of the Karg movies. In one of them, *Jungle Jeopardy*, I believe, Anna, as Kiela, had been tied to a stake in the center of the village, her hands bound and her arms pulled above her head. The evil hunters who had taken over the village planned to burn her alive. It was a scene that had done wonders for her appearance in the scanty outfit as she writhed from the flames, and when Karg had come riding to her rescue on the back of a mighty elephant, audiences all over the country had broken into wild applause. They applauded even louder when the unbound Anna skewered the leader of the bad guys with a spear thrown from atop the same elephant.

There appeared to be no one in the village now. As Karg would have said, it was quiet. Too quiet. I found myself wishing I had a roscoe, or that Anna had a spear.

There was a rustling noise at the back of one of the huts, and I saw Ruggles break through and sprint off into the jungle again.

"He's going back to the treehouse," Anna said.

I looked down at my ruined clothes and wished we'd just waited there for him.

"This way," Anna said, and we were off in hot pursuit.

When we came to the treehouse, the others were still there, but they were no longer looking down at Steele. They were all looking up at the treehouse.

"Ruggles?" I said.

"There," Zenko said, pointing up.

Anna Lonestar started for the rope ladder, but before she could reach it, Ruggles pulled it up and out of sight.

"What now?" I asked Anderson.

"I don't suppose we could just forget the whole thing," he said, and I figured someone had filled him in on Steele's sexual proclivities, if he hadn't known already. "Or we could still claim that Steele fell."

"Not with his killer on the loose," I said. "When there's a murder, someone has to pay. And this time it's Ruggles."

"This is going to make us look really bad," Anderson said.

"We'll worry about that after we take care of Ruggles," I said, and turned to Anna to ask how I could get up in the tree.

She was already walking toward another tree, with Benton at her heels trying to stop her.

"You Leos," he said to her. "Always wanting to be the center of attention. That young man might kill you. You must let someone else catch him."

He put a hand on Anna's arm, but she shook him off. I saw that she was headed for a large tree that looked easy to climb, and of course I'd seen it in the movies. In *Jungle Terror*, Steele had eluded his pursuers (a band of greed-crazed gold hunters) by climbing it, swinging to the treehouse on a vine, and bombarding them with coconuts. I wasn't at all sure that there were any coconuts in Africa, but that hadn't bothered the audiences. They'd loved the scene.

"Benton's right," I told Anna. "I'll go. It's what Gober pays me for."

It wasn't, really. What he paid me for was more along the line of what I'd done earlier that day, stopping scandals before they got started. But there was no use in thinking that way. Somebody had to go after Ruggles. Better me than one of the stars.

Anderson agreed. He said, "Let Ferrel do it, Anna. We can't afford to lose you."

For a second I thought she might object, but instead she moved aside. I took off my jacket and shoes and went up the tree. I felt like a kid again until I got to the branch where the vine was waiting. Ruggles wasn't going to treat me like a kid, not if he'd retrieved his hammer.

I tried not to think about that as I snatched the vine and jumped off the tree branch. As the air rushed past my face I thought about trying one of those jungle yells like Johnny Weissmuller did, but I thought better of it. Karg didn't have a yell, and I didn't want to infringe on another studio's property. Besides, I couldn't have yelled like Weissmuller, anyway.

My hands slid on the vine again, and I hit the railing of the treehouse with my stomach. By great good luck I folded in the middle and toppled onto the porch instead of falling back in the other direction.

Ruggles came rushing out and tried to make up for my good luck by kicking me off the edge. He got in a couple of solid blows to my ribcage, but at least he didn't have his hammer.

He did have a powerful leg, however, and the next thing I knew I was dangling above the jungle floor, hanging from the side of the treehouse porch by my fingertips.

I looked up at Ruggles, who smiled down at me as he raised his foot to stomp my hands.

I thought about telling him that he wouldn't get away with it, which he wouldn't have. But I didn't think he'd care.

"I'll break every finger you have," he said.

He would have done it, too, if Anna Lonestar hadn't come swinging across from the tree, her legs extended stiffly in front of her.

Her right foot took Ruggles in the nose.

Her left foot took him in the throat.

He gurgled and gasped as he stumbled back into the treehouse, clutching his face.

Anna landed lightly on the porch and looked inside to check on Ruggles. He must not have seemed to be a threat because she bent down and took my wrists. With both of us straining hard, I managed to get up onto the porch, where I lay and gulped air. It's not easy, dangling fifty feet above the ground. Or twenty feet. Whatever it was, it seemed like fifty to me.

Anna threw the rope ladder down, and by the time I'd recovered, Benton had joined us.

"I suppose it's a good thing she doesn't like to share the spotlight," he said.

"It's fine by me," I told him, and went in to have a look at Ruggles.

He wasn't doing well. His breath rasped in and out through his broken nose, and he kept pointing at his throat as if to say he couldn't talk. And he couldn't, which was just fine as far as I was concerned.

I left Anna and Benton with him while I climbed down to talk to Anderson.

Zenko was off to one side, comforting Martha Varner. I'd heard he had a talent for that sort of thing, so I left him to it and pulled Anderson aside.

"Here's the way we'll play it," I told him. "Ruggles was abusing Sidney, trying to get him excited for a scene or something. Steele, soft-hearted war hero that he was, intervened, and they got into a fight. Ruggles took out his hammer and killed him. Ruggles was captured by the heroic efforts of Anna Lonestar, who will no doubt go on to get top billing in her own series of jungle thrillers."

Anderson thought it over and said, "Not bad."

"Not bad? It's great. Steele dies a hero's death, the studio looks good, Anna Lonestar looks good, and I get a bonus. And maybe the undying gratitude of Anna Lonestar."

I smiled at the possibility.

"Benton has all her gratitude already," Anderson said. "Not to mention everything else."

"Oh," I said. "Well, there's still that bonus. And I'll get to see her in the movies. Gober really should do her series in color. And take a few more square inches off her costume."

"Why don't you tell him that," Anderson said.

"Maybe I will," I said, but of course I never did.

Kristine Kathryn Rusch

The Perfect Man

KRISTINE KATHRYN RUSCH is still best known for her science fiction and fantasy, for which she has won major awards and been widely lauded. But her mystery work, both the short stories done under her name and the nominated novels under the pen name Kris Nelscott, are fast becoming known to readers and booksellers, too. She was recently nominated for two Edgars in the same year—best novel and best short story. We certainly hope she keeps those elegantly wrought mystery stories, such as "The Perfect Man," which first appeared in *Murder Most Romantic*, coming as fast as she can write them.

The Perfect Man

Kristine Kathryn Rusch

Paige Racette stared at herself in the full-length mirror, hands on hips. Golden cap of blond hair expertly curled, narrow chin, high cheekbones, china blue eyes, and a little too much of a figure—thanks to the fact she spent most of her day on her butt and sometimes (usually!) forgetting to exercise. The black cocktail dress with its swirling party skirt hid most of the excess, and the glittering beads around the collar brought attention to her face, always and forever her best asset.

Even with the extra pounds, she was not blind-date material. Never had been. Until she quit her day job at the television station, she'd had to turn men away. Ironic that once she became a bestselling romance writer, she couldn't get a date to save her life. Part of the problem was that after she quit, she moved to San Francisco where she'd always wanted to live. She bought a Queen Anne in an old, exclusive neighborhood, set up her office in the bay windows of the second floor, and decided she was in heaven.

Little did she realize that working at home would isolate her, and being in a new city would isolate her more. It had taken her a year to make friends—mostly women, whom she met at the gym not too far from her home.

She saw interesting men, but didn't speak to them. She was still a small-town girl at heart, one who was afraid of the kind of men who lurked in the big city, who believed that the only way to meet the right man was by getting to know him through mutual interests—or mutual friends.

In fact, she wouldn't have agreed to this blind date if a friend hadn't convinced her. Sally Myer was her racquetball partner and general confidante who seemed to know everyone in this city. She'd finally tired of Paige's complaining and set her up.

Paige slid on her high heels. Who'd ever thought she'd get this desperate? And then she sighed. She wasn't desperate. She was lonely.

And surely, there was no shame in that.

Sally had picked the time and location, and had told Paige to dress up. Sally wasn't going to introduce them. She felt that would be tacky and make the first meeting uncomfortable. She asked Paige for a photograph to give to the blind date—one Josiah Wells—and then told Paige that he would find her.

The location was an upscale restaurant near the Opera House. It was The Place to Go at the moment—famous chef, famous food, and one of those bars that looked like it had come out of a movie set—large and open where Anyone Who Was Someone could see and be seen.

Paige arrived five minutes early, habitually prompt even when she didn't want to be. She adjusted the white Pashmina shawl she'd wrapped around her bare shoulders and scanned the bar before she went in.

It was all black and chrome, with black tinted mirrors and huge black vases filled with calla lilies separating the booths. The bar itself was black marble and behind it, bottles of liquor pressed against an untinted mirror, making the place look even bigger than it was.

She had only been here once before, with her Hollywood agent and a movie producer who was interested in her second novel. He didn't buy it—the rights went to another studio for high six figures—but he had bought her some of her most memorable meals in the City by the Bay.

She sat at the bar and ordered a Chardonnay that she didn't plan on touching—she wanted to keep her wits about her this night. Even with Sally's recommendation, Paige didn't trust a man she had never met before. She'd heard too many bad stories.

Of course, all the ones she'd written were about people who saw each other across a crowded room and knew at once that they were soul mates. She had never experienced love at first sight (and sometimes she joked to her editor that it was lust at first sight) but she was still hopeful enough to believe in it.

She took the cool glass of Chardonnay that the bartender handed her and swiveled slightly in her chair so that she would be in profile, not looking anxious, but visible enough to be recognizable. And as she did, she saw a man enter the bar.

He was tall and broad-shouldered, wearing a perfectly tailored black suit that shimmered like silk. He wore a white scarf around his neck—which on him looked like the perfect fashion accent—and a red rose in his lapel. His dark hair was expertly styled away from his chiseled features, and she felt her breath catch.

Lust at first sight. It was all she could do to keep from grinning at herself.

He appeared to be looking for someone. Finally, his gaze settled on her, and he smiled.

Something about that smile didn't quite fit his face. It was too personal. And then she shook the feeling away. She didn't want to be on a blind date—that was all. She had been fantasizing, the way she did when she was thinking of her books, and she was simply caught off-guard. No man was as perfect as her heroes. No man could be, not and still be human.

Although this man looked perfect. His rugged features were exactly like ones she had described in her novels.

He crossed the room, the smile remaining, hand extended. "Paige Racette? I'm Josiah Wells."

His voice was high and a bit nasal. She took his hand, and found the palm warm and moist.

"Nice to meet you," she said, removing her hand as quickly as possible.

He wore tinted blue contacts, and the swirling lenses made his eyes seem shiny, a little too intense. In fact, everything about him was a little too intense. He leaned too close, and he seemed too eager. Perhaps he was just as nervous as she was.

"I have reservations here if you don't mind," he said.

"No, that's fine."

He extended his arm—the perfect gentleman—and she put her arm through his, trying to remember the last time a man had done that for her. Her father maybe, when they went to the father-daughter dinner at her church back when she was in high school. And not one man since.

Although all the men in her books did it. When she wrote about it, the gesture seemed to have an old-fashioned elegance. In real life, it made her feel awkward.

He led her through the bar, placing one hand possessively over hers. This exact scene had happened in her first novel, *Beneath a Lover's Moon*. Fabian Garret and Skye Michaels had met, exchanged a few words, and were suddenly walking together like lovers. And Skye had thrilled to Fabian's touch.

Paige wished Josiah Wells's fingers weren't so clammy.

He led them to the maitre d', gave his name, and let the maitre d' lead them to a table near the back. See and Be Seen. Apparently they weren't important enough.

"I asked for a little privacy," he said, as if reading her thoughts. "I hope you don't mind."

She didn't. She had never liked the display aspect of this restaurant anyway.

The table was in a secluded corner. Two candles burned on silver candlesticks and the table was strewn with miniature carnations. A magnum of champagne cooled in a silver bucket, and she didn't have to look at the label to know that it was Dom Perignon.

The hair on the back of her neck rose. This was just like another scene in *Beneath a Lover's Moon*.

Josiah smiled down at her and she made herself smile at him. Maybe he thought her books were a blueprint to romancing her. She would have said so not five minutes before.

He pulled out her chair, and she sat, letting her shawl drape around her. As Josiah sat across from her, the maitre d' handed her the leather-bound menu and she was startled to realize it had no prices on it. A lady's menu. She hadn't seen one of those in years. The last time she had eaten here had been lunch, not dinner, and she had remembered the prices on the menu from that meal. They had nearly made her choke on her water.

A waiter poured the champagne and left discreetly, just like the maitre d' had. Josiah was watching her, his gaze intense.

She knew she had to say something. She was going to say how nice this was but she couldn't get the lie through her lips. Instead she said as warmly as she could, "You've read my books."

If anything, his gaze brightened. "I adore your books."

She made herself smile. She had been hoping he would say no, that Sally had been helping him all along. Instead, the look in his eyes made her want to push her chair even farther from the table. She had seen that look a hundred times at book signings: the too-eager fan who would easily monopolize all of her time at the expense of everyone else in line; the person who believed that his connection with the author—someone he hadn't met—was so personal that she felt the connection, too.

"I didn't realize that Sally told you I wrote."

"She didn't have to. When I found out that she knew you, I asked her for an introduction."

An introduction at a party would have done nicely, where Paige could smile at him, listen for a polite moment, and then ease away. But Sally hadn't known Paige that long, and didn't understand the difficulties a writer sometimes faced. Writers rarely got recognized in person—it wasn't their faces that were famous after all but their names—but when it happened, it could become as unpleasant as it was for athletes or movie stars.

"She didn't tell me you were familiar with my work," Paige said, ducking her head behind the menu.

"I asked her not to. I wanted this to be a surprise." He was leaning forward, his manicured hand outstretched.

She looked at his fingers, curled against the linen tablecloth, carefully avoiding the miniature carnations, and wondered if his skin was still clammy.

"Since you know what I do," she continued in that too-polite voice she couldn't seem to shake, "why don't you tell me about yourself?"

"Oh," he said, "there isn't much to tell."

And then he proceeded to describe his work with a software company. She only half listened, staring at the menu, wondering if there was an easy—and polite—way to leave this meal, knowing there was not. She would make the best of it, and call Sally the next morning, warning her not to do this ever again.

"Your books," he was saying, "made me realize that women look at men the way that men look at women. I started to exercise and dress appropriately and I . . ."

She looked over the menu at him, noting the suit again. It must have been silk, and he wore it the way her heroes wore theirs. Right down to the scarf, and the rose in the lapel. The red rose, a symbol of true love from her third novel, *Without Your Love*.

That shiver ran through her again.

This time he noticed. "Are you all right?"

"Fine," she lied. "I'm just fine."

Somehow she made it through the meal, feeling her skin crawl as he used phrases from her books, imitated the gestures of her heroes, and presumed an intimacy with her that he didn't have. She tried to keep the conversation light and impersonal, but it was a battle that she really didn't win.

Just before the dessert course, she excused herself and went to the ladies' room. After she came out, she asked the maitre d' to call her a cab, and then to signal her when it arrived. He smiled knowingly. Apparently he had seen dates end like this all too often.

She took her leave from Josiah just after they finished their coffees, thanking him profusely for a memorable evening. And then she escaped into the night, thankful that she had been careful when making plans. He didn't have her phone number and address. As she slipped into the cracked backseat of the cab, she promised herself that on the next blind date—if there was another blind date—she would make it drinks only. Not dinner. Never again.

The next day, she and Sally met for lattes at an overpriced touristy café on the Wharf. It was their usual spot—a place where they could watch crowds and not be overheard when they decided to gossip.

"How did you meet him?" Paige asked as she adjusted her wrought-iron café chair.

"Fundraisers, mostly," Sally said. She was a petite redhead with freckles that she didn't try to hide. From a distance, they made her look as if she were still in her twenties. "He was pretty active in local politics for a while."

"Was?"

She shrugged. "I guess he got too busy. I ran into him in Tower Records a few weeks ago, and we got to talking. That's what made me think of you."

"What did?"

Sally smiled. "He was holding one of your books, and I thought, he's wealthy. You're wealthy. He was complaining about how isolating his work was and so were you."

"Isolating? He works for a software company."

"Worked," Sally said. "He's a consultant now, and only when he needs to be. I think he just manages his investments, mostly."

Paige frowned. Had she heard him wrong then? She wasn't paying much attention, not after she had seen the carnations and champagne.

Sally was watching her closely. "I take it things didn't go well."

"He's just not my type."

"Rich? Good-looking? Good God, girl, what is your type?"

Paige smiled. "He's a fan."

"So? Wouldn't that be more appealing?"

Maybe it should have been. Maybe she had overreacted. She had psyched herself out a number of times about the strange men in the big city. Maybe her overactive imagination—the one that created all the stories that had made her wealthy—had finally betrayed her.

"No," Paige said. "Actually, it's less appealing. I sort of feel like he has photos of me naked and has studied them up close."

"I didn't think books were that personal. I mean, you write romance. That's fantasy, right? Make-believe?"

Paige's smile was thin. It was make-believe. But make-believe on any level had a bit of truth to it, even when little children were creating scenarios with Barbie dolls.

"I just don't think we're compatible," Paige said. "Sorry."

Sally shrugged again. "No skin off my nose. You're the one who doesn't get out much. Have you ever thought of going to those singles dinners? They're supposed to be a pretty good place to meet people. . . ."

Paige let the advice slip off her, knowing that she probably wouldn't discuss her love life—or lack of it—with Sally again. Paige had been right in the first place: she simply didn't have the right attitude to be a good blind date. There was probably nothing wrong with Josiah Wells. He had certainly gone to a lot of trouble to make sure she had a good time, and she had snuck off as soon as she could.

And if she couldn't be satisfied with a good-looking wealthy man who was trying to please her then she wouldn't be satisfied with any other blind date, either. She had to go back to what she knew worked. She had to go about her life normally, and hope that someday, an interesting guy would cross her path.

". . . even go to AA to find dates. I mean, that's a little crass, don't you think?"

Paige looked at Sally, and realized she hadn't heard most of Sally's monologue. "You know what? Let's forget about men. It's a brand-new century and I have a great life. Why do we both seem to think that a man will somehow improve that?"

Sally studied her for a moment. "You know what I think? I think you've spent so much time making up the perfect man that no flesh-and-blood guy will measure up."

And then she changed the subject, just as Paige had asked.

As Paige drove home, she found herself wondering if Sally was right. After all, Paige hadn't dated anyone since she quit her job. And that was when she really spent most of her time immersed in imaginary romance. Her conscious brain knew that the men she made up were too perfect to be real. But did her subconscious? Was that what was preventing her from talking to men she'd seen at the opera or the theater? Was all this big-city fear she'd been thinking about simply a way of preventing herself from remembering that men were as human—and as imperfect—as she was?

She almost had herself convinced as she parked her new VW Bug on the hill in front of her house. She set the emergency brake and then got out, grabbing her purse as she did.

She had a lot of work to do, and she had wasted most of the day obsessing about her unsatisfying blind date: It was time to return to work—a romantic suspense novel set on a cruise ship. She had done a mountain of research for the book—including two cruises—one to Hawaii in the winter, and another to Alaska in the summer. The Alaska trip was the one she had decided to use, and she had spent part of the spring in Juneau.

By the time she had reached the front porch, she was already thinking of the next scene she had to write. It was a description of Juneau, a city that was perfect for her purposes because there were only two ways out of it: by air or by sea. The roads ended just outside of town. The mountains hemmed everything in, trapping people, good and bad, hero and villain, within their steep walls.

She was so lost in her imagination that she nearly tripped over the basket sitting on her porch.

She bent down to look at it. Wrapped in colored cellophane, it was nearly as large as she was, and was filled with flowers, chocolates, wine, and two crystal wine goblets. In the very center was a photo in a heart-shaped gold frame. She peered at it through the wrapping and then recoiled.

It was a picture of her and Josiah at dinner the night before, looking, from the outside, like a very happy couple.

Obviously he had hired someone to take the picture. Someone who had watched them the entire evening, and waited for the right moment to snap the shot. That was unsettling. And so was the fact that Josiah had found her house. She was unlisted in the phonebook, and on public records, she used her first name—Giacinta—with no middle initial. And although her last name was unusual, there were at least five other Racettes listed. Had Josiah sent a basket to every one of them, hoping that he'd find the right one and she'd call him?

Or had he had her followed?

The thought made her look over her shoulder. Maybe there was someone on the street now, watching her, wondering how she would react to this gift.

She didn't want to bring it inside, but she felt like she had no choice. She suddenly felt quite exposed on the porch.

She picked up the basket by its beribboned handle and unlocked her door. Then she stepped inside, closed the door as her security firm had instructed her, and punched in her code. Her hands were shaking.

On impulse, she reset the perimeter alarm. She hadn't done that since she moved in, had thought it a silly precaution.

It didn't seem that silly anymore.

She set the basket on the deacon's bench she had near the front door. Then she fumbled through the ribbon to find the card she knew had to be there.

Her name was on the envelope in calligraphic script, but the message inside was typed on the delivery service's card.

> Two hearts, perfectly meshed.
> Two lives, perfectly twined.
> Is it luck that we have found each other?
> Or does Fate divine a way for perfect matches to meet?

Those were her words. The stilted words of Quinn Ralston, the hero of her sixth novel, a man who finally learned to free the poetry locked in his soul.

"God," she whispered, so creeped out that her hands felt dirty just from touching the card. She picked up the basket and carried it to the back of the house, setting it in the entryway where she kept her bundled newspapers.

She supposed most women would keep the chocolates, flowers, and wine even if they didn't like the man who sent them. But she wasn't most women. And the photograph bothered her more than she could say.

She locked the interior door, then went to the kitchen and scrubbed her hands until they were raw.

Somehow she managed to escape to the Juneau of her imagination, working furiously in her upstairs office, getting nearly fifteen pages done before dinner. Uncharacteristically, she closed the drapes, hiding the city view she had paid so much for. She didn't want anyone looking in.

She was making herself a taco salad with Bite-sized Tostitos and bagged shredded lettuce when the phone rang, startling her. She went to answer it, and then some instinct convinced her not to. Instead, she went to her answering machine and turned up the sound.

"Paige? If you're there, please pick up. It's Josiah." He paused and she held her breath. She hadn't given him this number. And Sally had said that morning that she hadn't given Paige's unlisted number to anyone. "Well, um, you're probably working and can't hear this."

A shiver ran through her. He knew she was home, then? Or was he guessing?

"I just wanted to find out if you got my present. I have tickets to tomorrow night's presentation of *La Bohème*. I know how much you love opera and this one in particular. They're box seats. Hard to get. And perfect, just like you. Call me back." He rattled off his phone number and then hung up.

She stared at the machine, with its blinking red light. She hadn't discussed the opera with him. She hadn't discussed the opera with Sally, either, after she found out that Sally hated "all that screeching." Sally wouldn't know *La Bohème* from *Don Giovanni,* and she certainly wouldn't remember either well enough to mention to someone else.

Well, maybe Paige's problem was that she had been polite to him the night before. Maybe she should have left. She'd had this problem in the past—mostly in college. She'd always tried to be polite to men who were interested in her, even if she wasn't interested in return. But sometimes, politeness merely encouraged them. Sometimes she had to be harsh just to send them away.

Harsh or polite, she really didn't want to talk to Josiah ever again. She would ignore the call, and hope that he would forget her. Most men understood a lack of response. They knew it for the brush-off it was.

If he managed to run into her, she would just apologize and give him the You're-Very-Nice-I'm-Sure-You'll-Meet-Someone-Special-Someday speech. That one worked every time.

Somehow, having a plan calmed her. She finished cooking the beef for her taco salad and took it to the butcher-block table in the center of the kitchen. There she opened the latest copy of *Publishers Weekly* and read while she ate.

During the next week, she got fifteen bouquets of flowers, each one an arrangement described in her books. Her plan wasn't working. She hadn't run into Josiah, but she didn't answer his phone calls. He didn't seem to understand the brush-off. He would call two or three times a day to leave messages on her machine, and once an hour, he would call and hang up. Sometimes she found herself standing over the Caller ID box, fists clenched.

All of this made work impossible. When the phone rang, she listened for his voice. When it wasn't him, she scrambled to pick up, her concentration broken.

In addition to the bouquets, he had taken to sending her cards and writing her long e-mails, sometimes mimicking the language of the men in her novels.

Finally, she called Sally and explained what was going on.

"I'm sorry," Sally said. "I had no idea he was like this."

Paige sighed heavily. She was beginning to feel trapped in the house. "You started this. What do you recommend?"

"I don't know," Sally said. "I'd offer to call him, but I don't think he'll listen to me. This sounds sick."

"Yeah," Paige said. "That's what I'm thinking."

"Maybe you should go to the police."

Paige felt cold. The police. If she went to them, it would be an acknowledgment that this had become serious.

"Maybe," she said, but she hoped she wouldn't have to.

Looking back on it, she realized she might have continued enduring if it weren't for the incident at the grocery store. She had been leaving the house, always wondering if someone was watching her, and then deciding that she was being just a bit too paranoid. But the fact that Josiah showed up in the grocery store a few moments after she arrived, pushing no grocery cart and dressed exactly like Maximilian D. Lake from *Love at 37,000 Feet,* was no coincidence.

He wore a new brown leather bomber jacket, aviation sunglasses, khakis, and a white scarf. When he saw her in the produce aisle, he whipped the sunglasses off with an affected air.

"Paige, darling! I've been worried about you." His eyes were even more intense than she remembered, and this time they were green, just like Maximilian Lake's.

"Josiah," she said, amazed at how calm she sounded. Her heart was pounding and her stomach was churning. He had her trapped—her cart was between the tomato and asparagus aisles. Behind her, the water jets, set to mist the produce every five minutes, kicked on.

"You have no idea how concerned I've been," he said, taking a step closer. She backed toward the onions. "When a person lives alone, works alone, and doesn't answer her phone, well, anything could be wrong."

Was that a threat? She couldn't tell. She made herself smile at him. "There's no need to worry about me. There are people checking on me all the time."

"Really?" He raised a single eyebrow, something she'd often described in her novels, but never actually seen in person. He probably knew that no one came to her house without an invitation. He seemed to know everything else.

She gripped the handle on her shopping cart firmly. "I'm glad I ran into you. I've been wanting to tell you something."

His face lit up, a look that would have been attractive if it weren't so needy. "You have?"

She nodded. Now was the time, her best and only chance. She pushed the cart forward just a little, so that he had to move aside. He seemed to think she was doing it to get closer to him. She was doing it so that she'd be able to get away.

"I really appreciate all the trouble you went to for dinner," she said. "It was one of the most memorable—"

"Our entire life could be like that," he said quickly. "An adventure every day, just like your books."

She had to concentrate to keep that smile on her face. "Writers write about adventure, Josiah, because we really don't want to go out and experience it ourselves."

He laughed. It sounded forced. "I'm sure Papa Hemingway is spinning in his grave. You are such a kidder, Paige."

"I'm not kidding," she said. "You're a very nice man, Josiah, but—"

"A nice man?" He took a step toward her, his face suddenly red. "A nice man? The only men who get described that way in your books are the losers, the ones the heroine wants to let down easy."

She let the words hang between them for a moment. And then she said, "I'm sorry."

He stared at her as if she had hit him. She pushed the cart past him, resisting the impulse to run. She was rounding the corner into the meat aisle when she heard him say, "You bitch!"

Her hands started trembling then, and she couldn't read her list. But she had to. He wouldn't run her out of here. Then he'd realize just how scared she was.

He was coming up behind her. "You can't do this, Paige. You know how good we are together. You know."

She turned around, leaned against her cart and prayed silently for strength. "Josiah, we had one date, and it wasn't very good. Now please, leave me alone."

A store employee was watching from the corner of the aisle. The butcher had looked up through the window in the back.

Josiah grabbed her wrist so hard that she could feel his fingers digging into her skin. "I'll make you remember. I'll make you—"

"Are you all right, miss?" The store employee had stepped to her side.

"No," she said. "He's hurting me."

"This is none of your business," Josiah said. "She's my girlfriend."

"I don't know him," Paige said.

The employee had taken Josiah's arm. Other employees were coming from various parts of the store. He must have given them a signal. Some of the customers were gathering, too.

"Sir, we're going to have to ask you to leave," the employee said.

"You have no right."

"We have every right, sir," the employee said. "Now let the lady go."

Josiah stared at him for a moment, then at the other customers. Store security had joined them.

"Paige," Josiah said, "tell them how much you love me. Tell them that we were meant to be together."

"I don't know you," she said, and this time her words seemed to get through. He let go of her arm and allowed the employee to pull him away.

She collapsed against her cart in relief, and the store manager, a middle-aged man with a nice face, asked her if she needed to sit down. She nodded. He led her to the back of the store, past the cans that were being recycled and the gray refrigeration units to a tiny office filled with red signs about customer service.

"I'm sorry," she said. "I'm so sorry."

"Why?" The manager pulled over a metal folding chair and helped her into it. Then he sat behind the desk. "It seemed like he was harassing you. Who is he?"

"I don't really know." She was still shaking. "A friend set us up on a blind date, and he hasn't left me alone since."

"Some friend," the manager said. His phone beeped, and he answered it. He spoke for a moment, his words soft. She didn't listen. She was staring at her wrist. Josiah's fingers had left marks.

Then the manager hung up. "He's gone. Our man took his license number and he's been forbidden to come into the store again. That's all we can do."

"Thank you," she said.

The manager frowned. He was looking at her bruised wrist as well. "You know guys like him don't back down."

"I'm beginning to realize that," she said.

And that was how she found herself parking her grocery-stuffed car in front of the local precinct. It was a gray cinderblock building built in the late 1960s with reinforced windows and a steel door. Somehow it did not inspire confidence.

She went inside anyway. The front hallway was narrow, and obviously redesigned. A steel door stood to her right and to her left was a window made of bulletproof glass. Behind it sat a man in a police uniform.

She stepped up to the window. He finished typing something into a computer before speaking to her. "What?"

"I'd like to file a complaint."

"I'll buzz you in. Take the second door to your right. Someone there'll help you."

"Thanks," she said, but her voice was lost in the electronic buzz that filled the narrow hallway. She opened the door and found herself in the original corridor, filled with blond wood and doors with windows. Very sixties, very unsafe. She shook her head slightly, opened the second door, and stepped inside.

She entered a large room filled with desks. It smelled of burned coffee and mold. Most of the desks were empty, although on most of them the desk lamps were on, revealing piles of papers and files. Black phones as old as the building sat on each desk, and she was startled to see that typewriters out-numbered computers.

There were only a handful of people in the room, most of them bent over their files, looking frustrated. A man with salt-and-pepper hair was carrying a cup of coffee back to his desk. He didn't look like any sort of police detective she'd imagined. He was squarely built and seemed rather ordinary.

When he saw her, he said, "Help you?"

"I want to file a complaint."

"Come with me." His deep voice was cracked and hoarse, as if he had been shouting all day.

He led her to a small desk in the center of the room. Most of the desks were pushed together facing each other, but this one stood alone. And it had a computer with an SFPD logo screen saver.

"I'm Detective Conover. How can I help you, Miss . . . ?"

"Paige Racette." Her voice sounded small in the large room.

He kicked a scarred wooden chair toward her. "What's your complaint?"

She sat down slowly, her heart pounding. "I'm being harassed."

"Harassed?"

"Stalked."

He looked at her straight on then, and she thought she saw a world-weariness in his brown eyes. His entire face was rumpled, like a coat that had been balled up and left in the bottom of a closet. It wasn't a handsome face by any definition, but it had a comfortable quality, a trustworthy quality that was built into the lines.

"Tell me about it," he said.

So she did. She started with the blind date, talked about how strange Josiah was, and how he wouldn't leave her alone.

"And he was taking things out of my novels like I would appreciate it. It really upset me."

"Novels?" It was the first time Conover had interrupted her.

She nodded. "I write romances."

"And are you published?"

The question startled her. Usually when she mentioned her name people recognized it. They always recognized it after she said she wrote romances.

"Yes," she said.

"So you were hoisted on your own petard, weren't you?"

"Excuse me?"

"You write about your sexual fantasies for a living, and then complain when someone is trying to take you up on it." He said that so deadpan, so seriously, that for a moment, she couldn't breathe.

"It's not like that," she said.

"Oh? It's advertising, lady."

She was shaking again. She had known this was a bad idea. Why would she expect sympathy from the police? "So since Donald Westlake writes about thieves, he shouldn't complain if he gets robbed? Or Stephen King shouldn't be upset if someone breaks his ankle with a sledgehammer?"

"Touchy," the detective said, but she noticed a twinkle in his eye that hadn't been there before.

She actually counted to ten, silently, before responding. She hadn't done that since she was a little girl. Then she said, as calmly as she could, "You baited me on purpose."

He grinned—and it smoothed out the care lines in his face, enhancing the twinkle in his eye and, for a moment, making him breathlessly attractive.

"There are a lot of celebrities in this town, Ms. Racette. It's hard for the lesser ones to get noticed. Sometimes they'll stage some sort of crime for publicity's sake. And really, what would be better than a romance writer being romanced by a fan who was using the structure of her books to do it?"

She wasn't sure what she objected to the most, being called a minor celebrity, being branded as a publicity hound, or finding this outrageous man attractive, even for a moment.

"I don't like attention," she said slowly. "If I liked attention, I would have chosen a different career. I hate book signings and television interviews, and I certainly don't want a word of this mess breathed to the press."

"So far so good," he said. She couldn't tell if he believed her, still. But she was amusing him. And that really pissed her off.

She held up her wrist. "He did this."

The smile left Conover's face. He took her hand gently in his own and extended it, examining the bruises as if they were clues. "When?"

"About an hour ago. At San Francisco Produce." She flushed saying the name of the grocery store. It was upscale and trendy, precisely the place a "celebrity" would shop.

But Conover didn't seem to notice. "You didn't tell me about the attack."

"I was getting to it when you interrupted me," she said. "I've been getting calls from him—a dozen or more a day. Flowers, presents, letters and e-mails. I'm unlisted and I never gave him my phone number or my address. I have a private e-mail address, not the one my publisher hands out, and that's the one he's using. And then he followed me to the grocery store and got angry when the store security asked him to leave."

Conover eased her hand onto his desk, then leaned back in his chair. His touch had been gentle, and she missed it.

"You had a *date* with him—"

"A blind date. We met at the restaurant, and a friend handled the details. And no, she didn't give him the information, either."

"—so," Conover said, as if she hadn't spoken, "I assume you know his name."

"Josiah Wells."

Conover wrote it down. Then he sighed. It looked like he was gathering himself. "You have a stalker, Ms. Racette."

"I know."

"And while stalking is illegal under California law, the law is damned inadequate. I'll get the video camera tape from the store, and if it backs you up, I'll arrest Wells. You'll be willing to press charges?"

"Yes," she said.

"That's a start." Conover's world-weary eyes met hers. "But I have to be honest. Usually these guys get out on bail. You'll need a lawyer to get an injunction against him, and your guy will probably ignore it. Even if he gets sent up for a few years, he'll come back and haunt you. They always do."

Her shaking started again. "So what can I do?"

"Your job isn't tied to the community. You can move."

Move? She felt cold. "I have a house." A life. This was her dream city. "I don't want to move."

"No one does, but it's usually the only thing that works."

"I don't want to run away," she said. "If I do that, then he'll be controlling my life. I'd be giving in. I'd be a victim."

Conover stared at her for a long moment. "Tell you what. I'll build the strongest case I can. That might give you a few years. By then, you might be willing to go somewhere new."

She nodded, stood. "I'll bring everything in tomorrow."

"I'd like to pick it up, if you don't mind. See where he left it, whether he's got a hidey-hole near the house. How about I come to you in a couple of hours?"

"Okay," she said.

"You got a peephole?"

"Yeah."

"Use it. I'll knock."

She nodded. Then felt her shoulders relax slightly, more than they had for two weeks. Finally, she had an ally. It meant more to her than she had realized it would. "Thanks."

"Don't thank me yet," he said. "Let's wait until this is all over."

All over. She tried to concentrate on the words and not the tone. Because Detective Conover really didn't sound all that optimistic.

The biggest bouquet yet waited for her on the front porch. She could see it from the street, and any hope that the meeting with Conover aroused disappeared. She knew without getting out of the car what the bouquet would be: calla lilies, tiger lilies, and Easter lilies, mixed with greens and lilies of the valley. It was a bouquet Marybeth Campbell was designing the day she met Robert Newman in *All My Kisses*, a bouquet he said was both romantic and sad. (Not to mention expensive: the flowers weren't in season at the same time.)

She left the bouquet on the porch without reading the card. Conover would be there soon and he could take the whole mess away. She certainly didn't want to look at it.

After all this, she wasn't sure she ever wanted to see flowers again.

When she got inside, she found twenty-three messages on her machine, all from Josiah, all apologies, although they got angrier and angrier as she didn't answer. He must have thought she had come straight home. What a surprise he would have when he realized that she had gone to the police.

She rubbed her wrist, noting the soreness and cursing him under her breath. In addition to the bruises, her wrist was slightly swollen and she wondered if he hadn't managed to sprain it. Just her luck. He would damage her arm, which she needed to write. She got an ice pack out of the freezer and applied it, sitting at the kitchen table and staring at nothing.

Move. Give up, give in, all because she was feeling lonely and wanted to go on a date. All because she wanted a little flattery, a nice evening, to meet someone safe who could be—if nothing else—a friend.

How big a mistake had that been?

Big enough, she was beginning to realize, to cost her everything she held dear.

That night, after dinner, she baked herself a chocolate cake and covered it with marshmallow frosting. It was her grandmother's recipe—comfort food that Paige normally never allowed herself. This time, though, she would eat the whole thing and not worry about calories or how bad it looked. Who would know?

She made some coffee and was sitting down to a large piece, when someone knocked on her door.

She got up and walked to the door, feeling oddly vulnerable. If it was Josiah, he would only be a piece of wood away from her. That was too close. It was all too close now.

She peered through the peephole, just as she had promised Conover she would, and she let out a small sigh of relief. He was shifting from foot to foot, looking down at the bouquet she had forgotten she had left there.

She deactivated the security system, then unlocked the three deadbolts and the chain lock she had installed since this nightmare began. Conover shoved the bouquet forward with his foot.

"Looks like your friend left another calling card."

"He's not my friend," she said softly, peering over Conover's shoulder. "And he left more than that."

Conover's glance was worried. What did he imagine?

"Phone calls," she said. "Almost two dozen. I haven't checked my e-mail."

"This guy's farther along than I thought." Conover pushed the bouquet all the way inside with his foot, then closed the door, and locked it. As he did, she reset the perimeter alarm.

Conover slipped on a pair of gloves and picked up the bouquet.

"You could have done that outside," she said.

"Didn't want to give him the satisfaction," Conover said. "He has to know we don't respect what he's doing. Where can I look at this?"

"Kitchen," she said, pointing the way.

He started toward it, then stopped, sniffing. "What smells so good?"

"Chocolate cake. You want some?"

"I thought you wrote."

"Doesn't stop me from baking on occasion."

He glanced at her, his dark eyes quizzical. "This hardly seems the time to be baking."

She shrugged. "I could drink instead."

To her surprise, he laughed. "Yes, I guess you could."

He carried the bouquet into the kitchen and set it on a chair. Then he dug through the flowers to find the card.

It was a different picture of their date. The photograph looked professional, almost artistic, done in black and white, using the light from the candles to illuminate her face. At first glance, she seemed entranced with Josiah. But when she looked closely, she could see the discomfort on her face.

"You didn't like him much," Conover said.

"He was creepy from the start, but in subtle hard-to-explain ways."

"Why didn't you leave?"

"I was raised to be polite. I had no idea he was crazy."

Conover grunted at that. He opened the card. The handwriting inside was the same as all the others.

My future and your future are the same. You are my heart and soul. Without you, I am nothing.

Josiah

She closed her eyes, felt that fluttery fear rise in her again. "There'll be a ring somewhere in that bouquet."

"How do you know?" Conover asked.

She opened her eyes. "Go look at the last page of *All My Kisses*. Robert sends a forgive-me bouquet and in it, he puts a diamond engagement ring."

"This bouquet?"

"No. Josiah already used that one. I guess he thought this one would be more spectacular."

Conover dug and then whistled. There, among the stems, was a black velvet ring box. He opened it. A large diamond glittered against a circle of sapphires in a white gold setting.

"Jesus," he said. "I could retire on this thing."

"I always thought that was a gaudy ring," Paige said, her voice shaking. "But it fit the characters."

"Not to your taste?"

"No." She sighed and sank back into her chair. "Just because I write about it doesn't mean I want it to happen to me."

"I think you made that clear in the precinct today." He put the ring box back where he found it, returned the card to its envelope and set the flowers on the floor. "Mind if I have some of that cake?"

"Oh, I'm sorry." She got up and cut him a piece of cake, then poured some coffee.

When she turned around, he was grinning.

"What did I do?" she asked.

"You weren't kidding about polite," he said. "I didn't come here for a tea party, and you could have said no."

She froze in place. "Was this another of your tests? To see if I was really that polite?"

"I wish I were that smart." He took the plate from her hand. "I was getting knocked out by the smell. My mother used to make this cake. It always was my favorite."

"With marshmallow frosting?"

"And that spritz of melted chocolate on top, just like you have here." He set the plate down and took the coffee from her hand. "Although in those days, I would have preferred a large glass of milk."

"I have some—"

"Sit." If anything, his grin had gotten bigger. "Forgive me for being so blunt, but what the hell did you need with a blind date?"

There was admiration in his eyes—real admiration, not the sick kind she'd seen from Josiah. She used her fork to cut a bite of cake. "I was lonely. I don't get out much, and I thought, what could it hurt?"

He shook his head. That weary look had returned to his face. She liked its rumpled quality, the way that he seemed to be able to take the weight of the world onto himself and still stand up. "What a way to get disillusioned."

"Because I'm a romance writer?"

"Because you're a person."

They ate the cake in silence after that, then he gripped his coffee mug and leaned back in the chair.

"Thanks," he said. "I'd forgotten that little taste of childhood."

"There's more."

"Maybe later." There was no smile on his face anymore, no enjoyment. "I have to tell you a few things."

She pushed her own plate away.

"I looked up Josiah Wells. He's got a sheet."

She grabbed her own coffee cup. It was warm and comforting. "Let me guess. The political conferences he stopped going to."

Conover frowned at her. "What conferences?"

"Here in San Francisco. He was active in local politics. That's how my friend Sally met him."

"And he stopped?"

"Rather suddenly. I thought, after all this started, that maybe—"

"I'll check into it," Conover said with a determination she hadn't heard from him before. "His sheet's from San Diego."

"I thought he was from here."

Conover shook his head. "He's not a dot-com millionaire. He made his money on a software system back in the early nineties, before everyone was into this business. Sold his interest for thirty million dollars and some stock, which has since risen in value. About ten times what it was."

Her mouth had gone dry. Josiah Wells had lied to both her and Sally. "Somehow I suspect this is important."

"Yeah." Conover took a sip of coffee. "He stalked a woman in San Diego."

"Oh, God." The news gave her a little too much relief. She had been feeling alone. But she didn't want anyone else to be experiencing the same thing she was.

"He killed her."

"What?" Paige froze.

"When she resisted him, he shot her and killed her." Conover's soft gaze was on her now, measuring. All her relief had vanished. She was suddenly more terrified than she had ever been.

"You know it was him?"

"I read the file. They faxed it to me this afternoon. All of it. They had him one hundred percent. DNA matches, semen matches—"

She winced, knowing what that meant.

"—the fibers from his home on her clothing, and a list of stalking complaints and injunctions that went on for pages."

The cake sat like a lump in her stomach. "Then why isn't he in prison?"

"Money," Conover said. "His attorneys so out-classed the DA's office that by the end of the trial, they could have convinced the jury that the judge had done it."

"Oh, my God," Paige said.

"The same things that happened to you happened to her," Conover said. "Only with her those things took about two years. With you it's taking two weeks."

"Because he feels like he knows me from my books?"

Conover shook his head. "She was a TV business reporter who had done an interview with him. He would have felt like he knew her, too."

"What then?" Somehow having the answer to all of that would make her feel better—or maybe she was just lying to herself.

"These guys are like alcoholics. If you take a guy through AA, and keep him sober for a year, then give him a drink, he won't rebuild his drinking career from scratch. He'll start at precisely the point he left off."

She had to swallow hard to keep the cake down. "You think she wasn't the only one."

"Yeah. I suspect if we look hard enough, we'll find a trail of women, each representing a point in the escalation of his sickness."

"You can arrest him, right?"

"Yes." Conover spoke softly. "But only on what he's done. Not on what he might do. And I don't think we'll be any more successful at holding him than the San Diego DA."

Paige ran her hand over the butcher-block table. "I have to leave, don't I?"

"Yeah." Conover's voice got even softer. He put a hand on hers. She looked at him. It wasn't world-weariness in his eyes. It was sadness. Sadness from all the things he'd seen, all the things he couldn't change.

"I'm from a small town," she said. "I don't want to bring him there."

"Is there anywhere else you can go? Somewhere he wouldn't think of?"

"New York," she said. "I have friends I can stay with for a few weeks."

"This'll take longer than a few weeks. You might not be able to come back."

"I know. But that'll give me time to find a place to live." Her voice broke on that last. This had been her dream city, her dream home. How quickly that vanished.

"I'm sorry," he said.

"Yeah," she said quietly. "Me, too."

He decided to stay without her asking him. He said he wanted to sift through the evidence, listen to the phone messages, and read the e-mail. She printed off all of it while she bought plane tickets online. Then she e-mailed her agent and told her that she was coming to the City.

Already she was talking like the New Yorker she was going to be.

Her flight left at 8:00 A.M. She spent half the night packing and unpacking, uncertain about what she would need, what she should leave behind. The only thing she was certain about was that she would need her laptop, and she spent an hour loading her files onto it. She was writing down the names of some moving and packing services when Conover stopped her.

"We leave everything as is," he said. "We don't want him to get too suspicious too soon."

"Why don't you arrest him now?" she asked. "Don't you have enough?"

Something flashed across his face, so quickly she almost didn't catch it.

"What?" she asked. "What is it?"

He closed his eyes. If anything, that made his face look even more rumpled. "I issued a warrant for his arrest before I came here. We haven't found him yet."

"Oh, God." Paige slipped into her favorite chair. One of many things she would have to leave behind, one of many things she might never see again because of Josiah Wells.

"We have people watching his house, watching yours, and a few other places he's known to hang out," Conover said. "We'll get him soon enough."

She nodded, trying to look reassured, even though she wasn't.

About 3:00 A.M., Conover looked at her suitcases sitting in the middle of the dining room floor. "I'll have to ship those to you. No sense tipping him off if he's watching this place."

"I thought you said—"

"I did. But we need to be careful. One duffel. The rest can wait."

"My laptop," she said. "I need that, too."

He sighed. "All right. The laptop and the biggest purse you have. Nothing more."

A few hours earlier, she might have argued with him. But a few hours earlier, she hadn't yet gone numb.

"I need some sleep," she said.

"I'll wake you," he said, "when it's time to go."

He drove her to the airport in his car. It was an old bathtub Porsche—with the early seventies bucket seats that were nearly impossible to get into.

"She's not pretty anymore," he said as he tucked Paige's laptop behind the seat, "but she can move."

They left at five, not so much to miss traffic, but hoping that Wells wouldn't be paying attention at that hour. Conover also kept checking his rearview mirror, and a few times he executed some odd maneuvers.

"We being followed?" she asked finally.

"I don't think so," he said. "But I'm being cautious."

His words hung between them. She watched the scenery go by, houses after houses after houses filled with people who went about their ordinary lives, not worrying about stalkers or death or losing everything.

"This isn't normal for you, is it?" she asked after a moment.

"Being cautious?" he said. "Of course it is."

"No." Paige spoke softly. "Taking care of someone like this."

He seemed even more intent on the road than he had been. "All cases are different."

"Really?"

He turned to her, opened his mouth, and then closed it again, sighing. "Josiah Wells is a predator."

"I know," she said.

"We have to do what we can to catch him." His tone was odd. She frowned. Was that an apology for something she didn't understand? Or an explanation for his attentiveness?

Maybe it was both.

He turned onto the road leading to San Francisco International Airport. The traffic seemed even thicker here, through all the construction and the dust. It seemed like they were constantly remodeling the place. Somehow he made it through the confusing signs to Short Term Parking. He found a space, parked, and then grabbed her laptop from the back.

"You're coming in?" she asked.

"I want to see you get on that plane." He seemed oddly determined.

"Don't you trust me?"

"Of course I do," he said and got out of the car.

San Francisco International Airport was an old airport, built right on the bay. The airport had been trying to modernize for years. The new parts were grafted on like artificial limbs.

Paige took a deep breath, grabbed her stuffed oversized purse, and let Conover lead her inside. She supposed they looked like any couple as they went through the automatic doors, stopping to examine the signs above them pointing to the proper airline. Conover was watching the other passengers. Paige was checking out the lines.

She had bought herself a first-class ticket—spending more money than she had spent for her very first car. But she was leaving everything behind. The last thing she wanted was to be crammed into coach next to a howling baby and an underpaid, stressed businessman.

She hurried to the first-class line, relieved that it was short. Conover stayed beside her, frowning as he watched the people flow past. He seemed both disappointed and alert. He was expecting something. But what?

Paige stepped up to the ticket counter, gave her name, showed her identification, answered the silly security questions, and got her e-ticket with the gate number written on the front.

"You've got an hour and a half," Conover said as she left the ticket counter. "Let's get breakfast."

His hand rested possessively on her elbow, and he pulled her close as he spoke. She glanced at him, but he still wasn't watching her.

"I have to make a stop first," she said.

He nodded.

They walked past the arrival and departure monitors, past the newspaper vending machines and toward the nearest restrooms. This part of the San

Francisco airport still had a seventies security design. Instead of a bank of x-ray machines and metal detectors blocking entry into the main part of the terminal, there was nothing. The security measures were in front of each gate: you couldn't enter without going past a security checkpoint. So different from New York, where you couldn't even walk into some areas without a ticket. Conover would have no trouble remaining beside her until it was time for her to take off.

She went into the ladies' room, leaving Conover near the departure monitors outside. The line was long—several flights had just arrived—but Paige didn't mind. This was the first time she'd had a moment to herself since Conover had arrived the night before.

It seemed like weeks ago.

She was going to be sorry to say goodbye to him at the gate. In that short period of time, she had come to rely on him more than she wanted to admit. He made her feel safe for the first time since she had met Josiah Wells.

As she exited the ladies' room, a hand grabbed her arm and pulled her sideways. She felt something poke against her back.

"Think you could leave me?"

Wells. She shook her arm, trying to get away, but he clamped harder.

"Scream," he said, "and I will hurt you."

"You can't hurt me," she said. "You can't have weapons in an airport."

"You can bring a gun into an airport," he said softly, right in her ear. "You just can't take it through security."

She felt cold then. He was as crazy as Conover said. And as dangerous.

"Josiah." She spoke loudly, hoping that Conover could hear her. She didn't see him anywhere. "I'm going to New York on business. When I come back, we can start planning the wedding."

Wells was silent for a moment. He didn't move at all. She couldn't see his face, but she could feel his body go rigid. "You're playing with me."

"No," she said, letting her voice work for her, hoping it sounded convincing. She kept scanning the crowd, but Conover was gone. "I got your ring last night. I decided I needed to settle a few things in New York before I told you I'd say yes."

Wells put his chin on her shoulder. His breath blew against her hair. "You're not wearing the ring."

"It didn't fit," she said. "But I have it with me. I was going to have it sized in New York."

"Let me see it," he said.

"You'll have to let me dig into my purse."

She wasn't sure he'd believe her. Then, after a moment, he let her go. She brought up her purse, pretended to rummage through it, and took a step toward the ladies' room door, praying her plan would work.

He was frowning. He looked like any other businessman in the airport, his suit neat and well tailored, his trenchcoat long and expensive, marred only by the way he held his hand in the pocket.

She waited just a split second, until there were a lot of people around from another arriving plane, and then she screamed, "He's got a gun!" and ran toward the ladies' room.

Only she didn't make it. She was tackled from behind, and went sprawling across the faded carpet. A gunshot echoed around her, and people started screaming, running. The body on top of hers prevented her from moving, and for a moment, she thought whoever had hit her had been shot.

Then she felt arms around her, dragging her toward the departure monitors.

"You little fool," Conover said in her ear. "I had this under control."

He pushed her against the base of the monitor, then turned around. Half the people around Wells had remained, and two of them had him in their grasp, while another was handcuffing him. Plainclothes airport police officers. More airport police were hurrying to the spot from the front door.

Passengers were still screaming and running out of the airport. Airline personnel were crouched behind their desks. Paige looked to see whether anyone was shot, but she didn't see anyone lying injured anywhere.

Her breathing was shallow, and she suddenly realized how terrified she had been. "What do you mean, under control? This doesn't look under control to me."

Security had Wells against the wall and were searching him for more weapons. One of the uniformed airport police had pulled Wells's head back and was yelling at him. Some of the passengers, realizing the threat was over, were drifting back toward the action.

Conover kept one hand on her, holding her in place. With the other, he pulled out his cell phone. He hit the speed-dial and put the small phone against his ear.

"Wait a minute!" Paige said.

He turned away slightly, as if he didn't want to speak to her. Then, he said into the phone, "Frank, do me a favor. Call the news media—everyone you can think of. Tell them something just happened at the airport. . . . No. I'm not going through official channels. That's why I called you. Keep my name out of it and get them here."

He hung up and glanced at Paige. She had never felt so many emotions in her life. Anger, adrenaline, confusion. Then she saw security lead Wells away.

Conover took her arm and helped her up. "What's going on?" she asked again.

"Outside," he said, and pushed her through the crowd. After a moment, she remembered to check for her laptop. He had it, and somehow she had retained her purse. They reached the front sidewalk only to find it a confusion of milling people—some still terrified from the shots, others just arriving and trying to drop off their luggage. Cabs honked and nearly missed each other. Buses were backing up as the crowd spilled into the street.

"Oh, this is so much better," she said.

He moved her down the sidewalk toward another terminal. The crowd thinned here.

"What the hell was that?" she asked. "Where were you? How did he get past you?"

"He didn't get past me," Conover said softly.

She felt the blood leave her face. "You set me up? I was bait?"

"It wasn't supposed to happen like this."

"Oh, really? He was supposed to drag me onto the nearest flight? Or shoot me?"

"I didn't know he had a gun," Conover said. "He was ballsier than I expected. And he wouldn't have taken you from San Francisco."

"You know this how? Because you're psychic?"

"No, he wanted to control you. He couldn't control you on a plane. I had security waiting outside. A few plainclothes cops have been around us since we arrived. He was supposed to grab you, but you weren't supposed to try to get away."

"Nice if you would have told me that."

He shook his head slightly. "Most people wouldn't have fought him. Most people would have cooperated."

"Most people would have appreciated an explanation!" Her voice rose and a few stray passengers looked in her direction. She made herself take a deep breath before she went on. "You knew he was going to be here. You knew it and didn't tell me."

"I guessed," he said.

"What did you do, tip him off?"

"No," Conover said softly. "You did."

"I did? I didn't talk to him."

"You booked your e-ticket online." His face was close to hers, his voice as soft as possible in all the noise. "He'd hacked into your system weeks ago. That's how he found your address and your phone number. Your public e-mail comes into the same computer as all your other e-mail. He's been following your every move ever since."

"Software genius," she muttered, shaking her head. She should have seen that.

Conover nodded. Across the way, reporters started converging on the building, cameras hefted on shoulders, running toward the doors. Conover shielded her, but she knew they would want to talk to her.

"Why didn't you warn me?" she asked again.

"I thought you'd be too obvious then, and he wouldn't try for you. I didn't expect you to be so cool under pressure. Telling him about the ring, pretending you were interested, that was smart."

One of the reporters was working the crowd. People were turning toward the camera.

"Where were you?" she asked. "I looked for you."

"I was behind you all the time."

"So if he took me outside . . . ?"

"I would have followed."

"I don't understand. Why didn't you tell me not to get the ticket online?"

"The ticket was a gift," Conover said. "I didn't realize you were going to do it that way. You told me when you finished. His file from the previous case mentioned how he had used the Internet to spy on his first victim. He was obviously doing that with you."

"But the airport, how did they know?"

"I called ahead, said that I was coming in, expecting a difficult passenger. I faxed his photo from your place while you were asleep. I asked them to wait until I got him outside, unless he did something threatening."

She frowned. More reporters were approaching. These looked like print media. No cameras, but lots of determination. "You could have waited and caught him at home."

"I could have," Conover said. "But this is better."

She turned to him, remembering the feel of the gun against her back, the screaming passengers, the explosive sound when the gun went off. "Someone could have been killed."

"I didn't expect a gun," Conover said. "And I didn't think he'd be rash enough to use it in an airport."

"But he did," she said.

"And it's going to help us." Conover watched another set of reporters run into the building. "First, his assault on you in an airport makes it a federal case. The gun adds to the case, and all the witnesses make it even better. Then there is the fact that airports are filled with security cameras. There's bound to be tape on this."

She frowned, trying to take herself out of this, trying to listen like a writer instead of a potential victim.

"And then," Conover said, "he attacked you. You're nationally known. It'll be big news. Our DA might have lost a stalking case against Wells, but the feds aren't going to let a guy who went nuts in an airport walk, no matter how much money he has."

"You set him up," she said. "If this had failed—"

"At the very least, I would have been fired," Conover said. "But it wouldn't have failed. I wouldn't have let anything happen to you. I didn't let anything happen to you."

"But you took such a risk." She raised her head toward his. "Why?"

He put a finger under her chin, and for a moment, she thought he was going to kiss her.

"Because you didn't want to leave San Francisco," he said softly.

"I get to stay home?" she asked.

He smiled, and let his finger drop. "Yeah."

He stared at her uncertainly, as if he were afraid she was going to yell at him again. But she felt a relief so powerful that it completely overwhelmed her.

She threw her arms around him. For a moment, he didn't move. Then, slowly, his arms wrapped around her and pulled her close.

"I don't even know your first name," she whispered.

"Pete," he said, burying his face in her hair.

"Pete." She tested it. "It suits you."

"I'd ask if I could call you," he said, "but I'm not real good on dates."

That pulled a reluctant laugh from her. "Obviously I'm not, either. But I make a mean chocolate cake."

"That's right," he said. "Let's go finish it."

"Don't we have to talk to the press?"

"For a moment." He pulled back just enough to smile at her. "And then I get to take you home."

"Where I get to stay." She couldn't convey how much this meant to her. "Thank you."

He nodded. "My pleasure."

She leaned her head against his shoulder, feeling his strength, feeling the comfort. It didn't matter how he looked or whether he knew *La Bohème* from *Don Giovanni*. All that mattered was how he made her feel.

Safe. Appreciated. And maybe even loved.

Stephan Rykena

Conscience

OUR NEXT FOREIGN story comes from Germany, where for
many there still remain deep scars from the last century. Stephan
Rykena, an author and lecturer in Germany, gives us his take on
one man's quest for answers to a question posed in a decades-old
newspaper clipping. A fiction staple in the German newspapers, he
recently published a collection of short fiction there. "Conscience"
was first published in the newspaper *Stadtanzeiger*.

Conscience

Stephan Rykena

W̶hen Frank, a friend of mine, stopped me in South Street in order to give me a brown envelope, I couldn't even guess that a very crazy story was waiting for me.

"Here, I think that's something for you," he said. "Stuck behind a mirror I bought at a garage sale two weeks ago. It's a part of a newspaper with a crime story, I think. You like writing crime stories yourself, don't you?"

It took some days until I had the time to have a look at the envelope. It contained a special edition of the *Vienna News* from April 18, 1949.

It was the second part of a crime-series with the title "The House of Horror."

It was cut in two halves right in the middle. Somebody had written something in the margin, which I couldn't read. The other five pages of the story were torn and parts were missing. So I didn't read the text intensively.

But on page seven there was an article that attracted my attention. *Legendary Chess Machine Found* was the headline.

> When workers tore down the ruins of the chocolate factory at Betzler Mountain they found, hidden in a secret chamber, a sophisticated copy of a human being, dressed in oriental clothes.
>
> After they had taken a close look at it, they found out that the body contained a very complicated apparatus of cog-wheels and other mechanical gear which they didn't understand.
>
> Only the director of the museum of science, who they took the strange figure to, recognized immediately that it was the famous chess machine of the all-around genius "Zatora," alias

Werner Hirch, by means of which he had saved the world-famous Jewish pianist Isaac Lensky from the concentration camp in Theresienstadt near Prague.

There was a photo which showed the inside of the figure.

This so called "chess machine" was a perfect construction which had been made in the last decades of the nineteenth century and which had only been improved by Hirch.

Achmet, as Hirch called his puppet, was said to be able to play chess as well as every good chess champion. Each person from the audience was allowed to play against Achmet. Even very good chess-players lost their games and so it was quite natural that there were soon rumors that Achmet was not a machine.

But even when skeptics opened different parts of the puppet they could find nothing but cog-wheels and metal. There wasn't enough space in the puppet, which was only the size of an ordinary grown-up man.

There were several contests in which even chess professionals tried to win against Achmet, but they usually failed.

Of course there was a person in the machine. It was Hirch's dwarfish step-brother Peter, a brilliant chess-player.

The two brothers were the ideal couple and toured with Achmet through the whole of Europe. Even a lot of famous Nazis invited them to their parties, without being able to find out about the secret. A tragic car accident in Paris, in which Peter was killed, ended Achmet's show appearances in 1940.

Hirch, who was also an excellent musician, earned his living from then on as a cello player in the Hamburg state orchestra which was transferred to Prague in 1941 because of the war. In Prague Hirch got to know Isaac Lensky, the Jewish pianist, and they soon became very good friends.

When Lensky was taken to the concentration camp Theresienstadt by the Nazis in 1942, Hirch "revitalized" Achmet and he managed to get an engagement for the camp during which he freed Lensky by using Achmet for one last time.

Hirch and Achmet have never been seen or heard of since that time.

After the war Lensky performed in every famous concert hall of the world, before he retired. He is said to have lived in Prague after his retirement.

I was very confused when I put the paper down. Why did anybody stick an envelope containing a piece of an old paper behind an antique mirror? And where did this old mirror come from? Curiosity had taken hold of me.

The crime story didn't make sense without the missing part.

Nobody had ever heard of a paper called *Vienna News* and I couldn't find anything about it on the Internet. There wasn't any paper with that name anymore.

A friend of mine who worked for the university in Hanover managed to make out the handwriting in the margin.

It said: Praha, Jachynova 23, Sholon, Seldomir.

It was just by chance that I had to travel to Prague on business four weeks later. I don't really know why I took the envelope with me. I had a lot of appointments but I managed to have a free Saturday for sightseeing.

Being a tourist for a day I went, of course, to the Jewish quarter in the city and suddenly there was this Jachynova Street that was mentioned on the paper.

It was at the outskirts of the Jewish quarter in the old part of Prague.

As I didn't know who this Seldomir Sholon was and what part he played in the whole game, I decided to do something very crazy and looked for the Jachynova number 23, which I found very soon.

An old door in a backyard led to a very rundown stairwell. On a weathered brass doorplate I could read "Sholon, S."

My heart was beating like a drum when I rang the bell. I heard the noise of slippers. A fragile, little old man opened the door and looked seriously at me.

About one hour later I left the house deeply impressed through the same door; I cursed my curiosity and decided never to tell anybody about what had happened.

Unintentionally I had made an eighty-one-year-old man tell me a secret which should better have gone into his grave with him.

S. Sholon, otherwise known as Isaac Lensky, had lived for fifty-nine years with a heavy burden.

"Well, you know everything, don't you?" he had asked very calmly and in perfect German, when I had shown him the brown envelope, while he poured a cup of tea in this poor, cold and nearly empty flat.

"Originally my confession should not have been found before my death, but the circumstances changed and I had to sell parts of my furniture. And—well—I forgot about the envelope. Have you already informed the police?"

I was totally dumbfounded and my hands became wet. I didn't know what to say.

"It was homicide, not murder," he went on. "We had not intended to kill him." He took his cup and drank. I fumbled for the piece of newspaper in the envelope.

"He suddenly woke up and I wanted . . ."

I held the newspaper pages right in front of his eyes. "I . . . I don't understand," I stammered. He put his cup back on the table.

"I think I explained everything in the letter," he said in a strong voice. "And if you've read the part of the crime story . . ." He stopped and frowned.

We sat there and looked at each other in silence.

"I haven't read anything but a story about a chess machine," I said hesitating. "There was no letter in the envelope and there is no need to explain anything." I took a sip from my tea-cup.

He smiled and nodded. "Let's take it as a sign." He rubbed his hands, because it was rather cold in the room. "I'm eighty-one now. Time for the truth, I think. And who knows where the letter really is now?"

He then told me about his escape from the concentration camp in the chess-machine.

"Werner had planned everything perfectly. The man in the machine, a certain Adolf Blahn who Werner had got to know during a chess tournament, played very well. After the last match we wanted to anesthetize him in a little room behind the main room and then we should change places. Werner wanted to get me out of the camp in the puppet. Everything was perfect. Unfortunately this Adolf Blahn woke up too early, just when I was about to climb into the chess machine.

"I smashed a chair on his head, he fell back with his head against a big oak table and died. We didn't have any time to lose, and so we hid the corpse in a cupboard and left the camp as we had planned.

"My life was saved while Adolf Blahn had lost his life."

The old man had sunk deeply into the huge, worn-out armchair he had been sitting in all the time.

"I'm glad that I have told you the story," he said in a low voice.

Two weeks after I had returned home I met Frank again in a café in South Street. He wanted to know what I had found out about his discovery from behind the mirror. I shrugged my shoulders and said that my inquiries had led to nothing.

Billie Rubin

Living Next Door to Malice

BILLIE RUBIN is the pen name of German author Ute Hacker, who lives in Munich, Germany. A trained bookseller, she worked for several years in bookshops and publishing houses, but is now employed in the information technology industry. She writes under several different names, including children's books (as Luisa Hartmann) and fiction (as Ann E. Hacker). Her fiction has been featured in several magazines and the Online Magazine of the Dublin Writers' Workshop. She also offers online workshops in creative writing, and more information on that can be found at *www.billierubin.de* or *www.utehacker.de*. Her story, "Living Next Door to Malice," was first published in the anthology *Teuflische Nachbarn*, or *Diabolical Neighbors*, and is about exactly that.

Living Next Door to Malice

Billie Rubin

L ooking back on my early studying days I cannot help but feel a shiver run down my spine though it's more than twenty years ago. I had moved from Lower Bavaria to Munich to study English and American Literature. My parents couldn't afford to buy an apartment in Munich and I wasn't exactly looking forward to heated arguments and fights with roommates, so I started looking for an affordable apartment on the outskirts. I found one in the East of Munich, then a sleepy nest, now the IT boom town. The apartment was a real snip: The friend of a friend of my parents knew the previous tenant, an elderly bachelor who mainly cared for quiet hobbies like reading and collecting stamps. I am convinced that only the fact that this friend of a friend vouched for me gave me the chance to have a look at the apartment. I fell in love immediately: an attic apartment in a two-story house with real wooden beams across a huge room, splitting it into two smaller spaces at each end and a larger section in the middle. Somehow I must have made a good impression because a week later I surprisingly received the contract.

Glad to have escaped the boring narrow-mindedness of Lower Bavaria I moved to Munich and wasted no time in making myself right at home. My landlords, a couple in their forties, lived on the first floor; the second floor was occupied by an elderly couple that I seldom met. Seeing the house from outside didn't tell you what treasures it contained: The landlord was a real wood fan and over the years had refurbished everything in wood. The wood lent a touch of coziness to the interiors without being kitschy.

My first year passed by uneventfully. I loved my apartment, concentrated on my studies, found a job in a café and went to see my family once in a while. My landlords, with the inconspicuous name of Miller, never bothered me, and as the ride to the university took less than twenty-five minutes it soon became clear to me that I would spend my whole student life in this house. The house was set in large grounds, which extended right up to a little stream that wound its way through the small town. I wasn't allowed to use or even access the garden but I didn't mind too much as I went to the Isar for swimming anyway. I would have loved to sit by the stream and listen to its steady murmur while reading or learning. However, that would have been more than unwise since I knew that Mr. Miller regularly dusted the banks with rat poison.

The first instances of harassment occurred during my second year. I had spent some weeks in England, leaving my apartment empty. All had been discussed with the Millers, so I was more than surprised when they told me that I shouldn't have let the apartment become neglected. I couldn't see more than a thin layer of dust and forgot about the incident. The second year brought more group activities at the university. We couldn't afford to go to a café each time we met, so we decided to take turns in gathering at our respective apartments. Whenever people saw my apartment for the first time, they stood and stared, stunned by its beauty. Needless to say, it became the most popular place of all. Okay, we weren't always very quiet but neither did we party. Nonetheless I had to listen to complaints from my landlords who had even kept a list of the number of people who'd visited or the frequency of flushing the toilet.

When I say my landlords I mean Mr. Miller. Of course I knew and had sometimes met Mrs. Miller, but whenever they wanted to tell their tenants something bad she sent him ahead. He wasn't such a bad guy, though not at all the stuff dreams are made of. Most times I felt sorry for him. The elderly couple on the second floor had told me that the grounds and house belonged to her and apparently there was a son from her first marriage who was to inherit everything. I don't know what kind of marriage they led but I often got the feeling that Mr. Miller was a cheap handyman. Sometimes I could hear them quarreling in their apartment and it didn't take much to imagine her running about their place like a madwoman.

I talked to Mr. Miller. I told him I wasn't looking for trouble but that I had to meet my colleagues from time to time. He showed some understanding and I promised to be more considerate. Weeks passed by without trouble, but then I fell in love with a guy and no longer spent my nights alone. It took some weeks before my boyfriend had a close encounter of the first kind; it was so impressive that from then on he refused to stay over for weeks. Again I talked to Mr. Miller. I explained the situation, asked for his understanding. Again some weeks went by without further trouble. Okay, they did tell me to use the toilet less frequently during the night, but otherwise we lived in peace. My boyfriend talked about living next door to malice, an allusion to a famous hit record, but I could imagine worse situations. Too many times had I heard my friends complain about permanent trouble in their sharing community. My situation wasn't that bad.

During the third year I changed boyfriends, a cat found its way to my doorstep and heartache and trouble started big time. Like a good girl I had asked Mr. Miller about the cat. He said yes, only to go back on his decision a couple of weeks later—definitely on his wife's behest. But Cat and I had become used to each other by then and we decided to ignore the revocation. My current boyfriend was a lawyer and advised me that it was legal to keep small pets like cats, even without expressed permission from the landlord. Cat wasn't allowed to leave the apartment as I was afraid she might eat some of the rat poison. For several months everything went well. When Mr. Miller asked about Cat I told him I had long before given her to a friend. He believed me.

Are you familiar with this feeling? You know, when you come home and sense that someone has been in your apartment? More and more I had the sneaking suspicion that during my absence somebody had been snooping around my rooms. It could only be the Millers. My parents had a key but they lived too far away to come that often. And they would have told me. Furthermore Mrs. Miller had started complaining about cat droppings on her doormat whenever she met me—unfortunately I met her very often now. Of course I was surprised about her discovery and asked her how this could be as we didn't have a cat in the house. After all, she couldn't possibly insist that Cat was still living with me without admitting that she'd been inside my apartment.

The lawyer friend was soon history, as my feelings briefly turned towards an older fellow student before choosing a colleague of my age. When my parents called one evening and asked me what the hell was going on I didn't suspect anything yet. Of course I told them nothing was going on. They repeated the angry call of my landlords who apparently more than once had used the words *Sodom* and *Gomorrah*. Furthermore they had mentioned my excessive abuse of cigarettes and alcohol, not to speak of the alarming frequency with which I seemed to change my men. I was speechless. Okay, so I was smoking heavily at that time and now and then I had even had a drink too many but to insinuate that I changed my partners more frequently than my underwear was taking things too far. It took me a while to calm my parents. I confronted Mr. Miller. He admitted at once that they would love to get rid of me. I wasn't the tenant a landlord wanted to have.

My first reaction was to move out. But then I told myself that I wouldn't make it that easy for them. I started setting up traps to prove their snooping around. Cat moved to a friend, not to calm down the Millers, but because I was afraid they might kill her. At least once a week I invited friends and more than once they slept on my floor. Of course we were not very considerate and "Living Next Door to Malice" became our favorite song. My landlords thought I was bad? Okay, I became bad. I became their personalized nightmare. Notice to vacate the premises came within days. I went to a lawyer and was told that they had been suing all their neighbors for years. My lawyer and I filed a counternotice.

However, the problem was solved in a completely different way than I had expected. It was an opportunity too good to be missed. It had been pouring rain for days and the quiet stream at the edge of the grounds had become a torrential river. I carried my rubbish to the collection point when I saw Mr. Miller standing at the bank facing the water. He was probably setting up new rattraps. I didn't think for a second, just acted on my feeling. I crept up on him and shoved him into the water. I didn't think of the consequences, just of the stupid expression he would make. But I still have this feeling in me that I wanted to happen what happened: The strong current immediately dragged Mr. Miller away from the bank. Only afterwards did I learn that he wasn't able to swim. His body was found one day later down the river near a small dam. I was petrified and pretty sure that the police would come at any moment to get me. The police came but they asked Mrs. Miller, who had reported her husband missing. They asked me if I had seen him and I replied truthfully, yes, I had seen him at the river when I carried my rubbish to the collection point. Afterwards, I said, I had gone to the university and not returned until late in the evening. I was surprised that Mrs. Miller didn't object. She must have known that I hadn't left the house the entire day. Anyway, she had completely changed from a madwoman to a desperate wife. Was it possible that she had had feelings for her husband after all?

I took advantage of the chaos during the following days and disappeared. Under the cover of night I had my furniture moved to a room in an apartment-sharing community. I moved out only some weeks later when I realized that my room neighbor was a notorious snorer. Lots of luck and a good portion of recklessness, which always comes in handy in a big city, helped me find a small apartment in one of these anonymous concrete blocks. Exactly what Cat and I needed. The room was small and dark, too hot in summer, too cold in winter, but it was my castle. Only selected friends were welcome and only after having announced themselves. Now and then I exchanged a nice word with my neighbors to the left. The folks in the apartment to the right of my place could regularly be heard fighting when they were drunk. But otherwise life was fine. A couple of months later though my left neighbor did start bothering me. His wife had locked him out and he wanted to get into their apartment via my balcony. We lived on the fifth floor but who was I to fight with this man? To avoid trouble I let him do as he pleased. You want to know if he arrived safely on his balcony? Sorry, but that's another story.

Tatjana Kruse

The Good Old German Way

TATJANA KRUSE is a member of the German writers' organization Syndikat, as well as the American group Sisters in Crime. She
has written three novels and more than twenty short stories, and
was recently awarded the Marlowe Award for the best German
short story. With stories like "The Good Old German Way" under
her belt, it's no wonder. Another masterpiece of European economy, this story, first published in the anthology *Briefe Aus Mos-
bach—Das Verbrechen Lauert Ueberall*, is a classic study of one
person's greed overwhelming her common sense.

The Good Old German Way

Tatjana Kruse

It's especially lovely in the prime of day, when the morning dawns—Schreckenstein Castle, somewhere between Schwäbisch Hall and Michelbach. The main buildings date back to the seventeenth century, erected on the ruins of a Hohenstaufen fortress. As I was later told, the old countess had to put all the antiques up for auction—no ghost with a reputation would want to haunt in these pitiful surroundings anymore—but even with only a few sticks of furniture the castle seemed to me more splendid than anything I had ever seen in my life.

I was on the run. Escaping my past as a beaten and humiliated housewife. My husband was no longer with us, and if it's true that one should not speak badly of the dead, then nothing else could be said about my deceased husband other than these two words: Thomas Hausmann.

"I see you're quite strong, my dear. Exactly what I need for my horses. I'm too weak for the hard work myself, I'm afraid."

Countess Agnes was on the sunny side of ninety. She lived alone at Schreckenstein Castle. Twice a week an old cleaning woman came by from the nearby town of Schwäbisch Hall, but she now wanted to retire. An ad that I'd discovered by chance in the *Haller Tagblatt* got me interested in the job. The prospect of being a lady of the castle, if only in my imagination, was more than I could resist.

"I won't dissappoint you," I said. "Shoveling manure or scrubbing the floors, I'll do whatever you want."

We got along quite well. I had to run the household and care for Arbor and Ajax, the two huge cold-blooded draft horses, the last of her late husband's breed. As the countess was almost blind, I did a cursory job cleaning the few rooms in the castle she still inhabited—she neither saw the dust clouds in the parlor nor the grease stains on the kitchen stove. Only when it came to her horses she tended to be fussy, so I cared for thems as if my life depended on it.

Taking the horses out for a ride was what I loved best—in the mornings it was Arbor's turn, in the evenings Ajax's. Each time I came back from Mount Einkorn and saw Schreckenstein Castle below me in the valley, my heart beat faster. Sometimes I even imagined that down there in the castle court a Prince Charming was playing his serenade on a lute. I loved this castle as if it were my own.

But those days of carefree bliss didn't last long.

"Still no horse droppings from Ajax!" The countess pressed her aristrocratic ear to the horse's belly. The horse stood with his head drooping, ribs heaving. A faint rumbling growl rolled up from the rib cage. "What's that noise in there?"

"I don't know. When I came into the stable this morning, Ajax was rolling on the floor. Dr. Völkl will be here right after her consulting hours."

For many years now the countess couldn't pay Dr. Völkl, but the spunky veterinarian came anyway. Maybe it flattered her that one of her clients was a real blue-blooded aristocrat.

"If anything should happen to my darling Ajax, I won't survive it," wailed the countess.

"Don't worry, Ajax will survive us all," I soothed.

But Dr. Völkl thought otherwise. "I haven't seen such a bad colic in quite a while. I'm afraid his intestines are totally entwined. His gases can't escape. Someday soon the intestinal walls will tear apart and the animal will die of massive intoxication in the abdominal cavity."

I must have turned green. If Ajax died, the countess might blame me and I would lose my job and thus my refuge. My uneasiness was replaced by a drymouthed dread. "Is there anything I can do?"

"You could walk him around. That's the best you can do."

Which I did, all night long, in slow circles. But the next morning, shortly after ten, Ajax died.

The knacker, a simple tight-lipped man, came an hour later. He heaved the dead horse onto the hydraulic platform of his truck. Then he drove away with Ajax to the carcass disposal plant to make soap from our beloved four-legged friend. The countess had definitely ruled out horse sausage, which enjoyed great popularity in these times of mad-cow disease.

Countess Agnes was deeply shaken, at least as shaken as Arbor, who missed his horse buddy, which is why I looked after him with special care.

However, I was completely mistaken about the countess. She didn't fire me. After two weeks she was almost her old self again, and when I came back from shopping one day, she was waiting in the parlor together with Traugott Wilfinger, her lawyer.

"My love, what would I have done without you these past two weeks?

Since you are here, I know that the horses and I"—she stopped in the middle of the sentence and her eyes got wet—"that the horse and I are in good hands. I want to show you my gratitude. As I have no living relatives, I want *you* to be my sole heir."

I have to admit I was nonplussed. I really hadn't bargained on that. I could see from the lawyer's eyes that he couldn't disagree more with the countess's decision, but right there and then the countess drew up her last will, and so—from one moment to the next—I was an heiress. Not a rich heiress, mind you, but still an heiress.

It was a true turn of events. Until that moment I loved to work on Schreckenstein Castle because I was grateful to have found such a nice refuge. But from then on nothing was the same. Greed reared its ugly head. Every evening I prayed, "Dear God, if you happen to be in the neighborhood, please let me inherit the castle right now!" But even though the countess was almost ninety she showed no sign of impending demise. And the heavenly powers obviously didn't want to interfere: the old lady survived a bad fall, absolutely unharmed. Every morning I asked myself how long it would take until this wonderful castle would be mine.

And then one day the idea struck me on horseback.

I felt sorry for Arbor but I had never been a true horselover and his death would serve a higher purpose.

In the Schwäbisch Hall library I read all about what harms horses and soon I found an indigenous plant that would slowly but surely poison Arbor. For nearly a month I systematically poisoned the old hack, who devoured everything as long as he got a lump of sugar before and afterwards.

In mid-December Arbor died. I found him dead one night in the stable.

I fetched the big carving knife from the kitchen and set to work. Slitting open the belly was easy, but carrying the stinking, slippery intestines on a shovel behind the stable and then piling the manure over it was an achievement of Herculean proportions. But as told before, I was strong.

When the countess came in late that morning to check in on her darling Arbor, my work was already done.

I whacked her head with the shovel—two well-aimed blows were all it took—and stuffed her body into the disemboweled carcass of the horse, which wasn't all that hard: Arbor was a giant horse and the countess was an extremely petite woman.

However, sewing up the carcass proved to be much more difficult than I had imagined. Thank God the horse had a wonderful winter coat with long bellyhair so one could see the seam only when looking for it. The knacker whom I called soon thereafter would undoubtedly notice nothing.

When the man arrived I told him that I was concerned about the well-being of the countess and that I hadn't seen the old dear since dinner the previous evening. He ventured that she might have found her horse dead in the morning and, in her distraction, ran into the woods. Or maybe she had drowned herself in sorrow—and the Kocher River had flooded during recent snow thaw.

What a wonderful idea—that was exactly what I told the police when I reported the countess missing that very day.

The woods were searched by police and the Bundeswehr, but of course the countess remained missing. The Kocher couldn't be searched by divers due to rough waters. The leader of the search party told me that we just had to wait until the countess washed up somewhere, then he gave me a paternal pat on the back.

It takes seven years before a missing person can be officially declared dead, which means that Schreckenstein Castle isn't yet mine—but I don't care. As future owner I'm allowed to live in the castle and nobody tells me what to do. The countess had some debts but I won't have to pay them until she's officially declared dead and I inherit the castle. Before that time something will come up, I'm sure. Maybe I'll turn the castle into a hotel. Or I'll buy some horses and give riding lessons.

It's only when I wash my hands with soap that I feel guilty. I don't mind the countess, she was older than God and had had a good life. No, I feel guilty because of Arbor—I hope he's now grazing in horse heaven and has forgiven me.

Anne Perry

The Case of the Bloodless Sock

ANNE PERRY is one of the most popular writers of historical mysteries in the world. Her novels, set in Victorian England, are the measure for all other historical series. The reason for this is simple. She is a first-rate storyteller. Whatever else you find in her novels—wonderful research, riveting set-pieces, a nice wry voice—she above all else keeps you turning the pages. Her short fiction is just as evocative and compelling as her books. In "The Case of the Bloodless Sock" she puts her own spin on the master sleuth himself, Sherlock Holmes, in a case as baffling as anything Sir Arthur Conan Doyle could have come up with. The solution, too, is just as clever, and more important, plausible. This story first appeared in *Murder in Baker Street*.

The Case of the Bloodless Sock

Anne Perry

There had been no cases of any interest for some weeks, and my friend
Sherlock Holmes was bored by the trivia that came his way. His temper
showed it to the degree where I was happy to accept an invitation from an
old friend, Robert Hunt, a widower who lived in the country, not far from
the handsome city of Durham.

"By all means go, Watson," Holmes encouraged, except that that is far
too joyful and heartening a word for the expression on his face that accompanied it. "Take the afternoon train," he added, scowling at the papers in
front of him. "At this time of the year you will be in your village, wherever
it is, before dark. Good-bye."

Thus was I dismissed. And I admit, I left without the pleasure I would
have felt with a more sanguine farewell.

However the late summer journey northward from London toward
the ever-widening countryside of Yorkshire, and then the climb to the
dales, and the great, bare moors of County Durham, improved my spirits
greatly. By the time I had taken the short, local journey to the village where
Robert Hunt had his very fine house, I was smiling to myself, and fully
sensitive to the peculiar beauty of that part of the world. There is nothing
of the comfortable Home Counties about it, but rather a width, a great
clarity of light, and rolling moorland where hill upon hill disappears into
the distance, fading in subtle shades of blues and purples until the horizon
melts into the sky. As I came over the high crest and looked down toward
the village, it was as if I were on the roof of the world. I had almost a giddy
feeling.

I had wired ahead to inform Hunt of my arrival. Imagine then, my dismay at finding no one to meet me at the deserted station, and being obliged
to set out in the darkening air, chillier than I am accustomed to, being so

much further north and at a considerable altitude, carrying my suitcase in my hand.

I had walked some four miles, and was worn out both from exertion and from temper, when an elderly man in a pony trap finally offered me a lift, which I accepted, and then arrived at Morton Grange tired, dusty and in far from my best humor.

I had barely set my feet upon the ground when a man I took to be a groom came running around the corner of the house, a wild hope lighting his face. "Have you found her?" he cried to me. From my bewilderment he understood immediately that I had not, and despair overtook him, the greater after his momentary surge of belief.

I was concerned for him and his obviously deep distress. "I regret I have not," I said. "Who is lost? Can I assist in your search?"

"Jenny!" he gasped. "Jenny Hunt, the master's daughter. She's only five years old! God knows where she is! She's been gone since four this afternoon, and it's near ten now. Whoever you are, sir, in pity's name, help me look—although where else there is to search I can't think."

I was appalled. How could a five-year-old child, and a girl at that have wandered off and been gone for such a time? The light was fading rapidly and even if no harm had come to her already, soon she would be in danger from the cold, and surely terrified.

"Of course!" I said, dropping my case on the front step and starting toward him. "Where shall I begin?"

There followed one of the most dreadful hours I can remember. My friend Robert Hunt acknowledged my presence, but was too distraught with fear for his only child to do more than thank me for my help, and then start once more to look again and again in every place we could think of. Servants had already gone to ask all the neighbors even though the closest was a quarter of a mile away.

In the dark, lanterns were visible in every direction as more and more people joined in the search. We would not have given up had it taken all night. Not a man of us, nor a woman, for the female staff was all out too, even gave our comfort, our hunger or our weariness a thought.

Then at some time just after midnight there went up a great shout, and even at the distance I was, and unable to hear the words, the joy in it told me the child was found, and they believed her unhurt. I confess the overwhelming relief after such fear brought momentary tears to my eyes, and I was glad of the wind and the darkness to conceal them.

I ran toward the noise, and moments later I saw Hunt clasping in his arms a pale and frightened child who clung onto him frantically, but seemed in no way injured. A great cheer went up from all those who had turned out to search for her, and we all tramped back to the house where the cook poured out wine and spices into a great bowl, and the butler plunged a hot poker into it.

"Thanks be to God!" Hunt said, his voice shaking with emotion. "And to all of you, my dear friends." He looked around at us, shivering with cold still, hands numb, but face shining with happiness. We needed two hands each to hold the cups that were passed around, and the hot wine was like fire in our throats.

We quickly parted as relaxation took over, and the nursemaid, chattering with laughter and relief, took the child up to put her to bed.

It was not until the following morning, all of us having slept a trifle late, when Hunt and I were sitting over breakfast that he looked at me earnestly and spoke of the mystery that still lay unaddressed.

"I am very exercised in my mind, Watson, as to how to deal with the matter for the best. Jenny is devoted to Josephine, the nursemaid. Yet how can I keep in my employ a servant who could allow a child of five to wander off and become lost? And yet if I dismiss her, Jenny will be desolated. The girl is all but a mother to her, and since her own mother died . . ." His voice broke for a moment and he required some effort to regain his composure. "Advise me, Watson!" he begged. "What can I do that will bring about the least harm? And yet be just . . . and not place Jenny in danger again?"

It was a problem that had already occurred to me, but I had not thought he would ask my counsel. I had observed for myself on the previous evening the nursemaid's care for the child, and the child's deep affection for her. Indeed after the first relief of being found, it was to her that she turned, even when her father still clung to her. It might well do her more hurt to part her from the only female companionship and care that she knew, than even the fear of being lost. She had already been bereaved once in her short life. In spite of last night's events I thought it a certain cruelty to dismiss the maid. Perhaps she would now be even more careful than any new employee would, and I was in the process of saying so, when the butler came in with a note for Hunt.

"This was just delivered, sir," he said grimly.

We had already received the post, and this had no stamp upon it, so obviously it had come by hand. Hunt tore it open, and as he read it I saw his face lose all its color and his hand shook as if he had a fever.

"What is it?" I cried, although it might well have been none of my affair.

Wordlessly he passed it across to me.

Dear Mr. Hunt,

Yesterday you lost your daughter, and last night at exactly twelve of the clock you received her back again. You may take any precautions you care to, but they will not prevent me from taking her again, any time I choose, and returning her when, and if I choose.

And if it is my mind not to, then you, will never see her again.

M.

I confess my own hand was shaking as I laid the piece of paper down. Suddenly everything was not the happy ending to a wretched mischance, it had become the beginning of a nightmare. Who was "M," but far more pressing than that, what did he want? He made no demand, it was simply a terrible threat, leaving us helpless to do anything about it, even to comply with his wishes, had that been possible. I looked across at my friend, and saw such fear in his face as I have only ever seen before when men faced death and had not the inner resolve prepared for it. But then a good man is always more vulnerable for those he loves than he is for himself.

Hunt rose from the table. "I must warn the servants," he said, gaining some control as he thought of action. "I have shotguns sufficient for all the outdoor staff, and we shall keep the doors locked and admit no one unknown to us. The windows have locks and I myself shall make the rounds every night to see that all is secure." He went to the door. "Excuse me, Watson, but I am sure you understand I must be about this matter with the utmost urgency."

"Of course," I agreed, rising also. My mind was racing. What would Sherlock Holmes do were he here? He would do more than defend, he would attack. He would discover all he could about the nature and identity of this creature who called himself "M." Hunt's mind was instantly concerned in doing all he could to protect the child, but I was free to apply my intelligence to the problem.

My medical experience has been with military men and the diseases and injuries of war; nevertheless I believe I may have a manner toward those who are frightened or ill which would set them at as much ease as possible. Therefore I determined to seek permission of the nursemaid, and see if I might speak with Jenny herself, and learn what she could tell me of her experience.

The maid was naturally deeply reluctant to pursue anything which might distress the child, of whom she was extraordinarily fond. I judged her to be an honest and good-hearted young woman such as anyone might choose to care for an infant who had lost her own mother. However the fact that I was a guest in the house, and above all that I was a doctor, convinced her that my intentions and my skill were both acceptable.

I found Jenny sitting at her breakfast of bread and butter cut into fingers, and a soft-boiled egg. I waited until she had finished eating before addressing her. She seemed to be little worse for her kidnap, but then of course she had no idea that the threat of that again, and worse, awaited her.

She looked at me guardedly, but without alarm, as long as her nursemaid stayed close to her.

"Good morning, Dr. Watson," she replied when I had introduced myself. I sat down on one of the small nursery chairs, so as not to tower over her. She was a beautiful child with very fair hair and wide eyes of an unusually dark blue.

"Are you all right after your adventure, yesterday night?" I asked her.

"Yes, I don't need any medicine," she said quickly. It seemed that her last taste of medicine was not one she wished to repeat.

"Good," I agreed. "Did you sleep well?"

The question did not appear to have much meaning for her. I had forgotten in the face of her solemn composure just how very young she was.

"You did not have bad dreams?" I asked.

She shook her head.

"I'm glad. Can you tell me what happened?"

"I was in the garden," she said, her eyes downcast.

"What were you doing there?" I pressed her. It was important that I learn all I could.

"Picking flowers," she whispered, then looked up at me to see how I took that. I gathered that was something she was not supposed to do.

"I see." I dismissed the subject and she looked relieved. "And someone came and spoke to you? Someone you did not know?"

She nodded.

"What did he look like? Do you remember?"

"Yes. He was old. He had no hair at the front," she indicated her brow. "His face was white. He is very big, but thin, and he talked a funny way."

"Was his hair white?" What was her idea of old?

She shook her head.

"What did you call him?" That might give some clue.

"Fessa," she replied.

"Fessa?" What an odd name.

"No!" she said impatiently. "P'fessa!" This time she emphasized the little noise at the beginning.

"Professor?" I said aghast.

She nodded. A ridiculous and horrible thought began to form in my mind. "He was thin, and pale, with a high forehead. Did he have unusual eyes?" I asked.

She shivered, suddenly the remembered fear returned to her. The nursemaid took a step closer and put her arms around the child, giving me a glare, warning me to go no further. In that moment I became convinced within myself that it was indeed Professor Moriarty that we were dealing with, and why he had kidnapped a child and returned her with a fearful warning, would in time become only too apparent.

"Where did he take you?" I asked with more urgency in my tone than I had intended.

She looked at me with anxiety. "A house," she said very quietly. "A big room."

How could I get her to describe it for me, without suggesting her answers so they would be of no value?

"Did you ride in a carriage to get there?" I began.

She looked uncertain, as if she could have said yes, and then no.

"In something else?" I guessed.

"Yes. A little kind of carriage, not like ours. It was cold."

"Did you go very far?"

"No."

I realized after I had said it that it was a foolish question. What was far in a child's mind? Holmes would chastise me for such a pointless waste of time.

"Was it warm in the room? Was there a fire?"

"No."

"Who was there, besides the Professor? Did they give you anything to eat?"

"Yes. I had teacakes with lots of butter." She smiled as she said that; apparently the memory was not unpleasant. But how could I get her to tell me something that would help find the place where she had been taken, or anything whatever which would be of use in preventing Moriarty from succeeding in his vile plan? "Did you go upstairs?" I tried.

She nodded. "Lots," she answered, looking at me solemnly. "I could see for miles and miles and miles out of the window."

"Oh?" I had no need to feign my interest. "What did you see?"

She described an entire scene for me with much vividness. I had no doubt as to at least the general area in which she had been held. It was a tall house, from the stairs she climbed, at least three stories, and situated a little to the west of the nearby village of Hampden. I thanked her profoundly, told her she was very clever, which seemed to please her, and hastened away to tell my friend Hunt of our advance in information. However I did not mention that I believed our enemy to be the infamous Moriarty.

"I have reason to think that the matter is of great gravity," I said as we sat in his study, he still ashen-faced and so beset with anxiety he was unable to keep from fidgeting first with a paper knife, then with a quill, scribbling as if he had ink in it but merely damaging the nib.

"What does he want?" he burst out in desperation. "I cannot even comply! He asks for nothing!"

"I would like your permission to go into the village and send a wire to my friend Sherlock Holmes," I replied. "I think he would involve himself in this matter willingly, and I know of no better chance in the world to detect any matter than to have his help."

His face lit with hope. "Would he? So simple a thing as a child who has been taken, and returned, with no ransom asked? It is hardly a great crime."

"It is a great crime to cause such distress," I said quite genuinely. "And the fact that he has asked no price, and yet threatened to do it again, is a mystery which I believe will intrigue him."

"Then call him, Watson, I beg you. I will have the trap sent around to the front to take you immediately. Ask him to come as soon as he may. I will reward him any and every way in my power, if there is any reward he will accept."

But I knew, of course, that the name of Moriarty would be sufficient to bring him, and so it turned out. I received a return wire within a few hours, saying that he would be there by the late train that evening, if someone would be good enough to meet him at the station. I spent the rest of the afternoon searching in the village of Hampden until I was sure that I had found the house Jenny had described, but I was careful to appear merely to be passing by on my way somewhere else, so if any watcher saw me it would cause no alarm.

In the evening I went to meet the train, and the moment it drew in and stopped amid clouds of steam, one door flew open and I saw Holmes's lean figure striding along the platform toward me. He looked a different man from the miserable figure I had left behind me in Baker Street. He reached me and said the one word, as if it were some magic incantation, his eyes alight. "Moriarty!"

I was suddenly afraid that I had miscalculated the situation, perhaps been too quick to leap to a conclusion. He so often charged me with precisely that fault. "I believe so," I said somewhat cautiously.

He gave me a quick glance. "You are uncertain. What makes you doubt, Watson? What has happened since you wired me?"

"Nothing!" I said hastily. "Nothing whatever. It is simply a deduction; not a known fact that it was he who took the child."

"Has any demand been received yet?" There was still interest in his voice, but I thought I detected a note of disappointment all the same.

"Not yet," I answered as we reached the gate to the lane where the trap was waiting. He climbed in and I drove it in silence through the winding, steep banked roads, already shadowed in the sinking sun. I told him of my conversation with Jenny and all I had learned from it, also my location of the house, all of which he listened to without comment. I was certainly not going to apologize to him for having called him out on a matter which may not, after all, involve his archenemy. It involved the abduction of a child, which as far as I can see, is as important as any single case could be.

We were within quarter of a mile of the Grange when I saw in the dusk the gardener come running toward me, arms waving frantically. I pulled up, in case he should startle the pony and cause it to bolt. "Steady, man!" I shouted. "Whatever has happened?"

"She's gone again!" he cried while still some yards from me. He caught his breath in a sob. "She's gone!"

Instantly Holmes was all attention. He leaped out of the trap and strode to the wretched man. "I am Sherlock Holmes. Tell me precisely what has occurred. Omit no detail but tell me only what you have observed for yourself, or if someone has told you, give me their words as exactly as you can recall them."

The man made a mighty effort to regain control of himself, but his distress was palpable all the time he gasped out his story.

"The maid, Josephine, was with Jenny upstairs in the nursery. Jenny had been running around and had stubbed her toe quite badly. It was bleeding, so Josephine went to the cupboard in the dressing room where she keeps bandages and the like, and when she returned Jenny was gone. At first she was not concerned, because she had heard the hokey-pokey man outside the gates, and Jenny loves ice-cream, so she thought that she had run down for the kitchen maid to find him." He was so distraught he was gasping between his words. "But she wasn't there, and the kitchen maid said she hadn't seen her at all. We searched everywhere, upstairs and down . . ."

"But you did not find the child," Holmes finished for him, his own face grim.

"That's right! Please sir, in the name of heaven, if you can help us, do it! Find her for us! I know the master'll give that devil anything he wants, just so we get Jenny back again, an' not hurt."

"Where is the hokey-pokey man now?" Holmes asked.

"Percy? Why, he's right there with us, helping to look for her," the gardener replied.

"Is he local?"

"Yes. Known him most of my life. You're never thinking he would harm her? He wouldn't, but he couldn't either, because he's been here all the time."

"Then the answer lies elsewhere." Holmes climbed back into the trap. "Watson may know where she was taken the first time and we shall go there immediately. Tell your master what we have done, and continue your search in all other places. If it is indeed who we think, he will not be so obvious as to show us the place again, but we must look."

We drove with all speed to Hampden and I took Holmes to the street parallel with the one on which was the house. We searched it and found it empty. We had no time to lose in examining it closely, and only the carriage lantern with which to do it.

"She has not been here tonight," Holmes said bitterly, although we had not truly dared believe she would be. "We shall return in the morning to learn what we may."

We left to go back to the Grange to continue with any assistance we could. It was in turmoil as on the evening before, and as then, we joined the others seeking desperately for the child. Holmes questioned every one of the staff, both indoor and outdoor, and by nearly eleven o'clock we were exhausted and frantic with fear for her.

I found Holmes in the kitchen garden, having looked once again through the sheds and glass houses, holding a lantern up to see what the damp ground might tell him.

"This is a miserable business, Watson," he said, knowing my step and not bothering to raise the light to see. "There is something peculiarly vile about using a child to accomplish one's purposes. If it is in fact Moriarty, he has sunk very low indeed. But he must want something." He stared at me earnestly, the lamplight picking out the lines of his face, harsh with the anger inside him. I have never observed him show any special fondness for children, but the anguish caused to a parent had been only too clear for all to see. And Holmes despised a coward even more than he did a fool. Foolishness was more often than not an affliction of nature. Cowardice was a vice sprung from placing one's own safety before the love of truth, known as the safety and welfare of others. It is the essential selfishness, and as such he saw it as lying at the core of so much other sin.

"But he wants something, Watson. Moriarty never does anything simply because he has the power to do it. You say the child was returned last night, and this morning a note was delivered? There will be another note. He may choose to torture his victim by lengthening the process, until the poor man is so weak with the exhaustion of swinging from hope to despair and back, but sooner or later he will name his price. And you may be sure, the longer he waits the higher the stakes he is playing for!"

I tried to concentrate on what he was saying, but I was longing to take up my lantern again and renew my effort to find Jenny. After my conversation with her this morning she was no longer merely a lost child, she was a person for whom I had already grown a fondness, and I admit the thought of Moriarty using her in his plot nearly robbed me of sensible judgment. If I could have laid hands on him at that moment I might have beaten him to within an inch of his life—or closer even than that.

I walked what seemed to be miles, calling her name, stumbling over tussock and plowed field, scrambling through hedgerows and frightening birds and beasts in the little coppice of woodland. But I still returned to the house wretched and with no word of hope at all.

We were all gathered together in the kitchen, the indoor staff, the outdoor, Hunt, Holmes and myself. It was all but midnight. The cook brewed a hot, fresh pot of tea and the butler fetched the best brandy to strengthen it a little, when there was a faint sound in the passage beyond and the door swung open. As one person we turned to face it, and saw Jenny standing white-faced, one shoe off and her foot smeared with blood.

"Papa . . . ," she started.

Hunt strode across the floor and picked her up. He held her so tightly she cried out with momentary pain, then buried her head on his shoulder and started to cry. She was not alone, every female servant in the place wept with her, and not a few of the men found a sudden need to blow their noses uncommonly fiercely, or to turn away for a moment and regain their composure.

•　　•　　•

Holmes was up before six and I found him in the hall pacing back and forth when I came down for breakfast just after half past seven. He swung around to face me. "Ah, at last," he said critically. "Go and question the child again," he commanded. "Learn anything you can, and pay particular attention to who took her and who brought her back."

"Surely you don't think one of the household staff is involved?" I dreaded the idea, and yet it had been done with such speed and efficiency I was obliged to entertain the possibility myself.

"I don't know, Watson. There is something about this that eludes me, something beyond the ordinary. It is Moriarty at his most fiendish, because it is at heart very simple."

"Simple!" I burst out. "The child has twice been taken, the second time in spite of all our attempts to safeguard her. If he has caused one of these people to betray their master in such a way, it is the work of the devil himself."

Holmes shook his head. "If so then it is coincidental. It is very much his own work he is about. While you were asleep I buried myself learning something of Hunt's affairs. Apparently he is the main stockholder in the local mine, as well as owner of a large amount of land in the area, but he has no political aspirations or any apparent enemies. I cannot yet see why he interests Moriarty."

"Money!" I said bitterly. "Surely any man with wealth and a family, or friends he loves, can be threatened, and ultimately, by someone clever and ruthless enough, money may be extorted from him?"

"It is clumsy, Watson, and the police would pursue him for the rest of his life. Money can be traced, if the plans are carefully laid. No, such a kidnap has not the stamp of Moriarty upon it. It gives no satisfaction."

"I hope you are right," I said with little conviction. "The amount Hunt would pay to have his child safe from being taken again would be satisfaction to most thieves."

Holmes gave me a withering look, but perhaps he sensed my deep fear and anger in the matter, and instead of arguing with me, he again bade me go and question Jenny.

However I was obliged to wait until nine, and after much persuasion of the nursemaid, I found Jenny in the nursery, pale-faced but very composed for one who had had such a fearful experience not only once but twice. Perhaps she was too innocent to appreciate the danger in which she had been.

"Hello, Dr. Watson," she said, as if quite pleased to see me. "I haven't had breakfast yet. Have you?"

"No," I admitted. "I felt it more important to see how you were, after last night's adventure. How do you feel, Jenny?"

"I don't like it," she replied. "I don't want to go there again."

My heart ached that I was obliged to have her tell me of it, and I was terribly aware that a whole house full of men seemed unable to protect her. "I'm sorry. We are doing all we can to see that you never do," I told her.

"But you must help me. I need to know all about it. Was it the same man again? The Professor?"

She nodded.

"And to the same place?"

"No," she shook her head. "It was a stable I think. There was a lot of straw, and a yellow horse. The straw prickled and there was nothing to do."

"How did the Professor take you from the nursery here?"

She thought for several minutes and I waited as patiently as I could.

"I don't 'member," she said at last.

"Did he carry you, or did you walk?" I tried to suggest something that might shake her memory.

"Don't 'member. I walked."

"Down the back stairs, where the servants go?" Why had no one seen her? Why had Moriarty dared such a brazen thing? Surely it had to be one of the servants in his pay? There was no other sane answer. It did not need Holmes to deduce that!

"Don't 'member," she said again.

Could she have been asleep? Could they have administered some drug to her? I looked at the face of the nursemaid and wondered if anything else lay behind her expression of love for the child.

I questioned Jenny about her return, but again to no avail. She said she did not remember, and Josephine would not allow me to press her any further. Which might have been fear I would discover something, but might equally easily have been concern that I not distress the child any more. In her place I would have forbidden it also.

I went down the stairs again expecting Holmes to be disappointed in my efforts and I felt fully deserving of his criticism. Instead he met me waving a note which had apparently just been delivered.

"This is the reason, Watson!" he said. "And in true Moriarty style. You were correct in your deduction." And he offered me the paper.

> My Dear Hunt,
>
> I see that you have called in Sherlock Holmes. How predictable Watson is! But it will avail you nothing. I can still take the child any time I choose, and you will be helpless to do anything about it.
>
> However if you should choose to sell 90% of your shares in the Morton Mine, at whatever the current market price is—I believe you will find it to be £1.3.6d more or less—then I shall trouble you no further.
>
> Moriarty.

I looked up at Holmes. "Why on earth should he wish Hunt to sell his shares?" I asked. "What good would that do Moriarty?"

"It would start a panic and plunge the value of the entire mine," Holmes replied. "Very probably of other mines in the area, in the fear that Hunt knew something damaging about his own mine which was likely to be true of all the others. Any denial he might make would only fuel speculation."

"Yes . . . yes, of course. And then Moriarty, or whoever he is acting for, would be able to buy them all at rock-bottom price."

"Exactly," Holmes agreed. "And not only that, but appear as a local hero as well, saving everyone's livelihood. This is the true Moriarty, Watson. This has his stamp upon it." There was a fire within him as he said it that I confess angered me. The thrill of the chase was nothing compared with the cost to Hunt, and above all to Jenny. "Now," he continued. "What have you learned from the child of how she left here?"

"Very little," I replied. "I fear she may somehow have been drugged." I repeated what little she had been able to tell me, and also a description of the stable, as far as she had been able to give one.

"We shall borrow the pony and trap and go back to the house in Hampden in daylight," he replied. "There may be something to learn from a fuller examination, and then seek the stable, although I have no doubt Moriarty has long left it now. But first I shall speak to Hunt, and persuade him to do nothing regarding the shares . . ."

I was appalled. "You cannot ask that of him! We have already proved that we are unable to protect Jenny. On two successive nights she has been taken from the house and returned to it, and we have never seen her go, nor seen her come back, and are helpless to prevent it happening again."

"It is not yet time to despair," Holmes said grimly. "I believe we have some hours." He pulled out his watch and looked at it. "It is only six minutes past ten. Let us give ourselves until two of the clock. That will still allow Hunt sufficient time to inform his stockbroker before close of business today, if that should be necessary, and Moriarty may be given proof of it, if the worst should befall."

"Do you see an end to it?" I asked, struggling to find some hope in the affair. It galled me bitterly to have to give in to any villain, but to Moriarty of all men. But we were too vulnerable, I had no strength to fight or to withstand any threat where the life of a child was concerned, and I know Hunt would sacrifice anything at all to save Jenny, and I said as much.

"Except his honor, Watson," Holmes replied very quickly. "It may tear at his very soul, but he will not plunge a thousand families into destitution, with their own children to feed and to care for, in order to save one, even though it is his own. But we have no time to stand here debating. Have the trap ready for us, and as soon as I have spoken with Hunt, I shall join you at the front door."

"What use is it going to Hampden, or the stable, if Moriarty has long left them?" I said miserably.

"Men leave traces of their acts, Watson," he replied, but I feared he was going only because we were desperate and had no better idea. "It might be to our advantage when we have so little time, if you were to bring a gardener or some other person who knows the area well," he continued, already striding away from me.

It was barely thirty minutes later that he returned just as the gardener drew the trap around, with me in the back ready to set out for the village. I had also questioned the gardener as to any local farms which might be vacant, and answer such slight description as Jenny had given me, or where the owner might either be unaware of such use of his stables, or be a willing accomplice.

"Did you persuade Hunt to delay action?" I asked as Holmes climbed in beside me and we set off at a brisk trot.

"Only until two," he said, tight-lipped. I know that he had had some agreement to achieve even that much time from the fact that he stepped forward in the seat and immediately engaged the gardener in conversation about every aspect of the nearby farms, their owners and any past relationship with Hunt, good or ill.

What he was told only served to make matters worse. Either the gardener, a pleasant chap of some fifty-odd years named Hodgkins, was more loyal than candid, or Hunt was generally liked in the region and had incurred a certain mild envy among one or two, but it was without malice. The death of his wife while Jenny was still an infant had brought great sympathy. Hunt was wealthy in real possessions, the house and land and the mine itself, but he had no great amount of ready money, and he lived well, but quite modestly for his station in life. He was generous to his staff, his tenants and to charity in general. Naturally he had faults, but they were such as are common to all people, a sometimes hasty tongue, a rash judgment here or there, too quick a loyalty to friends, and a certain blindness when it suited him.

Holmes grew more and more withdrawn as he listened to the catalog of praise. It told him nothing helpful, only added to the urgency that we not only find where Jenny had been taken, but far more challenging, we learn from it something of use.

We found the tall house again easily, and a few questions from neighbors elicited an excellent description of Moriarty.

We went inside and up again to the room that in the daylight answered Jenny's description in a way which startled me. It was indeed bright and airy. There was a red couch, but the grate was clean and cold, as if no fire had been lit in it recently. I saw a few crumbs on the floor, which I mentioned to Holmes as coming from the teacakes Jenny had been given.

"I do not doubt it," Holmes said with no satisfaction. "There is also a fine yellow hair on the cushion." He waved absently at the red couch while staring out of one of the many windows. "Come!" he said suddenly. "There is nothing else to be learned here. This is where he kept her, and he intended us to know it. He even left crumbs for us to find. Now why was that, do you suppose?"

"Carelessness," I replied, following him out of the door and down the stairs again, Hodgkins on his heels. "And arrogance."

"No, Watson, no! Moriarty is never careless. He has left them here for a reason. Let us find this stable. There is something . . . some clue, something done, or left undone, which will give me the key."

But I feared he was speaking more in hope than knowledge. He would not ever admit it, but there is a streak of kindness in him which does not always sit well with reason. Of course, I have never said so to him.

We got into the trap again and Hodgkins asked Holmes which direction he should drive. For several moments Holmes did not reply. I was about to repeat the question, for fear that he had not heard, when he sat very upright. "Which is the most obvious farm, from here?" he demanded. "That meets our requirements, that is?"

"Miller's," Hodgkins replied.

"How far?"

"Just under two miles. Shall I take you there?"

"No. Which is the second most obvious?"

Hodgkins thought for a moment or two. "I reckon the old Adams place, sir."

"Good. Then take us there, as fast as you may."

"Yes, sir!"

It proved to be some distance further than the first farm mentioned, and I admit I became anxious as the minutes passed and the time grew closer and closer to two. Holmes frequently kept me in the dark regarding his ideas, but I was very much afraid that in this instance he had no better notion of how to foil Moriarty than I did myself. Even if we found the farm, how was it going to help us? There was no reason to suppose he would be there now, or indeed ever again. I forbore from saying so perhaps out of cowardice. I did not want to hear that he had no solution, that he was as fallible and as frightened as I.

We reached the Adams farm and the disused stable. Holmes opened the door wide to let in all the light he could, and examined the place as if he might read in the straw and dust some answers to all our needs. I thought it pointless. How could anyone find here a footprint of meaning, a child's hair, or indeed crumbs of anything? I watched him and fidgeted from one foot to the other, feeling helpless, and as if we were wasting precious moments.

"Holmes!" I burst out at last. "We . . ." I got no further. Triumphantly he held up a very small, grubby, white sock, such as might fit a child. He examined it quickly, and with growing amazement and delight.

"What?" I said angrily. "So it is Jenny's sock. She was here. How does that help us? He will still take her tonight, and you may be sure it will not be to this place!"

Holmes pulled his pocket watch out. "It is after one already!" he said with desperate urgency. "We have no time to lose at all. Hodgkins, take me back to the Grange as fast as the pony can go!"

It was a hectic journey. Hodgkins had more faith than I that there was some good reason for it, and he drove the animal as hard as he could short of cruelty, and I must say it gave of its best. It was a brave little creature and was lathered and blowing hard when we finally pulled in the drive at the front door and Holmes leaped out, waving the sock in his hand. "All will be well!" he shouted to Hodgkins. "Care for that excellent animal! Watson!" And he plunged into the hall, calling out for Hunt at the top of his voice.

I saw with dread that the long case clock by the foot of the stairs already said three minutes past two.

Hunt threw open his study door, his face pale, eyes wide with fear.

Holmes held up the sock. "Bloodless!" he said triumphantly. "Tell me, what time does the hokey-pokey man play?"

Hunt looked at him as if he had taken leave of his wits, and I admit the same thought had occurred to me. He stammered a blasphemy and turned on his heel, too overcome with emotion to form any answer.

Holmes strode after him, catching him by the shoulder, and Hunt swung around, his eyes blazing, his fist raised as if to strike.

"Believe me, sir, I am deadly earnest!" Holmes said grimly. "Your daughter will be perfectly safe until the ice-cream man comes . . ."

"The ice-cream man!" Hunt exploded. "You are mad, sir! I have known Percy Bradford all my life! He would no more . . ."

"With no intent," Holmes agreed, still clasping Hunt by the arm. "It is the tune he plays. Look!" He held up the small, grubby sock again. "You see, it has no blood on it! This was left where Moriarty wishes us to believe he held her last night, and that this sock somehow was left behind. But it is not so. It is no doubt her sock, but taken from the first kidnap when you were not guarding her, having no reason for concern."

"What difference does that make?" Hunt demanded, the raw edge of fear in his voice only too apparent.

"Send for the hokey-pokey man, and I will show you," Holmes replied. "Have him come to the gates as is his custom, but immediately, now in daylight, and play his tunes."

"Do it, my dear fellow!" I urged. I had seen this look of triumph in Holmes before, and now all my faith in him flooded back, although I still had no idea what he intended, or indeed what it was that he suddenly understood.

Hunt hesitated only moments; then like a man plunging into ice-cold water, he obeyed, his body clenched, his jaw so tight I was afraid he might break his teeth.

"Come!" Holmes ordered me. "I might need you, Watson. Your medical skill may be stretched to the limits." And without any explanation whatever of this extraordinary remark he started up the stairs. "Take me to the nursery!" he called over his shoulder. "Quickly, man!"

As it turned out we had some half-hour or more to wait while the ice-cream vendor was sent for and brought from his position at this hour in the village. Holmes paced the floor, every now and then going to the window and staring out until at last he saw what he wanted, and within moments we heard the happy, lilting sound of the barrel organ playing.

Holmes swiveled from the window to stare at the child. He held up one hand in command of silence, while in the same fashion forbidding me from moving.

Jenny sat perfectly still. The small woolen golliwog she had been holding fell from her fingers and, staring straight ahead of her, she rose to her feet and walked to the nursery door.

Josephine started up after her.

"No!" Holmes ordered with such fierceness that the poor girl froze.

"But . . . ," she began in anguish as the child opened the door and walked through.

"No!" Holmes repeated. "Follow, but don't touch her. You may harm her if you do! Come . . ." And he set off after her himself, moving on tip-toe so that no noise should alarm her or let her know she was being followed, though indeed she seemed oblivious of everything around her.

In single file behind we pursued the child, who seemed to be walking as if in her sleep, along the corridor and up the attic stairs, narrow and winding, until she came to a stop beside a small cupboard in an angle of the combe. She opened it and crept inside, pulling a blanket over herself, and then closed the door.

Holmes turned to the maid. "When the nursery clock chimes eleven, I believe she will awaken and return to normal, confused but not physically injured. She will believe what she has been mesmerized to believe, that she was again taken by Professor Moriarty, as she was in truth the first time. No doubt he took her to at least three different places, and she will recall them in successive order, as he has told her. You will wait here so you can comfort her when she awakens and comes out, no doubt confused and frightened. Do not disturb her before that. Do you understand me?"

"Yes sir! I'll not move or speak, I swear," Josephine promised, her eyes wide with admiration and I think not a little relief.

"Good. Now we must find Hunt and assure him of Jenny's welfare. He must issue a statement denying any rumor that he might sell his holdings in the mine. In fact if he can raise the funds, a small purchase of more stock might be advantageous. We must not allow Moriarty to imagine that he has won anything, don't you agree?"

"I do!" I said vehemently. "Are you sure she will be all right, Holmes?"

"Of course, my dear Watson!" he said, allowing himself to smile at last. "She will have the most excellent medical attention possible, and a friend to assure her that she is well and strong, and that this will not occur again. Possibly eat as much ice-cream as she wishes, provided it is not accompanied by that particular tune."

"And a new pair of socks!" I agreed, wanting to laugh and cry at the same time. "You are brilliant, Holmes, quite brilliant! No resolution to a case has given me more pleasure."

"It was my good fortune she stubbed her toe," he said modestly. "And that you were wise enough to send immediately for me, of course!"

Joseph Hansen

Blood, Snow, and Classic Cars

JOSEPH HANSEN must tire of being tied to the "gay subgenre" of mystery fiction. While his novels and stories are sometimes concerned with homosexuality as a subtext, they are far more often focused on lives of all kinds being lived on all levels of Californian society. He has an anthropologist's grasp of how people relate to their work, for example; and how the American family has become a loose collection of drifters, much in the way that Ross Macdonald first pointed out in the 1950s and 1960s. He's also one hell of a literary stylist. In "Blood, Snow, and Classic Cars," first published in *Alfred Hitchcock's Mystery Magazine* in April, all of his talents come together in a story of a big murder in a small town.

Blood, Snow, and Classic Cars

Joseph Hansen

Talbot had let Hovis drive the Maserati tonight. Not to Madison, no, but to Randall Falls, the nearest town not too dinky for there to be some action. It was February. It had begun to snow, and while he'd showered and shaved, Hovis had dreamed of driving back here at midnight with somebody new from the bars, in this fantastic car, snow blown into high drifts beside the cleared highway, and gleaming in the moonlight on the branches of the pines.

He was driving home alone. No one he wanted was in the bars. That was okay. He was still young. He could take his time. And even alone, he loved the snow. It was beautiful, as if in some painting. Hovis sometimes daydreamed of going to art school to learn how to paint. But there was no hurry about that, either. This setup, living in Talbot's guesthouse rent free, was too good to leave. About all he had to do was keep the cars shiny.

The Maserati was built for speed, and since he'd met only one rattly pickup truck on the highway tonight, he let his foot weigh on the gas pedal and ate the thirty-five miles from Randall Falls to Talbot's sprawling ranch house in thirteen minutes. He geared down, swung the rumbling, low-slung classic off the highway past the dozen, snow-covered not-so-classic cars Talbot displayed down here, and his headlights flicked across a bundle of rags beside the drive.

He braked. People threw trash everywhere. Talbot hated that. Hovis would pick it up now and get rid of it before Talbot ever saw it. In foot-deep snow he bent over the bundle. And it groaned. He jerked his hand back. It was no bundle. It was a man. A leg kicked feebly, an arm tried to reach out. Hovis began to shake. And not from the cold. He bent closer, narrowing his eyes, trying to see. His mouth was dry. He moistened his lips. His own voice sounded alien to him.

"Gene?"

Heart thumping, finding it hard to breathe, Hovis crouched and folded back a sheepskin coat collar that hid the man's face. The wool crackled because ice crystals had formed on it. This was Talbot, all right. The moonlight made the blood look black. His hair was matted with blood. His hands were slashed. Blood was all over the back of the sheepskin jacket. Hovis ran for the Maserati, fumbled with the gearshift, killed the engine, began to whimper, got the engine started again, and careened up the long curved driveway to the house.

Lemke was new. That was why he was on nights from ten to six Monday through Thursday. Nothing much happened then. But something had happened tonight and he was in charge, so he handled it. The first thing he did when he got to the Talbot place was to look at the victim, radio for an ambulance, and take Polaroids. The second thing was to talk to Bobby Hovis, who had discovered the crime and dialed 911. Hovis bunked in Gene Talbot's guesthouse, had no visible means of support, and had been driving one of Talbot's expensive cars. He had alcohol on his breath and bloodstains on his clothes and on his hands. He was pacing up and down Talbot's long living room looking as if he were about to cry, but he didn't cry, and he didn't stop pacing even when Lemke told him to sit.

"I had his permission to drive the Maserati," Hovis said.

"I don't think so," Lemke said. "I think you took it without his permission, and when you got home, he was waiting down there for you and raised hell with you about it, and you're drunk and you shot him."

"That's crazy," Hovis said. "He's my friend. He's good to me. I wouldn't hurt him. I wish I'd gotten here sooner. I'd have helped him fight them off, whoever did it." He stopped and gazed wide-eyed at Lemke, holding his hands out. "Who would do such a horrible thing? Why?"

"Nobody liked him," Lemke said. "That's why. He was a degenerate, a drug dealer, jewel smuggler, child molester, pornographer, homosexual. If you don't know how this town felt about him, then you're the only one."

"Then arrest *them*, for Christ's sake," Hovis said. "Why me? Two perverts with one stone, is that it?"

Lemke blinked. "You want to explain the blood all over you?"

"He was alive. He groaned. He reached out. He moved his legs. I thought—I don't know. I thought he wanted me to help him up."

"Robert Hovis—" Lemke detached the never-before-used handcuffs from the back of his belt "—you are under arrest for aggravated assault against the person of Eugene Squires Talbot."

"I had three beers," Hovis said. "Three lousy draft beers."

"Turn around," Lemke said. "You have the right to remain silent." He yanked Hovis's arms behind him. The handcuffs clicked. "Anything you say can and will be used against you in a court of law . . ."

•　　•　　•

Shattuck came in at six because he hated being home alone. Mornings were the worst. The two kids were off at college. And his wife was dead. Breast cancer. Only ten weeks ago. A house should be full of life first thing in the morning, excited voices, coffee smells, bacon sizzling.

He showered, dressed, entered the kitchen only to cross it to the garage door. He drove along streets of tall old frame houses, under big, winter-naked trees standing in snow, to eat breakfast at Mom's Diner on Main Street—for the talk and laughter, not the greasy food. The old joke was right: *Never eat at a place called Mom's.*

Then he drove straight to the sand-colored stucco building marked RANDALL COUNTY SHERIFF'S DEPARTMENT, the Percival substation of which he, a lieutenant, age forty-eight, was in charge. He pushed in through thick glass doors out of the cold, a massive man, six foot four, two hundred fifty pounds, and hung up his jacket and fur hat. Lanky Deputy Lemke was watching him from his desk like a kid. Was that pride on his farmboy face? Or fright?

"Something to tell me, Avery?" Shattuck said.

And Lemke came eagerly into his office to tell him. He was so excited he couldn't sit down. He talked in a breathless rush, waving the papers in his hand. The arrest report. He'd been writing it for hours. He needed hours. He was slow on a keyboard. When he ran out of speech, he laid the report in its folder on the desk. Shattuck put on reading glasses and began turning the pages.

"Why didn't you phone me when the call came in?" he said.

"Middle of the night. I didn't want to wake you up," Lemke said. "I mean, a man was down. It didn't sound like something all that big and important. I figured I could handle it." He straightened with pride. "I did handle it. Caught the perpetrator redhanded."

"And the weapon?" Shattuck said. "You have the weapon?"

"I don't. But Talbot keeps guns around, lots of guns. Whole town knows that. Why wouldn't Hovis carry one of those?"

"Well, did he? Did you find it on him?"

Lemke shifted from foot to foot. "It must be someplace out there in the snow. Couldn't see it in the dark."

"Yup." Shattuck sighed and picked up the telephone. "You did make sure the injured man got to the hospital, right?"

"First thing," Lemke said.

"Good." Shattuck punched the hospital number. Not in Percival. In Randall Falls. He had to wait, and while he waited, he read more of Lemke's report. After a while, not a recording but a human being spoke to him, he asked questions, got answers, said thanks, and hung up. "Sit down, Avery."

Lemke peered at him, scared. Shattuck did not have a poker face. His disgust was showing, even to as dense a subject as Lemke. "The man was shot six times at close range with a .22. Then his skull and hands and back were hacked with a hatchet. Or maybe it happened the other way around."

"He did look pretty awful," Lemke said.

"You don't say," Shattuck said. "All right, you didn't find the gun. So tell me, did you find a bloody hatchet?"

"Hovis had blood on him," Lemke said stubbornly.

Shattuck tapped the report. "But it shows here that you dragged poor Miz Durwood out into the cold from home to check the Internet—" craggy Edna Durwood was the oldest employee here, and the only one on the payroll who could use the Internet "—and Hovis has no criminal record."

"He was drunk," Lemke said. "Talbot chewed him out. He lost it. You know how hysterical they get."

Shattuck grunted. "So you booked him and fingerprinted him."

Lemke brightened. "Yes, sir. You bet. And locked him in a cell."

"And faxed your report over to Randall Falls?"

"Oh no, sir." Lemke was shocked at the thought. "I wouldn't send it without you signed off on it, sir."

Shattuck handed it to him.

"Good. Then you can just put it in the shredder, now. All copies, Avery. And we'll forget it ever happened."

Lemke was dumbfounded. "The shredder? Why?"

"Because you made a mistake, and unless we destroy all record of it and humbly beg Hovis's pardon, odds are ten to one that Talbot's tireless defenders at the Civil Liberties Union will sue your ass, my ass, the whole county's ass, for false arrest and illegal detention."

Lemke said, "But he did it, lieutenant. It had to be him. He was the only one there."

"He was the only one there, Avery," Shattuck explained, "because the assailant ran off. Hovis phoned 911 and waited around for you. That didn't suggest to you that maybe he wasn't the assailant? That's what it suggests to me. Load two shovels in the trunk of a patrol car, pick up Deputy Schneider at his house, and the pair of you drive back to the Talbot place and search for those weapons. Let nobody near the house or the grounds, and do not say one word to anybody. I don't care how many TV cameras and microphones they have. Not one word, understand?"

Shattuck drove Hovis home so he could change into clothes that weren't bloodstained. Lemke and Schneider had strung between tree trunks broad yellow ribbons that said CRIME SCENE on them, and were turning the snow over around the cars down by the road. He lifted a hand to them in passing. While Hovis changed, Shattuck went into the main house and looked at the engagement calendar on Gene Talbot's dusty desk. Whoever came up here and maimed him didn't have an appointment. He roved through the sprawling house looking for the fabled gun collection. Paintings, figurines, cut glass, but no guns. Talbot was a reader. Shattuck ran his gaze over the shelves. Brazil. Sunken treasure. Lost mines. Jewels and gems. Horse breeding. *The Male Nude in Art.* And of course classic cars. He stepped out into the cold sunshine and pulled the door shut so it locked.

Next he needed to get Hovis off the absorbing subject of himself. Driving up here from the substation, Shattuck had learned about Hovis's strait-laced parents, his boyhood, high school years, single year of college, his 7-Eleven and Wal-Mart jobs. All in Madison. And how, after he came out to his folks and they changed the locks on the doors, he began staying nights with strangers picked up in parks, coffeeshops, bus stations, and how this had led him out of Madison to other towns and at last to Percival, where he met the legendary Gene Talbot.

Now Hovis sat beside Shattuck again, smelling of soap, and Shattuck was driving him to the hospital to see his friend, benefactor, lover. Shattuck still winced at that word in this context. But the long, clean-swept highway curving through pine-grown hills to Randall Falls offered more time for talk. And Hovis talked. If he were sore at what Lemke had done to him, he didn't seem to mind opening up to Shattuck. He was either guileless or a damn good actor.

"Sometimes he wants company in the evenings, and I stay with him and we—" Hovis was blond and blushed easily "—like, watch, um, videos."

Shattuck laughed without amusement. "I know all about those videos. Hauled a truckload of 'em out of there a few years back. There was a trial about it. He has a Constitutional right to keep them. We hauled 'em all back."

Hovis was quiet for a while, watching the snowy landscape out the car window. Then he went on. "Usually, if I want to go out, he doesn't mind. I can take any car I want as long as he says okay. I don't like to take the really rare ones in case I have an accident. But last night I took the Maserati because I wanted to score and it makes an impression, all right?"

"But it didn't," Shattuck said. "You came back alone."

Hovis shrugged. "Snow kept people home. The bars were half empty."

"The doctors say he hadn't been lying out there long when you found him," Shattuck said. "Try to remember. Did you see anybody around?"

"Nobody," Hovis said. "I mean, even this highway was empty. Once I got out of Randall Falls, I didn't meet but one car all the way back."

"What kind of car?" Shattuck said. "Where, exactly?"

"Old white pickup," Hovis said. "Just before I crossed the bridge, okay?"

"Notice who was in it?"

Hovis thought for a second. "Some high school kid," he said.

"Get a good look at him?"

Hovis turned red. "I was seeing how fast the Maserati would go."

"We had a teenage witness once, claimed Talbot threw parties with high school boys. Wild, naked parties? Drink and dope?"

Hovis marveled. "What? Get serious! He swore this in court?"

"His parents wouldn't let him. County attorney had to drop the case."

"Well, I never saw any boys. Sure, friends come now and then. From out of town. Weekends, mostly. Sometimes they party. But they're Gene's age."

"Make me a list."

Shattuck stopped at the hospital entrance and Hovis got out, but before he closed the door, he bent down to add, "One thing was a little weird. The kid driving that truck—he didn't have any jacket. And I mean it was cold last night."

Shattuck parked in the hospital lot under a leaning, snow-clad pine tree. In a slot marked with some doctor's name. Nice thing about driving a sheriff's car. You could park any damned place you chose.

He had to ask a few busy people, but he at last found out where Eugene Squires Talbot was. And here came Hovis down the hall, carrying a big bunch of plastic-wrapped flowers and looking stormy. "Whoa," Shattuck said, and took his arm. "What's the matter?"

"They won't let me see him." Hovis pointed with the bouquet back down the corridor. Gathered outside double doors marked Intensive Care Unit stood a middle-aged woman, a young woman, and a young man. "Claim they're his damn family," Hovis said. "Flew in from Chicago. Say if I don't stop trying to see him, they'll call Security and have me thrown out. Why?"

"This way." Shattuck led him to chairs clustered around a low table in an alcove. "Sit down. Cool off." And Hovis sat, clutching the flowers so hard his knuckles were white. Shattuck sat facing him. "That's his ex-wife," he said. "And his daughter. I don't know the man. Maybe the daughter's husband. Time flies."

"He never told me he was married," Hovis said.

"It was a long time ago," Shattuck said.

Hovis laid the flowers on his knees. "Yeah, well. 'Ex-wife,' isn't that what you said? They're divorced. So what gives her the right to shut me out?"

"I'm not sure she has the right," Shattuck said. "Maybe the daughter has. She didn't divorce him. There's no such thing as an ex-daughter."

"It's because I'm gay, isn't it? Well, so is Gene Talbot gay. They think if I don't see him that's gonna change him back? I want to see him." Hovis stood up, dumped the flowers, picked them up. He peered down the hall to those double doors. "Hold his hand, tell him I'm here, tell him I'm sorry I wasn't around when he needed me." He looked at Shattuck. "What the hell are they to him? He never talks about them. I'm here. I'm his goddamn friend." Tears came into his eyes. "I love him. Not sometime years back. Now. And he loves me."

"Yes, all right," Shattuck said. "Wait here. I'll see what I can do."

He went down the corridor, past the pale-faced family, and pushed into the unit where the glaring air was filled with antiseptic smells and voices and the beeping of monitors. Green-clad, white masked, harried staff moved, grimly purposeful, among beds hidden or half hidden by curtains. For a second he got a glimpse of Talbot. He'd never seen anybody hooked up to so many wires, tubes, machines. A nurse carrying a clipboard noticed him. "Sheriff?"

"How's Gene Talbot doing?"

"His heart is strong. It's senseless, since the rest of him is broken beyond repair, but it keeps pumping away." She was a worn-looking woman who had perhaps only a year or two ago been pretty. Her laugh was brief and dry. "But whoever said the human heart made sense?"

Shattuck said, "Robert Hovis is here, the friend who found him last night, and he's very upset. They were close. Lived together. He wants to see him, speak to him. Family's digging in their heels. Can you—?"

She shook her head, her smile regretful. "I can't change hospital rules, sheriff. You're here only because of your badge. And I'm afraid you can't stay. Whatever you need to know officially, you can learn at the desk."

Shattuck blinked. "So the family can't come in, either?"

"No one but medical personnel," she said.

"All right. Thank you." Shattuck turned away. "I'll tell him."

She touched his sleeve. "Oh, and sheriff—no flowers."

Edna Durwood didn't have to read and clip the local papers, the daily Randall Falls *Reporter*, the weekly Percival *Press*, but she did. It was no part of her job description. But often there wasn't a lot of action in this office, and it helped to pass the time. So it cheered her up when Shattuck laid on her desk the flowers Hovis hadn't known what to do with, and asked her, "Have you got a file on Gene Talbot?"

Steel-rimmed glasses with thick lenses perched on her witchy nose. She glared at him through them. But he'd surprised her, and she smiled, a rarity. He couldn't recall when he'd last seen Edna Durwood do that. She sniffed, "Do you know anybody in this town who's been in the papers more?" She took off her mouthpiece-earpiece rig, got up, and marched off to fetch the folders. She laid them on his desk, and went to put the flowers in water.

Shattuck went through the clippings briskly because he remembered much of the fact and fancy they detailed. The oldest was brittle. It was a dozen years back when Gene Talbot had jumped into print. At that time he lived in Randall Falls, where he owned a thriving new car dealership. He had driven his wife and two girls to Madison to catch a flight to Chicago to visit her parents.

Then he had stopped off at a gay bar, where he'd picked up a fair young stranger and taken him home to Randall Falls for the weekend.

This youth was not what he seemed to be. He had a gun and, poking it into Talbot's ribs, had ordered him to drive to his bank and withdraw all his savings in cash and make the blue-eyed boy a present of them. Talbot as instructed walked into the bank with the youth close at his side, but when he got to the teller he told her what was going on. The youth didn't shoot Talbot dead as he had threatened. Instead, he tried to run away, but a security guard caught him.

Unluckily, he told the police, public defender, judge, and whoever else would listen, exactly how and why he happened to be with Gene Talbot that day. Talbot's wife left him, taking along the kids. The good folk of Randall Falls decided to buy their new cars from someone better-behaved. And Talbot sold the dealership, bought the ranch house outside Percival, and settled there to live, surrounded by his collection of classic cars. He wanted to breed racehorses, but Percival's zoning laws wouldn't let him.

This didn't slow him down. He raced through town in Bugatis, Aston Martins, Ferraris, even a 1933 Auburn for a while. He always wore flash clothes the like of which Percival had only glimpsed in magazines. And on weekends he threw parties. Percival knew this because of all the expensive if not classic cars—not one of them carrying a woman—that went tooling out the highway to Talbot's place. The place was so isolated that anything at all could have gone on there and nobody not invited would have seen or heard.

Percival didn't need to see and hear. Gossip filled in for lack of witnesses.

It wasn't good-hearted gossip. It was mean-spirited and squalid. Shattuck came to hate the talk, and to avoid it if he could. But he wished Talbot would tone down his behavior and buy his liquor out of town. He bought a lot of booze, Wild Turkey, Glenlivet, Tanqueray. And champagne. Taittinger, Clicquot, God knew. By the case. Art Gillespie at Economy Liquor had never seen anything like it. He didn't complain, but he sure as hell did tell everybody.

Then the foreigners started coming. Easily spotted by their chauffeur-driven stretch limousines and the costumes of the passengers. Indians in turbans, Egyptians and Arabs in flowing robes, Africans in kaftans. Japanese. South Americans. And the legendary cars that had stood around Talbot's low-roofed, rangy house on its hill, like prize bulls in a feedlot, were carried off on trucks, as many as six masterpieces at a time.

It would figure, said the fellas at the barber shop, the gals at the beauty parlor, that if Talbot had been rich before, and everyone was certain he had, by now he must be a billionaire. Then he added to the excitement and speculation by leaving town for a time. A travel agent in Madison had a sister in Percival, and she said Talbot had flown to Brazil, to buy land there, and raise thoroughbreds.

The FBI thought different. They thought he had flown down to pick up cocaine in exchange for some of the cars he'd shipped out earlier. Shattuck, of course, was told what they thought.

It turned out they were wrong. Talbot had been flattered to have their attention and, while denying he was ever a courier, pretended to know a lot of Latino drug dealers. The FBI had investigated his leads. They were all brag, no substance. Talbot told one investigator that while he never dealt drugs, he occasionally used them. Recreationally.

"I doubt it," the agent in charge had told Shattuck in disgust. "Yeah, he's got ten thousand acres of land in Brazil. Wasteland. No water. You couldn't raise lizards there, let alone horses. And those cars of his—half of them are put together out of junked parts, slicked up, and sold as untouched originals." He wagged his head over the farewell beer Shattuck had bought him at the Hofbrau on Main Street. "But what a con man he is. Jesus. What a sweettalker. And you know, I think he believes his own lies. He doesn't live in the world we live in. He dreams it up and thinks it's real."

How true this was came out later when Talbot bought a 1953 Cadillac Eldorado convertible from its owner, gave him fifty thousand in cash and the rest, thirty thousand, in diamonds. The seller sued. Experts testified the diamonds were trash. The court agreed. Talbot claimed he'd been deceived about the diamonds. And he still wanted the car, so he mortgaged his house to make up the shortfall. Percival raised its eyebrows. Talbot wasn't a billionaire, after all. Still, Shattuck thought, he probably had a buyer in some far corner of the world willing to pay him more than the market price.

He stayed afloat and the town kept gossiping about him, and he was back in court a few more times, most notably when some kid told a teacher that Talbot was taping naked sex among high school boys at his home and selling the videos over the Internet. Shattuck, since the sheriff needed to be reelected about that time, was ordered to turn the ranch house upside down. He found a lot of videos that surprised him. Stuff those boys were doing he'd never even heard of at their age. Some of it not till now. But Talbot denied he'd made the videos, said he'd bought them from other sources. And the people couldn't prove he hadn't. The defense could prove the claims about the Internet were false. The Civil Liberties lawyers had a gleeful time establishing Talbot's first amendment right to own and enjoy the videos. And the sheriff was elected again, anyway.

Shattuck lifted his head and looked at the clock. He'd wasted an hour on this stuff. And learned nothing. He turned over the rest of the clippings, only glancing at them. All stuff he knew. But what was this final one? Datelined last week. A funeral writeup. From the Percival *Press*, with the usual typos and misspellings. JURGEN JENSEN BURIED AT 34. Shattuck frowned down the room at Edna, who was fielding a phone call. She hung up, and he asked, "What's this Jensen funeral thing doing in the Talbot file?"

"I didn't know where else to put it," she said. "He's the only person ever died of AIDS in Percival. And you know who dies of AIDS well as I do. Only other gay man we've got here is Talbot."

The office was at the back of the tall white frame church. Nobody had shoveled the walk alongside the building, so Shattuck kicked through snow to the five steps that climbed to the office door, on which a neat sign read COME IN. He went in. It was colder inside than outside, where a pale sun was shining. Doors stood open on three offices, but nobody was in any of them. Still, maybe someone was in the building—he heard organ music.

He found the chancel, squeezed his bulk through a narrow door, and climbed corkscrew stairs to the organ loft. Thirtyish, skinny, the organist wore a ponytail, jeans, and a T-shirt stenciled with a picture of Jerry Garcia. At the sight of Shattuck he raised his hands in mock fear. "My name is Denis Du Pre," he said. "and I didn't do it."

Shattuck said, "You didn't play for Jurgen Jensen's funeral?"

Du Pre's cheerfulness died. "Not what he would have wanted. I played groany old Calvinist hymn tunes. What his parents wanted. They sat there, stiff as wood, with their white-bread daughter and her son. They were uncomfortable. Church full of gays and lesbians. But the boy was broken up. Big kid, hockey player, straight-A student, class president. Crying like a four-year-old."

"Over an uncle? Any idea why?"

"He'd been kind to him. Years ago. When the parents broke up."

Shattuck gazed down at the rows of empty pews. "Jurgen your friend?"

"Last couple of years, yes. After he got HIV. We have to help each other."

"So you know his other friends," Shattuck said.

Du Pre grew wary. "Some. Why? What's this all about?"

"Gene Talbot is in the hospital. Intensive care. He was assaulted last night. With a hatchet, among other things. He obviously had an enemy. Did he have any friends? Was Jurgen one of them? Was Talbot at his funeral?"

"No way. Jurgen knew him, but they didn't socialize. Jurgen didn't like him." Du Pre's laugh was brief and humorless. "Does anyone?"

Shattuck cocked an eyebrow. "Are you adding to my problem?"

Du Pre was appalled. "Oh no. Forget I said that. Talbot is the kind who makes us all look bad, and he was resented for that. But no gay did this, sheriff. A hatchet? That is pure bigotry, pure hate crime. Is he going to live?"

"I doubt it," Shattuck said.

Du Pre's mouth twisted. "And when you catch the one who did it, his lawyers will plead him not guilty by reason of mental defect. He'll be a victim, not a killer. All he needs is medication, not punishment. No one will remember poor, awful old Gene Talbot."

Shattuck dug a card from his pocket. "As soon as the news is out, there'll be talk." Thin fingers took the card. Sad eyes studied it. Shattuck said, "In your crowd, you may hear things I wouldn't." He started down the twisted stairs, feet too big for the narrow treads. "If you do, phone me, all right?"

Du Pre sounded panicky. "What do you expect me to report?"

"Shouts and murmurs, especially murmurs." Shattuck edged himself out the tiny doorway into the chancel, took a step, then stopped and called up to the organ loft, "What's that nephew's name?"

"French. He'd come to the hospital to see Jurgen. Sulky. Wouldn't shake my hand. But that's the name he gave. Larry French."

"I left Avery, uh, Deputy Lemke, off at home," Brun Schneider told Shattuck. "It was a long shift for him. He was real tired." The red-haired, pop-eyed young deputy stood holding a blue fleece-lined windbreaker jacket. Cheap. You could buy them anywhere, and millions did. "Digging up all that snow didn't turn up anything. But this was in the river. You know. By the bridge there? Avery spotted it when we was driving across. Caught in the reeds. Frozen there." He turned it over in his hands. It was still a little bit stiff. "Looks like blood here. Inside."

"Take it to the washroom," Shattuck said.

In the washroom he laid it on a hand basin and peered at it closely while it dripped on the vinyl floor. It did look like blood. Washed to a thin pink by the river, but maybe the lab in Randall Falls could make something of it. He sent Schneider after a plastic bag. When he came back, Shattuck had him hold open the bag, and he dropped the jacket into it. He said, "I don't suppose in your excitement, you and Lemke remembered the hatchet, did you? You didn't wade in up to your ass in frozen slush and poke around for the hatchet, did you?"

"You think the assailant wrapped it in the jacket?"

"I think that's how the blood got on it," Shattuck said.

"Yeah, right. Well, I guess I can go back with hip boots."

"And a rake." Shattuck took the sack away from him. "You do that."

Schneider pushed glumly out of the washroom, and Shattuck followed and said, "At a guess, how many beat-up white pickup trucks would you say there are in Percival and vicinity?"

Schneider stopped, turned, grinned at him. "You're kiddin', right?"

Shattuck sighed and nodded. "I'm kiddin', Brun."

The list Bobby Hovis had made for him of men who had come to Gene Talbot's house on odd weekends was not long. After he had dropped the jacket off for analysis at the sheriff's station in Randall Falls, he went to find the men. None of them had heard what happened to Talbot last night, he watched them sharply as he told them, and he judged they were truly shocked. Had Talbot told them of threats to his life? Had he spoken the name of anybody he was afraid of?

"No" from the dentist, reedy, balding, pink and white, in the expected crisp white jacket. "No" from the veterinarian, stocky, with black bristly brows over bright blue eyes. In his store dogs never let up barking, and Shattuck wondered what the man did not to be stunned by silence at home at night.

"No" from the third man, who sold men's wear in a shop that signed itself Savile Row. He looked like the image of a beautiful youth in a snapshot that sunlight had damaged. He was, Shattuck guessed, in his mid-fifties. Like the others. Like Talbot. Maybe ten years younger was the slight, nervous man in a green apron and yellow rubber gloves who with his mother operated a florist shop in a busy corner. He took Shattuck behind a tall, glassed refrigerator filled with irises and orchids and whispered his negatives, seeming worried that his mother might discover his sexual bent. Even this late in the day.

The Tool Room was open, but without customers. The bouncy bartender bubbled over with chuckles. His Elvis pompadour and long sideburns, the way he rolled up the short sleeves of his loud Hawaiian shirt to hold a pack of Marlboros, the wooden match he chewed, and the cigarette he kept ready behind his ear, only showed how time had passed him by. His arms and chest bulged, all right, but it was fat making the shirt too small for him, not muscle. Not lately, not for a long time. He stopped joking when Shattuck told him what had happened to Talbot. He staggered backward, sat down hard on a stack of beer crates.

"I told him those South American drug dealers were dangerous. I warned him. He just laughed. And now look what's happened." He began to cry.

"Those drug deals were fantasies," Shattuck said. "I wish they'd been real. Then I'd have somebody to go after for this."

The barkeep blew his nose, dried his eyes. "Fantasies?"

"The FBI proved that," Shattuck said. "Years ago."

"Well, he certainly made me believe him."

"That was his stock in trade." Shattuck started for the door. It was old fashioned, with a big oval of glass in it. Sun glaring off the snow outside made him squint. He turned back. "Jurgen Jensen? He ever come in here?"

"All the time." The bartender stood up. "Till he got too sick. AIDS. What a waste." He lit a cigarette and bleakly watched smoke drift in a shaft of sunlight. "He was bright and funny, but he was also good and kind. Really. Everybody adored him. Funeral was only last week. I was there. So were all his friends. In Percival of all places. I thought that ugly church would fall and crush us."

"He and Gene Talbot never came in here together?"

The bartender almost reeled. "You don't know what you're saying. No way. Those two had nothing, but I mean nothing, in common."

"When Jurgen was a kid, Talbot never, uh, took him to bed?"

Headshake. "Gene likes 'em beautiful but dumb. Jurgen wasn't dumb."

•   •   •

It was just five but dark and already very cold again, somewhere in the twenties. Lights were on indoors at the Paychek place. But from the sound of it, so was the television set, and Shattuck had to ring the chimes and knock a long time before a porch light went on and Janos Paychek, a hefty, beard-stubbly man in sweats, opened the door. He looked sore. Then he took in that this was a uniformed peace officer, and he looked startled. Then he looked alarmed. "What's wrong? Something happened to my kids? They only went to the—" He shut his mouth when Shattuck held up a clear plastic bag for him to see.

Shattuck asked, "You lose this? It's got your name carved into the haft."

Paychek scowled, squinted at the hatchet, reached out.

"Uh-uh." Shattuck stepped back. "Don't touch."

Paychek said, "Yeah, it's mine. Where'd you get it?"

"Somebody threw it in the river," Shattuck said. "Last night. Just after a bloody crime out at the Talbot house."

"Oh, hell." Paychek was a pale man to start with. Now he turned paler. "It was on the news. You think I did that?"

"I don't know what to think," Shattuck said. "You know Mr. Talbot?"

Paychek shrugged. "Buys gas from me sometimes. But I don't know him. Not how you mean. I mean, he's a drug dealer, keeps guns around, he's a pervert. Everybody knows that. Hell no, I don't know him."

"What kind of car do you drive, Mr. Paychek?"

"A 1989 GM pickup." Paychek was shivering, rubbing his hands. He looked behind him into the glowing warmth of his living room. But he decided against inviting Shattuck in. "It's freezing. Let me get a coat, okay?"

Shattuck said, "What color is your pickup?"

"Used to be cherry red," Paychek said. "Kind of rust color now. Look, I wasn't even in town last night. Me and the wife was clear over to Appleton. Her folks' place."

"I'll need to check on that," Shattuck said. "What's their name?"

"Henrickson. Hank and Sophie." Paychek gave a street address. "Old man's got prostate cancer. Do I get my hatchet back now?"

"It has to go to the police lab, first," Shattuck said, "to see whose blood is on it. And whose fingerprints. If any. I doubt even an axe murderer would forget to wear gloves in this weather."

"It wasn't me," Paychek said. "Somebody stole it, didn't they?"

"Maybe," Shattuck said. "Thanks for your time."

He trudged back out to the patrol car. As he started to get into it, a rust-colored pickup truck with bags of groceries in the back jounced squeakily in at the Paychek driveway. A pair of girls about ten or twelve were riding in the cab. They wore red and yellow striped stocking caps. The driver was a longhaired teenage boy with Paychek's pale skin. He was trying to grow a Mark McGwire beard. As he sat waiting for the garage door to go up, he stared at Shattuck. Out of curiosity or fear? Hard to tell. Shattuck motioned to him.

The kid switched off the engine but not the lights. He got down out of the truck and came at a slouchy walk. The girls gave glad cries and followed him. They stood in front of Shattuck in a bunch. The girls didn't exactly stand. They wiggled. And giggled. Their cheeks were rosy with the cold.

The boy scratched his scraggly beard. "What do you want?"

"The answer to a question," Shattuck said. "Where were you last night?"

"Right here," the boy said. "Babysitting them."

"We rented *The Lion King*," the smaller girl said.

"For the forty-zillionth time." The boy nodded at the bagged hatchet in Shattuck's hand. "What's that?"

"Someone tried to kill a citizen with it last night. It belongs to your father. But he was in Appleton. That's why I wanted to know where you were."

"Pizza Hut," the boy said. "Video store. And here. That's all."

"You want to tell me your name?"

"Ernie." The boy gave a sour laugh. "My folks claim they didn't mean it that way, but it's some kind of joke. Ernie Paychek; right?"

"If you say so," Shattuck said. "Thank you. Goodnight."

Ernie slouching, his sisters skipping, they went off across the brown, snow-patchy lawn to the red pickup. Shattuck opened the trunk of the patrol car and dropped the hatchet into it and slammed the lid down. The pickup rolled into the garage and the garage door closed. Shattuck got into the patrol car and drove off.

When he got up in the dark at five, he could see out the window that it was snowing again. The street lamp showed him that. He flapped into a bathrobe and went to the kitchen. He brewed a pot of coffee and switched on the radio for news. The Talbot murder was there, among storm warnings, lame jokes, and raving commercials. ". . . lies in a coma. Lieutenant Ben Shattuck stated yesterday that the sheriff's department is using all its resources to find the person or persons responsible for the coldblooded gunning down and brutal beating of the wealthy classic car collector."

Shattuck showered, shaved, put on a fresh uniform, boots, sheepskin jacket, fur hat, and went out, not through the garage this morning but through the front door. This was because he'd driven the patrol car to Randall Falls last night, to leave the hatchet at the lab and to stop at the hospital for an update on Talbot. He was still alive. The ICU staff told Shattuck it was a miracle. Bobby Hovis was sitting in a waiting area. Stained plastic coffee cups were stacked one inside the other on the low table in front of him. A magazine was open in his lap. He wasn't reading it. He was staring straight ahead at nothing. He looked drained. Shattuck sat down facing him.

"You've been here too long," he said. "You need sleep."

It took Hovis a moment to recognize him. "Did you find out who did it?"

"Not yet. Tell me something. The boy in the white pickup—did he have long hair and a beard?"

"A beard?" Hovis peered. "Hey, he was blond, sixteen, seventeen."

"Why don't you let me drive you home now?" Shattuck said.

Hovis shook his head. "He could wake up. I have to be here for that."

"They'll call me," Shattuck said, "and I'll call you. I promise."

"Yeah. Well, look, truth is I don't want to be out there alone. I don't know who this monster is. He could come back." He glanced down the hall. "If they throw me out, there's motels across the street. That way I can be here as soon as the doors open in the morning."

"You all right for money?" Shattuck reached for his wallet.

"Gene never let me run out." Tears came to Hovis's eyes. He blinked them back, made an effort to smile. "Thanks anyway. I'll be okay."

Once he'd reached Percival, Shattuck had felt too damned tired to bother fetching his own car from the station parking lot, too tired even to park the patrol car in his garage. He'd left it on the street. Now he stepped out into the falling snow, pulled the door shut behind him, and scuffled along the white-blanketed front walk to the brown car. It looked oddly slumped. This was because its tires were flat. He crouched to see why. Slashed. He smiled. Hell, he must be closer to solving this case than he'd thought.

When Lemke brought him his car, Shattuck headed for Mom's Diner. But the bright windows of the place that normally cheered him up sent him on past this morning. He didn't want to hear the gloating of the breakfast crowd over the Talbot beating. And he didn't want to field their prying questions. Not even if he had answers, and he didn't. He had picked up two Eggs McMuffin and an apple turnover at the drive-by window of McDonald's and brought them here to his desk. Faxes lay on the desk. They were from the police lab in Randall Falls. The blood on the jacket and hatchet was AB negative, an uncommon type that matched Talbot's. Good. But there were no fingerprints on the hatchet. The maniac had been mindful of the cold. He'd worn gloves.

Edna Durwood brought Shattuck a mug of coffee. The mug had Boss stenciled on it. "Thank you," he said and blew at the steam.

"Welcome. The Appleton police canvassed the Henricksons' neighbors, and they say the Paycheks were there the way they claim." She started off, then turned back. "Oh, and Captain Baer wants you to call him right away."

"Will do." But Shattuck was a big man and needed nourishment to get moving, so first he ate the two little egg, cheese, and ham sandwiches and the apple turnover, washed them down with coffee, and wiped his mouth and fingers on tiny paper napkins. Then he picked up the receiver and punched Baer's number. "Ben Shattuck," he said. "What's up?"

"What kind of citizens you producing over there in Percival?" Baer said. "Two A.M., one of 'em started roaring around in circles in the hospital parking lot, yelling and firing an automatic rifle at the moon. Whoopee! So, as you can imagine, all the hospital people ran to see. Or ran to hide. Or ran outdoors to up their chance of getting shot. Just one cool character remembered to get on the phone to us. But time we got there, the fun was over."

"Anybody get a look at the driver?"

"He was wearing a ski mask," Baer said.

"Anybody write down a license number?" Shattuck said.

"Now, what do you think? But they did agree on the vee-hicle. It was a beat-up white pickup truck."

"I'm so pleased to hear that," Shattuck said.

"You'll be even more pleased to hear that another individual in a ski mask ran into Intensive Care the minute the hoo-rah began in the parking lot, while the medics were all spinning their wheels or bumping into each other. And shot off a pistol. Six times. In the general direction of Eugene Talbot."

"Oh my God," Shattuck said.

"Can you believe?" Baer said. "Not one bullet hit him. Twenty-twos, like night before last. But these didn't go into his skull. They went into the wall, the ceiling, the floor. Oh, and one blew the valve off an oxygen tank."

"So he's still alive?" Shattuck said.

"Probably outlive us both."

"And ski-mask got away?"

"And ski-mask got away. The ICU people were focused on that oxygen tank nobody could turn off. And I don't like to say it, Ben, but my night troops—they're not too swift. Both ski-masks got away."

"In their goddam white pickup," Shattuck said.

"Cheer up," Baer said. "Only a few hundred of those in Randall County."

Shattuck grunted. "And one more firearm than we needed."

The one more firearm, it turned out, was from the collection of Herb Many Horses. Herb was important in Indian affairs thereabouts, had all his life liked hunting deer, and had more than once been chairman or whatever they called it of the Randall County branch of the National Rifle Association. At one time and another he and Ben Shattuck had sat on committees together. Or had butted heads on TV and in the public print over gun issues. Now he came through the front doors, a broad-faced, broad-shouldered, big bellied, brown-skinned man wearing a mackinaw and a matching hat with earflaps. He didn't stop at the reception counter where Deputy Schneider presided but pushed the little wooden gate and went directly to Shattuck.

He didn't say good morning. With a disgusted look he laid creased papers on the desk.

"These are the registration papers for an AK-47 I owned."

"Past tense?" Shattuck said. "What happened to it?"

"Some son of a bitch stole it. Got in through a basement window. Not worth locking. It's too small for a man. Had to be a kid. Screen's just lying there in the snow. What would a kid want with a weapon like that? Kick would knock him on his ass first try."

"Maybe the kid let some grown-up in through the front door."

Many Horses took off his hat. "Busted the glass out of the cabinet and reached in and took it. Naw, only one set of wet footprints. Little ones." His brows knitted. "Must've happened when I was over to Randall Falls. Them Ojibwas. They get a problem, I never knew them to solve it theirself yet. Got to drag every Indian in the U.S. and Canada into it."

"Sit down," Shattuck said. "I've got a story to tell you." He sketched in words what had happened at the hospital last night. "Descriptions made it sound to Captain Baer like an AK-47. To me, too. Maybe it was yours. Who knew about it, Herb? Who knew you owned one?"

"Family, is all," Many Horses said. "My oldest son, George—he give it to me for Christmas. So that's what, six weeks? No strangers in that time."

"Kids?" Shattuck wondered, "small enough to get through that window?"

Many Horses frowned, flipping the earflaps of the hat on his knees. "Just my grandkids. But if they want something from me, all they got to do is ask. They know that."

"Not for an AK-47, though."

"They wouldn't want it," Many Horses said. "They'll get their own guns when they get the right age. They know that. I taught 'em. Taught 'em everything about guns. How to clean 'em, how to carry 'em safe, how to shoot. I know you don't believe in that. But it's my way, the Indian way, the American way."

"And stealing what you can't pay for is the human way. Herb, you have to protect that collection of yours better. A glass-front cabinet? Seriously?"

"Nobody ever stoled none of 'em before," Many Horses said. "This ain't no high crime area, Ben. This ain't Milwaukee, this ain't Chicago."

"Not yet." Shattuck stood up. "Ask Miz Durwood to copy these. You can take the originals back home. Deputy Schneider will take your report, and you can sign off on it. Only take a few minutes."

"Yellin'? Shootin' in the air from a pickup truck?" Many Horses rose, put the hat on, picked up the papers. "Sounds like teenagers on a beer bust."

"That white pickup," Shattuck said, "doesn't suggest anybody to you?"

"Suggests half the town. Used to drive one myself." And he went off, bandy-legged, in round-heeled cowboy boots.

•　　•　　•

Kevin Ralph was thirteen but still small enough to crawl through that basement window at his grandfather's. His mother brought him into the station at three thirty. It was snowing again, and the boy wore a parka and floppy galoshes. He was pale and shaken and kept repeating, "I'm sorry, I'm sorry." His young mother, in a white fake fur jacket and white shiny boots, was slim, big-busted, hawkfaced. Her expression was grim. She didn't answer the kid. Likely she'd heard his apologies all the way over here in the car and was tired of them.

Shattuck sat the two of them down. "What are you sorry about?" he said.

"I shouldn't have done it," the boy said. "But yesterday, after school, Ernie comes to me at my locker, and he goes, is it true my grandpa has a gun collection, and I go, it's true. And he goes, does he have an Uzi? And I go, no, but he's got an AK-47. And he gets real excited, and he goes, will I help him? Because he has to have it to capture this drug dealer he knows about. There's a big reward. And if I get him the gun, he'll split it with me."

"Ernie?" Shattuck frowned. "Ernie Paychek?"

"A big kid," Lorena Ralph said wryly. "A hero."

Kevin went on. "But today I heard what happened last night. In Randall Falls. At the hospital where that queer guy is dying that somebody tried to kill. And how this truck drove around firing off this automatic rifle, and I thought, Jesus, it must be Ernie that chopped the queer guy with the axe, and—" Kevin's voice broke, his mouth trembled, tears ran down his face "—and I got scared he lied to me, there wasn't no drug dealer. No reward. He got that off TV. He's just tryin' to murder this queer guy. And then he'll kill me, too, because I know."

"And so then, too late, he comes and tells his mother." Lorena Ralph scowled down at the weeping boy as if he were past saving. "Like he shoulda done in the first place before he ever broke in at his grandpa's." She grabbed his shoulder and gave him a shake. "Big kids are bad news, Kevin. How many times I gotta tell you—keep away from big kids?"

"I'm sorry," Kevin said again, hanging his head. "I'm sorry."

Shattuck caught the mother's eye. He lifted his chin and stood. She stood, too, a little uncertain. Shattuck touched the boy's shoulder. "We'll be back in a minute," he said, and led Lorena Ralph to the coffee room. She went in ahead of him, and he closed the door. "I want you to take him out of town. You have relatives anyplace that can put you up for a few days?"

Fear widened her eyes. "You think this Ernie would hurt him?"

"He might try," Shattuck said.

"Eau Claire?" she said. "I have a sister in Eau Claire."

"That's fine," Shattuck said. "Don't wait. Take him now."

In the biting cold, the early-closing dark, Shattuck knocked at the door of the Paychek house again, the back door this time, and didn't have to wait long at all before a woman opened it. She was fortyish, plain. Graying blonde braids wrapped her head. Her hands and apron were floury. She held a glass measuring cup. She blinked. "Sheriff?" she said. "You bringing back Janos's hatchet?"

"Not yet," Shattuck said. "It's got Gene Talbot's blood on it, Mrs. Paychek. We have to hold it for evidence. Is Ernie home?"

She turned to look at a white kitchen wall clock. "He oughta be. Truck in the driveway?"

"Not yet," Shattuck said. "Look, I can see you're busy, but—" he took a folded paper out of a pocket "—I've got a search warrant here. I need to look around inside."

Her mouth dropped open. "Search warrant? What for?"

"A gun, an automatic rifle. It was stolen yesterday. And the boy who stole it says he gave it to Ernie. I believe it was used in a crime last night. And I need to find it."

"Oh Lordy," she said. "Now it's guns, is it?"

Shattuck edged her a little smile. "Let's hope not. If I can look around, we'll see, won't we?"

"Ernie's a good boy," she said, not stepping aside to let Shattuck in. "Looks after his little sisters real nice. Even cooks breakfast for me sometimes. Sundays. Oh, I know he brags a lot to the other kids about bad stuff he supposedly does. But it's not true. It's just to make them, like, admire him, you know?"

"I know how that is," Shattuck said. "Can I come in, please?"

She set the measuring cup aside and jerkily wiped her hands on the apron.

"Well, sheriff, I'd rather Janos were here. My husband. I don't know . . ."

Shattuck stepped inside. It was warm as toast, and the cooking smells were wonderful. Lots of paprika. A Dutch oven bubbled on the stove. Bread dough lay on a floured board. "It'll be all right," he assured her. "I won't take long. Just show me Ernie's room, now, will you?"

A white telephone was affixed to the wall. She went to it. "I want Janos here." She took down the receiver. She was flushed and defiant. "I think I've got that right." She began pushing buttons. Her hand trembled.

"Absolutely," Shattuck said. "I'll just go ahead and search."

He clumped through to Ernie's room, opened some drawers, peered under the bed and into a closet that smelled of sweaty socks. But after he stepped on something and picked it up and it turned out to be a painty-headed screw, he knew where the gun was. Kevin Ralph's small-boy voice said in his head, *He got that off TV.*

Shattuck stood on a chair that creaked ominously under his weight and peered through the slightly tilted grill of an air-conditioning vent. Sure enough. He got down off the chair just as the woman came to stand scowling in the doorway of her son's room, and Shattuck's search became all show. Leaving the gun was dangerous, but that's what he did. And inside five minutes, with thanks and apologies, he was out of the house into the cold again.

He drove under big winter-stripped trees to the next block and parked. The street curved just right, so he could see the Paychek place from there. If it didn't commence to snow again. He talked to Edna Durwood on the radio, hung it up. This weather was wrong for a stakeout. He grew colder as the dark came down. But in twenty minutes the rust-red truck swung into the driveway, both men in it. Maybe the kid worked for his dad at the filling station after school. The truck rolled into the garage, and the door came down.

He checked his watch and turned on the heater. Just long enough to take the edge off the cold. He didn't want to exhaust the battery. He switched off the heater, turned up his collar, pulled down the earflaps of his fur hat, and waited. Another fifteen minutes passed. The garage stayed closed. Paycheks, father and son, were taking the news of his visit calmly, looked like. Or had she even told them? Maybe she'd wanted them to eat in peace first. Thinking how good that kitchen smelled made Shattuck hungry. Had he misjudged her? Wasn't she going to tell them at all? If not, why not?

He hadn't time to worry about it. Light glared off the rear view mirrors, making him squint. A patrol car pulled in behind him and parked. Its lights went off. A door slammed. And skinny, horse-faced Fritz Baer walked up beside him—hooded jacket, turtleneck sweater. Shattuck opened the window.

"You bring any food with you?" he asked.

Baer gave his head a wondering shake. "You always hungry?"

"I'll pick up a pizza." Shattuck started his engine. "Won't take me long. That's the place to watch." He pointed. "Number 522. The cowboy who staged the Wild West show in the hospital parking lot lives there. Ernie Paychek. Seventeen, long hair, little nothing beard. Drives a rust-red 1989 GM pickup."

"The one at the hospital was—," Baer began.

"White, I know. But what I believe is, sooner or later, maybe not till the family is asleep, Ernie will come out and drive off in the red one and lead us to the white one. And whoever that belongs to is who tried to kill Gene Talbot. Twice." Shattuck had halfway closed the window when he remembered. "Be careful, Fritz. I searched the house. He's still got that AK-47. I left it where he hid it so he'd think he's smarter than I am."

"I hope he isn't." Baer stepped back. "Anchovies, right?"

Shattuck touched his hat. "You're the captain," he said, and drove off.

By the time he got back to the Paycheks' street, snow had begun to fall again. He pulled up behind Baer's patrol car, switched everything off, lifted the warm pizza box off the passenger seat, opened the door, and got out.

He didn't close the door. There wasn't time. A white pickup truck with its lights off came roaring up the street toward him. Someone fairhaired hung out the window on the passenger side. That someone had an automatic rifle. The rifle began to stutter and spit fire. Bullets banged into the metal and glass of the patrol car. Shattuck dropped the pizza box, crouched behind the open door of his car, and yanked his 9mm from its holster. With crazily squealing rubber the white pickup careened past him. Bullets shattered glass over his head, and the fragments struck his fur cap, his collar, his shoulders. He pivoted and fired at the rear tires of the pickup. It held the street for a heart-stopping second, then tilted, jumped a curb, fell on its side, and crashed into a tree. Shattuck ran to the patrol car. Baer was bunched on the floor under the steering wheel. All angular elbows and knees, he pulled himself awkwardly onto the seat. He hadn't been hit.

"Sorry," he said. "He must have sneaked out the back way. On foot."

"You want to radio for an ambulance?" Shattuck said.

Doors began to open up and down the block, yellow light streamed out into the snowfall. Householders appeared, shrugging into coats, calling "What happened?" to each other.

"Everything's okay," Shattuck shouted. "Sheriff's already here."

Baer was talking on the two-way radio. Shattuck, to reassure the citizens, reached in front of Baer and switched on the bar of winking colored lights on the roof of the patrol car. Then, shaking splinters of glass out of his fur hat, he trudged up the snowy street to see who was in that silent white pickup truck.

By ten thirty Larry French, the big fairhaired, hockey-playing A student who had fired the AK-47 tonight lay in the Intensive Care Unit of the Randall Falls hospital in a coma, in a bed only six feet from Gene Talbot's. The smash-up of the white truck had fractured the boy's skull. His thin, washed-out mother, probably a nervous wreck anyway, sat in the waiting alcove in the hall across from a sour-looking man in a cheap suit who must have been her husband. She chainsmoked cigarettes. He worked a crossword puzzle.

Ernie Paychek, whose turn to fire the AK-47 had come last night, had broken an arm, a few ribs, and a good many teeth, but he was in a regular room. His mother and father were with him. They sat side by side on stiff steel chairs, staring numbly at their son. His face was bruised and swollen. His mouth was puffy. He was drugged for pain. But the doctors had told Shattuck that he could talk. And he did talk. What he said, to Shattuck, was unprintable.

Three hours later a broad, white, many-buttoned telephone yodeled on Fritz Baer's desk, where he and Shattuck were drinking coffee and writing up a report on a computer. Baer lifted the receiver, said his name, listened, and hung up. He looked at his watch. He stared at Shattuck. The expression on his long, lantern-jawed face Shattuck couldn't read.

"You're not going to believe this," Baer said.

"Try me," Shattuck said.

"Gene Talbot died at one oh-five."

Shattuck frowned. "That surprises you?"

"What surprises me," Baer said, "is that Larry French died seven minutes later." He watched Shattuck stand up and head for the coat rack at the end of the room. "Where you going?"

"Ernie Paychek will talk to us now," Shattuck said. "You coming?"

"He came over around eight," the boy said in the room where Shattuck and Baer stood like a pair of shadowy monoliths beside his bed. They had not turned on the lights. The only illumination came from a window. Landscape lighting reflected off snow. "He wanted me to go with him, but I couldn't. I had to babysit my sisters. He had ski masks for us. Gloves so we wouldn't leave fingerprints. A .22 was stuck in his pants. He said we'd break into the house. Talbot had all kinds of guns. Larry said he had to have an Uzi.

"I said, 'What for?' and he said, 'You can rule with one of those.'

"And then I went outside with him, and he saw this hatchet by the woodpile and threw it in the truck. 'What's that for?' I said, and he said it was in case the house was hard to break into. Then he got in the truck. 'See you after,' he said and drove off. Look, can I go to sleep now?"

"Soon," Shattuck said. "Did he come back?"

"Sure. I was surprised how soon. Like he'd been to the store or something. He said Talbot had been home. So Larry rang the doorbell and pretended he wanted to buy one of those junkers Talbot keeps down by the road. A Mustang. But it needed a lot of work. And Larry said thanks but no thanks and got in his truck and came back. So it was a big nothing.

"But I could see he wasn't telling me the whole story. He was pale and jittery and kept jumping up and walking around, grinning to himself. We were in the kitchen, right, and my sisters were in the family room watching 'The Lion Yawn,' but it's not all that far, they could see and hear us, and finally he grabbed me up and yanked me into the garage and said, 'I killed him, Ernie. I killed the rotten pervert. He kept talking all the way down the hill, joking, being charming, right? That voice. The lah-didah way they talk. It drives me crazy. And when he bent to unlock the Mustang, I pulled out the .22 and shot him in the back of the head. Filthy faggot. He was the one who gave Jurgen AIDS. My uncle. He was the one who killed him.

"'He fell down in the snow. He was all bloody, but he wasn't dead. He was reaching out. "Help me," he kept saying. "Something's happened to me. I need your help." And I just kept pulling the trigger till all the bullets were gone. "Die, you creep," I said. "Why won't you die?" But he wasn't dead. So I started kicking him. But he just grunted. He didn't die.

"'And then I remembered the hatchet. And I ran and got it, and I chopped him. Like chopping firewood. Just chopping at his head. And he put up his hands, and I chopped his hands. His shirt pulled up from his belt and I saw his back, and I chopped his spine. And finally he stopped moving. He didn't say anything more, didn't make a sound. He was dead. Christ, I'm glad. That son of a bitch. I'm so happy.' He stretched his arms up. 'Thank you, Jesus,' he said."

"What was so special about this Jurgen?" Baer said.

"When Larry's dad walked out when he was like nine or something, Jurgen, like, I don't know, filled in for him, right? He was Larry's mother's brother. And he was always around. He took Larry to hockey games, ice fishing, the Brewers. Then, when his mother married again, the husband didn't like a queer hanging around and told Jurgen to get lost. But Larry never forgot, and when he turned sixteen and his new so-called dad wouldn't buy him a car, he went to Jurgen, and Jurgen bought it for him. The white pickup. Who from? Had to be Gene Talbot, right?" In the aseptic darkness, Ernie Paychek laughed. "Isn't that what friends are for?"

"Talbot didn't sell pickup trucks," Shattuck said. "And he and Jurgen were never friends. Larry was mistaken, Ernie. His beloved uncle didn't get AIDS from Talbot. He couldn't have."

"Why not?" Paychek said. "They were the only two faggots in town."

"We've seen his medical records," Baer said. "Talbot was HIV negative."

Marcia Muller

The Impostor

MARCIA MULLER has arrived. Took a long time. Some would say too long. But now it's happened. And it's happened big-time for two reasons. She writes very well about both the middle class and the working class. And she does her work with a hard, clear eye that is neither selfish nor sentimental. She has an easygoing style that manages to work in a lot of social comment without getting in the way of the storytelling, which has been and always is first rate. "The Impostor" is set during the deflating bubble of the Internet boom, when everyone was scrambling to get out while the getting was good. Detective Sharyn McCone is hired to figure out who would claim to be someone he's not, just to crash a party in Silicon Valley. It was first published in *The Mysterious Press Anniversary Anthology*.

The Impostor

Marcia Muller

The house was in Daly City, a suburb abutting San Francisco to the south, which had been developed with an eye for practicality rather than style. There was nothing to distinguish this dwelling from its neighbors to either side: All were beige stucco with a garage on the ground floor, a picture window above, and stairs to the front door rising on the right. But inside, the resemblance to a conventional suburban home stopped.

For one thing, the living room was full of balloons that bobbed and stirred on the breeze that followed me inside. Gold lamé balloons, no less. Costumes in satin and sequins and velvet were crammed onto a rack in the foyer. Gigantic bags of confetti were stuffed behind the sofa; a rubber octopus leered from one corner; mouthwatering aromas emanated from the kitchen. In the cramped office to which my new client, Barbara Baldwin, led me, the computer screen showed a spreadsheet with substantial totals.

Baldwin cleared the screen and shut the machine off while motioning me toward a chair. She was a short, plump woman with frizzy red hair that looked as if it could radiate sparks; laugh lines around her mouth suggested she smiled often, but right now her brow was creased in a frown.

She said, "Thanks for taking the time to drive down here, Ms. McCone. We've got a huge party at the Hyatt Regency tonight, and they've requested a triple order of our Wildest Dreams canapés. Plus my partner's down with the flu, and I'm waiting for confirmation that the strolling minstrels will actually show up this time, and—well, I'm sure you don't want to hear about my problems. Not those particular ones, at least."

When she'd called to request McCone Investigations' services, Barbara Baldwin had explained that Wildest Dreams Productions were professional party planners who assumed responsibility for coordinating large corporate events. Apparently that included preparing hors d'oeuvres and corralling straying minstrels. I'd done some checking on the firm after I'd talked with her and been impressed: In five years Baldwin and her partner, Melanie Katz, had gone from a shoestring operation that catered neighborhood children's parties to a company that did more than two million dollars' business annually, and they kept their profit margin wide by continuing to work out of Baldwin's home so she could keep tabs on her young children—one of whom had been seated on a carousel horse watching TV cartoons when I'd entered. The kids loved the party props, my client had explained.

Now I said, "You mentioned a problem of a serious nature."

"Yes. Have you heard of Raffles?"

"You mean where you buy a ticket and—"

"No, it's a name. The alias of a man here in San Francisco, after the gentleman burglar of English literature. No one knows his identity, what he does for a living, or what he looks like. He's a party crasher by avocation."

"Unusual hobby. I take it he's crashed parties you've planned."

She rolled her eyes. "He's crashed *everybody's* parties. The man's an absolute master at it. They say he's in his late twenties, has a good social background, but his family lost its money and position a number of years ago. He regards it as a game to slip into the important corporate parties or upper-crust benefits, wine and dine himself, hobnob with celebrities and the rich, then slip out undetected. And he always leaves an engraved card with just the one word on it—Raffles."

"Does he wear disguises to keep from being identified?"

"Only a veneer of charm and good breeding. He's probably a familiar face to the people he encounters on the social circuit, and they don't identify him as a notorious crasher because his mannerisms and appearance make him seem to be one of them. He may even introduce himself by an aristocratic-sounding name."

I finished making a few notes and asked, "Do you have much trouble with crashers?"

"Yes and no. There's a hard core of about a hundred of them in the city who regard it as a kind of sport. They're young, semi-affluent, not very well connected socially, but with aspirations. And relatively harmless. Most of the time they're easy for the security staff to spot: They're not dressed exactly right; they make pigs of themselves at the buffet table and the bar; they don't appear to know anybody. When the guards corner them and ask them to leave, they go without protest. But lately they're becoming more sophisticated and skilled, and there's also been some theft."

"What kind of theft?"

"Oh, expensive party favors. Crystal. Silver cutlery. We're insured against loss, of course, but now—"

A woman in a clown's costume burst into the room. "It's too tight!" she wailed. "If I try to juggle in this I'll pop my buttons!"

Baldwin sighed. "Call Dress You and explain the problem. Tell them to give you another or make alterations on this one."

"At the last minute?"

"They'll do it. God knows we throw enough business their way."

The woman nodded and left.

Baldwin looked at me and asked, "Where was I?"

"There's been some theft."

"Ah, yes. But that's minor, compared to the Raffles problem. He's sent us a note indicating he has special plans for a party we've organized for this coming Saturday." She took a cream vellum envelope from her desk drawer and passed it over to me.

The typewritten address was that of Wildest Dreams' post office box. I slipped a card from it, saw "Raffles" spelled out in raised lettering. Beneath he'd typed a single line: "I will honor the Colossus.com party with my presence and take action that will astonish you."

"What's Colossus-dot-com?" I asked.

"A big new client. They're one of the hottest dot-coms in Multimedia Gulch, and the party's to commemorate the third anniversary of their founding. The partners, David Keith and Preston Freeman, are both Stanford graduates, under thirty, and about to become very, very rich when the company goes public. We've rented the entire Bakker Mansion on Octavia Street. Ordered the best champagne, liquors, caviar, seafood, filet mignon. The entertainment is big-name. If the party goes well, more business of this type is sure to come our way, and our kids will someday be able to afford the colleges of their choice. But if it doesn't . . ." She shuddered.

I asked, "Do you have any idea what this astonishing action that Raffles promises might be?"

"I can't begin to guess."

"Is there any reason this Raffles would want to ruin you or your partner?"

"As far as I know, he's never set eyes on either of us. We don't interact with the guests—legitimate or crashers—at our events."

"Do either of you know anyone who fits his profile?"

"Well, the hosts of the parties we plan. But they're mostly A-list, high-visibility people."

"Has the security staff at one of your events ever roughed up a crasher?"

"God, no! They're told to be discreet so as not to upset the guests. And the crashers don't want a scene, either."

"Okay, now: What exactly do you want me to do? McCone Investigations isn't a security firm, although we have good connections in that area. I can refer you—"

"We're not concerned about security for the event," Barbara Baldwin said. "We want you to identify Raffles and prevent him from ruining the party—and *us*."

• • •

I drove back to Pier 24½ on San Francisco's Embarcadero, a renovated structure in the shadow of the Bay Bridge where my agency occupies half the
second story. Instead of following the iron catwalk to my office at the far
end, I went the other way and stopped in to see Charlotte Keim, my best
operative in the financial area. Keim, a Texas transplant in her twenties, was
at her desk, twirling a lock of curly brunette hair around her index finger as
she frowned at her computer screen.

"Shar!" she exclaimed. "This data from the new client you assigned me
is driving me crazy. Somebody's been fiddling with his accounts like a musician at a barn dance, but I can't figure how."

I glanced at the meaningless columns of numbers on the screen. "If you're
hoping for input, you're talking to the wrong person. Even Humphrey would
be more helpful." Humphrey was the Boston fern that sat atop her file cabinet.

"Yeah, I know." She swiveled away from the offending figures. "So
what's up?"

"Have you heard of an outfit called Colossus-dot-com?"

"Who hasn't? Well, you, of course. They're an on-line service that provides fitness information, helps you tailor your exercise and diet programs to
your specific needs and then track how they're working. Company's been
around a few years now, and they're planning to float an initial public offering of their stock soon, although it's been delayed twice now. Probably, like
a lot of the dot-coms, they look better on paper than they do in fact."

"You know either of the founders?"

"Pres Freeman and Dave Keith? Sure. Oddly enough, I used to date
Pres. The two of them make a strange pair. Never agreed on which direction
the company was going to take from day one. Dave's really into making
money; Pres saw them as bringing proper health and fitness to the masses.
Dave invested most of the start-up money, so he wanted to call all the shots.
Around the time I was seeing Pres, they had a major blowup and Dave tried
to force him out. That would've ruined Pres; he's always been on shaky
financial ground. But I guess they smoothed things over, and the IPO will
finally go forward."

"You still see Pres?"

"Around, sometimes. We didn't date long. The man's a health nut and a
food snob. It drove him crazy when I'd eat pork rinds and drink bourbon
and Dr Pepper."

I stared at her.

"Right." Keim nodded. "The man doesn't know what's *good*."

When I got to my office I realized there was something else I should have
asked Keim and went back along the catwalk. There I found her with her
arms around my tall blond nephew, Mick Savage, who had both his hands on
her ass. I cleared my throat and they pulled apart, flushing.

"Office romances," I said, shaking my head in mock disapproval. Mick and Charlotte had been living together for a while now, and I was pleased with the way she'd domesticated my younger sister's wild son.

"Actually, she was sexually harassing me," he said.

"Good for her. Listen, have either of you ever crashed a party? I don't mean some beer bust, but a genuine upscale party?"

They exchanged glances.

"I'm asking because I've got a case involving a crasher."

"Well . . . ," Charlotte said. "Yeah, we have."

"But not often," Mick added.

"Tell me how you did it."

"First off," he said, "you've got to find out what kind of event it is, then dress to fit in. The first party we crashed was at the St. Francis Yacht Club, and security wasn't so hot. We just breezed through the door, had a couple of free cocktails and some canapés, and slipped out when we saw one of the guards watching us. The second time we got booted out of the Mark Hopkins ballroom before we even finished our first drinks. And the third time finished us." He shook his head ruefully.

Charlotte laughed. "That time was a benefit for charity at this mansion in Pacific Heights. We wanted to go because a lot of celebrities would be attending. I started talking to a couple on the sidewalk, complimenting the woman on her dress, and the people on the door thought we were with them and let us in without asking for our invitation. And the place was full of celebrities, huh, Mick?"

"Yeah. One of whom was Dad." My former brother-in-law, country music superstar Ricky Savage, lived in the city.

"What did he do?"

"Pointed us out to one of the security people, who escorted us to the door."

I smiled. Ricky must've loved the opportunity to put in his place the son who had given him more than a fair share of trouble. "So what's the appeal of crashing?" I asked.

"The challenge. The thrill of getting away with something. The really great food and drinks. Being around people you only read about in the papers."

"Like your own father."

"Well . . ."

"You ever hear of a crasher who calls himself Raffles?"

"He's legendary."

"Any idea who he is?"

"Nobody knows."

"Know anybody who could give me a lead on him?"

Mick shook his head and glanced at Charlotte. She said, "I think somebody interviewed him a while back, in that new on-line magazine called *Soiree*. The reporter might be able to help you."

I had a suspicion who that reporter would be. J. D. Smith, my old friend and former *Chronicle* reporter, had recently crossed over into the world of electronic journalism. J. D., who—in whatever medium—always managed to get the most interesting assignments.

"Haven't you ever heard of reporters protecting their sources?" J. D. said.

"Oh, come on." I cradled the phone against my shoulder and shifted in my chair so I had a better view of the excursion boats passing on the bay. "I'm not asking you to reveal the identity of someone who's given you information on matters of national security. This is a guy who sneaks into parties, for God's sake."

"The confidentiality rule applies across the board."

"Since when did you become so principled?"

"Since when did you become so *un*principled?"

Impasse. "Okay, let me tell you what your buddy Raffles has been up to lately." I explained about his note to Wildest Dreams Productions.

"So?" J. D. said. " 'Astonish' isn't a word that necessarily implies trouble."

"It doesn't imply lack thereof, either. At least not in that context."

"Look, Shar, I can't help you."

"I think you can. Why don't you call Raffles, tell him I want to talk with him about his plans?"

"I suppose I *could* put the ball in his court."

"Of course you can. And if you do, I'll consider your debt canceled."

"Debt? What debt?"

"You remember an evening three years ago when you announced there wasn't a cop within ten blocks, right before you started breaking into that sleazy lawyer's office? And the officer who was parked across the street watching you happened to be a friend of mine?"

"Jesus! I pay and pay—"

"And pay. Call the man, J. D."

There's usually a bite to April nights in San Francisco—and most nights at any other time of the year—but on this one the air was balmy. When the phone rang I was sitting on the backyard deck of my small earthquake cottage, glass of wine at hand. I picked up and a cultured male voice said, "Ms. McCone, this is Raffles. J. D. Smith suggested I call you."

"Thanks for phoning so quickly. I'd like to set up a meeting."

"I'm afraid that's impossible. I never allow anyone to learn my true identity."

"What about J. D.?"

"That's different. We're old friends."

"I can promise you the same confidentiality J. D. did."

"That's not the point. What if you were to encounter me while on the social circuit? You'd recognize me, perhaps give me away."

"I'm not likely to attend the same parties as you do," I said dryly. "My name doesn't appear on anybody's A list."

He hesitated. "It's not really necessary we meet, Ms. McCone. The reason I called is to assure you that I'm not the one who sent that note to Wildest Dreams Productions. I have no stationery like you described to J. D., only the calling cards. Both, of course, can be made up at any copy shop. Someone has usurped my good name, and it makes me angry. When you identify the individual, I'd appreciate you letting me know who he is."

Of course he would say that. "I'm not sure I believe you."

"And I can understand why you wouldn't. But think of it: Writing a note to forewarn someone that I plan to crash a party would be self-defeating. And, frankly, this particular fete is not on a par with the events I favor. Dot-commers don't interest me, except when I can get in on an IPO. And I've heard rumors that Colossus can't get theirs off the ground."

"You forget—the note was addressed to Wildest Dreams."

"I've never heard of them. I don't concern myself with the little people behind the scenes; it's the rich and powerful who count, and I intend to number among them one day."

He was vain, and vanity could be played upon. "So what should be done about this impostor?"

"As I said, when you identify—"

"By then he may already have taken his 'astonishing' action. It'll be too late to save your reputation."

Silence.

"If you really care about exposing this impostor, Raffles, I have a suggestion . . ."

For the rest of the week I delved into the lives of Barbara Baldwin and Melanie Katz, attempting to identify someone with a reason to want to ruin them. I had extensive conversations with both women, talked with Baldwin's former husband and two of Katz's former boyfriends, plus three dissatisfied clients and the owner of a rival party-planning company who felt Wildest Dreams had lured clients away from her in an unethical manner. None of the leads got me anywhere, but during our talks I did pick up on certain tensions between the partners.

Baldwin: "Melanie gets sick a lot, and I end up with most of the responsibility heaped on me. And I'm the one who's inconvenienced, because the office is here in my house and all the party crap gets delivered to me."

Katz: "Barbara wants to make the majority of the decisions, even though this is supposed to be an equal partnership, because she invested more money initially."

Baldwin: "Mel doesn't understand business and cost control. If I let her have her way, we'd be bankrupt within six months."

Katz: "Barb is looking to make a ton of money, and lots of times she cuts corners. We can't agree on what the company is supposed to be about. I know she'd like to buy me out, but I've got two kids to support and no other skills. Even if she paid me a good price I'd probably end up broke in a few years."

It made me glad I'd never taken in a partner.

On the night of the Colossus.com party I opened my door to a tall, slender stranger in his late twenties, with aristocratic features and finely styled dark hair. He wore a tuxedo and highly polished shoes and—when he saw me— a frown.

"No!" he exclaimed. "Absolutely not!"

I'd been extending my hand to him, but now I withdrew it and stepped back, amazed at receiving such a greeting from someone I'd never laid eyes on before. The man who called himself Raffles strode into my front hall.

"This will never do," he announced.

"What?"

"Just look at you!" He gestured dramatically from my head to my toes.

I glanced down at the red velvet dress that I always trotted out for special occasions.

"The key to dressing for these events," he said, "is understatement. Not red. Not velvet. Not short skirt, garnet earrings, or cleavage. Especially not cleavage. Where is your closet?"

Dumbstruck, I pointed toward the rear of the house.

Raffles grabbed my hand and dragged me through my sitting room and kitchen to the bedroom, where he threw open the closet door and started pawing through what could loosely be termed my wardrobe.

"No," he muttered. "No. No. Certainly not. Never!"

I watched him, turning the phrase "psychological abuse" over in my mind.

"Ahah!" he said triumphantly. "Here it is!"

The garment he brandished at me was a twenty-some-year-old black dress that I'd bought for the funeral of my godmother and never had on since. I'd saved it in case any of the other pious, proper individuals in my life died.

"Put this on," Raffles told me, brushing dust from its shoulders. "Where is your jewelry?"

Still taken aback, I pointed mutely to the box on the bureau. He rummaged through it and produced a pearl necklace and earrings that had been a college graduation present from my parents. I'd seldom worn them.

"These are appropriate. Now, shoes . . ." He glared down at my T-straps. "Don't you have any black pumps that are simple and elegant?"

As a matter of fact I did: Ferragamos, my one extravagant purchase of the past decade. I went to the closet and held them up for his inspection.

He sighed with relief.

I shooed him out of the bedroom so I could change.

"That was a novel experience," Raffles said.

"What was?"

"Presenting a bona fide invitation to get into a party."

We were standing in the foyer of the Bakker Mansion, a twenty-room Queen Anne Victorian that had once been a private residence and now belonged to a historical foundation which rented it out for special events. Formally attired partygoers deposited their coats at the checkroom, then moved through the archway to the front parlor, where a sting quartet played. Others carried flutes of champagne and plates piled high with delicacies from the buffet in the dining room. Still others ascended the wide staircase to explore the second-story rooms or to check out the big-name entertainment on the third floor. Raffles kept his eyes on the door, scrutinizing each arrival.

"I'm not sure I like being a legitimate guest," he said.

"Well, after tonight you can go back to your wicked ways."

"They're not really wicked—ah!"

"What?"

"That couple."

They were in their twenties and dressed simply but stylishly. The man said to the woman who was collecting invitations, "My mother's here, and she was supposed to meet us at the door, but we're late and I guess she got tired of waiting."

"I'm sorry, sir, but I can't—"

"Oh, there she is. Mom!" He waved toward the living room. A woman there waved back. The invitation taker glanced her way, but turned toward the couple before the woman frowned, not recognizing them. The couple was admitted immediately.

"Not bad," Raffles said. "For amateur crashers."

A few minutes later an elegantly dressed man appeared and began apologizing for having forgotten his invitation. When the woman said she couldn't admit him without it, he beamed. "My lucky day! Now I get to go home and veg out in front of the tube. Of course, my department manager'll be furious."

The woman hesitated, considering possible repercussions, then passed him through.

"Smooth," Raffles commented.

Within the next half hour he identified three more lone male crashers and then, as the flow of arrivals ebbed, we began drifting through the crowd, keeping tabs on them. In the middle parlor, Raffles spotted a heavyset man of around thirty, who was already beginning to show the effects of too much of the good life, downing champagne and holding court for a circle of admirers.

"Dave Keith," he said. "Just the man to tell me about that IPO. Watch this." He went up to the man and put a hand on his shoulder. "Great party, Dave."

Keith turned, trying to mask his confusion at not being able to place Raffles.

Raffles said, "Amory Thayer, Stanford, ninety-six." He drew me forward. "And this is Buffy Millhouse, of the Boston branch of the family."

Keith nodded and shook hands with both of us. "So what've you been doing since graduation, Amory?"

"This and that. Venture capital, investments. I've heard good things about Colossus-dot-com. When's your IPO?"

"Not for a while, unfortunately. I've got to . . . do a bit of reorganizing before that happens. You thinking of buying in?"

"Definitely."

Dave Keith's eyes warmed. "Well, splendid. You and I will ride the bubble all the way to the top."

"That we will. Great seeing you, Dave. We'll circulate now."

When we were out of Keith's earshot I said, "*Buffy*? Do I look like a Buffy?"

Raffles studied me. "Perhaps of the vampire-slayer type."

"Oh, thanks. While you were showing off back there, were you also keeping an eye on those crashers?"

"Yes. The fellow who said he wanted to veg out in front of the tube is over by the bar. The couple with the nonexistent mom are stuffing themselves at the buffet."

"And I can see the other three, but security's closing in on one of them."

"Well, that makes our job easier. Ah, I see Preston Freeman. Let's say hello to the other half of the team."

Freeman was the opposite of his partner: He had the lean physique of a mountain biker and was standing alone near the fireplace, looking ill at ease and sipping at what appeared to be mineral water. When Raffles introduced himself as Amory Thayer, Stanford '96, Freeman regarded him with open bewilderment. Even after Raffles introduced me and complimented him on the anniversary party, Keith's partner seemed uncomfortable. I couldn't imagine such a man dating Charlotte Keim.

Raffles said, "I was just talking to Dave, and he indicated your IPO's been delayed."

Freeman looked at him for a moment, then nodded. "Yes, delayed." He glanced around the room at his guests and put on a smile that fit him about as well as his obviously rented formal wear. After an awkward silence he said, "Would you excuse me, please? I need to speak with the caterers."

Raffles watched him walk toward the staircase, then said to me, "He has the social graces of a turnip."

"Well, a lot of these high-tech people don't relate very well."

"I suppose not. Ah, there goes our well-stuffed couple. They're being shown the door."

"That leaves three men who arrived alone. Your impostor could be any one of them."

"My odds are on the fellow who said he wanted to veg out. He's almost as smooth as I." He glanced around. "They're all in the vicinity of the buffet."

"And so's Dave Keith, helping himself to Wildest Dreams canapés and jumbo prawns. At least one of the partners is enjoying the party."

As I watched, a waiter went up to Keith and handed him an envelope. I heard him say, "This was just delivered by messenger." Keith ripped it open, read the message, and frowned. Then he set his plate down and excused himself to the people he was talking with. He headed for the staircase.

"Damn!" Raffles exclaimed softly. "Security just apprehended my prime suspect."

I glanced toward the door, saw the crasher being quietly escorted out.

"Damn!" Raffles repeated. "I wanted to tell that impostor what I thought of him for appropriating my good name. He was using me for his own purposes, and I'd like to know—"

"Be quiet." I'd begun to feel a peculiar uneasiness. Words and phrases that I'd heard over the past few days were filtering through my mind.

At odds about the direction . . . invested more money initially . . . call all the shots . . . looking to make a ton of money . . . buy out . . . force out . . . end up broke . . . on shaky financial ground . . . do a bit of reorganizing . . . IPO . . .

Partners, complaining about partners.

"That wasn't your impostor," I told Raffles. "And Wildest Dreams isn't his target. And you don't go upstairs to talk with the caterers."

"What? What does all that have to do with—"

I hurried to the staircase, pulling him along with me.

Upstairs the rooms glowed with light and guests wandered from one to another, stopping to exclaim over the exquisite decor and costly artworks. From the third floor came the percussive beat of a well-known rock band. I scanned the hallway, saw that a door at its far end was closed, a handwritten PRIVATE sign taped below a brass plaque that said "Renoir Room." I ran to it, threw it open.

Preston Freeman stood on a chair in front of the fireplace, about to lift off the painting that hung above the mantel. Dave Keith lay on the floor, blood oozing from his head. A stained poker leaned against the hearth.

Freeman heard me come in and turned, nearly losing his balance. His face froze in shock.

Raffles stepped up behind me. I said, "There's your impostor."

Freeman leaped from the chair and scrambled toward the door, but Raffles intercepted him and dragged him down. Freeman tried to knee him in the groin, then aimed a kick at my shin as I rushed to help. His foot connected solidly; my leg gave and I fell smack on top of both of them. We flailed around—a many-limbed creature intent on destroying itself—until I got Freeman's arms pinned. Raffles squirmed out from under us, glared at Freeman's inert form, and sat on him.

In the struggle one of us had torn Freeman's jacket pocket. A card and a note protruded from it, the card engraved with the word "Raffles." I took out the note by its edges so as not to smear any fingerprints and read: "Mr. Keith: Meet me in the Renoir Room. I have important information about Mr. Freeman that will clear the way for you buying him out of Colossus.com. A Potential Investor."

I set down the note and closed the door against the crowd that had gathered outside, then said to Freeman, "You were taking the Renoir down so it would look as if your partner was killed when he surprised a burglar. You planned to take away the note and leave Raffles's card in order to implicate him."

Raffles's face darkened with anger. "And I wouldn't have *dared* come forward to proclaim my innocence because there would be too much evidence against me. Besides, why would I? No one knows who I am. But now they will." He grabbed Freeman by the hair and thumped his head against the floor. "Damn you! You've spoiled everything!"

Freeman groaned and muttered something.

"What?" Raffles thumped his head again.

"He told me there wouldn't be any IPO. He wanted me out of the company. But his buyout offer was so low I couldn't have lived a year on it. I was counting on that IPO. I've got debts, big ones. To the kind of people who don't forgive money owed."

Gambling debts, I thought, and almost felt sorry for him.

Behind me Dave Keith moaned and stirred. I went over and helped him sit up. His being alive didn't surprise me; scalp wounds always seem worse than they are because they bleed a lot, and when I'd first seen him I'd noticed the rise and fall of his chest.

It surprised Freeman, though. He turned his head, conflicting emotions passing over his face. Probably relieved that he wouldn't be charged with murder and sick because Keith would be able to testify against him.

Dave Keith stared groggily at his partner for a moment, then said, "Happy anniversary, Pres, you son of a bitch."

Edward D. Hoch

The Problem of the Yellow Wallpaper

EDWARD D. HOCH is the Grand Master of short crime fiction, and it's not just by the sanction of the Mystery Writers of America either, although the award they gave him in 2000 doesn't hurt. Since the mid-1950s, he has supported himself almost completely by writing short stories, a claim nobody else can come close to making. Listing his various series characters would require a separate book. He writes in a wide range of styles, voices, subgenres. He's even created several of his own subgenres along the way. After all this time, one would think he'd have run out of ideas by now, but they just keep coming, as varied and inventive as the first ones. And all the better for his decades of experience. He certainly makes his stories look easy, but it's taken a bit of time to polish his craft to that diamondlike shine that glitters in each one of his stories. "The Problem of the Yellow Wallpaper" was first published in *Ellery Queen's Mystery Magazine* in March. Enjoy.

The Problem of the Yellow Wallpaper

Edward D. Hoch

Much as I hated to see Mary Best depart from my office to become a Navy nurse in that glowering November of 1940, I was delighted when my former nurse April moved back to Northmont. Her husband had been called up for eighteen months of reserve duty, and she arrived on the train from Maine with her four-year-old son Sam in tow, looking not a day older than I remembered her. It would be the beginning of two of the most eventful years of my life. (Old Dr. Sam Hawthorne paused to wipe something from his eye before continuing his narrative, and his guest might not have been mistaken if he thought it was a tear.)

April had been a plump, jolly woman of thirty when I hired her shortly after my arrival in Northmont. Now, in her late forties, she was a happily married woman and the mother of a wonderful little boy. Perhaps I was predisposed to like him, since Sam Mulhone had been named after me, but a few minutes of playing with the boy at the station had made us fast friends.

"It's good to have you back, April," I told her, and meant it.

"You're sure I'm not putting someone else out of a job?"

"Far from it!" I assured her. "With Mary gone off to the Navy, I really needed somebody in the office. It was good of her to make the arrangements with you."

April nodded. "The Navy took Mary and my André at virtually the same time." She hung on to young Sam's hand as I guided them to the parking lot where my Buick waited. She smiled when she saw it. "A nice car, Sam, but I can remember your Pierce-Arrow Runabout."

"I was younger then." I opened the trunk and hoisted her bags inside.

"Weren't we all!" She helped Sam into the front seat and then slid in herself while I got behind the wheel. She'd rented a nice apartment only a few blocks from my office at the hospital, and I drove her there from the station.

I'd made arrangements for a dependable neighborhood woman to look after Sam while April worked, with the understanding that she could bring him to the office any day the woman wasn't available. April hadn't wanted to make the long drive from Maine with her son, so a friend was bringing her car down the following week, with more of her clothing and possessions.

I helped her get settled and then invited her to my house for Thanksgiving dinner the following day. "You and your son can't be alone on the holiday," I reasoned.

"Oh, Sam, we had our Thanksgiving last week!" We'd had two years of confusion and anger over the holiday, ever since President Roosevelt changed the date to the third Thursday in November instead of the fourth.

I merely smiled. "Well, I guess you could celebrate both days. A lot of people in Northmont do."

So April and young Sam had a second Thanksgiving dinner before she plunged into the daily chores of the office. After dinner that night, while her son slept on the sofa in my living room, she said, "Fill me in on what's been going on. I know you and Mary were quite close for a time."

"We were," I answered with a sigh. "It was one of those things that reached a point where neither of us wanted to take the next step. I hope that's not why she joined the Navy, but it might have been a factor."

"Is there anyone else now?"

I smiled at the question. "We have a woman veterinarian with a new place outside of town, over toward Shinn Corners. Her name is Annabel Christie and she calls the clinic Annabel's Ark. We've become friendly, that's all."

"And how's the crime rate? Are you still saving Sheriff Lens's hide on a regular basis?"

"Oh, the sheriff is a good man. He'll be happy to see you back. I still help him a little when I can."

"You're much too modest, Sam. You always have been. How about our patients? Anything unusual?"

"A Dutchman named Peter Haas claims he has a crazy wife. There's no one in town who can treat her but he won't send her away. I'm going over there tomorrow morning. You may want to ride along."

"How crazy? Does he keep her locked in the attic?"

"As a matter of fact, he does."

Peter Haas and his wife had come to America from Paris in search of a better life. They'd been fearful of Hitler's rise and what it might portend for the future of Europe. Haas had been in the diamond business, and I assumed it was the profits from those past dealings that enabled him to live with his wife in one of our town's largest homes, a lavish three-story Victorian house dating from the turn of the century, complete with kitchen and servants' quarters in the basement and a small carriage house out back. They lived there alone, though a maid came in to clean and cook for them.

Haas himself met us at the door that Friday morning, the day following our traditional Thanksgiving. He was a tall, slender man with thinning hair who wore metal-rimmed eyeglasses that he often removed as he spoke. I knew from his medical record that he was forty-four years old. His wife Katherine was twenty-nine but appeared older. I'd started treating her for nervous depression about a year earlier and her condition had grown steadily worse with time. I detected a slight hysterical tendency and urged him to seek help in Boston, where practicing psychiatrists were readily available.

Today, as I introduced him to April, he seemed especially distraught. "She's been peeling off the wallpaper in her room. I don't know what I'm going to do, Dr. Hawthorne."

"Let's go take a look."

He led us up two flights of stairs to the third-floor room that had been her bedchamber since early October when he had twice found her running nude through the garden at night. "Katherine," he called out as he unlocked the door, "Dr. Hawthorne's here to see you."

"Come in!" she sang out, almost too cheerfully.

We entered the bedroom and I felt that I was seeing it, for the first time, through April's eyes. The big double bed sat with its head against the far wall, between two barred windows that looked out on the rear garden and the carriage house. To our right were two more windows facing toward the center of town. These also were barred. One window was open a bit for fresh air, and all were covered by window screens to keep out summer insects. The wall to our left was blank, covered, as were the other walls, with faded yellow wallpaper of an unattractive flowery design. It had been ripped away in places and left dangling from the wall, exposing the bare plaster. The only other pieces of furniture in the room were a nightstand, a straight-backed chair, and a wardrobe.

Katherine Haas sat upright in the center of her bed, wearing a pink negligee tied in a bow at her throat. It was the sort of garment a young woman might wear, and it contrasted sharply with the lined and haggard face above it. There was little doubt that she was ill. "I've been waiting for you, Doctor," she told me at once. "I have a whole new set of symptoms to tell you about."

"Let me give you an examination first." I took out my stethoscope and listened to her heart and lungs. They seemed fine, and her temperature was normal. We talked for a few minutes while I introduced April, then I said, "Suppose you tell me what the trouble is."

"Mainly it's the dreams, Doctor. They come on me every night, closer to nightmares than anything else. I dream there's a prisoner in these walls, inside the wallpaper, trying to claw her way out."

"Is that how it got torn?" I asked.

"I suppose so. I can't remember clearly."

We chatted a while longer and I wrote out a new prescription, more to comfort her than to do any real good. Once outside, I watched Peter Haas locking the door and asked, "Is that really necessary? Keeping her locked up only makes matters worse."

"You didn't have to chase her through the garden in the middle of the night," he replied bluntly. "I did."

"Then take her to Boston, for God's sake!" I urged. "I can give you the name of a fine man there."

"I believe she can recover better here," Haas said, running a nervous hand through his thinning hair.

"How? Locked in an attic room?"

April spoke up for the first time. "Mr. Haas, why are there bars on her windows?"

He sighed, seeming thankful for a question he could answer. "I understand the room was once a nursery, and later a playroom for small children. The owner had the latest safety devices for summoning servants in case of an emergency, and the bars were to keep the children from climbing onto the roof."

"I see."

The full import of her question suddenly became clear to him. "Did you think I had the bars installed?"

"I just wondered about it," April said. "The room seems like a jail cell."

The Dutchman turned to me with anger in his eyes. "Does this woman mean to insult me?"

I tried to soothe him. "Of course not. We're both concerned about your wife, that's all. She needs the sort of treatment I can't give her."

By the time we'd reached the door he'd calmed down a bit. "When will you be back, Doctor?"

"Tuesday morning, to see if that new prescription is doing any good."

Back in the car, I had to listen to April's views on the subject. "Sam, you can't allow that poor woman to suffer another day like that. It's like—it's like a story I read once. I might have it in one of the books I brought along."

I shook my head as I drove back to the office. "I'm at my wits' end," I admitted.

"Is there anyone in Boston who'd be willing to come here to examine her?"

Suddenly I remembered an old classmate of mine who'd become a psychiatrist. Doug Foley. I'd visited him a few years back on one of my infrequent holidays. "There is somebody, but he's in New York."

"Could he come up on a weekend?"

I thought about it. Like me, Doug Foley thrived on a challenge. He just might be willing to make the trip. "I can ask him," I decided.

I reached Doug in New York later that afternoon and he agreed to take the train up to Stamford the following Saturday morning, assuming there wasn't an early-December snowstorm. I would meet him at the station for the two-hour drive to Northmont. He'd stay overnight with me and return to New York on Sunday afternoon. Meanwhile, April had a suggestion.

"She's alone too much in that room. No wonder she's starting to imagine things about the wallpaper. Do you think we could get her a pet, perhaps a cat? They're soothing for people."

"It's an idea," I agreed.

I had invited Annabel Christie to dine with me that evening at the Northmont Inn. The old Ferry House was long gone, and this was now our only claim to a real country inn. As with most people, our conversation turned first to the war news. It had been a bad month for England, with the city of Coventry all but wiped out by German bombers. A naval battle between British and Italian warships was raging off Sardinia in the Mediterranean, but it was too soon to know the outcome.

Annabel looked especially fetching that evening, wearing a light brown dress that went well with her blond hair and hazel eyes. It was hard to believe I'd known her only about ten weeks, having met her when unusual circumstances arose at her veterinary hospital, Annabel's Ark. Over dinner I told her about Katherine Haas and her problems. "My nurse April wonders if having a pet cat might help her. Do you have any strays at the Ark right now?"

"I have a perfect little kitten, only a few weeks old. She was born at the Ark and the owners gave her to me as partial payment on their bill. I call her Furball, but that can be changed. She's mostly black with white paws."

"Do you think it would help?"

She shrugged. "It might."

"I feel sorry for her husband."

Annabel scoffed. "Any man who would keep his wife locked up like that deserves a horsewhipping, not sympathy."

"My friend Doug will be here next weekend. I'm hoping he'll have some suggestions."

I picked up the kitten on Monday morning and drove over to the Haas's house alone while April settled in at my office. Katherine was in her locked third-floor bedroom and seemed little different from the previous week. When I presented her with the black and white kitten she seemed genuinely pleased. "It's yours," I told her. "You can name it whatever you want."

"How can I thank you, Dr. Hawthorne? This is one of the nicest things anyone has ever done for me."

"You can thank me by getting better. Have you been taking your medicine?"

She glanced over at her husband, who stood near the door. "I have. I think it's helping me."

"How about the dreams?"

"N–No, I haven't been having them the last few nights."

It seemed to me that more of the yellow wallpaper had been torn and scratched away since my Friday visit. We left Katherine playing with her kitten on the bed and went back downstairs. "She's been at the wallpaper again," I observed.

He nodded with a sigh. "She denies it. She insists there's a woman behind the wallpaper, trying to get free. She must be having the same dream, even though she won't admit it."

I rested a comforting hand on his shoulder. "I have a friend, a classmate from medical school, who has a psychiatric practice in New York City. He's visiting me next weekend and I'd like him to see Katherine. He might be able to help her."

He hesitated a moment before agreeing. "Very well, if you really believe it might help."

"I'll telephone you on Saturday after my friend arrives. His name is Dr. Doug Foley."

The first week in December was a busy one for Northmont's hospital and medical staff. The beginning of the month, often accompanied by plunging temperatures and snow, seemed to signal the onslaught of all manner of colds and flu each year. Though the polio season was pretty much past, there were plenty of other worries for nervous parents. In a week as busy as that, April and I gave little thought to Peter Haas and his wife.

It wasn't until Friday, the afternoon before Doug Foley's arrival, that April remembered the story she'd been going to show me, in a twenty-year-old anthology entitled *Great Modern American Stories*, edited by the author William Dean Howells. It was a horror story, "The Yellow Wallpaper," by Charlotte Perkins Gilman, about a situation very similar to that of Katherine Haas.

"What a ghastly tale," I said when I'd finished reading it. "I only hope we can save Mrs. Haas from a fate like that."

"The part about the barred windows and the wallpaper is what reminded me of it. I feel as if the story has come to life right here in Northmont."

"It is an odd coincidence," I admitted. "Can I borrow this book until tomorrow? I'd like Annabel to read it."

I let Annabel read it after dinner that evening, but her reaction was quite different from April's and mine. She closed the book and set it down. "You read this as a pure horror story?"

"Isn't it?"

"Sam, it's a story about feminine consciousness, about a woman imprisoned by male authority. The woman she imagines trapped in the wallpaper design is the nameless narrator herself. Her husband treats her like a child and is unresponsive to her needs. She suffers some natural depression following the birth of their baby, and he treats her in the worst possible manner."

I could see what she meant, and perhaps she was right. "You shouldn't be wasting your time on animals," I told her, only half in jest.

Saturday morning was cold and sunny as I drove down to Stamford to meet Doug Foley's train. We were both still in our early forties, though I could detect a slight graying of his hair since the last time we'd gotten together. When I mentioned it, he laughed and said, "It's good for business. People don't like to reveal their innermost secrets to a callow youth. Every time I notice a few more gray hairs I increase my hourly rate."

"What do you think about the war?" I asked as we drove. "My office nurse just joined the Navy."

"We'll be in it," he predicted. "Maybe within a year. But you and I are both over forty. The draft doesn't want us. Now tell me about this patient of yours."

"I'll show you my file on her at the office. Katherine Haas, age twenty-nine, although she looks older. She and her husband moved to Northmont from Paris a few years ago when Hitler first started threatening the rest of Europe. They bought the largest Victorian mansion in town, but appeared very little in public. I started treating her for mild depression about a year ago, but her condition has worsened. After a couple of episodes of her running naked through the garden at night, her husband confined her to a third-floor room with barred windows. Almost from the beginning, I recommended he seek psychiatric help for her in Boston, but he wouldn't hear of it. I don't know how he'll react to your visit, but at least he's agreed to let you see her."

Doug shifted uncomfortably in his seat. It was a long ride after an hour already spent on the train from Grand Central. "Unfortunately, we're still viewed by many people as something akin to witch doctors. Freud and Jung aren't exactly the Mayo brothers."

"I do appreciate your coming all this distance, Doug. Naturally I'll compensate you for your time."

Foley waved away the offer. "It's good to get out in the country sometimes. In Manhattan, we get too many patients unhinged by the sheer pace of things. They simply can't cope with life in a metropolis." He glanced out the car window at the barren fields spotted here and there with a trace of snow. "I don't expect that's a problem up here."

Although my office was only open half-days on Saturday and April could have gone home at noon, she was still rearranging files when we arrived. "I'm waiting for my friend Ellen to arrive with my car and more of my things," she explained. "I'll be going shortly."

"I thought Mary's filing system was pretty good," I said, observing the stack of folders on her desk.

"It was, Sam, but everyone does things differently. I learned a lot managing our hotel with André."

I explained to Doug that April's husband had been called to active duty with the naval reserve and the three of us fell into conversation until her friend pulled into the parking lot with her car. After they went off, I located Katherine Haas's folder in the stack and showed it to Doug. He read it over twice with a grim, intense expression on his face. "I think we'd better go over there now," he decided.

"Don't you want lunch first?"

"It can wait."

On the way over he asked me about April. "She was a great help when I first came here to set up a practice," I told him. "She's different now, with her own way of doing things, but that's probably good. I'm lucky to have her back, even if it's only for eighteen months."

"The way the war in Europe is developing, her husband might be away a lot longer than that."

I hoped for April's sake he was wrong about that.

Peter Haas met us at the front door of his house and ushered us inside. "Pleased to meet you, Dr. Foley," he said after I'd made the introductions. "I'm afraid my wife is having a bad day."

"What's the trouble?" I asked.

He led us through the hall to the stairs, and I caught a glimpse of their maid dusting the parlor. "She won't let me come in, claims she'll hide in the wallpaper if I open the door."

At the third-floor room I knocked softly. "Katherine, are you in there?"

"Go away!" she said from the other side of the locked door. "Don't come in here."

"This is Dr. Hawthorne, Katherine."

"I know who it is. Go away." Her voice was low, but close by.

"A friend of mine is here from New York. I think he can be a big help to you."

"No!" she almost screamed it. "He'll lock me away!"

"Aren't you locked away now?" I tried to reason with her through the door. "Dr. Foley can help you."

"The wallpaper—" Her sentence was cut short by a sort of gasp.

I turned to her husband. "There's no reasoning with her. You'll have to unlock the door."

Haas took a deep breath and fitted the key into the lock. As soon as I heard the bolt slide free, I turned the knob and opened the door. I saw at once that even more of the yellow wallpaper had been peeled away. It hung in great hunks from the plaster walls.

The room appeared to be empty and I quickly looked behind the door as Haas and Doug Foley entered. "She must be under the bed," Haas said.

But she wasn't. She wasn't anywhere. The black and white kitten sat on the center of the quilt, the only living thing in the room.

I opened the wardrobe, which contained only one dress and a night-gown. I walked around the room, tapping the solid plaster walls. I tried the windows, but the bars and screen held firm.

Then, looking back at the wall opposite the windows, I noticed something that sent a chill down my spine. It was the blurred face of Katherine Haas, staring out at me from her wallpaper prison.

"Looks to me like it was painted with some sort of watercolors," Sheriff Lens said as he examined the face on the wallpaper an hour later. I'd summoned him at once, after determining that Katherine Haas had indeed vanished from that locked and barred room. "Was your wife a painter, Mr. Haas?"

"Not in a good many years. When we first met, back in Paris, she used to do watercolors along the Seine."

While we'd waited for the sheriff's arrival, Doug and I had been over every possibility. We'd searched the house from top to bottom, paying special attention to the third-floor storage rooms, but we'd found nothing. Katherine Haas had faded away as if she'd never existed.

Going over her room with me, Doug could only shake his head in frustration. "She had nothing here! No personal possessions, no books, no cosmetics, not even a mirror!" He turned angrily on the woman's husband, who stood watching us from the doorway. "Did you even allow her to go to the toilet?"

"Of course. I took her downstairs several times a day. She ate her meals with me. I just could not trust her out of my sight unless she was locked in here."

"And now where is she?"

"I don't know," he admitted. "In another world, perhaps. I hope it's a better world for her."

He gave the same answer to Sheriff Lens, and the sheriff wasn't any more satisfied than Doug Foley had been. "Did you kill your wife, Mr. Haas?"

"What? Of course not! How could I? These two gentlemen have been with me every minute."

"I mean before," the sheriff said, glancing over at me. "That voice Doc heard could have been a recording or something."

But I objected to that possibility. "She spoke directly to me through the door," I pointed out. "She answered what I said. We carried on a brief conversation."

We went back to searching the room. We poked and prodded the bed, pulling it away from the wall. We searched the wardrobe for a hidden compartment and pulled that out from the wall, too, but there was nothing. Sheriff Lens had a new suggestion. After establishing just where we were standing in the hall while I conversed with Katherine through the door, he asked, "Mr. Haas, is there any chance you're a ventriloquist?"

"Of course not!"

I had to agree. "It was his wife's voice. I'd stake my life on it. She was in this room and now she's gone."

We went downstairs to the parlor, where Sheriff Lens was clearly uncomfortable with the Victorian bric-a-brac. After running his finger over a silver tea service, I saw him wipe away the dust with a sour expression. "What about the maid?" he asked. "I caught a glimpse of her arriving."

"She must be down in the servants' quarters," Haas replied. He walked over to the wall and called out, "Rose, can you come up here for a minute?"

I couldn't catch her reply, but when the young maid presented herself I realized it was Rose West, daughter of a local hardware dealer, who'd graduated from high school the previous June. "How are you, Rose?" I greeted her. "I didn't know you worked here."

"Hello, Dr. Hawthorne. I'm trying to earn money toward college. I'm at my dad's store mornings and I come here from two to six to clean and help prepare dinner." She glanced from me to Sheriff Lens and finally to Peter Haas. "What is it? Has something happened to Mrs. Haas?"

"She's disappeared," her employer told her. "Katherine is gone and we can't find any trace of her."

Rose's mouth dropped open. "I hope she hasn't hurt herself."

"We don't know," Sheriff Lens said. "Did you see anything when you arrived, anything unusual?"

She shook her head. "Everything was the same. I saw nothing of Mrs. Haas."

"Did you ever visit her in her third-floor room?"

"Sometimes when she wouldn't come down for dinner I'd take it up to her. Mr. Haas came along to unlock the door."

"What can you do, Sheriff?" I asked him. "This whole situation is beyond belief."

He could only shrug. "Nothing, Doc. I can't see that any crime has been committed."

"The woman is gone!"

"A missing person. She probably squeezed between those bars on the windows."

"They're only five inches apart, Sheriff," I pointed out. "And they're covered with window screens."

"Let's wait a day. My guess is she'll turn up, none the worse for wear."

As we were leaving, Haas said, "You'd better take the kitten. There's no one to care for it now."

Driving back to my house, I could only apologize to Doug. "Looks like I got you all the way up here for nothing."

"Don't worry. It was a good excuse to get away from the city."

Annabel Christie insisted on preparing dinner for us both, and we spent a pleasant evening at her apartment. I tried to return the kitten, but she thought I should keep it. "You can call him Watson," she suggested. Later, when she mentioned the story about the yellow wallpaper, Doug insisted on reading it.

"Well?" she asked when he'd finished. "Is it a story about insanity or the subjugation of women?"

He could sense there'd been some disagreement about it. Wisely, he answered, "Both, I think."

The following day at the railroad station we shook hands. "Keep me informed of developments," he said. "I can make another trip up here if necessary."

"Thanks, Doug."

"And Sam—"

"Yes?"

"Annabel Christie is a fine young woman."

Monday passed, and then Tuesday, without any sign of the vanished Katherine Haas. When I phoned Rose West she told me that Peter Haas seemed remote and preoccupied on her daily visits. He ate very little, and even suggested he might be leaving town in the near future.

The news from Sheriff Lens was a bit more interesting, even if it seemed to contribute nothing toward solving the mystery. He'd been looking into Katherine Haas's background before she and her husband arrived in Northmont and had discovered some interesting facts. "It was her father, not her husband, who'd been the diamond merchant in Europe," he told me on the phone. "When he died, fourteen years ago, the family money was left in trust for her until she turned thirty. Checks from a Swiss bank are deposited to her account on the first of each month."

"So her money has been supporting them both," I said, thinking out loud. "That's interesting. What happens to the trust fund if she dies before turning thirty?"

"The whole thing goes to a convent of nuns in Spain. No wonder he kept her a virtual prisoner. He was afraid she'd run off."

"Perhaps." But suddenly I was thinking of another possibility. "How much will she receive on her thirtieth birthday?"

"Those Swiss banks won't release information like that, but you can be sure they wouldn't handle it unless it was a sizable sum."

"Thanks for the information, Sheriff. Any word on her yet?"

"Not a thing. I've sent a missing persons report out to police departments and sheriff's offices throughout New England and New York."

"I doubt if that'll do any good. I don't think she ever left that house."

"Then where is she, Doc?"

"I wish I knew."

April had finally gotten the files arranged to her liking, and when I hung up she had a raft of questions to ask me. One was about Katherine Haas. "What are these papers in French that were in her folder?"

"Her medical records. She brought them with her when they moved here from Paris. My French isn't very good, but it didn't really matter. She was in good health at the time."

She studied the top sheet. "André taught me French when we were first married. I can read most of this." Then, "Didn't you tell me she painted a picture of herself on the wall of that room?"

"Apparently. Haas said she used to do watercolors along the Seine when they lived in Paris."

"That's odd. Look at this." She was pointing to a French word in the second paragraph: *daltonien.*

I shook my head. "What does it mean?"

"Color-blind."

"Oh?"

"Certainly it's not impossible for a color-blind person to be a painter, but you don't find too many of them. Did she ever mention it to you?"

"No. And until recently she seemed in perfect health."

But I thought about it the rest of the afternoon. I thought about how Katherine Haas could have gotten out of that room, and where she might be. Finally, that evening, I phoned Sheriff Lens.

"I'm going to see Haas. Do you want to come along and make an arrest?" I asked.

"Haas killed his wife, didn't he?"

"Yes."

"I knew it! I'll pick you up."

I didn't tell him anything else on the short ride back to the Victorian house. We parked a few houses down the street and went the rest of the way on foot, not up to the big house but around back toward the carriage house. I was guessing now, but I could think of no other possibility. The door was unlocked and we entered quietly. I could hear voices from the second floor. As we started up the steps a squeaky tread signaled our arrival.

In an instant Peter Haas appeared at the top of the stairs, holding a revolver. "Who's there?" he asked.

"Sam Hawthorne and Sheriff Lens, Peter. You'd better put down the gun."

Someone else had appeared behind him in the doorway and I saw that it was the missing woman. Her hand was to her mouth in alarm.

Sheriff Lens turned to me. "I thought you said he killed his wife, Doc."

"I believe he did. This woman is not Katherine Haas."

•   •   •

Perhaps my words were a charm of some sort, or perhaps Haas simply realized that it was all over. He lowered the revolver and turned back into the room as we followed. It was the woman we'd known as Katherine Haas who asked the question. "How did you know?"

We followed them into the little upstairs room and Sheriff Lens took the gun from Haas's hand. "I didn't at first," I admitted. "I went about it the wrong way, concentrating on how you got out of that room instead of the real question, which was *why*. The sheriff and my nurse April supplied me with some key facts about that. The sheriff told me that Katherine Haas had a trust fund until she reached the age of thirty. You'd both been living off that fund for years. Then April was filing some old medical records and found one from France that said Katherine Haas was color-blind. It's unusual but not impossible for a color-blind person to be a painter. That got me thinking about the self-portrait she'd painted on the wallpaper. What did she paint it with? There were no paints or brushes found in that room, no cosmetics, not even a mirror. It would be quite a trick for a color-blind artist without paints or a mirror to create a self-portrait of her face. And there were other things, too. This woman seemed older than Katherine's stated twenty-nine years. And the whole business of that locked and barred room with the torn wallpaper seemed inspired by a fifty-year-old short story."

Sheriff Lens was growing impatient. "Whatever her real identity, Doc, how could she have gotten out of that room? And why would they bother with such trickery?"

"I'll answer your second question first, because the *why* is the key to the whole thing. If we assume Haas killed the real Katherine before coming to America, it clarifies what followed. She was receiving a large monthly check from a trust fund, so it was important to him that the checks continue to arrive. It had to appear that she was still alive. It wasn't too difficult to forge her endorsement on the checks. He must have had plenty of samples of her signature. And by moving to America he avoided contact with family and friends who knew the real Katherine. But there was a problem on the horizon—the real Katherine's thirtieth birthday was approaching. The Swiss bank would require proof positive of her identity, possibly fingerprints, before surrendering the trust fund's principal to her. Haas hoped the supposed mental problem would be a way to delay her appearance, but then I insisted on bringing Dr. Foley up to examine her and they knew that wouldn't work. Katherine had to disappear until they had time to work out their next move. Nothing else would do. If they faked her death the trust fund would automatically go to those Spanish nuns."

"Why couldn't he just have her run away?" the sheriff wanted to know.

I glanced in Haas's direction. He was standing with his eyes tightly shut, as if refusing to grasp the reality of the moment. "She couldn't remain missing forever or he'd be suspected of killing her. It would be a repeat of

Paris, where he had to leave the country and come here with a new Katherine Haas. This way they concocted a mystery, possibly even a supernatural event, to give themselves time."

"How?" Sheriff Lens asked again.

"When Doug and I arrived at that third-floor door, she was already gone from the room."

"But you talked to her through the door!"

"Big old houses with servants' quarters had to have a way of summoning the servants when needed. Most used a bellpull, but some had a system of speaking tubes like you see on ships. You told us the family had safety devices to summon servants if there was an emergency with the children, and I imagine this was one of them. The speaking tube was right inside the door, and by speaking loudly into it our Katherine's voice sounded as if it was on the other side of the door. We should have known the house had such a system because we saw Haas use it to summon his maid Saturday. We just didn't realize what he was doing when he walked over to the wall and called her."

"But why didn't we see this speaking tube when we searched that room?"

"That was the real reason why more wallpaper had been peeled off and hung in strips. One of those strips was hiding the speaking tube and we never noticed it."

The false Katherine spoke again. "How did you know all this? What did we do wrong?"

"Besides that suspicious painting on the wall, only one thing. When I arrived on Saturday with Doug Foley I glimpsed a maid dusting the parlor. But it wasn't Rose West, whom I recognized later, because the sheriff saw her arrive about two, her usual time. And I noticed the parlor was still quite dusty. You were lurking downstairs, dressed as a maid, until we were in position for you to use the speaking tube. Then you hurried off to hide in this carriage house, which is why Doug and I found no one when we searched the house before the sheriff and the real maid arrived."

The authorities held Peter Haas and the false Katherine while the Swiss bank and the Paris police were notified. But Paris had fallen to the Germans six months earlier and no one there showed any interest in the case. Haas insisted the real Katherine had died accidentally and there was no way to prove otherwise. They were released and quickly left town, though we heard later that the Swiss bank had hired detectives to track them down and recover the payments from the trust fund.

I kept the kitten, Watson, because it reminded me of Annabel.

Dick Lochte

In the City of Angels

DICK LOCHTE'S intelligent, evocative novels and short stories have won him praise for many years now. He is one of those careful stylists who know exactly when to speed it up and when to slow it down, the way masters such as Graham Greene and Raymond Chandler did. He is always listed as among the most important writers of his generation. His noir novella, "In the City of Angels," first published in the anthology *Flesh and Blood*, is just one very good reason why.

In the City of Angels

Dick Lochte

Jee-zus," Wylie said. "He's giving it to her good."

Mace stared at the punk sitting beside him at the window of the dark room, his night-vision binoculars trained on the apartment building across the courtyard. He guessed Wylie was in his early twenties. Twenty-five, tops. Greenish blond crewcut showing black at the roots. There was enough light from the moon and the glowing pool in the courtyard two stories below for Mace to make out the head of a blue and red serpent tattoo poking above the neckline of Wylie's loud Hawaiian shirt. At Pelican Bay prison, Mace used to watch an old con named Billy Jet stick needles full of dye into the flesh of some of the other cons. There wasn't much else to do there, except get tats or watch other guys getting tats. As far as Mace knew Wylie had never served time, so the snake didn't make any sense to him at all.

The window occupying Wylie's attention wasn't the one they were there to watch, but that point seemed to be lost on him. He licked his slightly feminine lips and said, "Oh, ba-bee, don't use it up all at once."

Mace stubbed out his cigarette and picked up his binoculars. He aimed them at a set of windows one floor up and to the left of Wylie's point of interest. The main room was still empty. Angela Lowell was somewhere to the right, probably in the bathroom, since the bedroom was still dark.

"Swear to God," Wylie said, "this sure beats the beater flicks all to hell. I could go for a little hormone fix myself."

"Keep me posted," Mace said.

"Whoa. Here comes Mr. Backdoor Man."

"I didn't know better," Mace said, staying focused on the Lowell apartment, "I'd take you for some snot-nose kid on his first trip to a riding academy."

"Oh, yeah?" Wylie said, obviously stung. "Well . . . go fuck yourself."

"You're the one who's turned on," Mace replied calmly.

"What turns you on? Little boys?"

Angela Lowell entered her living room dressed in a robe, rubbing her dark hair with a towel, her handsome face shiny from night cream. She crossed the room and moved just past the wide window and out of sight.

"Since you asked," Mace said, "professional behavior turns me on."

Angela walked back into his line of sight carrying a thick book. A coffee-table book. Probably an art book, Mace thought. She was an art appraiser, an artist herself.

He liked the way she moved, a graceful glide. He couldn't see her feet, but he imagined they were bare, luxuriating in the soft texture of the carpet.

"You saying what? That I'm not a professional?" Wylie asked, more hurt now than angry.

"I'm saying you should keep your mind on the job."

Angela turned out the living room light. Mace started a countdown. One hundred. One hundred and one. One hundred and two. One hundred and—A light went on behind the bedroom drapes.

Mace lowered his binoculars and placed them on the table. "She's tucked in," he said.

Wylie was glaring at him. "So you don't think I'm a pro, huh?"

In point of fact, Mace thought he was a hopeless jackass. He'd formed that opinion five minutes after meeting him that afternoon. But he didn't know how long they'd be cooping, so he said, "Right now, I'm jet lagged, bone tired, and pissed off at the world in general. If Paulie Lacotta gives you a paycheck, you're a pro. Okay?"

Wylie nodded, but he still wasn't happy. "I'm pro enough to stay out of the joint," he said.

"Good point," Mace said. "Okay if I fade for a while?"

"Do what you want," Wylie said, raising the binoculars.

Mace was on the cot, just starting to drift when somebody knocked.

He sat up and watched Wylie, a gun in his hand, moving for the door. Mace started to call him off, then thought better of it. Maybe the kid would shoot somebody, then Mace could catch the next flight home.

"Me," Paulie Lacotta said from the hall.

Wylie fumbled the gun back into his belt rig and unlocked the door.

Lacotta brought the smell of booze and cigar smoke into the dark room with him. Even in double heels he was five inches shorter than Wylie's six-one or six-two, a stocky guy wrapped in an Italian suit worth a couple thou, cut to emphasize his shoulders and hide a thickening waist. His nut-brown face had once been slick-handsome, but it was starting to sag at the jowls.

It was nine years since Mace had last seen him.

Lacotta approached the cot, opening his arms. "C'mere, you son of a bitch," he said, grinning.

Mace got to his feet and accepted the inevitable bear hug. When Lacotta was through physically bonding, he stepped back and gave Mace a head-to-toe. "You're lookin' good, amigo."

The tan. The hug. Now "amigo." Jesus. "You, too, Paulie," Mace said. "Really living la vida L.A., huh?"

Lacotta beamed proudly, as if Mace had paid him a high compliment. "You know it, dude." He turned to the windows. "My girl been behaving?" he asked.

"Been in all night," Wylie said, his eyes darting nervously to Mace as if he half-expected to be contradicted.

"Good." Lacotta removed a gray ostrich-hide wallet from his pocket and slipped a twenty from it. He held it out to Wylie. "Go get us some ice cream, willya?"

Wylie took the bill reluctantly. "What kind of ice cream?"

"Kind? Spumoni. That's what we used to eat, huh, Mace?"

Mace didn't think he'd ever eaten spumoni or any other ice cream with Lacotta. "That's the stuff," he said.

"Where do I find spumoni at midnight?" Wylie whined.

"They got a dozen Italian restaurants within shouting distance," Lacotta said. "Just make sure it's got plenty nuts and fruit."

Wylie seemed uncertain. He said, "I'll . . . be back."

Lacotta moved to the window. When he saw Wylie cross the courtyard, heading for the underground parking, he asked, "How's the kid doing?"

"Even at his tender age," Mace said, "I don't think I'd have worn that beach boy shirt on a shadow job. Snake's a nice touch."

Lacotta crossed the room to the cot and sat on it, looking disappointed. Without thinking about it, he adjusted the crease in his trousers. "I don't suppose you could call shit like that to his attention?"

"You're beautiful, Paulie," Mace said, lighting a cigarette. "Not only do you bring me in cold and saddle me with a green punk, now you want me to give him lessons."

"The kid's a legacy. His old man was Leo Giruso."

"Leo, huh? Like father, like son. Where'd he get the name Wylie?"

"I dunno. Read it in a book, maybe?"

Mace rolled his eyes.

"Okay, so you don't like the kid," Lacotta said.

"It's not just him. I don't like this whole setup."

"Hey," Lacotta said with a little heat behind it, "you did me a good thing a while ago, but I figure I kinda made up for it. Your old man kept his ranch in Montana, right?"

Mace nodded.

"And didn't I put some dough aside for you every year you were away?"

"That you did."

"So now I ask you for an assist and you bust my balls?"

Mace moved to the window and frowned out at the night. "Who is this Lowell woman anyway?"

"Since when you start asking questions like that?"

"Since I started sitting around empty apartments, peeping in windows like some goddamn bathroom idiot."

Lacotta got to his feet. "Yeah, well, like Bobby D. used to say, we all gotta serve somebody." He headed for the door.

"Hold on," Mace called.

Lacotta paused and turned to face him, scowling. "Angie and me . . . it's personal, okay? I just want to know what she's up to. Can you handle that?"

"What are you expecting her to do?" Mace asked.

Lacotta winked. Not much of an answer. "You and the kid enjoy the ice cream," he said, heading out.

"Where's Mr. Lacotta?" Wylie asked.

"He got tired of waiting," Mace said, slipping into his jacket.

"I had to go all the way to fucking Westwood," Wylie whined. "And it's melting."

"Stick it in the freezer, then. And make sure to keep checking the Lowell window till I get back."

"Where the hell *you* going?"

"Out. Get you anything?" Mace smiled. "Cookies to go with that ice cream?"

Mace parked his rental in a lot behind the Happy Burger on Sunset. He moved with purpose down the Strip, maneuvering around the late-night dawdlers—GenXers with nothing better to do, hookers, pimps, members of the glitterati who'd dined unfashionably late, tourists looking slightly lost and anxious. He counted himself among the latter.

His quarry was sitting alone at a table in front of a restaurant that was called Charley-O's. When Mace had lived in L.A., it had been the Elegant Eggplant. Now there was nothing elegant about it. Certainly not the gaunt senior citizen sipping coffee and keeping his eyes on the passing parade. In the old days, he'd called attention to his remarkable similarity to the sixteenth president of the U.S. by wearing a stovepipe hat and morning dress. He'd conformed to the informality of the times. Mace found it vaguely disconcerting to see a graying Abraham Lincoln in sandals, jogging shorts, and a T-shirt that read "There's a party in my pants."

"Hello, Abe," Mace said, taking an empty chair. "You're looking breezy."

"Mace." The bony, chin-whiskered face broke into a smile. "Welcome back to the Big Enchilada. What can I do to celebrate? Got a sweet sixteener, tender as a mouse's ear."

"Thanks, but what I need is information," Mace said. "I've been out of the loop awhile."

"Heard you went to live on a ranch after you left Pel. For a city boy that could be like prison."

"Not really," Mace said.

"I guess not. How can I help?"

"You ever hear the name Angela Lowell? Mid-twenties. Brunette."

"Tits?" Abe asked.

The question annoyed Mace but he managed to reply, "Two, as I recall."

Abe furrowed his brow and stared at his coffee for a few beats. Then he unfurrowed and shook his head. "No bells ring. Want me to dig a little?"

"Yeah," Mace said. "Do I check in by phoning this place?"

Abe reeled off a seven-number combination. "My cell phone."

"Your cell phone," Mace repeated, dumbly.

Abe's long fingers reached into the pocket of his party-loving pants and retrieved a lime-colored cellular phone. "You *have* been out of the loop."

"I'm a fast learner," Mace said, and stood to go. "You used to be a man who could keep a secret. We haven't had this conversation, okay?"

"What conversation?" the gaunt man asked.

Mace was moving his key toward the door lock when he heard grunting and moaning inside the apartment. He opened up, the hall light falling on Wylie and a plump woman banging away on the cot.

The woman's bloodshot eyes popped open and saw him. She didn't say a word, but she stopped writhing under the skinny boy and just lay there. Wylie didn't seem to notice her sudden passivity. More likely, he just didn't care.

Temporarily ignoring them, Mace moved to the window. The Lowell apartment looked unchanged. He relaxed, turned, and noticed Wylie's holstered gun resting beside his pants on the carpet.

The woman watched him fearfully and silently as he freed the gun and pointed it at the back of Wylie's bouncing head. She still said nothing. Mace wondered if she were a mute.

Wylie's snake tattoo stretched from his neck down his back, curving at his waist and disappearing toward his lower stomach. Mace pressed the gun to a spot just above the snake's tongue and below Wylie's left ear and said, "Bang, you're dead."

Wylie made a noise like "Gah" and pushed in on the woman.

"Feeling better?" Mace crooned. He grabbed Wylie's left ear and gave it a nasty twist. The young man yelled as Mace led him by the ear off the woman.

"Lemme go, you fuckhead."

Mace did let him go, pushing him onto the foot of the bed. He stuck the gun behind his belt and said to the naked woman, "Out."

"But I . . . ," she began, not a mute after all.

"But nothing." He bent down and gathered her discarded clothes and six-inch pumps from the carpet. Gripping her by a fleshy arm, he yanked her from the cot.

"Hey. Wait a goddamn min—"

He dragged her to the open doorway. She tried to kick and bite as he pushed her into the hall. He threw her clothes and shoes after her and slammed the door on her curses.

Wylie was sitting on the cot rubbing his ear. "You're a real asshole," he grumbled.

"And you're a real pro," Mace said scornfully. "Yes you are."

The plump hooker began pounding on the door.

Mace picked up Wylie's pants and found his wallet. "How much you owe her?"

"Thirty."

There were two fifties and several twenties in the wallet. Mace took one of the fifties, opened the door, and threw the bill at the woman. "Keep the change," he said, and slammed the door again.

It shut her up.

Mace sat down at the table by the windows and stared at Wylie, who was pulling up his rumpled khakis. "I thought you was out gettin' *your* ashes hauled," Wylie said. Then his pout dissolved. "You gonna tell Mr. Lacotta?"

"What's the percentage in that?" Mace answered.

Wylie picked up his shirt and slipped into it on his way to a kitchenette counter where a bottle of Jim Beam rested next to a set of tumblers. He cracked the bottle.

"Do one for me," Mace said.

Wylie put a couple of inches into two tumblers. He walked to the table and sat, shoving one of the tumblers toward Mace. Mace shot his. The kid followed suit. "Mr. Lacotta says there's a future for me in the corporation."

Mace said nothing. He raised his empty glass. Wylie crossed the room, got the bottle, and brought it back to the table. He splashed a couple more inches of bourbon into their glasses.

"How long you been working for Paulie?" Mace asked.

"Six months."

"Like it?"

"Got me a title: Security Consultant. My own office. Check every week. Free time to screw off. Okay, so I gotta let my hair grow out and maybe burn off my tats. Still a good deal."

"What kinda jobs he been givin' you lately?"

Wylie thought about it. "Surveillance, mainly. Before Angela, I was keepin' tabs on this guy, Tiny Daniels. Me and another guy, we followed him for most of last month, day and night. We went all the way across the state and back again by friggin' car. This Daniels is scared to fly."

"Maybe he's too fat to fit in the seats," Mace said.

"You know Tiny?"

"He didn't used to be that hard to keep in your sights. He weighed in at three hundred pounds and he was in the office between mine and Paulie's."

"No shit? The fat man worked for the corporation? Times sure as hell have changed."

"You don't have to tell me," Mace said. "What's Tiny been up to?"

"Not all that much. Had a meeting at this place just outside Frisco. Commingore Inc."

"They make weapons," Mace said.

"Yeah, I know. Lissen, Mace, about the hooker. If you tole Mr. Lacotta—"

"Don't worry about it." Mace poured himself another shot. "Get some sleep. We'll switch at four."

Wylie nodded and moved to the bed. He sat on it, winced, and pulled a used rubber from under his thigh.

Mace leaned forward. "Oh, lemme get rid of that for you."

Wylie held out the contraceptive.

Mace turned away from him, chuckling at the kid's gullibility.

Angela Lowell is asleep. The thick art book she'd been reading lies nearly submerged in the bed's thick down duvet.

Mace stands beside the bed, watching her. She is only partially covered by the duvet. In peaceful sleep, she is achingly beautiful. Her right arm is raised high on the pillow. Her full right breast has freed itself from the ribboned neckline of her sheer gown.

Something—an intake of breath, the shifting of air—causes her to stir. She opens her eyes. Sees Mace . . . and smiles.

He bends over her. Her arms come up to meet him. Playfully, she pulls him down.

The mere touching of their lips ignites her. Her fingers tighten on his back. She breathes heavily, pressing her body against his. Her tongue, hard and hot and pointy-tipped, slips into his mouth. She begins tearing the clothes from his body. First his shirt, then his belted slacks. He tries to help but, almost angrily, she insists on doing the job herself.

He lies back on the bed as she undresses him. She smiles at his erection, touches it almost playfully, then caresses it.

He moans. It's been so long.

Someone calls his name.

"No," Angela shouts. "Not enough time."

In a frenzy, she straddles Mace, moving down his body eagerly until her body takes him in. He arches his back, feels the velvety softness yield—

•   •   •

"Mace," Wylie hissed near his ear. "Gotta get up."

Mace awoke from the dream to a room filled with glaring sunlight. Wylie whispered, "Mr. Lacotta just crossed the courtyard."

Mace swung his bare feet around to the floor. He was still groggy from the dream. "What time is it?"

"Almost eleven," Wylie said. There was a knock at the door.

"Why didn't you wake me sooner?"

"No reason to. She ain't goin' nowhere," Wylie said, heading for the door.

Lacotta entered, giving Wylie a manly punch on the arm. "How's the boy?"

"Fine, Mr. Lacotta."

Lacotta's grin faded at the sight of Mace sitting on the edge of the cot in his underwear. "You keepin' banker's hours, Mace?"

"Mace had the night watch, Mr. Lacotta. Just hit the sheets a couple hours ago."

"What's on your mind, Paulie?" Mace asked. "Your ice cream's in the—"

"Slip some clothes on. We'll go for a walk."

"Now this is beauty," Lacotta said as he and Mace strolled through Griffith Park. It was green and tranquil, bathed in sunlight. "Not like your friggin' Montana. Too cold in the winter, too hot in summer. I don't know how you can live there."

"Maybe I like extremes," Mace said.

A softball landed at Lacotta's feet. He picked it up, tossed it back into the game. Immediately, he began rubbing his shoulder. "What do you do with yourself back there?" he asked.

"Hunt. Fish. Read. Watch the news, mainly the weather."

"No jobs?" Lacotta asked.

"Not the way you mean it."

"Your time at Pel Bay, guys go bad in there."

"Guys go bad out here in your sunshine," Mace said, annoyed. "What's on your mind?"

"You're different. Maybe it was stir. Maybe playing hermit on your old man's ranch."

"I'm older," Mace said.

"Old age turned you curious, huh?"

"I get it. You've been talking to Abe. Honest Abe."

"You put my business out on the street," Lacotta said.

"If you'd tell me what the hell I'm supposed to be doing, maybe I wouldn't have to."

Lacotta nodded. "Yeah, maybe." He gestured toward an empty park bench. When they were seated, looking out at the softball game, he said, "I told you it was personal between me and Angie. Only jealousy isn't the big problem. Not that I'm Joe Don't Care. Remember the Irish broad who worked at the Raincheck?"

"Let's take it one romance at a time."

"Yeah, right. Well, Angie and me, we're going great until right around when the trouble started."

"You want me to ask what trouble?" Mace said. "Okay, I asked."

"I had this deal going. And it got cocked up. Right around then, Angie suddenly went unavailable on me and I went a little nuts, like I do. I even asked her to mar . . . Hell, I tried everything. She just wasn't interested. Then I went back to being my usual cynical rat-bastard self. I started thinking maybe the two things are tied in."

Mace frowned. "Tied in how?"

"You remember Tiny Daniels?"

"Hard to forget."

"The fat fuck was working for us, but he was cutting all these deals on the side. With the Russkies. The Chicanos. The gooks, even. Montdrago was madder'n hell, but he just let Tiny walk away."

"He suddenly get religion?" Mace wondered.

"Yeah, sure. The big man gets religion when the Holy Ghost gets his own talk show. Tiny tells Montdrago he's got some heavy insurance in place, can put him away. Could be a bluff, but it keeps the fat man breathing."

"And all this relates to Angela Lowell how?"

Lacotta squirmed on the rough bench. "I get word Angie's been keeping company with Tiny. So you see my position?"

"No," Mace said.

"I got to know: Did she have anything to do with the fuckup on the deal I had going? Has Tiny taken over the project? I got to know the answers before Montdrago starts asking me the questions. That's why I need you, Mace. Somebody outside the organization. A friend I can trust."

"How much does Wylie know?"

"Bupkis," Lacotta said. "Even if he does get the drift of things, he's still my guy. He won't fuck me over with Montdrago."

Feeling suddenly restless, Mace got up from the bench. Reluctantly, Lacotta followed behind him. "And if Angela *is* in bed with the fat man?" Mace asked. "You kill her?"

"No way," Lacotta said. "You tell me she's sold out to Tiny, then I'll know for sure what a fucking doof I've been. Then maybe I can get her out of my mind."

It didn't make sense to Mace. There was still more to the story. He was about to press when a tall African-American male, apparently one of the homeless army, staggered toward them.

"You gen'mens got a dolla' y' can spare?" he asked.

Lacotta gave the man a hard, get-the-fuck-away glare. He saw Mace reaching into his pocket and said, "Don't do that."

Mace got out his wallet and removed a dollar. He handed it to the black man who accepted it with a grin. He held the bill out to Lacotta. "Here. This fo' you."

"I don't want your fucking money," Lacotta said testily.

"It's fo' you. A dolla' to blow me."

"What?" Lacotta couldn't believe his ears.

"Man say you a dolla' blow job."

Furious, Lacotta grabbed the black man's coat. "What man?" he yelled.

The black man grinned. His left hand emerged from his coat pocket carrying a small pistol that he shoved into Lacotta's midsection. "The fat man. He say, 'Bye-bye, asshole.' "

With amazing speed, Mace's right foot connected with the pistol, knocking it aside just as it exploded.

Lacotta yelled and fell back, losing his grip on the black man.

Mace grabbed the gun. The black man tried to knee him in the groin, but Mace twisted his body and took the knee on his thigh. With his free hand, he punched the black man once in the stomach, once in the face.

The black man let go of the gun as he bent to the ground. Mace kicked him in the head. Once. Twice. It was all he could think about.

He felt somebody grab his arm. He swung around, fist cocked for the punch, and saw it was Lacotta. Even then, he almost took the swing.

Lacotta backed away. "Let's get outta here," he said.

Mace blinked.

The park was in silence. The ballplayers, the dog walkers, the strollers were all frozen, staring at them. The only thing in motion in the whole park was the black man getting to his feet and running away.

Cautiously, Lacotta took the gun from Mace's hand and slipped it into his pocket. He led Mace toward the parked car.

Mace got in, still dazed.

As they drove away, Mace asked, "You hurt?"

"Naw, maybe some burns," Lacotta said. He smiled, then started laughing. Soon he was laughing so hard tears appeared at the corner of his eyes. "I told you not to give that fuck the dollar, didn't I?" he said between bursts of nervous laughter.

Wylie was gone when Mace let himself into their room. He'd seen Angela Lowell's car in the parking area, but, as cavalier as Wylie was, he couldn't believe the punk would have deserted his post for no reason. He sat down and watched the Lowell apartment for a few minutes without seeing any sign of activity. Then he pecked out Angela's phone number.

When her answering machine clicked on, he hung up and went visiting. He used a pick to enter her apartment. He'd done the same thing the day before, just after he'd unpacked. He liked getting the feel of the place, experiencing the softness of the sofa, the scent of her bath soap, the way the light filtered through the bedroom curtains.

There were several framed pastels on the bedroom wall, signed with an *A*. Her work. A narrow street with book stalls. The statue of a lion. A stern-looking, elderly man wearing a high collar. Her father?

He investigated her medicine cabinet, casually browsed the pill bottles. None particularly interesting. Her two perfume bottles seemed almost untouched.

In the drawer of her bedside table he found an assortment of expensive contraceptive sheaths along with a spermicidal gel and a plastic case containing an IUD cap. There was also a vibrator for those lonely nights.

He made one more pass through the apartment and let himself out.

The rest of the day, he waited at his place, wondering where she'd led Wylie.

The phone woke him.

It was dark. He squinted at his watch. Nine-eighteen.

The voice on the other end was barely recognizable. "I . . . been shot. Tiny picked up the bitch . . . Followed 'em . . . Got jammed."

"Where are you, Wylie?"

"Point Dume." He coughed. "Twelve Oceanside Drive."

"I'll send an ambulance."

"No," Wylie shouted, and began coughing. "No. I'm okay . . . in the car. You come get me."

"On my way."

He pressed the tab to disconnect the call, wondering if he shouldn't just send the damned ambulance. The kid said he was okay. Maybe he wasn't as bad off as he sounded. Maybe a lot of things. He wished he had a gun. Worse came to worse, he figured he could use Wylie's.

The breeze off the Pacific was warm and briny as he turned off the Coast Highway onto Dume Drive. It had taken him nearly thirty minutes to get there. Wylie's car was parked on Oceanside, down the block from number twelve. Wylie wasn't in it.

The metal gate to number twelve was open a few inches.

Mace entered the grounds cautiously, not liking the creak of the gate. He moved down a stone walkway that cut through a Japanese garden to a modern beach house, all stone and metal and glass. As he approached the thick glass front door, a man stumbled toward the door on his way out.

He was short, stocky, and middle-aged. Mace had never seen him before. He was wearing black pants, shiny black shoes, and a white dinner shirt rapidly turning red at the collar. He tried to push the glass door open, but he hadn't the strength. His knees buckled and he sank to the flagstones.

Mace opened the door just as the man keeled over on his side. He'd been shot in the neck, a few inches below his sunken chin. No pulse. It was a near miracle that he'd made it to the door.

Mace patted him quickly, hoping to find a gun. No luck.

In the next room, the living room, he found two other dead men. The one staining the white rug was in his twenties, chiseled features, thin mustache. Also in dinner clothes. Shot twice in the chest. A gun was clutched in his left hand.

Mace had to break his index finger to pry the weapon free. He checked the clip. Two bullets left. He snapped the clip back into the gun and moved on to the other fatality.

It was Tiny Daniels, looking even fatter in death. He was seated on a massive leather chair, a broken wineglass near one of his patent-leather–shod feet. In his tux, he looked like a three-hundred-pound penguin. His eyes were open, giving his puffy face a look of astonishment.

There was a small hole in his black satin lapel. Mace touched his neck to see if there might be some pulse.

The fat man slumped forward, his upper weight tumbling him from the chair onto the carpet. Mace bent over the corpse to look at Tiny's face. Something glinted at the corner of the mouth.

Tiny's teeth were clamped on something. Mace worked a couple fingers between the teeth and pried out . . . a coin the size of a silver dollar. Some kind of specialty item. No writing. Just a man's face in bas-relief. He might have studied it longer, but a door slammed, followed by the sound of running footsteps.

Shoving the coin into his coat pocket, Mace raced through the cottage to the kitchen. The back door was open. It was the screen door that had slammed shut. As Mace went through it, its wooden frame splintered near his hand.

Ducking, he raised his gun. Too late. A tall figure, masculine he thought, slid over a cement wind wall separating the cottage from the sandy beach. Mace was poised to chase the figure when he heard a female voice call out, "What's happening down there?"

He moved back through the cottage to a stairwell and raced up to the floor above. "What's happening?" the voice asked again behind a closed door.

Mace didn't bother trying the door handle. He raised a foot, kicked in the door, and ran into the room, gun held high.

The room was dark. A wind off the water stirred gossamer drapes. Angela Lowell was in a rumpled queen-size bed. The sheet that had been covering her had fallen to her waist, revealing her naked breasts. Caution forced Mace to look away to make sure they were alone in the room.

That accomplished, he turned back to her. She regarded him with no emotion showing on her lovely, placid face. "Carlos?" she asked.

"No. Not Carlos."

"I see that now." She smiled at him. "I'm . . . awake." She slid to the side of the bed and sat there facing him, completely naked.

"We have to leave here," Mace said. "Put on your clothes."

"What clothes?"

He picked up a black dress from the floor and a pair of white silk panties. The panties were still warm from her body. He placed them beside her on the bed.

"Put the clothes on now," he ordered.

"I don't think . . . I . . . ca . . ." She slumped back onto the bed, eyes closed, breathing softly through an open mouth.

"Damn it," he grumbled and put the gun in his belt. He jammed the panties in his pocket and began to struggle the dress over her rubbery body.

He found her shoes and purse, but there were probably other things of hers he was leaving behind. Fingerprints, if nothing else, but that wouldn't matter if she was a frequent visitor to the cottage.

He hoisted her over his shoulder. She was a substantial, full-bodied woman. By the time he got her to his car, he was breathing like a porpoise. He dumped her onto the passenger seat and used the safety belt to keep her upright. He tossed her shoes onto the backseat and got behind the wheel.

Wylie's car was still parked in front. Still empty.

Mace drove away from it, humming a tune. He was surprised to realize it was "Oh where, oh where has my little dog gone."

Heading back to the coast highway, the girl beside him began to snore.

He called Lacotta from a gas station pay phone. "Tiny's out of the picture, permanently," he said. "If he wasn't just blowing smoke about having some life insurance, Montdrago had better call his lawyer or put on his running shoes."

Paulie began to squawk, cursing Tiny, then Angela, Mace, and finally himself. Mace listened for a while, trying to decide if it was an act. After five minutes he no longer cared. "Shut up for a goddamned minute," he shouted into the phone, and was half-surprised when Lacotta obeyed.

"I'm up to my chin in your bullshit," Mace said, watching the car parked just past the gas pumps. The girl's head was still angled forward, eyes closed. "Tell me what's been going on and where the girl fits in. Make it quick and simple."

There was silence on the other end for a couple seconds. Then Lacotta said, "There's this guy I know in Paris—ex-CIA. He came into possession of something very hot. He held this auction and—"

"What part of quick and simple don't you understand?"

"I'm trying to explain. This goddamned formula is gonna take us to a new generation of weapons. Smart bombs, shit. There are gonna be fucking *genius* bombs."

"Paulie," Mace said. "Get to the point in sixty seconds or I head straight to the airport."

"Calm down. Jesus. I'm the guy standing at the fucking precipice. I borrowed a shitpot of company loot to buy this goddamned formula. It was a lock. I'd already got a commitment from Commingore Industries that would net a very sweet profit."

"Only . . . ?" Mace said.

"Only this ex–CIA guy got cute. You know how they are. He baked the formula inside a coin that's made from the same shit the weapons are gonna be made of."

Mace saw Angela's head bob. She was too far away to hear him, but he didn't want her waking up alone in a parked car. "I'm hanging up," he told Lacotta.

"Whoa, whoa. I used Angie to mule the coin back here. Somehow Tiny found out and intercepted it."

"Why use her?"

"She goes over there four, five times a year, picking up art for her clients. The customs people know her. She's legit. Handles paintings worth big money. Straight as they come."

"Except that she sold you out."

"I'm not sure she did. I sure as hell didn't tell her about the formula. I sent her over there supposedly to pick out some paintings for me. I told you the seller was cute. He was using a gallery for a front. He put the fucking coin in a crate with the art she bought for me. Only it never got to me. Tiny had the shipment hijacked."

Mace felt his pocket getting a little heavier. "I don't suppose the inventor can just strike another coin," he said.

"Well, that's the thing. We're talking exclusivity here."

"Meaning your cute ex–CIA guy made sure there'd be only one coin."

"I tried to tell him that a white coat who could come up with something this valuable might have a few more good ideas in his head, but by then the body was already cold."

"Okay, I get it," Mace said. "Tiny wound up with the coin and the girl. And you wound up waiting for the monthly audit with your finger up your ass."

"Something like that. What the fuck do I do?"

"I'll let you know," Mace said, and hung up.

Angela opened her eyes just as he got behind the wheel.

"Who the devil are you?" she demanded, slurring a little. "Do you work for Tiny?"

"Nobody works for Tiny anymore," Mace said, driving through Santa Monica, heading east to Hollywood. "Not even Tiny."

"What do you mean? What am I doing in this car?"

"We're headed away from a bad situation. We left three dead men back there. Four if you count Tiny as two."

"My God," she said. "Did you . . . kill them?"

"No, ma'am. All I did was get you dressed and out of there before the cops dropped by."

She looked down at her dress.

He reached into his coat pocket and pulled out her panties. "These yours?"

She took them from him and, without hesitation, hiked up her skirt and slid them on.

"What drug were you on?" he asked.

"I . . . Demerol. I shouldn't drink with them, but sometimes I . . ." She decided not to finish the sentence.

"You didn't hear anything back at the house? Gunshots, shouts, anything?"

"No," she whispered. "Are you sure they're all dead? Tiny and Lew? And Carlos?"

"Tiny I'm sure of. I didn't recognize the other two gentlemen."

He moved the car around a creeper. From the corner of his eye he saw her turn to him. "Why . . . did you help me get away?"

"You didn't seem to be in any condition to be entertaining cops."

They drove in silence for a few minutes. Mace took the La Cienega exit and headed into Hollywood. "What was Tiny to you?" he asked. "Lover? Friend?"

"A friend, I guess. And a client. I . . . deal in art and sculpture. Tiny was a collector."

Mace reached into his pants pocket and got out the odd coin.

"Recognize it?" he asked.

She shook her head no. "It looks like a commemorative coin."

He grinned. "Commemorating what, I wonder?"

"Could I . . . ?"

He handed it to her. She studied it.

"Recognize the guy?"

She shrugged. "Nope. Where did you get it?"

"A dark, damp place," he said, holding out his hand.

She placed the coin in his palm and he slipped it back into his pocket.

"Where do I drop you?" he asked.

The Hollywood Boulevard of his memory had not been a particularly lovely streetscape. Now it was incomparably garish and ugly. Dark, looming buildings. Vacant movie theaters. Tattoo parlors. Fast-food joints.

While they paused for a red light, Mace watched male and female hookers hungrily work their way through the stalled traffic, plying their rough trade. The light changed and he started forward, almost hitting a huge man on Rollerblades. He was wearing a pink Mohawk, matching pink short shorts, and tube top, gliding across the boulevard with a boom box under one weight-lifter arm and a pink poodle under the other.

"What do you think?" Mace asked, indicating the apparition. "Too much?"

"Pink is always in style," she said.

The apartment complex was on a side street several blocks off of the boulevard. Pretending he'd never laid eyes on it before, Mace aimed the car into the circular drive and parked by the front doors.

"What now?" Angela said.

"You go inside and get on with your life," he told her. "The police may visit, sooner or later."

"What do I tell them?"

"The truth. You've visited Tiny's often but you weren't anywhere near there tonight."

Her fingers touched the door handle, but she seemed reluctant to leave. "I'd feel more comfortable if you came in. Just for a little while."

"Sure," he said.

They'd barely entered her apartment when she excused herself. He poked around the living room for a while. When she emerged from the bathroom wrapped in a white floor-length robe, he was at the portable bar, fixing himself a gin and tonic. "I'd like one of those, too," she said, leaving him again to enter her bedroom.

When he'd finished building the drinks, he called her name. She didn't answer.

He crossed the carpet to her bedroom.

She was lying in bed, covered by a sheet but obviously naked. Eyes closed. He was amused by how close the situation was to his dream. The only differences were that he was carrying two gin and tonics. And she wasn't asleep.

He placed the glasses on the night table next to the bed. He noticed that one of her pastels was missing from the wall. No surprise. Probably in the closet.

He stared down at her.

Her lips twitched. Then she grinned and opened her eyes. "I'm pretending to be Sleeping Beauty."

"I'm no Prince Charming," he said, and yanked the sheet away.

She grabbed his belt and the top of his slacks and drew him closer. "Charm isn't all it's cracked up to be."

She pulled him down onto the bed. It required very little strength on her part. She began undressing him, not frantically like in the dream, but slowly, sensuously.

He was perfectly content to let her do most of the work until his clothes were off, then he made his contribution. Tongue. Fingers. Exploring her amazing body.

Finally, with a moan, she pulled away and opened the drawer to her night table, extracting a contraceptive sheath. She had a lovely method of lubricating him.

He repaid the compliment.

Then they made love.

"The ice has melted," she said, sampling her drink an hour or so later. "I'll fix some new ones."

She returned shortly with two fresh g & t's. She held one out to him and placed the other on the table. "Have to freshen up," she said. "Be with you in a minute."

It was more like fifteen.

She'd brushed her hair and applied new lipstick. She was wearing a simple skirt and blouse. She looked great. Even better when she smiled. "Thirsty man, huh?" she said, indicating his nearly empty glass.

Mace nodded, but seemed to be having trouble moving his head. Trouble speaking, too. "I . . . I . . ."

She put one knee on the bed and reached over him to grab the glass before it slipped from his fingers. She paused to kiss him, pushing her tongue past his lifeless lips. It was a kiss more exploratory than passionate. She backed away as he struggled and failed to raise an arm to hold her.

"Relax," she told him. "The paralysis isn't permanent. In an hour or so you'll be good as new, assuming you live that long. Probably not."

He watched her pick up his pants and root through the pockets until she found the coin. She carried it to the light. "We looked all over Tiny's for this. You walk in and five minutes later, it's in your pocket. Well, you're supposed to be good." She held up his empty glass. "But not that good."

Someone called her name from the living room.

"In here," she called back.

Wylie sauntered in. "He drank the shit, huh?"

Angela didn't bother replying.

Wylie moved to the bed, grinned down at Mace. "You can hear me, right, asshole?" He laughed. "Don't bother trying to answer, Mister Professional." He turned to Angela. "That trank of yours is a beauty."

"Everything quiet at the house?"

"Well, yeah. So what's our plan now? We gonna have to take him all the way back there?"

Angela gave him a disgusted look. "What do you think?"

"I guess, if we want it to look like he pulled the trigger on Tiny."

"It would have been so much simpler if you'd just followed the plan," she said.

"You were the one said your fucking drug'd keep 'em all under for an hour. That little son-bitch—what's his name?"

"Lew," she said flatly.

"Yeah, Lew. He nearly did me while I was searching for the coin. Shot him in the fucking neck and he still didn't go down. Threw everything off. I wasn't set up for Mace when he showed."

"All you had to do was hold your ground and take him out," she said. "You panicked and ran out to hide in the dunes. Leaving me to improvise."

Anger showed briefly on Wylie's face. His lip curling, he said, "Least it gave you a chance to ride his hobby horse."

"Very poetic," she said. "You going to be able to carry him downstairs if he's dead weight?"

"He a better fuck than me?"

She gave him a look of contempt. "What's that got to do with anything?"

"Was he better?"

"We're poised on the brink of collecting more money than either of us can spend in a lifetime of vulgar extravagance. All we have to do is set up this fool. He and Paulie will pay the price for Tiny and we can walk away without ever having to look back. And you want to know if he was better in bed? Well, sonny, as far as I'm concerned, all you boys are in second place."

"You sayin' you're a dyke?"

She took a step toward him until she was in his face. Through clenched teeth, she said, "What I am is no concern of yours, snake boy. Now I ask you again: Can you carry him to the car or do we have to run the risk of taking him there at gunpoint?"

"I can fucking carry him," Wylie said, drawing the gun from his belt.

"That's Carlos's, right? It's got to look like Carlos shot him before he died."

"I know the goddamned plan," Wylie said.

"Use a pillow to muffle the sound."

"Yeah, yeah." Wylie reached past Mace for the pillow. Suddenly, Mace's right hand shot up and grabbed Wylie by the throat. His left twisted the gun free, not caring much either way if any fingers came with it.

Wylie yelled and Mace smashed the gun against the side of his head. As Wylie fell forward, Mace drove an elbow into the back of his head then leapt from the bed. He raced through the apartment, catching Angela at the front door, struggling with a lock.

"Too late," he said.

Her body slumped and she turned. "The stupid . . . he put on the chain lock."

"Just being cautious," Mace said.

"You didn't drink any of the gin?"

He shook his head. "Your improvising at Tiny's had some rough spots."

"I thought I did pretty well, considering."

"What was the plan? Wylie cleans house, shoots me, and you wait for the cops so you can give them an eyewitness account of my murder spree?"

She shrugged. "We weren't planning on killing anybody. We thought Tiny would give up the coin. But the fat bastard kept his mouth shut."

"That he did," Mace said.

"So, of course, the cool-headed Mr. Wylie had to shoot him. That's when he decided to set you up. He called you and we started searching the place. We didn't find the coin and one of Tiny's bodyguards woke up sooner than expected. It was a mess. But I thought I put on a pretty good show for you."

"Your panties were still warm," Mace told her.

It took her a second or two to realize what he was saying. "I should have left 'em on," she said. "It would have been okay, me stoned in bed with my panties on. I just thought it'd make a more interesting distraction."

"I was distracted all right," Mace said. "But I was also suspicious."

"Why?"

"I've been in this apartment before. You had a drawing hanging in your bedroom. It's the same guy who's on the coin. You design it?"

"No. I was told whose portrait would be embossed on it, so I looked him up. Did a sketch, just for my own amusement."

"Who's the old bird, anyway?"

"Count Basil Zaharoff," she said. "He was a liar, a cheat, a schemer. Supplied weapons to both sides in the Boer War, the Balkan conflicts, and World War One and wound up one of the wealthiest men in Europe. They called him the Merchant of Death."

"Born before his time," Mace said. "Just think of the fun the two of you could be having today."

"Just think of the fun the two of us could be having." She moved toward him.

"You never give up, do you?"

She licked her lips and ran her right hand up her side, fondling her breast. "I didn't think we were quite finished," she said. The hand went to the top button of her blouse, worked it free, and drifted to the next.

She was something, all right. But her eyes shifted for just the fraction of a second and that was enough.

He took a fast sideways step and the heavy metal sculpture Wylie swung made an arc through empty air and dug a chunk out of the plaster wall. Mace smashed the gun butt against Wylie's skull. The tattooed punk went down, but not all the way. He started to straighten and Mace hit him again, sending him to the carpet.

Angela headed for the door. "You won't make it," Mace warned.

She froze.

Somehow Wylie got to his feet.

"Boy, you're too stupid to live," Mace said, and drove the heel of his hand into Wylie's nose, cracking the bone and sending it up into his brain. Wylie's eyes rolled up in his head and blood spurted down over his lips and chin. He fell backward onto the carpet and stayed there.

Angela stared down at the lifeless man. "You . . . killed him," she said with a hint of wonder.

"It's what I'm good at," Mace said, lifting a cushion from the sofa. He pressed the muzzle of the gun into it and shot her twice in the general vicinity of her heart, assuming she had one.

"Well, that's that," Lacotta said to Mace, snapping his cellular shut and slipping it into his pocket. They were in a nearly deserted departure lounge at LAX.

Mace glanced at his watch. His flight was forty minutes late, which meant he was stuck with Lacotta for a while. "Your guys went over her room, right?" he asked. "I doubt they'll bother to dust it, but still . . ."

"They did a steam clean. You're clear." Lacotta smiled. "We're all clear. That was a beauty idea, putting Tiny and the other two guys on Angie's bill."

"It's what she and Wylie had in mind for me."

"This way, it looks like a lovers' quarrel, her going psycho and being taken down by one of the fat man's bodyguards before he faded. No connection whatsoever to the corporation."

"What are you going to do about the money you blew on the formula?"

"I think I'm gonna get lucky on that. When Tiny's 'insurance' surfaces, Montdrago's gonna have other things on his mind, like how he'll look wearing orange."

"Maybe Tiny was bluffing about the 'insurance,'" Mace said. When Lacotta's smile went sharklike, he added, "Oh, I get it. You'll make sure something surfaces."

"Gotta keep one step ahead," Lacotta said. "That's why I want you to move back here."

Mace shook his head. "That's not going to happen," he said.

"It'd be like the old days, amigo. You and me. Only now, we'll be in charge of things. Hell, I bet we could even find out what happened to the fucking formula."

"You'll do okay without me," Mace said. "And the world will surely be better off without its genius bombs."

He stood up.

"Where you going?" Lacotta asked. "Your plane's not in yet."

"Getting us a couple of soft drinks from that machine," Mace said. "Got some coins in my pocket I'd like to get rid of."

Honorable Mentions
Angela Zeman

The year 2001 had two months of "blue moons" and a once-in-a-lifetime comet show, so that must explain the oddities we had to face. Even Ed Hoch admits he has never heard of so many crazy circumstances surfacing in one year. I won't list them all, but a few arrived daily.

Here's a good starter: Mark Twain was a legitimate competitor (*Atlantic Monthly*)! Dorothy Sayers almost was one, until somebody realized her piece was a radio play (among other disqualifying factors). The distinguished *New Yorker* magazine submitted a story, and with that slight act acknowledged Edgar's growing significance. We received a sheaf of stories submitted by a magazine I'd never heard of, about which of course I immediately e-mailed Ed Hoch, who always knows what's happening in the short story world before the rest of us. He explained that *Handheld Crime* was published on Palm Pilots. The stories were pretty good, one was very good, but what mystified me was how long they were. I could only imagine a commuter on a train for an hour or more, scrolling through tiny screens crammed with words.

Years ago (Ed Hoch was chairperson then), I remember, we had a problem finding enough stories good enough to choose from, to award an Edgar. This year, several writers could easily have won (although in my opinion the winning story was truly and well chosen). Such quality work. Such creative ideas. We worked long and hard. When voting time for both the Robert L. Fish and Edgar Awards arrived, an eleventh-hour disqualification of a favored Fish story candidate forced us to start from scratch on that list, re-reading, re-thinking our choices. We discussed voting procedures, asking each other questions until arriving at decisions satisfactory to all.

This committee applied itself with a devotion to fairness, to meticulous choosing, to careful reading and re-reading. I ended up thinking of us as a gang. No Chair (or as Warren Murphy called me, "madam chairthing") with a committee of four, but a team. The Gang of Five. Ed Hoch, Meg Chittendon, Kate Grilley, Warren Murphy, and myself. As for the short story writers: Congratulations! Your creativity has made 2001 a year to remember. I wish you all could've won.

Honorable Mentions for:

Allyn, Doug, "The Saracen's Curse," *Alfred Hitchcock's Mystery Magazine*, November

Banker, Ashok, "Flesh Songs," *Futures*

Collins, Max Allan, "Kisses of Death," *Kisses of Death*

Collins, Michael, "The Horrible Senseless Murder of Two Elderly Women," *Fedora*

Lewin, Michael Z., "If the Glove Fits," *Ellery Queen's Mystery Magazine*, Sept./Oct.

Mayor, Archer, "Instinct," *The Mysterious Press Anniversary Anthology*

Mortimer, John, "Rumpole and the Old Familiar Faces," *The Strand Magazine*, issue VII

Rendell, Ruth, "Piranha to Scurfy," *Piranha to Scurfy and Other Stories*

Schofield, Neil, "Groundwork," *Ellery Queen's Mystery Magazine*, November

Womack, Stephen, "www.deadbitch.com," *A Confederacy of Crime*

The **Mystery Scene Magazine** *List of Honorable Mentions:*

Allyn, Doug, "Black Irish," *Murder Most Celtic*

Barnard, Robert, "Old Dog, New Tricks," *Ellery Queen's Mystery Magazine*, March

Braunbeck, Gary A., "In the Lowlands," *Murder Most Feline*

Cannell, Dorothy, "Bridal Flowers," *Love & Death*

Clark, Simon, "Fenian Ram," *Murder Most Celtic*

Deaver, Jeffery, "Lesser-Included Offense," *Ellery Queen's Mystery Magazine*, May

Estleman, Loren D., "South Georgia Crossing," *The Blue and the Gray Undercover*

Hills, Rick, "I'll Keep This Brief," *Alfred Hitchcock's Mystery Magazine*, November

Ing, Dean, "Inside Job," *Combat*

Jakober, Marie, "Slither," *The Blue and the Gray Undercover*

Law, Janice, "The Helpful Stranger," *Ellery Queen's Mystery Magazine*, April

Lindskold, Jane, "Slaying the Serpent," *Death by Horoscope*

Lovesey, Peter, "Murdering Max," *Ellery Queen's Mystery Magazine*, Sept./Oct.

Lutz, John, "Hobson's Choice," *The Blue and the Gray Undercover*

McGuire, D. A., "Full Moon, High Tide," *Alfred Hitchcock's Mystery Magazine*, April

Reeve, Paul G., "Chinese Puzzle," *Alfred Hitchcock's Mystery Magazine*, March

Resnick, Laura, "Homicidal Honeymoon," *Murder Most Romantic*

Robinson, Peter, "April in Paris," *Love & Death*

Sellers, Peter, "Avenging Miriam," *Ellery Queen's Mystery Magazine*, December

Williams, David, "The Rude Awakening of Sybil Flitch," *Ellery Queen's Mystery Magazine*, June

Williams, David, "The Gift of the Gab," *Ellery Queen's Mystery Magazine*, June

About the Editors

Ed Gorman has been called "one of suspense fiction's best storytellers" by *Ellery Queen,* and "one of the most original voices in today's crime fiction" by the *San Diego Union.*

Gorman has been published in magazines as various as *Redbook, Ellery Queen, The Magazine of Fantasy and Science Fiction,* and *Poetry Today.*

He has won numerous prizes, including the Shamus, the Spur, and the International Fiction Writer's Award. He's been nominated for the Edgar, the Anthony, the Golden Dagger, and the Bram Stoker Awards. Former *Los Angeles Times* critic Charles Champlin noted that "Ed Gorman is a powerful storyteller."

Gorman's work has been taken by the Literary Guild, the Mystery Guild, the Doubleday Book Club, and the Science Fiction Book Club.

Martin H. Greenberg is the CEO of TEKNO•BOOKS, the book-packaging division of Hollywood Media, a publicly traded multimedia entertainment company. With more than nine hundred published anthologies and collections, he is the most prolific anthologist in publishing history. His books have been translated into thirty-three languages and adopted by twenty-five different book clubs. With Ed Gorman, he edits the 5-Star Mystery line of novels and collections for Thorndike Press, and he is copublisher of *Mystery Scene,* the leading trade journal of the mystery genre.

In the mystery and suspense field, he has worked with at least fifteen best-selling authors, including Dean Koontz, Mickey Spillane, Tony Hillerman, Robert Ludlum, and Tom Clancy.

He received the Milford Award for lifetime achievement in science fiction editing in 1989, and in April 1995 he received the Ellery Queen Award for lifetime achievement for editing in the mystery field at the 50th Annual Banquet of the Mystery Writers of America, becoming the only person to win major editorial awards in both genres.

Dr. Greenberg received his Ph.D. in political science and international relations from the University of Connecticut, and was the founding chairperson of those departments at Florida International University from 1972 to 1975. He retired as professor emeritus of political science and literature after a twenty-year teaching and administrative career at the University of Wisconsin—Green Bay, where he served as the university's first director of graduate studies.